S.M. BOYCE

WRAITHFORGED

THE WRAITHBLADE SAGA
BOOK TWO

WRAITHFORGED: BOOK TWO OF THE WRAITHBLADE SERIES
Copyright © 2022 by S.M. Boyce. All rights reserved.

This book is a work of fiction. Names, characters, places, and incidents are either a product of the author's imagination or used fictionally. Any resemblance to actual events, locals, or persons, living or dead, is entirely coincidental. All rights reserved. No part of this publication can be reproduced in any form or by any means, electronic or mechanical, without expressed permission from the author.

Cover Illustration: Mansik YAM
Cover Design and Interior Layout: STK•Kreations
Art Direction: Bryce O'Connor

Trade paperback ISBN: 978-1-955252-27-0

Worldwide Rights
1st Edition

Published by Wraithmarked Creative, LLC
www.wraithmarked.com

This one's for you, Dan.
*As much my best friend
as you are my brother.
You breathe life
into stories, into art,
and into Saldia.
Thank you
for all you do
and all that you are.*

"When everything goes to hell, the people who stand by you without flinching—they are your family."
—*Jim Butcher*

CHAPTER ONE

THE WRAITH KING

Death spoke his name on the breeze.

The great ghoul lifted his bony head toward the setting sun as he listened to the winds of the dead. The fleeting whisper had been unmistakable, as it had visited him a handful of times thus far in his undead centuries.

He had yet to learn why, but the tides of this world always shifted when he heard it.

As a beam of sunlight hit him, he could almost feel its heat on what used to be his face. The Black Keep Mountains glimmered in the lingering rays of amber daylight, and ribbons of gold glistened in the rock as another dusk fell across his long-lost home. The timeless jet-black peaks pierced the clouds, scraping lines through the churning white fluff.

The bones of his hand clicked against each other as he curled his fingers into a fist. With the simple motion, the sunlit forest around him shifted.

Color drained from the trees, until only the muted browns of tree bark and discarded pine needles remained. The sky dimmed, and the bleak paint strokes of a white-washed world replaced the vibrant greens and blues. It was a world he visited often, an in-between where mortals could no longer see him, but where he could see all.

A massive silhouette passed over the ground, blotting out the sun in this dimension, in a domain everyone passed through at the end of their lives. As the shadow blurred across the evergreens, the wraith merely waited for Death to pass them by.

How curious.

When Death's shadow had disappeared over the horizon, the wraith returned to the land of the living. The southern wind tore through the trees, churning their fragrant leaves as the world carried on, oblivious to the danger of the Beyond.

He studied the forest, trying to remember what it felt like for a breeze to pass across his face. Even as the grass beneath him rippled like waves on the sea, he felt nothing but the icy surge of magic through the enchanted marrow of his long-dead bones.

Immortality had its price—one he had always been willing to pay.

The whisper floated past again, almost too quiet to hear as the God of Death spoke a new name and chose a new mark. A worthy one, since only the worthy deserved their names spoken by the Creator.

The slap of something wet hitting skin shattered the peaceful evening. Something shifted within the ghoul's ribs as his host neared—just a flicker, like a candle lighting, but one that nonetheless tracked his tether to this world.

Connor Magnuson stalked through the trees, his bloodstained boots making no sound as he ducked a low-hanging branch and tossed an apple into the air. A few droplets of water shot off the red orb as it spun, and Magnuson caught it with an effortless twist of his callused hand. He bit into it, the crunch snapping through the evening, and his dark gaze shifted toward the ghoul.

You grow fat and lazy, the wraith chided.

Magnuson just laughed.

How irritating.

"I'm fat and lazy, am I?" The man sat on a toppled log and leaned his elbow on one knee as he took another bite of his apple. "I spent three days combing through this overgrown forest for signs of predators. All that, and I barely slept. Studying the land to assess risk was a necessary precaution and a worthwhile delay. You will never convince me otherwise."

You wasted precious time, the ghoul said. *This land is safe, and you found nothing that could threaten your human pets. No living creature got in or out, just as I told you. Even the catacombs remain sealed.*

A miracle, really, given all the enchantments taxing Slaybourne's residual magic, but he wasn't about to admit as much aloud.

The rush of wings on the air cut through the steady chorus of the breeze, and a brilliant red sparrow landed on a nearby branch. Its body glowed with the fire of a star as it sang into the fading daylight. In its belly, light surged and faded in time with its rhythmic twittering. A soft hum buzzed in its chest as its magic swelled.

In his mortal lifetime, the wraith might have thought the tune to be enchanting. Mesmerizing, even, like the voice of an angel trapped in a tiny ball of feathers.

In death, however, it was just another noise.

As he held the half-eaten apple, Magnuson pointed at the bird. "You say there's no threat here, and yet the animals have changed over the centuries. They're not the same breeds that lived here in your day. You said so yourself."

True, the wraith begrudgingly admitted.

"There you go." Magnuson bit into his apple with a self-satisfied nod. "The delay was worthwhile. Stop complaining."

The ghoul studied the tiny sparrow as its crisp song sliced through the air. Though Magnuson had a point, the Wraith King wasn't going to admit it.

While the towering pines swayed overhead, Magnuson sucked in a deep breath of fresh air. His chest expanded, and his eyes briefly closed as he savored the day—a day the ghoul would never feel.

A white-hot flicker of envy snaked through the Wraith King's core before he could squelch it. He paced to distract himself, gliding back and forth above the grass.

I have only allowed you this reprieve so that you could recover from your duel with the Starlings, the wraith announced. *Get on your feet. We have much to do.*

"Oh, is that what this was? A reprieve?" Magnuson grinned and took another bite of his apple. "How considerate of you, Oh Merciful One."

Another prod. Another joke.

It was odd, really, how much the ghoul enjoyed their banter. He suppressed a chuckle and scanned the forest around them to keep himself occupied. If he had been told in his life how much he would one day appreciate a peasant's company, he would've killed the oracle foolish enough to lie to his face.

But they had no time for this.

Yes, it was a reprieve, the wraith countered. *A storm is coming, Magnuson. You're simply in the eye, and you cannot yet see the true scope of the devastation barreling toward you.*

"I know." The man's smirk faded, and he set his free hand on his waist as he studied the forest. He took a few final bites and tossed the apple core into the forest for the deer to finish.

Where is the Bloodbane dagger you procured from Zander Starling?

With an impatient sigh, Magnuson stood and lifted his shirt to reveal the weapon's ornate leather sheath strapped around his waist. Soft green light radiated against the hilt, and he tugged it loose. The light intensified as it left its casing, and an emerald glow illuminated his face while he studied it. "It's hard to believe such a tiny blade can inflict so much pain."

It is a unique enchantment, the wraith agreed. *And after we retrieve the second dagger, we can never allow anyone to create a third.*

"Think we're too late?" A frown tugged at the edge of the man's mouth as he examined a weapon that could kill even the simmering souls.

Doubtful, but we cannot underestimate how badly they want you dead.

"And you," Magnuson raised one eyebrow as he slid the glowing dagger back into its sheath.

A fair point, but the wraith didn't reply. His cloak billowed around him, its tattered fibers trembling in the waves of a god's wrath. Death was up to something, and the ghoul suspected there was more at stake than either he or Magnuson could imagine.

Together, they watched his pristine forest in a rare moment of silence. A deer wandered through the tree trunks on its way toward the apple core, its body half-submerged in the thick green foliage of an unspoiled woodland. The vivid sunlight briefly faded as a cluster of clouds cast a shadow across the idyllic scene, and the wraith allowed himself to savor this moment in a valley he had once feared he would never again see.

Life thrived here, now, in a land he had once destroyed.

Of all the hosts the wraith had endured in his undead life, Magnuson was the first to bring him home. It was a debt the wraith would repay in the only way he knew how: by forging this mortal man into a foe worthy of the gods and, perhaps, even the Creator.

But to conquer Death, one must be unafraid to die.

Don't get comfortable, Magnuson, the wraith warned. *There's still much for us both to discover. There's much we don't understand.*

The mortal snorted derisively. "I thought you knew everything."

This is no time for jokes, peasant, the wraith snapped. *Have you never wondered what I am? What you are? Think about it. Our magic does not obey the laws of this world. It cannot be replicated by any potion, nor explained by any book, save perhaps the Deathdread. Have you never wondered why?*

The Wraithblade's eyes narrowed briefly before they glossed over with thought. Evidently, he hadn't.

The ghoul grunted in frustration. *I told you, not long ago, that you are power incarnate. I meant what I said, but it comes at a cost. It's not your swords or your enhanced senses that give you this unlimited ability, but rather the simple fact that this world does not limit you. You are not bound by the laws of other men. What we must discover, Magnuson, is why—and what your limits truly are.*

Magnuson frowned. "Didn't Aeron Zacharias know?"

He thought he did, but he was wrong. The wraith shook his head, and the frayed edges of his hood drifted side to side with the motion. *I'll tell you a secret, Magnuson, something I have never told any of my hosts. Aeron Zacharias didn't make me. Not really. He used magic he could never fully understand and shattered natural laws that weren't meant to be broken to bring me back, yes, but the act of creation itself was beyond him. Whatever made me—and whatever fuels your power—it doesn't come from Saldia. Whatever it is, it bleeds into this world from the land of the dead. I know that much for certain.*

The man went still. He stood there, his face unreadable and stony as he waited for the wraith to continue, but there wasn't much more to say.

The Wraithblade had to become a master of war and death to survive in a world that would slit his throat at the first sign of weakness. Mastery of that caliber wasn't something a man could ever complete; it was an art, a lifetime pursuit, one a man had to commit to with every fiber of his being.

Much awaits us both, the Wraith King admitted. *I must ensure you are ready for the chaos to come.*

As the last threads of light retreated toward the horizon, the char of campfire smoke wafted past. The Wraithblade lifted his chin, and his nose flared at the scent.

Through gaps in the darkening trees, the orange glow of a campfire sprang to life. Silhouettes crossed in front of the flames, casting long shadows behind them, and the quiet murmur of conversation drifted through the forest as Magnuson's team settled in for the night.

"Chaos. War. Blood. I know it's all coming." The Wraithblade stared at the fire and cracked his knuckles. "The best I can do is prepare for it. Worry never did me any good, and it won't do me any good now. As for what's coming next, our prisoner most likely has the answers. Our little Starling guest let herself be captured, and I think it's high time we found out why."

I'm impressed, Magnuson. With a contented chuckle, the wraith gestured toward his host. *I didn't think you had it in you, but yes—a bit of old-fashioned torture sounds like a delightful way to celebrate coming home.*

The man just shook his head in frustration and set one hand on his waist as he watched the ghoul with a disappointed glare.

The wraith shrugged. *What?*

"You should know me better than that by now."

And what, precisely, is the alternative? You can't bluff her into answering.

"Of course I can." Magnuson pointed at the fire for emphasis. "Watch and learn, you old fart."

The man strode off toward the campfire without so much as a cracked twig beneath his boots to announce himself to the makeshift band of misfits he had collected thus far. As Magnuson disappeared into the shadows, the wraith rubbed the bony tips of his fingers against the hollow sockets that had once been his eyes and let out an exasperated groan.

Foolishly noble, as always.

Though the mortal man had accomplished much on his own, he would soon learn what it truly meant to be the Wraithblade. Hell itself would knock at Death's Door in its hunt for Connor Magnuson, and the wraith would see to it they were both ready to answer the call.

Regardless of what Death had in store for them, the monsters of Saldia's nightmares would soon learn to cower at the mere mention of this new Wraithblade's name.

The wraith would see to that *himself.*

QUINN

As darkness fell on the valley, Quinn Starling listened to the night.

In every direction around her, glowing meadow grasses swayed in a gentle wind and left emerald imprints on the air—a clear sign of a spellgust deposit nearby, and a considerable one at that. The soft whistle of a breeze through the meadow hummed with life and power, and twittering birdsong filled the sky. A shadow-drenched forest loomed just beyond the field, and somewhere among its oaks and pines, a horde of crickets trilled.

Surrounded by magic and drenched in an ocean of nature's music, Quinn almost couldn't believe what she already knew to be true: she now sat in the heart of the notorious Slaybourne Citadel.

A place of evil. A place of death. The home of a warlord whose horrific deeds outlived even his name.

And yet, it was beautiful.

That wench of a necromancer had fixed a new Bluntmar collar around Quinn's neck, and the infuriating enchantment cut her off from her magic. Quinn had planned for this, of course, but it didn't make her hate the damn thing any less.

It didn't matter. She didn't need her augmentations to observe. From the moment the Wraithblade had brought her here, she had watched his every move. The less she said, the more she heard.

Quinn may have been his prisoner, but she had come here with a purpose, and she had only to wait for one of them to make a mistake. With time, the Wraithblade would realize he shouldn't have let her in. This close, observing the things he didn't think she could see, she could do so much more damage than any weapon.

The time had come to learn who this man truly was.

For now, she would merely wait, ever silent and aware, for them to show her their true selves. That was all it took to regain the upper hand, after all. To find what a man truly hid in his heart, she had only to uncover what he wanted most.

If it turned out Saldia would suffer with him in it, she would find a way to slit his throat—even at the cost of her own life.

CHAPTER TWO
CONNOR

As the night wore on, Connor waited in the shadows beyond the campfire. With his arms crossed, he studied the trio sitting on fallen logs around the flames.

An orange glow danced across Quinn's face as the Starling woman stared into the crackling logs with her elbows resting on her knees. As she leaned forward, her low-cut collar revealed more of her cleavage, but he suspected it was a deliberate trick to distract anyone foolish enough to take the bait.

Firelight glinted off the metal collar around her neck. The silver circlet was now enchanted with all the power of a Bluntmar potion thanks to Sophia's quick work with an old cauldron they'd found in the rubble. As long as that collar remained locked around Quinn's neck, she wouldn't have access to any of her magic. As an extra precaution, however, he had taken her Firesword and hidden it in one of the entrances to the catacombs for safekeeping.

Quinn Starling was their prisoner—for now. With an enemy like her, he doubted his upper hand would last long.

Though he wanted nothing more than to find out everything she knew about him, he had chosen to wait, unseen, in the darkness. He had wanted to study her. To learn her intentions. To figure out her motivations or, if nothing else, to discover at least one weakness. He needed something, anything at all, before he tried to bluff his way into her head.

So far, he'd gleaned very little.

Behind her, the meadow grass pulsed with a faint green light. These mountains must've been overflowing with spellgust ore, once upon a time, but it surprised him to see lingering evidence of it after all these years. He figured the wraith would've mined it hollow in his days here.

An animal shifted in the muted green darkness on the other side of the fire—the Starling woman's pet vougel. It stretched its golden wings and yawned, its white fangs sharp and wet in the low light. From what he'd picked up in the taverns on his travels, war-birds like that were often beaten and drugged into submission, but not hers. Hers was different. Alert. Aware. It wore a helm like all the others, but its eyes were clear and crisp.

Whatever enchantment she had put on that helm, it wasn't a Bridletame. This creature could think for itself, and that made it even more dangerous than any of the mindless steeds in the Lightseer army.

So far, that tiger-bird lounging in the night beside her was her only weakness, but he wasn't about to hurt an animal just to make someone talk.

And, just like that, he was back at square one.

He'd never before faced a foe like her, and if he wasn't careful, she would gut him in his sleep. Whatever it took, he had to always remain two steps ahead of her.

Murdoc shifted on his log, his back still to Connor as the man leaned toward Sophia and whispered about the kind of pie he would like to make for her. She elbowed him hard in the side, and he grunted with poorly masked pain.

"Oh, I'm sorry," she whispered in a sickly sweet voice. "Did that hurt?"

Still doubled over, Murdoc forced a smile and shook his head. "Not at all, my darling."

She groaned in annoyance.

Connor sighed and rubbed his eyes, but Sophia could hold her own. If she needed Connor to intervene, he would make Murdoc stop, but the woman hardly needed saving.

He whistled, soft and low enough that only someone with a Hearhaven augmentation could notice. Sure enough, neither Quinn nor Murdoc looked up—but Sophia twisted in her seat until her dark eyes landed on him.

With a subtle twist of his head, he silently asked her to join him.

She stood as Murdoc leaned toward her again to whisper. The sex-obsessed rogue's smile faded as he watched her walk away.

"Was it something I said?" the former Blackguard asked.

Sophia ignored him as she brushed a few leaves off her skirts. In the darkness, her pale skin glowed almost as white as the stars overhead. She joined him in the shadows and rubbed her arms in the cold night.

"Yes?" she demanded with a twinge of irritation on the edge of her voice.

Puzzled, Connor glanced at the goosebumps on her arms as she hunched over for warmth. "You can summon ice that freezes men solid on impact, and yet you're uncomfortable on a cool spring night?"

"Easy for you to say. I've never once seen *you* shiver."

He shrugged. Fair point. "I need a Hackamore. I know you made an extra one."

"We only stole enough reagents for the one we gave Richard."

In the silence that followed, Connor raised one skeptical eyebrow and glared down at her.

The necromancer grimaced. "Don't give me that look, Connor. It's your fault I didn't make an extra one. As much as I would've loved to add to my collection, that potion is hard to make and I didn't want to risk our bargain any more than I already had at that point. I'm telling you the truth."

He frowned and let out a frustrated sigh. It would've been far easier to use a truth potion on the Starling woman, but he would have to make do. "What other potions do you have in that enchanted bag of yours?"

"To make her talk? I have plenty." Sophia listed them one by one and counted them on her fingers. "One to burn her skin. One to drown her from within. One to make it feel like you're flaying her alive. How creative do you want to get?"

The wraith chuckled, his voice echoing in Connor's head. *I enjoy her.*

Connor wrinkled his nose in disgust, and his eyes narrowed as he silently demanded that she rein in her bloodlust.

"Fine, be all noble and righteous." She shrugged and returned her attention to the fire.

Absently, almost too slowly for him to even notice, she ran her fingers over her chest. Her fingernail caught on the fabric of her dress, and a dim glow escaped from the folds of her gown.

Dull green, now, instead of the vibrant green of a healthy augmentation. The magic tethering her to this body was fading faster than he had expected.

"How much longer do you have?" he asked, careful to keep his voice low in the rare case Quinn had found a way to listen in.

Sophia's jaw clenched, and her back stiffened at the question. "Not long. You need to deliver on your end of the bargain."

"I said I'd get you bloody beauties, and I will."

"How?"

He pointed across the fire, toward Quinn Starling and her vougel. "If anyone in Saldia knows where to get them, she does. You'll have them in time, Sophia."

The necromancer didn't answer, and he wondered if she doubted him. If, after everything they had endured together, she assumed he would just let her die.

The thought stung.

He cleared his throat and walked toward the campfire. She would follow, and with time, maybe she would learn to trust him.

As Connor stepped into the light, he adjusted the silver swords in their sheaths on his back. It was a timeless intimidation tactic he had learned from his days with Beck Arbor, all those years ago, and it subtly reminded the opponent of who held the upper hand.

Quinn looked up from the fire first. Her tiger-bird sat upright as he neared, and Murdoc followed their gazes. Unfazed, Connor sat down on an empty stump by the flames.

"Find anything good, Captain?" Murdoc asked. "Some gold, maybe? Or a—"

In a puff of dark smoke, the ghoul appeared from the air behind Murdoc and smacked the man in the back of the head.

"*Ow*," Murdoc snapped. He spun around and glared up at the old ghost. "Why'd you do that, you ass?"

Instruct your pet not to raid my home, the wraith demanded. *Nothing here is for him to take.*

"Behave, children." Connor gestured between the two of them. "Don't make me come over there."

The wraith crossed his bony arms, and though he didn't reply, his empty eye sockets remained focused on the back of Murdoc's head.

"Perhaps try not to insult the ghost that can kill you in your sleep," Sophia suggested as she took her seat on the log beside Murdoc.

Murdoc shrugged. "If he was going to kill me, he would've done it already."

Don't be so sure, scoundrel.

Connor snapped his fingers. Both Murdoc and the undead king tilted their heads toward him, but he focused his glare on the wraith. "That's enough."

The old ghoul growled and slipped away into the night, grumbling nonsense under his breath about royalty and the respect he used to receive.

Murdoc rubbed his jaw. "No, if I was going to worry about anyone, it would've been Zander Starling. Thank the Fates he's finally dead. Good riddance." He paused, and his gaze darted toward Quinn. "Uh, no offense."

Her hazel eyes drifted slowly toward him, but she didn't respond.

"Zander's a hard man to kill," Connor said. "We can't assume he's really dead until we find a body. Or, at least, what's left of it."

"You're joking, right?" With a chuckle, Murdoc gestured in the vague direction of the only path in or out of Slaybourne. "Zander was dragged off by blightwolves, Captain. The man may be strong, but he's dead. There's no way he's powerful enough to survive that."

"I won't believe he's dead until I see the corpse." Connor shifted his attention to Quinn. "Wouldn't you agree?"

Though the rest of her remained eerily still, her hazel eyes darted toward him. Listening intently. Acutely aware of not just what was being said, but of what was left unsaid. Without question, she was a dangerous prisoner to keep this close.

After a moment's pause, she merely nodded.

You should kill her. The wraith's chilling voice echoed in his head, painfully loud. *Extract what you can from her and dispose of her quickly. She sees more than you suspect, and you cannot afford an enemy to know as much as she will by the time we're through with her.*

"No," Connor answered under his breath. "Stop intruding."

Sophia cracked her knuckles, the sound barely audible over the sizzle of the fire. "I think it's time our little guest starts earning her dinners."

"The Starlings are the wealthiest family on the continent, right?" Murdoc pointed at their redheaded prisoner and shifted his attention to Connor. "Let's just ransom her back to her soft life of privilege. The Fates know we could use the kind of coin we could get for her."

A fair point, and not a bad idea if he could time it right. Connor sat with the option, mulling it over like a fine wine. If a Lightseer emissary was on the way, he had to play his cards carefully to get the most out of the deal without invoking the wrath of the Starlings.

He leaned forward and rested his elbows on his knees as he held the Starling woman's intense gaze. "I assume you Lightseers have some sort of failsafe in place for predicaments like these. Your father must know you've been captured by now."

"Most likely." Her soft voice broke the air, shattering it almost, like the pop of a fire. Though she watched him intently, her stony expression remained unreadable.

After three days of her complete silence, he hadn't expected her to actually speak.

He cleared his throat to mask his surprise. "When will he send a messenger for negotiations?"

She laughed. Her eyes crinkled with delight, and the smile on her face melted away the cold mask of indifference she'd worn seconds before—but her laughter didn't make a lick of sense.

With a deep frown, Connor cracked his knuckles. "I didn't say anything funny."

Her laughter slowly faded, but the smile lingered. "Think of it from my father's perspective, outlaw. Teagan Starling is widely considered to be the greatest Lightseer to ever live, and as such, he has a reputation to uphold. Two of his children have disappeared mid-mission, including the future Master

General of the Lightseers. For all he knows, we're both dead. You're the one connection between our two missions, and you happen to be the most wanted man in Saldia. He won't negotiate, Wraithblade. He won't send an emissary, and if you know what's good for you, you won't harm a hair on my head."

"That's ridiculous," Murdoc said with an impatient huff. "If he doesn't send someone, how does he expect to get you back?"

"Because he's coming himself." Those green eyes of hers swept across everyone gathered at the fire before they settled once again on Connor. "You beat me once before, Wraithblade. You even survived a fight against Zander. That takes skill, certainly, but do you really think you can win against Teagan Starling himself?"

Connor didn't move. He watched her face for signs of a lie, but she held his gaze with all the confidence of a hustler cashing in a winning bet.

She wasn't lying, which meant a horde of Lightseers were probably already on their way here—with the most brutal Starling in history leading the charge.

CHAPTER THREE

CONNOR

Despite the sizzling heat rolling off the flames, an icy chill snaked through everyone seated by the campfire.

As Connor waited for the Starling woman to elaborate, he did his best to strangle the primal impulse to bolt to his feet and slip into the night. Beside him, Murdoc and Sophia went deathly still, both of them frozen at the thought of Teagan Starling on the warpath.

Quinn leaned forward, studying Connor through gaps in the flickering fire between them. She didn't have to say a thing for him to imagine the massacre that lay in store for them all if they ever met Teagan face-to-face.

I told you we were in the eye of the storm, the wraith said, still unseen even as his voice floated through Connor's head.

"Shit," whispered Murdoc. "The Lightseers—coming here? And with Teagan leading them on—Oh, *shit.*"

"Well said," Sophia whispered.

Murdoc combed his fingers through his thick hair as he stared into the campfire. "Captain, what the hell do we do?"

"We stay calm," Connor ordered with a quick glare over his shoulder at the man sitting nearby. "Quinn, tell me how much time we have before your father mobilizes."

"Why should I?"

In a whishing blur of skirts and metal, Sophia drew a dagger from a hidden sheath around her calf and hurled it through the flames at the Starling. Unfazed, Quinn leaned ever so slightly to the right to let it whizz past her ear. Her red hair shivered as the blade whistled by, but she never took her eyes off Connor.

Sophia let out a string of curses and, seconds before she could throw the second blade, Connor snatched the glimmering metal dagger out of her hand.

"Sit the hell down, damn it!" he demanded.

"You're playing nice," Sophia hissed under her breath. "She will kill us all the second she can, and you should—"

In a rush of popping joints and flexing muscle, he stood. He stared down at her, shoulders squared and fists at his side as he dared her to finish that sentence.

She didn't.

"Don't undermine me again," he warned in a gravelly voice.

Her jaw tensed, and her gaze drifted away from him as she silently surrendered. With a flick of her hand, she summoned her enchanted dagger, and it whistled through the air as it returned to her palm. He tossed her the second blade, and she effortlessly caught it.

"Personally, I'd rather enjoy watching a Lightseer starve," she grumbled as she returned to her seat.

At least one of you is entertaining, the wraith interjected. *Let the necromancer torture the Starling girl already so that she can let off some steam.*

Connor ignored both Sophia and the wraith, opting instead to focus the full intensity of his furious glare on Quinn. "Look, Starling. You can make this difficult and painful for yourself if you want. I'm fine with that. What we have here, however, is a chance for you to make this easy on us both. Either way, you're going to tell me what I want to know."

The Starling warrior's pink lips twisted into a subtle smile, and she met his intense stare with one of her own. "Fine."

Connor paused, waiting for the trap.

It couldn't possibly be that easy.

"You want to know what's going to happen?" she asked.

He nodded.

"You're going to die."

"Let's try that again." He crossed his arms and narrowed his eyes in warning. "This time, add in a bit more detail."

With a gloating twist of her lips, her gaze swept across his body. "Alright, then. You want details? Fine. The last time my father fought a Wraithblade, it took three months to fully mobilize Lightseers from across the continent and another two months to reach the warfront. It was a brutal battle that lasted for weeks. We lost, though, so perhaps you and your little ragtag team stand a chance at lasting a little while longer."

Despite the Bluntmar collar around her neck, she relaxed. As she fell silent, she watched him carefully. Her posture, her tone, her grin—she had to be taunting him.

What she didn't realize, however, was that she had actually told him something useful.

Her father had lost his war against King Henry, the last Wraithblade, and now Connor knew why—the Master General of the Lightseers had made one crucial mistake, and he probably wouldn't do it again. Teagan had taken his time to muster his full forces, thinking sheer numbers would be enough to conquer his enemy, but that had given Henry time to master his powers in those precious early weeks of his connection to the Wraithblade.

Connor stiffened and absently tapped his finger on his jaw as he sifted through his thoughts. Now that he had her talking, he needed to carefully phrase his questions to get to the heart of what he wanted to know. "What kind of general is Teagan?"

"Haven't you heard the stories?" Quinn tilted her head in confusion. "Brutal. Merciless. Efficient. He's—"

"Oh, enough with the games!" Sophia interjected. "Connor, this is bad. You've never faced Teagan, but I've studied him extensively. He's an accomplished warrior who works with speed and strong fronts to flush out stragglers and kill every last opponent. He's going to assume we have both Zander and this pain in the ass over here." Sophia pointed an elegant finger at Quinn. "He's not going to risk a long, drawn-out campaign if he thinks the two of them are behind enemy lines."

"So, your name's Connor." Quinn watched him, and her stony expression returned almost instantly.

Connor sighed and glared at Sophia, who grimaced with regret.

Damn it. She was better than this. With her magic fading, it seemed like her good judgement was vanishing along with it. He would need to be careful of the tasks he gave her until they repaired her augmentation and cemented her connection to her body.

Quinn already knew too much, but what was done couldn't be changed. He had to plow onward, and with time, he would have to figure out what to do with her. He didn't want to needlessly kill, but he also couldn't risk her running back to her father with everything she had learned about him and his team.

He would have to figure that out later, perhaps after he figured out why she had let herself be captured.

As he internally scrutinized what she had said, a horrifying thought hit him like an arrow in the back.

On his way to Slaybourne, Teagan Starling would travel past the Finns. It was inevitable.

Those good people lived off the beaten path, but even they had to go into town on occasion. Rumors traveled quickly through the taverns along the southern road, and he had no guarantee his connection to them would remain secret. The average sheriff might not piece the clues together, but Teagan employed the best of the best.

With the Lightseers after him, the Finns were in danger, too.

"You." Connor pointed at Quinn as he regained control of the conversation. "How long would it take for Teagan to mobilize his fastest, most elite team? Something moderately sized, but which can move quickly on those things." He gestured to the vougel behind her, who perked up as everyone around the campfire stared at it.

Both she and Zander had ridden their tiger-birds into the Decay, so the creatures could clearly survive out here. It made the most sense for Teagan to do the same, since time was of the essence and money was never an issue for the Lightseers.

She frowned. "A week or less."

"How many?"

"A hundred," she said with a shrug. "Maybe more."

"And how fast do they move?"

"Fast."

"Be specific."

Quinn sighed impatiently and tapped her fingers on her thigh as her eyes glossed over with thought. "Lunestone to Bradford in three days."

"That's a seven day trip on foot, and if…" Murdoc trailed off into incoherent grumbling and took a long swig from his flask.

"Right," Quinn said with an exasperated huff. "That's why I said he's *fast*."

Connor stood and paced along the outer rim of the firelight as he ran calculations in his head. Given that speed, it would take roughly twenty days for a small army to travel from Lunestone to Slaybourne. The larger the team, the slower they would move.

Though Slaybourne's location had been lost to the centuries, Zander had been waiting for him. That meant at least some of the Lightseers had always known how to get here, but there was no telling if they truly knew the fastest way.

Lots of unknowns, and lots of maybes. He hated this—the not knowing. It left too much to chance.

"Twenty days," he muttered. "Thirty if we're lucky."

Murdoc spit out his whiskey, and a fit of coughing followed. In a halfhearted attempt to help, Sophia patted his back with a stiff hand, as though afraid to catch a disease if she touched him for long.

"Twenty days? How is that even possible?" Murdoc wiped his mouth with the back of his hand as he stared up in barely masked horror.

"You clearly don't know Teagan Starling," Sophia whispered. Her gaze drifted to the ground, and her shoulders stiffened with fear.

Connor studied their captive and scanned her face for any reaction, but she once again studied him, cool and indifferent, giving nothing away.

It didn't matter. The math made sense. If Quinn had wanted to catch them off guard, she would've stretched out the timeline so that they thought they had more time to prepare than they truly did. As far as he could tell, she was either spinning tales about her father's abilities as a scare tactic, or she was telling the truth.

Twenty days. It wasn't enough time to do anything, much less fortify the crumbling ruins of an ancient fortress.

He wanted to continue his interrogation, but preparing for an onslaught was far more urgent. It wouldn't do any good to have all the answers if her father dragged an army out here to kill them before they could do anything about it.

He needed to come up with a plan, and their prisoner didn't need to hear this part.

"Wraith, watch her." Connor pointed to Quinn and her vougel before shifting his attention to Sophia and Murdoc. "You two, come with me."

In a puff of dark smoke, the ghoulish figure of the Wraith King appeared beside Quinn. The smoke rolled over her face, but to her credit, she didn't even look at the ghost as Connor led the others away from the fire. She watched them, silent once more and aware of far too much.

As they walked out of earshot, Sophia shuddered and rubbed her arms for warmth. "This is bad, Connor."

"It is," he agreed.

"Twenty days," Murdoc muttered as he scratched his head. "Fates be damned. Captain, what are our choices here?"

"Not many," Connor admitted. "We could run, but that puts us out in the open. At least here we have the enchantments, Death's Door, and the walls to protect us. We're going to face him eventually, so we may as well choose where we fight."

"Maybe she's lying." Sophia shrugged. "Maybe she's trying to get under our skin. If we're in a panic, we'll make poor choices. She could just be playing with our minds."

Connor shook his head. "What else would Teagan do? His children are missing and the entire continent is watching to see what he'll do next. Back in Oakenglen, even we heard the rumors about where Zander had gone, which means everyone has heard by now. Word travels fast, especially in the cities. Zander found Slaybourne, and that means his father can as well. He's going to try to make an example of us. She might be lying, but it's still a good point. It would've been in her favor to tell us he would send a messenger, only for an army to show up in the messenger's place. We would've been unprepared."

"Then why tell us the truth?" Sophia's brows twisted in confusion as she looked up at Connor. "Why not lie? I would have, in her shoes."

He rubbed the back of his neck, but he had no idea. "She let herself be captured, Sophia. She's up to something, and we need to figure out what she's after before she finds it."

The necromancer let out a string of curses as her slender fingertip tapped anxiously against her ruby-red lips.

"How about this?" Murdoc curled his thumb through a belt loop and pensively rubbed his beard. "We meet them halfway. We find a suitable war zone, set traps, and kill the stragglers."

"They're flying here, idiot," Sophia snapped. "And we have no idea how many of them there will even be."

"You can still trap them if you're clever." The former Blackguard looked over his shoulder at Quinn Starling, seated by the fire. "It's all about the bait you use."

The three of them went silent as they followed Murdoc's gaze.

"It's too risky," Connor said, killing the idea before it could take root.

Sophia closed her eyes and took a settling breath. "Then it sounds like our only real choice is to stand our ground."

"I agree." As his enhanced eyes acclimated once again to the darkness, Connor studied the distant perimeter walls. The lingering enchantments in this place protected them from whatever tried to fly overhead, but only ruins remained of the once-great buildings inside. With a forest full of game and a lake of fresh water to the east, they could wait out a siege. The walls, however, had to hold against an onslaught for that to work, and he had no idea how long the walls would last or how many reinforcements would join the first wave of soldiers as the weeks wore on.

"We need to find mercenaries," Murdoc said. "Mercenaries don't always want gold, you see. I know some guys from my time as a hired sword, and I could get us a decent army. Not as good as the Lightseers, but enough to—"

Connor shook his head. "I don't trust someone who can be bought."

Murdoc snorted derisively. "You hired me!"

"No, you owed me a life debt. That's different."

The former Blackguard opened his mouth to reply, but his eyes glossed over with thought, and he quickly shut his mouth once more. "Hmm."

"If not mercenaries, then what?" Sophia snapped. "We have to do *something*. I'm good, but even my potions can only get us so far."

There is a way. The wraith's grim voice shattered Connor's focus.

With a subtle twist of his head, he shifted his attention toward the ghoul hovering by the campfire. Quinn studied Connor and his team from behind the flames, but from that distance, she had no way of reading his lips. She had to be watching his body language and expressions, still trying to learn more about him and his team as the days wore on.

Behind her, the ghoul floated at the edge of the shadows, half-submerged in the night. *There is powerful magic in the catacombs beneath the citadel. Before I died, I built an enchantment that had no rival. There are powerful artifacts hidden all across this continent, and I needed only one of them—a power source strong enough to fuel my creation. In my time with Henry, I finally found one. We can make it there and back within the twenty days, but only if we leave soon.*

Connor shook his head. "Too risky."

"What?" Murdoc asked, likely because he'd only heard Connor's half of the conversation.

"Be quiet." Sophia smacked Murdoc's arm. "Let them talk."

Only a fool dismisses that which he doesn't understand, Magnuson. At least see what I built in the catacombs before you decide to discard it.

"It's too risky," Connor repeated, more firmly this time. "But leaving now, when there's so much at—"

I challenge you, Wraithblade, the ghoul interrupted, and the undead king's grim voice hit him like waves crashing against a cliff. *I challenge you to see what awaits in the tunnels. There are two weapons down there unlike anything you have ever seen—one which you must conquer, and one which you must claim. If you fail to master either of these weapons, then you were never ready to take on the mantle of Wraithblade. If you succeed, you will have the power and resolve to become Teagan Starling's equal.*

It was quite a claim.

Connor chewed on the wraith's words. They hummed in his brain long after the ghoul had stopped speaking, and as the crickets chirped in the night, he simply lost himself in thought. He sifted through all the ways this could backfire. He tried to come up with a better plan, but all his ideas fell apart upon closer examination.

He had precious few options.

With a resigned sigh, he set his hands on his waist and nodded. "Show me."

That is the correct decision. The ghoul groaned with irritation. *Though, one day, you will learn your manners and stop trying to give a king commands.*

"Don't hold your breath."

To his surprise, the undead wraith chuckled.

Murdoc's gaze shifted between Connor and the specter hovering by the fire. "What's the plan, Captain?"

"I'm not sure yet," he admitted. "You two stay here with our prisoner and her tiger-bird. We can't risk her breaking free of that collar."

"She won't." Sophia dismissed the idea with a flick of her wrist.

"She did once already," Connor pointed out. "Back when Murdoc and I first found you, remember? If she hadn't eventually gotten that collar off, somehow, she would be dead."

Sophia pursed her lips but didn't answer.

Connor absently scratched at his jaw as he thought up new ways to mess with the Starling woman's mind. "Spin whatever tales you want about the ghoul and his ability to go unseen. Let her think she's being watched."

"Gladly." Murdoc rubbed his hands together and grinned with mischievous delight.

"And you," Connor added with a stern glare at Sophia. "Don't kill her or the tiger. No blood."

The necromancer frowned and rolled her dark eyes.

"Sophia, I mean it." He raised one eyebrow, and his voice lowered an octave in warning.

"Yes, fine. Fine." She waved her hand as if to tell him to get on with what he had to do. "I won't touch a single hair on her privileged little head."

It wasn't exactly a glowing reassurance that she would behave, but it was good enough. Between the two of them, they would be able to keep Quinn Starling in line.

Murdoc gestured toward the fire. "If we're staying here, then where are you headed, Captain?"

"I'm not sure, yet," Connor admitted. "It seems like there might be something in the catacombs that can help us. I need to take a look."

"The catacombs?" Murdoc shook his head. "Nope. No, I don't like this. I'm coming with you. I know you can handle yourself, but we have no idea what's down there."

"No." Connor scratched at the growing stubble on his jaw and scanned the mountains again. "I need you to stay here with Sophia."

Whatever awaited Connor in the catacombs, it was as much a chance for the Wraith King to test his limits as it was a chance to find something that could properly fortify Slaybourne. Anyone who joined him would be at risk, and he needed to focus on whatever the ghoul had in store for him down there.

As much as he would've liked backup, he had to do this himself.

Teagan Starling was on his way. According to the stories that traveled with merchants along the main roads, the man left only ashes and corpses in his wake. Death and destruction would find its way here, no matter what Connor did.

There were those on this continent who thought of Teagan as a reincarnated god, but Connor knew better. Powerful? Yes. Rich beyond imagination? Absolutely. Feared by any sane man and ruthless in combat? Without question.

But, like any man, Teagan Starling could still bleed.

CHAPTER FOUR

TEAGAN

The candle on Teagan Starling's desk popped and fizzled in the otherwise painfully silent office.

The Lightseer Master General sat at his desk, half-submerged in shadow as the candle's chaotic dance cast swirling ribbons of light across his stern features. With his elbows on the table and his fingertips pressed together in front of his face, his eyes glossed over with thought.

Across from him sat two empty chairs. Both Quinn and Zander should've been there at some point during the day, begging for his forgiveness, and yet both had failed him.

Starlings didn't lose, but he now found himself dangerously close to losing his two greatest possessions in the world: these two children. His eldest son would one day take his place, and his youngest daughter—the gem in the Starling crown, and one the entire continent envied—would define his legacy. Quinn's marriage had the potential to win the Starlings the most coveted crown in the empire, and Zander's time as Master General would forever be compared to his own.

Without them, Teagan Starling would be remembered as a failure. The tomes of history would write of him as the man too swept up in his own self-image to secure the longevity of the family name. His own descendants would speak of him as an example of what not to do, just as his father and grandfather had spoken ill of the ancestors who had failed to secure land rights that would've established the Starlings as the rightful monarchs of Oakenglen long ago.

He had to fix this.

A jolt of scorching-hot hatred shot through his temple and down to his heart. He winced as it burned within him, raw and all-consuming, and he cracked his neck to relieve the tension.

One man stood at the center of this mess: the Wraithblade.

A thin ray of pale blue light slowly crept along the rug as Saldia's twin moons inched across the night sky. His chair's mahogany legs scraped against the hardwood floor as he stood and debated his options.

Two letters waited on his desk, but he had already memorized both. Short and to the point, one update from Colonel Freerock explained that Zander had never arrived in Hazeltide. It assured him the Discovered, which Zander had been ordered to interrogate in the Hazeltide dungeons, was contained for now while the Lightseers guarding it awaited new orders.

It was no secret, of course, where Zander had gone instead. The rumors had spread through the castle like wildfire, but the infuriating young man had acted too quickly for Teagan to intervene. By the time the rumor had reached his office—and it of course hadn't taken long—Zander was already gone.

Teagan had debated flying after his fool of a son and dragging him back to Lunestone by his ear if he had to, but he had learned a lesson about the Wraith King in his time fighting Henry: no wise man rode alone into a battle against a simmering soul, no matter how talented he thought himself to be.

For Teagan to follow his son into the Decay, he needed to bring an army.

If Zander had waited even a week, Teagan would've let the boy lead the charge into battle. They would've gone together at the head of a great army, and they would've squashed the new Wraithblade's uprising before it had even begun.

But then, Zander would've had to share the glory. Now, his irreplaceable son might be dead.

Teagan winced. Unwilling to entertain the thought for even a second, he buried it deep in his soul, next to the other withered parts of himself he rarely reflected upon.

He opened the drawer in his desk, and a soft green glow spilled into the room from its depths. A bottle lay on a black pillow, and the facets along its surface glistened as he lifted it to the candlelight. Ribbons of green and blue light danced across the ceiling as he studied it in more detail, and for a moment, he doubted what he had discovered in the ancient texts of Lunestone's archives.

It seemed impossible, really, for a bottle like this to contain magic as powerful as the Wraith King.

Carved from pure spellgust and enchanted with a powerful spell from the archives, bottles like these had been used before. When placed in vaults carved from spellgust ore, the vial could hold the abomination prisoner for centuries.

Without the Bloodbane daggers, this would be Teagan's only way to contain the wraith.

He groaned in frustration and put it away. Zander should've had two of these with him when he left for the Decay, but none had been recorded in any of the enchanters' logs. Perhaps Zander didn't even know these existed. The fool had access to the vast history of forbidden knowledge stored beneath Lunestone, and yet he rarely visited the vaults.

No patience. No foresight. Just blind ambition. When this disaster was finally over, Teagan would have to burn the last traces of insubordination out of his idiot son.

The corner of a second letter poked out from underneath the first—a short summary on Quinn's failure to return by her deadline. He had assumed she would take longer to complete the mission once she inevitably failed, but she had always followed protocol whenever she asked for an extension.

Letters. Updates. Any contact at all would've reassured him that his precious little girl was alive, but he'd heard nothing.

All current intelligence on her last known location suggested she had gone west, but Teagan knew better. If that were true, she would've been home by now because his spies assured him no one fitting either Quinn's or the Wraithblade's description had ever ventured that far. None of the Shade folklore had made it out west, either, and that nonsense followed him like breadcrumbs in a forest. The only thing out west that could kill his daughter was Freymoor, but she knew better than to return to that cursed fallen kingdom.

No, something or someone had detained her, and it didn't take a scholar to deduce who was responsible.

He growled, low and deep, and massaged his temples in frustration. He had wanted to break her of her warrior habit, but now he wondered if his plan had worked a little too well. He wondered what else in her would break if she had indeed become the Wraithblade's captive.

Thankfully, his children were hard to kill. He had seen to that himself, and he suspected they were both still breathing. The question, of course, was where they had gone.

Teagan threw open the rich velvet curtains blocking the moonlight and stared out at the lake beyond his castle. A shimmering blue glow danced across the water as each wave reflected starlight. Slowly, with his full focus on the thoughts swarming through his mind, he paced a familiar path across the well-worn rug.

Though he would never admit it to any living soul, he had made an egregious error. Something unforgiveable. Something his father would have broken his bones for allowing to happen.

The moment this catastrophe had begun, Teagan should have dealt with the peasant himself. He had underestimated a commoner and expected Aeron's abominations to remain contained due to the fear of public retribution should any Wraithblade ever dare speak the truth, but Teagan's pride had blinded him to reality.

The simmering souls consumed their hosts. Every time. Peasant or king, the magic Aeron Zacharias had brought into this world played by different rules. Though Teagan still didn't quite understand what they were—nor, he suspected, did the Great Necromancer, back in the day—he knew full well what they *weren't*. These weren't enchanted items or potions that obeyed the laws of Saldian magic. They were something more, something entirely foreign to this land and perhaps even this world, and they were never supposed to rise from the cobwebs. Now, they threatened the continent's very salvation. They threatened Teagan's children. Otmund's ploy to kill Henry might well have cost Teagan his future.

More importantly, they threatened his seat of power. No man on this continent could ever be seen as his equal.

Though he hated to consider it, Celine had been right—these monstrosities could no longer be contained. The simmering souls needed to be destroyed, once and for all.

Every last one of them.

For that to happen, he needed Celine to comply. She had been far easier to control before she had become queen, and though he hated her, he hated the simmering souls more. That common revulsion would secure their partnership.

And if it didn't, he would remind her of the life she led before she became queen. He would see to it she recalled all the debts she still owed, both to him and the Lightseers.

"You must know I'm on the way," he muttered to the far-off Wraithblade as he paced. "You must have them both. I bet you've already interrogated them. Used a Hackamore, if you can afford one. Made them tell you everything."

Teagan's children knew him better than anyone, and he had to operate on the assumption that they had unwillingly divulged his process. He could reach Slaybourne with a small army in just a few weeks.

But not even his children knew all his secrets, and Teagan had not been idle.

His best engineers had already been ordered to Charborough at the edge of the Decay to build him something legendary. It would be the sort of military advancement worth adding to the history pages, and it would be immortalized alongside his name.

The merlins.

Only a fool went into a war without a backup plan, though, and he couldn't depend exclusively on fairly new technology. He needed to find the Wraithblade's weakness. Every man had at least one, and Teagan knew the perfect man for the job.

By the time the Lightseers reached Slaybourne, he would have everything he needed to crush the Wraithblade—and that infernal wraith—once and for all.

His ear twitched as the soft rustle of footsteps in the hallway broke his focus. Seconds later, knuckles rapped on the door to his office.

With a settling breath, he pressed his thumb hard into his left temple to recenter himself. The pressure eased a bit of the tension in his skull, and the creases of concern in his forehead disappeared.

Common folk saw in him what they wanted to see—namely, a benevolent champion leading the charge against the darkness. It served him best when he wore a mask that indulged their fantasy of who he truly was.

He practiced his warm and comforting smile for a second or two before he allowed the serving girl to enter, careful to ensure the skin around his eyes crinkled with what would appear to her as genuine compassion.

"Come in, Aida," he said when he was ready.

A young woman with long brunette braids pinned to her head walked into the study with a smile plastered on her youthful face. A carafe of wine, a goblet, and a plate covered with a silver dome shifted slightly on the tray she carried, nearly toppling off as she fought to balance it all, but he didn't care. He'd hired her for her looks and legs, not her serving ability.

"You need to eat, sir," she said as she shot him a playful glare from under her thick lashes. "It's been hours."

"Thank you." He nodded with practiced sincerity and gestured toward his desk.

The carafe of red wine clinked against the empty glass on the tray as she set it on the table. "Lord Jasper is here to see you, sir. Should I send him in?"

Finally.

Teagan stifled an impatient sigh and, instead, simply nodded.

"I know how busy you get, sir." With a flourish, she lifted the silver dome off the plate to reveal an elaborate stack of grapes, strawberries, and cheeses. "Please remember to eat."

"I will, my dear."

She flashed a brilliant smile and tucked the now-empty tray under one arm as she made her way toward the door. With her back to him, his gaze drifted down her back as he examined her figure once again. He enjoyed watching her leave more than he enjoyed their half-baked banter. Perhaps he would order her to his office again later tonight so that he could relieve some of his tension before he left for this campaign.

After she disappeared into the hall, Teagan poured himself a glass of wine and sipped it as he watched the open door. With a man like Charles Jasper, it was wise to never turn one's back on the entrance.

Sure enough, the subtle creak of a floorboard followed shortly after—so quiet that he would've mistaken it for a mouse in the walls if he hadn't known who was about to pay him a visit.

Men like Charles Jasper could steal through the darkness as well as any wraith, equally overlooked and every bit as deadly. Only Quinn's stealth rivaled Charles Jasper, and it still unnerved Teagan how often he couldn't hear either of them coming.

He once again rubbed his left temple as he swapped his metaphorical masks, given that the facade he wore around Lord Jasper differed slightly from the one he always donned for Aida. While she needed a warm and approachable father figure to feel at ease, Charles needed to see an authoritative commander. The assassin did his best work when Teagan indulged bits and pieces of classified intelligence—just enough to pique interest, but never enough to give the man ammunition.

Masks. Lies. Illusions. Every person in Teagan's life needed a different one, but he had mastered this exhausting art long ago. He lived for those moments where he could drop the charade, but to preserve his legacy and public image, only those who wouldn't survive the encounter ever witnessed the real Teagan Starling.

Without so much as a footstep to give away his position, Charles rounded the corner and paused on the threshold. His long silver beard ended in a well-groomed point over his chest, and the carefully tailored mustache above his mouth curled at both ends. He bowed his head in respect, and those cold blue eyes of his swept across the desk as he undoubtedly tried to scan for information he shouldn't know.

"A pleasure, Master General." The assassin shut the door behind him, and a soft ribbon of emerald light shot through the wood as the closed latch reactivated its silencing enchantments.

Teagan merely nodded in a stiff welcome.

Charles stroked his beard as he scanned the office, and his gaze hovered for an extra second or two on the bookshelf along the far wall. "I see you added a few new titles to your collection. Engineering, by the looks of it. Are you building something remarkable, my Lord?"

With a resigned sigh, Teagan grabbed the book on his desk that contained his sketches of the merlins and tucked both letters into its pages. "Your powers of observation never cease to amaze, Charles."

"Could it pertain to why you wanted to see me?" The retired assassin paused in the center of the room, and his heels clicked together as he clasped his hands behind his back. "What can I do for you, Master General?"

Teagan took another sip of wine, and this time, he took the moment to carefully study the assassin before him. Squared shoulders. Raised chin. Steady gaze. The man wore a cape too heavy for the late spring season, even at night, and Teagan could only imagine the weaponry Charles had brought with him tonight.

His Lightseers always confiscated everything they could find, of course, but men like Charles had more weapons up his sleeve than most soldiers carried with them into battle.

The man's paranoia made sense, though. The assassins of the Unknown were rarely called to their master's office in person, and they usually disappeared shortly afterward.

Teagan set his wine on the desk. "I'm not going to kill you."

"That is a relief, sir." Charles didn't move, however, and his expression didn't change. "Are we going to swap war stories, then?"

"No." The Master General set his fingertips on the desk in front of him as he stared the assassin dead in the eye. "I'm bringing you out of retirement."

At that, Charles lifted one eyebrow in surprise. "That would be unprecedented, sir."

"These are unprecedented times," Teagan admitted. "Besides, we both know men like you don't really retire."

The assassin's head tilted, just slightly, in restrained irritation. Teagan took another sip of wine to hide a victorious smile, as he rarely managed to get under the man's skin.

"A fair point, sir." Charles gave a stiff nod, as if acknowledging a point earned in a fencing match. "However, I gave you my heir. I was under the impression that relieved me of my…" He paused, his eyes glossing over as he searched for the right word. "Obligations."

"You did." A muscle twitched by Teagan's eye, and it took effort to keep his tone calm. "But then your heir left to become queen without filling her own… *obligations*."

Charles didn't reply. Those cold blue eyes focused intently on Teagan, and after a moment of silence, the man nodded once in surrender.

Good. Now, to business.

Teagan plucked a grape from the cluster on the plate before him. "I'm sure you've heard rumors of a man called the Shade by now. He's something of a folk hero in the south."

Focused and alert, Charles merely nodded again.

"Find out everything you can about him," Teagan ordered. "His name. His home. His training. The boy has dual blades, and I need to know how a peasant learned to fight so well. More than anything, however, I need his weaknesses—family, lovers, mentors. Anyone he cares about. Find them and bring them to me alive. I've chosen two rendezvous points for us along my army's route to the Decay. It's imperative you give me updates at each of these times. Here are your orders."

With a sharp tug, he plucked a folded piece of parchment from under the pile of letters on his desk and slid it slowly toward the assassin.

"Understood."

"None of my officers will know you're assisting," Teagan reminded him. "No one can see you at any point in your mission."

"They never do, sir."

"It's imperative you move quickly." Teagan paused, his eyes narrowing as he met the assassin's frigid gaze with one of his own. "I cannot head out into the Decay without knowing the Shade's weakness, Charles. Do not make me wait on you."

"I wouldn't dream of it, my Lord."

A small army trudging across the Ancient Woods took time, both to muster and to coordinate. Worse, they would have to travel along the southern road to establish supply chains that would support the inevitable siege to follow.

The retired Unknown stared out the window at the lake beyond Lunestone. A vein pulsed in his temple, and Teagan narrowed his eyes in suspicion.

"Is there something else you want to say, Charles?"

At first, the assassin didn't speak. His jaw clenched, and he swallowed hard. "This Shade of yours left for the Decay, sir. He's headed to Slaybourne."

Teagan grinned. "I'm pleased to see retirement hasn't softened you."

"Ah, so you already know." Charles forced a thin smile. "My question, then, is how might I best prepare for such an arduous journey? No one returns from the Decay. What awaits us out there that could be worth risking the life of a Lightseer Master General?"

Teagan had to admit he sometimes envied the speed with which Charles could adapt to the change of tone in a conversation. Though the man spoke as if he cared about Teagan's life, the truth bubbled deep below the surface, in the words he never would've dared say out loud.

Charles knew Teagan would only drag him back into the field for something truly dangerous. For something that could kill even one of the Unknown.

"War." Teagan stared out at the moonlit lake. "And, if this peasant has any idea of what's good for him, he will give me both of my children, alive and well."

"From what I've heard, sir, he doesn't seem like an ordinary peasant."

"He's not." Teagan's icy hatred stormed beneath his impenetrable mask of cool indifference. "But he will die like one."

CHAPTER FIVE
CELINE

Footsteps echoed through the darkness. The gentle trickle of water dripping into a puddle joined with the echoes, falling in a steady rhythm, like a withered waterfall somewhere out of sight. A man screamed, his voice muffled by a thick wooden door. Moments later, a woman sobbed, but the crack of a whip cut through her whimpers. Silence followed, interrupted only by the repetitive shuffle and scrape of feet on stone.

The cascade of sound blurred together in the somber corridor beneath Wildefaire Castle. These tunnels acted like veins, feeding into and protecting the glittering empire that spanned the northwest mountains. Down here, the charms and enchantments etched into the walls masked these sounds from the outside world.

The wicked came here to die—whether by choice or by chance.

A queen had no place in a labyrinth like this, but Celine had never been an ordinary monarch. She had visited these corridors many times before, and today's errand couldn't wait.

Draped in hand-spun silk that practically glowed in the firelight of each sconce she passed, she glided through the tunnel as though headed to a gala. Though she wore nothing on her head, it would not remain bare for long. Her crown waited in Oakenglen, and though she had resigned herself to retirement, the time had come to retrieve what no one else could properly wield.

Her golden skirts stirred up dust along the floor, and hints of a stain crept along the bottom-most hem like ink spilled on parchment. Her silk shoes passed over the stone floor without a sound, ever the huntress even when she had nothing to hunt.

Old habits.

The man behind her, however, sucked in air through his whistling nose as though his sinuses had fractured from his strained attempt at silence. His breaths skipped through the air like a river rock across a pond, and it took active restraint to keep from stabbing him in the neck out of sheer irritation.

Aidan Belfry, Celine's new assistant, trailed in her wake. A clever man, or so she had been told by her cousin Queen Whitney, and one who would have to prove his value before Celine believed him to be worthy of her time. She needed a shrewd man to run her errands—one with enough spine to do what had to be done, but enough self-preservation to remain obedient.

That was where she had erred with Otmund. Though he had always been clever, the fool had thought himself her superior simply because he had taught her a few tricks over the years.

It wouldn't take long for Otmund to discover how wrong he had been.

The stale tunnel ended in a single wooden door with an iron handle. Behind her, Aidan cleared his throat, no doubt ready to beg her pardon and slip ahead of her so that he could open a door she was perfectly capable of opening herself.

A trite gesture. It meant nothing, and she had no patience for wasted words.

Her delicate fingers curled around the metal handle, and the rough iron scratched at her palm as she pulled open the door. Aidan let out a strangled little sound, like a man on the end of a rope, but she ignored his surprise.

It wasn't his fault, after all. As a wealthy merchant's son raised in a land of glamours and lies, he had probably mastered the art of chivalry before he could even read. The Wildefaire court thrived on tradition and gallantry, but the real world didn't operate by these pretentious laws.

If he passed her test tonight, he would soon grow accustomed to impropriety.

A cold draft shot past her as she entered the prison cell beyond the door. In each corner of the room, a flickering sconce cast amber light into the windowless space. Thick stone encased the room from the floor to the rafters.

In the center of the cell, a man hung from chains that had been bolted to the ceiling. Blood pooled beneath him, and the crimson puddle reflected his bruised body back to him. As Celine studied her new prisoner, a single red drop fell from his broken nose, and the impact cast ripples that broke his reflection. His head and wrists hung limp in the shackles, and his long brown hair shrouded his eyes in shadow. His arms hung above his head, bound and tied just as she had instructed, and his legs bent to the side at an unnatural angle. It gave him a twisted appearance, like a dancer frozen mid-jig.

Behind her, Aidan quietly gasped.

A jolt of irritation froze her midstride. The fool had broken her first two rules: obey, and do it quietly.

Lips pursed, she glared over one shoulder to find him gaping at the man in chains, his eyes as wide as a maiden who had just learned what lurks in a man's pants.

With her delicate hands clasped in front of her, Celine raised one eyebrow in question. By now, he'd already been warned about what fate awaited the assistants who had failed her over the years. If he were to remain at her side, he would need to get used to the sight of blood.

Aidan's eyes darted toward her, and he cleared his throat. Though his face paled, he set his hands behind his back and stared at the back wall, as though the room were empty.

Smart man. At least he learned quickly.

Just as she had requested, a row of glittering silver knives lay on a table by the door. She resumed her silent march and, on the way to inspect the daggers, hooked her finger in one of the chains from which the man hung. He spun, his shackles rattling from the sudden movement, and the hook overhead creaked in protest as the man's weight tested its rusted rotation.

He groaned and coughed. Blood spattered against the floor, missing her foot by inches.

"Oh good." Her gentle voice floated through the air, as soft and soothing as a lover reciting a poem to her beloved. "For a moment there, I thought they might've killed you too soon."

"Won't do you no good," he slurred. "I'll never talk. Never—never talk to—" He wheezed and coughed again. "Not a chance in hell that I'll—"

"—talk, yes," she finished for him with a bored little sigh. "Are you an assassin or a parrot?"

The chains slowly rotated him toward her, but he craned his head around his twisted torso to get a better look. As his tethered body pivoted on the hook above like a broken performer twirling on puppet strings, his green eyes peered through the greasy threads of his hair. "That voice—"

"Correct." She lifted her chin as though congratulating a knight returning home from war. "You've found me."

He watched her, silent even as his body creaked and swayed in the chains. Bloodstained clumps of his hair still hid much of his face, but it couldn't hide the bruises or the crusting brown blood caked along his nose. Though he met her gaze, his nose flared with fear. The edge of his mouth quivered. His eyes shook, their whites stained pink from his torment so far, and he studied her with the horror of a man meeting Death.

Once upon a time, she had savored the fear. Back then, she had almost been able to taste it. In the moment or two before she killed her targets—in those precious seconds when they had realized they were going to die, and that they couldn't do a damn thing about it—she used to smile. To watch grown men shiver when they found themselves alone with her, well, it gave her back all the power she had lost in her youth.

But not anymore. Like any decadent delight, it had become cloyingly sweet. Predictable and practiced, like a play she had rehearsed one too many times.

Celine turned her back on her new pet and lifted one of the daggers off the table. She tilted it this way and that, examining the dazzling silver blade in the low light from the sconces. The amber glow glinted along the metal, sharp and sleek. These had either been specially crafted for her use tonight, or they had been so expertly polished that any trace of blood and gore had long been removed from them.

Interesting. She would have to get the name of Whitney's weaponsmith. He was clearly a master, and she rather enjoyed collecting adepts.

"Do your worst, woman." The assassin's whisper crackled, broken by a fleeting tremor of terror. He went to speak again, but this time his breath caught in his throat.

The edge of her mouth twisted downward, and she waited to feel the customary surge of pleasure as their match of wits and resolve continued. In the lifetime before she had become queen, she had dearly enjoyed these little games. The banter. The back and forth. The thrill of discovering what it took to break a strong man.

Deep down, she had hoped that at least a flicker of that familiar joy would've returned now that she had indulged her old ways, but the game couldn't even make her feel that anymore.

It couldn't make her feel *anything*.

Standing here, bleeding information from an assassin sent to kill her in her sleep—it was nothing but a tired theatre production in a playhouse riddled with broken seats from accommodating too many patrons over the years. It was a performance she had long ago abandoned, and to return to the stage felt like shining candlelight on cobwebs.

Pointless.

After all these years, this tired old play simply bored her.

A pity, really. All her life, she had been a flawless actor in this theatre of war and blood. She had delivered her lines on cue, crossed to the little mark on the floorboards, and gestured to the crowd with a well-rehearsed flourish. She had played her part to perfection, killed everyone she was told to kill, and no one but Otmund and the Starling patriarchs had ever known her name. Both she and her father had been handsomely rewarded for her time on the stage—until she married Henry, anyway.

Henry had changed everything.

"I'm not afraid," the assassin lied.

His shaky mumble broke her daze, and she briefly closed her eyes. Her lungs filled, and a decadent rush of energy swam through her. Air. Life. Breath. A reminder that Hell hadn't come for her yet. A sign that she still had time to do what had to be done.

Delicately, as though it were a sleeping child, Celine returned the dagger to its place on the table. Masterful as these pieces were, they served only as props on her stage. The real weapons had always lain dormant in her dress, tucked away in every crevice and fold, as much a part of her as the bare skin beneath her skirts or the braided star-white hair on her head.

Perhaps she should've said something menacing. Something derisive, or something that would make him tremble even harder.

Instead, she let the silence weigh between them.

"Celine." The tangled assassin's chapped lips cracked as he said her name. "Don't do this."

That, of all things, stirred something within her. Something deep. Something lurking far below, but it was enough to intrigue her.

Very well.

"Why shouldn't I?" She clasped her hands in front of her, just as she had done so many times in the royal court, and she studied him with a bored tilt of her head. "You came to kill me, didn't you?"

His eyes narrowed in answer.

She gestured to the cell around them. "I assume things didn't go quite to plan. General Davarius must not have prepared you properly."

The assassin's lips parted ever so slightly, revealing bloodstained teeth through the coarse brown hairs in his overgrown beard. To his credit, however, he remained otherwise unfazed. That had been his only tell, his only lapse in judgement to give away the lie, but it had been enough.

He scoffed. "You don't understand what's at stake if—"

"Have you figured it out, yet?" she interrupted. "Do you know why he sent you to slit my throat?"

The stranger shook his head. "Why won't you listen? He didn't send me, Celine. There's more at play than you realize, but I need you to *listen*."

She chuckled, and for the first time in a while, the barest hint of a true smile tugged at the corner of her lips. At least the general had been smart enough to send a tantalizing tease her way. The over-familiarity. A soft-spoken man strung up in chains. The laughable idea that the world could operate in any capacity without her knowledge of its inner workings.

It was like a present waiting to be unwrapped. The mystery. The suspense. The itch for something new, something exciting, or even something forbidden.

In her younger days, the trick might've worked, but not now. Not after everything she had witnessed in those bloodstained walls that had once belonged to scoundrel royalty. Oakenglen—and Henry—had changed her.

Celine's new pet insisted Henry's former General of War hadn't sent him, and it was time to put that claim to the test.

"I'm a threat," she explained. Silently, without even letting her skirt swish across the floor, she inched toward him and lowered her voice to a whisper. "I have many enemies, young assassin, but there are only four who know the truth of what I am. Of what my father raised me to be."

With a flick of her wrist, she summoned a thin blade from the depths of her sleeve. It slid into her fingers without even a rush of air to betray its arrival. The dagger glistened, its curved edges stunningly sharp, and it rested in her palm like a feather fallen from a hawk.

She lifted it in front of his broken nose. As firelight danced across the silver, his battered face went pale. Her gaze lingered on those terrified green eyes of his as they widened with recognition, and it was all the proof she needed.

"Five," she corrected, and she whistled softly to taunt him with feigned surprise. "It would appear that *five* people know the truth. What else did General Davarius tell you? Why did he pick you for this mission, little assassin?"

"I don't know what—"

"You're not one of us," she interrupted, already bored with his attempts to lie. "If you were, you wouldn't have broken this easily. You wouldn't have betrayed fear. I wouldn't have been able to get anything out of you at all. You made it farther than I expected you to go, so I can at least admit you're good." She leaned in, until her mouth was barely an inch from his ear, and the rusty stench of crusting blood burned her nose. "But I will always be better."

A strangled sob escaped his throat, like a beast clawing at the bars of a cage, and his jaw clicked shut as he tried to bury it.

"It's smart to be scared." She hooked her finger through another link in one of his chains and spun him again, mainly just to watch him twirl. "And there's no point in you trying to lie anymore. General Davarius is the only one who could have sent you. My father would never betray me, and if he had known you were coming, he would've killed you himself. Teagan needs me, and Zander isn't self-aware enough yet to realize I pose a threat to him. After the stunt Otmund pulled with Henry, that old buffoon doesn't have the contacts necessary to acquire an assassin of your caliber. That leaves Henry's two generals. General Barrett doesn't know what I am, which means General Davarius must have sent you. What I can't figure out, however, is where you came from." She paused to consider where a talented assassin like this could've possibly learned the trade in secret. "He trained you himself, didn't he? Is that it?"

The assassin's eyes narrowed in defiance. The chains rattled as he tightened his bruised hands into fists.

Celine let out a delicate little sigh as she pieced it together. "You poor thing. He didn't just train you. He *raised* you, didn't he? Found you on the street and gave you a way out of poverty?"

"Just get it over with," the assassin whispered.

"Soon," she promised. "Once you're useless."

Her voice never shifted in timber, nor did her expression change, but her new assistant whimpered—quietly, and just once—from his place by the door.

Because she had more urgent matters to address, she pretended she hadn't heard anything.

With the painfully sharp tip of her feather-like dagger, Celine lifted the assassin's chin until he met her eye once more. "He knows I want the throne back, and I'll admit he was right to send you. I'm going to ruin all of his plans. I know about his coup back in Oakenglen. Barrett and Davarius always squabbled, but their fear of Henry kept their bloodlust at bay. With him gone, their little civil war is starting, and it's up to me to squelch it before it becomes a thorn in my slipper."

Diffusing the first threads of a civil war would delay her efforts against the simmering souls, and the thought of letting the new Wraithblade become more powerful scorched her soul. Yet again, she would have to navigate powerful men as they stabbed each other in the backs to keep anyone from taking the scraps of power they had accumulated thus far. As always, she would be forced to clean up their mess.

Always.

A jolt of anger stabbed her through the heart, and a scowl broke through her gentle mask. Her brow furrowed, and the thrilling hum of her Buzzbright augmentation purred beneath her skin, aching to be released.

With her free hand, she grabbed the assassin's blood-crusted collar and yanked him close. The stench of week-old sweat mingled with the rusty haze of blood in the air as he swung toward her face. His green eyes shook, but by now he must've known what would happen next.

Even she played into the Fates' hands, sometimes.

"You petty fools have always squabbled," she whispered to him. "None of you care about the wraiths. None of you realize what's at stake, and I don't care about saving you anymore. I tried to bring you all peace. You had unity, and you squandered it. You had order, and you wished it away because you can never be satisfied. What happens to you lot is your own damn fault, and now all I want is my revenge. All I want is the simmering souls, finally gone, and for good this time."

He didn't answer. He just stared up at her, eyes wide. In his final moments, his training had failed him. She saw past the assassin, past his swordplay, past his tolerance for pain and torture. Where others saw a battle-hardened killer, she bore witness to the trembling child deep within.

And as her rage subsided, nothing replaced it but the numb boredom to which she had become accustomed in her semi-retirement.

She released his collar, but brown flecks of his dried blood stuck to her palm. The chains creaked, and his bodyweight carried him back and forth over the floor like a gory pendulum.

The feather-blade glinted in her hand, and she ran her thumb along the edge. It teased her skin, raising goosebumps of dread-drenched delight as it threatened to cut her.

The sensation helped her think.

Celine needed an army to face the Wraithblade. He would inevitably rise to power, same as Henry, same as they all had throughout history—only this time, she would stamp him out for good. There would be no *next* Wraithblade. This one would be the last, even if she had to call on favors from the Fates themselves to make it happen.

Her army waited in Oakenglen, but she could not take the throne until she knew for certain the soldiers would obey—even the little assassins like this one, raised in the underbelly of the castle to serve the crown. When the dust settled, they would all serve their purpose in life by bending the knee to her.

More important even than an army, however, were the Bloodbane daggers. It was time to recover hers from Otmund. The would-be puppet master had known the consequences of failing to fulfil his end of their bargain, but he had thought himself immune to her wrath.

The fool.

"Uh, y-your Majesty?" Aidan's voice shook, and his fearful tenor broke her reverie.

Celine's heart skipped a furious beat at the interruption. She didn't answer. She didn't even move, save for her eyes as they drifted toward him. Three times, now, he had interrupted her, and that tested her patience.

Though it didn't seem possible, even more color drained from his lily-white face when their eyes finally met. His mouth opened like a dying fish gasping for breath, and his gaze shifted from her face to her hand and back. He stuttered, trying and failing to form words.

She followed his slack-jawed stare to find the tip of her feather-like dagger embedded in her finger. A crimson stream of blood trickled from the wound and wove its way through the lines in her palm. It poured out of her hand like a macabre stream, and red dots stained the skirts of her golden dress.

With her other hand still on the hilt of the tiny weapon, she stared down at the self-inflicted wound. As always, she felt nothing. No pain. No sensation other than the light breath of warm metal against her skin.

Just... *nothing*.

In her youth, she had thought of this as a gift from the Fates. Proof that her father had chosen the right child to take his place in the Unknown. A blessing, one that proved she would one day become a legendary warrior of light.

But she had already lived that life, and now she would give anything to simply *feel*.

The dagger slid from her skin, and more blood rushed forth as she removed the silver dam holding it back. With a settling breath to slow her racing thoughts, she ripped off a thin strip of cloth from her skirt and wrapped it around her finger.

Her favorite gown, ruined.

Bit by bit, the world returned. A prison cell. Sconces on the walls. A table of daggers and a rancid man, bound in chains and hanging from the ceiling by a hook. She had come here for something specific, and she had finally found it.

"Tell me something," the assassin said under his breath. "Before you… you know…"

Celine frowned as she used her feather-blade to trim the ends of the glittering gold bandage. Usually, this was the time when her marks began to beg and plead. They had realized these would be their final moments, and they wanted to taste a few more breaths of life.

But not him. He intrigued her.

"Go on," she said, her tone even and calm once again.

"I didn't believe him when—." The assassin coughed, and splotches of red hit her gown. She grimaced in disgust, but she didn't move.

After all, it was just blood, and the gown had already been ruined.

"I didn't believe him when he said you were the Silent Knight." The assassin swung gently now as the chains slowly found their equilibrium. "I always thought Henry's famous bodyguard was a myth. You know, a legend for the kids. I was just a boy during the war, but everyone heard the story of the knight who rode at the king's side. The one who never removed his helmet, even at feasts in the lands they conquered, all in the service of his lord and king. He fought like a demon. Soldiers who saw him in battle swore he had come back from the dead, just to serve Henry. The man in that suit of armor had broad shoulders and didn't even carry a sword. How could that have been you?"

At first, she didn't answer. He watched her as the chains clattered around him in his steady swaying. His hair drifted, back and forth, but his eyes never wavered.

Celine tilted her head ever so slightly and watched Aidan through the corner of her eye. These were the risks of becoming her assistant—to hear things no one was meant to know, things mortals had to take to their graves with them. As long as Aidan proved himself to be useful, she would allow his heart to keep beating.

"Was that really you?" the assassin pressed.

She nodded, only once, and cut the final piece of excess cloth off her new bandage.

His eyes didn't widen with surprise, and to that at least, she felt a flicker of gratitude. In his final moments, he had seen through the fog of rehearsed lines and finally witnessed the theatre beneath it all.

Her pet's gaze roamed her delicate frame. "But how?"

"You know what I am. You know what the Unknown are capable of. Would you expect any less?"

His gaze drifted to the floor, and his eyebrows tilted up in resignation. "I suppose not."

"Had you believed him, would you have done anything differently?"

The young man nodded. "I would've run. I would've left Saldia and never looked back."

"Life is full of regrets, I suppose." She grabbed the nearest chain and tenderly slowed the assassin's swinging to a halt. "Davarius knew the consequence of sharing these secrets with any living thing. If he truly cared about you, he never would have told you any of this."

"I'm his best." The assassin swallowed hard. "I've never failed him. Not once."

"Until now." With the feather-blade, Celine affectionately lifted a clump of bloodstained hair out of the young man's face. "If it's any consolation, he wouldn't have sent you if he thought you would fail. There's too much riding on your success."

His jaw tensed, but he didn't reply. There was nothing left to say.

No use dawdling, then.

Her dagger slid deep into his throat, and she sliced across the vital veins and pipes with names she had never bothered to memorize. He choked as blood spurted from his neck, and his eyes rolled back into his head as he drowned in it.

She waited for the remorse she had been told she should feel, but yet again, nothing came.

With a little sigh, she wiped her blade against her already ruined dress and slipped it back into her sleeve. The swish of her skirts mingled with the assassin's desperate gasps for air as she walked toward the door. Aidan blocked the exit, immobile and mute, his body tense and his eyes locked on the dying man strung up in chains behind her. Her new assistant's chest barely moved, as though he were afraid he would suffer the same fate if he so much as took a breath.

"Come along," she said with a nod to the door. "Walk ahead of me, this time. It would seem there's much for us to do before I can retake Oakenglen."

A slurred jumble of words poured out of his mouth. They vaguely resembled a coherent sentence, but even she didn't know what he had been trying to say. As the dying assassin gargled for air, Aidan offered her a silent, jostling bow of obedience before doing as he was told. The door creaked as he yanked it open, and his footsteps echoed down the corridor once again while he led the way into the shadows.

Her eyes settled onto the back of his neck as she shut the door behind her. The assassin's strangled gasping faded to silence, and the steady drip of distant water returned.

She waited for Aidan to look over his shoulder. To flinch, perhaps, or even run. Except for Otmund, all of her past assistants had looked back the first time. They had hesitated at first, but ultimately they had surrendered to their impulse and peered over one shoulder to offer her victim a pitiful farewell.

To her surprise, her new assistant never once looked back.

How curious.

As they walked in a tense and somber silence, Celine brushed off her bloodstained skirts—more out of habit than need. The crimson stains had ruined this dress, of course, but her cousin would provide another, just as she had provided another assistant when the last one had failed.

This Aidan fellow would require further study. If the time came, like it eventually had for all the others, at least he would be easy to kill.

Just like Otmund.

CHAPTER SIX

ZANDER

ain.

It was all Zander could fathom.

In the numb recesses of his mind, he hid from it. He shoved away the sharp bursts of agony pumping through his body with every heartbeat. The lightning shocks in his skull. The sting in his throat as he fought for and earned every breath. If he built a wall around his mind to distance himself from the misery, he could make it home.

Just barely, but he would make it.

Trees whizzed by in his periphery, but little registered to him beyond the blurring greens and browns of a night-lit woodland. Blue moonbeams. Dangling moss. The faint screech of something alive, far off in the distance. His eyes watered and burned, but he did his best to blink away the exhaustion.

Huffing breaths mingled with the steady thrum of paws against the dirt as his stolen steed carried him through another forest. His brain splintered as jolts of lightning—real or imagined, he couldn't be sure—shot through his skull.

Numb it, he told himself. *Tune it out.*

As he rode the silver blightwolf alpha toward Lunestone, his delirium scrubbed away the edges of reality. It seemed at times as though he had become the blightwolf, as though he could feel the rough pricks of crushed twigs under his claws, as though the night air filled his massive lungs, fueling him back to a world where he once again had control.

He snapped awake. His body tilted left toward the ground, dangerously close to falling. Only muscle memory from his decades of riding experience had kept him in his seat and, battered as he was, even that wouldn't hold him for much longer.

In a pang of panic and impulse, he tightened his grip on the wolf's silver fur and pulled himself upright. His biceps flexed. His core tensed, and his entire body screamed in protest with the movement.

"Ignore it." The words slurred as he said them, but he didn't care. He repeated them under his breath until his voice blended into the rush of wind around him, like a sick and twisted mantra.

—ignore it—ignore it—ignore it—

His Rectivane hadn't healed enough of his injuries. As close to death as he had come, he needed at least one more vial—a full one this time—and several days in the healing ward back at Lunestone. His body couldn't take much more abuse, and yet he had no choice but to ride.

Ribbons of moonlight filtered through the canopy overhead. The soft leaves of the Enchanted Woods tainted the blue moonbeams with a silver stain. Dappled flashes of light skittered across the ground as the forest tilted and danced in the wind.

Though the open fields outside of Oakenglen would've offered a faster and smoother ride back to his father's castle, Zander had abandoned them in favor of the cover only this forest could offer. No one needed to know he'd procured a blightwolf—or that he had been so gravely injured.

Never in his life had he come this close to death. With augmentations that surpassed even his sisters' power, he and his father had no equals.

Until now, anyway.

No. Not ever. He seethed at the very idea of calling a peasant his equal.

Like his father, Zander had to remain the superior man, unrivaled. Such was both his birthright and the unwavering expectation his family placed upon him.

He sucked in a sharp breath to quell his burning resentment at how his battle with the Wraithblade had gone. His only victory had come from retreating on his own terms. He had lost the wraith. He had lost the Bloodbane dagger. He had lost everything, and his duel with the blightwolves had nearly killed him.

But failure was never truly an option—not for a Starling. In the end, when all was said and done, his family never truly lost.

His blightwolf sidestepped a log. Instinctively, Zander gripped his knees tighter to keep his seat, but the jarring movement sent ripples of agony down his legs. The two wounds he'd been given from his own Bloodbane dagger, stolen by that infuriating son of a *whore*, sizzled in unison. Both his shoulder and side blistered, the days-old injuries as painful now as when they were new. It felt as though something were writhing within him and ripping him open from the inside-out. Beneath his bloodstained shirt, heat sizzled across his chest and down his arms.

As the wolf reached a stretch of uneven underbrush riddled with short, sloping hills, each of the beast's steps sent a fresh tremor of agony up Zander's legs and into his core. He grimaced and choked down an agonized scream.

Face the pain and laugh at it. His father's voice echoed through his mind, feeding the bubbling resentment that fueled him onward. *A Starling endures.*

A familiar howl pierced the air—distant, almost hollow, and yet far too close for comfort. Deep in his chest, his heart skipped a beat in fear despite his lifetime of war.

He peered over his injured shoulder into the shadow-drenched woods behind him, but no bloodstained teeth glowed in the darkness.

And yet, that howl had been the unmistakable and timeless southern omen of death. A cry only the people of the Ancient Woods truly understood. One he shouldn't have been able to hear from this distance.

"Your kind never leave your territory," he said to his new pet as they thundered through the underbrush. "What made that sound? It couldn't have been your pack."

"It was," the blightwolf alpha answered between its gasping breaths. "They're slaves to the hunt, same as me. Same as you."

It peered back at him as they ran, and its foggy eyes sharpened, clear as day. The shift lasted only a second or two before its eyes returned to the milky white of a creature consumed by the Bridletame curse, but Zander had seen it nonetheless.

Impossible.

The bewitched helm remained planted in its skull. The broken band of gold still sat on its brow, and the spellgust stone in the center cast a brilliant green glow across its forehead. This enchantment had been designed to force even a dragon into mindless obedience, and not even a blightwolf should have been able to think for itself while wearing one.

Zander narrowed his eyes in suspicion. His mind buzzed at the impossibility of what had just happened, and his fingers dug into the wolf's hide as the alpha returned its attention to the path ahead.

It couldn't have overpowered the magic in the enchanted helm. That simply wasn't feasible.

"What are you hunting, human?" the wolf asked as they bounded through the forest.

It darted around a gnarled old pine with ease, and Zander leaned with the movement to keep his seat even as a fresh jolt of pain shot down his legs.

Zander kicked it sharply in the side to remind it of its place. "You will address me as your Master."

It chuckled, and the raspy wheeze in its laughter reminded him of a dying man's breath. "So you hunt respect, then? Power, perhaps? Have you so little of both?"

Zander gritted his teeth to stem the rising surge of irritation, and his nails broke through the wolf's hide as he debated whether or not he had the patience to restrain himself from just killing it.

Despite the ache in his battered shoulder and the deep stab wounds in his torso, Zander braced himself to use what little energy he had to spare. With a grunt of effort and a grim scowl, he drew his sword and smacked the flat of the blade against the side of the alpha's head. The thud of steel on bone reverberated through the forest, and the wolf stumbled from the sheer force of the strike.

This reminder of Zander's raw power always put wayward beasts in their place. This wolf had been an alpha in its day, but now its only purpose was to serve.

The wolf skidded to an abrupt stop. Dirt and grass kicked into the air from under its feet, but Zander remained on its back through sheer force of will. Jolts of pain skittered up his spine as he leaned backward to keep from flying over its neck.

In the cloud of dirt and dust it had kicked up, the beast shook its head. Its ears pinned back against its skull as it growled with pain, but its eyes remained closed.

"You mutts." The swish of metal on cloth hissed through the air as Zander sheathed his sword. "If your blood wasn't so useful in potions, I would've exterminated the lot of you by now."

The silver blightwolf twisted its massive head around and watched him with a milky white gaze. It bared its teeth, its lips trembling as it growled, low and menacing.

Zander's hand tightened again on the hilt of his sword as he frowned with confusion. It had given him a bit of lip, certainly, but that wasn't uncommon in the beginning when taming a truly powerful beast. It had insulted him, but it had continued to obey his order to ride. It had left behind its pack and followed his every command.

It had no power to defy an order.

"Move." He lifted his sword partway out of its sheath—both as a warning and as a precaution.

"No," it barked.

The blightwolf violently bucked. It tucked its head toward its chest and threw its hind legs into the air with the force of a boulder rolling downhill.

Though Zander had ridden or killed nearly every creature known to Saldia, the sheer force of the kick snapped something in his lower back. A blistering bolt of pain ripped clear up his spine and into his skull. His vision blurred. The trees and stained moonlight melted into nothing more than streaks of color, and his grip on the silver wolf's fur loosened.

A blast of cold air pelted his face. Seconds later, he hit the ground so hard that he rolled. The violent thrust sent him tumbling over the dirt. Grass filled his mouth, and he choked on the soil's musky blend of carrots and rust. A rush of white-hot pain shot down his left shoulder, and heat burned through his skull as though something had tried to bury into his eye socket.

In that moment, he snapped.

It wasn't the shock of a mount breaking through the Bridletame helm. It wasn't the shame of retreating from the Wraithblade. It wasn't the pain of his Bloodbane injuries or even the humiliation he would endure when he returned to his father as a failure.

It was the fact that absolutely *nothing* had gone to plan.

This vile creature had now added yet another delay to this miserable retreat when he needed to regroup and heal instead of milling about in a decrepit woodland, taming monsters. He needed a medic and a potions master, for the Fates' sake, and he needed at least one thing to work in his favor.

He was Zander Starling, damn it all, and a Starling got his way.

The blightwolf's insolence ignited the untapped rage deep within his soul. Fractured and furious, Zander was finally able to dip into the anger that every man possessed—the reserves. The cauldron of resolve and determination, fueled by spite and revenge, that could get him through anything.

And he *burned* with it.

Still tumbling across the dirt, Zander tapped into instinct and his years of brutal training under his father's watch. He rolled onto the balls of his feet, and his boots carved deep gouges into the soil as he skidded backward. With a half-mad scream of agony and effort, he drew his sword from its sheath and drove it deep into the earth. His blade kicked up rotting leaves and chunks of dirt, but it was all he could think of to slow his momentum. His palm slipped on the hilt, and he could barely keep hold of it.

Eventually, he slid to a stop.

With the fury of a shattered man that had nothing left to lose, he glared up at the silver alpha. Eyes narrowed. Skull aching. Injuries screaming. The beast had pushed its luck, and not even the allure of having a blightwolf as a pet could save it now.

It didn't matter how this thing had managed to defy him. Zander didn't care. He would saw off its legs and make it eat them to survive. These beasts lived to inflict pain and feed off fear, but it would soon learn he was a master of both.

The blightwolf waited seven yards away, its head low in warning even as it watched him with those vacant, milky eyes. The fur on its haunches stood on end, and the forest's low light glinted off its fur like moonbeams along metal. The green spellgust stone glowed in the helm on its forehead, as strong as ever.

A growl rumbled through the air, seemingly from every direction.

Where he should have felt concern or even panic, Zander felt nothing but the inferno of his hatred. He was lost in it, consumed by it, beyond redemption and far beyond caring what happened next.

If the other blightwolves had reached them, so be it. He was a Starling, and he would find a way to overcome.

He glanced around the clearing, expecting to see teeth glinting in the low light, but he and the alpha were alone.

How odd.

As an eastern breeze snaked through the leaves overhead, Zander steeled himself for a second duel even as the hair on his arms stood on end in warning. Everything about this was wrong. Something deep in him cried for him to retreat, but the rage drowned out the omen.

Besides, only a fool would run in his condition. He had precious little energy left, and he had to use every ounce of it wisely.

The wolf snarled, its lip quivering as beads of drool snaked down its dagger-like teeth.

Tenderly, careful not to further damage whatever had snapped in his back during his fall, Zander stood. His vision snapped in and out of focus even with the simple motion, but he scowled at the blightwolf to keep his attention focused on something other than the pain. Once on his feet, he raised his Firesword and tapped his thumb lightly on the hilt.

A silent command to ignite, and his sword always obeyed.

Instantly, *Valor* roared to life. Its enchanted flames billowed around the magnificent blade as he straightened his back and leaned into his stance. An orange glow flickered to life in the small clearing as he stared down the beast of Saldia's nightmares.

"I'm going to enjoy killing you," Zander confessed. A shrill ringing echoed in his ears, and his jaw tensed as he prepared for war.

The wolf chuckled, and the edges of its sneer twisted into a sinister smile. "So close to death, and yet he still makes threats. He is fearless, I will grant him that. Perhaps your time with me has finally come to an end, Farkas."

Zander frowned with confusion as he studied the blightwolf's vacant eyes, and for a fleeting second—just one—the rage fueling him dimmed. A chill snaked down his battered spine, and he wondered yet again if they were not, in fact, alone. He scanned the darkness for another monster lurking in the shadows, but found nothing except for the trees and a painfully quiet evening beyond the crackling circle of orange light.

Tension pulled at his neck and biceps, but his breath came evenly as the fire within his soul overtook him once again. The air thickened with anticipation. His bloodstained grip tightened on his Firesword as he did his best to figure out what game this creature was playing.

He gave the beast a sidelong glance. "What the hell are you—"

"I wasn't speaking to you, human." The blightwolf's sneer dissolved in an instant, and it snapped impatiently at the air between them.

When its jaws clomped shut, an impulsive burst of pain shot down Zander's left shoulder, and he couldn't help but stare at its massive teeth.

In the orange glow radiating from *Valor*, the blightwolf's form shimmered. Its edges blurred and hummed. A shadow rolled across the silver-stained woodland behind it, obscuring the silhouettes of nearby bushes and underbrush. A cricket chirped its half-hearted song, alone in its chorus, and a violent gust of wind kicked through the canopy as something stepped from the blightwolf's body.

The movement struck Zander as simply *wrong*.

A violation of nature, like watching a soul leaving a corpse.

This second form, whatever it was, cast a dark sheen over everything behind it—translucent, like a mirage shivering on the horizon, somehow both real and not truly there. Its shadowy paw flattened the ground in front of the alpha as the hovering blob of darkness escaped the blightwolf. A second paw followed.

The low growl in the clearing grew louder. In a blinding rush, the shimmering form sharpened.

A second blightwolf stepped out of the first. Its piercing yellow eyes, now focused on Zander, glowed even brighter than *Valor's* flame.

Zander froze in place, unable to believe what was happening. Unable to understand. His mind went numb, and for a blissful moment, he couldn't feel anything—not the rage, not the pain in his skull, not even the two Bloodbane wounds slowly eating away at his flesh.

He felt only the shock of frigid disbelief.

Before him stood a second blightwolf made of shadow, yes, but a twisted one. Spikes of metal protruded from a gnarled hump on its back. Its fur—if it could even be called fur—stuck out at odd angles, longer than it should have been, as though a power-mad alchemist had sewn obsidian swords to the hide of a mutated carcass and tricked the Fates into granting his abomination life.

At twice his height, the shadow towered over him. Its long black teeth protruded from its mouth, and it studied him with the half-starved intensity of a predator that had stumbled upon its favorite prey.

With the shadow wolf no longer in its body, the blightwolf alpha went still once more. The growling in the clearing faded completely. The green spellgust gem in the golden hilt glowed brighter than ever, and the silver blightwolf stared at Zander's boots as though it once again awaited his orders. Perfectly obedient, just as any mount wearing the Bridletame helm should be.

Zander had seen many things in his life. He had slayed the dragons that disobeyed him and shown their hearts to their brethren to earn their respect. He had ridden wyverns that once ate men whole, only to beat them into submission through his sheer force of will. He had sliced off the stingers of man-eating scorpions, only to present them later to kings and lords as presents for them to hang on their walls. Necromancers pissed themselves at the mere mention of his name.

Yet never in his life had he seen something like this.

He stood, immobile, in a surreal blend of wonder and disgust as the second blightwolf solidified before him into the sort of twisted demon that couldn't be real. Into something children made up to justify their fears of the dark.

"Curse the Fates," he muttered as he studied the thing, his body and mind still numb with bewilderment. "What are you?"

The shadow didn't answer. Instead, its yellow eyes darted toward the silver wolf behind it. With a flash of jet-black teeth, it ripped the glowing green helm out of the alpha's forehead and spat the hunk of metal and spellgust onto the ground.

Damn it.

The thud of the helm hitting the dirt broke the icy spell this creature had cast over him. His blistering fury returned, and Zander's nose creased with revulsion as it undid his work.

The shadow wolf lowered its head, and its attention returned to Zander as it slunk to the edge of the clearing. It circled, weaving through the trees without so much as a glance backward. He had expected the shadow to attack, but it merely watched from a distance as the alpha came to.

Across from him, the silver blightwolf snarled as its eyes slowly cleared and the last of the Bridletame curse faded from its blood. Its claws dug into the dirt, and its eyes darted toward him, as bright and focused as ever.

His grip on *Valor* tightened as his heart drummed a steady beat with anticipation. He had faced impossible odds before and won. It was simply what Starlings were expected to do. What *he* was expected to do.

Win.

The silver wolf snarled, but its ear twitched toward the shadow circling them. The alpha's head turned toward the demon, its growl fading to silence, and the two beasts locked eyes—as though they spoke words he couldn't hear.

With it distracted, he had an opening to attack. His body tensed in preparation as he scanned its stance. Its throat was exposed, and he could—

The silver wolf's cold gaze shifted again toward Zander, and his window of opportunity passed far more quickly than he had expected.

The alpha bristled. "He says it is time to prove how badly you want to live, little human."

In the silver night beyond the orange ring of *Valor's* firelight, the shadow wolf's glowing yellow eyes left blurred imprints on the darkness as the beast walked. The spikes along its back gleamed in the moonlight, and it silently circled them both.

"And who exactly is he?" Zander asked, not bothering to mask his disdain. "A Starling has nothing to prove, least of all to creatures like you."

The alpha barked, the sound grating and rough on the still air, like a whistle blown in a match to call out a cheating player on the field. "He is the Feral King, you damned *fool,* and you are but a plaything to us both."

Zander froze in place. The claim almost seemed too incredulous, too wild even for these monsters, but he didn't dare let the cold numbness creep back in. If he did, he would lose access to the raging inferno of his reserves, and he would lose the inevitable fight to come.

Heat from his Burnbane fires simmered beneath his skin, and he once more studied the pacing shadow and its glowing yellow eyes.

The twisted demon lowered its head as it finished its first lap around the clearing. It stalked toward him, ignoring everything else—the wind, the alpha, the overbearing silence that proved this woodland knew something had gone terribly wrong in the night.

Zander shifted his weight and raised his sword between them, but he would need a miracle to win this without a Bloodbane dagger.

It seemed this was no ordinary shadow, but a second wraith. Another unholy king, cobbled together from a graveyard and unleashed on this continent by Aeron Zacharias himself.

This couldn't get worse.

No victory against the peasant. No dagger to defend himself. No advantage in the brewing war against the simmering souls. That damned Wraithblade had ruined it all. The peasant had stolen everything that mattered, and more importantly, the fool had stolen from a Starling.

This—all of this—was the Wraithblade's fault. That reminder fueled Zander's rage. It gave him access to his reserves for a little while longer.

Only time would tell if it would last long enough to make a difference.

Bit by bit, pawprint by muddy pawprint, the Feral King closed the distance between them. As it stalked closer, it grinned, and its teeth gleamed in *Valor's* blazing inferno.

When faced with an embodiment of the things that terrorized men in the dark, even the most hardened soldier would've dropped their sword. They would've fallen to their knees in terror and begged for their lives, sobbing and tripping over themselves for a few more precious seconds of life.

Not Zander. He had been born and bred to kill the darkness, no matter the cost. Even if a portal to Hell opened beneath his feet, Zander would find a way out of this and claw his way back to his corpse.

Survival was the only way of life he knew.

"Interesting." Though the silver blightwolf spoke, the Feral King's yellow eyes snared Zander until it felt as though the abomination was merely using the alpha as a mouthpiece.

"What is?" Zander demanded, his tone firm.

"You face certain death, and yet you do not look afraid."

"Because I'm not." He met the monster's glare the way he would face any threat—with his stance firm and his sword ablaze.

It sneered, and light glinted off those soot-black teeth. "I've watched humans over the centuries, and they're all the same—except for a rare few. The ones like you, little warrior of fire. You and your kind, I have watched from afar. You in particular, I wish to study more. You hold many secrets, and I will have them all."

"I won't tell you a damn thing." Zander took a careful step forward, ready to end this. He had vowed to destroy the simmering souls, and one way or another, and it seemed as though the Fates wanted him to start with this one.

"We will see," it said with a wicked sneer. "Now, my little plaything, show me how hot those fires burn. Show me how brutal you Starlings truly are."

CHAPTER SEVEN
ZANDER

The first threads of dawn finally broke through the Enchanted Forest's silver-green canopy. The leaves shivered in the day's drowsy sunbeams, casting a soft blanket of light across the overgrown tangles of thorns across the forest floor. Birds twittered and sang. The slender birches rested in the quiet morning, still as the sky after a fresh snowfall.

A ragged hum pierced the serene landscape.

The sound shook and quivered, uneven and rough, but nothing in the woodland seemed to notice. A flock of finches cut through the leaves and landed on the forest floor to peck for fallen nuts. Two fanged squirrels scampered across a gnarled old branch, their fluffed tails twitching as the pair hunted for shiny things to steal.

The world blurred briefly, as though a fog had darted by and burned off in a matter of seconds. An ache pounded like a drum in Zander's skull, and his mind cleared in a violent rush as he finally came to.

He sputtered and gasped for air. His eyes squeezed shut, but that only made the pain in his head worse. His forehead stung with all the fire of hornets in his brain, and a steady throb of red light pulsed through his eyelids.

Something scratched at his lungs, as though he had inhaled tiny shreds of steel that carved him hollow from the inside out with every breath. Something hot and wet pooled in his mouth, and without even pausing to consider his dignity or pride, he spat it onto the ground.

When he finally blinked the world back into focus, he was on his hands and knees, staring down at a tiny puddle of blood in a boot print. His hands framed either side of it, with his fingers and palms pressed hard into the grass. A red drop fell from his mouth into the rippling pool as he stared at his hazy reflection floating on the surface.

He narrowed his eyes, trying to remember what had happened. Death waited in the shadows—he knew that much. Something in the back of his mind told him to stand, to find his sword and to *fight*, but he couldn't remember what he had been fighting. Something wanted to kill him, but he couldn't remember what he had called it.

A shadow, maybe. No, that didn't make sense. A demon, perhaps. Or a wolf.

He coughed again. The bite of iron and rust coated his tongue. He ran the back of his hand across his mouth to clear away the blood.

His chest ached. Piercing jolts of pain shot through his head with every movement. He tried to stand, but his legs wouldn't obey. He teetered and fell on his elbow, and another bolt of agony ripped through his shoulder. He gritted his teeth and forced himself to breathe through the misery.

He had to get ahold of himself. To snap out of this and get on his Fates-damned feet.

Throughout this life, in so many training sessions that he had lost count, his father had pushed him harder even than this. He had been thrown to the edge of death and brought back, again and again, all in the name of protecting his family.

It fell to Zander to grow the enduring legacy he had inherited, and he was nothing without his name.

A Starling was strong.

A Starling persevered.

If Zander could survive his father, he could survive anything.

A numb prickle shot across his abdomen and slowly faded—but as it disappeared, the mind-blistering pain returned. In his left side, something burned with all the fires of hell. The same scorching fury roared across his left shoulder. Something poured down his right arm, hot and wet. He brushed it away with his hand, but it didn't leave. Instead, a strange red goo clung to his fingers, stretching between them like sticky webbing.

Blood.

His blood.

He studied his right arm, and his vision blurred again as a red cascade bubbled from three long gouges in his bicep—three lines that reminded him of claw marks.

It came back to him, then.

The Feral King.

The blightwolf.

The brutal fight for his life.

Images rattled through his skull, and each hit him like a blow to the head. Only bits and pieces of it remained, like shreds of memory that had been chewed and spat out. Teeth. The chomp of a jaw inches from his face. The snap of bones. The whimper of a dog. The crackle of flame, and the charred stench of burning fur.

And through it all, those floating yellow eyes in the darkness.

Foggy black and gray circles bubbled at the edge of his vision as he fought to stay awake. His lungs screamed for air even as his chest ached with every movement. His shirt clung to his back, fused to his skin from all of the blood and sweat, but he didn't care. Even the worst filth could be washed away after a victory.

He tried again to push himself onto his feet, but the ground seemed to tilt underneath him. His head spun, and he lost track of the sky. Before he could even get his feet under him, his arm gave out, and he fell.

His head hit the cold dirt with a hollow thud. A shrill scream echoed in his ears, almost like a voice, but he couldn't make sense of it.

As he opened his eyes once again, the tip of a leaf sank into the pool of blood beside him. Ripples broke across the still surface like waves on a lake. He stared at it, unable to hear anything other than the ringing in his ears.

No excuses.

No respite.

He had to finish this, no matter the cost.

A heavy fog churned in his brain. He groaned and raised a shaky hand to rub his face. The stinging in his eyes worsened, and his heavy eyelids drifted closed. The ground supported his weight, and never before had he felt so comfortable.

So calm.

The cold soil against his cheek began to warm. A gentle wind meandered through the leaves like waves crashing on a shore, soft and steady, quiet and soothing.

If only he could rest, he would have more energy.

He just needed sleep. A little nap, in the scheme of things, would be fine.

Even a few minutes would help. He could certainly afford that much.

A pang of dread shot through him like a spear of ice to the heart. His eyes snapped open, and he caught himself seconds before he drifted off. The jolt cleared his head like a cold shower, and the ringing in his ears faded to almost nothing.

To sleep now meant surrendering to death, and he wasn't ready to go. Not yet. Not after everything he had endured. Not after everything he had sacrificed to make it this far.

It took a few moments to finally blink away the daze, but the trees finally came into view once again. Leaves. Dappled sunlight on the soil. Tangles of thorny underbrush. Spatters of blood across the bark. Claw marks in the trees. Chunks of fur floating in yet another crimson puddle, not far away.

"The alpha." His voice came out as more of a wheeze than coherent words, and he sputtered as something wet blocked the back of his throat. He coughed until the blockage cleared, but he didn't bother to look at what came out.

He didn't know how much blood he had left in him, and he didn't need to watch any more of it leave.

Though he still couldn't stand, he craned his neck and scanned the meadow again for signs of his opponent. At first, he caught only moments in time as his vision drifted in and out of focus. A rabbit peering out from a bush. A bloody handprint on a tree trunk. His sword sticking out of the earth, its spellgust gem glittering with raw power.

With an agonized groan, he pushed himself onto his palms and rested his remaining weight on his knees. He stayed there, leaning on all fours like an animal until his vision finally sharpened long enough for him to get his bearings.

At the edge of the bloodstained clearing, the silver blightwolf lay beneath a weeping willow. The tree's long green branches shielded half of the massive creature, though the beast's tail and hind legs protruded from beneath the wall of pale leaves.

An impossibly dark shadow darted through the sun-filled gaps between the willow and a nearby oak. Zander squinted, trying to make sense of it through his hazy thoughts.

Spikes protruded from the shadow's twisted back. The dark wolf's silhouette obscured the forest beyond it for only a moment before it disappeared behind a cluster of fir trees.

The Feral King.

It had watched all night, but it had never once engaged. Thus far, it had merely supervised the fight to the death, but it would inevitably attack. He had to figure out the beast's game, and soon.

This abomination had called him its plaything, but it would soon learn the truth. He had become a boogeyman in the night to all who threatened his family's seat of power, and it would come to fear him, too.

He refused to die out here, like a peasant eaten by the forest. He deserved a better death than that.

A flash of light in the corner of his eye blinded him. A ripple of pain shot through his skull, and he grimaced. He raised one bloodstained hand to block out the glow until he could make sense of where it had come from. A loose lock of his fire-red hair hung in his eye, scratching at his skin, but he didn't have the energy to brush it away.

Sunlight glinted off a dagger within arm's reach—one of his, one he usually kept in his boot. A layer of dirt glazed the once-vibrant silver handle, and a dark red sheen coated the blade.

Fine. The dagger wasn't his Firesword, but since he could barely stand, crawling a hearty distance away from his target to get a better blade would be foolish. This pathetic little dagger—something he usually drew as an afterthought in his battles—would have to do.

He grabbed the knife. The movement toppled his balance, and he fell yet again. This wouldn't work. He needed leverage, something to carry him until he regained sensation in his legs.

Even as his fingers slipped along the hilt, he drove the blade into the dirt. With the dagger firmly planted in the soil, he pulled on it to drag himself forward. His bicep flexed with the effort, and the dagger tilted toward him as it nearly slid out of the earth—but he still managed to drag himself a bit closer to his mark.

Inelegant, but effective.

As he hauled himself across the ground, the silver blightwolf didn't move. If it heard him coming, it didn't have the strength to stop him.

Good.

He drove his dagger into the soil again and dragged himself forward, closing the gap between them, inch by painful inch.

Not much farther now.

A gentle breeze parted the willow branches, like a maid pulling aside a curtain to reveal the day outside. The broken blightwolf stretched across the grass at the base of the trunk. Its side rose and fell with each ragged breath. Smoke wafted from lingering embers of burning fur on its back. A long gouge in its side ran from its shoulder to its rump. Deep slashes covered its legs to the point where he couldn't tell bloodstained fur from exposed muscle.

Almost there.

A gouge across the beast's eye trailed down to its snout. Its tongue lolled out of its open mouth, and drool oozed onto the flattened grass beneath its head. The wounded eye didn't open as Zander neared.

Fragments of a plan hovered just out of reach. He gritted his teeth as he dragged himself over the final few yards between him and the alpha, trying all the while to remember what he had been trying to do. His mind buzzed and rippled as his body threatened to quit on him.

Not yet, he silently demanded. *You can't fail me now.*

The plan. He had to remember.

He stabbed the dagger into the soil, and the memory hit him, then: the Bridletame helm. Even to his delirious mind, the idea of trying to fix or strengthen it seemed like a fool's errand, but he couldn't just kill the alpha.

If he did that, the Feral King would do what every simmering soul did when it lost its host—fuse with the closest living thing.

With *him*.

His arm roared in protest every time he stabbed the dagger into the ground. He grunted with the effort of hauling himself across the bloodstained grass, and the blightwolf flinched at the sound of his voice. Through the thin gaps in the willow's canopy, the wolf's ears pivoted toward him, and it tried to lift its head.

It failed.

The beast whimpered and fell back onto the grass, immobile except for the rise and fall of its belly as it struggled for air.

"Serves you right," Zander spat, his words slurring together.

After what felt like ages, he finally reached the edge of the willow. With its claws close enough to touch, he did his best to give the sharpest points on the blightwolf's body a wide berth and hauled himself toward its head. With its swollen eye closest to him, he pulled himself farther, until he could see its whole face.

When he finally swatted aside the willow branches to reach the thing's head, its one good eye was already watching him.

Waiting.

Ready.

It gave a half-hearted snarl, but the growl turned into a sputtering wheeze halfway through. A robin twittered overhead, and the blightwolf's ear twitched on impulse toward the birdsong. It twitched again, away from them, this time toward something Zander couldn't hear over the ringing in his head.

The blightwolf's wheezing became a quiet chuckle. Raspy gasps punctuated the laughter as it built, louder with every second, growing stronger as the brutal beast's entire body shook with every breath.

"Gone mad, have you?" Zander spat blood onto the grass as he scanned the field for the helm. The dagger's warm metal hilt weighed on his palm, far heavier than it should've been.

"On the contrary." The blightwolf closed its good eye and chuckled as its breathing slowed. "I finally won."

"Stupid, vile thing." Zander leaned on his elbows, managing to raise his body just enough to glare it in the eye.

It had lost, and it had lost badly.

"You humans are blind as bats," it said, still laughing. "Even with all that power."

Inches from death, and yet it still had the gall to laugh in his face.

A bead of sweat—or maybe blood, he couldn't tell anymore—fell into Zander's eye, and he rubbed it away with the heel of his palm. His vision blurred, and as he blinked away the haze, the looming shadow of the Feral King appeared briefly through a gap in the willow tree's branches.

A distant howl echoed through the forest. He tilted his head to figure out where it had come from, but it seemed to surround him. As quickly as it had come, it faded to almost nothing, and the twitter of birds drowned out the lingering echoes as the forest ignored the approaching danger. The ringing in his ears grew louder as he strained to listen, still trying to pinpoint where the howl had come from.

"Damn it," Zander muttered under his breath. "They're here."

"All I had to do was distract you," the wolf said through its wheezing laughter. "I knew I wouldn't make it out of this clearing alive, but I didn't care as long as I took you with me. I hope I live long enough to watch them rip you apart. I want to hear you scream, Starling. I want to know what your fear tastes like."

Oh, *shit*.

An avalanche of cold dread crashed through Zander as he finally pieced together this thing's plan. It had worn him down to allow the rest of the pack time to catch up to them. It had never intended to survive their fight, only to make his retreat impossible. Now that its helm was gone, the other blightwolves wouldn't hold back. They would do what they had wanted to do back in the Decay, and they would rip him to shreds.

He had been played.

The alpha's grim laughter grew louder, though it was more strained wheezing than anything else, and it watched him with all the mirth of a man watching a comedy.

It relished this moment. It savored his horror.

Beneath Zander's broken body, a subtle, almost unnoticeable rumble shook the ground. He set his palm on the dirt as the approaching tremor of a stampede reached him.

He cursed under his breath. Stiffening, he scanned the forest. A surge of agony ripped through his spine with even the slightest twist of his head, however, and he was forced to stop. He gritted his teeth and shut his eyes to ride out the waves of pain, but it was no good. Even if he still had the drive to fight, this thing had broken his body.

Climbing a tree would've been his best bet at survival, but he could hardly stand. In his battered state, getting high enough in the branches to remain out of reach of a blightwolf would've been impossible.

He couldn't run. He couldn't seek cover. Even with his considerable power, he couldn't fight. Not anymore. Not after the duel that had siphoned the last of his energy and left him unable to even stand.

For the first time in his life, Zander Starling had run out of options.

The thought struck him as unnatural. Surreal. Wrong, on so many levels, to think he might actually *lose*.

With his wealth and lifelong training, he had never lost. Not really. Not in the end. Even his defeat against the Wraithblade had come on his terms. He knew when to withdraw to fight his way to victory another day.

But here, alone in the wilderness, he had run out of tricks.

He had nothing.

Unless...

Zander peered over his shoulder at the edge of the clearing. The Feral King didn't show itself, but he could practically feel its eyes on him as it paced through the trees. He could sense its path as the hairs on his neck stood on end, always wary of the atrocity of nature lurking nearby.

Simmering souls gave their hosts incredible power and new abilities. Most notably, the Wraith King had given Henry the ability to heal faster and more completely, even from the gravest of wounds.

Perhaps the other simmering souls could grant a similar healing ability.

If so, his only way out of this mess was to do the unthinkable.

The rumble beneath his palm grew louder, and the vibrations carried up his arm.

When facing impossible odds, his father had taught him to look for all options, even the unsavory ones. There was always a choice, somewhere in the rubble, that could mean the difference between failure and survival.

And here, today, the only way out of the forest was through the Feral King—not in killing it, but in stealing it for himself.

Maybe it had known all along how this would end. From the beginning, it had pitted him and the alpha against each other. It had likely known all along that the duel would end this way.

Perhaps this abomination just wanted to see which choice he made.

Fates be damned. It had played him, and either way, it would win.

No, be rational, he chided himself. *Think your way out of this.*

The blightwolves obeyed the alpha, and now he knew why—the silver wolf had the power of the Feral King behind it.

Perhaps Zander could take that power for himself and force the blightwolves to obey *him*.

Desperate as it was, the idea repulsed him. He was destined to become the Great Lightseer. Destroying the simmering souls would give him the leverage he needed to cement his place in history and outshine even his father. For a Lightseer, infamy was the only way to become immortal.

To fuse with the very darkness he sought to eradicate went against everything he stood for. It violated everything he had been raised to believe about himself and the world.

The rumble beneath his palms became a quake. His mind hummed with half-baked ideas as he fought to concoct a better solution, but nothing else came to him. He had run out of time, and he had to choose between his morals and his life.

There are plenty of noble Lightseers in the grave, son, his father had told him once.

It was the night he had first received his Firesword. His Father had set those calloused hands on Zander's shoulders and, for the first time, said he was proud of all Zander had accomplished thus far.

He was finally worthy. He was finally good enough.

They were honorable, yes, but they're still dead, my boy, his father had warned. *Those men and women carried Lightseer secrets to the grave. I trained them to live by that code to protect you, Zander. To protect the Starling name. It's time you learned the truth, son. You and I live by a different code because we are what the Lightseers protect. You are the future of Lunestone. You are their future, Zander, and you are mine—which means the darkness in this world will hunt you until your final breath. If you must one day choose between death and dishonor, don't you dare choose death.*

Zander went absolutely still. Even as the vibrations in the ground shook his arms, he sat with the weight of what he was about to do.

Wondering if he could truly bring himself to go through with it.

You are the future of Lunestone.

His father's voice echoed again in his mind, as sharp and stern as it had been that night all those years ago.

Don't you dare choose death.

CHAPTER EIGHT
ZANDER

As the rumble of paws against the dirt became a thunder, Zander's grip on the dagger in his hand tightened.

His heart raced with the impossibility of what he had to do to survive, but the alpha was right. No matter what Zander did at this point, he wouldn't be able to evade a pack of blightwolves. Neither he nor the alpha could even stand.

The Fates had forced him into a corner, and he would rather betray his Lightseer Code than die as some blightwolf's breakfast.

As he slowly accepted the inevitable, his breathing settled. His pulse evened out. He relaxed, despite the pounding ache in his skull and jolts of pain down his legs.

He stared at the patchy grass beneath him, and though his vision blurred once again, his mind had never been more clear.

When he had first headed to Slaybourne, he had been willing to make the ultimate sacrifice—to carry the Wraith King if the need arose. It had been the worst case scenario, of course, but it was something he would've done if all else failed.

Here and now, all else had failed.

He would do what he had always done—overcome. The tomes of history would remember him as the Great Lightseer, even with this setback. He had little doubt of that. He would twist the simmering soul to do his bidding, but he would never succumb. He hadn't come this far to be remembered only as the prodigal son who could've been great.

The Starlings were unconquerable, even by the worst of the darkness.

Fusing with the enemy would be only temporary. If anything, it was an advantage. A chance to observe the abomination up close and learn its weaknesses. When the other simmering souls were destroyed, Zander would find a way to remove this one's stain from him and destroy it, too.

He scowled at the alpha. Its laughter faded, and now it could only suck in greedy, rattling breaths. A howl pierced the air, and this time, a flock of birds scattered from the treetops.

Close. Too close.

Using his forearms, Zander crawled closer to the blightwolf's face. The dagger's hilt slipped in his palm, but he tightened his fingers to keep his grip on it. A bolt of pain shot up his arm with the movement, but he steeled himself against the discomfort and ignored it as best he could.

—ignore it—ignore it—ignore it—

He reached the wolf's skull in seconds and raised the dagger. It didn't look up. Its good eye remained shut. It chuckled on the out breaths and wheezed with each inhale as it barely clung to what little life it had left.

As he held the weapon in his right hand, he set his left palm on the dirt to steady himself. The rumble of paws beneath his hand vibrated up his forearm.

He was out of time.

The dagger's steel glinted in the sunlight as he set the tip of the blade against the base of the wolf's ear. His sister Victoria had taught him her theories about this weak spot on a blightwolf's skull, back when they had caught and drained their first blightwolves. She had found the theory in an old book, and she had been delighted when it worked.

It seemed so long ago, now, that she had asked him to track down some wolves for her experiments. So long ago that she had brewed that first bubbling green concoction with nothing more than a half-baked idea and all the wealth in the world to try it for herself, consequences be damned.

The alpha didn't seem to notice the blade pressed against its skull. Its ear twitched, but it didn't resist. At this point, it couldn't do a damn thing to stop him.

Maybe it knew that. Maybe it didn't care.

He drove the blade into the beast's brain. Bone snapped. The hulking terror of the night went limp, and it let out one last wheezing exhale as its lungs deflated. He gagged on the rancid rot of its dying breath.

Lying beneath the weeping willow, the blightwolf seemed almost asleep. All of the hatred dissolved from its face as the tips of the soft green willow branches petted its tangled silver fur.

And yet, nothing happened.

Zander's chest heaved with effort as he studied the vacant woodland. The crickets went silent. In the painfully still air, an old oak creaked somewhere nearby, and even the willow branches went limp as the breeze died. He cocked one eyebrow in disbelief as he surveyed the canopy, wondering if he had done something wrong.

Perhaps the wolf had conned him. Perhaps that twisted beast hadn't been the Feral King at all. Perhaps he would have to concoct another plan in the seconds before the blightwolves arrived.

He cursed under his breath and forced himself onto one knee as the gashes in his side bubbled with fresh blood. A small river trickled down his arm as he set his palm on the rumbling dirt, and he glared up at the willow tree, wondering if he could find a way to haul himself into the branches in time.

In his periphery, a shadow rose from the alpha's head and hovered above the dead blightwolf. Its warping edges blurred and shimmered, and Zander squinted as he watched the pulsating mass rise from the beast's corpse.

As his mouth parted in wonder, it darted toward him.

Everything in his body screamed at him to duck. To twist out of the way. To let it sail by and evade it at any cost.

Though it took effort, he forced himself to remain still.

To take it.

The pulsating black mass hit him hard in the chest and kicked the air from his lungs. The force knocked him backward, and his head slammed hard against the dirt.

Something he couldn't see reached into his ribcage and dug its claws into his heart.

The surreal sensation lifted him off the forest floor and hurled him backward through the trees. Brown blurs whizzed past as he grappled to control the vile enchantment tearing into him. Blisters of pain bubbled and burst behind his eyes, and his vision faded completely. He gritted his teeth, fighting back an agonized yell as something clawed its way into his very soul.

Agonizing and disorienting, yes, but also somewhat familiar.

After all, he and pain were old friends.

On your feet, boy. His father's voice boomed in the back of his head, louder than the agony.

Any lingering sensations of his legs or hands dissolved into nothing as the claw in his chest dug deeper. His jaw ached from gritting his teeth, but he couldn't stop. He had no control over his body. Not anymore.

Be a man! his father's warbling voice demanded. It echoed, wet and distant, as though Teagan Starling had yelled at him from below the waves.

Zander's head hit something hard. A rock, maybe, or the cold stone tile floor in the sparring room back in Lunestone.

He bit back furious tears, ten years old again and lost in the memory of his father summoning more fire into his massive, callused palm.

Face the pain and laugh at it, boy. Or would you rather train with the women?

Hatred blurred with his shame. Zander wasn't good enough to be in the royal training hall, not really, but he had to at least try to earn his place here.

A fist hit his jaw with a thunderous crack. His brain shook in his skull. Seconds later, before his vision could clear, the cold bite of steel plunged into his bicep. Something hot and wet rolled down his arm.

It was too much. He bit back a sob. He wanted to find his mother, to get one of her Rectivane potions and heal, but a boot crunched his ribs. He screamed and fell again to the ground, those frantic tears hot and heavy as they tried to break free, but he refused to cry. Not in front of his father. Not now.

A Starling doesn't cry, boy.

He swallowed hard, and the tears disappeared.

You want to quit?

No, sir.

Not now.

Not ever.

Zander's leg slammed into a rock, and the jolt of pain shocked him back into the forest, back to the blightwolf, back to the Feral King and the shadow that had hit him in the chest. He forced his eyes open to find a hurricane of colors smearing around him, like a child's failed attempt to fingerpaint.

Nothing made sense. The sky had vanished, and he couldn't see the ground.

The claw tightened its grip around his heart, and Zander yelled his own twisted battle cry to block out the pain. Something clutched his lungs, squeezing as it tried to suffocate him from within, but he tensed his body until he could force a breath.

Just one. Even a single breath was a victory.

Nothing would dominate him, not in the end. Nothing would stop him. Nothing and no one—not even Aeron Zacharias himself—would come between him and all he had left to do in this lifetime.

His back slammed into something hard, and a splintering crack cut through the air. He couldn't tell if a tree had broken or if his spine had fractured, but he didn't care anymore.

Whatever it took, he would get back to Lunestone eventually. Whoever he had to kill, whatever he had to become, it would all be worth it in the end.

The hurricane in his head slowed to a gust, until the blurring smears of color finally—blissfully—settled. The smearing color became hazy silhouettes that darted between blurry brown pillars, but he still couldn't make sense of it all.

Though his vision slowly returned, the pain in his body only worsened. The grip on his heart squeezed until he couldn't feel his own pulse anymore. The agony in his chest and left side built to a crescendo as the fires of the Bloodbane injuries boiled him alive.

His revulsion at having to debase himself to such a low to survive overwhelmed the misery.

Don't you dare choose death, Zander.

"I didn't!" he screamed. He didn't care who heard him. He didn't care how demented he sounded, or if he had even formed words. "And even if the Fates themselves come for me, I never will!"

That broke the spell.

The grip on his lungs disappeared. He gasped for air, and this time, it seeped into his lungs. Relief flooded through him. Though his throat still ached with every breath, the unseen claw released his heart.

His head cleared in a rush. The shrill screech in his ear quieted to almost nothing, and the rustle of wind through leaves soon replaced it. As the minutes passed, the peaceful chirp of distant birdsong joined in with the chorus of a forest at its best.

He gulped in breath after greedy breath. Slowly, carefully, he curled his fingers into a weak fist. Sensation rippled up his arm. The numbness in his legs faded, and he curled his toes. The sizzling tension in his back was gone, and the thumping in his head slowed like a dying man's pulse, until it, too, finally stopped.

How badly do you want to live? The voice didn't sound like his father's anymore, but through the ringing in his ears and his own battle cry piercing the air, he couldn't place it.

A dull alarm buzzed in the back of his hazy mind, and a jolt of urgency shot through him. After all, he didn't have long before the pack of blightwolves found him, and he didn't know what to expect when they did. Even if his attempt to steal the Feral King had worked, he didn't know how they would react to discovering their murdered alpha beneath a willow.

Despite how tired and bruised as he was, he didn't have the luxury of taking even a moment to recover.

With a groan, he rubbed his face and blinked away the final foggy blurs. The simple movement shook him, pushing his battered bones to the limit, but at least he could move. His eyes adjusted to the sunshine, and the fuzzy brown pillars sharpened to tree trunks.

But he wasn't alone. Not anymore.

Half a dozen blightwolves studied him from between the trees. A gentle breeze ruffled their metallic fur as life returned to the forest. They towered above him with their dark eyes already locked on his face.

Ears alert and still as statues, they waited.

Zander stiffened. He needed a weapon, and his Firesword would serve him best. He scanned the forest around him, but he didn't recognize this stretch of trees. A broken line of shattered branches traced the path he had taken through the forest as whatever the Feral King did to him had dragged him along the ground. The meadow was long gone, as were the willow and the alpha. His Firesword lay somewhere far beyond this place, and it couldn't help him now.

Of the six blightwolves standing around him, a black one stood nearest. It watched him more intently than the others, as though it alone knew what he had done, and he held its gaze to buy himself some time. Gingerly, he felt around the grass beside him, only to discover that the small dagger he had used to kill the alpha was gone, likely somewhere between here and the silver blightwolf's corpse.

With a few glances around the woodland, he took stock of his opponents. Two brown wolves and a white one stood between the trees to his left, and three jet-black beasts stood to his right.

Yet, none of them moved. They simply examined him from afar, immobile and silent in a forest they didn't own. Two fanged squirrels scampered up a tree behind the largest of the black wolves, and a bird sang in the branches above them as the woodland came to life.

Time to regain his ground.

Zander pushed himself to his feet, and the six blightwolves stepped back in unison. He teetered, just once, and caught himself on the nearest thing—the towering oak that had stopped his flight through the woods. Its bark scratched at his palm as he leaned his full weight into it, unwilling to fall back down. Refusing to show weakness.

Whatever it took, he had to at least *stand*.

Through sheer stubborn grit, he rose to his feet and leaned his back against the oak for support. His legs ached, but at least he could feel them again. His head swam, but at least his vision didn't blur.

It was progress.

He was already healing, and even faster than he had seen Henry heal in his time with the Wraith King. He studied his hands, and though bloodstained dirt crusted his fingers, the bruises from his fight with the alpha had faded to almost nothing.

Astonishing.

His desperate, twisted plan had worked. Whatever the Feral King had done to him, it seemed as though it had begun to restore his strength.

Good. At least the atrocity was useful. Now, he needed an exit strategy. A way past the small circle of wolves before the rest found him.

As his strength seeped slowly back into his bones, he risked a quick scan of the forest—but with every glance, yet another blightwolf stepped into view. He lost count as dozens of them circled his tree, and his mouth set into a grim line as his opportunity for escape dwindled to nothing.

For whatever reason, none of them growled. None of them snapped at him. None of them even came close, except for the massive black wolf standing almost within reach. They all simply watched him, their metallic fur glistening like thousands of multi-colored swords in the morning sunlight.

Zander took a settling breath as he adjusted his weight against the tree and debated his options. It was time to see if his desperate ploy had truly paid off.

"You, there." In an effort to feign a full recovery and mask the pain lingering in every muscle, he merely nodded toward the black monstrosity that towered over the others as it stared down at him. "Take me to Lunestone."

The blightwolf didn't move or acknowledge that he had spoken. It didn't even blink.

Zander narrowed his eyes in warning, but before he could speak, a dark chuckle echoed in his head, as grim as the voices he had concocted for the gremlins in his childhood bedtime stories. It rippled through his brain, and he flinched with surprise. The voice reached into him, traveling down his spine, coiling around him from within like a sea serpent twisting around a ship.

Though he tried to keep his eye on the black blightwolf and remain in command of the moment, the rippling voice built to an overwhelming crescendo in his head. He pressed his fingertips against his scalp to relieve the pressure, but the crushing sensation of a tentacle coiling around his brain only worsened as he tried to fight it.

My wolves are not so easily bought, Zander Starling.

The voice rumbled like a storm in his mind, and he grimaced with disgust at the abomination's brazen violation of his thoughts.

Given how much he had endured and how little he had slept in the past few days, he almost lost control. Fire pushed against his palms, desperate to be freed and aching to destroy something. To burn someone alive if that was what it took to let off some steam.

None of the legends had prepared him for this. He had seen the way Henry looked at the wraith, as though they spoke words no one else could hear, but he had never imagined what the sensation would be like. The lack of control. The voice, unbidden, bouncing around in his mind as if it belonged there. As if it had planted wicked thoughts on its visit.

As if it owned him, now.

But his father had taught him, in all their countless sparring sessions, that showing even a hint of weakness meant losing the battle before it had even begun. He would not lose to this atrocity of nature, and he would never let it know the depths of his raw loathing for it and its creator.

It took everything he had left, but he swallowed the impulse to torch the nearest living thing. His magic sputtered beneath his skin, but he kept it at bay through sheer willpower.

"Get out of my head," he demanded, his voice far calmer than he truly felt.

I rather like it in here.

He scowled, his nose wrinkling with disgust at its audacity. This time, a thin flame broke through his defenses and erupted over his palms. Fire rolled over his fingers, and his arm shook as he fought to restrain himself from letting the inferno loose.

A Starling always persevered, and this would be no different.

With a soft crack of his knuckles, he closed his hand into a fist. The blaze extinguished, and he let out a settling breath as he regained control.

Go on, Starling, the grim voice said in his ear. *Destroy everything you see. Burn this forest to the ground, if you must. I want to see what you can do.*

He spun around with his fists raised, ready for a fight and expecting to spot the Feral King behind him.

The gathered blightwolves took another wary step back as they studied him in silence, their ears perked and focused as they waited, but the shadow had yet to appear. The sharp whistle of birdsong floated by, oddly out of place in the circle of mythical monsters.

"Show yourself," Zander ordered.

In a moment, it answered. *First, you must tell me what you want most.*

"I won't play your games." His jaw tensed, and his back ached from the sheer effort of restraining his magic. "Step out here and face me, you coward."

Coward, is it? The unseen abomination laughed. Its raspy cackle floated through his brain, overriding his focus and skewering his own thoughts on its way. *You crave power and respect, that much is obvious, but what else? Do you want their loyalty? Do you want them to die for you?*

"Of course," Zander spat. He glared at the wolves around him, knowing full well he wouldn't stand a chance if they attacked. He could stand, sure, but his body still begged for rest.

Good. You're less of a fool than I thought.

Zander bristled at the gall of this creature. He wanted it to step forward so that he could break its jaw and maybe rip off an ear, but he took a shallow breath to settle his temper.

That didn't work, of course, but it did give him a moment to clear his head.

This beast couldn't be dominated in the same way as a mortal one. If he wanted this plan of his to work, he had to be patient. Admittedly, patience had always been one of the few things that had never come easily to him, but he had to try.

They want to eat you. The faceless voice chuckled again. *And yet, I'm fused to you now. I have a new plaything, and they don't dare kill my playthings until I grow bored. As you can imagine, they're quite upset.*

Zander wanted to tell the thing not to get comfortable, but he held his tongue.

True loyalty is rare. The voice in his head echoed, the words lapping over each other like ripples colliding in a pond, and Zander grimaced as he fought to make sense of it. *A man can be bought or seduced, but a blightwolf's devotion to their alpha is unyielding. Unwavering. Insatiable. It is powerful because it comes* at such a hefty price. With that in mind, dear plaything, how can a man earn the loyalty of the very things that want to rip out his throat?

As Zander's gaze swept across the wolves, he didn't reply. They hadn't eaten him, and that at least worked in his favor.

Answer me, the voice said dryly. *My playthings are only fun when they speak to me.*

He bit back another scathing retort, but his attempt at patience wouldn't last much longer. This thing was practically begging him to kill it, and he didn't want to play into its hands again. One way or another, he had to regain the advantage.

"I assume you have a point," he finally answered. "I was waiting for you to get to it."

So impatient.

"If you only knew," he muttered under his breath.

Very well, plaything, here it is," the rippling voice said. *I have granted you a right to trial. The only blightwolf law is that of respect, and the alpha must earn it from every living member of the pack. That means no alpha, not even Farkas of the Dark Fogs, earns the title without completing the Kurultai. Our pack is wide and travelled, so all four factions will meet for the event. Prove yourself in the arena, and every blightwolf will die for you. Prove yourself, and they will forgive all you have done.*

"An arena?" He scoffed, doubtful that some tournament could change every mind in the pack.

You don't believe me, the abomination said with a curious tilt to its voice.

Zander shook his head, and the black blightwolf closest to him growled in warning. He met its unflinching gaze. If any of them were to attack, this one would clearly reach him first.

Its dark face scrunched, and its long snout wrinkled as its snarl grew louder. With his back firmly planted against the tree for balance, Zander lifted his fists again and allowed the fire in his hands to crackle to life in answer.

None of that, now, the faceless voice said with a patronizing chuckle. *Each of them wants you dead, Starling, for what you have done to their brothers and sisters. You have taken fifteen blightwolf lives when only the alpha has that power. You did what only Farkas was permitted to do, and the price for your actions is death. They will give you hell in the Kurultai, and you will either earn your place among them or die in your attempt.*

"And if I refuse?" His gaze never strayed from the black wolf before him.

They will watch from afar, waiting for me to grow bored, and with time I will grant them what they want. What will it be, Starling? Their loyalty, or a lonely trek back to a home I will only destroy?

Zander entertained the idea as he stood there, surrounded by the very pack of blightwolves he had tried to drain for their blood. Victoria would've sacrificed a hundred servants to even stand this close to them, much less have their complete loyalty.

The thought intrigued him, to say the least.

Though the haunting specter in his head presented this as a choice, Zander knew better. He couldn't continue on to Lunestone until he figured out how to control his new connection to this atrocity. He had no idea what this thing would do if he left the isolation of the woods. Most likely, it would test his authority at every turn. Henry had controlled his simmering soul through the promise of blood, but even that had failed in the end.

No, Zander couldn't be around another human—much less a Lightseer or, worse, his family—until he could bend the Feral King to his will and keep it hidden. If anyone discovered it, he risked the same fate as Henry even with the power of his family name behind him. Perhaps his father would understand what he had done, but no one else would.

After fusing with the Feral King, his body already hurt less. Even the blistering agony of the Bloodbane wounds in his side and shoulder had begun to fade. Given the proper time to recover, he would be at his peak once more. He could delay and stall their travel until he was refreshed, and if he eventually chose to step into the arena after all, he would do so at his full power.

"And you?" he asked the faceless voice. "How does one earn your loyalty?"

Become the alpha, of course.

Zander could almost taste the lie as it reverberated through his mind. His fists tightened, and the billowing flames in his hands burned hotter.

What will it be, Starling?

His gaze drifted to the ground as he thought through the many ways this could go wrong. He had little information to go on, and yet, the blightwolves hadn't attacked. If they were going to swarm him, they would've done it by now.

Perhaps he truly had earned himself a temporary ceasefire. Only a fool would surrender the opportunity to learn more about the beasts Saldia feared most. He could discover their dens, their laws, and any number of ways to manipulate them to his will or destroy them once and for all. Provided the Feral King was telling the truth about blightwolf loyalty, completing this test would also mean controlling the creatures that terrified even the Lightseer elite. To march through Oakenglen with the wolves in tow would force every nobleman and king to bow before him, and he would have whatever army or throne he asked for.

The loyalty of the blightwolves would guarantee him everything he had ever wanted.

More importantly, it would grant him an alternative means of studying the abomination. Whatever he gleaned would be fodder to use against it when the time came to destroy it.

"I need to retrieve my Firesword first," he demanded.

Of course.

"Very well." He relaxed his stance and shook the fire from his hands. "I'll indulge you."

The voice didn't answer.

He frowned and scanned the woodland, waiting for another rippling echo to pierce his thoughts, but nothing came. Above, the leaves clapped together in a brief rush of wind as the otherwise silent forest waited for the intruders to leave.

A puff of dark smoke erupted midair, roughly ten yards ahead. The black mist coiled in a strikingly similar way to the Wraith King, but instead of a skeletal figure draped in a robe, twisted metal spikes emerged from the inky shadows. A flash of sunlight glinted off the jagged spear protruding from a mutated hump. The shadows of the churning black fog swallowed all light around it, as though the Fates had summoned a portal to the next life.

Yellow eyes appeared first in the darkness. A massive paw emerged next from the haze, and it flattened a small white flower as the Feral King's claws sank into the dirt. The simmering soul's glowing eyes focused on Zander, as though it knew his mission was to destroy the very thing he had become, but he stood taller at the challenge.

You intrigue me. The Feral King's yellow eyes narrowed as the last of the black smoke faded into the sunlight. *With all the blood on your hands, I can hardly wait to see what you destroy next.*

Oh, there was *plenty* Zander wanted to destroy. Slaybourne. The Wraithblade. Maybe Quinn, too, for good measure. Yet here he was, stuck wandering the backwater woods with these feral savages for the foreseeable future.

Every moment spent on this detour gave his enemies more power. His father would ride for war, and the inevitable clash in the Decay would be the stuff of legend.

Zander would miss it *all*.

He didn't know how long he would be gone from Saldia, nor could he guess how much of it would survive in his absence.

With a settling breath, he clenched his jaw and steeled himself against what lay ahead. To survive—to master the darkness—he had no choice but to walk beside it.

In his silence, the wretched Feral King studied him with those glowing yellow eyes. Unfazed, Zander met the beast's gaze, just as he had both times he'd faced the Wraith King. And in that moment, as before, he felt nothing.

No fear.

No dread.

Just the icy knowledge of what had to be done, and the unwavering willpower to do it.

CHAPTER NINE
CONNOR

In the depths of the catacombs beneath Slaybourne, only the crackle and pops of Connor's torch filled the silence. Its orange circle of firelight stretched into the shadows and illuminated every imperfection in the tunnel's stone floor.

Ahead of him, just out of reach and at the edge of the light, the Wraith King led the way through the darkness. The ends of that tattered old cloak floated behind him, its frayed ribbons caught on the winds of the dead in an otherwise stagnant tunnel. The old king's hood covered his cracked skull, and the aged bones of his hands appeared as bright white flashes in the gloom.

Step by whisper-silent step, Connor descended into the depths of the ancient fortress. The hair on his neck and arms stood at attention, acutely aware that the darkness hid something else, something *other*, and his mind played tricks on him in the oppressive quiet.

No matter how high he raised the torch, he could never spot the ceiling or the walls. Only the floor, and only the ghoul ahead of him. Whatever tunnel the wraith had chosen stretched taller and wider than he could guess—if this was indeed a corridor at all. It seemed at times as though the wraith merely drifted from cavern to gaping cavern.

They'd been walking for hours through an endless black that swallowed most of his torchlight, and its soft amber glow illuminated only a few yards at a time. The darkness engulfed the light as though it were hungry, as though the shadows were a single, living thing and its eons in the wraith's catacombs had left it starved.

As the minutes passed, Connor tracked their path in his mind, always aware of the way out. For all he knew, the walls down here could shift and change on their own, but knowing the path they'd taken gave him at least some reassurance. Folk stories told all sorts of tales about the Wraith King, and even Connor didn't know which of them were true. Not yet.

Only the wraith understood this place.

"Which weapon are you showing me first?" Connor's voice carried down the chillingly quiet corridor in a haunting echo.

The one you must conquer. In the depths of these ancient tunnels, the wraith's voice warbled with the drowning echo of a man being pulled out to sea. *It is the more dangerous of the two challenges. If it kills you, then you would never have been able to defeat Teagan.*

Connor frowned. "Thank you for the vote of confidence."

This is a matter of efficiency. The latter challenge will take much longer. If you are unfit to fight the Lightseers, I must discover as much now and adapt my plans.

Connor's grip tightened on the torch in his hand, and his palm creaked against the leather strap as he nearly splintered the wood with his enhanced strength. His shoulders ached with the tension of everything the ghoul had left unsaid.

A quiet hum filled the air and killed their conversation. It buzzed, soft and almost too distant to hear. He raised the torch to cast its orange circle of light farther down the corridor in an effort to keep an eye on any threats—ideally with at least a few moments to spare before whatever it was tried to eat his face.

Nothing. The torchlight illuminated more of the same stone floor he had been staring at for ages. He and the wraith were alone in the darkness and haunted by that incessant hum. The air itself sparked and fizzled, crackling as though it would light on fire at any moment.

"Do I—" His voice thundered through the darkness, and he shut his mouth on impulse to keep the noise to a minimum. He cleared his throat and tried again, this time muttering under his breath to keep from announcing himself to whatever monstrosities the ghoul had stowed away in these catacombs. "What's wrong with the air? Do I need to put out the torch?"

Don't be ridiculous. What you're feeling is merely an enchantment on this stretch of the tunnels.

Connor scanned the barren floor, wondering what in the Fates' name could make the air fizzle like that. "What the hell did you do to this place?"

I fortified it. It takes quite a bit of magic to contain a beast as powerful as the one you're about to face.

"A beast? That's the weapon?" Connor scoffed. "And just one? What creature could possibly turn the tides against Teagan Starling?"

Be careful of the assumptions you make about the world and its creatures, Magnuson, the wraith warned. *There are many in Saldia who say the same thing about you.*

Connor frowned, but he didn't reply.

The enchantments in these corridors are tied to the magic on Slaybourne as a whole. I designed it that way as a failsafe, in case I was unable to break the beast's will.

As the air thrummed around them, it all suddenly made sense. Connor rubbed his eyes with his free hand and grumbled in frustration. "That's why Slaybourne's defenses are failing. That's why there was new growth at the entrance of Death's Door. Containing this creature—and whatever other enchantments you tied into Slaybourne's magic—has been chipping away at its power for centuries."

The thought has occurred to me, the wraith admitted. *Perhaps I made an error in my design.*

"Perhaps?" Connor asked with an exasperated gesture toward the darkness ahead. "Eventually, Slaybourne's magic would've failed. This and whatever else you have trapped down here would've broken free."

Correct. I think we have fifty years left at most, and that's without any strain on the fortress.

"Fantastic," Connor said under his breath.

It is less than ideal, the ghoul agreed.

"Tell me what's down here. Tell me everything you have squirreled away in these tunnels."

With an irritated groan, the undead king pivoted midair. The man's skull glowed white beneath his hood as the holes where his eyes used to be reached into Connor's soul. He hovered off the ground, his legs long gone as he floated in the endless void beneath Slaybourne.

Instead of answering, the Wraith King pointed at something in the shadows ahead. Connor tensed and narrowed his eyes in suspicion, but he ultimately indulged the ghoul and walked closer.

First, the torch's amber light caught on the jagged stones of a rocky black wall—the first wall he'd seen since stepping into the darkness. He lifted his torch higher, half-wondering if the ghoul was setting him up for some sort of trap.

After all, it seemed in character for the dead idiot to put him in a life-or-death situation, just to teach Connor some half-baked lesson about power.

Something glittered at the edge of the firelight, and the sudden flash of gold almost blinded him. Metallic fibers glinted in the orange glow, and as he stepped closer, something flat and taller than him materialized from the darkness. A long shadow stretched up the imperfect stone toward the ceiling he still couldn't see, and it took a moment to process the rushes of color that appeared beneath his torchlight.

A tapestry.

"That's the secret?" Connor lifted a dubious eyebrow. "You liked art? Art is a rich man's hobby. There's no need to hide it all down here."

For a moment, the wraith didn't answer. The old ghost just hovered there, staring at him with those empty eye sockets, until a frustrated groan fluttered through the back of Connor's mind.

You infuriate me.

"The feeling is mutual."

Connor reached the tapestry and held his torch high enough to get a good look. The wraith disappeared into the shadows beyond the torchlight as the tapestry came into full view. Gilded threads glittered in the first light they'd seen in centuries. In the intricately woven scene, silver and white clouds churned over the edge of a cliff, and shadows darted into the mists. Winged creatures flew through the air, suspended in time as they blocked out the sun.

Horns. Scales. Claws. The gold fibers woven into their legendary bodies glowed in the firelight, and the old myths returned to Connor in a flood of staggering disbelief.

Dragons.

Dozens of them.

"You have…" Connor trialed off as his mind struggled to process the unspoken confession in the wraith leading him here, of all places. "Are you trying to tell me you have a dragon stored away down here?"

The wraith emerged from the oppressive darkness. The undead king hovered in the air to Connor's left, and the amber firelight cast strange shadows across the pockmarked bone of his skull.

The ghoul simply nodded.

A dragon.

Even a few short months ago, Connor would've said it was impossible. Now, however, after his time fused with the Wraith King, the word didn't hold the same meaning.

The beast chips away at Slaybourne's reserves, Magnuson. In the old days, it wouldn't have mattered. There was enough spellgust ore in this mountain to sustain it for eons, I thought, and I could always bring in new magic when it was needed. Now, however, I feel Slaybourne fading faster than I ever anticipated. I suspect this creature is the primary cause.

"Then I don't have a choice." Frustrated as all hell, Connor rubbed one eye with the heel of his palm. "If the defenses are failing around Slaybourne, then I have to handle this now. We can't risk the defenses fracturing when Teagan gets here."

Exactly.

Connor let out a string of curses under his breath.

The hint of sulfur stung his nose, and he lowered his chin to follow the odor. The orange light from his torch bent as it met a black basin bolted to the floor, roughly fifteen yards from the wall. A metal lid covered a circular pot at one end, and a thin rectangle of black steel followed the floor into the shadows. He lifted the lid, and a ripple broke across the surface of a dark liquid in it. He sniffed again to confirm his suspicion.

Heady. Musky. A hint of rust, the tang of metal, and the choking sting of sulfur. Definitely lamp oil.

Time for some real light.

He set the lid on the ground and tossed the torch into the basin. Fire erupted on impact. The flames blazed down the center of the corridor, following the length of the narrow basin, and warm light burst to life in the hall. The ceiling towered over him, easily ten times his height, and thirty men could've marched side by side on their way through.

The flames glinted off something brilliant and gold, and Connor shielded his eyes with his arm. When the ache in his skull faded, he peered over his elbow to find a pair of golden doors farther down the hallway. The gilded entry stretched from the floor to the ceiling, and two circles of iron, each as large as his head, served as its handles.

As the flames continued to race down the length of the basin of the cavernous hall, more and more tapestries appeared on both sides of the imposing corridor. Dozens. Hundreds, even.

"Where did you get all of these?" Connor asked.

I stole them.

"Of course you did," he muttered. "Who did you steal them from?"

The dragons. Their artisans are truly masters.

Connor tilted his head back and gave the ghoul a once-over. "You're telling me they can weave with those claws of theirs?"

The younglings can. From the research I've done into their kind, the young ones have hands similar to ours before their claws grow in. A few of the tapestries have unique fibers, though, which I suspect means the occasional human is allowed into the temples to observe.

"Temples?"

The wraith nodded. *The legends you know are lies, Magnuson, and the dragons lie to themselves just as much as we lie about them. These tapestries taught me that. Each masterpiece captures a taste of dragon culture. Bit by bit, decade by decade, they taught me everything I needed to know to break the dragons I lured to me.*

Connor pointed to the golden doors, which he assumed housed their scaly guest. "All except one, apparently."

The wraith huffed impatiently, but he didn't disagree.

In silence, they scanned the hall. Sure enough, each and every tapestry featured a dragon in some way—flying, fighting, sleeping. These pieces of art told the story of the legendary creature now stored away in these tunnels, and he still couldn't quite believe what waited for him beyond those doors.

A dragon.

After years of believing they were gone, if they had ever existed at all, he was about to see a *dragon*.

CHAPTER TEN

CONNOR

If Connor's six-year-old self had known he would one day come face-to-face with a living, breathing dragon, the boy would've collapsed in a gleeful little heap.

Even now, after all Connor had endured, a grin spread across his face, as wide as any child's.

A dragon.

You're smiling like an idiot. Have you finally gone mad?

The wraith's voice in his ear snapped him from his happy daze, and he cleared his throat to cover his momentary lapse in judgment. The ghoul was an ass, but he had a point.

Connor needed to focus.

He tried to stuff down all the fanciful wives' tales he'd heard through the years about treasure and talons so that he could decipher the very tapestries the ghoul had used to conquer these mythical beasts.

In the flickering firelight, the scene on the first tapestry shifted from an eerie landscape of cliffs and fog to a dragon's brilliant flight through the sun. Though there weren't any humans for him to estimate its relative size, the legends claimed that a full grown dragon could swallow a man whole.

Vile things made of shadow and darkness, these dragons—or so the old stories said. Born for blood and battle, they would eat anything that came close.

The dragons depicted in this scene, however, had golden scales. The fibers twinkled and shone in the crackling firelight, giving the effect of an enchanted glow. Some had their eyes closed as they turned their faces toward the sun. Others spun through the clouds, dancing with the sky, the hint of a smile along their scaly faces. They seemed almost—well, *happy*. Peaceful. Free.

An odd emotion for the fire-breathing demons of legend to feel.

His feet passed silently over the dust-covered floor as he turned his attention to the next tapestry. In this scene, dragons sat in a circle with their eyes closed. Trees surrounded them with unnatural precision. The trunks formed a wall of sorts around the dragons, and the branches arched toward the sky like a makeshift roof. A circle of sunlight broke through the leaves and cast a spotlight on a white dragon with a regal curve to her neck. She towered over the others, while flecks of gold and silver shimmered in her scales.

"Are they—"

Meditating. The ghoul laughed, as though it were the most ludicrous thing he had ever seen. *Creatures of war, lying to themselves about the light they wished could live within them.*

"Lying, or looking?" Connor muttered, mostly to himself.

He continued down the wall of art, and the next tapestry portrayed a single dragon up close. A golden line separated the dragon's head into perfect halves. On one side, the beast's eye remained closed. Dazzling clouds filled the sky behind it, and sunbeams broke through the fluffy white day to cast soft rays across a verdant field. Golden threads glimmered along its scales, and its horns all but glowed with a light of their own.

The other half, however, burned with hatred. It snarled, its lip curling over its jagged teeth. Its eye blistered with crimson fibers, as intense and vibrant as if the dragon could climb from the tapestry at any moment. Smoke blocked out the sky behind it, and the once-vibrant horizon was cast in a murky darkness almost as black and hollow as the catacombs. Only scorched streaks of ashy woodland remained of the landscape behind the creature.

This. The wraith tapped his bony finger on the fiery half of the dragon's face. *This is the truth at every dragon's core. Deep within, their feral nature still thrives. They have deluded themselves into containing it, but it's always within reach. They believe that to lie to oneself is the ultimate failure of life, and I used that to break them. They've lied to themselves for all of time, trying to act enlightened when they are, in fact, nothing more than primitive beasts that deny their own power. Once they have a taste of their feral natures, they can never go back.*

Connor wrinkled his nose in disgust. "You conquered dragons by pushing them to their feral side, then? You tortured them until they snapped?"

The ghoul nodded.

"How many?"

Two, before this one came. I was so close to having a third, but it resisted me. It's stronger than the others. But don't worry, Magnuson, I did most of the work for you. Once you push a dragon over the edge, they're just another animal to break. That part's easy.

"Just when I thought you couldn't sink any lower."

There you go again, clutching your pearls. The wraith waved his bony hand dismissively. *A warlord's throne is built on bones. The sooner you accept that, the easier your ascent will be.*

Connor bit his tongue. There was a time for arguments and being right, but this wasn't it. This dragon's containment threatened Slaybourne's safety, and he had to stay focused, even if he wanted nothing more than to knock the ghoul's head clean off his body to teach the undead man a lesson.

"What was different about this dragon?" he asked instead.

It's hard to know for certain, the ghoul admitted. *It's royalty, and as far as I could tell, that means it was more dutifully trained to control its feral side. It had a better understanding of the darkness than the others. It resisted me, but that only made me want it more. I got close. I did everything I could think of to push it over the brink, but it clung to its so-called enlightenment. I nearly lost an arm and both legs before I retreated.*

"Has the dragon been in there all this time? How could it have possibly survived this long?"

It's in stone sleep, thanks to an enchanted chamber lined with spellgust. The beast waits inside, perfectly preserved since the day I sealed it away.

The ghoul disappeared in a cloud of smoke, and a second puff of darkness erupted farther down the hallway. The dark mist curled over the set of massive doors, and flickering firelight from behind the wraith danced with its reflection along the gold. A bony hand emerged from the shadows as the wraith materialized, and he set his long-dead palm flat against the entry.

You must succeed, Magnuson. There is no room for failure. When you awaken the creature, it will not realize any time has passed at all. It will still be trapped in the past. When it wakes, it will still be hovering on the edge of its feral side, sitting on the cusp, and you can take advantage of that weakness.

Disgusted but not surprised, Connor rubbed the back of his neck and forced himself to take a settling breath. The Wraith King had been a colossal asshole in his life, and sometimes Connor had to remind himself that the ghoul had only just begun to redeem a lifetime of evil deeds. Only time would tell if the wraith succeeded in being anything other than a selfish bastard.

"How did you manage to get a dragon down here?" Connor scanned the towering ceiling above, and now the wide hallway made far more sense. "How did you find one, for that matter?"

They were rare, even in my day, the ghoul confessed. *It came to Saldia from the Barrens looking for something. I can't recall what it was, but that was never important. I used its hunt as a lure to get it down here.*

Connor rubbed his brow as he scanned the walls of artwork. For what it was worth, the wraith hadn't lied. A dragon as an ally truly could turn the tides in his conflict with the Starlings. It would mean power. Prestige. Influence. Respect from the people and the ruling class—or maybe just their fear.

He looked over his shoulder at the tapestry of a dragon divided in two—the monk and the murderer.

It couldn't be that simple. Dragons had ascended to myth and legend for a reason, and there had to be more to their story.

The wraith rarely saw the world as it truly was, and Connor suspected this was no different. The dragon inside that room had been tormented and pushed to the edge of what it could handle, and Connor had to choose: kill it, or push it over.

The first threads of a plan began to form, but Connor didn't trust it. Not yet. To conquer a dragon and send it over the edge went against everything he believed in, but he also couldn't bring himself to kill a legendary creature in cold blood.

There had to be another way.

As he studied the dragon's serene and peaceful half, he considered a third option: perhaps, if he played his cards right, he could coax it back from the brink. He frowned as he mulled this new option over, mainly because it was such an unknown. He didn't know if pulling it back to sanity would work out better or worse for him in the end.

Before he opened those doors, he needed a plan. A real one. A solid one, something he could rely on. And for that to happen, he needed to better understand the creature that waited for him.

"Wait," he said under his breath as his head spun with ideas. "War can break a man, so it must do the same to a dragon. How can they protect themselves if pain could push them into their feral nature?"

The ghoul sighed impatiently. *It doesn't matter, Magnuson. What matters is that you get in there and break its will.*

"Indulge me, then."

Why?

"You want me to succeed, don't you?" Connor bluffed. He held the ghoul's gaze, half-wondering if the undead king would even answer.

The wraith watched him for a moment. Those empty sockets that served as eyes were cold and empty as he stared Connor down. Connor didn't waver, and he didn't look away as the flames crackled beside them. He let the stillness linger because sometimes the silence told a man more than words ever could.

The ghoul let out a strangled sigh of defeat. *Dragons avoid war. If they have no other choice than to fight, they acknowledge that they may lose some of their brethren to the feral bloodlust in the process. That's why royalty trains so diligently to master their feral natures—it allows them to protect the clan.*

Connor turned his back on the ghost to hide a small smile of victory at the edge of his mouth. Apparently, the wraith wanted him to succeed after all.

With time, he might teach the undead king how to properly bluff, but he rather enjoyed being able to wring answers out of a man who had once been royalty.

Come, Magnuson. It is time.

"I need a minute." Connor studied the tapestry of the dragon split into its two halves once again. Something about it didn't sit right with him, and he wrestled with everything he had learned so far as he fought to figure out what about this smelled off.

Fear is beneath you, the wraith chided. *You have only to—*

"Will you stop talking for two minutes and let me think?" he snapped.

The ghoul grumbled under his breath and threw his bony hands into the air in resignation.

As the flames roared behind Connor, everything he had heard so far churned through his mind. A dragon waited on the other side of this wall, suspended in stone sleep, and he had no choice but to wake it. The mythical creature had come here looking for something, but the ghoul had forgotten what. The beast hovered on the edge between sanity and madness, and both outcomes posed equal threats to him and his team.

He knew one thing for certain: Saldia would burn if he let it free.

His gaze drifted to the dragon's peaceful half. Eyes closed, body glowing, this sort of creature had sentience. If that half of the dragon was still in there, perhaps he could make a deal with it. Whatever it had come to Saldia to find might still exist, and Connor might be able to help.

The wraith wanted him to break this magnificent creature like a horse, but the ghoul had given plenty of terrible advice before. Woven into a majority of these tapestries were stories of peace and home, not brutality and war. Judging from what he had seen so far, there was nobility in these creatures—and perhaps even a bit of dragonish humanity.

But if he opened that door and failed, he risked unleashing a feral hellbeast on the team he had vowed to protect. Slaybourne's defenses would most likely keep the dragon contained and away from the rest of Saldia, but walking into that room and breaking its stone sleep still put everyone in the valley at risk.

If it came down to saving the dragon or his team, he would choose his team.

Of course, he had to consider the worst case, too. If it somehow escaped the citadel, he would unleash hell on Saldia. Hundreds or maybe even thousands would die, and there were so many ways this could go wrong—but he didn't have the luxury of waiting. Its stone sleep had drained so much of

Slaybourne's defenses already, and with Teagan on the way, he couldn't risk letting the enchantments on the catacombs fail.

He had to handle this now.

The golden threads composing the peaceful dragon's scales shimmered, brighter than ever. These creatures created art and meditated, for the Fates' sake. If he could bring it back from the brink, he could reason with it.

He knew what he had to do. He would help it remember itself, and when the two of them could have a rational conversation, he would strike a bargain. Both Murdoc and Sophia had made deals with him, so perhaps this beast of legend and lore would do the same.

And if it refused—if it insisted on war and blood—he would kill it. Only if all else failed would he push it over the brink and give the ghoul what the undead man wanted most.

His jaw tensed. He was almost disgusted with himself for even considering what he was about to ask, but he had to know. "How do I make a dragon go feral? How do I push it over the edge?"

Look for the eyes, the wraith answered. *When they burn red, the dragon is yours. Until then, punish it. blister it. Break it. Hurt it until it loses touch with everything that made it sentient. Remind it of its raw power, of what it truly is, of how freeing it is to let the beast take over. Then, tame it as you would any mount. Show it your power and force it to respect you.*

Connor didn't answer. He didn't need to. He didn't want to do that to any living thing, but at least he knew what to do in the worst-case scenario.

More importantly, the ghoul's reply had also given Connor everything he needed to do the opposite. To bring it back, he would have to speak to it, reassure it, and calm it down until it regained its connection to what made it sentient. He would remind it of its connection to its magic, to its brothers, and of how fiercely dragons fought to contain their feral selves.

"What's the dragon's name?"

The ghoul shrugged. *Is that relevant? Stay focused, Magnuson. Don't get soft on me.*

"Don't you worry about that," Connor said dryly.

His boots kicked up dust as he crossed to the doors, and when he reached it, he flattened his palms flat against the golden surface. A piercing chill sank into his skin, into his bones, and it cleared the last threads of doubt from his mind. He took a calming breath, and the relief of air in his lungs flooded his body.

I challenge you, Wraithblade. The wraith's words echoed in his head—muddled, distant, and nothing but a memory. *If you succeed, you will have the power and resolve to become Teagan Starling's equal.*

Connor couldn't fail. He had too much at stake.

When you open the doors, the seal will break. The ghoul's voice snapped Connor back to the present. *You won't have long to overtake the creature before it's fully alert.*

"And if I need to seal it in stone sleep again?"

Shut the doors. The wraith gestured to the entry. *But I warn you—you have, at most, a handful of opportunities to do so. It takes a great deal of power to activate the enchantment, and a great deal less to maintain it. Every time you close the doors, you risk breaking Slaybourne's lingering defenses.*

"No pressure," Connor muttered. "Look, when I go in there, I want you to stay out of sight. You'll make everything worse if the dragon can see you."

A decent idea, Magnuson, the wraith admitted with a proud nod. *A moment of surprise may be all we need to push it over.*

It wasn't what he had meant, but he let the wraith think whatever was necessary to keep the undead king hidden.

Connor's biceps flexed as he pushed against the doors. They swung open, far lighter than he had expected, and they slammed hard against the walls. A resounding boom cracked through the corridor. The flames behind him cast a line of orange light across the floor, and his shadow stretched across the rocky terrain beyond the threshold. His eyes strained to peer into the endless black beyond the firelight.

A breath rolled past him, as though the room itself were alive. In the silence that followed, something heavy thrummed through the air—nothing tangible, nothing to be heard or seen, but there nonetheless. The tension weighed on his chest, warning him of impending doom.

Slowly, like stars popping to life in the night sky, green dots of light shimmered into existence across the towering ceiling. One by one, the green specks blurred together into ribbons of spellgust that snaked across the jet-black ceiling. They glowed with an unmistakable brilliance, and though he'd never seen raw spellgust ore before, nothing else in Saldia glimmered like that. The soft, green light cast a faded glow across the stone floor, like the first threads of an emerald sunrise breaking through a starlit night.

The soft radiance illuminated a silhouette in the center of the cavern. It towered over him, easily four times his height, but it didn't move. It didn't breathe. If he hadn't known what awaited him beyond the golden doors, he would've thought it was an ordinary rock carved into a peculiar shape.

Connor took his first step over the threshold. As his boot hit the stone floor, two amber eyes appeared in the shadow.

A low growl vibrated through the cavern. It trilled and shook like the slow, sharp warble of a predator assessing its prey.

The shadow lowered its massive head, each of its glowing amber eyes as big as Connor's face. A yellow glow flickered to life along its head, radiating in coiling circles up to the tip of its two horns. It stretched its wings, and shards of rock broke off its body as it awoke. That piercing gaze studied him, and the ground beneath his battered boots vibrated in time with the soft clicking in the back of its throat. Firelight from the hallway glinted off a single claw as it reached forward, and the blisteringly sharp talon carved a trench into the stone floor.

Something this large could've easily carried off a barn by itself—and perhaps whatever animals were unfortunate enough to be inside at the time—but Connor didn't budge.

He stared it down, same as he had done countless times before when a predator had stalked him through the Ancient Woods. The fanged tree lizards. The horned bush snakes. The humpback coyotes. They had all come for him, hunted him, bitten him and done their best to eat him alive, but he had survived, every time. He had slaughtered them all in that gnarled old woodland, and every last one of them had unknowingly prepared him for this moment.

As twisted as the wraith's warning had been, the old ghost was ultimately right: if Connor couldn't defeat this dragon, he didn't stand a chance against Teagan Starling.

In his years before encountering the ghoul, he never would've imagined himself capable of facing such a deadly foe. But tonight, he would either leave this room with an ally, or everything he had fought for thus far would crumble beneath him.

CHAPTER ELEVEN

CONNOR

In the catacombs deep beneath Slaybourne, Hell awoke.

The ancient magic coursing through Connor's veins burned within him, aching to be freed. The shadow swords. The shield. His enhanced senses, speed, and strength.

But he waited. For this to work, his timing had to be perfect.

A spasm shot through Connor's hand as he resisted the urge to summon his blades. His fingers drummed on the air as the cavern rumbled around him. Broken rock skittered across the floor, missing him by inches, but he held his ground.

He watched as the towering shadow loomed over him, growing bigger with each moment, but he was aware of everything—every falling pebble, every tremor through the ground, every breath his opponent took.

He saw it all, and yet he forced himself to wait.

The raw spellgust ore in the walls glimmered and glistened as the waking giant threatened to send the ceiling crashing to the floor.

The dragon huffed, and plumes of dust churned through the air around its face as its amber gaze scanned the rest of the cavern. Its pupils dilated, and a burst of light shot from its forehead to its horns. Each horn curled around itself, as thick and long as Connor's leg.

"Its eyes aren't red," he muttered to the ghoul, careful to keep his voice quiet enough to go unheard by the beast. "Gold, but not red. Is it close to the edge?"

Very, the Wraith King answered.

If the old stories were to be believed, this creature had magic unlike anything he could fathom. Fire. Lightning. The madness of a storm, to be summoned at will. Dragons had faded to half-forgotten lore because men didn't want to think of what the world would be like if they had to share the world with beasts like this.

Connor had heard similar myths before, though, about the beasts in the Ancient Woods. Foreboding tales were told to drive folks away from danger, but those tales had been the lure that drew him into the gnarled old oaks where monsters roamed. In the horrors of the shadows, he had hidden from both the men who hunted him and the past that had haunted him.

Sparks skittered across the dark beast's body in an oddly familiar way. The sensation broke his focus, and despite the danger, he stared intently at the scampering embers.

Nothing about this should feel familiar, but it could be the key to figuring out how to win. Whatever the cost, he had to remember—and soon.

As he struggled to place where he had seen that before, the dragon took a wary step closer. Its heavy claw shook the cavern, and Connor sank deeper into his stance to steady himself as the ground threatened to give out underneath him.

"You." The great dragon's voice rumbled like thunder. The very word vibrated clear through to Connor's bones. It grabbed his very soul and shook him, as though trying to wrench it from his body, and the wall of sound stole the breath from his lungs.

It was like speaking to a *god*.

The very word emanated raw power. Control. Dominance. In the overwhelming boom of a voice that could pierce the soul, many a man would have pissed himself.

Connor, however, saw the moment for what it was: the true beginning of their duel. He summoned his shield. In a rush of shadow, he released the magic in his blood, and the lustrous metal sang to life as it weighed on his left forearm. He stretched out the fingers on his right hand, and on command, one of his dual shadow blades settled firmly into his palm. Its weight reassured him of his power, of his strength, and in that moment, he knew the ghoul had been right about one more thing—the word "impossible" meant nothing to him anymore.

He stood between the door and the dragon, the lone line of defense against a creature that could topple empires.

Its long neck stretched toward him, and its mighty head tilted to one side. Those glowing amber eyes examined him closely. "You are not the one who challenged me."

In answer, Connor merely shook his head. Only the creak of his hand tightening on the leather strap of his shield broke the silence that followed.

The dragon snarled. Its lips curled upward, revealing moon-white teeth that contrasted sharply with the inky black scales covering its face. The trilling warble returned to the cavern, and the ground quaked. Its mouth hovered too close for comfort. A bead of sweat rolled down Connor's bicep as he slowly raised his sword.

Wait for it, he told himself. *Wait and listen.*

"You look similar. You smell similar, and yet you are not the one I want. How can this be?" Its voice boomed like thunder through the cavern, and its head shook with rage. "What have you done?"

"I've stopped him," Connor answered. "He can't hurt you anymore. I came here to—"

It slammed one massive claw against the ground. The stone trembled. A chunk of rock broke off the ceiling and shattered along the edge of their makeshift arena, but Connor held his ground. If he moved, he risked giving the dragon a clear path to the exit—something he couldn't afford to allow.

The dragon raised its head, and the snarl became a threatening growl. "What fool of a human thinks he could hurt a dragon prince? I do not fear him, nor do I fear you!"

A prince.

The wraith had been right, then: this dragon was indeed royalty, and now Connor knew a little bit more about this beast.

First of all, this dragon was not an "it," but a "he."

"I want my vengeance," the dragon demanded. "I want the blood I am owed. I will eat him, even if I must dine on his crypt!"

Connor grimaced. That certainly didn't sound like something he would expect to hear from the monk-like creatures in the tapestries. Until he reminded the dragon of its regal nature, it wouldn't act like a prince at all—the beast would remain an unfeeling, vengeful "it," just as the wraith wanted.

Mindless. Hateful. Full of spite.

The dragon took another step, and the stone cracked under Connor's feet. He grunted and sank deeper into his stance to hold his ground.

"Step aside!" the dragon bellowed.

"That's enough!" Connor's sharp tone cut the air just as powerfully as the beast's voice had moments before.

The creature's head snapped back as though he'd backhanded it, and in the seconds that followed, the amber glow in its eyes dimmed ever so slightly.

Progress.

"Get a hold of yourself!" Connor squared his shoulders as he stared the beast down. "You've been asleep for centuries, and the Wraith King has no crypt. You won't get vengeance, and you won't get blood. Now, calm the hell down!"

In the back of Connor's mind, he could practically feel the wraith bristle. *Magnuson, what are you—*

The dragon snarled, apparently unhappy with the answer. "Centuries? That imbecile imprisoned me for *centuries*?"

The wraith huffed at the insult. *He's even more of an ass than I remember.*

"Then you two will get along swimmingly," Connor muttered to the ghoul.

"All that time, wasted." The menacing clicks of the dragon's guttural growl cut through the silence between each word. The light in its eyes flickered between amber and a soft yellow as it fought to process what he had said. "Hundreds of years of my search, lost."

There was a sense of loss in its voice. Of sadness.

Of *grief*.

Connor lowered his shield in an effort to appear less threatening. He needed to calm it down and speak to the sentient creature of legend still locked somewhere within. "Tell me your name."

"My name?" The dragon's eyes narrowed, and the blazing amber glow returned. The ceiling trembled with the weight of its voice as the prince of beasts glared at him. "You do not care about my name, and you will not con me as he did. He dragged me down here, to a land I could not burn, to a land devoid of sky. He tried to muzzle me. To control me."

"Yeah," Connor said with a frustrated sigh. "But I won't. Just breathe and tell me your name."

"My name…" Its growl hummed through the air, thicker than the magic had been, heavier than the silence once was. The glow in its amber eyes flickered again, and for a moment, its eyes became a soothing black, as smooth and serene as a river rock.

The prince of dragons was still in there, just below the surface.

With a sinister snarl, the dragon shook its head, and the amber glow burned again in its eyes. "You carry his scent, and you carry his sword. You carry his legacy, which means you must also bear his guilt. If I cannot have what I am owed from the Wraith King himself, I will take it from you!"

It begins, the wraith said.

Damn it.

Connor braced himself for the fight of his life.

The dragon charged, its tail snaking along the ground after it, and Connor raised his shield in preparation. The creature wanted him, not a way out, and he could use that to his advantage. His weight shifted to the balls of his feet, and at the last second, he jumped. The dragon roared in frustration and dragged its claws through the stone, kicking up rocks and debris as it slid across the floor. As the creature passed beneath him, Connor slammed his shield hard on the top of its snout. Its scales clanged as he hit it, like the clash of two swords in the midst of a battle.

His boots landed hard on the rocky ground, and he rolled. In seconds, he was ready to go again.

The dragon snarled and blinked away the shock of his blow. Fast as lightning, the dragon tilted its head and snapped at him. He twisted his body, and with a grunt of effort, he slammed the flat of his blade hard against the tip of its nose. Black flame crackled over its scales, and for a moment, the fire illuminated its full face. Light glimmered across the jet-black scales like an aurora through the night sky, soft as silk and harder than steel.

Majestic. Raw. Powerful.

The dragon shook its head, and its eyes shifted in and out of focus. It took two dazed steps backward, tilting slightly off balance as it fought to regain its footing.

Each time its feet railed against the ground, stones broke off the ceiling overhead. A rock crashed into the ground to Connor's left, a little too close for comfort. Even as he studied the dragon for signs of the next attack, he kept a wary watch in his periphery.

Just in case.

He twirled the sword in his right hand, ready for the next blow, and sank into his stance. The distant crackle of the fire beyond the open doors reminded him of everything at stake, and he let out a slow breath as he waited.

The legendary creature bared its teeth and launched toward him, impossibly fast. He barely rolled out of the way before it could bite off his head. The chilling chomp of its jaws snapping at the air reminded him of all the times creatures had bitten him throughout his years in the Ancient Woods.

As he jumped once more to his feet, he took a cautious step backward to put a little more distance between them.

It snapped at him again, and he lifted his shield with moments to spare. Its teeth caught on the edges. The white spears protruded over the top and bottom of his shield, almost close enough to pierce his arm. The metal groaned under the dragon's raw power, as though it would break at any moment if he didn't act soon.

A breath of hot air rolled over Connor. The creature huffed again, and this time a wall of black smoke hit him in the chest. It clogged his nose, suffocating him, and his eyes watered as he gagged on the smoke. The beast slowly closed its jaws and leaned into him. Though he stood his ground with his heels firmly planted against the rock, his tattered boots slid slowly toward the door.

If it escaped, he would fail. Time to see if all that prattle about being *power incarnate* actually meant anything.

With the shield as his only protection against the dragon's teeth, Connor dismissed the sword in his right hand. The blackfire blade dissolved in a rush of dark smoke that blended with the dragon's breath, and he cocked his right arm as he prepared to land a blow to its face.

The dragon's eyes narrowed, daring him to do it.

Since discovering the wraith, he had fought some of the strongest Lightseers in Saldia and won. He had stolen silently through the night and even killed a brutal man in the forbidden circles reserved for Oakenglen's elite. He'd stared a blightwolf in the eye and survived. To date, he had survived injuries that would've killed anyone else.

Deep in his core, to the depths of his very soul, he finally understood. As infuriating as the Wraith King could be, the undead man was right about one thing—the limits of mortal men didn't apply to Connor Magnuson anymore.

With every ounce of strength he could muster, with more power than he had used to stab Zander Starling with the Bloodbane dagger, he punched the dragon in its nose.

It roared with anger and pain. Another wave of blisteringly hot air blasted his face, but in its scream, it released his shield.

Though his eyes stung from the dragon's smoking breath, Connor dove out of the way and rolled across the uneven rock. He slid to a stop as the dragon clawed at its face, its eyes tightly shut from the pain.

A second wave of those dazzling sparks raced along its body and up its neck in that oddly familiar manner.

This time, he remembered.

Those wild flashes of light dancing over the dragon's scales reminded him of none other than Zander Starling.

When the Lightseer had summoned lightning, similar sparks had covered the man's body. And here, now, those same flashes of light scampered across the dragon's scales with the fire and magic of an augmentation.

How curious.

Strange, certainly, and something to revisit later—but it also gave him an idea.

Zander had tried to roast him alive with that lightning, and it would've worked if not for Connor's shield. The metal had protected him from the worst of the attack. Sure, it had hurt like hell, but he'd been able to push through the pain to close the gap between them.

The dragon's eyes snapped open, burning with amber hatred, and its pupils dilated as it focused its full attention on him. It reared its head, its body tensing for something, and Connor shifted his weight to the balls of his feet in preparation.

Whatever this prince of beasts had in store for him, he would need to be able to duck out of the way. Given the creature's unholy speed, he probably wouldn't have much time to do it.

It screeched. The shrill scream echoed endlessly in the cavern, deafening and every bit as brutal as any blow to the face. Connor winced in pain, but he held tight to his shield.

A burst of lightning shot from between its teeth. The air snapped and crackled. A thunderous boom rocked the cavern, and an arc of blistering light carved its way through the air toward him.

Shit.

Connor didn't know if that had been the wraith's voice or his own thought, but it didn't matter.

He threw himself to the side. The hair on his arms stood on end as the lightning missed his chest by inches. He slid across the rock, kicking up dust. He had misjudged his own strength, and now he tumbled across the ground at a blinding speed, giving the dragon a clear opening to the door. Its head tilted toward the exit, all too aware of the opportunity he had mistakenly given it.

Damn it all.

No time to think. He had to act.

His body moved on impulse and muscle memory. With a grunt of effort, he pressed his fingers together and shoved his hand into the rock like a dagger to the heart. He didn't even pause to process what he'd done—he just did it in a desperate bid to stop the creature from escaping.

To his surprise, his fingertips broke through the stone. A stabbing pain, like a scorpion's stinger through his skin, snaked up his arm. The pain hit him again and again, pulsing with every heartbeat, but he didn't let go.

To date, he had endured far worse.

His hand in the stone slowed him to an immediate stop. As dust churned around him, he stared at the gouges he'd made in the floor. His brow knit in confusion. For a moment, he forgot about the early death looming overhead and savored the ease with which his bare hand had broken through solid rock.

Like a shovel through freshly tilled earth.

A smile crept across his face despite the dire situation.

I saw that grin. The wraith's voice reverberated in Connor's mind. *You're learning to control your power. I believe some gratitude is in order.*

He frowned with irritation, but at least the dead king's voice had broken the spell.

A bolt of blinding light cut through the air, and he reflexively ducked. The rock behind him shattered as the blast of lightning hit it.

Connor glared up at the dragon. It now stood between him and the door, their positions reversed. The flickering light from the hallway cast its orange line over the threshold, but the dark silhouette of the beast's wings blocked most of the corridor beyond.

In the low green light from the spellgust overhead, the edges of the dragon's mouth curled in a subtle sneer as it stared down at him. Sparks scurried over its scales once again, but this time, ribbons of golden light also swam through its scales like snakes through murky water.

The dragon roared, and its voice carried its blistering frustration. Its pain. Its rage. The sound clawed at Connor's chest, as though the dragon within the feral beast were begging for help.

"Take it easy," he said, doing his best to keep his voice calm.

Magnuson, you can't be serious! The wraith's voice blasted through his skull, as loud as though he were shouting in his ear. *You would dare to talk it down? To pull it back from the brink, after all I endured to get it this far? You could have everything, if only you conquer this mindless beast! If only you would listen to me!*

Unfazed, Connor kept his weight on the balls of his feet and his eyes locked on the dragon before him as its tail twitched.

"You've given me a lot of bad advice since we met," he told the ghoul.

"But this is easily the worst. I'm not going to break it, not when there's a chance to bring it back."

You conned me into giving you answers, you ass. You can bluff your human pets, but don't you dare do it to me!

"Stop whining." Connor pushed himself to his feet and tried to tune out the ghost in his head.

He needed to focus on the dragon, not an old fart's feelings.

Unbelievable. The ghoul let out a string of curses that slowly faded to silence.

"I HAVE HAD ENOUGH OF YOU HUMANS!" The dragon's booming voice cascaded through the cavern, and a stalactite broke off the ceiling from the sheer sound. It crashed against the floor, shattering to pieces, and the earth trembled from its fall. "YOU WEAK AND BROKEN THINGS. YOU STEAL AND YOU PILLAGE, BUT IT'S NEVER ENOUGH. YOUR GREED CONSUMES YOU. SO LONG AS ANY OF YOU LIVE, YOU THREATEN ALL OF DRAGONKIND. I WILL DESTROY EVERY ONE OF YOU, IF THAT'S WHAT IT TAKES TO PRESERVE THE PEOPLE!"

As it spoke, the amber glow in its eyes darkened to a burnt orange hue. The sparks scampering along its scales doubled, and smoke billowed from its nose.

"This is bad," he muttered.

The dragon prince within was losing, and the feral beast had come one step closer to victory.

Maybe Connor was too late.

The more it spoke of war, the more lost it became. He had to end this, and he had to do it soon. It was closer to the brink than he had realized. Rational conversation wouldn't work, at least not until he found a way to calm it down. If it wouldn't pause long enough to listen, he would have to force it to be still.

So be it, then. Time to do what he did best—throw it off its game.

CHAPTER TWELVE
CONNOR

With an emerald glow rolling across its silky black scales, the half-mad dragon screamed. Its shrill roar split the air and nearly cracked open Connor's skull. He gritted his teeth and raised his shield once more. With his brows furrowed and his thoughts racing, he switched to his backup plan: piss it off.

If he could irritate the beast, he could trick it into making mistakes. Tiring it out would give him a chance to pin it down and *force* it to listen to him.

Of all the insane ideas he'd had in his life, this was probably the most likely to get him killed.

A flash of red light shot through the dragon's eyes and faded back into the amber glow.

Might as well get this over with.

"Do you plan on hitting me at any point?" He grinned with all the mischievous ire of a schoolboy.

The dragon's eyes narrowed at the taunt, and a stream of black smoke rolled out of its nose. With his shield still on his left forearm, Connor shook out his right hand. His fingers buzzed with anticipation as he prepared for the next attack. He shifted back and forth on his feet, ready to dance.

A slurry of yellow light skittered over the dragon's scales, and the vibrant glow in its horns burned ever brighter. It dug its claws into the rock, no doubt bracing itself for another burst of lightning.

This time, Connor was ready.

Before the beast could unleash its onslaught of supernatural death,

Connor charged. There wasn't a chance in hell he would outrun the blast, but he didn't need to.

He just needed to get closer.

A crackling boom shattered the cavern. Rocks broke off from the ceiling and smashed to the ground like hail. An arc of blinding yellow light split the air, coming right for him.

Now.

Connor dropped to the ground, raised his shield over his head, and slid underneath the lightning. It sizzled above him, sparking and fizzing with the almighty power of a storm, but the shield protected him. The hair on his arms stood on end as he skidded over the rocky floor of their arena. The burst of light blinded him, and he winced as he was forced to look away.

Tiny pops of lightning scurried over the interior of his shield. The metal groaned, threatening to buckle. Rocks dug into the exposed skin on his arms as he came to a stop, but he gritted his teeth through the pain.

As quick as it had come, the stream of lightning ended. Hollow imprints of the light floated in his vision, and he blinked to shake them away. As his eyes readjusted, he found himself surrounded by black scales. A sloping neck hovered over him, close enough to touch as the dragon lowered its mighty head. It stared at the spot where he had stood moments before and growled with unearned victory, apparently convinced it had obliterated him.

How cocky.

He had to act fast. From this vantage, he could either crawl over to its soft underbelly or attack its head.

Choices, choices.

Connor rolled to one side and jumped to his feet, careful to stay in its blind spot as it scanned the far wall for possible hiding places. Its horns left glowing trails of light in their wake as its head shifted back and forth. Connor crept slowly closer, still waiting for the perfect moment.

The horns slowed and reversed. In seconds, its head would sail over his.

He tightened his hold on his shield, and as the dragon's head came within reach, he slammed the edge of the enchanted metal into the bottom of the beast's jaw. He yelled with the sheer effort of the blow, giving it everything he had, and it hit bone with a resounding crack.

Metal clanged. Vibrations shot up his arm. The dragon's head shook like a gong, and it stumbled backward, dazed. Its claws dragged across the rock, etching long gouges in the stone as it tried to keep from falling.

Unlike the dragon, Connor didn't pause to savor his victory.

He charged, close enough that he could reach its head before it let loose another blast. It blinked away its daze and snarled. Its mouth opened wide, like a cave lined with glistening white teeth, and a yellow glow built in the back of its throat.

If that burst hit him, he didn't think even his enhanced healing would be enough to save him.

In the seconds before it unleashed the next stream of lightning, Connor jumped. He sailed into the air, higher than he had expected to go. A dazzling yellow arc sliced through the air underneath him, and once more, the cavern drowned in brilliant light.

The glowing amber eyes shifted up toward him, a second too slow, and he used them as his guide. The gap between them closed, and he dismissed the shield in his left hand. His stomach lurched as he fell toward the dragon's face. With no time at all to spare, he summoned his blackfire swords into his palms and bellowed his own brutal war cry, throwing everything he had into the blow.

The flat sides of both blades slammed hard against the dragon's muzzle, followed by the hearty twang of steel hitting steel. The dragon's head gave under his blow, and they hit the ground with a boom that ricocheted off the cavern walls. Black flames billowed into the air, and those glowing amber eyes disappeared in the enchanted fire.

And, for the first time since the dragon had awoken, the cavern was still.

In the aftermath, nothing moved. Connor's chest heaved as he sucked in air. He had pushed his body beyond every limit he thought he'd had, and it ached.

He waited, listening for the dragon's breath or voice through the soft patter of falling pebbles, but nothing came.

The fire in his swords fizzled and popped as the dust cloud settled.

Through gaps in the murky brown mist, the dragon's head appeared in a small crater beneath him. It let out a slow breath, and he firmly pressed one foot on its snout.

Its great eyes opened, glaring up at him even as they failed to focus.

Good. It wasn't dead.

In the fury of their fight, he'd lost control of his sheer strength. The dragon had tried to roast him several times already, but it was still worth saving.

It growled in warning, still ready to fight, but he didn't give it a chance to catch its breath or clear its head.

"Fine!" he shouted at it. "You want blood? I'll *give* it to you!"

He dismissed one of his shadow blades. It dissolved in a puff of smoke, and he slammed his now-empty fist into the creature's skull. His voice echoed off the cavern walls, same as the dragon's snarls had not long before, and the blow drove its head deeper into the crater. It roared with rage and pain, but the fire in his blood warned him not to stop.

To not show mercy.

Not yet.

He dismissed his second blade as well and pummeled the dragon with a left hook. His knuckles cracked. Jolts of agonizing pain shot down his arm, but he didn't care.

He cocked his right arm, ready to go again. Ready to hit it as many times as he needed to, so long as it stayed down.

Right jab. Left hook. Right. Left. Again and again, he nailed his bare fists hard against the dragon's face. It growled and screeched, and its skull drove deeper into the rock with each blow.

Don't kill it, the wraith chided. *Watch your anger. Don't let it consume you.*

As Connor's chest heaved from the effort of fighting a living legend, he ignored the dead man's warning.

Rock dust churned around them like a midnight fog, obscuring everything in sight. The dragon's dark scales lay beneath his left fist, nothing more than a barely visible circle of darkness as he paused to catch his breath.

The dragon's amber eyes appeared through the dust cloud, watching him, and he met its challenge. Air scraped against his throat, the pain sharp and raw, but he cocked his right arm again. It was a wordless threat, one that carried the weight of blood and broken bones as he dared the dragon to move.

"Tell me your Fates-damned *name!*" He tensed his core and cocked his arm, ready to land another blow if it so much as growled again.

It didn't move. It didn't answer. It simply watched him, those glowing eyes narrowing as Connor sucked in breath after dusty breath. The brown cloud of powdered rock hung in the air, and he wished it would disperse already. Never once taking his gaze off the dragon, he spat out a pebble in an effort to clear his windpipe.

The air shifted, and he felt the threat before he saw it. The dust cloud churned, and the dragon's tail soared toward him. A spike sliced through the dust cloud, inches from his face, and he threw himself backward as it sailed past.

Connor hit the hard stone floor as the tail disappeared again into the murky fog.

The dragon snarled and pushed itself to its feet. Its wings beat the air, churning the dusty cloud that lingered in the wake of their fight, which made it impossible to see. Before he could even stand, the dragon disappeared into the haze.

Damn it.

He scanned the dust storm, both his eyes and ears straining for a clue as to where it had gone. The leathery snap of wings came from seemingly every direction.

Yet again, the tension in the air shifted—a warning of an incoming attack, and this time, not even he could move fast enough.

The rock-solid frame of one of the dragon's wings hit him hard in the chest. It kicked the breath out of his lungs, and he sailed backward. His body smacked against the wall, and the crack of splitting rock reverberated through the cavern. The green light from the spellgust overhead blurred, and for a moment, he saw dazzling stars.

This wasn't working.

The dragon's silhouette appeared in the dust cloud, and it landed with a deafening thud. The ground trembled beneath each of its hulking steps as it neared.

Connor racked his brain for another idea and tried to understand why this had failed so far. He thought again of the tapestries, of their golden fibers, of the skies and cliffs of each landscape.

It hit him, then—the missing piece.

He dragged me down here, it had said. *To a land I could not burn, to a land devoid of sky.*

The sky had been featured in every tapestry except for one. In the only scene without a sun and open clouds, the dragon had been feral.

The beast's tail sailed through the dust cloud, and Connor rolled to the side seconds before it crashed into the rock where he'd been standing.

Connor pushed himself to his feet and stared up at the hulking behemoth. "Wraith, how long has it been down here?"

Before I enchanted the doors? The ghoul's voice broke through his mind, grim and echoing. *Eight months, give or take. I stopped counting after a while. It took seven months to even break into its feral state.*

Connor cursed under his breath and ducked another swing of its tail through the dust cloud. No wonder the dragon had gone mad. From what he'd seen thus far in the very tapestries the Wraith King had used to break dragons' will, they needed the sky. To be stored away from the sun for almost a year had likely cut it off from everything that could calm it down.

No wonder nothing he had done so far had worked.

As the dust finally settled, he spotted the orange light from the corridor beyond the double doors. The dragon's massive head tilted toward it, studying the exit, as though debating its escape.

And yet, it stayed.

The nearly feral beast craved blood—his blood—even as the dragon prince trapped within it longed for freedom.

He had tried to calm it down by talking to it. He had tried a show of force. Short of killing it, he had only one more shot at bringing it back from the brink.

He had to let it see the sky.

A low warble filled the air, and that eerie clicking came once more from the back of the dragon's throat. Connor's head buzzed with all the ways this could fail, but he had to make his choice.

Deep down, he knew he had to let it taste the stars.

His jaw tensed with stubborn resentment as he considered the alternative. He couldn't do that, not until he was sure there was no other way to fix this mess the wraith had dumped in his lap. If he lost control once they were topside, either he or Slaybourne's defenses would kill the creature. It wouldn't break free. He would see to that himself.

To make this work, he had to fully commit.

So be it.

"Don't you want to see the sky?" he yelled. His voice bounced off the stones, louder than any roar.

The beast snarled in response, and another flash of red light burst through its glowing amber eyes.

Magnuson! The wraith's voice was tight with warning. *Don't you dare. I worked too hard for you to ruin this!*

"It's out there!" Connor ignored the wraith and pointed to the open doors. "You and I can dance all night long down here, or you can fly again. Which do you want more?"

Its head pivoted toward the exit, and the clicking trill became a soft and pensive growl. The amber glow in its eyes faded briefly, replaced by that soothing black sheen, and it lowered its head as it considered the option.

"Do it," Connor said softly—too quietly for it to hear. He inched forward, ready to run toward it the second it bolted toward the door, but he didn't want to risk drawing its attention before it made its move. "Just *go*, damn you."

The blazing amber glow returned to its eyes. It snarled, spread its wings, and bolted for the doors.

Finally.

Connor's heart skipped a beat, and he raced toward the dragon. Its head lowered as it neared the exit, and he eyed a spot along the base of its neck that would provide him the best leverage.

Now or never.

As it passed by, he hurled himself toward it, flying through the air from the force of his jump. His stomach churned, and for a moment, he wondered if he would miss—if the dragon would figure out his plan and ruin everything.

His chest hit the dragon's neck so hard that he nearly vomited his dinner. He grabbed hold on instinct, even as his head spun from the force of his landing. His wayward steed wriggled underneath him, but he wrapped his legs around the base of its neck and held tight with both arms.

The dragon growled and shot him an irritated glare over its shoulder as they reached the golden doors. One amber eye peered back at him, but it had nowhere to go.

You damned fool, the wraith shouted in his head. *Get off its neck so that we can shut the doors! I was wrong. You were never ready to do what must be done. Seal it away before—*

"Shut your damn mouth!" Connor shouted.

The dragon roared, its voice dwarfing his, but he didn't care. This was happening, one way or another.

The creature of legend tore through the open doors, and its feet crushed the fiery basins lighting the hallway. Flames erupted as the basins toppled, but the dragon hardly seemed to notice. Its body slammed against the wall, and its claws left deep gouges in the dusty floor. Tapestries crumpled to the ground, knocked from their nails, but it didn't slow even as the fires ate away the masterpieces. It snarled and barreled ahead, its body already angled toward the exit.

Toward the sky.

It knew, deep in its bones, where to go. It knew the way out, and that alone gave Connor a thin ray of hope that his plan would work.

Its wings curled tight against its body as it barreled through the massive corridor. Its tail smacked against the walls, knocking over tapestries and kicking over the basins of fire mounted to the ceilings.

It seemed a shame and a waste to lose the tapestries. With a furious dragon on the loose, however, he had to prioritize self-preservation over preserving ancient art.

The dragon roared, the sound deafening in the confined space, and vibrations traveled up Connor's arms as he held tight to its neck. If it managed to knock him off its back, it would inevitably impale itself on Slaybourne's defenses, and that alone kept him rooted in place.

He gritted his teeth and steeled himself as they charged into the darkness, and the same thought rumbled on repeat through his brain.

This had better work.

CHAPTER THIRTEEN
MURDOC

As dawn finally broke, Murdoc lay on the steep slope of a hill near the campsite and stared up at the receding stars. The twinkling silver dots faded as soft yellow and orange sunbeams crept across the sky. The meadow grass hummed with a faint green light, and a blade of grass tickled his ear as he lay in a meadow. He let it sway back and forth, scratching at his skin, because he couldn't bring himself to move.

Frowning and lost in thought, he could only listen—and wait.

The ground beneath him rumbled yet again, longer and louder than before. The earth shook with the venom of a volcano about to blow, and his core tensed on impulse. He set one hand flat on the dirt beside him, and his eyes glossed over as he ignored the clouds meandering by overhead. His full focus remained on the tremors coursing up his back and through his body.

The vibration faded. Yet again, silence followed. He strained his ear, eager for a clue as to what the hell was happening.

A piercing scream cut through the air, and he winced as the shriek rattled around in his brain. He sat upright, brow furrowed with concern, but nothing ran out of the woods at him. In the distance and off toward the lake, a flock of birds startled into the sky, but most of the animals had retreated from the meadow the moment the quakes had begun. Crumbled black stone buildings lay in piles around him, and the meadow grass bent in a gentle wind.

The scream lingered, shrill and distant, for several moments. Bit by bit, it faded into the wind before dissolving entirely into the rush of clattering leaves in the nearby forest.

Tense and uneasy, Murdoc balled his hand into a fist as he debated what to do. His knuckles cracked from the tension coiling in his body. As he scanned the valley, the breeze blew his loose hair into his face, and his attention shifted to the ground beneath his palm.

His gaze swept across the peaks, and he did his best to track the path the rumble had taken. As far as he could tell, it was headed right for them.

Nearby, someone sucked in a sharp breath, but he hadn't heard anything to imply someone was walking toward him.

No footsteps. No broken twigs.

Nothing.

His years of training as a Blackguard soldier kicked in, and he drew his sword. The swish of metal on cloth broke the still morning. In a fluid, practiced motion, he shifted his weight and pivoted onto his knee as he angled his blade toward whomever had snuck up on him. His other leg swung out to the side, balancing him as he prepared to defend himself and his new home.

At the base of the hill, Sophia leaned against a tree. Her hand rested on her stomach, and she grimaced in pain. She leaned her head against the trunk, chest heaving.

Shit.

The Starling woman must have escaped. If their prisoner had hurt his future wife, not even the captain would be able to save her from Murdoc's wrath.

He bolted down the hill and scanned the field, looking for any indication of where the Starling warrior had gone, only to find Quinn lying beside the now-dead fire with her head resting on her scrunched up jacket. With her arms exposed, dozens of augmentations hummed with a steady green glow across her pale skin. Her tiger-bird lay beside her, and the fur on its face shivered like meadow grasses in the breeze as it lifted its head to scan the horizon.

Confused, Murdoc slowed to a light jog and scanned Sophia's face for clues as to what was going on. Her eyes snapped open as he neared, and as their gazes met, she stood a little taller. She winced with the movement and swallowed hard, as though trying to hide her pain.

"What's wrong?" His voice, firm and commanding, shattered the otherwise silent morning.

"Nothing." She pushed off the tree and tucked a lock of her dark hair behind one ear as she surveyed the horizon—looking everywhere but at him.

"Sure." With a frown, he sheathed his sword.

The ground rumbled again, the vibrations stronger than any that had hit so far. Sophia swung her arms out to get her balance, and he grabbed her shoulders to keep her upright. To his surprise, she didn't bat him away. Instead, she leaned into him as she grappled for support.

Something was *definitely* wrong with her.

Over by the smoldering embers of their fire, the tiger-bird stood, and its head towered above the tall grass around it. It scanned the mountains, but ultimately its gaze settled on the ruins of a temple at the top of the nearest hill. What little remained of the black stone building shook. Chunks of rock broke off the ancient structure. A crack splintered through its massive pillars, and as the strain proved to be too much, the top half shattered. The broken ruin rolled down the hill like a boulder, and though it passed harmlessly between Murdoc and the campfire, the rumble only grew louder.

Murdoc glared up at the temple, and his jaw clenched with worry. Connor had been gone all night, hunting for some unnamed terror the wraith had stored down there. He had expected the captain to have returned by now.

Over by the long-dead campfire, Quinn Starling finally sat upright. She leaned back on her palms and scanned the horizon, same as her vougel. They both watched the sky with the same wary suspicion, as if they shared the same mind.

"She knows something about this," Murdoc said under his breath. His eyes narrowed in distrust as he studied her.

"Maybe," Sophia whispered back, though her dark gaze remained locked on the temple ruins.

"What sort of weapon makes the ground shake like that?"

She shrugged. "I've never felt anything like this. Whatever it is, it's big."

The tremor intensified. Trees groaned around them, threatening to topple. Leaves broke loose of their branches. The last flock of birds scattered into the air, racing toward the lake at the far end of the valley, and Murdoc scowled again at the temple ruins.

This time, the vibrations didn't fade. They grew stronger with each passing second, closing in on them, and the ground threatened to give out under their feet. Murdoc sank into his stance, desperate to keep his balance, but even he couldn't stay upright. He fell and landed hard on one knee as Sophia grappled for something to hold onto. He wrapped one arm protectively around her waist and leaned his other hand into the grass at their feet, bracing himself as he waited for the quake to end.

At the top of the hill, the last surviving block of jet-black stone slid off the temple's already-decimated roof. It shattered against the ground, and smaller boulders tumbled down the hill toward them. Murdoc rolled, pulling Sophia with him, and they dodged the nearest boulder before it could flatten them.

And still, the tremor worsened. The rumble of shattering rock deafened him, as loud as any thunder, and he winced as his ears rang.

Murdoc eyed the ruins yet again, and he wanted nothing more than to defy orders. Connor had instructed him to stay put and guard Quinn, but this couldn't be good. For all Murdoc knew, their captain was trapped down there, crushed in a cave-in or worse.

Connor was the closest thing to a friend he had, and damn it all, he would defy orders if that was what it took to save the man's life. Whatever the cost, even to himself, he couldn't let Connor die.

Sophia craned her neck as she stared up at the top of the hill. Creases of worry appeared in her forehead, and it appeared she had the same thought he did.

That settled it, then.

He leaned his mouth toward her ear. "Stay with the prisoner. Don't let her out of your sight."

Sophia's stunning eyes snapped toward him, and she bristled. "Murdoc, don't you dare."

But he was already gone.

He jumped to his feet and ran toward the hilltop. A thick cloud of dust plumed around the crumbling temple, and he squinted to protect his eyes. Through the murky fog, he scanned the ground any chance he could, always wary for any more of the falling stones.

The ground shook violently. He stumbled, and a rock whizzed past his head. He tried to catch himself, but the quaking earth rattled him. He fell to his hands and knees. He tried pushing off the grass, still struggling to right himself and aching to reach the temple in time to help.

A surge pulsed through the ground, rippling the grass like water, and a wall of energy hit him in the chest. It shot him backward, and he tumbled down the hill. He dug his fingers into the soil to slow himself, and as he slid, he looked up at the temple in an effort to come up with a better plan.

He didn't get the chance.

Stone shattered. A wall of black dust shot into the air. A backlit silhouette burst from the temple and into the sky, taking half the crumbling building with it. Rocks shot in every direction and hit the ground like hail.

A boulder launched at him. It careened through the air, right for his face. Running on instinct and muscle memory, he darted to the left moments before it crashed against the ground and left a dent in the soil where he had been. Smaller rocks whizzed past him, and he ducked them one by one.

As the massive silhouette broke free, the earth finally stopped trembling.

The figure and the dusty haze it had brought with it blocked out the sun. Wings stretched wide. The silhouette cast an eerie shadow through the cloud of debris, and with the sudden darkness came a chill. Its tail writhed underneath it, and a long neck reached for the last of the receding stars.

A thick layer of ash coated Murdoc's face as he went deathly still. He stared up at the thing in awe, wondering what the hell it could be. Its wings easily stretched twenty yards across, maybe more, and it towered over him like a creature of nightmare.

As the dust settled, sunlight glinted over its dazzling silver claws. Lights skittered across its scales, and through the murky mist, it took a moment to recognize the lights as tiny flickers of lightning. The silhouette's neck craned toward Murdoc as it flew upward, and two glowing amber eyes appeared in the cloud of debris.

That snapped him from his awestruck daze.

The creature roared, and the forest trembled. Murdoc winced as the wall of sound broke across his face, and he covered his ears. His brain went fuzzy, not entirely capable of processing what he had seen, and a single word swam circles in his mind.

Dragon.

"Fucking hell," he muttered to himself, still half-numb from his shock. "That's a Fates-damned dragon."

The roar cut off abruptly, and the muffled grunt of a man lifting something heavy broke through the air. Murdoc stiffened as he recognized the voice, and he pushed himself to his feet. He once again drew his sword, determined to help regardless of the cost.

A yellow light built in the center of the shadow. Along the edges of the light, he noticed a vague outline of a row of sharp points that resembled impossibly large teeth.

Fun.

Murdoc balled his free hand into a fist and squared his shoulders, as ready as he would ever be for whatever the hell he was about to face.

In an abrupt and jarring movement, the yellow light jerked upward. The motion cleared a section of the dust cloud, and the dragon's jet-black head appeared through the murky fog. Lightning shot into the sky from the beast's mouth, and Murdoc flinched as he realized how close to death he had just come.

Seconds ago, that magic had been aimed at *him*.

The beast writhed in its fury. Its wings beat the air, churning the dust and clearing it in seconds. It twisted, rising into the sky, and its head bent back again. This time, Murdoc caught sight of a man sitting at the base of the dragon's skull, holding onto its horns.

Connor.

With his knees wrapped around the base of the dragon's neck, the captain said something in a low tone, calm but firm, as the beast squirmed beneath him. The man grunted with effort, but Murdoc couldn't make out anything he said—he was too far away. The dragon's head bent back again, and the curves of Connor's biceps flexed in the dawning sunlight as he forced the creature to do his bidding.

Murdoc's hold on his sword loosened in his shock, but he reflexively tightened his grip before it could fall out of his palm. Connor had skill and strength, obviously, but this was another level altogether.

This was the power of gods, imbued into a mortal man.

"Need help?" Murdoc shouted up at his captain.

Before Connor could answer, the dragon's wings snapped against the air and carried the man fully out of earshot. It roared, and as the ground quaked from the raw power of its voice, it spewed another blast of lightning into the sky. The arc of fizzling energy shot through the clouds, frying the air, and the hair on Murdoc's arms stood on end.

The beast shook its head, unable to knock Connor off, and it bolted toward Death's Door. Something in Murdoc's neck snapped as he followed its blindingly fast speed, and he winced as he tenderly rubbed the base of his head.

Fates be damned, that thing was going to kill his friend. He didn't know how, but he had to reach them.

He had to help.

Murdoc pushed himself to his feet and raced after them, even as the blindingly fast dragon flew farther and farther away. The distance between them grew with each of his steps, but he pushed himself harder. Faster. He ran across the meadow in the direction they had gone, not caring what it took to get there. He gritted his teeth, pushing himself harder than he had ever gone in his life.

As he neared the forest on the far side of the hill, however, a rush of black shadow rolled out of the trees. He skidded to a stop, kicking up grass and clumps of clover in his attempt to keep from slamming into whatever had suddenly appeared. He fell hard onto his back as the coiling darkness rolled over his legs.

A haunting skull appeared in the inky black fog, its hollow eyes focused squarely on him.

The Wraith King.

Once, long ago, Murdoc might've pissed himself in terror just looking at this thing. But he had been around it long enough that the last traces of his fear had been burned away.

"Move, damn it!" He pushed himself to his feet and looked again at the dragon, but the canopy blocked any hope of seeing them from this angle.

The hulking specter before him held out a bony hand, the palm flat against the air—a silent command to stop.

"Are you insane?!" Murdoc shouted at the infuriating dead man. "He needs my help!"

The wraith shook his skeletal head. Those hollow gaping holes somehow focused on Murdoc, as though they were peering into his heart and mind all at once. The specter's cloak shifted, and a bony arm appeared from beneath the tattered cloth. He pointed at something over Murdoc's shoulder.

Murdoc followed the wraith's finger, only to discover the dead man had pointed at the campfire. At Sophia, sitting on one of the logs, her face scrunched and focused as she stared after the dragon. At Quinn, who stared after Connor—not with horror or surprise, but grim concern.

Murdoc cursed under his breath and brushed the lingering dirt off his face. He glared back at the campsite, knowing full well what both the wraith and Connor truly wanted him to do.

He looked back at the Wraith King, who stared at him with a surreal intensity despite the lack of eyes, as if trying to make his silent point with nothing more than a vacant stare.

Murdoc groaned in frustration, but he spread his hands wide in surrender. "She won't escape."

The dead king nodded, just once, and dissolved into the wind. Where seconds before there had been a hulking specter of war and death, now there was nothing more than the edge of a forest beside a field littered with debris from a cracked and crumbled temple.

"Good luck, Captain." Murdoc's words faded into the wind, same as the old ghost had, but it was all he could do at this point. "Looks like you might need it."

CHAPTER FOURTEEN
CONNOR

A mad gale whistled over the dragon's head, blinding Connor as he clung to the base of its skull. It flew like the dogs of hell chased it, as though its very life hinged on its escape. The beast's wings sliced at the air, propelling them faster and faster toward the wall.

Toward Slaybourne's defenses.

Toward the deadly enchantments that would kill it if it dared to fly out into the Decay.

He was running out of time.

"Stop!" he shouted.

The wind drowned out his voice. The dragon didn't even look back as it barreled toward the edge of the Black Keep Mountains.

He let out a string of curses that were swallowed by the rushing air. The dragon shook its head, and though his knees pinched tightly against its neck, he slid. His heart leapt into his throat as he inched down its long neck, and his arms wrapped impulsively around its throat. It screamed into the air and snapped back at him, but from this vantage, it could only bite the wind as they whizzed past.

Before he could stop himself, he looked down.

Far below, the canopy sped by in a dizzying green blur. A gap in the forest opened up, so briefly he barely noticed it, and a sharp collection of rocks gathered in the center of the meadow like a boobytrap waiting to spear him through the back.

Hot acid burned the back of his throat, and his stomach lurched. The dragon bobbed on a draft of air like a buoy out at sea, and he gritted his teeth to ride out the waves of nausea.

Death's Door loomed ahead of them. The inner-most gate rose above the valley like a monolith marking the only exit. The mountains met the door on both sides, and if he were to open it, a narrow walkway carved into the mountains would lead to the outer gate and the Decay beyond it.

The dragon, however, angled upward. It banked toward the clouds, ready to sail over.

As the wind howled, Connor peered back at the dragon's wings. He needed a way to slow it down, perhaps even to ground it long enough to talk some sense into the damned thing. The wings pumped, the dragon's entire body moving with each crack of its leathery hide on the air, and its scales glistened like dark gems in the sunlight.

An idea shocked his system, so sudden and violent that it rooted him in place. If he controlled its wings, he could force it to crash somewhere between here and the exit.

As Death's Door neared, he racked his brain for a better plan, but nothing came to him.

Now or never.

Without a moment's pause to doubt himself, he inched backward. Each movement threatened to throw him off its back, so he crept along the inky black scales with precision and care. Carefully, almost painfully slow given how little time he had left, he clung to the protruding spikes of the dragon's spine and shifted his way down toward its wings.

The dragon snarled, no doubt feeling his movement along its body. It slowed and snapped its wings once against the air, and the brutal movement catapulted them directly upward.

Below, the forest shrank away, and Death's Door receded until it blended into the black mountain rock around it. Any icy blast of air hit his face as they raced toward the clouds, impossibly high, and his body tensed with dread. He clung to the dragon for dear life, and the sheer force of his grip on its body indented its rock-hard scales.

It slowed as they reached the lowest cloud. Its wings folded over its body as it leaned backward, pivoting Connor toward the ground. He held tighter to the spikes along its back, refusing to be hurled off even if it meant ripping off parts of its body.

As its nose broke through the soft white fluff above them, the dragon growled softly. Happily. The sensation rumbled under Connor's hands like a cat's gentle purr, and a pulse of hope shot through him.

Deep down, the dragon prince could still be rescued. His plan could still work.

Its wings brushed the cloud, suspended and still now that it had paused to savor the sky, and their momentum reversed.

They fell.

Connor's stomach lurched. His fingers dug into the dragon's scales, but the beast didn't seem to care. It pointed its nose toward the ground. Wings tucked in tight, it dove toward certain death.

As they fell, the dragon rolled. The distant forest floor blurred into a kaleidoscope of color interspersed with streaks of black rock and green fields. Connor clung to the beast, his muscles screaming. His body ached. His knees and shoulders burned with the effort of clinging to a creature that wanted nothing more than to hurl him off into the forest far below.

Still, he held tight and squeezed his eyes shut to keep himself oriented. Bile rose into the back of his mouth, but he did his best to keep it at bay. Icy wind bit at his face.

Finally, blissfully, the spinning stopped. The blurs solidified once more, but the ground neared at a dizzying speed.

Out in the Ancient Woods, he had seen birds do this, on occasion, when a fanged squirrel tried to sneak up on them and steal their eggs. It would climb on their backs to break their wings, but the birds who acted faster always survived. They would dive out of the tree and, at the last second, they would change direction, sending the squirrel flying toward the ground.

Most of the time, the squirrel didn't get back up.

He muttered obscenities as they barreled toward the canopy. The closer they got, the more details he could pick up in the ocean of green below them—gaps in the branches, the rustle of the wind through the leaves.

Any second now, it would shift direction, and his momentum would throw him off its back.

With no time to lose, he crawled the final distance to its wings, which were still tightly tucked against its body. With one hand still gripping the dragon's spiky spine, he grabbed the bony frame of its right wing with the other.

He was nearly ready. Next, he had to find a place to land where they could talk like civilized beings.

He scanned the ground below and, to his relief, spotted a flat stretch of rock along the deep channel that stretched through the mountain between each of the two gates that comprised Death's Door. As long as he didn't slide off the edge and into the road hewn into the mountainside, he could find a way to land them somewhere along the top of the cliff.

It would take some maneuvering, but he would have the upper hand. It didn't, however, give him much leeway. The edge of the outer wall loomed ever closer. This stretch of rock would place them closer to the Decay than he would've liked, but they were nearing the cliff edge and he was running out of time.

As they plummeted toward the valley below, he tracked how close they were to his target and did his best to gauge the distance. His grip tightened on the top curve of its wing, and his fingers spasmed as his sense of self-preservation screamed at him to open the wing already.

"Steady," he told himself.

Admittedly, he'd never done something like this before, but the wraith had brought a wealth of firsts into his life. Downing a dragon would just be another surreal addition to the list.

He had far less leverage without both of his arms wrapped around the massive dragon's spine, but he would have to make do. As the cliff neared, and he muttered a half-hearted prayer that this would work.

Sparks fizzed across its scales. They hit Connor in waves, and he sucked in air through his teeth as each one hit him. The buzz blistered through him, hot and fast. His ears rang, louder with each arc of light that shocked him, but he couldn't do a damn thing about it until they landed.

With his focus on the rapidly approaching mountainside, he waited. He had to time this perfectly. One miscalculation, one lapse in judgement, and he would send them both crashing straight into the stone mountain. At this speed, it would flatten them both.

There was no room for error. Not now.

It snarled and looked back at him, its glowing eyes narrowing as it finally realized what he was about to do, but it was too late.

The cliff neared, finally in range.

Connor gritted his teeth and grabbed the bony frame of the dragon's wing. With all his enhanced strength, he pried it away from the creature's body. It resisted him, testing his strength and pushing his limits, but it eventually gave. The dragon roared with pain as he manhandled its wing, but the leathery sail ultimately obeyed. It snapped open, slowing their descent instantly and pivoting them to the left.

They banked hard as he forced the dragon closer to the cliff. The sheer rock loomed ahead of them. Even as the beast pushed against him, fighting him every step of the way, he tilted the wing upward and adjusted their trajectory as best he could.

His fingers ached, seconds from giving out. His arms flexed as he resisted the powerful creature, and he roared with the effort of resisting a dragon's strength.

The cliff barreled toward them. In seconds, they would crash into it. He braced himself for a rough landing, but as he peered over the dragon's head, he got another wild idea.

Seconds from impact, the dragon roared in frustration. Connor tilted his shoulders toward the dragon's skull, careful to aim himself as best as possible to end this.

There would only be one shot at this.

No going back now.

The dragon's chest hit the rock first. Black boulders launched into the air, and fresh plumes of dust rolled over them both. The impact launched Connor forward, just as he had expected, and he sped toward the glowing horns protruding from the thick dust swirling around them. As the dragon lifted its head, roaring in pain and fury, Connor brought his fists together over his head and aimed for the spot between its eyes.

This would hurt them both.

With its snout aimed up toward the clouds, Connor drove his clasped fists at the spot between its glowing amber eyes.

The impact rocked him, as if he had punched a thick iron door immune to even his magic. Pain splintered up his arms, and he grimaced in agony as he rode the shockwave. The blow launched the dragon's head straight down into the rock, and the battered mountainside quaked from the force.

Connor tucked his head and rolled across the flat stretch of cliff. His momentum carried him across the jet-black stone, and his boots kicked up pebbles as he slid. Mostly out of instinct, he drove his hands into the mountain to slow himself. His fingers carved a channel through the rock, and another bite of pain shot up his arm from the effort—but it worked.

As he gradually slowed to a stop, his body ached. His eyes stung. He longed to rest, to sleep, to take a break from this brutal battle of theirs, but he pushed through it.

This close to the end, he couldn't stop *now*.

In the murky haze that lingered after their crash, he lost sight of the dragon. Its tail swept through the dust, churning it like a fog on the ocean, and the dragon's soft growl rolled through it like thunder.

He waited, daring it to move. Daring it to test his patience even more than it already had.

Two golden eyes appeared in the settling mist, burning like suns, and his heart skipped a beat. They blinked rapidly, still disoriented, and stared directly at him before they shifted toward something to his left.

He peered over his shoulder, careful to keep the dragon in his periphery. Barely fifty yards away, the cliff ended. Beyond, the Decay stretched to the horizon, and the ash-strewn ruins of the decimated new growth beyond the gate marked where he and Zander had dueled just days before.

Their crash landing had taken him far closer to the edge of Slaybourne than he had intended.

The dragon snarled and darted past him toward the cliff edge. It just wanted to escape. It didn't know the danger lurking beyond the wall.

"Stop!" Connor shouted. "It'll kill you!"

The beast shook its massive head, still dazed, and dug its claws into the mountain rock as it ran. Its wing hit him hard in the chest as it passed, knocking the wind out of him, and he launched backward.

For a few seconds, he saw stars. He coughed and sputtered, trying his best to force himself to his feet.

The dragon's tail swept overhead as it closed the distance to the wall, and that snapped him out of his daze. The dust hovering around them cleared in a rush of wings, and the edge of Slaybourne's walls appeared through the murky fog.

The dragon leaped into the air. Only its tail remained in reach, and Connor did the only thing he could think of.

He grabbed it.

With all his might, he pulled on the dragon's tail. The beast snarled in anger, but he dug his heels into the rock and yanked it back. In the same second, its head passed over the edge of the wall.

A soft, subtle tremor shook the ground beneath Connor's feet. From somewhere in the rock, somewhere hidden and beyond maybe even the wraith's understanding, a jagged black spike shot into the air, aimed directly for the dragon's head.

Connor unleashed a strangled battle cry as he leaned everything he had into his hold on the dragon's tail. Finally, mercifully, his desperate ploy worked. At the last possible moment, the dragon shifted direction. The spear, once aimed for the soft spot underneath the dragon's jaw, missed by inches. The jagged weapon shot past the beast's nose and passed harmlessly into the sky.

More soft rumbles followed, and a flurry of spears shot after the first. The resulting effect resembled a pulsating wall of deadly stone between them and the Decay. Safe within the boundary of the wall, however, the dragon hit the ground hard. The mountain shook from the sheer weight of it collapsing against the earth, and its tail went limp in his hands. Both Connor and the beast froze, still as statues as they watched the wall of death that had almost snared them both.

The last harpoon whizzed into the air after the rest, and the world went eerily still. The wind howled through the ravine below, and the dragon let out a single, huffing breath.

Connor's chest heaved from the effort of what he had just done, and he shut his eyes in momentary relief to savor the impossibility of yanking a dragon from the sky.

This world does not limit you, the wraith had said last night. *You are not bound by the laws of other men. What we must discover, Magnuson, is why—and what your limits truly are.*

At this point, Connor couldn't even *guess*.

CHAPTER FIFTEEN

CONNOR

Stunned into silence, both Connor and the dragon waited on the edge of Slaybourne. A soft whistle hummed through the air from somewhere above them.

Connor tensed, instantly on edge once more, and stared up at the clouds as the first spike fell back toward the earth. It sank into the charred ruins beyond the main door and hit the ground with a thump. One by one, the other spikes fell in droves, like a wall of arrows shot from the heavens to spear the godless ground beyond Slaybourne.

The dragon, however, didn't move—it sat there, still as death itself, and a cold bolt of dread shot clear through Connor's bones.

He let go of its tail and sprinted toward its head. He must've been wrong. He must've been too slow, or too late, to save it. One of the spikes must've hit it, after all.

When he reached the dragon's snout, however, he found it staring blankly ahead. Its eyes had dilated in its dazed confusion, and as far as he could tell, it had lost itself in the trauma of a near death experience. The amber glow in its eyes faded, and the soothing black returned.

"Good," Connor said softly, his chest still heaving from the effort of pulling a beast of legend from the sky.

It snarled, and its eyes flashed briefly gold. Its gaze darted to him, and its lips curled back in warning.

"You ungrateful *ass!*" he snapped.

He had saved this damn thing's life, and it still wanted to fight him. It still saw him as food, or worse.

As he glared the stupid beast down, something in him snapped.

It growled, and that ominous clicking came again from the back of its throat. It bared its teeth, but before it could do anything else, he grabbed its snout with both hands and shoved its face into the rock. He'd acted on impulse, lost in his frustration and bubbling rage, and he no longer cared what happened next.

The moment had snared him, and he was utterly lost in it.

His biceps flexed with the sheer effort of holding down a beast of this size, but he was close to cracking. He was close to letting the damn thing fly over the walls and get itself killed.

His patience was *gone*.

"Look at yourself!" he shouted as it squirmed beneath his grip. "Look at what you've let yourself become! Since I was a boy, I've heard the legends about your kind. I read every story I could get my hands on about the noble dragons of the old days. I was told you represent power. Magic. The forces of nature. I heard that even the storms fear you because you can master their chaos. Fates above, you infuriating thing, even *nature* fears you. But this is what I find when I finally meet one? You're a breathing titan brought to life, you stupid twat, and yet you've reduced yourself to nothing more than a petty carnivore!"

He backhanded it in the middle of its forehead, and its whole body shook from the force of his blow. As it blinked rapidly to clear its head, he once again grabbed its snout, and his grip only tightened.

"Get ahold of yourself!" he added, his voice carrying the full weight of his disappointed fury.

Its eyes went wide with surprise, and for a moment, it went dangerously still.

"Is this what you want? Really?" Connor nodded to the edge of the wall, toward the spikes covering the long-dead ground beyond his fortress. "Is this how you want to die? This is a mountain few even know about. Your final battle isn't here. If you want to go down in a blaze of glory, I can arrange that, but you're going to die if you keep resisting me. I'm trying to help you, damn it! Don't waste your life in a fight you could never win!"

In the back of Connor's mind, the wraith chuckled with pride.

The clicking noise in the back of the dragon's throat slowly faded, replaced only by the heaving huffs of its bewildered breath.

"You're a prince, damn it all," Connor added, glaring it down. "Act like one!"

At that, it looked away in shame. It blinked rapidly, and the amber glow in its eyes dissolved into a soothing and endless black. The yellow ribbons of magic disappeared from its horns and spine. It lowered its tail, and though its wings remained spread wide, it relaxed beneath his palms. Its claws receded from the rock and slid back into its feet.

As it all but surrendered, Connor braced himself for another attack. For a trick. For something, anything at all, to fly at him and nail him in the chest again.

He wasn't quite ready to believe it was over.

The dragon watched him with eyes as smooth and dark as the depths of the ocean. In the silence that followed, only the howl of the wind through the passage into Slaybourne filled the air. The amber glow didn't return, and the dragon didn't try to escape.

"Are you back?" Connor raised one eyebrow in suspicion. His chest ached from the tension in his core, but he wasn't going to back down until he was certain.

"I am." The dragon's resonant voice sent vibrations up Connor's arms as it studied his face. "But I do not understand why. You reek of the Wraith King's magic, and yet you undid what he has done."

Infuriatingly, the wraith added.

Connor ignored the ghost, and his intense gaze remained locked on the dragon. "If I let go, what will you do?"

"Rest," The dragon admitted. "I am so very tired."

"As am I," Connor admitted.

Carefully, almost reluctantly, he lifted his hands off the dragon's snout. The legendary creature let out a weary sigh, and the huff of air stirred dust under its nose. Small tornadoes of debris spun to the edge of the wall before they dissolved into the air.

Still, the dragon didn't move.

"You have a name." Connor set his hands on his waist as he stared it down. "Do you remember?"

The dragon growled softly, and its eyes narrowed as it studied him with equal intensity. "I AM NOCTURNE, PRINCE OF THE DRAGONS, KING OF THE NIGHTLANDS, PROTECTOR OF WARRIORS AND MONKS ALIKE."

"I'm Connor." He cleared his throat awkwardly as he debated how much information to give the creature. "Connor Magnuson."

Tell him your title, damn you, the wraith snapped. *If you're going to treat this thing like an equal, at least make certain it understands that this is your domain. It is a prince, but you are a king.*

Connor waved away the wraith's demand with a flick of his wrist. He had more important matters to discuss.

The ghoul let out an infuriated groan. *Honor the custom, you fool! You'll have to get used to it sooner or later.*

"CONNOR." The dragon spoke his name as though he were tasting it. "I ASSUME YOU BROUGHT ME BACK BECAUSE YOU WANT SOMETHING FROM ME."

"What makes you say that?"

"YOU HUMANS ALWAYS DO."

"That's fair." Connor rubbed his eyes and sat on a nearby boulder, his chest still heaving from their duel. He leaned his elbows on his knees and stared out over the Decay, still marveling at how close they had both come to death today. "Look, the enchantment holding you was wearing down Slaybourne's defenses. I needed to break it to keep my home safe."

Don't tell it that! the wraith snapped.

"He," Connor corrected under his breath, his tone quiet but firm. "Not 'it.' He."

The ghoul grumbled obscenities, but didn't reply.

"WHY DIDN'T YOU PUSH ME OVER THE BRINK?" The dragon gave a half-hearted nod over its shoulder, back toward the valley. "DOWN THERE IN THE TUNNELS, I WAS CUT OFF FROM THE SKY AND CLOSE TO GONE. I'VE ALREADY FORGOTTEN LONG STRETCHES OF OUR DUEL. YOU COULD HAVE FINISHED what the Wraith King started."

"It wouldn't have been right."

The dragon prince lifted his mighty head, and Connor tensed impulsively at the sudden movement. His fingers stretched wide, ready to summon his shadow blade if the need arose, but he forced himself to wait.

The creature's head swept toward him. Those massive black eyes neared, as did those teeth. The prince of beasts came close—too close—and it took everything in Connor to resist driving one of his swords into the dragon's skull.

Nocturne tilted his head until only one eye was visible, and he brought it close enough for Connor to touch. The dragon studied him, that glistening black eye both soothing and surreal. It gleamed in the early sunlight, and as he stared into it, the inky black iris seemed to go on forever. It swallowed any light that came close, almost absorbing it, to the point where Connor nearly lost touch with the world around him. He felt suddenly naked, as though the dragon were peering into his soul and seeing more than any living creature ever should.

Nocturne hovered there for only the Fates knew how long, studying the unseen, discovering things not even Connor knew about himself yet.

They stood there, suspended, for what felt like ages.

After a while, Connor shut his eyes, and that broke the spell. Though the dragon's breath rolled over his right arm, he resisted the overwhelming urge to attack.

"What are you doing?" he asked.

"Observing."

Connor raised one dubious eyebrow. "Find anything good?"

"Yes," the dragon prince answered. "And no."

Connor frowned, uncertain of whether or not that had been an insult.

Nocturne shifted his weight, and the massive head finally moved away. The dragon reclined on the stone and rested his jaw against the rock beneath them as he stared off at the horizon. "Dragons are creatures of nobility and truth. We can see through lies, even those a man tells himself. I see more of you than you realize, Connor Magnuson, but there is more I must learn."

"And what exactly do you need to learn about me?"

"You want something from me," the dragon answered. "Tell me what it is."

"Alright." Connor stretched out his neck, stiff as it was from their little flight through the clouds, and a surge of relief shot through him. "I want to make a deal."

The ghoul sighed impatiently. *Of course you do.*

Nocturne narrowed his massive eyes, skeptical, and waited for Connor to continue.

With a gesture out toward the Decay, Connor ignored the wraith's jibe. "This is my home. A threat has been made against it—against me—and there's war coming this way. I want help defending what's mine."

"And why would you ask for my help? I am trained in war, but I do not enjoy it."

"I figured," Connor admitted, still piecing together the threads of his plan as he went along. "I brought you back to right an old wrong, not to force you into debt or servitude. You don't owe me anything for that."

You are a Fates-damned idiot, the wraith snapped.

"I know you came here looking for something," Connor continued, refusing to acknowledge that the ghoul had spoken. "Whatever it is, maybe it's still out there. Maybe I can help you find it."

"I see." The dragon paused as he considered the offer. "I came here looking for some of my people. Dragons began to go missing in the southern borders of this land you call Saldia. It was my task to rescue them if I could, or at a minimum, discover what had become of them."

With a frustrated sigh, Connor rubbed his eyes. "No dragons have been sighted around here in centuries. I don't know if I can help you find them, but I have connections. Friends. Even if we can't find them, I can probably help you figure out if they were ever here."

If Sophia didn't have answers, she would know someone who did—or they could always squeeze something useful out of Quinn Starling.

"And in exchange?"

"You help me defend my home and my team. While you're here, you're my guest, and that means you do as I say. You can't go rogue. You can't leave my sight, or I won't be able to protect you. There are worse fates waiting for you out there if you were to fly through Saldia on your own, trust me."

"And then?"

"You go home. If we find any of your fellow dragons, you take them with you."

"That is all you want from me?"

Connor nodded. The wraith groaned at the missed opportunity to negotiate for more, but Connor didn't care. He wasn't the sort to wring every last coin out of someone just because he could.

He took what he needed, and nothing more.

"You are strange."

"Am I, now?" He smirked and raised one eyebrow in surprise.

Nocturne closed his eyes and sucked in a deep breath as a sunbeam broke through the clouds and landed on his neck. "You seem to be a man of honor, despite your connections to the brutish king who ruled here. Are you his descendent?"

Fates forbid, the Wraith King muttered. *To lose my tenacity and ferocity through my line would be the ultimate stain on my name.*

"I'm not the Wraith King's descendant," Connor answered with a grin, still refusing to acknowledge the dead king's commentary.

Truth be told, he was probably enjoying the wraith's frustration a little too much.

Sunlight filtered through the clouds, warmer now than in the early dawn, and the world around them brightened as the sun finally awoke. A soft hum buzzed in the back of the dragon's throat, almost like a happy little purr. "If you are not the Wraith King's descendant, why do I see traces of him in your soul?"

"Ah, that." Connor scratched the back of his head, wondering how the hell he was going to explain this. "Because—"

The wraith appeared beside him in a puff of black smoke. The dark mist churned over the rock, and the dead king crossed his bony arms as he stared

Connor down.

He met the ghoul's gaze, unfazed.

Nocturne's eyes snapped into focus, and he jumped effortlessly to his feet. His wings spread wide, and he snarled in warning. Sparks ricocheted across his silky scales, and a soft amber glow burned in his once-peaceful eyes.

"You," he seethed, glaring at the Wraith King. "I would know that scent anywhere."

Damn it all to hell.

Connor jumped to his feet, wondering if the wraith had undone all of his work just to spite him, but the amber glow in Nocturne's eyes had a different intensity this time. It didn't engulf him, but it instead rippled like water in a pond, floating over the inky black eyes beneath.

Nocturne still had full control. As a royal, he had better connection to and control over his feral side.

Time for Connor to test his newfound influence and the strength of their little truce.

"Stop," he ordered.

Nocturne roared, and a blast of hot air hit Connor in the face. The dragon prince tilted his mighty head toward him, however, and the amber glow faded the moment their eyes met. The sparks receded, and though he remained coiled to pounce, he didn't move.

A stressful and uncertain alliance, perhaps, but an alliance nonetheless. The prince had obeyed.

Connor couldn't deny the ribbon of glee snaking through him at the thought that a dragon had just obeyed a direct order.

He set his palm on the dragon's neck to soothe the prince's fury. The regal creature flinched under his touch, but ultimately didn't move away. Heat radiated from the silky scales, and Connor almost couldn't believe he'd had enough power to take something like this down.

"He is my enemy," Nocturne let out a slow growl as he watched the wraith hovering before them.

"I know." Connor patted the dragon's neck again, and this time, the low growl faded to silence.

The idea of protecting a creature like this seemed almost ludicrous, but he couldn't imagine what Zander or Otmund would do if they got their hands on Nocturne. There were men—and women—who would use the prince's power to decimate the continent.

He frowned. There were plenty of people who assumed any Wraithblade would do the same. That he would use his strength to destroy everyone and everything. The Starlings expected him to play the villain, and no logic or reason would ever sway them.

It didn't matter. To his dying breath, he would do everything he could to prove them wrong.

The wraith pivoted toward Connor. *You ruined everything. You undid all of my hard work, and for what? A truce this ravenous thing could break at any moment?*

"He," Connor corrected again.

You ignored everything I said to do! the ghoul snapped. *If you truly wish to embody power incarnate, you cannot dismiss my wisdom and experience again!*

"I would take a sane, rational prince over a broken hellbeast any day."

Nocturne snorted, and his eyes narrowed as he glared down at the wraith. "I dislike him immensely."

Connor laughed. "You're not the only one."

I swear, Magnuson, you're impossible. With his skeletal fingers, the ghoul pinched the bone between his empty eye sockets. *One of these days, you will learn to listen to me.*

"I doubt it." Connor ran his hand across Nocturne's impossibly soft scales. "It's when I agree with you that I'm concerned for my sanity."

CHAPTER SIXTEEN

QUINN

With her elbows resting on her knees, Quinn closed her eyes and lost herself in thought.

Though the Bluntmar collar around her neck cut her off from her magic, she didn't need the Hearhaven augmentation to enjoy the woodland chorus in these first hours of a new spring day. The rush of clattering leaves blended with the twittering birdsong as the rumbling finally faded and life returned, bit by bit, to the forest.

Something shuffled through the meadow grasses, and she peered through one eye as a rabbit hopped past her foot. Its little tail stood out from the verdant field around it, a streak of white against the green, and it paused a short distance away to inspect her. Its nose sniffed at the air as it studied her face, and when she didn't try to eat it, it rummaged through the nearby grass for its breakfast.

Innocent creatures. Glowing golden birds. A vibrant garden rife with enchantment and littered with ruins of a long-dead empire.

None of this made any damn *sense*.

Based on everything she had heard through her life, this land should have been a salted graveyard where nothing could grow. By all accounts, the Wraith King had destroyed this valley and left it barren, and yet life somehow thrived here.

As did, apparently, a dragon.

Her shoulders stiffened with fear as she relived the mythical beast bursting from the ground. She shut her eyes again as a second rush of terror hit her, followed by yet another lightning shock of disbelief. Numb awe crept into her bones once more, and she rubbed her tired eyes as she recounted the stunning detail around the monster's face. The glowing horns. The silky black scales. Those burning amber eyes.

And Connor, firmly planted on its back.

The way he had ridden the dragon should have been impossible. Quinn had grown up surrounded by the greatest warriors in Saldia, but never in her life had she seen someone harness that much raw power before.

Not even her father.

The thought chilled her to her core. There was clearly more to the Wraithblade than she had suspected.

And the *dragon*. Tavern rumors and old wives' tales suggested that dragons still existed somewhere beyond the Barrens, but no one had ever returned with proof—mainly because anyone who left in search of them never came home.

If the Wraith King had managed to preserve a dragon in the depths of this twisted citadel, Quinn wasn't sure she wanted to know what else lay dormant beneath her feet.

A sharp sting shot through the back of her eyes, and she groaned as she massaged her aching temple. Blaze had kept guard through the night to give her some much-needed rest, but her eyelids still drooped with exhaustion. It didn't matter how much sleep she got or how little she moved. Her exhaustion bit into her soul, and she figured all of this was by design.

The Bluntmar collar drained her. Even holding her head upright tested her strength. Her neck ached, and her back strained with the effort of maintaining her weak and meager slouch. As she sat in the glowing meadow grass, she leaned her weight into her elbows while the enchanted metal siphoned more and more of her energy.

In the prisons beneath Lunestone, even the weakest prisoners could at least stand with relative ease when wearing a Lightseer's Bluntmar collar. They had always appeared a little tired, certainly, but not weak.

Nothing like *this*.

This had to be the necromancer's doing. That wench must've enchanted it to be something more than just a regular Bluntmar, somehow.

"Get ahold of yourself," Quinn whispered, chiding herself for letting weakness show. She clenched her jaw, tensed her core, and forced herself to sit taller. She refused to give the necromancer the satisfaction of knowing how much effort it took just to sit upright.

Around her neck, the Volt clinked against her Starling Crest pendant as she adjusted in her seat. The sheer weight of the charmed medallion pulled on her neck, and though it was harder to bear now that she had lost access to her Strongman augmentation, she refused to take it off.

This collar had to be broken, and soon. Enduring it for a few days had already pushed her beyond her limits, but she hadn't wanted to draw any attention to herself while the Wraithblade's suspicions were high.

After several uneventful days, however, he had begun to lower his guard. She could practically see his thoughts shifting to more urgent matters. He had left her alone, for the most part, and as the days passed, he had cast fewer sidelong glares in her direction.

Of course, his straying attention could've easily been a trap, but it hardly mattered. At this point, Quinn had already observed far more than the Wraithblade or the ghoul could imagine. The collar had given her an excuse to stay quiet and conserve her energy. Always listening and always eager for someone to make another mistake, she had absorbed everything she could about this odd collection of misfits he had acquired.

For starters, the Wraithblade had a name—Connor. Though she had yet to uncover his surname, she had monitored the way he interacted with his two companions. From what Quinn had gathered, both of them must've been deserters.

The woman, Sophia, possessed the enchanted blades that were only crafted for the Nethervale elite. The man, however—Murdoc—had been harder to identify. After a bit of studying, she figured he had most likely been expelled from the Blackguard Brotherhood. He fought like a trained soldier, but he had yet to use magic despite ample opportunity. If someone without magic wanted to fight, only the Blackguards would take them in.

That meant Connor had surrounded himself with criminals. How fitting. Most of the men she knew would've treated these two as servants, but not Connor. No one had been ordered to build the fire, clean game, or do other menial chores to make his life easier unless he was already consumed in another task of greater importance. As he had surveyed the valley, he had focused first on finding them all a safe place to sleep. Not once had he asked them to do something he hadn't already done himself. He found them water, hunted them game, and even showed the necromancer where to find berries when she complained of eating nothing but meat. He had grumbled and poked fun at her the whole time, of course, but he had still done it.

And now, with the dragon's escape, he had put himself in harm's way to keep them out of it. This Connor fellow, for whatever reason, cared about these felons.

Of everything Quinn had expected to find out here, of all the horrors she had prepared herself to see, she hadn't anticipated *that*.

As the dull ache in the back of her skull sharpened into blistering pain, Quinn groaned and set her head in her hands. Several hours had passed since the dragon had burst from the ground, and yet Connor still hadn't returned.

She scanned the valley through the gap in her fingers, fully expecting to see him riding into the clearing at any moment, but nothing sped toward them from the distance. Clouds rolled peacefully through the topaz sky above, and the forest around them danced with a gentle breeze.

Debris littered the grass around her from the dragon's escape, and her two remaining captors sat beside the black pit that had once been their fire. They spoke in a low tone, but without access to her Hearhaven augmentation, she couldn't hear a word of it.

Murdoc leaned toward the necromancer, frowning with concern as he studied her face. Though Quinn could only see Sophia's back from here, the woman's soft voice followed, and her shoulders drooped ever so slightly.

Another nugget from Quinn's observations: the necromancer was deathly ill, and she didn't have much longer to live. Whatever had happened to her, whatever she had done, she needed a skilled healer. But as the collar pressed hard against Quinn's throat and drained more of her energy, she couldn't quite bring herself to feel sympathy for the woman. Perhaps she could exploit this should the opportunity for a negotiation arise, but without more information, she didn't know of anyone who could help.

Except Tove, of course. Tove Warren had figured out every complex problem Quinn had ever given her. Quinn didn't want to drag her only friend into this mess, but if she and Connor were able to strike a deal, Tove was the only one she could trust to help.

Her training told her to sit, to wait, to listen more, but Quinn had already seen everything she needed to see. Any more observation would waste valuable time.

Next, she needed to poke at his weak spots. A man like this, with access to such limitless power, needed inhuman morality to resist the allure of *more:* more power, more soldiers, more land.

That was the black pit into which Aeron's abomination had lured every Wraithblade thus far. No matter how much they acquired or how powerful they became, it was never enough.

It was likely that, with time, this Wraithblade would fall into the same trap.

A sharp jolt of pain shot from her eye, clear through to the back of her head, and she winced. Her thumb pressed hard into her brow, but the ache only worsened.

To hell with waiting. The collar had to come off *now.*

She stood, and her head spun from the sudden movement. Black dots peppered her vision, and she teetered as she fought to keep her balance. She braced herself and forced a slow, steady breath to keep from upchucking her dinner. The Volt slid down her chest and settled into her cleavage, and it gave her some measure of comfort to know a weapon even deadlier than her Firesword rested between her breasts.

From deep in the meadow nearby, Blaze lifted his head. His furry white face popped above the shivering grasses as his ears perked to attention. The wind played with the soft white and gold fur on his features as the vougel watched her, ready to follow, but she lifted her hand in a subtle command to stay put.

Over at the dead firepit, Murdoc's gaze shifted her way. "Where exactly do you think you're going?"

Sophia looked over her shoulder, and though her brows pinched with annoyance, she couldn't hide the bags under her eyes or the weak slump of her posture.

"Privy," Quinn said simply.

"Nature's call, huh?" Murdoc gestured to the overgrown woodland behind him with a mischievous little smirk. "You're in luck, my good noblewoman. We offer only the finest accommodations for such a proud and esteemed guest. Pick whichever tree you like!"

Despite her dire situation, she chuckled quietly.

"Five minutes." The necromancer's voice sliced through the air, her tone sharp with warning. "One minute longer, and I'll freeze your vougel alive."

Blaze growled, and Quinn whistled once to make him stop. The snarl faded as he instantly obeyed, but he watched Sophia with all the intense focus of a hungry dog. His tail twitched back and forth above the grasses with barely restrained irritation.

Like Quinn, he wanted nothing more than to rip this infuriating woman open, but they would both have to resist the urge. As long as Sophia was under Connor's protection, killing her came with consequences Quinn didn't want to face.

Not yet, anyway.

As her head swam from whatever the Bluntmar collar was doing to her, she focused her full attention on walking in a straight line. The clattering applause of shivering leaves in the canopy replaced the rush of the wind through the grass as she stepped into the forest. Birds twittered as she put distance between her and the campsite, and she kept a careful watch over her shoulder as Murdoc returned his attention to the ever-weakening Sophia.

If the necromancer hadn't been fading so quickly, Quinn doubted she would've been left to wander on her own. Murdoc seemed to have an unrequited soft spot for the woman, which meant he wouldn't leave her side. Sophia could hardly stand, much less keep watch, so she was hardly a threat. But between the Bluntmar collar and her beloved vougel held hostage, they knew they had the upper hand.

For now.

When they were finally out of sight—and with only five short minutes to break this powerful enchantment around her neck—she forced herself to sprint through the woods as she hunted for a good spot to break the collar. Trees blurred past her on all sides, but a few towering pines wouldn't muffle the inevitable snap of an enchantment breaking.

She bit her lip, rapidly scanning every inch of the forest she passed. Based on what little she knew of Sophia, the five minute warning had merit. That necromancer might actually try to kill Blaze if she got the chance, and may the Fates help the woman if she tried.

Up ahead, Quinn finally caught sight of a cluster of boulders jutting from the forest floor. She ducked behind them so that they stood between her and the now-distant campsite. With one hand against the cold stone for balance, she knelt on the ground. Her head spun, and each breath scraped against her throat as she fumbled for the Volt.

It rested in her palm, warm and heavy—her salvation from this blasted collar.

With her free hand, she fought with the metal circlet around her neck until she located the lock. In seconds, the bottom-most tip of the pendant settled into the keyhole, and she braced herself for what would come next.

It would hurt like hell for lightning to hit metal pressed against her skin, but in her time fighting the elite necromancers of Nethervale, she had endured far worse.

She twisted the Volt ever so slightly, just enough to create a single short burst, and a small arc of lightning ripped out of the base of the pendant. A sharp crack cut through the forest, as loud as thunder, and her ears popped from the sheer weight of the sound.

An agonizing shock snapped through her body. It crackled through every vein, every pore, through every hair on her head. Her neck tightened until she could feel the tendons pressing against her throat.

Lean into the pain, her father used to say. *Embrace it.*

She stifled her agonized scream, grimacing instead as the torment boiled her blood. Her lungs refused to work. Her heart lost track of its own rhythm and thudded in a crazed, discordant melody.

Tears? Really? Her father's voice rattled around in her brain as the agonizing current cooked her from the inside out. *Are you my daughter or not, Quinn? A Starling doesn't cry.*

The charred stench of burning meat curled through her nose, and she ground her teeth together as she fought to ignore the pain.

A Starling doesn't cry.

In a rush, the burst of lightning released her. She fell to the ground in a heap. Her chest heaved as her lungs labored for air. Her ears rang. Her vision blurred. Bursts of sharp pain shot through her body with every beat of her heart, and she flinched each time they hit. Leaves stuck to her face, and sweat dripped down her neck.

She didn't have time to waste on recovery, but she couldn't even lift her head.

"Get up," she hissed at herself.

The sharp crack from the Volt's magic would inevitably attract her captors' attention, even from this distance, and she couldn't let them find her like this.

She tried to push herself onto her hands and knees, but she fell again to the dirt. Heaving for air, she tried again. Though her arms shook, she managed to stay upright this time. Loose hair and a few fragments of bark stuck to the sweat on her brow, and she wiped her face against her trembling shoulder to clear it away.

As the pain slowly receded, the collar slid off her neck and hit the dirt with a dull thud. She waited, exhausted and aching, for her magic to return.

It hit her in a blinding rush.

She let out a strangled little gasp as her blood ignited with raw, unfettered power. Fire from her family's trademark augmentation flickered and snapped through her chest. On impulse, she stretched her fingers toward the canopy, and the wind shifted direction as her Airdrift charm took it over.

Her augmentations flared to life, one by one, in a blinding cacophony, and she was once again whole. As relief flooded her body, clear down to her toes, a broad smile broke across her face.

"That's more like it," she whispered.

Thanks to her Eyebright augmentation, her vision sharpened once more.

The tiniest flecks of mica and bark mixed into the soil beneath her hands came into clear focus. The open Bluntmar collar lay beneath her, and the Volt's powerful blow had snapped it at the lock in one clean line.

"Perfect." She grinned. It would never work again, but she could still close it.

Without warning, the lightning of her Voltaic augmentation crackled through her fingers. Sparks skittered across her hands, wild and uncontrolled. She growled in frustration and fought to reign in the one magical ability that her father and brother flaunted, but which she had never been able to tame.

She balled her hands into fists as the wild magic nearly overtook her in this moment of weakness. It pushed against her palms, begging to be freed, but she restrained the chaotic energy with a series of steady breaths and muffled curses.

As her strength finally returned, she brushed the last of the leaves from her hair. Though she wanted nothing more than to melt down that damned collar with her Burnbane fires, she lifted the circlet and set it loosely around her neck. The hinge creaked as she wrapped it around her throat, and her body tensed on impulse even if she knew deep down it would never again lock. It would, however, stay around her neck and appear functional as long as she didn't abruptly move.

It was the perfect disguise. With the broken keyhole tucked away behind her hair, no one would know it had ever come off.

Now, at least, she could observe her mark with a clear head. There was still much to learn about this Connor fellow before she made her next move. Namely, she needed to know what he really wanted and the lengths to which he would go to get it.

Hell, after watching him ride a dragon into the sky, she didn't even know what he was capable of anymore. Perhaps he had no limits at all.

The thought sent a chill down her spine.

Her test would be simple—she would offer him a deal. There had to be plenty of things he needed. The point was to get him to leave so that she could both study him outside of Slaybourne's walls and look for opportunities to escape when the time was right. Out there, she would have ample opportunity to test his motivations, his weaknesses, and his greed.

Even good men could succumb to the allure of ultimate power. For all she knew, this kindness of his was nothing more than a mask he wore to fool others. Before long, she would know everything there was to know about Saldia's new Wraithblade.

And if he fails my test…

Quinn stilled and rubbed her tired eyes. Dueling someone who could conquer a dragon hardly seemed wise, but she had never backed down from a fight before. Whatever the outcome—whoever this man truly was—she refused to let Saldia burn.

Her father was coming, and his brewing conflict with the Wraithblade would scorch the earth. She had as little time to decide her place in this war as Connor did to prepare for it.

CHAPTER SEVENTEEN
SOPHIA

As the southern wind rolled through the trees above, the tail end of a muted roar lingered in the air. Nothing else seemed to notice—not even the tiger-bird lounging by the matted patch of grass where Quinn Starling had been lying moments before. The shrill scream faded, and only silence followed.

Connor's duel with the dragon had ended, but Sophia couldn't tell which of the warriors had won.

Her body buzzed with disbelief. Still in a half-numb daze, she kept curling and straightening her fingers just to feel something.

The dragon changed *everything*.

If Connor had a dragon, this little three-person army of theirs could conquer the continent. With conquest came power, and it meant she could become so much more than a mere necromancer in exile. He could elevate her in society and give her everything she had ever wanted in life. Perhaps he could even kill her uncle, once and for all, and give her the Beaumont crime family so that she could burn it to the ground herself.

Her mind hummed with ideas, and she loved them *all*.

This mountain range held secrets, dark ones, and she could feel its magic beating like a dying pulse just out of reach. The enchantments keeping this place alive had ancient roots, powered by something even she didn't understand, and she couldn't fathom what other dire beasts lived in the depths beneath the fortress.

It held such immense possibility, and she hated to see wasted potential.

Even as the spring day warmed, a shiver raced down her back. She rubbed her hands on her arms as she tried to retain what warmth she could. Murdoc had given up trying to milk her for answers on her rapidly depleting energy, and he now lay on the grass beside her with his hands behind his head as he stared up at the clouds. She silently cursed herself for letting her weakness show, but it couldn't be helped.

Not until she healed this miserable augmentation-gone-wrong.

Another shiver raced through her, and she gritted her teeth in an attempt to suppress it.

It didn't work.

"Curse the Fates," she muttered. She stood, trying to get her blood moving again, and a hint of warmth crept up her toes with the movement. Her head spun as she stood too quickly, and she paused, half-bent over, until the buzzing black and white dots faded.

To hell with it. One way or another, she had to get warm, her pride be damned.

Without caring what she looked like, Sophia shook out her hands and bounced back and forth on her feet as she stared after the route Quinn had taken moments before. "Murdoc, make sure that Starling woman is back in two minutes. I need to take a walk."

"Anything for you, my love."

She didn't even have the energy to reply. With her head still spinning, she trudged off into the woods. She hugged herself tightly, but it didn't help. Another chill swept through her, and she did her best to simply ignore it.

As she stepped past the first row of elms and into the tree line, a soft pang hit her in the chest. It rippled and pulsed like a shot of ice to the heart. Tension pooled beneath the augmentation between her breasts, coiling like a snake about to bite. It curled and twisted, tighter and tighter.

Until it snapped.

The pain decimated her. It festered and boiled like a blister. Her knees gave out, and her stomach lurched as she stumbled. One shoulder hit the nearest trunk hard. Black dots buzzed through her vision, and even as she tried to blink them away, the forest around her became a confusing labyrinth of shadowy tree trunks.

Her red lips parted, but she had nothing to say as she rode out the agonizing wave. She gasped with grief and confusion, staring at nothing as she tried to make sense of it all.

Nothing like that had ever happened before, and it couldn't be a good sign.

Out of sight and earshot from the others, she leaned her full weight against the tree that had caught her. Her eyes fluttered closed, and in the soft rustle of the leaves above her, she turned her attention inward toward her borrowed body.

Another jolt of pain hit her hard, deep in the bones beneath her augmentation. Her body convulsed as she rode out another miserable tsunami of anguish, but this one crashed through her harder than the first. Something hot sizzled in the gaps between bone and muscle, as though something altogether foreign had wriggled under her skin and was now writhing within her, trying to flay her alive from the inside out.

Her knees hit the damp ground, and a sharp jolt of pain shot up her legs. A breeze rolled over her exposed neck as her hair slid to one side, and the spring air hit her skin like frost. Even as she burned from within, tiny specks of ice crawled up her fingers and toward the palm of her hand.

"N-no," she stuttered, staring down at the encroaching frost. "N-not yet. It can't have started so soon."

The spots in her vision finally receded, but lingering dark splotches buzzed in her periphery. Her breath caught in her throat, and for a terrifying second, she couldn't breathe. When the air did come, it tasted like salt and rust. She grimaced and spat, trying to get the taste out of her mouth, and she set a hand on her chest to steady her racing heart.

Her teeth chattered. The blistering fire within finally faded, and sensation slowly returned to her fingers. She tapped them against the dirt, grateful to feel anything at all.

Sophia's end had begun. Based on her observations from studying the rats on which she had initially tested her augmentation, this would be only the first episode of many as Death slowly ripped her soul from this body.

Sweat slicked her face. With a trembling groan, she ran the back of her hand over one cheek to wipe the worst of it away.

In all her years at Nethervale, showing even the slightest weakness had meant an early grave. The vulnerable found quick ends in that tower, deep in the northeastern swamps. Her time there had taught her well. Its cruelty had forged her into a survivor unlike any other, and she refused to die.

Through Connor's hunt for answers, she had indulged his detours on the assumption that she would have more time. To ensure he kept his end of their bargain, she needed to be strong enough to enforce it.

Now, however, she wouldn't stand a chance against him if he refused. As much as she hated to admit it, he had the power to decide her fate, and she wasn't certain what choice he would make. It would be easiest for him to let her die, of course, and it was the choice anyone in Nethervale would've made in his position.

Even her.

She stared at the dirt beneath her fingers, but her eyes wouldn't focus. Sophia needed a plan, and for the first time in years, nothing came to mind.

In Nethervale, she had fought for the right to merely exist. In her parent's home, she had been a near-worthless bartering chip against a society that thought of her as disposable. In Richard's grasp, pinned against the wall and helpless, she had been nothing more than entertainment in his tedious life of excess.

From the day she was born, Sophia had never mattered to anyone. To belong in any sense of the word struck her as a foolish fairytale, the sort of sunshine with a seedy underbelly—and one that dragged its prey from their beds when they felt safest.

And now, she had more at stake than ever before. One misstep, even one blunder, and Sophia would lose her battle with Death. She needed Connor, and by now, he knew it. The question was what he would do with that much power over her.

As foolish as it was to admit out loud, she wanted to believe she mattered to Connor. To Murdoc. To this little team they had formed. Connor had given them all so much, but she still didn't dare let herself do the unthinkable.

To trust.

In the deepest, most withered depths of her soul, she wanted to believe he had meant what he had said back in the forest outside Murkwell. She wanted to be part of a team—*his* team—but childish dreams like that could get her killed.

A bird flew by, and the curled feathers in its long tail hummed with a soft golden glow. The little sparrow rested on a branch above her as sunlight streamed through the canopy of a paradise the world once thought had been lost to ruin and decay.

At best, Sophia had another two months before this body gave out on her. More likely, she had only weeks left to her name. They needed to get the bloody beauties and the secrets in Aeron's journal, or she was as good as dead.

Hell, maybe it was too late. It would take time to decipher his journal, and that assumed they would even be able to open it. Maybe she was dead, really, and she had just been delaying the inevitable all this time. Richard had said as much, back when he first discovered what she had done. He had found her old body on the floor and tried to see her new face for himself.

You're nothing but a ghost in someone else's corpse, he'd told her.

She grimaced as his words bounced around in her head, and she finished it out loud, just to rob his memory of the pleasure of making her feel so worthless yet again. "I'd say you're barely even human anymore."

As sick and twisted as he had been in life, he wasn't wrong.

When most of the pain had finally faded, Sophia held her side as she stared up at the sunbeams breaking through gaps in the canopy. She closed her eyes and savored the cool spring air of yet another day she had stolen from Death.

"You can't have this body back," she whispered to the long-dead soul of the girl she had killed to become Sophia Auclair. "I'll cling to this carcass with everything I have left."

To her dying breath.

Try as she might, Sophia couldn't bring herself to simply wait and see what he did. She couldn't just trust him and hope for the best, even if she wanted nothing more than to believe he would keep his word.

She needed to know, one way or another, what choice he would make.

If he chose well, he would be the first on the continent to earn her trust. If he failed, he would prove he was just like all the others, and she would disappear into the night to salvage what she could from the rubble that had once been her life.

And though she couldn't bring herself to admit it, the battered child deep within her knew the truth: if he betrayed her, too, there would be nothing left to live for in this broken, heartless world.

CHAPTER EIGHTEEN

CONNOR

A sunbeam hit Connor square in the face, and an orange light filtered through his closed eyelids. With a drowsy groan, he rolled onto one side to avoid the sunshine. It followed him, and he squinted up at the sky. The shade from the jagged boulder under which he slept had disappeared as the sun crawled across the sky, and his skin baked in the spring afternoon.

Damn it.

"Guess I'm awake," he muttered.

He yawned and rubbed the sleep from his eyes, but they ached with exhaustion. He needed more than a short nap to recover from a duel with a dragon.

A dragon.

The words bounced around in his skull, and his heart skipped another happy beat in surreal joy at encountering a living legend from his childhood fantasies.

It still didn't seem real.

Careful not to smack his head against the rock above him, he sat upright and grimaced in the harsh sunlight hitting the dark stone that made up the outer walls of Slaybourne. He lifted one arm to block out the blinding light and tried to gauge the time. It had to be close to noon at this point.

Finally. Though the wraith didn't appear, the grim voice rippled through Connor's head like an echo through a dark cavern. *As thrilling as keeping watch over the dragon was, the scaly lump of fat slept the whole time. You both need to get on your feet. There's much to do.*

"Yeah, yeah." Connor waved away the ghoul's concern as he stifled another yawn. Some venison and a fresh beer would've been a great start to the day, but not even that would stifle the dull thump of exhaustion still rattling through his head. He had been up all night with barely any rest, and he felt as though he could sleep for weeks.

As annoying as the wraith sometimes was, though, the old ghost had a point.

Connor pushed himself to his feet, and as he stretched, his muscles popped in protest. His body ached from his duel, and it took all of his remaining willpower not to find a new patch of shade and lay back down.

The ground rumbled, soft and low, and a pang of unease chased away his exhaustion at the sensation. He sank into his stance, fully expecting the quake to grow, but it faded. A second later, it came again, and his brows furrowed with confusion. He scanned the cliff around him as the gentle rumble came once more.

Curious, he followed the vibrations around a curve in the rock to find the dragon curled around himself with his tail tucked under his massive head. Nocturne lay on the sunbaked rock, and as he snored, another gentle quake shivered through the rock under Connor's feet. A thin black coil of smoke wafted from his nose, and those jet-black eyes remained shut.

Wary of what a sleeping dragon might do if startled awake, he paused a fair distance away and crossed his arms. "Nocturne, you need to get up."

The dragon snorted, and the snoring faded into soft breathing. The beast of myth and legend opened one eye, but otherwise didn't move.

"Come on." Connor nodded back toward the valley. "Let's go."

"I was locked underground for almost a year and then frozen in stone for centuries." The dragon's voice boomed across the mountainside, so rich and loud that the vibrations echoed in Connor's chest. "I require more time to recover."

With that, the dragon's eye closed again, and the snoring resumed.

"We don't have time for this." Connor snapped his fingers impatiently. "I need you to—"

The snoring grew louder, nearly drowning out his voice entirely, and the dragon peeked briefly through a half-opened eye before covering his head with his wings.

Connor chuckled. "Alright."

Ass, the wraith said, still unseen.

"He has a point," Connor admitted. "If I'd gone through everything you did to him, I would probably need some sleep, too."

A puff of black smoke rolled over the ground to his right, and flashes of bright white bone appeared from within the haze. The Wraith King emerged from wherever he went when he disappeared, and the long-dead king crossed his arms as he glared at the dragon without answering.

Connor sat on the edge of the cliff and dangled his legs over the deep ravine below. To his left, the exterior gate of Death's Door led out to the Decay. His eyes followed the channel through the mountain, all the way to where it let out at the inner gate and the valley beyond. This chasm through the mountains connected the two gates of Death's Door, but the wraith had mentioned traps when they first entered. Only the ghoul and the Fates knew the true extent of the hellish snares waiting down there to lure unsuspecting visitors to their deaths.

The high sun cast a spotlight into the chasm, illuminating the many piles of bones far below. Even at noon, thin shadows darkened the depths of the channel and the long-faded stone path that had once led the way into the Wraith King's kingdom.

One way in. One way out.

There are trails throughout these mountains. The wraith glided over the edge of the cliff and hovered above the steep drop to the chasm below. With a bony finger, the dead king pointed toward the far side of the ravine, at the cliff opposite theirs. *The paths are now worn and lost, but they should be easy enough to reclaim. Soldiers used to man them any time I allowed visitors to enter. This channel gives you complete control over your domain, Magnuson. If anyone were to break the outer gate, ten thousand arrows could kill them in an instant.*

"Impenetrable," Connor admitted with an impressed whistle. "With enough soldiers manning the walls, of course."

A true fortress. The ghoul nodded, his voice swelling with pride. *With the lake to the east and the vast forest at its center, there's enough food and water in this valley to sustain your subjects through any siege.*

Connor's jaw tensed, and he curled his fingers into an uneasy fist. "If Teagan Starling is really on his way, that will come in handy."

It's not just him, the wraith said. *He will be the first of many.*

"Let them come." Connor leaned back and rested his hands on the jet-black cliff. As the warm stone heated his palms, he stared out over the Decay and followed it to the bleak horizon.

You will never again know peace. Still hovering over the void, the wraith pivoted and followed Connor's gaze to where the sky blurred into the brown haze of the endless desert. *Every day, for the rest of your life, you will have to prove you're worthy of seeing another sunrise.*

"That's nothing new." He sighed. "At least, not for me."

When the wraith didn't respond, Connor peeked out the corner of his eye to find the ghoul staring not at the horizon, but down at the shadowy chasm below. Checking on a trap, maybe, or staring at the long-dead bones of the people he killed.

It occurred to Connor, then, that the wraith may not have been talking to him at all.

This place held memories for the ghoul. Lots of them. Coming here must have brought him back to a different time, when he was a different man who had no idea what would become of him.

The wind howled through the channel, and a gust of hot air hit Connor in the face. He grimaced, but it passed almost as quickly as it had come. Out in the Decay, beyond the outer gate, ash and dust spun in little tornadoes as the wind carried off most of the evidence of his fight with Zander Starling.

I conquered the continent, the ghoul said after a while.

The dead man's reverberating voice in Connor's mind shattered the peaceful day, but he waited for the Wraith King to continue.

It's strange, the specter admitted. *Coming here has brought back memories I thought I'd forgotten. It's made me relive things I wanted to stay dead.*

Connor's mouth set into a grim line. He probably understood that better than most.

His gaze drifted out of focus as he thought again of his long-lost home at the edge of the sea. After all these years, no one back in Kirkwall would've recognized him. He could've easily returned, and yet he had given the place a wide berth.

After a few moments of silence, he opted not to reply. He had nothing to add, anyway, and no comfort to offer. He had his own haunted past, and he had run from it for years. Besides, the Wraith King wasn't the sort of man who needed someone else to fill the quiet stretches in a conversation.

What do the stories say about how I died? the ghoul asked.

"You must've heard them by now."

Humor me. I want to know what the peasants say.

Connor smirked at the subtle jibe, but he didn't take the bait. "According to the old stories, no one knows. You just disappeared, and you took your entire citadel with you into the Decay."

The wraith nodded. *Good.*

"Why?"

It's better than the truth.

Connor's grin faded.

There's something you need to know, Magnuson, about me. About the last lesson I learned as a mortal man.

Sitting there on the edge of a cliff, Connor stiffened as he watched the undead king. "I'm listening."

On thirteen separate occasions, I nearly died in combat. That would've been a soldier's death, a good death, but I wanted immortality. I met Death a few times, but I crawled my way back. I lived. And in the end, after all that war, after running out of battlefields to fight on, I died here, in my bed. He scoffed. *The injustice.*

The ghoul's bony fingers wrapped around his hood, and he lifted it off his head. The crack in his skull ran across the bone, clear and prominent in the brilliant daylight. His skeletal finger traced the line from start to finish, and he sighed.

In those final years, I had begun thinking about heirs. My hunt for immortality hadn't gotten far, and if I failed, I needed a competent prince—or, hell, princess—to ensure my legacy lived on. I had my choice of women, but only a handful truly fascinated me. Of them, only one kept my attention as the years passed. I enjoyed her. I found that, for some reason, the world made more sense with her in it.

"You were in love," Connor pointed out.

The wraith scoffed, but he didn't disagree. *One summer night, I held her in my arms as the insects buzzed through the open balcony. As we laid there, I felt almost… happy. Almost at peace. It was something I had been hunting all my life, without ever realizing what had been missing. She set her head on my chest, and I kissed her forehead. I felt her hand on my neck, and I thought she was asleep until she slit my throat.*

Connor's head snapped back in surprise. His mouth gaped open, but he didn't know what to say.

I didn't have any Rectivanes nearby. I'd gotten soft, thanks to her. In that moment, I knew I was going to die, and I decided to take her with me. Even as I choked on my own blood, I strangled her. She grabbed a rock she had hidden under the bed and gave me this. The ghoul pointed to the crack in his skull. *Her devotion had been a lure, all along. A trap, years in the making, and a truly masterful deception. With her last gasping words as we died together, in the bed she and I had shared for so many years, she finally told me the truth. She had never loved me. I had murdered her brothers and father in some western war. After she lost them, she had done whatever it took to win the trust of a monster so that she could kill their murderer herself.*

With his thumb pressed against his jaw, Connor stared down at the void beneath them without really seeing anything. He tried to imagine what it must've been like, to lay next to a woman who he thought was devoted to him, only to have her reveal it had all been a lie.

I offer this to you not for pity, but as a warning, the wraith explained. *This is your chance to learn from my greatest mistake. Any love you let yourself have must still be guarded. Any trust must come as a result of complete control.*

Connor frowned, and he didn't reply. He doubted he could change the dead man's mind.

But he didn't agree.

Back in Kirkwall, Connor's father had never controlled his mother. They argued, on occasion, but they had always been equals. He had protected her, and she had given him light. Purpose. Happiness.

She had filled his life with the sort of joy that died in a cage.

A man is his legacy. The wraith gestured across the skeletons below as he pointed back to the valley. *What does mine say of me?*

As the ghoul stared down at the destruction he had left behind, Connor silently studied the dead man's skeletal face. For the first time, he saw more than an abomination infused with the Great Necromancer's dark magic. He could finally see past the legendary warlord feared by the pages of history.

Here, now, he witnessed the Wraith King as a man: flawed, imperfect, arrogant and a royal ass, but still a man who had something left in him worth redeeming.

Connor sat with everything the ghost had told him so far. "My father used to say a man's legacy isn't made of the achievements he leaves behind. He always told me it's built from the caliber of people who remember him and how he made them feel."

The Wraith King didn't reply.

"You left behind destruction," Connor said. "You broke people. Ruined them. Took everything from them and shattered what you couldn't steal. You were legendary enough to be remembered in song, but at what cost? What's the point of building a castle if it's just going to crumble when you're gone?"

Shockingly, that doesn't make me feel better, the wraith said dryly.

Connor shrugged. "I'm not going to sugarcoat it. Not with you, anyway. You did a lot of harm in your life, and there aren't many who remember you fondly. My point is that you're still here. You have a chance to build a new legacy. Even you aren't immortal, thanks to the Bloodbane daggers. Maybe you should think about your legacy in a new light. Think about it—as a wraith, you have a second chance most people don't get. What are you going to do with it?"

The bones of the skeletal king's left hand coiled into a fist, but otherwise, he didn't move. *I have never paused to question that before.*

"Now's your chance, then."

Hmm. The ghoul's head pivoted on his spine as he scanned the valley beyond the inner gate of Death's Door. *I want to know how much Zacharias truly learned about what I am, even after he stored me away in that damned bottle.*

"He shoved you in a bottle?"

The ghoul nodded. *Before he knew if it was safe to fuse with me, he locked me away in a bottle made of spellgust and enchanted with a potion not even I understand. It kept me weak and at bay. When my first host found me, centuries ago, I learned Zacharias had been killed a decade after he brought me back. He could have learned so much in that time, but without access to his notes, I had no way of knowing.*

"Henry conquered the continent." Connor rubbed the back of his neck as he mulled it over. "He controlled the Lightseers, and they've had the Deathdread all this time. Why didn't he demand they give it to him?"

I tried, the Wraith King said, exasperated. *For most of our time together, he feared its power. I suspect he dreaded what he might become if he knew where to find the other simmering souls.*

"Huh."

The dreaded King Henry had pillaged whole towns and forced the Lightseers to bend the knee. It seemed strange, wrong even, to think of the man as afraid of anything, much less a book.

There is so much the Deathdread can tell us both, Magnuson. Before I decide what to do with this so-called second chance of mine, I must understand what I truly am.

"That's fair," Connor acknowledged. "It's important, but it can't be what we search for next. Sophia is fading fast. It's too much of a risk to go all the way to the Mountains of the Unwanted on the hope that the Deathdread has the information she needs to recover. There has to be someone else on this continent who can help her."

We both know who has that information.

Connor nodded. "I think the Starling woman has quite a bit more she can tell us."

Agreed.

"We'll get the Deathdread eventually. I promise you, one way or another, we will answer those pesky questions of yours."

The ghoul flexed and curled his fingers repeatedly. A stretch of awkward silence followed before he mumbled something incoherent.

"What was that?"

Thank you, the wraith snapped impatiently. *I said thank you, damn it all.*

Connor grinned. "Is it really that hard to show a bit of gratitude?"

The phantom groaned in irritation and waved away the playful jab with a flick of his bone-white wrist.

With a quick scan of the sky, Connor guessed at the time again. The afternoon stretched on, and yet the soft and rumbling snores from Nocturne continued. He glanced over one shoulder to find the behemoth still curled on his sunbaked rock, and Connor rubbed his face in frustration.

They had too much at stake to sit here and sleep all day. Perhaps he could leave the dragon here for the second leg of his journey. He eyed the wall of arrows embedded in the Decay beyond the outer gate of Death's Door. One of them toppled as a strong gust rolled over the dead dirt.

Nocturne knew what awaited him if he tried to leave Slaybourne on his own.

"Come on." He swung his legs back from the cliff and pushed himself to his feet. "I think it's time you show me the other weapon."

Finally. You're going to like this one.

Connor chuckled and took one last glance back at the sleeping dragon. "We'll see."

CHAPTER NINETEEN
CONNOR

A narrow spiral staircase led Connor into the depths of the Black Keep Mountains, not far from Death's Door. His shoulders brushed the walls on both sides of the stairwell, so he tilted his body to make the walk a bit more comfortable.

With his muscled bulk, it didn't truly work, but he tried nonetheless.

Specks of green spellgust ore embedded in the black stone walls cast a pale glow across the ancient, hand-carved steps. The enchanted flecks splattered the walls like stars obscured by a thick layer of clouds—present, yes, but offering precious little light.

Even with his enhanced vision, Connor could only make out about five steps at a time. Shadows swallowed everything beyond that, and the frayed ends of the wraith's cloak dipped in and out of the darkness as the undead king led the way.

The second weapon awaited him, somewhere at the end of this narrow staircase. Given his first task had been to face a dragon, he couldn't fathom what else the wraith had in store.

One you must conquer, the wraith had said, *and one which you must claim.*

The edge of one of the stone steps cracked beneath his boot, and he instantly shifted his weight to his heels as the lip of the stair broke off. His palm rested against the icy stone wall for balance as the chunk clattered as it rolled down the staircase. It cast a hollow echo through the narrow corridor, and Connor kept to the base of each step as he continued.

We have arrived, the wraith said from deep in the darkness.

Seconds later, Connor's boot hit the final step. An iron door emerged from the shadows, and the ghoul in front of him disappeared into a cloud of churning black smoke. The mist whipped against the door as the wraith passed through without him.

Connor chuckled, and his voice carried up the empty stairwell. "What, is the door too heavy for you to open?"

The wraith sighed heavily. *Ass.*

The iron handle stung Connor's palm as he grabbed it, cold as a block of ice, but he fought off the chill snaking up his arm and shoved his shoulder against the door. The metal groaned in protest. Its rusty moan reverberated off the walls and drowned out the fading echo of his voice.

It resisted, at first, so he shoved his shoulder against it again—harder this time. It swung inward, its ancient hinges groaning in protest, and a rush of stale air rolled over him as he stepped over the threshold.

The air shifted. Though he could see only darkness, it felt as though the ceiling in this next room had disappeared entirely. As his eyes adjusted once more, speckled flecks of green blinked to life along the walls, interrupted here and there by large rectangular stretches of black. He squinted, trying to figure out if they were doorways, but ribbons of gold and silver shimmered in the dim light.

Tapestries. Had to be.

"What are all these?" Connor gestured to the walls. "You genuinely loved art, didn't you?"

Hardly, the wraith answered with a bored tilt to his voice. *I hung a tapestry for every king I conquered. They're nothing but memories, now.*

"Sure," Connor said dubiously. "Look, it doesn't make you less of a man to like art. You can just admit—"

At the end of the hall, two silhouettes loomed within the shadows. Connor tensed on instinct. He sank into a fighter's stance, ready to summon his shield at a moment's notice, and the fingers of his right hand drummed on the air as he prepared to summon one of his shadow blades.

He hadn't expected company. Not down here.

The silhouettes stood side by side, still as stone, but unmistakably human. Their broad shoulders blocked out the speckles of light behind them, and the rounded edge of a shield in each man's left hand cast an ominous shadow across the wall.

The wraith chuckled. *Jumpy, are we?*

In a rush of dark smoke that churned across the floor, the wraith reappeared. His bleached white bones practically glowed in the corridor's low light, and his skeletal fingers stretched wide as he beckoned Connor closer.

"Statues?"

Close, the ghoul admitted.

Shoulders tense and still ready for a fight, Connor took several cautious steps closer. As he neared, more and more detail came into focus. Rusted shields. Helmets, resting squarely on decayed skulls. Exposed jaw bones with a few missing teeth. Skeletal fingers, not unlike the wraith's, wrapped around ancient spears.

Soldiers, guarding their post even in death.

"You sick bastard," Connor said, his voice gravelly and deep.

You make assumptions when you should shut your mouth and listen, the wraith chided. *These men weren't chained here. They stayed of their own free will. My army was loyal to me above all else, even the Fates themselves. They did what I commanded, regardless of the order, because the reward was great: immortality.*

Connor wrinkled his nose in disgust. "Why lie to them?"

The wraith leaned toward him, so close that Connor could glare directly into the gaping holes that used to be his eyes. *Did I?*

Before Connor could answer, the wraith set his bony palms against the set of double doors between the two guards. The iron edges glowed green at his touch, and with a gust of air not unlike a heavy sigh, they swung open in unison.

A long, slow creak echoed past, and Connor winced as the grating noise assaulted his enhanced ears. A bright green glow crept across the floor from the room beyond, and he lifted one arm to shield his eyes from the sudden light. A sharp twinge pierced the back of his eyes, and he squinted until they could adjust.

When the stabbing pain behind his eyes finally faded, Connor peered over his arm to find another towering cavern beyond the doors. Glittering green gems covered the towering ceiling like stars in the night, brilliant and bright, and they cast an enchanting glow across the rocky walls.

He stared up at the ceiling in awe. "Is there any room in these mountains that isn't enchanted with raw spellgust ore?"

No, the ghoul answered. *With as much as we have here, it would've been a waste.*

The doorway ended in a cliff, and a stone bridge crossed the inky black depths. Connor peered over the ledge, but the shadows continued on forever. "What's down there?"

You don't want to know.

He frowned, but the wraith was probably right.

The specter led the way across the bridge, and as Connor followed, he scanned the cavern to get his bearings. On the other end of the bridge, piles of gold lay strewn haphazardly around the edge of an enclave. A giant map of Saldia hung from the far wall, and even from this distance, he noticed small holes burned into the map where cities should have been. Two pairs of double doors, each carved from solid spellgust, framed the giant tapestry of Saldia.

In the center of the enclave, centered beneath the map, a raised platform held a pedestal carved from the same black stone in the walls. On a dark pillow atop the platform sat a glittering golden crown.

Halfway across the bridge, the wraith paused. He stared out over the abyss, and Connor followed the ghoul's gaze to a cage suspended over the endless void below. Trapped inside, a skeleton lay slouched against the bars with a slender tiara resting on her long-dead brow.

The wraith stared at her, and in the silence, Connor studied the undead king. The specter didn't move. He didn't so much as sigh or ball his fist in anger. He simply examined the corpse, and Connor figured this was what had become of the man's wife.

"How did she get down here?" he asked.

Every king, even the ones who go soft, establishes orders for what must happen if someone assassinates him. My soldiers knew what had to be done, even as Death took us both. Come, Magnuson, the ghoul said as he resumed his path across the bridge. *She doesn't matter anymore.*

As tempting as it was to call out the wraith's lie, Connor kept his mouth shut.

Once they had crossed the bridge, the ghoul floated to the pedestal and hovered behind it. His cloaked body was framed by the massive map on the wall as he stared down at the crown. With his bony fingers, he lifted the bejeweled circlet. Flashes of green light snaked across the polished gold with each movement. Round gemstones sat in the base of the crown, and a spike not unlike a spearhead rose from each gem, all of them perfectly spaced apart in a crown worthy of any warlord.

As he held it, the wraith's skull pivoted toward Connor. *This is what you needed to see.*

"Your crown?" He joined the wraith by the pedestal and raised one eyebrow skeptically. "You didn't bring me all the way down here to lecture me on how my power is my greatest weapon, did you?"

The wraith chuckled and, instead of answering, haphazardly tossed the headpiece to him.

Connor caught it with ease. It weighed against his palms, a little heavier than he had expected. Despite himself, and though he knew better than most how these things corrupted men, he studied it more intently. Among the spellgust gems glittering at the base of each spear, a single black stone sat nestled at the front of it. The dark stone somehow glowed and glittered, brighter even than the spellgust, but he had never seen a gemstone like this. Hell, he had never even seen a crown before, much less held one in his hands.

Many men in Saldia would burn their own families at the stake to claim something like this.

The thought snapped him from his daze, and his jaw tensed as he glared down at it.

You will wear that, the wraith said. *Sooner than you think.*

Connor scoffed and set the headpiece on a nearby pile of gold. "I don't think the deer care that I'm their king."

The wraith groaned impatiently and, instead of answering, tossed the pillow from the pedestal onto the nearest pile of gold. With the pillow gone, a brilliant green glow sliced through the air beneath his face and cast its emerald light clear into the recesses of his skull.

A set of stairs at the base of the platform led up to the pedestal, and Connor climbed them to find out what the hell the wraith wanted him to see.

In the flat surface underneath where the pillow had been, a divot roughly the size of his fist had been carved into a block of spellgust stone inlaid in the otherwise jet-black pedestal. It waited, painfully vacant, as if something important had been removed.

"I don't understand," Connor admitted. "How is this a weapon? What exactly am I supposed to claim, here?"

This was never about the crown, the wraith answered. *But, yes, I did bring you here to discuss power. There is an ancient artifact called the Soulsprite, and when it is finally placed here, it will activate the enchantments I spent decades carving into this mountain. I was told in my time that this artifact had been reclaimed by the Fates, but I never believed that. Something this powerful doesn't just disappear; it goes into hiding. And if it was in hiding, I knew I would eventually find it.*

Connor narrowed his eyes skeptically, not entirely fond of where this was heading. "What does it do?"

The wraith's skull tilted toward him, and for a moment, the specter simply watched him in silence. *For starters, it proves you wrong.*

He laughed and crossed his arms. "How do you figure?"

You assumed I lied to my men. The ghoul pointed back at the exit, toward the skeletal soldiers still guarding the entrance to the vault, even in death. *The Soulsprite—and the enchantments I built into this fortress—will bring them back. They will finally be invincible, just as I promised they would be.*

Connor took a step back in surprise, and his boot hit the stair with a muffled thud. He stared at the open doors as he recalled the dead men standing outside. "Are you serious?"

I am. You will have an undead army, Magnuson. They're bound by the ore in these mountains, and though they cannot leave Slaybourne, they will be the perfect guardians of this great land. As they did with me, they will obey your every command.

Connor's brows furrowed as he contemplated what that would truly mean—the good, the bad, and the ugly. An undead army, even one limited to defense, would prove immensely valuable.

No more mercenaries. No more threats against his new home.

Provided, of course, that they actually listened. This only worked if the wraith had done everything perfectly in his time fortifying Slaybourne. An undead army running amok in Saldia would only cement the continent's hatred of him.

I wanted them to be able to travel, the ghoul confessed. *I wanted to use them to conquer the world, but that magic is beyond even me.*

"Thank the Fates," Connor muttered.

The ghoul grunted with irritation, but didn't reply.

Connor stared again at the empty pedestal and rubbed his jaw as he lost himself in thought. "If you made even one mistake—"

I didn't.

He narrowed his eyes and glared at the ghoul, making his point without a saying word.

I didn't, the wraith said again, more firmly this time.

Connor shook his head, but he didn't need to repeat himself. Not with the wraith. The ghoul knew the consequences of making an error in such powerful magic. "You said you know where the Soulsprite is?"

Freymoor.

With a groan, Connor turned his back on the wraith and set his hands on the back of his head. Just as quickly as his hopes were raised, they had been dashed. "So much for that, then. Freymoor is a twenty-day journey from here on foot, maybe more, and we would have to go through Oakenglen check points to reach it. Even if Nocturne flies us there, we could never make it there and back in time. It's not possible."

You damn fool, the wraith snapped.

Connor glared at the ghoul over one shoulder, daring the ghost to say that again.

Unfazed, the specter towered overhead, blocking out much of the world around Connor, and spread his arms wide. *Listen to yourself. Not possible? Have you lost your mind? You brought down a Fates-damned dragon!*

Connor's shoulders relaxed ever so slightly, and he waited in silence for the wraith to continue.

You can no longer limit yourself like a mortal man. The specter gestured to the exit and to the dead men standing guard. *Burn the last of the peasant out of you if you must, but start thinking like the king you have become!*

As the wraith's voice boomed in his head, Connor's back straightened. He stood taller, the weight of the ghoul's words heavy on his shoulders. Though his mind still raced with the risk of embarking on a journey like that now, of all times, he eventually nodded.

Though he hated to admit it, the ghoul had a point. Doubt only limited his potential. Never in his life had he suspected he could bring down a dragon or battle the Starlings and win, and yet he had already accomplished both.

But still, Freymoor of all places—and in only twenty days. With Sophia's fading health and the Finns in harm's way, he didn't see how they could manage.

That's better, the ghoul said, apparently seeing something in Connor's expression. *Back to business. I admit, this task of ours carries hefty risk. Freymoor is, shall we say, not fond of me.*

"Is anyone?"

This is serious, Magnuson. The wraith waved away the jibe with a flick of his wrist. *There's magic in Freymoor that defies the laws of this world in ways that are eerily similar to my powers. Enchantments seep over from the death dimension, but only in the Blood Bogs. It's a dangerous place of ancient magic, and this artifact will not be easy to obtain.*

"The timeline still doesn't work," Connor pointed out. "If Teagan gets here before we return, we will have no way back into Slaybourne and we won't be able to place the Soulsprite. This isn't about what's possible—this is about being smart and understanding the risks involved."

And what is our alternative, Magnuson? The wraith shrugged. *Wait for him to come with his army and hope our new ally decides to help after all?*

Fair point.

"Hmm." Connor paced the small stretch of stone around the edge of the pedestal as he debated his options. "Say this works. Say we get the Soulsprite and get back before Teagan reaches Slaybourne. Is this truly going to be enough to defeat the Lightseers?"

The wraith hesitated. Though the stretch of silence didn't last long, it was enough to cast doubt on whatever he said next. It spoke volumes of the uncertainty. Of the unknown.

Yes, the wraith eventually said.

Connor frowned and, after a moment spent studying the wraith's vacant skull of a face, he resumed his pacing.

"To leave," he muttered to himself, "or to stay."

Both options carried immense danger, and he had to face the truth. Nocturne's prison had drained a significant amount of Slaybourne's magic, and Connor wasn't confident the walls would hold when Teagan inevitably attacked. While a dragon ally would prove immeasurably helpful, Nocturne hadn't committed to fighting on his side in the inevitable battle.

They had a truce, after all, not an official bargain. Not yet.

Connor needed a surefire way to defend the citadel if the worst came his way. It needed power. It needed renewal, and from what little he knew of this new artifact, the Soulsprite was his best chance of surviving this war with Teagan Starling.

Damn it.

"Alright," he finally conceded. "I don't like this one bit, but it's the best idea we've got."

I appreciate your enduring faith in me, the ghoul said dryly.

Connor grinned. "I'm sure it's mutual."

We must leave at once.

"No, we need a plan," he countered. "If it's twenty days one-way, we need to know how fast a dragon can fly. Provided, of course, he's willing to take us at all."

Ah, yes. One moment. The wraith disappeared in a puff of black smoke.

The churning black cloud rolled down the steps surrounding the pedestal, and Connor's gaze swept the cavern as he tried to figure out where the ghoul had gone. In the silence, the distant drip of water echoed through the void from somewhere far below.

Arms crossed, he frowned as he waited.

After a few moments, another rush of inky darkness rolled across the ground at his feet. The air shifted in the now-familiar sign that the ghoul had reappeared, and Connor glanced over one shoulder to find the ghoul holding a scroll sealed with red wax.

"What's that?"

The recipe for an obscenely powerful augmentation called the Fogsbane, the wraith answered. *This scroll is precious. If you lose it—or if anyone but the augmentor who inks you and the dragon reads it—I will figure out a way to murder you.*

Connor grunted in annoyance. "Just tell me what it does."

The wraith offered him the scroll. *This augmentation will give you a mental link to the dragon.*

Speechless and not entirely certain such a thing was even possible, Connor took it. The ancient parchment scratched at his fingertips, frail and almost decayed, and he marveled that it had survived this long without crumbling to dust. Paper this old risked cracking when unrolled, and he did his best not to crush it in his palm.

Both of my dragons had this augmentation. The wraith tapped the seal on the scroll to emphasize his point. *It is unnaturally powerful. It lasted for years longer than an ordinary augmentation, and it allowed me to command them in battle, even from a distance. Feral dragons let me in instantly, but I'm not certain how it will work with a conscious one. You truly did make this harder than it needed to be.*

"Will you stop harping on that? It's done."

Fine. The ghoul grumbled impatiently. *Since you refused to conquer the damn thing, you must convince the beast to stay. Having a dragon will change the tides for us.*

Connor studied the scroll in his palm as he sifted through everything he had learned down here. With his brows furrowed in thought, he debated what he could possibly say to make Nocturne want to stay, or how he could convince the Lady of Freymoor to give him something as ancient and powerful as the Soulsprite. Just as the ghoul had wanted him to force Nocturne to go feral, the wraith would probably urge him to steal it. He snorted in annoyance, but a pang of concern drowned even that as he thought about his alternatives. With precious little time before Teagan arrived, he didn't know if he could manage all of this before his deadline.

Truth be told, he had no idea what he would ultimately have to do to protect his new home, and these were uncharted waters.

A flash of gold in his periphery snapped him out of his daze. The crown rested on a pile of coins, tilted and askew on its new perch, and he watched it with somber reverence. He was king of this abandoned pile of rubble, and he wouldn't let Teagan burn what remained.

CHAPTER TWENTY

OTMUND

In the heart of Everdale—a pristine city of white cobblestone and gray brick houses far too close to Lunestone for comfort—Otmund pulled on his leather gloves. The expertly tanned hide creaked against his fingers, and his heart skipped an anxious beat as he sat with everything he had learned tonight.

Finally, like a long-overdue gift from the Fates themselves, he had discovered the perfect bait to lure the Wraithblade to him.

During his years of research in the vaults, a strange artifact had often been mentioned in passing, but never named. Something powerful. Something the Wraith King had always sought in life, and something which he was rumored to want even in death.

No one had ever known what this mythical artifact was—until now.

He stepped over his informant's corpse as she stared up at him, her eyes still open. Blood trickled from her tear ducts, and a loose lock of gray hair stuck to her blue lips.

Tonight had been useful, and everything he had learned pointed him to one city: Freymoor.

The fallen kingdom had always held secrets and treasures—all of which he had tried over the years to steal—but he had only found trinkets. The city's truly powerful artifacts remained hidden in the Blood Bogs, and only a native could navigate that treacherous swamp. Few people ever left that cursed place, and even fewer actually knew the secrets of Freymoor's former royal family. Until tonight, he had never been able to find one of the castle's servants.

But now, he had all the answers he needed.

The Wraith King wanted something called the Soulsprite. If the Wraithblade had indulged the ghoul enough to return to Slaybourne, that meant the peasant would eventually seek out the Soulsprite as well.

If Otmund were to stand a chance against the Wraithblade, he had to get the Soulsprite before his opponent.

The Lord of Mossvale paused at the door and pivoted on one heel. Two of his new elite necromancers stood behind the woman's corpse, their faces void of any emotion as they watched him with their hands clasped behind their backs. The shorter of them fidgeted as he caught her eye, as though she were resisting the urge to say something, while her taller counterpart wisely kept his mouth shut.

"Get rid of the body," Otmund demanded as he set his gloved hand on the doorknob.

The female necromancer, whose name he had never bothered to learn, raised one slender eyebrow and tucked her blonde hair behind one ear. "As you wish, sir."

Otmund resisted the urge to smile. What obedient little pets he had—and they were perhaps even more obedient now that he had sent Nyx on a little errand for him. Maybe he needed to send her away more often.

The taller necromancer slipped his pack off one shoulder and studied the dead informant's corpse. The top of his rucksack fell open, and firelight from a wall sconce glinted along several sharp metal blades inside.

With that handled, Otmund threw open the door and stalked into the hallway. His boots thudded against the wooden floor of the inn where they had found the long-lost traitor that had given Henry all he'd needed to storm the city.

He doubted Freymoor would notice—or care—that she was dead.

Two additional necromancers keeping watch outside left their post by the door to join him. They flanked him, and the hoods on their heads cast long shadows over everything but their mouths. They matched his pace with ease, just as he so often saw the palace guards do with King Henry back when that bastard was still alive.

Loyal. Quiet. Obedient. Perfect in every way, except of course for the fact that he was working on borrowed time.

He absently scratched at the fading augmentation on his forearm, but it would last a while longer. He needed to finish this job before he got it redone. Illegal as his favorite spell was, he only trusted one augmentor to do it properly, and Dewcrest was in the opposite direction to where he needed to go.

A delay now could mean the difference between success and failure. In his race against the Wraithblade, every lost grain of sand in the hourglass counted against him.

It had taken ages to find this old woman, since most of the ladies in waiting to the old royalty of Freymoor had disappeared into the night with new faces and new names. With them had gone any hint of what lay dormant in the bogs.

It was a stroke of luck to find this one. In fact, she was the only one he had ever caught wind of in the twelve years since Freymoor's downfall.

Otmund frowned as they reached the stairs. He didn't trust luck, and his heart skipped another anxious beat at how easy this had been. He was good, of course, but this woman had practically fallen into his lap. For his spies to recognize her in the first place, they would've needed information none of them should've had. Perhaps the necromancers were even better than he had given them credit for, or perhaps his paranoia would save his life.

For all he knew, this might've been a trick on Nyx's part to lure him into a deadly situation. He wasn't certain, yet, but what little he had read in the vaults about what this fabled artifact could do corroborated with what tonight's quarry had told him about the Soulsprite.

She had also left him with an ominous warning—that the people of Freymoor were building an army. He'd heard rumors of someone in the fallen city recruiting soldiers under Oakenglen's nose, but until now, he'd never had proof.

A wall of noise hit him, snapping him from his spinning thoughts, and he pulled his own hood over his head as he reached the bottom of the stairs. With his eyes focused on the exit, he did his best to ignore the drinking songs washing over the drunken mob in the tavern below the inn. Someone shouted nearby, the words slurred and unintelligible, and the men around him laughed.

An insult, probably, and one most likely directed at him. Even with a hood over his head, Otmund stood out in a crowd of peasants like these. A fine wool cloak stained with the finest dyes in Saldia could never blend in with the browns and beiges these banal folk seemed to prefer.

Damn peasants.

Rather than order the necromancers to kill the man, however, Otmund chose to ignore the jibe. Making an example of a drunk would hardly get him to Freymoor faster.

When he reached the door, he shoved it open with his shoulder and tried again to focus on what lay ahead. Everything pointed toward the Soulsprite being the answer he had sought for so long, and all evidence suggested the Wraithblade would eventually come looking for it.

As suspiciously easy as this had been, he didn't have the luxury of time to wait out any unseen opponents in the shadows. It wouldn't be long until Teagan realized how much of a role Otmund had played in Zander's hunt for the new Wraithblade, and he needed control of the ghoul before the young man's father realized the truth.

Otmund had pulled on too many strings. In his efforts to become the next Wraithblade, he had forced too many of his puppets to dance at once and called in too many favors. He had pushed every limit, tested every weakness, and played every card in his hand. The sands in his hourglass were almost empty, and only the wraith could refill it.

No matter. Soon, the peasant would be just another puppet on a string, dancing before the puppet master.

As was the case with all of Otmund's toys, it was just a matter of time.

CHAPTER TWENTY-ONE
CONNOR

As Connor rode Nocturne through the late afternoon sky, he ran his hand along the dragon's silky scales. Seated at the base of the dragon prince's neck, he leaned with each gentle tilt of Nocturne's body as they flew on the air currents above his fortress.

The beast of legend expanded beneath him with every breath, and fiery heat simmered beneath each scale. Wind whistled past, deafeningly loud, and it drowned out his voice every time he tried to speak. He had abandoned any hope of steering the massive beast the moment they'd taken flight. If Nocturne chose to stay, he would definitely need to get the wraith's telepathic augmentation. He hated the idea of another voice in his head, but a dragon didn't seem like the kind of mount who would allow him to use reins.

For now, it didn't matter. Since his was the only campsite among the rubble, it wouldn't be hard to spot.

The wind rushing over Nocturne's back hit Connor in the face, every bit as crisp and fresh as spring water straight from a stream. Soft gray clouds stretched across the endless desert, and the brilliant blue sky opened above them.

He closed his eyes and smiled as his inner ten-year-old beamed with joy. Riding a dragon wasn't just a dream come true.

This felt like *freedom.*

They banked to the left, and Connor's eyes snapped open as he instinctively leaned with the dragon's tilt—only to find the legendary creature watching him through one eye.

"I saw that smile." Nocturne's booming voice broke the wind, and a plume of dark smoke rolled from his nose as he huffed with laughter.

Connor lightly smacked the dragon's hide and studied the bright green treetops below to hide his grin.

The valley stretched on for miles, its forest vast and overgrown. Glowing green meadows whizzed underneath them as they flew. Ahead, the tree line stopped at the largest of the fields, and shattered ruins of the black stone temple they had destroyed littered the hillside. Long trails of flattened grasses ended in chunks of black rock, and a gaping crater bored into the top of the hill. The tunnel had collapsed on itself, and the cave-in now blocked access to one of the entrances to the catacombs.

More importantly, however, were the three figures waiting at the edge of the forest. Murdoc's long, dark hair shook as he waved his hands, and Sophia's pale face trailed their route across the sky as she gaped up at them.

Only Quinn remained seated, hunched over on her log as she studied the dragon's every movement through the sky.

Nocturne circled the meadow and banked downward. Connor's stomach lurched as they dropped in altitude, and the whistling wind became a roar as they picked up speed. They hit the ground with a resonant thud, and the tall meadow grasses shivered as the dragon's feet sent a vibration clear through them.

Before Connor could even dismount, Nocturne lowered his head to eye level and charged Murdoc.

The former Blackguard squared his shoulders as he stared the regal creature in the eye, and though his hand rested on the hilt of his sword, he thankfully didn't draw it.

"Hey now." Connor smacked Nocturne's shoulder. "At least introduce yourself first."

The dragon snorted, and a plume of dark smoke rolled across Murdoc's feet as Nocturne studied him with one scrutinizing eye. "I like this one."

Murdoc cleared his throat and took a wary step backward. "'This one' has a name."

Connor kicked one leg over Nocturne's back and slid down his side. His boots hit the ground with a thump, and he stretched out his back after the long flight. Relief flooded through his shoulders and down his back as he loosened his muscles. "Murdoc, Sophia, this is—"

"I am Nocturne, prince of the dragons, king of the nightlands, protector of warriors and monks alike." Nocturne's voice shook the ground, and even the trees trembled under the might of his voice.

"Hello," Murdoc said weakly as he studied the dragon's fangs.

Sophia wandered closer, her arms wrapped tightly around her body despite the warming spring day, and her face paled even more as she stared up at the dragon. Her red lips parted, and she blinked in wonder.

Connor's smile fell as he studied her face. Every time he saw her, she looked worse.

She was running out of time, and he didn't have much longer to fulfill his end of their bargain.

Dark smoke rolled across his boots, and the Wraith King glided from the murky haze. With his hood over his skeletal face, he stared off toward the tree line.

As the ghoul emerged from thin air, Murdoc flinched and cursed under his breath. "I hate it when he does that."

Our guest has seen too much, the wraith said, ignoring Murdoc entirely.

Connor followed the specter's gaze to find their Starling prisoner, sitting contentedly on the log by the firepit with her tiger-bird at her side. Though the vougel watched the dragon, its neck arched and wings half-spread in concern, Quinn studied Connor. She stared, as though she could glean his every secret merely from how he held himself.

Reluctantly, he agreed with the Wraith King's observation. Quinn Starling had seen far too much.

In my day, she would've been in the dungeons by now, strung up by her ankles. The ghoul waved his hand through the air in disgust. *You cannot be soft with a prisoner like her. Your noble heart will get you killed if you let her use it against you.*

Connor didn't answer.

"You had us worried, Captain," Murdoc's voice broke through Connor's thoughts, and the former Blackguard clapped him on the back. "You need to tell me *everything*. Holy hell, Captain. A dragon!"

"This dragon has a name." Nocturne smirked, and his teeth glistened in the sun.

Connor nudged the dragon in the side, and the beast's massive body gave somewhat under his shove. "Behave."

"A living dragon." Though Sophia spoke, her voice cracked with awe. Her eyes widened as she studied his magnificent face.

Murdoc leaned closer and lowered his voice to the barest whisper. "That thing's not going to eat my future wife, is it?"

"He," Connor corrected. "Not 'it.' And no, you all are safe."

"We are now, you mean." Murdoc shot a sidelong glance at him. "You're certainly full of surprises."

"It keeps life interesting." Connor shrugged. "Did our captive behave herself while I was distracted?"

"Distracted?" Murdoc snorted and stared up at the beast again. "A light workout, was it?"

Connor chuckled, but he needed the man to focus. "Did Quinn give you trouble?"

"Right." The former Blackguard crossed his arms as he finally turned his full attention away from the dragon. "No issues, for the most part. There was a strange cracking sound during her privy break. I thought she might've been up to something, but she claimed a tree branch fell and nearly speared her through the heart."

"Pity it didn't," Sophia grumbled, mostly to herself as she stared up at the dragon.

"A branch, huh?" Connor raised one eyebrow skeptically.

"Couldn't verify it, Captain," Murdoc admitted with a shake of his head. "The Bluntmar collar is still on, though, and she hasn't tried anything. I'm not sure what to make of it."

Beside him, the wraith didn't move. The ghoul studied their captive with an unwavering focus, his hands behind his back and still as stone. Only his cloak billowed around him, ever shifting in the winds of the dead.

And, for once, the ghoul didn't interject himself into the conversation.

How refreshing.

"Stand still." Nocturne's dark eye narrowed as the dragon examined Murdoc. A rush of warm air rolled past them as he breathed, and the ground shook again as he meandered slowly closer. "There is more in you I wish to witness."

Murdoc violently shuddered and raised one hand to block the dragon's piercing gaze. "What in the Fates' name was that? It felt... it was like you could..." Unable to finish his thought, the former Blackguard winced in discomfort and turned his back on the dragon. "Captain, what the hell is he doing?"

Connor frowned and raised a stern finger at the dragon in warning. "You need to start warning people."

Nocturne growled with annoyance.

"It's best not to fight it," Connor added under his breath as he patted the former Blackguard on the back. "You might as well get it over with."

Murdoc groaned in frustration, but he ultimately looked the dragon in the eye. "Get on with it, then."

As his friend squirmed uncomfortably under Nocturne's gaze, Connor rubbed his tired eyes. His head buzzed, foggy and full of fuzzy thoughts he couldn't quite wrangle. He didn't know what he needed more after a drawn-out fight like that—sleep, food, or enough water to flood a farmhouse. His stomach growled with hunger, the pain so intense it made him nauseous.

But he couldn't rest. He had to push through.

Nearby, Quinn leaned her elbows on her knees, her eyes narrowed in focus as she watched Nocturne's every move.

No time like the present, the wraith said, breaking his silence.

Connor took a settling breath, but nodded. "Time to find out what else she knows."

In a few easy strides, he closed the distance between them, and her hazel eyes shifted toward him. Her expression didn't change, and even with a dragon in their midst, she remained cool and collected.

Unruffled by a living legend—or simply unsurprised. He couldn't tell.

Beside her, Blaze growled in warning as Connor neared. The vougel's ears pinned against his head, and his snout wrinkled with his snarl. Unruffled by the tiger's threat, he glared it down, never one to back down from a challenge.

To his surprise, however, Quinn whistled. At the short, sharp command, the creature's snarl instantly stopped, and it rested its head on the ground as it waited patiently for him to draw near.

Interesting.

"Congratulations on your new pet," she said dryly.

He didn't answer. He hated how much she had already seen. Worse was how much she must've learned about him and his team over these past few days. Somehow, he needed to detain her until everything she knew became obsolete. He couldn't possibly let her go, but he didn't know how much longer he could contain someone with her level of skill.

No matter the measures they took to restrain her magic, it all seemed unlikely to last.

She had let herself get captured, which meant she probably wanted something from him. He needed to figure out exactly what that was, ideally before she found it on her own. It was time to discover for himself if taking her alive had been a wise move or a massive mistake.

When he reached her, he scratched at the stubble on his jawline to buy himself a little more time to figure out the best approach. In the tense silence that followed, however, light glinted off the metal collar around her neck.

Through the thick curls of her fire-red hair, the collar's broken lock glinted again in the sunlight. She shifted her weight, and as she adjusted in her seat, her hair hid the collar once more.

The *gall*.

He went dangerously still as, internally, he fumed. They had confiscated everything on her, save for the two pendants locked around her neck with an enchantment Sophia hadn't been able to break.

No weapons. No pack. No potions. And yet, somehow, she had broken the collar while he was away. She could've taken his team hostage or used them as leverage against him to demand her release.

To her credit, she hadn't, and that only confused him further.

His eyes narrowed as he debated on how to play this, but he had only one choice—remind her who she had decided to challenge.

The silence stretched on as they both waited for the other to break first. Her shoulders slouched, and her head hung weakly, so she could certainly play the part of powerless captive well. Whatever her plan, she wanted him to think she was still cut off from her magic, and he figured he could still use this to his advantage.

"Is this the part where you interrogate me further?" Quinn tilted her head as she studied his face. "Torture? Dungeons? All that fun stuff?"

He ran his tongue over his back molars as he ignored the bait. He had been watching her for days, now, same as she had been watching him. By now, he had a decent idea of how to handle her.

Time to see if he could bluff a Starling.

"Torture, huh?" He raised one eyebrow at her challenge. "Is that what you would do to me, if the roles were switched?"

Her cocky smile fell. "That's not my style."

"Not sure I believe, you," he admitted.

She shrugged. "Doesn't matter if you do or don't, Connor."

The edge of his mouth twitched with irritation that she knew his name, but it only proved that she knew too much for him to release her.

He glanced over his shoulder and whistled to get Nocturne's attention. The dragon's head snapped toward him, and Sophia let out a long sigh of relief as he released her from his piercing gaze.

Connor motioned for Nocturne to join him. With slow and steady steps that sent shockwaves through the ground, the dragon lumbered over.

"Here's how this is going to go," Connor explained as he towered over her. For added effect, he crossed his arms over his thick chest and intently glared her down. "I'm going to ask a few more questions, and you're going to answer them honestly."

"Ah, yes." She chuckled. "Willingly give you classified secrets for free. That's certainly in my favor."

"It is."

"How do you figure?"

"Because you're not very useful otherwise." He gestured over his shoulder. "I found a lot down there in the catacombs. If you're just going to be difficult, I could lock you in any number of rooms. Hell, I might even forget you're down there."

She frowned and held his gaze as Nocturne's long shadow fell across them both. A chill snaked over his arms as the dragon blocked out the sun, and the creature's massive head appeared at Connor's side.

"That was a lie," the prince of dragons observed with an air of confusion. "What I don't understand, however, is why you would lie about killing her."

Connor briefly shut his eyes in unrestrained irritation and shot a sidelong glare at the infuriating dragon who had called his bluff against an enemy.

"I cannot see much in you, but I did see traces of nobility and honor." Nocturne's eye narrowed in challenge. "It is difficult for me to believe you would let someone starve to death, down in those catacombs."

Quinn chuckled as Connor groaned with frustration and set his head in one hand.

Damn it all.

The dragon glanced between them, more confused than ever. "What did I misunderstand?"

"It's called a bluff," Connor said through gritted teeth. "And you're not supposed to call me out on it."

The wraith sighed impatiently and shook his cloaked head.

If a life in the Ancient Woods had taught Connor anything, it was how to adapt to new situations. It wasn't too late to salvage this, and he could still make her talk.

"As you can see, my new friend sees through lies," he informed Quinn, though he shot one last scowl at the dragon beside him. "And he's going to tell me when you lie, too."

Her smile fell, and she went dangerously still.

"Let's begin." He smirked, once more in control of the conversation. "Why are you here?"

"You captured me," she said dryly.

"Don't play coy," he warned. "I'm not in the mood."

A muscle twitched in her neck, but she let out an impatient sigh and stood. With a lingering glance at the dragon, she set her hands on her hips and raised her chin in defiance. "Because I don't understand a damn thing about you, Connor. The Lightseers told me you're an assassin, but the southern towns call you the Shade. You're a folk hero to them, and that doesn't make a lick of sense."

The Shade.

It rang a hazy, distant bell for him, and it took a moment to remember that the kids he saved from the blightwolves had called him that. It was some folk legend from the Ancient Woods, something that predated him by decades, but they had given him the title nonetheless.

He shook his head. "I'm not the Shade."

"Doesn't matter." Quinn waved away his protest with a flick of her thin wrist. "You've saved people along the road, and they think you're a hero. Now, why would an assassin do that, I wonder? What's in it for you?"

Connor raised a skeptical eyebrow. "I assume you have theories."

"I see through you." Her voice dropped to a dangerous octave, and she took a menacing step forward. "I see the game you're playing with other people's lives. I see you trying to build a following through manipulating old legends. You've even conned a dragon into believing you're noble. I see you trying to play hero, but I bet you didn't tell any of them what you are. You can't, and you know it."

"And what exactly am I?"

"Host to one of the Great Necromancer's abominations." Her gaze shifted to the Wraith King, whose bony fingers wrapped around his sword at her audacious insult.

Connor stepped between the two of them. "Enough! You—" he pointed to Quinn. "Show him some respect. And you—" he glared at the wraith. "Get ahold of yourself."

This is foolish. The wraith huffed as he released his grip on the hilt of his weapon. *She is too obstinate for questioning. Give me an hour to do this my way, and she will sing for us if we ask.*

"Stop it," Connor warned in a low, gravelly tone.

The wraith let out a disgusted groan and disappeared into a puff of black smoke.

"You want to know why I helped those kids?" Connor squared his shoulders as he met her furious glare. "Someone has to step in when Lightseers like you won't do your damn jobs. The Ancient Woods are dangerous, and we haven't seen a Lightseer patrol along the southern road since Henry took over. You lot forgot your duty to the people and became his private army, so don't give me any of that *shit*."

Quinn flinched as if he had smacked her, and she cradled her right hand to her abdomen as if his words had caused her pain. As her fingers curled into a fist, he caught the briefest glimpse of a long scar across her palm.

Interesting. Given the rumors about the Starlings' mastery of potions, no wound should've been able to linger long enough to leave a scar. Apparently, there was more to Teagan's youngest child than met the eye.

"Look," she said quietly. "As fun as our banter has been, I have things to do. I don't want to be trapped here anymore than you want me around."

He snorted derisively. "I'm not going to let you go."

"Only an idiot would," she admitted with a shrug. "I don't trust you, and you don't trust me. That's fair, but I have another solution that could work for us both. I'm sure there's a long list of things you want, so I'm going to make you a deal."

How interesting.

Usually, he was the one striking bargains, not the other way around. No one had offered him a deal since his days with Beck Arbor.

"All I want are my sword and a safe way home." Her eyes darted briefly toward the forest, and a vein briefly pulsed in her temple.

He cast a sidelong glance at Nocturne, who nodded quietly. For whatever reason, she had just lied to them both.

Connor didn't respond. He let her stew in the silence that followed and studied her body language for more tells, but she didn't move. Aside from that brief twitch, she didn't give any indication of discomfort.

How curious.

For whatever reason, she didn't want to go home. It made a strange sort of sense, given how she and her brother had been at odds in the middle of a deadly battle. Hell, Zander had implied she was a bastard and tried to kill her when Connor had taken her hostage.

Apparently, Teagan's children didn't get along.

Negotiating with a Starling was like playing with fire, but it was his mess, and he would deal with it like a man.

"I gave you my terms, so tell me what you want." She spread her arms wide, as though inviting him to dream big. "I can probably make it happen."

He sat with her offer. Between Sophia's fading health and the wraith's insistence on getting the Deathdread, he and his team had quite the shopping list. In a negotiation like this, however, giving away his desires meant giving her yet another opportunity to dissect his plans and analyze his weaknesses. He couldn't allow her to figure out any more about him than she already had.

True, she could probably get him whatever he wanted, but she would have to join them when they went to retrieve it. The moment he let her leave Slaybourne, she was a flight risk. If she escaped, she would return to her father with far more intel than he wanted his enemy to possess.

This bargain could mean the difference between life and death in his battle against Teagan, and he had to tread carefully.

If anyone would stab him in the back after making a deal, it was a Starling.

CHAPTER TWENTY-TWO
CONNOR

Connor rubbed his thumb against the stubble on his jaw as he thought through the risks of making a deal with Quinn Starling. Boots shuffled across the grass as he inwardly debated, drawing nearer, and Murdoc appeared at his side moments later. A pale Sophia joined them shortly thereafter.

Everyone was here, and they were all just as curious as he was to find out what this Starling knew.

"You don't want to go home," Connor eventually said, calling Quinn's bluff. "Tell me what you're really after."

Her brows furrowed, but she didn't otherwise betray her discomfort, and she didn't answer.

"Last chance," he warned. "Those dungeons might not be a bluff after all if you keep wasting my time."

Quinn muttered obscenities under her breath, but as she looked once more at the dragon, she ultimately groaned in defeat. "Fine. *Fine*, damn it all. I want the truth. I want you to take a Hackamore and answer my questions until they're done."

Sophia cackled, and even Connor laughed at the ludicrous request. "Why in the Fates' name would I ever do that?"

The Starling warrior crossed her arms in defiance. "Because I will do the same for you."

Now *that* intrigued him.

She had plenty of secrets in that brain of hers, and a Hackamore would be the key to unlock them all—provided he asked the right questions.

Though he didn't like the idea of her rummaging around in his head, there was something unique about her compared to the rest of the Starlings and Lightseers who had hunted him across the continent. Whereas Zander would've probably killed Murdoc and Sophia once he had gotten free of the collar, Quinn hadn't done a thing.

Thus far, she had merely observed everyone around her.

"So, you want the Hackamores and your sword." Connor shifted his weight as he probed for the truth. "What else?"

"That's it." She crossed her arms as she laid out her terms in this would-be deal. "Along with the freedom to leave with Blaze if I so choose."

If I so choose.

Though easily overlooked, the words spoke volumes. They lingered on the air, heavy with implications, and they told him more than any conversation ever could.

She had lied because she didn't *want* to go home.

He sat with that. "When I'm certain you're no longer a threat, then yes. You and your tiger-bird can leave."

What?! The Wraith King's voice echoed through his head.

Connor didn't answer. He would deal with the ghoul's tantrum later, as he had chosen his words carefully. Declaring she could leave when he no longer considered her to be a threat gave him ultimate control over the matter.

Her brows knit together as she scanned his face, as though she didn't fully trust what he had said.

"There's a caveat," he warned. "If you attempt to escape before I say you can leave, then our entire bargain is off. Understood?"

She nodded.

"Here's the second caveat." His voice dropped an octave, and he studied her hazel eyes as he leaned in. "If, at any time, I see you as a threat to me or my team, our truce ends then and there. If you threaten any of us, even once, I will end you. It will be swift, it will be painful, and not even you will see it coming."

Quinn stiffened, and an icy chill snaked through the field. He held her gaze, firm and unrelenting, as he let the warning sink into her bones.

"Do you really think it's wise to threaten me, outlaw?" Quinn squared her shoulders, and Blaze growled softly at her side.

"It's a fair warning," he corrected. "And it's the only one you'll get. I'm no idiot, Quinn Starling. You surrendered with fight left in you, and I aim to find out why. In the meantime, I won't harm you unless you give me reason. And trust me, princess, you do *not* want to give me a reason."

He reached for the collar around her neck, and she reflexively grabbed his wrist. Her touch sent a shockwave up his arm, and for a second, he wondered if she had used her lightning augmentation on him.

His blades hovered just beneath his skin, aching to break free, but nothing happened. No pain shot through his body. The brief jolt of energy slowly faded, and the muscle in his forearm flexed beneath her touch.

The two of them froze in place, her fingers wrapped around his wrist and their eyes locked as each dared the other to do something stupid.

He looped his finger underneath the broken collar and slipped it off her neck with a gentle tug. The iron circlet landed in his palm, and she tensed. Though her eyes darted toward the collar in his hand, he never looked away.

Caught, the wraith said.

To her credit, she waited patiently for him to move. Her grip on his wrist loosened, and he tossed the enchanted shackle aside. It landed with a thud in the grass, and he crossed his arms again as he studied her.

"Noted," she said stiffly. "Are you going to keep threatening me, outlaw, or do I finally get to hear your terms?"

He flashed a mischievous smile. This was his chance to raid the coffers, and after what she had put them through so far, he intended to milk this for everything it was worth.

However, he still had to be careful about how he worded his demands. Though she needed to know what he wanted, she didn't need to know how he planned to use it.

"Well, outlaw?" She prompted with an irritated twitch of her eyebrow. "What do you want?"

"A lot," he admitted.

Murdoc chuckled. "You might need to write this down."

Her hazel eyes darted toward him, but she didn't reply.

"A master augmentor." Connor raised one finger as he began to count each of his demands on his hand. "A potion master. A Hackamore for you to take when I tell you to."

She frowned.

"Access to bloody beauties," he continued, still listing off his demands. "The Deathdread. Safe passage into and out of Freymoor."

"Freymoor?" Murdoc whispered under his breath. "Captain, what's in—"

"Later," Connor said quietly.

The former Blackguard gave him a rigid nod, but didn't comment. After Connor's visit into the bowels of the Black Keep Mountains, they had quite a bit to discuss.

"And lastly, you're going to help me find Otmund." Connor stood a little taller, knowing full well she would resist this one.

Quinn stiffened, and though she didn't reply, a small dimple appeared in her cheek as she pursed her lips. As far as he could tell, she didn't know anything about the Bloodbane daggers, nor did she realize Otmund had one. Without question, however, she could guess what would happen to Otmund after Connor found him.

He was asking her to help him kill a nobleman, and she damn well knew it.

Though he had already asked for a lot, most of his requests had gone unspoken. The potions master would craft the Hackamore and whatever other potions Sophia needed to refill her stores. The master augmentor, along with the bloody beauties, would both heal her and create the telepathic augmentation he needed for Nocturne.

"Alright," she said calmly.

Connor's brows rose in surprise. He hadn't expected it to be that easy. "You can get all of it?"

"Maybe." She crossed her arms. "At a minimum, I know someone who can get you most of your list."

His eyes narrowed in suspicion. "I think we're going to need some collateral to ensure you don't lead us into a trap."

She frowned. "Such as?"

"Your vougel."

Quinn had one known weakness—her tiger-bird. If the vougel remained here, Connor had a much better chance of keeping her in line.

"Never in a million—"

"You don't get a say in this." He pointed at the broken circlet lying in the grass at their feet to remind her of just how little he trusted her. "If you think I'm going to let you roam free with your mount and your magic, then you're out of your Fates-damn mind. The tiger-bird stays, and that's final."

She curled her fingers so tightly that her knuckles cracked, but she nodded stiffly in surrender. "If anything happens to him—"

"Blood," Sophia interrupted with an eyeroll. "Murder."

"Chaos and death, right." Murdoc waved away the Starling's threat. "We know."

"Does that change who you're planning on taking us to?" Connor asked, his gaze still focused on their prisoner.

She let out an irritated sigh. "No, it doesn't. I'm taking you to the only person I trust with my augmentations. She's a master augmentor and potion master, so that takes care of two items on your wish list." Quinn's gaze shifted to Sophia. "Let me guess. You're the one who needs bloody beauties, aren't you? You think it'll cure whatever illness you have?"

"It's adorable that you think we're going to answer," he quipped.

"How many?" the Starling warrior asked, ignoring him.

"Twenty," Sophia answered.

Quinn laughed. The skin around her eyes crinkled with joy, and she buried her face in her hand as her shoulders shook with laughter.

With their prisoner distracted, Connor glared at Sophia through the corner of his eye. The sharp look said everything he needed her to know, all without him speaking a single word.

Stop being greedy.

"Fine." Sophia grumbled under her breath. "Five, with roots."

"That's better." Quinn wiped a tear from her eye. "It'll still cost you a fortune."

"I think you mean it'll cost *you* a fortune," Connor corrected.

She frowned. "I can help, but this is going to fall on you. Your list is long enough without asking me to front that kind of coin," she added with a nod to Sophia.

"That depends," he countered.

"On what?"

"On how many other items on my list you can get me."

In a negotiation, every concession had to come with a cost, and he wouldn't let Quinn walk out of this with a good deal.

"My contact can get five. She's a professional." Her cold gaze shifted to Sophia. "No matter what you screwed up, she can fix it."

The necromancer bristled. "Listen to me, you infuriating—"

"Enough," Connor said gently.

Sophia let out a strangled scream of frustration and stalked off toward the burned out firepit.

Connor sighed and leaned toward Murdoc, speaking in a hushed tone. "Keep an eye on her, will you?"

"Already on it, Captain." Murdoc nodded and jogged off after the necromancer.

"Though I must eat soon, I will remain for now," Nocturne announced. A hot breath shot through his nose, and he laid on the ground beside Connor. A tremor shot through the earth as he settled on the grass. Quinn's vougel flapped his wings to retain his balance as the dirt shook beneath them all.

When Sophia and Murdoc had jogged out of earshot, Connor fired a withering glare at Quinn. "Stop antagonizing her."

"She makes it too easy."

"I mean it." His eyes narrowed in warning. "As for the other items on my list—"

"There are conditions." She held up her finger, as if to tell him not to get excited. "For starters, I won't get you the Deathdread."

"You're not in a position to—"

"I am," she interrupted. "Since you're holding my vougel hostage to ensure I don't betray you, I'm in a bind. It means I need you alive to get him back, and we would all be walking into a deathtrap if we headed for the Mountains of the Unwanted. I wouldn't be allowed past the Hazeltide sentries without a Regent. I don't have clearance."

"But you're a Starling."

"Doesn't matter." She shrugged. "I'm still not a Regent."

Damn it.

Fine. He would have to find another way in, and he could question her about it along their route.

"You said conditions." He glanced her up and down. "Plural."

"I did. My other condition is that I won't help you kill Otmund."

"I didn't ask you to."

She barely restrained an eyeroll. "Right. Because you're just going to have tea with the man who sent the Lightseers after you."

"Why do you care what happens to him?"

"He's a Lightseer Regent," she said bluntly, as though it were obvious.

The thin vein in her temple pulsed again, and her eyes twitched—subtly, almost imperceptibly, but he saw it nonetheless.

Another lie—albeit, a white one.

"She is protective." Nocturne tilted his head in curiosity, examining her with that overwhelming gaze. "But also angry. He is like family, yet he has betrayed her."

Quinn sucked in a breath through her teeth and squeezed her eyes shut. "I hate it when you do that."

Nocturne's eyes narrowed. A low growl rumbled through the meadow, and a soft tremor vibrated through the ground beneath their feet. "You are not exempt from the honesty you demand of others."

Her lips parted in surprise, but she didn't respond.

Connor set his hands on his waist as he stared her down. "You should be more worried about the company you keep, princess, than you are about my intentions."

That snapped her out of her daze, and her nose wrinkled with disdain. "And what do you know about the company I keep?"

"I know Otmund's a coward." A buzzing energy shot through him as he relived the night he'd fused with the wraith. Connor paced the small stretch of flattened grass by her log, unable to stand still any longer. "What do you know about the night he tried to kill me, Quinn?"

She didn't flinch. "You murdered ten soldiers, and then you tried to stab him in the heart."

"Wrong." Connor jabbed his finger in the air to punctuate the word. "They tried to kill an innocent woman and her daughters, and I intervened. Besides, I killed nine soldiers, not ten. How do you think Otmund opened that Rift to limp back home with his tail between his legs?"

He let his question linger in the silence that followed.

She scowled, even as she pieced it together. "You're lying."

Connor looked at the dragon. "Am I?"

"He is not."

"Huh," Connor said sarcastically as he returned his attention to Quinn. "Go figure."

"Otmund is a scholar," Quinn said fiercely. "He doesn't have it in him to kill someone."

Connor laughed. He couldn't help it. "Princess, I watched him slit that last soldier's throat. The man had a patch on his eye. Otmund stayed in his blind spot until it was too late, and he dragged that dying man onto the Rift. I was broken, nearly dead, and I couldn't move fast enough to stop him."

Quinn didn't reply. The muscles in her neck tightened, and her eyes slipped out of focus as she sat with everything he had said.

"Think long and hard about who you're protecting," he warned, his voice gravely and low. "Think about who you are at your core, and how noble these so-called allies of yours really are. Because I'll take that into account when I decide where you fall on my list of enemies."

Her cold eyes darted toward him as she met his warning with a silent one of her own.

"You sit with that," he ordered. "And we can discuss Otmund another day."

"Fine," she said dryly. "Are we done?"

"Not quite. Tell me what you know about Freymoor."

"It's the oldest city in Saldia." She set her hands on her hips and tilted her head impatiently. "There are literal libraries filled with its history, so you're going to have to be more specific."

"The former princess, then. Is there anything she wants?"

"Ah." A knowing smile spread across the Starling warrior's face. "You want one of her artifacts for yourself?"

"Answer the question," he said curtly.

"She won't cooperate," Quinn warned. "King Henry spent years trying to force her to reveal what's in the Blood Bogs, but he never got anywhere. Freymoor and its people are clever, outlaw. Cleverer than you."

I truly hate this woman, the wraith interceded. *But she's right about Freymoor's fallen princess.*

Connor's ear twitched as the wraith spoke up. "Oh?"

"Oh?" Quinn's frowned with confusion. "What—"

Connor held up one hand to silence her as he waited for the wraith to continue.

Henry left the king's daughter alive because of the legends around that place, the ghoul explained. *He wanted the artifacts her family hid in the bogs, and rumor has it only royalty can access the mists without losing their way. He needed at least one of them alive to get him what he wanted. He figured he could break her over time.*

Fantastic. The one person they needed on their side must've loathed the Wraith King with every fiber of her being.

I warned him to stay away, the wraith continued. *Freymoor is the sort of land that doesn't stay conquered for long, and it is vengeful against its enemies. He refused to listen. Learn from his mistake, Magnuson.*

Interesting. The wraith wasn't just wary of this place; he feared it.

"What kind of defenses does she have?" Connor asked.

Quinn crossed her arms and let out an impatient sigh. "Are you talking to me now?"

He tilted his head in annoyance and gestured for her to continue.

"You've demanded a lot already." The Lightseer shook her head. "I'm not going to give away state secrets just because you want to know."

"There's always the dungeons."

Nocturne snorted impatiently, and a plume of dark smoke shot out his nose.

"You're no fun," Connor muttered to the dragon.

"I am aware."

"Fine." He turned his attention back to Quinn. "What will you tell me, then?"

"That you shouldn't bother." She shrugged. "Someone has taken over Freymoor, and no one knows who it is. There are rumors, of course, but nothing we can substantiate. Is it her advisor? The former military generals who went missing without a trace? An unknown new player? No one can say, but the former princess isn't going to give you what you ask for—even if she wants to."

"How do you know so much about her?"

"Tracking her activities was my first assignment as a Lightseer."

That piqued Connor's interest. "So you *can* get us in."

"Of course I can." Quinn crossed her arms. "But it will be a mistake, and it will probably get you killed. Since I want to see Blaze again after this shopping trip of yours, I need you alive."

More rare reagents grow in Freymoor than anywhere else, except perhaps on Troll Island, the wraith interjected, though he still hadn't reappeared. *Freymoor's knowledge of potionmaking and magic rivals any master I've seen in Oakenglen. If the Starling woman's augmentor can't save Sophia, the potion masters in Freymoor can. We must go there, Magnuson. Between the Soulsprite and your fading necromancer, there is simply no other choice.*

"We're going," he announced. "You'd better find us a safe way in and out, Quinn."

She shook her head and pinched the bridge of her nose. With the movement, the pendants around her neck slipped out of her shirt, and they hung against her deep neckline—the Starling crest, and a strange golden pendant with spears around its blue stone, like rays of a sun.

The only items they couldn't confiscate when they'd captured her.

"I don't know how you broke free," he said with a nod to the broken collar on the ground. "I figure you won't tell me, and that's fine, but you made a mistake. You showed your cards, and I know there's a weapon on you somewhere right this minute. I'll be watching you, Quinn. Whatever it is and however it works, I guarantee you don't want to use it on me."

"No?" she asked coyly. "Why is that, outlaw?"

He leaned in, until his mouth hovered by her ear, and she stiffened beside him. The scent of jasmine and honeysuckle rolled off her hair, but he saw through her beauty and wealth to the deadly warrior underneath.

"You're good, Quinn Starling," he acknowledged. "But I'm better."

CHAPTER TWENTY-THREE
CONNOR

The hazy blood-orange sun peered through two jet-black peaks as another day in Slaybourne came to a close.

Connor stepped into a sunbeam as he closed the southern-most entrance into the catacombs. He'd hidden Quinn's weapons and other belongings out here, specifically because he knew she would never find them on her own.

With her pack slung over one shoulder, he took a few unlicensed practice swings of her flawless Firesword. Orange light from the setting sun glinted off its blade, and he marveled at its craftsmanship. Light as a twig and perfectly balanced, the sword sliced through the air with a soft whistle. The glistening green gem in its hilt glowed with the fire of a star. Nearly the size of an eyeball, the stone itself must've cost a small fortune to create.

No wonder she wanted it back.

Tell me you've thought this through. Black smoke rolled across Connor's boots as the Wraith King appeared beside him. *Returning your enemy's supplies and her greatest weapon seems more stupid than your plans usually are.*

Instead of taking the bait, Connor smirked and swung the sword again. "We might need her potions on our trip. She can have the pack in Slaybourne, but I'll carry it after we leave. As for the sword, does it matter? She clearly has a powerful weapon on her already. How else could she have broken the collar?"

The wraith grumbled. *Fair point.*

"If she's going to betray us, I'd prefer she tried it sooner rather than later."

A wise choice. Otherwise, you might get attached, like you did with the other two.

Connor's jaw tensed, and he opted against replying.

A shadow soared over the grass as Connor crested a hill, and he glanced skyward as Nocturne banked on an air current. The dragon's eyes shut with bliss as he spun on the wind, reconnected with the sky.

Connor took a deep breath of the fresh mountain air, grateful he was able to bring their prince of darkness back from the edge.

"Giving her the sword back is a sign of good faith," he added as he resumed his trek toward the campsite. "Nocturne and I watched her through the entire interrogation. She told the truth, or at least most of it. There's more to her than meets the eye."

Yes, the Wraith King conceded. *But will that get you killed?*

Connor's smile fell, and he sighed as he sat with the question. "She's playing prisoner right now. I know it. She's testing the waters, but I'm testing her right back. If I discover she's a threat, she's dead."

You swear it?

He nodded. "I don't care if her father's on the way. If she puts my team in danger, not even Teagan's wrath can protect her."

Good.

At the base of the hill, Murdoc kicked a rock across the grass as he paced, still waiting for them to return. Connor made his way down the hill toward him, and the man met him halfway.

"Captain," the former Blackguard said in welcome. "A word?"

"What's on your mind, Murdoc?"

"This whole augmentor business." The former Blackguard gestured toward the trees, in the vague direction of the lone exit from Slaybourne. "Are you sure this will work? Sophia doesn't have much time left. Everything she has told me thus far—though I'll admit it's not much—requires the Deathdread. It's supposed to have the answers she needs. Why would we trust some augmentor on our prisoner's say-so?"

"We're not," Connor assured him. "There's no guarantee Quinn's augmentor can do this, but there's no proof the Deathdread can, either. Sophia told me as much herself. If the augmentor fails, Freymoor can help us."

"But will they?"

"I don't know," Connor admitted. "But it's the best plan we've got. Going into the Mountains of the Unwanted will take more time than we have. It's too risky to go in there on a hunch."

They trudged through a thin line of trees and into the glowing green meadow they had chosen as their campsite. At the opposite end, Sophia stood at a cauldron she had found in the rubble. The fire underneath it cast thin ribbons of smoke around the edges of the pot, and she glanced up at them as they approached. Without a word or gesture of welcome, she scowled and returned her attention to the bubbling concoction before her.

"She's upset," Murdoc said.

"You think?" Connor asked dryly.

As they neared, he cast a quick scan of the meadow for their prisoner. At the far end of their campsite, Quinn lounged on a log with her eyes glossed over with thought.

"Freymoor, is it?" Sophia raised one eyebrow skeptically as the two men neared. "Have you lost your damn mind, Connor?"

He grinned. "Maybe."

She grimaced in disgust, apparently not in the mood for jokes.

Murdoc cleared his throat nervously. "Captain, we don't have much time. I don't see how we can get all this done. Freymoor is one hell of a trek from here."

"By foot," Connor reminded him.

Nocturne's shadow sailed past, dwarfing them in a brief chill as he blocked out the sun. Connor squinted upward as the dragon glided over the trees and dove into the forest. The canopy shivered, and a distant thud echoed through the valley as he landed somewhere out of sight.

"Wait." Murdoc smiled as he pieced it together. "The dragon's going to be our draft horse?"

"Don't say that to his face," Connor warned. "But yes, and he's a hell of a lot faster than any horse."

"Will he carry me in his claws?" Murdoc rubbed his hands together gleefully. "I want to feel like I'm flying."

"Focus," Connor chided. His voice dropped to a whisper as he cautiously glanced at Quinn, but he had no idea what she could really hear now that she had access to her augmentations. "There's something else we need from Freymoor. With Teagan on his way, we must reinforce Slaybourne. There's an artifact in the bogs that can help us protect this place for good."

Sophia shook her head. "We're in a fortified mountain fortress. It's stupid to leave now."

"No," he corrected. "It would be stupid to stay in its current condition."

Sophia and Murdoc both frowned and waited for him to continue.

"The enchantments that secured Nocturne drained most of the residual magic here," he explained. "The wraith said it probably wouldn't have had enough magic to reseal him in his tomb if I'd failed last night."

"Shit," Murdoc muttered.

"Exactly," Connor admitted. "When Teagan arrives, there's no telling what manpower and weaponry he will bring with him. He knows he's coming to a fortress, and I can guarantee he will come prepared."

"And we're defenseless," Sophia muttered, rubbing her face.

Not defenseless, the wraith huffed. *The exterior protections are still active, and—*

"Close enough to it," Connor interrupted with a sidelong glare at the hovering specter.

"You don't know what you're getting yourself into," Sophia warned. "Freymoor has secrets not even the necromancers have dared try to uncover. I'm not sure if our little princess over there explained this to you, but dozens of Lightseer spies have disappeared into those bogs."

"How do you know?"

"Because Nethervale lost dozens of our elite soldiers, same as they did." Her voice dripped with icy disdain. "Nyx won't go to Freymoor, and rumors say Teagan won't either. They're afraid of it, and we should be, too."

"Why would the Lady of Freymoor heal Sophia or give us this artifact?" Murdoc asked. "Do we have anything she wants?"

"No idea," Connor confessed as he clapped his friend on the shoulder.

"But everyone wants something. Once we figure out what it is, we strike a deal."

"You and your damn deals." Sophia shook of her head. "We don't have time to waste on this… this… no, I can't even call it a plan, Connor."

"Thank you for the vote of confidence," he said dryly. He crossed his arms, knowing neither of them would like what he was about to say next. "And speaking of delays, there's one detour we need to make on the way to Oakenglen."

"Are you joking?" Sophia stared up at him incredulously. "We're under an obscene time restraint as it is, and you want to add more to our list?"

"This isn't negotiable."

"What could possibly be important enough to—"

"My family," he interrupted. "Or the closest thing I have to one, anymore."

Both of his teammates went silent. Only the soft whistle of the wind through the trees and the gentle pop of the cauldron's fire filled the silence.

"I know it's a risk," he admitted. "But they're out there, between us and Teagan, and kids talk. There's a chance someone will realize they're connected to me, and I can't let that happen. After what they did for me, I can't… I won't…" He cleared his throat and looked away. "I have to do this. If you don't want to come, wait here until I get back."

"Are you kidding?" Murdoc laughed. "I'm not going to miss a chance to fly on a dragon."

"Sophia?" Connor prodded.

"Of course I'll come." The necromancer ran a hand through her long black hair and sighed. "But I don't like this one bit."

"I don't either," he confessed. "But this is what we have to do to secure Slaybourne."

Her dark eyes snapped toward him, and she simply watched him for a moment. "You're sure?"

"This will work," he promised, seeing through her concern. "I made you a promise."

"I know," she said quietly, and yet her unspoken fear lingered in the air.

You made a promise, but can you really follow through?

His jaw tensed at the friction between them, but he'd already made up his mind. He wasn't an orphaned boy wandering aimlessly through the Ancient Woods anymore. Quinn Starling had the sort of influence to deliver almost any miracle they asked for, and his growing abilities as the Wraithblade gave him the power to ensure she met her end of this bargain.

"You two pack up what food and water you can store." He happily swung Quinn's sword, and it whistled as it sliced through the late afternoon. "I'm going to go give our prisoner her weapon back."

Sophia grimaced. "Honestly, I can't tell when you're serious and when you're just trying to get a rise out of me."

He chuckled, but didn't reply.

As he marched toward their prisoner, he snuck a glance over his shoulder at the team that had already risked their lives for him. They stood by the cauldron, talking in hushed tones. Murdoc playfully nudged Sophia and whispered something in her ear. A small smile spread across her face, and she tilted her head to hide it from him.

One way or another, the three of them would solve this. Together. Even if Sophia doubted what Connor could do, he refused to let her die. No matter the cost.

He always protected his own.

CHAPTER TWENTY-FOUR
QUINN

In the amber aftermath of another day, Quinn adjusted the pack on her shoulder as she returned to deliver Blaze the bad news.

A soft growl snaked through the meadow as she approached the towering grasses where she had ordered him to wait, and she couldn't hide the subtle grin pulling at the corner of her mouth as she scanned the glowing field for her pet. She paused midstride, her ears attuned to the soft rumble humming through the overgrown field. Her eyes fluttered closed, and she tilted her head to listen for the crunch of dirt under a paw, or the snap of a twig as he stalked her.

Any time they played this game, the furry lump always gave himself away.

The soothing rustle of wind through the meadow grasses blended with the swish and sway of the forest's distant canopy. A bird twittered, and in the pauses between its song, Blaze's growl faded into the muted roar of this timeless paradise.

To her left, pebbles rolled across the ground, so softly she almost missed it.

Her attuned senses focused on a patch of towering grass to her left. She peeked through one eye, careful not to give herself away, and the briefest flash of white filtered through the glowing green blades.

"You lose, Blaze." She grinned with victory. "I saw you."

The grasses stilled. A flock of glowing red birds flew overhead, their feathers snapping on the air as they passed, and yet her vougel remained hidden—excellent impulse control on his part, and a marked improvement from the first few times they played this game, back when she was just a girl.

As the silence stretched on, she began to piece together his strategy.

Blaze probably figured he could wait her out. Let her get comfortable. Watch her lower her guard or doubt herself. It made sense, given how he had witnessed her use that technique time and time again on the marks they had hunted together through the years. Tricking a criminal into thinking they had the upper hand against a Starling always got them talking. It dragged out their attacks, gave her time to recover, and usually revealed something that would shift the tides in her favor.

Hell, even the Wraithblade had fallen for that trick, back when she had first tried to detain him.

People saw what they wanted, especially when they looked at her. No one would ever admit it, of course, but she had learned long ago that most people love the sound of their own voice more than victory.

Slowly, she knelt and slid her bag off her shoulder. With a slight twist of her body, she blocked the vougel's view of her pack and slipped her canteen from its depths. With a flick of her thumb, she popped off the cork and waited—armed and ready.

Deep down, she figured he only played this game because he secretly liked this part.

The patter of paws over dirt broke the peaceful silence, but she acted faster. She flicked the canteen in his direction, and a spray of water hit her pet in his white and gold face. He slid to a stop, kicking up dust, and his eyes narrowed in disappointment as beads of water dripped from his now-soaked face.

Quinn laughed and sealed the canteen before grabbing a clean rag from the depths of her pack. Blaze collapsed into a puddle of drenched disappointment at her feet and pouted, his tail twitching in irritation at the loss. Her rag soaked up most of the water as she dabbed between his eyes.

"Don't be a sore loser, Blaze," she chided.

He growled softly and batted her head with his paw. The soft pads at the base of his feet brushed against her cheek, heavy and rough. The movement threw her momentarily off balance, and she laughed.

Though he still wouldn't look at her, he set his massive head in her lap and purred. Her fingers wove through the thick fur on the crown of his head. Their connection opened, as it did every time they touched, and she savored the rush of his emotions as they came through—happiness, devotion, affection.

And, toward the end, just a ribbon of fear.

Quinn's smile fell even as the giant winged tiger closed his eyes and leaned into her nails, purring louder now. She scratched behind his ears, careful to hit his favorite spots, but even a predator as fearsome as Blaze had every right to be afraid.

Over by the burned-out fire pit, Connor knelt by a log and refilled his own bag from the piles of supplies he had stacked on the nearby logs. He glanced her way as she watched him from afar. Those intense eyes of his didn't give away a hint of emotion, despite those furrowed brows.

"Bad news, buddy," she said softly to her pet. "You have to stay here."

Blaze snorted and rolled onto his stomach, his ears pinned to his head as he stared at her in disbelief.

"I know." She sighed and rested one arm on her propped knee. "I don't like it either, but right now we don't have a choice."

His attention snapped to Connor, and he snarled. His teeth glinted in the fading sunlight as he made his opinion on the matter known.

She whistled once, sharp and loud, to nip this in the bud. The vougel's rumbling growl instantly stopped, and this time, Blaze shifted his furious gaze back to her. She frowned and tilted her head without a word, silently admonishing his tantrum.

Her pet relaxed. He tucked his wings away as he reluctantly stood and brushed his heavy head against hers. She closed her eyes and leaned into his fur, holding both sides of his face as they sat there for a moment, their connection open once more, simply feeling.

The loss. The concern. The fear of never seeing each other again.

"I want you to explore," she whispered to him. "I want you to master every nook and cranny of this place, but don't go over the walls. You saw what happened to Zander's mount when he tried to infiltrate this fortress."

Blaze snarled, the roar sharp and loud in her ears with her forehead still pressed against him, and she gently ran her fingers along his jaw to soothe his concern. Though Zander had never bonded with any of the vougels, Quinn couldn't imagine such a horrible thing happening to hers.

A surge of concern and protectiveness rushed through their connection, and she held him tight. She had come here for answers, and she was so close to getting them.

"We started this together," she said under her breath, reminding him of why they were here. "And that's how we'll finish it. You and me. Understood?"

His low growl faded into gentle purring, and he moaned softly in resignation. Though she wanted nothing more to defy Connor's demand that she leave Blaze behind, she understood why he had done it. Her truce with this new Wraithblade could shatter at any moment, and Blaze was collateral he could use to ensure she didn't kill them all in their sleep.

Connor was smart, and that just made him all the more dangerous.

CHAPTER TWENTY-FIVE
TEAGAN

The rhythmic clink of Teagan's armor matched his steady stride through Lunestone's main hall. Wide enough for twenty men to march side by side, the towering corridor led to the dual iron doors and the courtyard beyond them. Flawless white banners, easily as tall as a commoner's home, lined the dark stone gaps between each gold-framed window on either side. The first rays of dawn cast thin sunbeams across the azure horse of the Lightseer crest that had been embroidered onto each flag.

Teagan adjusted the white and gold armored gauntlet on his left hand as two servants opened the wide double doors leading out to the courtyard. The elaborate armor weighed on his shoulders, and though it had taken four servants to lift the chest plate over his head, he wore it with practiced ease. The golden horse on his chest plate cast a dazzling reflection across the blue carpet leading toward the doors, and he stifled an impatient grumble at the theatre of it all.

Pageantry, all of it, but it served him well.

White and gold. Noise and fanfare. Though he preferred to handle his business in private—primarily to reduce the number of witnesses—this nonsense had its function, and performances like the one awaiting him in the courtyard had been organized for a unique and crucial purpose.

Only a rumor could fly faster than the winged tigers in his cavalry, and peasants loved to talk. For that reason alone, he had ensured as many of the Lunestone servants as possible would witness this takeoff. When the Wraithblade heard of the army coming for him, even the Wraith King would piss itself.

Now, Tegan had to inspire the masses to die for him.

As he approached the bowing men on either side of the open doors, he pressed his thumb into his left temple to relieve a bit of the tension pooling in his forehead.

Relief fluttered through his skull. The simple release gave him the clarity and focus to shift into the persona he always wore in public, when there were too many variables to don unique masks for everyone present.

The reserved but confident leader. Cool. Collected. In control of every moment but as deadly as any wildfire.

The steady chatter of a hundred men talking over each other hit him as he jogged down the main stairs. Golden light flashed across the cobblestone road as the sunlight hit the gilded armor of two dozen officers standing at attention in the grass circle at the center of the courtyard.

The best of the best, all awaiting his orders.

With a quiet grunt of satisfaction, Tegan took a quick inventory of the well-organized chaos of the final moments before his army took flight. The hum of a hundred conversations buzzed through the air, tense and laden with just the right amount of panic as they all raced to meet his deadline.

Countless servants clad in dark blues or muted browns scurried like ants across the dark stone road, each carrying sealed leather packs or crates of supplies on their way through the open iron gate and out to the field beyond his castle. Flashes of gold and silver skittered across the ocean of winged tigers as squires made the final adjustments to a hundred beasts' armor. Soldiers jogged in tightly formed units past the distant stables, and they all dashed across the network of well-worn routes of his vast island fortress.

Perfection.

When he reached the rows of officers waiting for him in the courtyard, a young man with short blond hair removed his helmet and stepped forward. His hand snapped to his forehead in a sharp salute, and he stared dead ahead as he waited to be addressed.

"Colonel Freerock," Tegan said as he reached the officer. "Report."

The man nodded and lowered his salute. "Every elite soldier from Oakenglen to Everdale has been called to duty, sir. One hundred and seven in all."

"That will suffice." Teagan scanned what he could see of the large field through the open iron gate. "Colonel, come with me. The rest of you, collect your units and prepare to leave. We move out in ten minutes."

"Yes, sir!" the officers said in unison.

The flawless rows of soldiers splintered as they jogged off toward the field. As seasoned as these soldiers were, they raced past the huffing servants and reached the field in seconds. Some of them whistled for their unit's attention, while others barked orders that blended into the chaotic hum of preparations.

Colonel Freerock stepped effortlessly in stride with Teagan as they headed for the gate. The elite soldier walked with his chin raised and his hands behind his back, but the deep lines of worry in his forehead betrayed an unspoken doubt he desperately wanted to share.

Teagan sighed and massaged his left temple as he adjusted his mask for a private conversation. Though only in his early thirties, Colonel Rowan Freerock's rise through the ranks had been legendary, even for the son of one of Teagan's highest-ranking generals. His father, the late General Freerock, had died in their war against Henry, and Teagan had seized the opportunity to mold the man's orphaned son into yet another zealous Lightseer. Rowan and Zander had grown up together, and that had given Teagan ample opportunities to learn Freerock's weaknesses.

So long as he treated the colonel like a surrogate son, the soldier devoted his every waking second to the Lightseers and, more importantly, to Teagan. Rowan Freerock had no life or purpose beyond the Lightseers, and that ensured the man's lifetime devotion.

And, of course, the sort of blind loyalty that could never be bought.

"Rowan," Teagan scolded, careful to use the soldier's first name to create a fabricated sense of affection and trust. "You always scowl like that when you disagree with a decision I've made."

"Apologies, sir." Freerock cleared his throat and distracted himself by watching a maid with frizzy braids falling from the pins in her head as she scurried by with an armful of bread loaves.

"Out with it, Colonel."

"As you wish, sir." Freerock took a slow and steady breath as he prepared to speak his mind—something few Lightseers were ever afforded the opportunity to do in the Master General's presence. "From what you've told me, this enemy is a serious threat. Dangerous and akin to our, shall we say, *previous* opponent."

The previous opponent—code for Henry Montgomery, the fallen king of Oakenglen whom only a few among the elite knew was dead.

It still astonished Teagan that any loyalists to Henry remained after all the evil that man had done over the last twelve years, but those bastards had infiltrated nearly every inch of Saldia. Even within his own ranks, he never spoke ill of the king except among the soldiers he completely controlled.

"Of course this enemy is dangerous." Teagan adjusted the long blue cape attached to his polished armor. "Why else would I have ordered this many elite soldiers to war, even when several of them were taking well-deserved leave?"

As the two of them reached the edge of the courtyard, a squire guided a golden vougel along the main road that connected Lunestone's castle to the Starling family's private stables. Gold from head to toe, the winged tiger watched him with milky white eyes as the two spellgust gems in its helm glowed vibrantly green.

Tempest. Teagan's personal favorite. A vougel this strong needed more magic than the others to control, but with the number of times it had saved his life in battle, the beast was well worth the cost.

"Exactly, sir." Colonel Freerock glanced over his shoulder as the squire leading Tempest walked far enough behind them to remain out of earshot. "We're leaving Lunestone with a barebones military presence by taking this many soldiers."

"There are more than enough soldiers remaining behind to secure Lunestone, Colonel, and more on the way in a matter of days."

"It's less than I would like, sir," Freerock confessed. "If you give me even just one more week, I can double our unit and simultaneously ensure a conservative defense force here at home. Two weeks, and I can gather everyone who isn't currently stationed in crucial roles. When we leave today, it means we will be facing a deadly opponent with a fraction of our forces. Shouldn't we hit someone this deadly with everything we have?"

"Don't you think I considered that, Colonel?"

"I'm sure you did, sir."

The unspoken tension remained on the air, and Freerock's scowl didn't fade.

For the sake of security, Teagan rarely shared the nuances of his plans with others. Freerock, however, had deep roots within the lower ranks of the army. In the thick of battle, he always remained calm. He'd begun to build something of a legend for himself as a man without fear, and when the soldiers panicked, he became their courage.

If the man had these doubts, it meant the others did as well. Best to squash the discontent early.

Teagan's father had taught him that, ages ago.

"Tell me, Colonel, how many men it takes to kill one of the Lightseer elite."

"When outnumbered, and given our unrivaled magical ability?"

"Yes, Colonel."

"Anywhere between five and fifteen, sir, depending on whether or not the opposing force has augmentations."

"Precisely." Teagan nodded to a nearby cluster of Lightseer soldiers, each adorned in their elite silver armor with the trademark blue horse insignia on their chests. "I handpicked each of these soldiers. I keep them close to Lunestone because they are superior even to their fellow elite, and I needed an army that could assemble on a moment's notice for situations just like this. That includes you, Colonel. It's one of the reasons I insisted you live in my family's wing of Lunestone."

Teagan cast a sidelong glance at the young man to test the effectiveness of the subtle compliment, one that had always inspired the colonel to go above and beyond in the past. As expected, Freerock's back straightened, and he couldn't hide the prideful smile tugging at the corners of his mouth.

"Deadly strength," Teagan continued. "War-hardened skill. Speed. Those are the factors that will win us this war, Colonel, before it even begins. Every elite soldier here has a vougel they've trained and flown into battle, but the foot soldiers don't. The core army would slow us down. Travel light, use the towns to resupply, and build a supply chain along the southern road for the foot soldiers to follow in the rare chance we fail. I always have a contingency, soldier, and this mission is no different."

A light sparked in Freerock's eye, and he grinned as he finally understood. "The other soldiers will follow, then?"

"If needed, and only once I've given the order. We have other enemies in Saldia, even stronger ones than this opponent, and I cannot risk bringing all of our forces to a fight the elite should be able to win on their own. Lunestone is our haven, and I can never risk it being taken in my absence."

"A wise choice, sir, but shouldn't we bring even a few more units? It would—"

"We've given our opponent enough time to prepare as it is," Teagan interrupted. "With our strength, augmentations, and a few other key resources I'll secure along the way, this man is as good as dead."

Between the merlins and Lord Jasper's hunt for the Wraithblade's weaknesses, the peasant didn't stand a chance.

Freerock raised one curious eyebrow and snuck a sidelong glance at Teagan. "Key resources, sir?"

The Master General simply grinned. "You'll see, Colonel."

"I look forward to learning more." Freerock cleared his throat. "But, uh, if I may offer one more concern?"

"Go on."

"Slaybourne, sir?" A muscle by the colonel's eye twitched. "The Decay has killed more people than any battle ever has."

"You're correct," Teagan conceded. "And I will not let two of my children be added to those numbers."

Freerock swallowed hard, and he focused his attention ahead of them as they reached the edge of the gathering military.

Teagan let out an exaggerated sigh and paused midstride, careful to remain out of earshot of the gathered soldiers that had, one by one, started to look his way. He studied Freerock over the bridge of his nose and lowered his voice to give the impression of a burdened man imparting a great secret.

"Colonel, my son is out there, and so is my youngest daughter. The future of Lunestone and, by extension, the continent is currently shackled to the wall in that madman's dungeons. The two of them would never divulge key secrets willingly, but you know firsthand the extent to which our enemies will go to pry information from those of us who have it."

Freerock stiffened, and his scowl deepened at the mere thought.

"They will not return to us the same as when they left," Teagan continued in a hushed voice, dipping his toes into just the right amount of drama as he wove his lies for the colonel to pass on to the army. "Our new enemy is brutal, and I guarantee you that rotting husk of a man is doing everything in his power to break them both. With all of that in mind, Colonel, do you truly believe we have even one more week to spare?"

"No, sir," Freerock answered.

"Good," Teagan said with a self-satisfied nod. "You understand. That said, your criticisms are fair. I already ordered the captains remaining behind to coordinate the ground troops as they arrive. Reinforcements will be ready to depart along the southern road as soon as I send word for them."

"Will they encounter issues when they pass by Oakenglen, sir?"

Before he could hide it, the edge of Teagan's mouth twitched in irritation. He cleared his throat and tilted his head to hide the break in his mask, and he used the brief moment to recenter himself.

"Oakenglen troops are a concern," he acknowledged. "I ordered any soldiers that join us later to quickly pass the Capital and camp instead in Murkwell. I can't risk an altercation because some loyalist idiot on the wall thinks we've come to attack."

"A wise move, sir."

Of course it was. Teagan still hadn't heard from Celine, which meant she likely intended to become a thorn in his side.

That infuriating woman. He would probably have to kill her, soon, and that unfortunately meant he would also have to kill her father. A regrettable loss, given Charles Jasper's skill, but one Teagan considered worthwhile.

His conflict with Celine, however, would have to wait. Zander and Quinn were more important even than the Oakenglen crown, and he would raze all of Saldia if that was what it took to get them back.

"Listen closely, son," Teagan said quietly, careful to use the term he knew the orphaned young man had always craved.

Freerock leaned in, his eyes focused and his full attention on Teagan as he breathlessly waited for whatever came next.

"This isn't just about my children being tortured," Teagan whispered, grimacing for a bit of added theatre as he spoke of what the two of them must've endured thus far. "Henry attacked us before we even understood the depths to which he had gone to control key cities and supply lines across the empire. This time, it's different. This aspiring warlord is a peasant, for starters, and he doesn't have the resources our last opponent had. We have the advantage this time. We can stop him before he amasses power, but only if we move quickly."

The colonel gave him an eager nod.

"Get to your vougel," Teagan ordered. "Rally the last of the troops and wait for my signal."

Freerock gave him a sharp salute and jogged into the fray as Teagan did his best to keep from smirking in victory.

How he loved to watch them dance.

"Let's ride!" the colonel yelled to the throng of soldiers.

One by one, an ocean of glittering blue and silver armor stretched before Teagan as the army climbed onto their steeds. Other officers echoed Freerock's order, and the command rippled through the gathered army like a shout echoing through a deep cave.

The squire holding Tempest approached Teagan from behind, and the unaugmented boy's feet scraped loudly across the loose rocks in the cobblestone path. With one last sweeping look across the brilliant army gathered before him, Teagan snatched the reins and hoisted himself onto Tempest's back. He set his hand against the vougel's neck, and at his touch, the one-way connection between them opened.

Quinn coddled her pet with charms and enchantments he wouldn't never otherwise allowed if he'd intended to keep her in the army long-term. She had never understood the unflinching obedience required to fly a vougel into war.

His eye twitched again at the thought of his daughter, and his mask came dangerously close to fracturing. He drove his thumb again into his left temple, and the ripple of relief that followed cleared his mind enough to recover the persona his soldiers craved—that of a man capable of unequaled destruction.

Fury simmered within him, blisteringly cold, but he was familiar with this sort of hatred. In his more passionate youth, he had often lost himself to the all-consuming fires of his rage, but time and experience had evolved it into something far more devastating. Cold fury like this sharpened his focus and cleared his mind. With time, Zander would realize how to wield his own anger as his greatest weapon, as had all the Starling masters throughout history.

That and that alone gave him hope that his son would one day be man enough to lead this army.

Decorated in glistening armor every Lightseer dreamt of one day earning for themselves, the gathered warriors prepared to fly. A lull settled across the field. Soldier and civilian alike waited in a breathless hush for him to speak. The elite watched in somber respect for their leader, while the servants stared in stunned silence at the spectacle before them.

"When we are faced with mountains," he shouted across the gathered throng, "what do we do?"

"Flatten them!" the soldiers answered in unison. The voices boomed through the air and overpowered even the lake's waves as they crashed across the rocky shore.

"Impossible odds?" he asked as he continued their ritual wartime chant.

"Overcome!" they answered.

Every soul within earshot now watched the field intently. They gaped out at the army and at him, but he had prepared for this moment. With a flourish, he unsheathed *Sovereign* and held the dazzling Firesword in the air.

"It is the charge of we, the Lightseers, to face the darkness even kings fear!" His voice carried effortlessly across the whisper-silent field. "And, once again, this great land begs for rescue. A tyrant has risen in the south, far deadlier than the foes we have conquered before. He is a peasant, pretending to be king. A commoner who has stolen magic beyond his understanding or control. This novice will set fire to the world in his relentless hunt for *more*—more power, more coin, and more enchantments than any sane man can wield without losing his mind!"

Lies, of course, but the soldiers had no reason to doubt him. When Henry had first risen to power, Teagan had rallied them in much the same way. Pinning unsolved crimes on the enemy always stirred his soldiers' ire, and that cemented their resolve to die if that was what it took to secure victory.

"He calls himself the Shade," Teagan continued. "This outlaw has even conned the simple people of the southern towns into thinking he's some sort of folk hero. On our route to his door, we will warn them all of the truth. You will explain to them the danger in letting him live, and you will ensure he never again has a safe place to hide along the southern road. Remind them that this man has robbed every potion shop from Oakenglen to Lindow. Explain to these poor people that this man has kidnapped daughters and wives alike, all for his private use!" Teagan paused, and in the lull that followed, he let the soldiers' imaginations fill in the gaps between his lies. "Remind them that this man has already killed one of our own Lightseer Regents in his desperate bid for more power!"

He spoke, of course, of Richard Beaumont.

Back when Teagan had learned what had become of Richard, he had, in fact, applauded the mysterious killer. Teagan's assassins had been trailing the crime lord's nephew and were beginning to discover clues to a more nefarious past than any had suspected. The murderer had simply beaten Teagan to the punch and saved him the trouble of cleaning up afterward.

It didn't matter who had truly used that Duvolia potion to freeze Richard Beaumont solid. The truth would die with the peasant Teagan had framed for Richard's murder, and he would finally be able to put this mess behind him.

With his Firesword, Teagan pointed toward Oakenglen on the horizon. "Our enemy hides beyond the southern forest, in the cursed lands even the Fates abandoned eons ago, because he thinks that will shield him from justice. He thinks we fear the midnight beasts of the Ancient Woods. He thinks we will never find him, deep in that cracked hellscape of the Decay. He thinks we're cowards."

A ripple of laughter swelled through the gathered soldiers, and Teagan grinned along with them.

"He is wrong," the Master General continued. "For we are the champions of light in a dark and unjust world. He knows the threat we pose to him, and as such, he has captured two of our own in an attempt to force us to surrender. He has taken my daughter and, yes, even my son."

A murmur snaked through the soldiers, and Teagan allowed it. He wanted them to understand their opponent's power. If he could capture Zander, he had true ability, and only a fool would underestimate him.

In the coming battle, these soldiers needed to bring their best.

"But a Lightseer is hard to kill." As soon as Teagan spoke, the hum of conversation instantly faded. "We fight for our own, and we will not leave the Decay without them. The fool has underestimated the single greatest military on this continent, and he won't realize the extent of his error until we slice off his head!"

The soldiers cheered.

"Duty before all else!" With a twist of Teagan's hand, an inferno erupted over *Sovereign's* blade. "It is our duty, then, to fight for the future! For a land free of tyranny! Throughout the ages and through every passing dynasty, Lightseers will stand on the battlefront until the last of the monsters are slain!"

The warriors' cheers grew to a deafening pitch, until it drowned out even the crackle of flame on Teagan's sword. The deep, thundering vibrations of their voices shook the very ground.

He frowned, careful to appear focused and furious, even though he wanted nothing more than to beam with pride at the raw display of power.

It was time.

With a sharp kick, his vougel launched into the sky. Tempest's wings snapped against the air as the other Lightseers followed in a brilliant display of shimmering armor and feathered wings.

By now, the Wraithblade must've known he was coming, but that peasant had never faced an opponent like Teagan. When he finally kicked down Death's Door and took his first steps into Slaybourne, he would come with all the power of Hell behind him.

CHAPTER TWENTY-SIX
NYX

As the midnight hour dragged on, Nyx Osana pressed her back against a cold stone wall in the eastern wing of Lunestone. A chill seeped through her shirt as the roughly hewn blocks of Teagan's castle pressed into her spine, but she held her position. After what she had endured to make it this far, failure wasn't an option.

This wing served as the living quarters for some of the Lightseer officers, and as such, she had to expect company at any moment. Carefully and with painful precision, she shut the heavy wooden door to one of the officers' suites behind her. The thin line of light from the hallway slowly faded as the bolt latched without even a click to announce her presence, thanks to the custom Prowlport potion she had used to silence her entry.

These fools didn't stand a chance against *her*.

She stood in a narrow foyer with rich silver tapestries hanging from the walls on either side of her. Ahead, a simple stone archway led to a sitting room with a marble hearth. Fire fizzed and popped in the fireplace, and opulent blue sofas with white filigree covered most of the azure rug beneath them. On the wall to her right, a massive mirror with a black frame reflected the hallways beyond the den, and though much of its surface had fogged with age and neglect, nothing moved in the blurred shadows of what lay in wait around the bend.

She craned her ear and closed her eyes as she leaned into her enhanced senses and felt for threats in the cluster of rooms beyond the entry. Her ears twitched as, somewhere in the walls, a mouse scurried across a beam. A muffled conversation leaked under a nearby door, the muted voices almost impossible to discern from each other.

Somewhere close by, sheets rustled across skin, and a woman let out an airy little sigh. The clink of glasses interrupted the lingering sound, and the soft rumble of men talking followed shortly after.

Nyx frowned. Her mark apparently had company tonight.

Out of habit, she patted the bag of potions and daggers on her shoulder, and the muscles in her back tensed with anticipation as she slipped through the shadows by the main door. As much as she wanted to burn her enemy's home to the ground, she had come here with a singular purpose, and no one could know she had been here until she was already long gone.

Ordinarily, Nyx would have never dared infiltrate this fortress at all, much less an officer's wing, but her spies around the island fortress had given her the sort of news she couldn't ignore.

Teagan Starling had left yesterday with every available elite soldier, and it would take several days for reinforcements to arrive. That left a narrow window of opportunity for her to break into the most secure fortress on the continent, and she had to use her time wisely.

Lunestone held so many secrets, and she wanted to get her hands on all of them. With such a narrow window, however, she had to prioritize, and there was one treasure she wanted above all others: the forged evidence Otmund was using to blackmail her into obedience.

It had taken a dozen slit throats to finally uncover that the letters were, in fact, real. To discover that Otmund had actually spent the time and coin to create such elaborate forgeries infuriated her more than if he had been lying to her face. The efforts he had gone to, all to bend her to his will, pushed the boundaries of anything she thought he was capable of.

When this was over, she would savor every second she spent torturing him for what he had done.

She let herself daydream for a moment as she tried to choose which agony he would endure first: a few of his body parts skinned while she held a mirror so he could watch, or perhaps a few dips into her boiling spring, just to see which of his parts fell off first.

So many choices.

Nyx paused at the interior archway, her heightened senses alert for any signs that someone had discovered her. No footsteps came down the hall, and though she ached to dart into the corridor, she forced herself to listen and wait a little longer, just to be sure.

Around her neck, a ring of spellgust threaded on a leather chain shifted beneath her shirt. She frowned, unused to wearing jewelry. As it nestled against her bare skin, the enchantments on its glowing emerald surface sent a single pulse of energy through her breasts. If someone killed Otmund before she got the chance, this little trinket would break, all thanks to some of the blood she had stolen from him while he was sleeping.

The fool should never have let her into his home, no matter how much he thought he controlled her. He had overestimated how much power he truly had over Nethervale. Given his preoccupation with the Soulsprite and Freymoor, he hadn't noticed her slip away on her own little errand, and that was his greatest mistake.

Somewhere within the suite, men laughed, and Nyx took a cautious step backward into the foyer's shadow. She wrapped one hand around the hilt of a dagger strapped to her thigh and tugged ever so slightly—just enough to hear the soft rustle of steel over leather as she prepared to throw it.

Never one to take a risk, she curled her other hand into a fist and tapped into the icy magic of her Crackmane augmentation, lest she need it.

A latch clicked somewhere deep within the labyrinth of rooms inside, and the muffled laughter faded. No footsteps thudded through the suite. The quiet night stretched on, and as far as she could tell, her mark remained blissfully unaware of her.

She took that as her cue.

Thanks to her custom-crafted Prowlport augmentation, her boots slipped over the carpet without a sound. Not a shuffle. Not a breath. This was how she preferred to operate: overlooked and unnoticed. She enjoyed it when people forgot she existed, as it made her work easier.

With whisper-silent steps, she stole across the living room and into the dark corridor that connected the entryway to the rest of the suite's many rooms. A lone sconce at the far end of the hallway fought against the shadows, and in the darkness, she finally relaxed. Her breath came easier, and the many augmentations pulsing through her veins pressed against her palms, each aching to be freed.

Aside from the flickering sconce, the only other light came from under one of the seven doors in a narrow stone hallway lined with portraits. A shadow crossed through the thin beam, and she instinctively paused until it passed.

As a Lightseer officer, her mark—and his guests—likely had Hearhaven augmentations. Even after a few drinks, their enhanced hearing would detect the slightest creak of a floorboard, so she took extra care to test each step with a practiced tap of her boot.

When she neared the door, glasses clinked again. The glug of liquid pouring from a bottle blended with the low-level chatter of three—no, four distinct voices.

In any duel, she always did her best to retain the element of surprise. Even one second's warning could mean the difference between life and death.

The crackle of fire in the sconce a few yards off filled the silence as she reached into the pack on her shoulder and fished out one of the vials from its depths. The rich blue potion of a carefully crafted Prowlport recipe sloshed against the glass as she tugged off the seal, and its cork left with a soft pop. She set her thumb over the opening and splashed the potion against the knob and hinges, careful all the while to keep her attention on the muffled conversation within, lest they suddenly decide to join her in the hall.

As the royal blue potion dripped off the hinges, she stowed her vial in her bag with precise movements. Every second mattered. Where most necromancers hurried, she relished the art of it all.

The nuance.

The skill it took to infiltrate Teagan's domain.

Nyx raised her hands and pivoted both palms toward the ceiling. At the silent command, her two enchanted blades slipped from the small sheaths strapped to her wrists and hovered, ever so slightly, above the heel of her palm. The daggers resembled the tiniest spearheads, but their appearance belied their devastating power. Laced with a quick-acting poison, anyone they cut wouldn't survive long enough to bleed out. An unearned kindness, perhaps, but she couldn't risk her victims firing any spells at her while she killed their friends.

Two blades. Three targets. One mark to keep alive for questioning.

Easy.

With a well-practiced kick against the drenched knob, she broke open the door. Only the thud of her boot on the entrance announced her as the latch broke under the enhanced strength of her Strongman augmentation. The entry flew open, and before it could even slam against the wall, she scanned her opponents to decide how she would kill them.

Two men with gray beards sat in the leather seats closest to the door, their black suits already wrinkled from how long they had been sitting. They craned their necks to look at her, their bushy eyebrows raised in surprise even as their bloodshot gazes lagged behind their movements.

Drunk. Old. Probably retired. Low risk threats. Easily neutralized.

Another man sat on the wooden desk by the far window, holding a glass as he intently watched the whiskey pouring into it. His clean-cut suit had thin creases along the pantlegs from its perfectly pressed and steamed treatment, and the stubble along his strong jaw would've charmed many a woman out of her dress. His biceps tested the fabric restraining them, and the top button of his shirt sat open as he eyed the whiskey with a relaxed smile.

Young, mid-twenties. Fighter's build. Likely an idealistic young officer who would die defending the others. Primary threat.

The fourth man—her mark—poured a heady bourbon from a frosted crystal bottle. The aroma wafted through the air, tempting even to her, and she figured she would have to take a souvenir with her when she left. She recognized this man from the description her spy had given, right down to the twisted bend in his nose from an apparent childhood injury. A red ribbon at the base of his neck held back his long brown hair, and flecks of dandruff peppered the clean part down the middle of his scalp.

No visible augmentations, but she would attack him last regardless. She needed that one alive.

All four men looked up as she entered, their eyes wide with surprise in the half-second she took to survey them. In their shock, they didn't even move.

The door finally slammed against the wall. The muffled thud—or maybe the glint of her blades in the firelight—broke her temporary spell over them.

It didn't matter. They hadn't moved fast enough.

With a wicked grin, she spread her fingers wide to give the floating daggers enough room to fly. Nyx hurled the blades hovering in her palm, one by one, at the two men by the door. The metal darts shot deep in their throats. They gagged and reached for their necks, but they had barely a second left before the Arcenium poison kicked in. Their drinks clattered onto the rug, spilling whiskey across the crimson wool. Red rivers cascaded through their fingers while they gasped uselessly, staring at each other as they choked to death on their own blood.

The man sitting on the desk stood and threw his drink at her, most likely as a distraction while he summoned an augmentation into his palms. With a bored tilt of her head, she ducked the glass and tugged on the invisible tether connecting her to the two Nethervale Daggers lodged in the older men at her feet. The glass shattered against the wall, spraying her with whiskey as this third soldier summoned fire into his palm.

Fire. She almost laughed in his face. No one wielded the Burnbane augmentation better than the Starlings, and she had studied the best methods to combat their flames in her decades at Nethervale. Ordinarily, she might have indulged him in a little hand-to-hand combat, but she was on a tight schedule tonight.

He threw a fireball at her head, and she spun in a graceful twirl to avoid it. With the movement, she summoned her enchanted blades to her. They spun around her head in a dazzling twirl that matched her own movement, splattering blood across the wall in elegant spray of deadly beauty. The motion picked up all the momentum she needed, and as she aimed for his chest, the blades flew at him with nothing more than a delicate flick of her wrist.

The daggers burrowed deep into his chest, and she stalked toward him just as the fire in his palm fizzled out. He staggered backward and tripped over the desk, landing hard on the ground as he scratched at the two blood-stained holes in his shirt. He gaped up at her, eyes wide with disbelief even as he slowly started to relax. His head leaned backward, and his gaze shifted to the ceiling as the poison in her blades finished her job for her.

Instead of summoning a spell of his own, the fourth man dropped the crystal bottle and raised his hands in surrender. The bottle thudded on the rug, and a single crack splintered across its side as whiskey poured onto the floor from its uncorked opening. Eyes wide, her mark trembled under her glare, and now she understood what he and Otmund saw in each other: an unwavering sense of self-preservation.

She restrained the impulse to roll her eyes. Cowards.

It made sense, of course. To protect his forged blackmail, Otmund had chosen a guardian who would never leave Lunestone—just as he had relied too heavily on the assumption that she would never dare infiltrate this place.

Nyx never took her eyes off her mark as she pressed her palms flat, calling her daggers back to her without a word. In her periphery, the blades darted out of the third soldier's chest on their way back to her. The silver blurs flew through the air and only slowed when they reached her open palms, where they hovered. Crimson splatters dripped onto her skin, warm and wet, and she let herself enjoy the sensation.

"P-please don't kill m-me," the lone survivor stuttered.

"Do you know who I am?" She dropped her voice an octave for nothing more than the thrill of intimidating a coward.

He nodded, slowly at first, but faster the longer she stared at him.

She narrowed her piercing green eyes. "Then you know why I'm here."

Her mark nodded again and, this time, pointed to the top drawer in his desk. He smacked his lips and tried to speak, but he mouthed wordlessly instead.

Fine. She would do it herself.

Nyx stepped over the corpse of the younger man who never got to enjoy his drink and opened the drawer to find a sealed envelope lying on top of a pile of papers. With a practiced tilt of her hand, she dismissed her blades, and they slid back into their sheaths on her wrists. With a brief glance at her trembling mark, she pulled out the letter and popped its seal. Her ears twitched as she listened for any changes in his shuddering breaths, and she gave herself a few seconds to scan the pages neatly tucked inside.

But with each word she read, her rage burned hotter.

She stiffened as she scanned the forged letters detailing her budding alliance with the Wraithblade. Their plans of attack. The routes they had taken. The negotiations. Detailed maps even outlined various potential routes on the warpath they would one day take to recapture Saldia from the Lightseers. Had Teagan received this, it truly would have been her undoing.

She glared at her mark. "Where are the other copies?"

He shuddered, and the last bit of color drained from his face. "There are no other copies, I swear to you. I made those myself, but please don't kill me. Otmund forced me to do it. I harbor no ill will toward you, Lady Osana."

She chuckled, and for a moment, she considered letting him live just for that little act of respect. No one had called her a lady in many, many years.

"Please," he whispered. "Please, I don't want to die. I won't say anything." He whimpered and pressed his palms together in a sniveling prayer.

Of course he wouldn't. Dead men couldn't bear witness to the horrors she left in her wake.

With a twist of her hand, she launched her right dagger at his face. It sailed out of its sheath without warning, nothing more than a silver blur. It carved through his forehead and shot out the other side as his eyes widened with shock. His mouth fell open, and he slowly tilted backward. A narrow river of blood streamed down his broken nose from the fresh hole in his head, and his lifeless body slumped onto the floor alongside the fallen soldiers he had so quickly betrayed.

Nyx tugged on the invisible tether to her blade, and it circled back to her as she flattened her palm and allowed it to return to its sheath. The blade nestled into its leather holster, snug and safe, as she eyed the aftermath. The two older men lay slumped over their armchairs, their heads craned back as blood dripped from their lifeless fingers onto the rug. The younger soldier lay sprawled across the floor behind her, and the papers she had come here to recover were strewn across the desk.

How fun. She stretched her arms toward the ceiling, and something popped in her lower back. A rush of relief snaked up her spine from whatever she had just released, and a contented grin spread across her face as she set her hands on her hips.

It felt nice to be back in her element.

Now, to get rid of the evidence. With no time to spare for sentimental drivel, she collected the packet of forgeries. The letters weighed in her hands, at least three dozen pages of evidence that must've taken ages to complete. She effortlessly sidestepped the corpses and shut the shattered office door behind her. In one of the dark rooms along the suite's interior hallway, the rustle of skin across sheets came again as the woman of the house tossed in her sleep.

Nyx frowned, wondering how much the woman knew, and figured it would be best to play it safe. On her way out, she would slit the woman's throat, too.

More important, however, were these forgeries. She crossed to the fireplace in the main sitting room and threw the papers onto the crackling logs. The edges curled and browned as the only contingency Otmund had left burned to ash. Nyx set her forearm on the mantle and leaned against the hearth as she stared into the fire and watched his hard work burn.

She wouldn't leave until every last bit of ink had been scorched to ash. Not even a scrap of the parchment would remain, and it would be like this had never existed in the first place.

Her eyes glossed over, and the flame burned white imprints into her vision as she considered what to do next. As much as she wanted to ransack this fortress and steal whatever she could find, it still had guards, and she couldn't risk getting caught in any of its traps. Unlike Otmund, greed wouldn't be her undoing. She had to get out of here before sunrise, and she had precious few hours left to do it.

For now, she would keep playing Otmund's little game. She and her elite soldiers would obey his whims and wishes until the perfect moment presented itself. Then, and only then, would Otmund realize he didn't have a single ally left in this world to protect him.

Finally, at long last, she would make *him* dance for *her*. Locked away in the depths of Nethervale, he would scream until she grew bored of his voice.

CHAPTER TWENTY-SEVEN
CONNOR

After two days spent preparing for their journey and three full days on Nocturne's back, Connor finally stood in the Ancient Woods not far from the Finns' treehouse. They had seen the distant rooftops of Bradford on the horizon, and he'd even caught sight of the cathedral ruins in the moonlit ocean of leaves.

How strange, to be back here. The eight years he had spent surviving in these woods, looking for odd jobs and tracking deer through the underbrush, already felt like another life.

Ever aware of how much time they had left, the countdown to Teagan's earliest arrival date ticked steadily in the back of his mind.

Fifteen days remaining, worst case.

His boots flattened the patchy grass underfoot as he studied the forest. Tension still pulled on his shoulders from their nonstop flight through the darkness. He stretched his arms above his head, and his joints popped while he stretched out his back.

Nocturne was faster than heading out here on foot, thank the Fates, but a full night of flying left him more sore than a day's walk. At least he'd gotten the long overdue rest after his ordeal in Slaybourne's catacombs.

As the dragon towered over the forest floor, his horns caught on the branches. They stirred the canopy with each subtle movement of his head. The prince huffed in irritation and slouched his long neck until his body cleared the leaves, but it didn't do much good.

A dragon that big couldn't hide very well in a forest, apparently. Connor made a mental note, but he didn't have many options when it came to hiding a creature this large along their route.

Dawn filtered through gaps in the leaves overhead. Soft yellow sunbeams pierced the canopy, casting dappled shadows across the patchy grass, and the familiar buzz of spring insects hummed through the air. The croak of a lone frog pierced the serene woodland, followed by the distant trickle of the stream that flowed from the Finns' waterfall.

The distant scent of smoke wafted by, charred and distant. A campfire, perhaps, or the Finns starting breakfast.

Connor set one hand on the back of his head and stretched out his neck, wondering all the while how in the Fates' name he could possibly explain his dragon to them. If they came with him to Slaybourne, he would eventually have to tell them the truth of what he had become that night by the cathedral.

His throat tightened at the thought.

"Curse the Fates." Murdoc slid off Nocturne's back and stumbled as his legs turned to pudding. His knees shook from their long ride, and he lost his balance. The former Blackguard shuffled sideways and slammed into a tree.

Connor chuckled. "Don't you think you're milking it a bit?"

"Back in a bit, Captain." Murdoc jogged off toward a cluster of trees. "I've got to take a royal piss. Might be a few days."

"We don't need updates."

"Can't hear you!" the man shouted over his shoulder. "I'm taking a piss!"

With a shake of his head, Connor just laughed.

Idiot.

Quinn slid off next, and her boots hit the ground without a sound. Instantly balanced and apparently unaffected by the long flight, she studied the surrounding forest and stretched her arms over her head. Her joints popped as she leaned into the stretch, and she took in her surroundings without so much as a glance toward Connor.

His smile fell as he again debated blindfolding her to keep the Finns' location a secret, but guiding a blindfolded Lightseer through an underbrush riddled with roots and ditches would only slow them down. Besides, even if they said no, he would insist they find a new place immediately and never tell anyone where they went.

Even with a dragon, this plan of his seemed impossible. He kept looking for something he could cut to save time, but he couldn't compromise on a single thing.

Get the Finns to safety.

Save Sophia.

Retrieve the Soulsprite, and then fly like hell back to Slaybourne.

Easy.

Connor sighed as the weight of everything he had to do settled between his shoulder blades.

Nocturne's majestic head pivoted as he looked back at the lone passenger who hadn't yet dismounted. At the base of his long neck, where his body blocked the worst of the wind, Sophia fussed with the rope that had secured her to one of the dragon's protruding spines. Connor crossed his arms as he watched the spectacle, and she cursed under her breath as a knot formed in the wild tangle of rope around her waist.

Quinn smirked and leaned against a tree to enjoy the show.

With an irritated groan, Connor gestured up to the necromancer. "Quinn, you could've helped her before you dismounted."

The Starling warrior's grin only widened. "I made a bargain with you, not her."

Fair point.

Nocturne's head tilted in curiosity as he studied the necromancer on his back. "Do you require assistance?"

"Oh to *hell* with this!" Sophia summoned ice into her palms and grabbed the rope's worst tangle. The fibers froze solid at her touch, and when she squeezed her hands, the rope splintered into a thousand pieces. She hurled the remnants into a nearby tree and slid down the dragon's back with a furious huff.

When her boots landed on the uneven ground, she stumbled. Connor caught her shoulders to help her get her balance, but she brushed his hand away.

"I'm fine," she snapped.

"You're not," he said quietly.

In his periphery, Quinn watched them, as cool and collected as ever. Her expression didn't change, and her smooth features didn't give any indication of whatever was going through her head.

That was her goal, he figured. Always watching. Always observing. Always seeing far too much.

There's really no time for this nonsense. Black smoke rolled across the dirt as the wraith emerged from wherever he went when he wished to go unseen. *We should be at the augmentor's by now, not wandering through the forest.*

"We're not wandering. I know exactly where I'm going."

You know what I meant, Magnuson.

Footsteps crunched along the grass nearby, and Connor instantly recognized the long, steady strides of Murdoc's gait. The former Blackguard sighed happily and clapped his hands together as he joined them in the small clearing. "Much better."

"Time to move out, then. You." Connor pointed at Quinn. "Up front where I can see you."

She let out an irritated sigh, but complied.

With his prisoner ahead of him, he cracked his knuckles and grabbed her shoulder to steer her through the forest toward the Finns. Though he scanned the woods out of habit, his gaze always returned to the back of her neck. His magic simmered beneath his skin, ready to attack the second she did something stupid.

If she so much as reached for a dagger or spread her fingers to summon fire, he would be ready, and she would die.

Nocturne followed, and the dragon's feet sent a tremor through the ground with each hulking step. Even with his long strides, he trailed behind them as he ducked around the giant oaks and fought to find gaps between the trees. Branches snapped with every twist of the prince's head, and Connor raised one eyebrow in annoyance as he looked at the dragon over one shoulder.

"As if you would move more quietly, in my position." Nocturne snorted with irritation, and a stream of black smoke shot from his nose.

The smoke joined with a lingering cloud of gray haze that hung in the canopy, thick and heavy, and Connor frowned with concern as he followed the trail. It wove through the trees, leading the way toward the Finns' treehouse.

With every step, the ashy char of burning wood worsened. Sophia coughed and waved her hand in front of her face to clear away the haze. The wind kicked up, carrying new scents through the forest.

Rotting wood. Burnt meat. The rusty tang of blood.

A jolt of dread shot clear down Connor's spine.

Fates be damned. They were too late.

He tried to tell himself it was just the stove, that Kiera had tried a new recipe or maybe started teaching one of the children to cook, with disastrous consequences, but everything in him warned against believing in a fantasy.

The dark haze thickened, blocking out whole sections of the canopy as they walked. Murdoc grabbed the hilt of his sword, and his shoulders tensed for a fight. "That's a lot of smoke, Captain."

"Find out what's going on," Connor ordered. "The house is dead ahead. Go around to the north before circling back, and keep to the outskirts. See what you can find."

Murdoc darted off into the forest without a word, and the fading rustle of someone passing through bushes filled the silence.

Without a word, Connor looked at the wraith through the corner of his eye in a silent command to join Murdoc's scouting party. The ghoul nodded, apparently understanding the gravity of the situation even though he despised mortals, and the specter disappeared into a cloud of black fog.

Connor pushed against Quinn's shoulder, and thankfully, she didn't resist his hurried pace. The distant crash of a waterfall mingled with the clatter of leaves rustling in the wind. Both Nocturne and Sophia trailed behind them as the silence stretched on.

He couldn't speak. He could barely think. He could only focus on the treehouse and hope that his gut instinct was wrong. That the Finns were fine, and he would laugh with relief in just a few minutes.

By the time they finally stepped into the clearing by the waterfall, he had lost track of Sophia. A humid mist rolled off the falls and coiled through the air, carrying with it the metallic stench of blood, so thick it nearly choked him.

An aftermath awaited them.

In the rippling surface of the small lake at the base of the falls, a severed hand bobbed in the water. Blue splotches dotted the palm, and its fingers curled as though it still held a sword. Dozens of footprints littered the muddy bank by the waterfall, and a red puddle under the treehouse rippled with each of Nocturne's thudding footsteps.

Thick spirals of dark smoke trailed from decimated piles of wood along the ground. A chair leg poked from one of the fires, and a half-singed doll lay in another. Nearby, deep cuts in several oaks along the tree line exposed the pale flesh underneath the bark. Though he still kept a firm grip on Quinn's shoulder to root her in place, he ran his free hand across one of the cuts, trying to place what had made it.

An axe, judging by the length and depth. In fact, the mark reminded him of all the times he'd used Ethan's axe to chop firewood.

Red stains coated several of the other trees, and clumps of dried slobber stuck to the nearby bark.

Those damned blightwolves had already licked this place clean.

A wooden handle stuck from a nearby bush, and Connor yanked it free of the brambles. Ethan's axe weighed in his palm, and he scoured the rest of the field for more clues. He found four additional swords scattered through the rubble, all of them as clean as the day they were made and coated in a thick layer of blightwolf drool.

Connor's blood ran cold. His grip on Quinn's shoulder tightened, but he barely noticed until she sucked in a sharp breath through her teeth.

"Stay on the bank." Dark and deep, his voice reminded him of a growl more than words. He released her, primarily because she knew the consequences of using this moment against him.

Dark shadows rolled over his forearms as he stepped into the center of the clearing and summoned his dual blades. In his bones, his magic thrummed, ready for a fight. He tightened his grip on the hilts, and his knuckles cracked from the tension in his arms. His body hummed with energy, desperate for something to kill so that he could vent this brewing dread, but nothing in the forest moved.

If Teagan had done anything to the Finns, there wouldn't be a negotiation. There wouldn't be a chance for redemption, and not even his bargain with Quinn could save the man's life.

There would only be *blood*.

The wind kicked through the dead-silent canopy, and overhead, the treehouse swayed. Crimson droplets trickled into the large puddle beneath it. He examined the underside of the house as another drop of blood seeped between the floorboards and fell to the ground.

He shot one look over his shoulder at Quinn. To his surprise, she no longer watched him with cold indifference, but rather with a thinly veiled look of horror. Her lips parted in shock, and her body stiffened as she took in the scene.

"Go." Her eyes darted toward him, and she nodded toward the treehouse. "I won't move."

She had better not.

Nocturne's head emerged from the canopy as his rumbling footsteps slowed. He wordlessly scanned the aftermath, and a low growl rumbled in his chest.

"Watch her," Connor ordered.

The dragon nodded.

Muscles tense and barely able to restrain his fury, Connor dismissed his blades in a rush of dark smoke. He climbed the ladder at the base of the treehouse, taking two rungs at a time and barely caring whether they were rotted or safe. Any time one of the rungs broke, his fingers dug into the tree instead, carving a handhold out of sheer will and stubborn grit. He barely felt it.

The stench of rotting meat rolled off the treehouse like a macabre fog, and he hauled himself onto the porch even as bits of the last rotten rung crumbled in his hands.

Across the curling floorboards, the front door stood open. The table had been smashed in half and thrown against the wall. One of the chairs lay in the corner by the exit, the lone piece of furniture to survive whatever had happened here.

In the kitchen's shadows, two figures lay on the floor.

Connor didn't pause. He raced toward them, and the stench of rotting meat worsened the second he crossed the threshold. His eyes watered from the overwhelming stench. Flies buzzed through the air in dizzying arcs, the hum of their wings louder than the wind in the canopy outside. Blood covered everything—the walls, the floor, the bodies.

He knelt beside the familiar figures, still unable to believe this was happening, and he gently rolled each of them onto their backs.

Ethan and Wesley.

Both men rolled limply as he adjusted them. Their eyes were closed. Their cold skin sent a numb chill up his arm from the mere touch, and to his utter horror, Ethan's left leg had been chopped off at the knee. White puss oozed from the poorly cauterized wound and pooled on the floorboard.

This couldn't be happening.

This couldn't be real.

The muscles in Connor's neck tightened as he stared down at them in shock, unable to process any of it. Refusing to believe what was right before his eyes. Unable to believe they could be dead.

Though Wesley's face had a faintly blue tint, the boy took a shallow breath. It was sparse, almost undetectable, and for a second Connor doubted what he'd seen. His heart panged with hope anyway, and he set his fingers against the boy's neck in search of a pulse.

It beat, slow but strong.

Thank the Fates.

Next, he checked Ethan. The man's heart also beat, though the pulse thumped so softly it barely registered at all.

These two were running out of time, and to save them, he needed one *hell* of a miracle.

CHAPTER TWENTY-EIGHT
CONNOR

The Finns were dying.

As Ethan and Wesley lay on the debris-littered floor of their decimated kitchen, Connor had no idea how to save them.

"SOPHIA!" he shouted, louder than he had ever spoken in his life. "Get up here *now*!"

Without waiting for her to arrive, Connor lifted Ethan in his arms. His biceps bulged as he carried the massive man, but due to his enhanced strength, he barely noticed Ethan's weight. He kicked open the door to the first room—his room, the one the Finns had promised would always be available should he want it—and set Ethan on the mattress. Bits of yellow straw poked through the lumpy sheets, and the man's bloody wound stained the white fabric with crimson splotches that seeped along the threads.

Someone else's footsteps thudded against the porch boards as Connor returned for Wesley. Wide eyed and bewildered, Sophia charged into the room just as he lifted the boy into his arms.

She scrunched her nose in confusion. "What are you doing?"

"Heal them," he ordered, ignoring her question. "Start with Ethan."

"Who's Ethan?"

"In there." With his hands full, Connor nodded toward the first room's open door and the eerily still man lying on the mattress.

"Heal *that*? Connor, he looks dead already, and even magic can't grow back a leg."

"I don't care!" he roared as he carried Wesley down the hallway. "Do it!"

He slammed his shoulder into the nearest door, but it wouldn't open. In his arms, Wesley grimaced in his sleep as the force shook him. Connor tried again, and on the other side, something heavy shifted. The door gave way, and piles of broken furniture slid across the ground. Nothing remained but splintery wood and torn fabric.

Mumbling obscenities under his breath, Connor tried the next door, only to find the room in almost identical chaos. His muttered vulgarities grew louder as he stalked toward the last door in the hall, and he eyed the ladder mounted to the wall at the far end of the corridor. It led to Fiona's room in the attic, and though he didn't want to try climbing a ladder with Wesley in his arms, he would do it if he had to.

As he kicked open the final door, he thankfully found a room relatively untouched by the destruction. An overturned chair lay in the center of the room beside a pile of blankets, but the straw mattress still had its sheets, and a book still lay on the lone nightstand beside the bed.

He set Wesley on the mattress. When the boy's head hit the pillow, he coughed, and blood splattered into the air.

There is little to go on. The Wraith King's voice pierced Connor's mind like an arrow, and he flinched in surprise as the ghoul joined him. Black smoke rolled across Wesley's legs as the ghoul emerged from the churning darkness. *The only trail was mostly destroyed by the blightwolves. Nothing else remains nearby. Nothing alive, anyway.*

"Check the attic." Connor snatched a blanket off the ground and threw it over the boy in an attempt to do something useful. "Check every nook and cranny in this house. If the girls are here, we need to find them. They might not realize it's us."

The wraith groaned in irritation but disappeared into the black smoke he had brought with him.

"Connor!" Sophia shouted, panicked urgency in her tone.

He barreled down the hallway toward her, wondering what fresh hell had hit them now.

She sat at Ethan's beside, her pack already emptied across the floor.

Connor set his hands on either side of the doorframe as he scanned the mess. "What is it?"

"It's going to take everything I have just to heal him." Sophia lifted a bottle filled with sprigs of white yarrow. Though her eyes remained on the reagent, she absently nodded toward Ethan as she spoke. "I can't do anything to help the boy, so you'll have to get that Starling woman to help him."

He gritted his teeth, hating to rely on the enemy.

"No choice." Sophia set the bottle aside and grabbed a glowing jar of spellgust. "They don't even have a proper cauldron. I'm doing my best. Tell that Lightseer not to touch the fire in the stove. That's mine."

Connor didn't waste time replying. His footsteps thundered over the floorboards as he charged to the porch and leaned over the railing. Quinn paced along the waterfront, her arms crossed and one finger tapping against her lips as she mumbled quietly to herself.

Her head snapped up toward him as he emerged from the house, and he gestured for her to join him.

She jogged toward the ladder and climbed it as quickly as he had. Seconds later, she hauled herself onto the porch. "What's the issue?"

Too furious to speak, he gestured for her to follow and led her into the house.

He couldn't believe they had reached this crossroads. To ask the woman he had run through with a sword to heal someone close to him—everything in him screamed that this was foolish.

And yet, he had no alternative.

He led his prisoner to the room in the back and stepped aside as she entered. Without a moment's pause, she leaned over Wesley and set her hands on either side of his head. Her eyes closed, and for a moment, she sat there in silence.

"Heal him," Connor ordered.

She shot him an annoyed glare over her shoulder, but nodded. "Give me my bag. This will take time."

He expected her to stretch out her hand and dare him to call her bluff. He expected her to use the moment against him. To negotiate more, maybe, or use the urgency to her benefit. Anyone he had ever met along the southern road would've stood there, milking him for everything he was worth, but she turned her back to him and shoved the nightstand out of her way. It clattered onto the floor as she made space around Wesley's bedside and dragged the chair to his side instead.

With an irritated sigh of defeat, he slung the pack off his shoulder and offered it to her. Not even looking his way and still focused on Wesley's face, she grabbed it.

He didn't let go.

With everything at stake, he wanted her to look him in the eye before he left her unsupervised with a pack filled with powerful Starling potions. He needed to know what she was really feeling right now, and what her intentions could possibly be.

Quinn tugged on it again, and when it didn't budge, she finally met his glare with one of her own. Her brows pinched with confusion, and she huffed with impatience.

Most of all, however, her eyes shook with concern—and with fear.

"Connor, we don't have time for this," she said quietly. "He's dying."

For whatever reason, she cared about Wesley's life. It didn't seem entirely possible, but maybe there were a few decent Lightseers in the world, after all.

As he held her eye, his earlier promise lingered, unspoken, between them. He didn't have to say a damn thing for her to know exactly what would happen to her if any harm came to the Finns or to Connor's team during this escapade.

Satisfied, he released his hold on the bag, and she threw it on the bed. The flap fell open, and the bottles inside clinked together as she turned her back to him and got to work.

The merciful choice is death, is it not? Dark smoke rolled across the floor as the Wraith King appeared once again at Connor's side.

As Quinn reached into her bag, she recoiled in surprise at the specter's sudden appearance. Though her nose wrinkled in disdain as the ghoul crossed his bony arms over his hollow chest, she returned to her pack and tugged out one of the glowing green potions.

Still too furious to speak, Connor simply ignored the undead specter.

This one and the father are hurting. The wraith gestured to Wesley with his bony finger. *Isn't it kindness to simply end their suffering? That's what you noble fools do, isn't it? Show mercy?*

Connor closed his eyes to keep from shouting at the ghoul and forced himself to simply shake his head in barely restrained anger. "You've come along way, but you've got a long ways still to go."

As Quinn ignored them both, the ghoul simply shrugged.

"Did you find anything?" he asked.

No. These are the only survivors in the house. There's no other bodies and no one hiding, though the blightwolves may have scavenged the others.

The treehouse creaked, shifting as someone climbed the ladder. That had to be Murdoc, then, and he could only hope the man had found something the wraith had missed.

With a final glance at Wesley, Connor stepped out into the hall. Murdoc's boots thudded over the threshold, and the two of them met in the kitchen as the wraith floated down the hallway at his own pace.

Murdoc gaped at the splintered and bloodstained remains of what had once been the Finns' table. The former Blackguard rubbed the back of his head, lost in thought and his face pale.

"Three are missing," Connor said. "Anything out there?"

"Nothing." Murdoc swallowed hard as he surveyed the destruction in the kitchen and the lone fire in the hearth. "Some old tracks, but that's it."

"How old?"

"Can't tell. The blightwolves destroyed most of the useful clues."

"Damn it!" Connor punched the wall, and his fist broke clear through the wooden panels. He stormed back and forth through the kitchen with his hands on the back of his head, kicking aside broken furniture as he tried to think through what to do. "It's too much of a coincidence that the men remained here, but the women are all missing. I don't think they were—" He cleared his throat, unable to finish that horrible thought out loud. "Kiera and the girls must've been taken alive."

"By who?" Murdoc kicked one of the toppled chairs. "The damned wolves ate our evidence."

"No, think about it." Connor's fingertips dug into his scalp, but the bursts of pain cleared his head. "Lightseers would've captured or killed everyone, especially if they knew the Finns' ties to me. Any magic user would've drained the bodies for blood, so that rules out necromancers. That leaves bandits or slavers."

"Bandits would've killed everyone," Murdoc interjected.

"Exactly. This was a slaver attack." Connor's jaw tensed, and his nose flared with unrestrained hatred as they finally figured out who they were up against. All this time, he had been worried about the Lightseers coming after the Finns, but the forest hurt them before Teagan even had the chance.

Deep in Connor's soul, something snapped, and it snapped *hard*.

He went deathly still as his hatred sizzled into an ice-cold ferocity. A lever flipped somewhere deep within his core.

A lot of people were going to die for this. He would kill them all himself.

"Murdoc, stay here and help with whatever those two need." He gestured to the hallway. "Quinn, too. She's healing Wesley."

"What about you, Captain?"

"I'm going to find Kiera and the girls." Connor's gaze darted to the former Blackguard, and the man went still at something in his expression.

"You're leaving me with a Starling?" Murdoc's voice lowered to a whisper, and he peered anxiously down the hallway. "She has her magic and her Firesword, Captain. This isn't a good idea."

"Bluff her," Connor ordered. "Tell her the wraith is watching. Between that and Nocturne, she will behave."

Without waiting for confirmation, Connor strode out to the porch and jumped over the fragile railing. He hit the ground with a heavy thud, and the soft dirt gave way beneath his feet. His enhanced body absorbed the blow, and he barely felt the pain.

He scoured the ground. Eyes sharp. Head clear. Even if the wolves had destroyed most of the evidence of where they'd gone, there had to be something useful.

There always was, hidden somewhere in the aftermath.

Though the prints in the mud around the riverbank blended together, he crouched and studied as many of them as he could clearly see. Most of the heels dug in deeper than the toes, and a rough pattern emerged from the chaos. It led through the trees, along a path of matted grass and snapped twigs to the east.

Toward Dewcrest.

In his time in the pubs along the southern road, he had occasionally heard rumors of a vibrant slave trade in Dewcrest. From what little he knew of it, they tended to separate families and auction them off in underground markets.

If he didn't find them first, he would never see Kiera or the girls again.

At the base of a nearby trunk, at the roughly height of a child's waist, someone had carved a deep nick into the tree. He ran his thumb across the shallow cut and followed the length of it, debating whether it had been accidental or intentionally made.

With his knee pressed into the cold soil for balance, he scanned the nearby trunks until he saw another mark like this one. He knelt beside it and, sure enough, the same shallow cut marred the trunk. This one sat in a small cluster of trees that would've been scarred if the nick had been accidental, and yet only one of the trees had been marked.

Whoever had made this didn't do it on accident. Though he didn't have much to go on, he figured one of the captured Finns had left a trail for him to follow.

Thank the Fates.

He ran the back of his hand across his brow to wipe away sweat as he scanned the forest. Sure enough, three more marks led the way through a larger section of trampled underbrush that forked off in two directions in a faked trail to the south. Without the guide, that decoy would've otherwise slowed him down.

Fiona was too young to have done this, and Kiera couldn't have reached these areas on each tree without being noticed.

This had to have been Isabella. What a brave kid.

Branches snapped overhead, and Connor summoned a blackfire blade on impulse as he scanned the canopy. Nocturne's head angled toward him as the dragon neared, and a single heavy thud rocked the ground with the prince's footstep. Connor's shoulders relaxed, and he dismissed the blackfire blade with a sigh of relief.

"You are in pain."

"No, I'm furious." Connor stood and brushed off his hands.

"Anger masks true emotion. It is never the only thing one feels."

With a frustrated grunt, he waved the dragon's philosophical babble away and focused on the path ahead. He didn't have time to listen to a monk waxing poetic right now.

"I understand the grief that comes with losing family." Nocturne stared out at the forest. "The pain dilutes logic and distances us from reason. You cannot go alone. I will help you find them."

"No, I need you here." Connor pointed at the treehouse behind them. "I need you to keep Quinn in line."

"Hmm." Nocturne narrowed his dark eyes and tilted his head as he studied Connor.

"It's not a lie."

"Nor is it the whole truth."

No, it wasn't, but Connor wasn't about to elaborate.

Unfazed by the dragon's challenge, he raised one eyebrow and met the prince's gaze. More than anything, Connor wanted the dragon prince to stay here because he didn't want witnesses. If Nocturne saw what Connor intended to do to the people who had hurt the Finns, their already shaky truce might not survive the bloodbath.

"I'm trusting you, Nocturne," he finally said. "Keep them all safe, and don't let Quinn out of your sight."

"I swear it," the dragon promised. "But I must know what you plan to do when you find those responsible."

No sense lying.

"I'm going to slit some throats." Connor cracked his neck and stared out at the path Isabella had left for him. "And this time, I don't plan on showing a thread of mercy."

CHAPTER TWENTY-NINE
CONNOR

Amber sunlight filtered through gaps in the forest's canopy as another day came to a close. The warm light cast an orange glow on the underside of the leaves. The heady musk of bark and soil swam through the air as the heavy springtime evening stretched on.

With a flick of his hand to swat away a cluster of gnats, Connor crouched amongst the trampled underbrush along the route the slavers had taken. Though the nicks had ended here, clues as to their path still littered the forest. Isabella's marks on the trunks had guided him through the worst of the forked paths the criminals had taken to discourage trackers from following.

From the trail thus far, Connor figured there had to be at least a hundred people total in the slavers' band. He'd detected children's footprints alongside larger boots, but he still couldn't piece together how many fighters he would face.

More than he'd ever faced in his life, most likely. It took quite a few people to keep that many prisoners in line.

The blightwolf tracks had turned off in another direction entirely shortly after leaving the treehouse, and he took solace in the hope that the wolves had opted not to stalk the large group through the forest.

He frowned, squinting as he scanned the footprints in the dirt, but they didn't tell him anything new. The smaller unit that had attacked the treehouse—twelve survivors, he wagered, and four casualties thanks to Ethan and his axe—had met up with a much larger group roughly an hour after leaving the waterfall. Most of the prints in the center of the muddy path shuffled, and divots in the dirt from tripping over roots suggested they either carried heavy loads or dragged their feet from exhaustion or injury. The footsteps along the edge had better definition to them, suggesting a more confident gait and familiarity with long treks through rough terrain.

These bastards kept their prisoners in the middle, shepherding them like sheep and forcing them to serve as pack mules for what could only be a growing collection of stolen goods.

He had passed two blackened fire pits thus far, indicating the larger group moved at a glacial pace and had already stopped twice to camp since leaving the Finns' treehouse. With his endurance, familiarity of the forest, and all-around lighter load, he would swiftly catch up to them.

With each passing hour, the trail grew warmer. He'd already found dozens of snapped twigs, and their pale green interior suggested the group had passed through recently. The prints were fresh, untainted with the crisscrossing prints of deer or bears, and he began to think he might actually catch up to them before dark.

A relief, since tracking quarry at night carried the risk of missing crucial details, even with his enhanced eyesight. Whatever it took to find Kiera and the girls, though, he would do it, even if it meant tracking them for days. He had already survived the blightwolves twice, and with the Finns' lives at stake, he would take his chances in the woodland night.

With the trail so fresh, he slipped his mask over his nose and mouth to hide his face in the event he ran into a scout lingering behind the rest of the party. The setting sun leeched the warmth from the day, and even as a chill fell upon the forest, he continued his hunt.

In the underbrush, the fading light glinted off something lying in a thicket. Curious, he pulled aside a low-hanging branch to find a small kitchen knife with a simple wooden handle. Dents pocked its thin steel, and shallow scratches ran the full length of the blade from all the times it had been sharpened.

Most notably, a thin line of blood had dried along the metal. Given how the trail of marks along the trees had ended here, this had to be what Isabella had used to make them.

They had found her out.

He growled, low and deep, as he picked up the knife. His massive palm dwarfed the tiny blade. For the little girl's sake, he hoped the blood wasn't hers.

I'm at the edge of our connection, the Wraith King told him from up ahead. *Nothing yet. Move your lazy ass so I can see farther.*

Connor groaned in annoyance and slipped the small blade into a pouch strapped to his waist before continuing along the trail. The more he focused on the tangible things in front of him—the broken blades of grass, the headless stuffed bear cast aside in the underbrush—the longer he could drown his rage.

His blood didn't just boil.

It *burned.*

Deep in his chest, his anger popped and fizzled like boiling fat in an oven. His body ached with the sort of bloodlust he had only heard about in stories. Every muscle tensed, tighter with each passing second. His knuckles cracked with every subtle movement, and his joints popped from even a simple stretch. Short bursts of pain shot up his forearm each time he balled his hand into a fist, but he didn't care. He did it again and again, regardless, just to do something with all of this energy.

He had never felt this sort of hatred before. Even when his real family died back in Kirkwall, even when he'd seen his father's head on a spike in the town square, even when he had found his mother and sister's scorched corpses in the ashy cinders that had once been their family home, it was grief that had drowned him, not anger.

Maybe it was because he hadn't had the power to do anything, back then. Now, however, he could rip out spines—and when he finally encountered those responsible for the aftermath at the treehouse, he intended to do just that.

Found them, the wraith said.

The two simple words cleared Connor's head. Any lingering uncertainty faded. The hatred cooled to a simmering rage, cold and furious, and he sprinted along the path to catch up to the ghoul. As he ran, the savory aroma of seasoned roasting meat reached him first. Though the spicy scent triggered a fierce rumble in his stomach as his body demanded fuel, he ignored it.

Burdened with the vast power the Wraith King had unintentionally given him, his body always craved something—food, water, sex. By now, he had grown accustomed to stifling the urges.

A tendril of smoke rose into the darkening canopy, and Connor slowed as he neared it. The buzz of a dozen conversations bubbled through the air, interspersed with the occasional clink of metal.

When the thin trail of smoke thickened to a plume and the conversations became loud enough that he could pick up occasional words, he knelt behind a cluster of honeysuckle bushes and peered through the blooming branches to take stock of his opponents.

Fifty men and six women sat on various logs and rocks around a raging bonfire in the center of a dirt clearing. Dressed in browns and blacks, they all carried at least one sword, all of which rested in the sheaths buckled around their waists. Eleven slavers had quivers on their backs, but only three held their bows over one shoulder. One of them rotated a deer on a spit over a second, smaller flame while the others milled about in the growing dusk. Most of them sat in groups of three or four, while a few rowdier ones in the center laughed and shoved each other roughly by the crackling pyre.

The six women intrigued him. He studied their faces, uncertain of whether they were criminals, too, or if they had been chosen as the night's entertainment. Two of the women wore long brown dresses, but the other four wore tight-fitting pants and similar tunics to the men. They each carried swords strapped around their waists, but none of them danced. None of them had bruises on their faces from being slapped, and none of them carried trays of meat or were dragged into the men's laps. The six of them mingled by the fire, talking amongst themselves in hushed tones, armed to the teeth and looking every bit the part of a warrior.

Not prisoners, then. They had chosen this life, and they wouldn't get a shred of mercy, either.

At the edge of the clearing, at least sixty silhouettes sat in the night's approaching chill, far beyond the orange circle of firelight. Metal chains around the trees glinted in the last beams of a fading sun, and quiet sobs filtered through the growing darkness.

The prisoners, huddled together in the cold while the slavers gathered around the fire.

His hands steadied. His breath slowed. His vision sharpened in the low light, and he went deathly still as he searched for three familiar faces in an ocean of strangers.

No luck.

As he leaned his palm against the dirt for balance, a puff of dark smoke rolled over his hand, and the wraith appeared in the growing shadows behind him. The undead king's dark cloak melted into the forest's shadows as he crossed his arms and studied the gathered throng.

"Find anything useful?" Connor asked in a hushed tone.

Twelve sentries, mostly on lone patrol. A few are in pairs.

"Hmm." He ran a quick tally in his head. "Have you ever fought off sixty-eight bandits at once?"

This is hardly a challenge, Magnuson. The wraith's bone-white skull pivoted toward him, and those holes that served as eyes swallowed the light. *Not for a man who pulled a dragon from the sky.*

Right.

An echo of one of Beck Arbor's many lectures bounced through the back of Connor's mind like a hazy warning, hazy and almost out of reach. He frowned with concentration as he sifted through the memory until, at last, he snatched it.

Sometimes respect is the best choice, the former king's guardsman had told him, once. *Other times, you must choose fear, and you must be brutal to survive. You must slit throats and draw a line in the sand no sane man would cross.*

The muscles in his neck tightened, and he sat with his former mentor's wisdom. Back then, he hadn't understood the depths of the lesson Beck Arbor had shared with him—but now, the words rang painfully true.

Connor Magnuson had become power incarnate, and it was high time he wielded it like the king he was becoming.

"Kill the sentries," he ordered the ghoul. "Stay quiet. Stay hidden. Make it quick."

Will I finally get a bit of war? The Wraith King sighed impatiently. *By now, you must realize these criminals are irredeemable and unworthy of adoption.*

Something in Connor's neck popped as he shifted his weight and stood. Without a glance backward at the ghoul, he slipped behind a tree to ensure he wasn't seen by anyone around the fire. "You'll get your blood."

It's about damn time, the wraith grumbled.

With the cloth still covering his nose and mouth, Connor stole through the forest—silent, deadly, and every bit the assassin Teagan Starling had claimed him to be. He charted the camp's perimeter and circled the now-distant bonfire as he searched for the sentries the Wraith King had spotted.

As he passed a cluster of birch trees, the first of the slavers' lookouts leaned against an ironwood's dark gray trunk. The bandit crossed his arms and leaned his head against the tree as he gave a half-hearted scan of the forest around him. Bored, he blew a raspberry and shifted his weight before looking over his shoulder at the warmth of the fire.

Now or never.

Connor used the sentry's moment of distraction to slip silently through the underbrush and sneak into the man's blind spot. With a twist of his hand, he summoned one of his shadow blades into his palm and inched closer with each whisper-silent step. The enchanted sword's dark steel glinted in the last sunlight, but he opted against summoning its usual blackfire since he needed silence.

As he finally crept up behind the guard from behind, he covered the man's mouth with his left hand to keep him silent. The lookout went rigid in his grip, but Connor slit the man's throat before he could even let out a muffled scream.

Tonight, there would be no mercy. Not for these people. Not after what they had done to the Finns.

The sentry gargled and grabbed his bleeding throat, and with a quick twist, Connor snapped the man's neck. The lookout collapsed into a heap, and Connor rolled the corpse into a nearby bush to hide it before he stole again through the darkness.

Ahead, a backlit silhouette stood a short distance from the cluster of prisoners. As Connor neared, the silhouette crouched.

Concerned he had been spotted, Connor darted behind a tight cluster of trees and blended again into the shadows.

And he waited.

When no arrows sailed by and no one shouted for backup, he slipped again through the underbrush, drawing ever closer.

"...else I'd do it now," a man said quietly.

Connor's ear twitched as he neared the crouching figure. Two thick oak trees behind the silhouette framed a narrow view of the distant bonfire and the dozens of slavers clustered around it. He studied them to ensure no one had wandered off toward the sentry he had just killed, but those gathered around the flames seemed more focused on the chunks of venison one of the bandits had begun to ration among them.

"Maybe when we get to Dewcrest, I'll buy you for myself, huh?" The voice pierced the night, louder now. The stranger laughed, and a woman whimpered. Metal rattled in the brief lull that followed.

"I love that sound you make," the slaver whispered. "Make it again."

As Connor peered around a thicket of brambles, he spotted a man holding a young woman by the jaw. He leaned over her as she sat on the ground, her frayed nightgown splayed across the dirt, and her loose brown hair covered most of her face. She pressed her shackled hands against his chest and whimpered again as her skin went painfully white from his tight grip on her face. Her brows pinched together in pain, but he only dragged her closer to him. He sneered, his nose wrinkling with a blend of disgust and desire as he looked her up and down, but his gaze lingered on her terrified eyes.

These slavers had no shame.

Not even the leaves rustled as Connor stepped out of the shadows. Without warning, he stabbed the man through the gut with his dark blade, and he covered the man's mouth with his free hand to stifle the inevitable scream. The bandit lurched as the blade tore him open, and Connor tossed him into the forest to spend his final moments writhing in the dirt.

The shackled girl yelped. She collapsed into a trembling heap and broke into tears. With her knees hugged tightly to her chest, she buried her face in her dress.

Shocked and unnerved by her reaction, Connor froze.

Trembling with horror and crying so hard she could barely speak, she stuttered with each shaky word. "P-please don't hurt me. P-please, for the love of the Fates, don't hurt me. P-please—"

With a heavy sigh, he took a wary step backward. This poor girl. He couldn't imagine what she had endured.

"I'm not going to hurt you," he said softly.

To reassure her, he set his empty hand on her shoulder, but she flinched at his touch. Her hands trembled, and the shackles jingled as she weakly held them in front of her like some sort of shield.

She finally looked at him, then. Through her dirty licks of hair, sniffling, she watched him with the same horror he had seen on Isabella's face as the blightwolves had howled in the night.

The girl's sheer terror nearly snuffed out his bloodlust entirely.

This stranger didn't see him as a hero at all. Hell, rescuing her from an abuser had sent her into hysterics. Even now, as he tried to reassure her she was safe, she couldn't stop sobbing. To her, he was as much a monster as these slavers.

The thought gutted him.

He let out a slow breath. His work wasn't done, and he had a long night ahead of him. As much as he wanted to correct the misunderstanding, he couldn't comfort each terrified prisoner he encountered tonight.

"How do I free you?" He pointed to the shackles around her wrists, opting not to touch her this time.

"I just want to go home. I just—"

He dismissed his blade in a rush of dark smoke and held her shoulders as gently as he could. The young woman peered up at him through stands of her frizzy hair. A smattering of freckles dusted her nose, and though he tried to soften his expression, her eyes only widened with breathless fear.

Yet again, he had to ignore the gutting disappointment of someone he had saved watching him with all the fear of a victim looking death in the eye.

"I want to help you get home," he promised. "I'm trying to free you. All of you. Now, tell me where the keys are."

She blinked in dazed astonishment and, nervously, pointed at the boot sticking out of the underbrush.

Connor released her. In an effort to keep from spooking the girl, he stood as slowly as he could manage and pushed aside the low-hanging branches on his way to the slaver. He knelt at the corpse's side and patted the man's pockets until he caught the jingle of keys on a ring.

As he returned, she shuffled weakly backward to try to put space between them, and her metal shackles rattled with the movement. She gaped up at him, lips parted as if she wanted to scream but didn't have the strength to make a noise.

Connor unlocked her shackles, and they hit the dirt with a muted thud. She rubbed her wrists, but her eyes never wavered from his face.

He pointed to the branches above their heads. "Get into the trees. Stay quiet. Don't leave until morning, no matter what you hear. You'll be safe as long as you stay up there. You understand?"

The girl nodded weakly, but she didn't move. Though freed, she watched him like a mouse frozen in a cat's hungry gaze.

He held one finger to his mouth as a final reminder for her to stay silent and disappeared into the shadows once more, trying all the while to forget the look of terror on her face.

Not once, in his eight years in the Ancient Woods, had anyone he'd saved ever looked at him that way.

But he couldn't dwell on it. Not now. He needed to focus.

As he reached the cluster of prisoners, he did his best to shove the gutting sensation of her haunted horror deep into his soul. He scanned the crowd of prisoners again, hoping to find the three he had stalked through the Ancient Woods to rescue.

Precious minutes passed as he slipped through the shadows, hunting for Kiera and the girls, but he didn't spot them. His breath came in short bursts, and with each unfamiliar face, his heart thudded a little harder in his chest.

Until, finally, he spotted Kiera's familiar braids.

She sat closer to the edge of the tree line than most of the prisoners. With her back against a gnarled old oak, she gently cradled Isabella and Fiona as the girls rested their heads against her chest. She soothed them, her voice barely audible over the other prisoners' hushed whispers.

From this vantage, he couldn't see Fiona's face, but the firelight cast a harsh orange glow across Isabella's features. A thin line of blood had dried around a large cut on her cheek, and she sniffled as the three of them shivered in the cold night.

As he stared at the mark on her face, the full flame of his hatred returned—and this time, it *consumed* him.

He crept up to the trio and, in his relief, nearly spoke—until he remembered the girl's panicked sobs from earlier. Standing in the shadows, almost close enough to touch them, he racked his brain for how to do this without making them scream.

Nothing came to him—nothing good, anyway.

In the end, he tugged the cloth off his face so that they could recognize him. Isabella rarely spoke, and he knew she wouldn't scream, but the other two would. With as tense and on edge as they must've been, they could easily alert the slavers of his presence without realizing what they'd done until it was too late.

With no better options, he slid from the darkness and held his hand over Kiera's and Fiona's mouths. All three of them stiffened with fear, but Isabella only gasped quietly with surprise. Kiera and Fiona both craned their heads to look at his face, and he hated that they all trembled under his hands.

It took another second for them all to understand, but their eyes quickly lit with recognition. Moments later, Fiona wriggled out of his grip and wrapped her tiny arms as far around his torso as they would go.

"Thank the Fates," Kiera whispered as he released her. A tear slid down her cheek, and her lip quivered.

Wordlessly, he held one finger to his mouth as a reminder to be quiet. His body was still rigid with anger, and he stole a glance at the distant circle of slavers to ensure no one had heard her.

Busy as they all were with their venison and conversation, none of the criminals looked his way.

Good.

By now, the wraith had probably killed the other sentries, and that at least bought him some time. He fished the keys out of his pocket and unlocked Kiera's shackles.

He wanted to comfort them, but he didn't know what to say. Nothing seemed suitable. Nothing redeemed him for leaving them alone in the first place.

The only thing he could do now was ensure these bastards never hurt the Finns again.

"Connor." With her wrists finally free of the shackles, Kiera ran her hand through his hair and studied his face, as though she didn't quite believe he was real. "Bless the Fates. I thought we'd never see you again. How did you—"

"No time," he warned her with another wary glance at the slavers by the fire. "Free the others and get into the trees. I'll buy you a few minutes to get everyone to safety. No matter what happens, none of you can leave the trees until morning. I can't risk the slavers taking any of you hostage, and anyone who runs might become dinner for the predators who are already on their way because of that damned fire. Understood?"

Kiera nodded, and another tear rolled down her cheek as she smiled. Though they had precious little time, she hugged him tight. As she set her face against his shoulder, her trembling touch weakened his resolve. He sighed heavily and relaxed into her arms.

Her calm and soothing touch reminded him of how his own mother used to hold him at night, long ago when he was small. It reminded him of the power she'd had, all those years ago, to chase away his childhood fears of the dark.

Kiera sniffled and wiped her cheek as released him. Though she smiled at him one last time, she finally ushered her youngest girl off into the shadows. "Fiona, baby, you're faster than I am. Tell everyone I'm coming with the keys. Isabella, come here, dear."

But the Finns' middle child didn't listen.

Isabella launched herself at Connor. Surprised, he froze in place—until she wrapped her arms around him and held him in the tightest hug he had ever experienced in his life. She clung to him, sniffling as she pressed her face into his neck. Hot tears seeped into his shirt as she sobbed, shoulders heaving, and her panicked grip on him only tightened.

With a pained sigh, he hugged her back. "You're a brave girl. You know that?"

"I don't feel brave," she whispered, her voice shaking. "I feel scared."

"Sometimes, it's hard to tell the difference," he admitted.

She looked up at him, tears still streaming down her face, and that long cut along her cheek sent another shockwave of fury clear into his bones.

"Who did that to your face?" He swallowed hard in an attempt to keep her from seeing his boiling hatred.

Isabella peered over her shoulder and scanned those gathered by the bonfire. The painfully long seconds passed in silence, until she pointed at a woman wearing a long dress. Her tightly laced bodice accentuated the deep line of her cleavage, and she cackled at something a nearby man said as the fire cast its orange glow across half her body.

"I'll take care of it," he promised.

"It's time to go, honey," Kiera said gently as she reached for her eldest living daughter.

Isabella nodded and set her small hand in her mother's. With one last look over her shoulder, Kiera smiled again in teary gratitude.

Before they left, however, he leaned toward her ear and lowered his voice to a whisper. "Don't let the girls see what I'm about to do. For that matter, I'd rather you not see it, either."

Her face went pale, and her forehead creased with worry.

"Promise me, Kiera."

"I promise," she whispered.

With that, Connor slipped again into the woods. He circled the edge of the forest, careful to scan the trees for any lingering sentries the wraith might've missed. As the prisoners' hushed chatter faded into the gentle buzz of insects in the underbrush, he intently studied the fighters gathered around the fire pit. He tried to ignore the rumble in his stomach as they passed out slabs of venison, but the heady aroma of meat only intensified.

Beside him, dark smoke rolled through the shadows between the trees. As though he knew no other way of making an entrance, the skeletal Wraith

King glided from the murky depths like he had found a portal from hell.

It is done, the ghoul announced.

"Good." Connor leaned one shoulder against a nearby tree, as close to the circle of firelight as he dared go without being spotted.

Will you spare any of them?

"Hadn't planned on it," he admitted.

Spare one, the wraith advised. *Let him—or her, I don't care—tell others what will happen to them if they cross you.*

"Hmm." Connor scowled at the heartless bastards who'd tried to destroy the closest thing to a family he had left. "I guess we'll see how generous I feel."

Well? The ghoul gave him a once-over and impatiently crossed his bony arms. *What are you waiting for?*

"I want to give the prisoners enough time to unlock the shackles and get into the trees."

A mistake. They are not warriors, nor do they know how to survive in this forest. One broken branch could unravel—

"I'm not worried," he interjected. "After what they've been through, they know what's at stake."

The wraith grumbled incoherently at being interrupted. *I assume you have a plan of some sort, then.*

"Of course." Cautiously, Connor scanned the slowly thinning cluster of silhouettes beyond the firelight. To his relief, only a handful remained on the ground.

Good. Not much time left to wait.

"You stay hidden while I approach," he explained to the ghoul. "We're going to find out who's in charge. We'll find out their buyer's name, if they have one, and then we'll kill them all."

A suitable plan, I suppose.

"You have a better idea?"

Of course.

"And that is?"

You need to learn the art of using a man's fear against him, the wraith said with a wide gesture toward those gathered by the fire. *Part of that is theatre.*

It's waiting to show your cards until he thinks he knows what will happen. It's throwing him off balance and using the moment to your advantage. Therefore, you must wait to summon your swords until they attack.

"Fine," he conceded. "We'll try it your way."

Will you hold me back? the wraith pressed. *Are you prepared to let me truly have my blood, or are you going to show more of that infuriating mercy?*

At first, Connor didn't reply. As he debated his options, he put the cloth over his nose and mouth once again to hide his face. He surveyed the slavers as they finally finished the last meal of their short, brutal lives.

"Have your blood," he finally answered. "And take as much of it as you want."

A wicked laugh echoed in Connor's skull, but he didn't acknowledge the Wraith King's murderous glee. His attention settled on the woman who had given Isabella that scar.

He had a very special death planned for *her*.

CHAPTER THIRTY

CONNOR

A chill wind blew through the trees surrounding the slavers' bonfire. Long shadows stretched across the dirt from the gathered throng as the flames shuddered behind them in the gust. A swell of rattling leaves drowned out the distant croak of bullfrogs, and the rush blended with the swell of the cicadas' song.

With his full attention on the fire, Connor cracked his knuckles and walked into the clearing.

Calm. Focused. More certain than ever of what had to be done.

At first, his footsteps fell too silently for even those on the outskirts to notice, and no one looked his way. As his boot passed into the orange circle of firelight, however, a cluster of six nearby bandits looked up from their venison.

The smart ones drew their swords as he approached. He scanned their faces, taking in every detail, looking each one in the eye, knowing they would all be dead within the hour.

A murmur snaked through the slavers, and it filtered all the way to the trees where the prisoners had safely escaped into the canopy. By now, Kiera and the girls were in the highest branches and finally safe. Or, rather, as safe as one could be in the Ancient Woods.

Tonight, they would witness what he was, and he could only hope he didn't lose them for it.

The murmured warnings finally reached those closest to the fire, and anyone who wasn't already on their feet now stood. Dozens of fighters sauntered closer, so confident in their numbers that some sneered as they sized him up, as if he were the fool for stepping into their den. The fire behind them cast dozens of long shadows across Connor's feet as he paused just out of reach, as close to them as he could go without attacking outright.

In the name of theatre—and to make that damn wraith happy—Connor let the forest's serenade fill the silence for a few minutes. The slavers leaned toward each other, debating his intentions in hushed whispers. His ear twitched as he caught snippets of their overlapping conversations.

"…reckon he's here to buy one?"

"…helluva bloke. Look at that chest…"

"…only an idiot would rob *us*…"

True to his word, the ghoul remained silent and unseen, no doubt observing the scene so that he could critique it all later.

"Who's in charge?" Connor bellowed.

The hushed conversations stopped abruptly as his voice echoed through the clearing. His glare combed over their faces, and several of them shifted uneasily. Firelight glinted off dozens of drawn swords, and a green glow from their augmentations cast an eerie light across several of the bandits' faces.

"Sorry, lad, we're not hiring." A cluster of men in the center stepped aside as a gruff man with a bald head and thick sideburns shoved his way through them. He took a long draw on his cigar, and its burning tip cast a brief orange glow across his backlit face. The stocky man set one hand on his hip and glanced Connor up and down, as though unimpressed with what he saw. "And you can't buy any of the girls. They're all spoken for."

Connor's eyes narrowed, and the bones in his wrist cracked as he balled his hand into a fist. "By whom?"

"You're asking questions that'll get you killed, boy," the man warned. "Can't have you jabbering to the local lawmen about what you found out here, can we?"

"Who bought them?" Connor asked again, his voice gruff with unspoken warning.

"You're not very bright, are you?" The man laughed and took another draw of his cigar. "Guess I have to kill you, then. Since you're about to die, it doesn't rightly matter who bought the girls, does it? It's seventy against one, kid, and those aren't good odds."

"Sixty-eight," Connor corrected, unfazed by the man's threat. "But you're down to fifty-six, now that I've killed your sentries."

The man's lips parted in shock, and his eyes narrowed with suspicion as the cigar nearly fell to the ground.

Enough banter.

Connor summoned his shadow blades, and this time, he let the blackfire rage across the dark steel. Plumes of smoke rolled over his forearms as the swords settled into his palms.

Perfect timing, Magnuson. The ghoul laughed, as though he were watching a well-choreographed comedy. *Look at their faces!*

Panicked mutterings swept across the gathered slavers, and even their leader went still. In the treetops, a few women screamed, and several more began to sob.

"Give. Me. A. Name." He emphasized each word as he gave the criminals their final warning.

The leader shook his head, slowly at first, but the glowing orange tip of his cigar burned streaks of light in the darkness in front of his face. "Can't make me talk."

"Suit yourself."

"Kill him!" The bald man's voice shook as he grabbed his cigar and used it to point at Connor. "Now, you dolts! Now!"

At first, no one moved. He took stock of his opponents with a quick scan across the crowd, and he figured their reservations wouldn't last.

The cluster of six men closest to him glanced at each other, as if confirming they wouldn't abandon the others to death. Apparently reassured, all six of them charged.

To his right, another cluster of four bandits glowed with augmentations—three men and a woman. The woman's hands spread wide as ice blistered across her palm, and though the others also raised their hands in front of them, nothing happened. Somewhere at the back of the crowd, a lone bow's string tightened, like a whispered warning.

Fine. Eleven-on-one sounded like good odds to him.

His mind raced, faster than the steps of those approaching.

Three of the six sword-wielding slavers would reach him first, and the other three would reach him only seconds later.

He had, at best, another five seconds before the augmented bandits hit him with whatever hellstorm they planned to unleash on him.

The lone archer would unleash his arrow at any moment.

So be it.

As the first wave of armed men reached him, Connor's dual swords rested lightly in his palms—soothing and familiar extensions of his body, ready for war.

He swung in a tight formation Beck Arbor had taught him years ago. The technique was meant to slit throats, but his black blades could halve a tree.

The enchanted metal sliced easily through bone. With one swipe, his right sword decapitated two of them. He spun with the movement, his feet perfectly balanced on the dirt, and his left blade cut the third slaver's head clean off as well.

He didn't even pause as he sidestepped their falling bodies, and he locked eyes with the nearest bandit as he readied for the slaughter to come.

The next slaver's mouth parted in shock. He raised his sword to swing, but he hesitated as his companions fell to the ground.

Killing a man carried consequence, and any time he had to kill someone, Connor remembered what Beck Arbor had told him about murder all those years ago.

If you're going to take a life, at least look the man in the eye while you do it. Own the gravity of what you've done.

But here, tonight, he couldn't. There were too many, and their deaths came too quick.

A bolt of ice flew through the air at him, and his laser-sharp focus tracked its movement.

Honed with the intuitive knowledge of war thanks to his connection to the Wraith King, his instinct took over. He instantly dismissed the blade in his left hand. As the dark smoke rolled across his forearm, he summoned his shield instead. With a careful sidestep, he shifted to the left, baiting one of the swordsmen to step into harm's way.

The trap had been set. Now, to see who fell for it.

One of the three surviving swordsmen skidded to a stop and took the bait. As he followed Connor's movement, no doubt thinking he had an opening that didn't exist, the fool stepped between Connor and the ice in the second before it hit. The bandit arched his back, screaming as the crackle of ice spread across his skin.

Four dead, and only seconds had passed. Furious and focused, Connor moved through the warzone with ease.

The last two swordsmen swung in unison, and he raised his shield as their blades clanged harmlessly across its enchanted metal.

His ear twitched with warning, and something slithered across the ground behind him. He glanced over his shoulder as a vine launched out of the earth, shooting clumps of dirt sailed into the air. His shield blocked a second blow from one of swordsmen, and he hacked at the vine with the remaining shadow blade still in his hand. The pale root went limp, and the half of it he'd cut off fell harmlessly at his feet.

Frankly, the archer should've fired by now. And aside from the lone vine, the magic users hadn't done much to help the swordsmen. They were either incompetent or, more likely, using the swordsmen as a distraction while they built up to something big.

He peered over the edge of his shield as one of the two remaining swordsmen sliced at his face. Connor raised the shield to meet it, and the steel clanged harmlessly across the metal once again.

Without waiting for the slaver to recover, he dismissed the sword in his right hand and used the billowing smoke to obscure his fist until the last second. With the shield over his head, he landed a jab in the man's sternum. Ribs cracked. The slaver collapsed to the ground and vomited.

Connor didn't wait for the bandit to finish upchucking his dinner. He summoned his sword once again and sliced the man's head clean off.

The lone survivor of the swordsmen swung, screaming a half-mad battle cry, but Connor easily ducked the blow. He sank to one knee and drove his sword into the man's stomach. With a twist of his hand, he sliced through the bandit's torso. Splatters of blood coated the dirt as the last of the original six crumpled into a bloody heap.

Six down. Four left—or five, if he counted the archer who still hadn't fired.

Through the corner of his eye, one of the four augmented bandits lifted his hands and spread them wide. In response, vines launched from the dirt by Connor's feet and wrapped around his leg.

Good. He'd finally figured out which of them controlled the roots.

Dismissing his sword, Connor used the cloak of black smoke from the disappearing blade to hide his hand as he grabbed a dagger from his belt and hurled it at the man. The silver blade landed in the vine master's throat and embedded to the hilt. The vines around his leg went limp, and the bandit stumbled backward into the trees.

Seven dead.

In the past, he would've stopped there. He would've made a show of it and bluffed his enemies into surrender, if possible.

Not tonight. Every last one of them would die.

A ripple of panic filtered through the survivors, and in his peripheral vision, many of them took wary steps backward. A few—the smart ones—bolted into the forest and abandoned their fellow criminals to his wrath.

I will kill the stragglers, the wraith offered. *Save some heads for me to lop off, will you?*

Connor nodded in silent agreement.

Barely any time at all had passed since he'd first entered the clearing, and he didn't have much longer before the others swarmed him.

These criminals had to fear him, and that meant a truly flawless performance. He had to use every moment, every breath, really, to strike terror into their hearts. Beck Arbor and the Wraith King wouldn't have agreed on much, but that was one lesson both men had tried to teach him.

He charged the augmented group, and his enhanced strength gave him the speed he needed to quickly close the gap.

With a quick, sidelong glance, however, he searched again for Isabella's attacker. The woman stood by the fire with her arms crossed as she watched the display. She scowled at him and watched his every step, just a hair out of reach. He would have to get a little closer, but his plan for her would still work.

The whistle of an arrow interrupted his thoughts, and he raised his shield to block it. The arrow bounced harmlessly off.

About time. He was beginning to think he had imagined the bowstring in the first place.

Dead ahead, the woman with ice in her palms yelled with effort as she hurled another frosty burst at him. The two magic users on either side of her grabbed at the air and leaned backward, as though they were pulling an invisible rope.

Abruptly, the steady wind in the clearing shifted, and the ball of ice shattered. Fragments launched in every direction, and a thin sheet of ice coated everything they touched.

Connor would take the most damage if he let it hit him, too.

With his shield covering his head and most of his torso, he dropped to his knees and skidded across the growing sheet of ice. Some of the fragments slammed against his shield, but its radiant heat burned them to mist with a sharp hiss.

When the last fragment hit the ground, he rolled and launched to his feet. The whole ordeal had brought him close enough to touch, and their eyes went wide with fear.

The whistle of another arrow sailed through the air. He grabbed the nearest bandit—one of the men controlling the air—and pulled the slaver between him and the arrow. The metal tip embedded deep in his skull.

Eight dead.

Connor tossed the man's body at his fellow criminals. The corpse barreled through them, and they fell. The blue glow in the woman's hands briefly faded, and Connor seized the moment.

The wraith had gotten enough theater, and it was time to end his demonstration of power.

He dismissed his shield and summoned both swords once again. Without even breaking a sweat, he drove both of his shadow blades into the small gap between the two bandits and sliced outward, taking their heads in a single motion.

But he wasn't done. Not even close.

In those lingering moments before their bodies fell to the ground, he dismissed his right sword and reached into the pouch where he had stowed Isabella's knife. Though it wasn't a throwing dagger by any stretch of the imagination, he took aim at the woman by the bonfire and launched it at her forehead. Her eyes went wide in the second before it hit her, but she didn't move fast enough.

No one in the clearing would be able to.

Isabella's little knife embedded into the slaver's skull and sank right to its cracked wooden hilt. The woman went limp, and her eyes rolled backward. She collapsed to the ground just as the decapitated corpses beside him hit the dirt with a thud.

There. Eleven.

Back in the meadow by the decaying cathedral ruins, ten of the king's guard had been a life or death challenge, and it was a fight he had come dangerously close to losing. Here, he wasn't even winded.

The whistle of a third arrow sliced through the air, but he didn't duck out of the way. He didn't even summon his shield. As it reached him, he simply caught it. His palm burned briefly as the wood seared his skin, but the arrowhead stopped two inches from his face.

It took real talent to hit a bullseye. What a shame this archer had chosen to waste such skill on a despicable profession.

A deadly quiet settled over the forest, and even the wind died down. Connor stretched out his neck, letting it sink in that killing eleven people had been a light workout. As a sliver of relief snaked down his spine from the stretch, he fixed his glare on the portly man who had ordered the rest to kill him.

The leader's cigar fell from his mouth and plopped onto the dirt at his feet.

It was an unspoken surrender. Swords clattered to the ground as several of the bandits dropped their weapons, and for a moment, Connor considered accepting it. His father had taught him the value of mercy, and it seemed wrong to fight someone who had no intention of engaging.

But these people had chopped off Ethan's leg. They'd left Wesley to die in a pool of his father's blood. They'd cut Isabella's face.

Not one of the Finns had wanted to engage, either, but these bastards hadn't shown their victims mercy.

His grip on his swords tightened, and that boiling hatred burned brighter than ever. Surrender wouldn't save these cowards. Connor had no intention of leaving any survivors, even if the wraith wanted him to do so.

The sour stench of urine rolled past, and he resisted the impulse to shake his head in disappointment. He hadn't even shown all his cards, yet, and at least one of them had pissed themselves in fear.

"Looks like the odds are still uneven," he said as his gaze swept across the gathered slavers. "I guess it's a good thing I didn't come alone."

The wraith's dark laughter filled his head. *Masterfully played, Magnuson.*

Dark shadows rolled across the ground on the opposite side of the bonfire. Those at the far end of the clearing panicked and spun on their heels. Heads snapped back and forth between Connor and this new menace, as though uncertain of which they should fear more.

The ghoul emerged from the shadows, and firelight pierced the darkness under the undead king's hood. That skeletal face studied the lot of them, and the gaping holes that served as his eyes scrutinized them as he passed silent judgement. He wrapped his bony fingers around the hilt of his sword, and with the swish of cloth over metal, he drew his ageless weapon.

"Kill them all," Connor ordered.

Drunk on bloodlust, the wraith's ghoulish laughter swelled in his head. He didn't give the phantom many opportunities for unrestrained murder, but tonight he would see what the Wraith King could truly do.

He didn't want to consider these cretins as human, but each of them had a past. Each had mothers. Fathers. Families, even. He had no idea what had driven them to this life, and he didn't want to find out.

Fellow men or not, this was his line in the sand—and every slaver here had crossed it.

CHAPTER THIRTY-ONE

KIERA

Screams pierced the pitch-black night.

Kiera sat on a thick branch in the canopy with her back against the trunk. As the screaming grew louder, she clutched her two girls tightly. If not for Fiona and Isabella, these past few days would have broken her will to live. The blood. The brutality. The death. Ethan's body, lifeless and still, as a slaver drove a sword into him. Wesley's screams as the cruel bastards had carted her away.

Her throat stung. Her eyes burned. She stifled a sob and tried desperately not to remember.

With what little courage she still possessed after everything they had endured over the last few days, she tried to hide the tremor in her hands. Her girls shivered, their fingers digging into her dress, and she wished she could whisk them away from all of this. They were still children, and babies deserved sunshine.

They didn't need to know how brutal the world could be.

A hot tear rolled down her cheek, but she didn't dare let go of them to wipe it away. Fiona sniffled, her head buried in Kiera's abdomen, but Isabella didn't make a sound. She didn't cry. She didn't whimper. She merely trembled, silent as her wide eyes glossed over, and that terrified Kiera more than the screams echoing through the night.

"Cover your ears," she whispered to them, wishing all the while that she could do the same for herself.

Beneath her branch, on the forest floor far below, a sobbing man crawled across the dirt. Despite her best judgment, her heart twisted at the thought that he was someone's son. Regardless of whatever terrible choices had led him to join a band of slavers, she wanted to think someone loved him. That someone, somewhere, missed him.

Ethan had always called her a bleeding heart, and maybe it was true. Maybe she cared too much.

A shadow bolted through the underbrush toward the man. He screamed, and his sobs ended with a wet gurgle, like a current bubbling through a river. Kiera squeezed her eyes shut, and her grip on her daughters tightened.

With her eyes still closed, the final memories of the charred wreckage of their home replayed. She remembered Wesley's gut-wrenching scream and felt the surge of heart-splitting fear as that man drove a sword into Ethan's body.

She had to choose between the horrors outside and the horrors within. The Fates could be so cruel.

A knot formed in her throat as she fought back the tears, and a few escaped as Wesley's haunting scream blended with those of the bandits dying below her.

Her jaw clenched, and she forced herself to open her eyes.

Beneath her perch, the deathly specter flew through the night. Its tattered cloak nearly blended into the shadows, almost impossible to see, and only the flash of its bone-white hand around a sword gave away its position. The specter disappeared into a rush of black smoke, and it took everything Kiera had left in her to keep from shutting her eyes again in raw terror.

"No!" a man said, somewhere below her. "Please, don't—"

The wet slash of a blade through meat cut him off, and something wet splattered against a nearby bush.

Trapped as she was in this tree as death stained the forest red around her, it felt as though this had gone on for ages. She scanned the trees, and in the shadow-drenched canopy, terrified faces shivered among the leaves. Most of these other women were mothers, too, and they all held their children close. In the tree next to hers, four young women no older than Connor huddled close and sobbed into each other's shoulders as the wind shook their precarious shelter.

In the center of the clearing, the abandoned campfire raged on. It crackled and popped, the logs around it now empty, save for a dozen forgotten rucksacks and a few half-finished chunks of roasted meat laying in the dirt. She stared at the flames, letting the brilliant light burn imprints on her vision and half-wishing it would burn away her memories of the last few days if she just stared long enough.

Bit by bit, the screams faded. The sobs continued, but only from the trees. Somewhere in the shadows, that horrifying phantom slashed again through the underbrush, but she no longer heard anything for it to hunt.

Somewhere down there, hidden in the shadows between the trees, Connor was hacking his way through the people who had torn apart her home.

The thought numbed her to the core, and instead of processing what she had already seen him do, she focused on the bonfire's flame.

A silhouette bolted through the tree line, toward the fire. A man stumbled and fell onto his hands, and he slid a few feet as the firelight illuminated the blood in his mud-brown hair. He dug his fingers into the dirt and tried to stand, but his knee gave out on him, and he fell once more to the ground.

As he lay on the dirt, chest heaving, the air shifted, as if Death himself had arrived.

Kiera stiffened, paralyzed by the sensation and lost to the fear it dredged from the depths of her soul. Not a thing had changed. No one else had arrived, and yet she knew in the core of her being that a creature of inhuman power had joined them. Something to fear. Something to obey.

A *god*.

Another silhouette appeared at the edge of the woods, his broad shoulders illuminated by the raging black fire covering both of his soot-black swords. Kiera went still, like a deer stunned into silence, and she held her daughters' heads to her chest to make sure they couldn't see.

A towering man stepped from the forest, and the fire cast long shadows across the streaks of blood on his face. He glared down at the slaver, his dark eyes narrowed and fierce. With all of the crimson splatters across his brow and jaw, she could barely recognize him.

Connor.

Kiera gasped, quiet as a mouse, as she stared down at him in horror. It was almost impossible to fathom this change in who she thought he was. This man had saved her family. He'd sat at their table and eaten their food. He and Ethan had brought home firewood and spun tales by the stream. He'd stood inches from her daughters and soothed their fears in the night.

And yet, here in this bloodstained woodland, his mere presence sent a ribbon of dread clear to her toes.

The whimpering bandit on the ground by the fire wept in terror and rolled onto his back. He shuffled awkwardly backward across the dirt, trying and failing to get away as Connor stalked closer. Blood trickled down the man's neck from a gash behind his ear, and red drops fell to the ground with each feeble attempt to put space between them.

As Connor loomed over him, the slaver finally froze in place, too terrified to even move. A dark puddle appeared beneath his trousers, leaking slowly down the gentle slope toward the tree line.

Connor leaned in, his nose wrinkling with disgust as he glared down at the bandit. "Where?"

"D-D-Dewcrest," the slaver stuttered. "The alchemist there promised to buy whatever we brought him. That's all I know! I swear!"

Kiera stiffened, scowling even as she shook with fear, at the idea of being sold. Of being referred to as a *what,* instead of a *who.*

"Please," the slaver continued. "Please, sir, I don't want to die."

Connor raised one of his blades, and the flickering black fire coating its steel popped in the air before the man's face. "Then you should have chosen a different profession."

The criminal whimpered and squeezed his eyes shut as he braced himself for the inevitable.

The silence stretched on, and Kiera's gaze darted to Connor's face as he glared down at the quivering bandit. Sword outstretched, fire blazing along the steel, it seemed as though he would slit the man's throat right in front of her.

With a rush of black smoke, the swords in his hands disappeared. He walked to the slaver's left side and crouched, now far closer to the man's face than before. The bandit sobbed, but when the blow didn't come, he finally peered through one eye. He flinched as he realized Connor had gotten so close, and he stared up in gaping horror.

"The Ancient Woods are under my protection," Connor said, his voice gravelly and dark. "Every one of your fellow slavers died tonight, but I'm going to let you live because you have a job to do for me. You're going to tell every slaver, every bandit, and every criminal on the continent that they are not welcome here. If they come, what I've done tonight will seem merciful compared to what I will do to them."

A terrifying chill snaked through the campsite, worse than any frost or snowfall. Kiera's heart skipped beats as she watched in helpless silence.

Connor stood and pointed off at the forest in a silent command for the criminal to leave. The slaver nodded profusely and scratched at the ground as he tried to stand. After a few awkward stumbles, he finally pushed himself to his feet and bolted off into the night.

Standing by the fire, Connor watched the man leave. Kiera, however, could only stare at him in a blend of emotions she couldn't name.

Awe, perhaps, or horror.

After a moment, his gaze shifted to her, and she flinched in surprise. As their eyes met, his intensity faltered. His shoulders relaxed, and moments later, his gaze shifted to the ground. He tugged off the cloth over his mouth and used it to wipe away the blood on his brow, but it only left crimson smears.

This was a side of the man she had never seen before—hell, a side of *men* she had never seen before, not even among the slavers. The violence. The devastation. It didn't seem possible for a single person to have done this. She had known he was strong, but she could never have dreamed he possessed so much skill.

Against her better judgement, and despite everything he had done for their family, she felt the slightest ribbon of fear for her children's safety.

His gaze swept again across her face, and he frowned with concern as he stuffed the blood-soaked handkerchief into his pocket.

She grimaced, caught in her moment of weakness and fully aware that her doubt had probably strangled his heart. She knew Connor well enough to know he would never forgive himself for letting them see this side of him.

The trees rustled as several women scampered down the trunks. They screamed as they ran into the shadows, preferring the unknown terrors of the Ancient Woods to facing Connor. He sighed in disappointment and rubbed his temple as the women shrieked.

No. Kiera had to make this right.

"Enough!" she shouted from her perch in the trees.

Her voice pierced the women's terror and froze them in place. Several of them looked around, some frozen mid-step, and it took several moments for them to all find her in the canopy. They watched her, the whites of their eyes almost glowing in the low light.

"Stay here," she whispered to her daughters.

Terrified, her children merely nodded as she kissed each girl's forehead and slipped off her branch. Her boots splashed into something wet, and she chose not to investigate it.

After what she had seen tonight, she doubted she would like whatever she found.

"He won't hurt us!" she shouted again, not giving a damn what else heard her in the night. After the screams and blood Connor and his wraith had spilled, any monsters in the Ancient Woods had already caught their scent.

"He won't hurt us?" one woman asked, her voice meek and distant. Kiera couldn't even place where it had come from.

"How in the Fates' good name would you know?" A second woman demanded. The voice carried from the shadows, and though Kiera didn't see any of the women so much as blink, she figured the question already weighed on everyone's mind.

Kiera looked again at Connor, who stood by the fire and watched her with a somber stillness. She smiled at him, her eyes crinkling with gratitude as the fear slowly melted away. "Because he's my son."

She walked toward him, careful to sidestep a blood-soaked corpse on her way, and wrapped her arms around his broad torso. He just stood there, letting her hold him as she fought back tears of relief.

It was finally over.

"Thank you, Connor," she whispered to him as she held him tightly. The knot in her throat tightened, and she wouldn't be able to restrain the tears much longer. "I thought I would lose them, too. I thought we were as good as dead. Thank you for finding us."

She hesitated, not certain she should finish her thought, but after tonight she had to tell him the truth.

"I'm so grateful you came back," she added with a shaky sob.

He sighed—with relief or resignation, she couldn't tell—and wrapped his bloodstained arms around her in return.

"I never should've left," he said quietly.

CHAPTER THIRTY-TWO
CONNOR

The night dragged on, and the incessant buzz of flies mingled with the suffocating rot from oozing corpses. Their pungent odor choked the air like a crimson fog.

Connor sat in the canopy, and he leaned with the tree beneath him as the forest swayed in a gentle wind. The breeze carried the putrid stench from below, stirring the foul blend of charred flesh and scattered ash that lingered on the clearing long after the massacre. Blood dripped from the remains, attracting the sort of creatures only the Fates understood, but neither he nor any of the survivors could risk leaving.

Not now. Not until morning.

As soon as the surviving prisoners had calmed down enough to go back into the safety of the trees, he'd put out the fire and climbed one of his own. Though he had intended on staying awake to monitor the night for predators, the girls had insisted on being in his tree. To spare Kiera and the girls from staring down at the worst of the horrors on the ground, he'd chosen an old pine far from the tree line that still gave him a narrow view of whatever happened in the clearing.

We left a truly impressive aftermath, the wraith said with a dark chuckle. *That was the most fun I've had in years.*

Connor grimaced with disgust, but he didn't bother replying. With the ghoul keeping watch on the forest, the undead king probably wasn't even within earshot.

He, Kiera, and the girls sat in a towering pine with two thick clusters of branches that served as lumpy seats. He sat in the lower of the two clusters with his back against the trunk and one arm wrapped tightly around Isabella. The little girl nestled into the crook of his arm, curled into a ball and with her hands wound as far around his torso as they could go. Her forehead pressed against his side, and she sniffled quietly in her sleep. Even when unconscious, her tiny fingertips dug into his shirt, as though she were afraid he might disappear while she slept.

He couldn't imagine why Isabella had asked to stay with him instead of with her mother in the cluster above. Thick layers of grime coated his clothes, and even he couldn't stomach his own stench anymore. He reeked of blood and sweat, and though he had managed to wipe the worst of it off, he would inevitably have to burn these clothes. Too much blood had seeped into the fibers to redeem them.

Yet the little girl stayed, her face pressed into his filthy shirt.

Barely an arm's reach away, Kiera cradled Fiona's head to her chest and gently patted the little girl's hair. In the rush of shivering leaves around them, she softly shushed her youngest daughter's whimpers until they faded.

Sobs filtered through the trees from the dozens of oaks and pines protecting the survivors. He had wanted to spare them the horror of a night spent overlooking the aftermath, but wandering into the woods for even a short distance would entice predators to pick them off, one by one.

Exhaustion tugged on Connor's eyelids. He leaned the back of his head against the tree, his ears attuned to the macabre chorus of the forest, and his breath steadied as he debated whether or not he could afford to sleep. Fates knew he needed it. The battle with the bandits had burned through most of his reserves, and his stomach roared for food or water. The daylight hours he'd budgeted for rest and recovery had been spent tracking the slavers, and now he didn't know when his next meal would come.

In the darkness, in those moments before sleep when even the worst of the world seemed to melt away, he saw Kiera's face again. He relived her terror as she watched him decide that last slaver's fate. He remembered how she'd held her girls closer, as though she feared for their safety with him near.

His eyes snapped open again, and his chest tightened as he chased the memory away.

Through gaps in the dark emerald leaves of the next tree, two wide eyes watched him in terror. A young woman, barely twenty, gasped with horror when he met her gaze. She quickly leaned back in her seat, and the forest's shadows swallowed her whole.

He grumbled in frustration and slouched against the trunk. He hated the way they looked at him—like he was the real monster in the night.

Of the sixty-odd prisoners he had liberated, a quarter had already defied his order to stay in the safety of the trees. Some had apparently bolted before he'd even finished killing the slavers, and more had run off in the aftermath.

Hell, he couldn't really blame them. Covered in blood, with swords that could cleave a tree, he must've looked every bit the part of a new conqueror, coming to take them to an even worse life than the slavers had in store. Though he and Kiera had tried to reason with them, fear made people do foolish things, and few realized how many fanged beasts lurked in the midnight forest.

As a wanted man, he couldn't even escort them to the nearest city to ensure they made it to civilization safely. All he could do was tell them to wait until morning to leave and follow the southern road to Bradford.

Unable to sleep, he stared out at the bloody dirt visible through gaps in the branches. The blue moonlight cast a soft glow across the corpses littering the ground.

Noble intentions or not, it took a degree of savagery to kill that many people in one night. Even he hadn't known he had the capacity for that much death.

To be power incarnate comes at a cost.

The wraith had told him that not long ago. This world didn't limit him, and not even the wraith knew what Connor's limits truly were.

Something slithered through the bodies, its hundreds of feet clacking across the rocks in the soil, and two quivering antennas felt across the still figures. The slinking shadow paused at one of the corpses in the middle of the clearing, and the smack of teeth ripping through meat followed.

A michera. Interesting. He hadn't seen one of those since the night he'd met Murdoc and Sophia.

The rustle of branches filled the night, and he sighed with disappointment as two more women climbed down a nearby tree trunk and darted of into the underbrush without even glancing back over their shoulders.

These frightened people had no idea what awaited them out there. To have survived all this, just to end up as a predator's dinner—it didn't seem right.

Some predators enjoyed the chase, and others refused to eat anything that was already dead. Any hungry animal couldn't deny the feast he'd left for them in the clearing, though, and he could only hope the michera, blightwolves, and other beasts of the forest would be too fat to give chase.

"How many will wait until morning?" Kiera's soft voice pierced the creak of their old pine's branches as she stared off at the fleeing survivors.

Connor shrugged. In the end, these women had to make their own choices. It would waste precious time for him and the wraith to hunt them all down one by one and drag them back to safety.

"I wish they had waited." The gentle woman sighed, and the outline of her frizzy braids shifted as she shook her head in disappointment. "You even offered to take them to your new land. I thought more of them would've taken your offer."

"They don't know me like you do, Kiera," he reminded her as he closed his eyes and tried again to sleep. "I can't imagine what they must think I am."

Demon.

Murderer.

Monster.

For a while, Kiera didn't respond. Exhaustion weighed on him, and in the darkness, he tried to drown out the memories of the treehouse. Of Wesley coughing up blood. Of Ethan, lying on the floor, pale as death and missing a leg. Of the nauseating odor that reminded him of fetid eggs and piss. Of Kiera, clutching her girls tighter as she witnessed something he'd tried so hard to shield them from ever seeing.

The tree swayed beneath them, creaking and groaning as the wind carried the stench of rust and rot skyward.

"They're just scared," she whispered.

They should be, he wanted to say. He blinked himself awake and stared into the darkness, opting instead for silence.

"I wish you'd been there." Kiera's voice cracked, and she barely stifled a sob. "When... when they..."

A muscle in his jaw clenched, and he did his best to swallow his guilt. "I do, too."

"I can't stop thinking about how it would've gone differently." She sucked in a sharp breath and tilted her head to hide her tears. "Maybe you would've pointed out the flaws in the house before it was too late. Maybe you would've known they were coming."

"Is that how they found you? The house?"

She nodded. "We had forgotten all its quirks. The creaks. The weak points. Bits of it were falling off every day, and we knew we needed to move. We just had to find a place. Building a house takes time, even for—"

Kiera choked on a sob and, with one hand still firmly around Fiona, she buried her face in the other.

Lost in her grief, she couldn't even say Ethan's name.

Connor gritted his teeth to stifle the surge of hatred that boiled within him, and a headache throbbed in the back of his skull as he suppressed it. He wanted to fix this. He wanted to tell her it would be okay. That they would survive.

He wanted to tell her he had the best healers he could find helping them, but he didn't want to lie. He didn't want to give her hope, only for it to be ripped from her again if Sophia and Quinn failed.

Before he'd left, he had told Isabella the house was safe. He had promised it would protect her, and ultimately, it had been their undoing.

The Fates could be so damn cruel.

Worst of all, Connor hadn't been there when they needed him most. The guilt ate him from within. It strangled his chest and left him breathless, but he couldn't do a damn thing about it.

"Did... did the wolves..." She sobbed again and ran the back of her hand across her cheek to wipe away the tears, unable to even finish her question.

"No," Connor answered flatly.

He couldn't bring himself to say more.

Beside him, Isabella squirmed in her sleep. She whimpered, her eyebrows scrunching as she fought off another terrifying dream. It reminded him of when he was little—back then, his sister's nightmares woke the whole house, and the whole family often converged on her room to soothe her. His mother would pet her hair, and his father would whisper reassurances as she drifted off to sleep.

Uncertain of what else to do, he did his best to mimic what they had done, all those years ago.

He cradled Isabella's head in his massive palm, and his hand covered much of her hair. At his touch, she relaxed, and her death grip on his filthy shirt loosened.

Given the nightmares he had endured for years after he'd lost his family, he couldn't imagine the demons plaguing her dreams right now. Though he debated waking her, tomorrow would be a long day, and she needed rest. Not even he could rescue her from her nightmares, however much he wished he could.

Nightmares had to be faced, or they would fester.

"Those horrible people…" Kiera sucked in a sharp breath, her face red from trying so hard to choke back tears.

They streamed down her face anyway.

With Fiona still asleep on her chest, she stared up at the twin crescent moons through a gap in the leaves and finally surrendered to the grief. Her brows scrunched in her deep mourning, and the tears left streaks down her travel-stained face.

It gutted him. With a tilt of his head, he did his best to hide his pained grimace, but he couldn't respond.

He didn't know what to say.

"I hate them, Connor." Kiera wiped away the flood and struggled for air through the sobbing. "I've never hated anyone or anything this much in my life. I hate them for what they did to Ethan. I hate them for dragging me away while Wesley screamed for me. I hate them for cutting Isabella's face so that only the worst buyers would want her. I hate—"

Kiera couldn't finish. The tears broke through even her hatred, and she lost herself in them.

"I just *hate*," she sobbed.

Though she was too far away for him to hold her, he set his free hand on her ankle and gently squeezed. In the trees above a bloodbath that had already begun to attract scavengers, he let her cry. He let her burn off the anger, free of judgement, until the sobbing abated.

It took ages, and even then, he knew the grief would return.

"Thank you," she eventually whispered, her voice breaking. "For being here. For finding us. I thought we were done. I thought the Fates had abandoned us."

He sighed and released his hold on her. "I wish I could've stopped this from ever happening."

"It wasn't yours to stop." She sniffled and wiped her nose on her sleeve. "You had to leave. I know you're not just a man anymore, Connor. Whatever happened by the cathedral, it changed you."

He stiffened, his forehead creasing with concern as she got dangerously close to the truth.

"I saw it that night." With a vacant stare, she looked dead ahead. Her shoulders slumped, and though she held tightly to her youngest daughter, she shook her head with careless surrender, as though nothing mattered anymore.

As though it had come time to tell him what she had always wanted to say, and it was too late for there to be consequences.

"The ghoul," she continued in a cracked whisper. "Death himself, I thought. The night you saved us, I thought I was seeing what happened when people die. I assumed he had come for me. But then…"

She trailed off, and for several minutes, only the rustling leaves kept them company.

"But then I saw it at the old house," she continued. "Just glimpses, so quick it almost seemed like a trick of the light, but my eyes are sharp. I saw it between the trees, like a specter stalking the lot of us. And then, one day, it simply disappeared." Her tearstained gaze finally shifted to him. "It left when you did, Connor."

All this time, she had known.

His breath came quicker as he sifted through his options. The tightness in his chest worsened, until every breath became a chore, but he steeled himself for the worst. "Who did you tell?"

"No one." Kiera shook her head, and her vacant stare shifted away from him again. "After we lost Kenzie, Ethan finds it so hard to trust other people. That he let you into our home is a miracle, and one I never thought I would live to see. I didn't want him to lose faith in you, and he doesn't appreciate magic like I do. Wants nothing to do with it. Doesn't understand. He—" She pinched her eyes shut as she caught herself speaking of her husband in the present tense and let out a long, slow breath. "I won't say he's dead, Connor, not him or Wesley. Not until I see for myself."

"Nor will I," he promised, though he refused to give her false hope.

She nodded absently and leaned her head back against the tree. The rip of meat off bone cut through the night, and in the clearing, something wet plopped onto the dirt.

"That rage." Kiera's eyes shut, but her whisper sliced through him like a weapon. "That hatred on your face, Connor, that wasn't anything like what I feel. It was worse. I saw it consume you, out there, and I hope you never feel it again. It was terrifying to witness. At first, I thought I'd lost you to it."

Fates be damned. Of everything she had said—of all the guilt he'd drowned in since he'd first discovered the decimated treehouse—that hurt him the most.

He shut his eyes to steel himself against the surge of remorse. He had come to save them, not scare them. Tonight, however, he'd tapped into his potential. Out there in the clearing, he had slaughtered so many people that he hadn't even been able to look them all in the eye.

Killing them had come almost too easily. All the power in the world meant nothing if wielding it corroded what made him human.

"What is it, then?" Kiera's eyes shook as she studied his face. "The magic you have? That ghoul?"

He shook his head and stared out again at the moonlit clearing filled with corpses. Even if she deserved to know, he couldn't tell her with this many witnesses in the nearby trees. Given Slaybourne's history and the wraith's connection to it, he would have to tell her eventually. For now, however, he remained silent.

He had terrified her enough for one night.

When the silence had stretched long enough that she took it as his answer, she sighed. "It doesn't matter, dear. Whatever it is—whatever you are—you're one of us. I will always be grateful to you. You're family, Connor, and family is for life."

A knot formed in his throat, and he swallowed hard to bury it.

A howl pierced the forest, and the steady vibration of paws against the dirt vibrated through the trunk of their tree. The sobs and whimpers in the canopy grew louder, but he had already warned them how dangerous noise could be when faced with the predators of the Ancient Woods.

Still nestled in the crook of his arm, Isabella went stiff. Her fingers clutched his bloodstained shirt, tighter than ever, and she began to tremble. He looked down to see her eyes wide open as she stared straight ahead, listening intently to the approaching horror.

Since she had one ear already pressed against his shirt, he covered the other with his palm. She didn't need to hear this.

Yips and howls overlapped each other, building to a crescendo as the thunder of paws neared, and figures darted through the woods. A massive silhouette bolted underneath his branch, and he stiffened on impulse as snarls floated through the air.

He couldn't see the whole clearing from this vantage, but he watched as towering blightwolves descended on the corpses. Growls blended with the sickening crunch of snapping bones, and their chaotic frenzy engulfed even the relentless buzz of the flies. He tried to tally the wolves he could see, but they swarmed and writhed in a shadowy mass that made the feat impossible.

He lost count around fifty.

The slurp of tongues lapping up blood blurred with the ravenous onslaught of glistening teeth. A severed arm flew through the air as each beast competed to eat the most. The blightwolves nipped and snapped at each other, never in one place for more than a few seconds, and the overwhelming snarl of the forest's most fearsome carnivores swelled until it drowned out even the wind.

Look at them all. The Wraith King's haunting voice broke the spell the wolves had put on Connor, and he let out a slow breath as he watched them feast. *I count a hundred, Magnuson, and it sounds as though more are on the way.*

Though the wraith wasn't within view, Connor nodded to himself. He'd never seen this many of them at once, and that concerned him.

"Something happened," Connor said quietly.

Something dire, the ghoul agreed, apparently close enough to hear him after all.

The wolves knew something Connor didn't—and that left a foul taste in his mouth, far worse than any blood.

CHAPTER THIRTY-THREE
QUINN

Through gaps in the canopy beyond the treehouse window, Quinn caught glimpses of Saldia's twin moons and a smattering of stars in the midnight sky. Never for a whole moment, of course, since the heavy forest blocked out most of the world beyond this crumbling structure lodged between the branches, but enough to gauge the time.

She sat in a rickety chair on the first floor, her elbows resting on her knees as she hunched over with her head in her hands. The ache of exhaustion and a stressful night of hearing two innocent people scream in pain tugged on her weary eyes.

As much as she wanted to sleep, she didn't trust the necromancer enough to try. That woman had clearly trained in Nethervale, and no one ever came out of that place with their soul intact.

On the bed beside her, the boy whimpered. Quinn shifted, just a little, and rested her head on one fist as she scanned his face. He twitched again in his sleep, his forehead creasing as he fought off yet another nightmare, and she gently ran her hand through his hair to soothe him. His sweat coated her fingertips, but he relaxed the moment she touched him.

Poor kid. Though she didn't have proof that these people were indeed innocent, everything she had seen thus far made her fairly certain none of them had deserved what happened here.

Her open pack sat on the bed beside him, and the dim light of the single candle on his bedside table cast a soft orange glow across the dwindling jars in her bag. She had given him one of the few Starling Rectivanes she had left, and that alone had sewn up most of his wounds. Even still, he walked the thin line between life and death. He hadn't spoken, and he hadn't so much as opened his eyes since they arrived.

Given the severity and age of his wounds, not even the most powerful healing potion in Saldia could do anything else for him now. There was nothing left for her to do, and yet, she couldn't bring herself to leave. As much as she needed some fresh air to clear her head, she could only sit there, staring at the floor as her skull ached with fatigue.

With her luck thus far on this mission, the boy would awake the second she stepped out. After what he had endured, he deserved better than to wake up alone.

A sharp sting pierced the back of her tired eyes, and she mumbled obscenities in frustrated surrender to the throbbing headache. With a grunt of annoyance, she lifted her bag onto her lap and rifled through her remaining potions for a cure. A small, custom-sewn cloth protected each of the carefully catalogued vials, and she briefly tilted each one to get a view of the custom labels she had crafted to protect her stores from thieves.

Rectivanes, to heal. Brackenbanes, to melt objects on contact. A Fieldmane, to rapidly grow food should the need arise.

"Damn it all," she muttered under her breath, eyes still stinging. "Where is it?"

Her knuckle knocked against the familiar blue vial with a four-leaf clover drawn on the label, and she let out a sigh of relief. Her Dazzledane charm—just the boost of energy she needed.

The cork left the vial with a soft pop, and Quinn held the shimmering silver potion to her lips. The liquid crackled on her tongue, vibrant and lively, and a ripple of numbness snaked down her fingers as it poured down her throat.

After Connor had taken her pack, she had been forced to go without this fizzling burst of life and energy for days, perhaps when she had needed it most. Her shoulders relaxed, and as her breathing slowed, her heart rate calmed as well. The stinging in her eyes faded, and the draining ache of a sleep-deprived mind seeped away.

Quinn shivered with delight, her eyes still closed, and she let the bottle linger at her mouth. The thought of taking that second, forbidden sip left her throat parched, as though she hadn't had a drink of water in days, and it took immense effort to cork the bottle once again.

One sip, and only once per day—it was all she had ever allowed herself, and she wouldn't lose her self-control tonight. A boost of energy could quickly become addiction, if she wasn't careful, and a potion wouldn't be her undoing.

Connor could return at any moment, and Quinn needed to remain vigilant. She couldn't let herself sleep just yet.

The boy's head shifted on the pillow, and his breath steadied into an even rhythm. As she sat beside this stranger the Wraithblade cared so much about, she marveled at how surreal this all was at its core.

At this very moment, she sat in a treehouse not unlike the one she had encountered before she had even known what she was hunting. Back then, shortly after she had been assigned to bring Connor back in chains, she had wondered if the house belonged to the assassin's family only to immediately dismiss the thought.

And she had been so very wrong.

For all her time as the Wraithblade's captive, she hadn't been in any real peril. Though she was still unclear on his motives, he was definitely not the man her father claimed him to be.

It made her question not just Teagan's word, but all of history. Her ancestors had written much of it, and all the books in Saldia agreed on one thing—Aeron Zacharias had created abominations, creatures of darkness and death that consumed what light remained in this world. No man with a wraith had ever been remembered as a good one. He was always a tyrant. A warlord.

A killer.

She absently rubbed her jaw, lost in thought and wondering what really happened the night Henry died and Connor acquired the wraith. Maybe he had told her the truth, or maybe he had killed Henry in cold blood. Perhaps she would never know.

Perhaps...

Quinn sighed and set her face in her hands once again as her thoughts raced in circles. Perhaps it didn't even matter anymore.

With her eyes now shut, her ears compensated for her missing sight by focusing on every creak of the dilapidated house around her. Underneath her boots, the structure swayed in the wind like a boat on the sea. Though she had always hated sailing, she had been on enough ships to intuitively bend with each movement.

Beside her, the boy whimpered again, and the swish of sheets over skin broke through the house's groaning melody. She reached for the kid again, and this time, he grabbed her hand. His fingers squeezed around hers, tighter than she had been expecting, but he didn't wake. He winced and sucked in air through his teeth, his back arching as he fought off another wave of pain, and a bead of sweat dripped down his nose.

Quinn wanted to give him another potion. She wanted to snap her fingers and chase away his pain, but even magic had its limits. It was up to him to duel with Death and make it through the night on his own. His grip on her palm tightened with each passing second, and she squeezed it back to offer what little comfort she could.

"Hush." She brushed a damp clump of hair out of his face. "Everything's fine. You're safe."

A lie, maybe, but one he needed to hear. The grim reality of it all was that this boy and his father would likely not survive the night. It was cruel and unfair, but Connor hadn't gotten here in time. If she had encountered them on her own, she would have done what she could, but the law was clear—the Fates made these decisions, not man. Death was their agent, their vessel, and it was the duty of the Lightseers to maintain the natural order.

Any Lightseer who brought someone back from the dead would be executed by Teagan Starling himself.

That was the law they all lived by, and that alone contained the chaos.

A muscle in her eye twitched, and she shook her head to chase away the grim thought. She had seen miracles before, and only the Fates got to decide what happened to these two. Not her.

As she stroked the boy's hair, the candlelight cast flickers of light across the scar on her palm—the reminder of her father's lies and the purpose she had lost.

The Lightseers had their code, sure, but Quinn no longer had to obey it. She had abandoned her mission in search of the truth, and along the way, she had violated almost every sacred oath she had taken when her father had given her *Aurora*. The more she learned, the more liars she discovered, and the more she lost faith in Saldia's people. In her family.

In herself.

"What's the point of any of this?" she asked the sleeping boy before her. "This world belongs to warlords and conmen, kid. What power does the truth even have?"

Out in the hall, the heavy thud of a man's boots on the floorboards interrupted her internal debate, and her ear twitched as she lost her train of thought.

Murdoc.

With a groan, Quinn rubbed her eyes and stood. The boy released her hand and rolled onto his side, and his shoulder rose with the steady rhythm of his settling breath. If Murdoc agreed to watch the boy for a while, this would be a good time to get some fresh air.

She stepped into the hallway, and her boots made only the barest scuff across the floorboards as she headed down the only passage through the house's many rooms. At the end of the corridor, Murdoc rested with his back against the wall, and he stared intently at the floor. His eyes glossed over with whatever thoughts consumed him, but he didn't look up as she neared. Even when she stood barely a yard away, he hadn't moved.

Whatever he was thinking about must've been weighing on him for quite some time to consume him so completely.

Quinn cleared her throat, and the man jumped backward at the sound. When his eyes finally darted toward her, he let out a soft string of curses.

"You're too damn quiet," he muttered.

"Thank you," she said dryly. "Stay with the boy while I get some air."

He frowned and raised one eyebrow at her tone.

"*Please.*" She resisted the impulse to roll her eyes. "I don't want him to wake up alone."

The skin around Murdoc's eyes crinkled as he studied her face, and he grinned. "Being around us finally made you go soft, eh?"

Quinn didn't have the energy for banter, so she waved away the taunt.

He brushed past her and, without turning around, pointed vaguely over his shoulder. "I suggest you stay put on that porch, princess. The wraith is out there, and that dragon will eat you if you try to run."

"Doubtful," she muttered, too quietly for him to hear.

As the house once again settled into its creaking melody, her Hearhaven augmentation picked up on someone breathing in the room nearby. The closed door muffled the ragged sound, but each scratchy breath reminded her of an animal in its final moments, unable to move and desperately trying to draw in just enough air to survive a little longer.

The father.

Not even the finest healers in the capital could have done what Connor asked that necromancer to do. It seemed as though she had staved off death for now, and that alone was a miracle. But even if his heart kept beating, that didn't mean the man would have a life.

"Damn it," a woman muttered from somewhere behind the closed door. "I know it's in here somewhere."

The necromancer. Good, at least Quinn wouldn't have company during her reprieve.

On her way through the kitchen, she massaged her forehead and debated what to do with this moment of isolation. Sure, she could escape—dragon or no—but Connor still had her vougel, and she still had unanswered questions.

For now, it served her to stay.

The wobbly front door squealed as she stepped onto the rickety porch, and she winced from the shrill sound. The top of the canopy swayed around her, the leaves rustling like waves on the ocean, and the cold bite of a spring night zapped a bit more energy back into her bones. Overhead, the twin moons cast their soft blue glow across the sky, and their gentle light seeped into the forest.

After chaos came a bit of calm. A moment of peace and wonder, to give the world a bit of pause and a chance to guess what would come next.

Quinn shut her eyes and drank in the darkness. Loose curls bounced along her nose in the wind, but she let them flutter. Her skin prickled as the cold woke her up, and her blood pumped harder.

The crunch of wood and the snap of shifting branches cut through the peaceful lull. Her eyes snapped open, and her fingers curled as she prepared to summon her Burnbane fires.

Connor didn't make that much noise.

To her left, a massive silhouette shifted in the darkness and arched toward her. It sifted through the shadows, blending with them, becoming them, almost, as the forest hid its features from view.

Quinn settled into her stance, never one to back down from a fight, and she set her palm on *Aurora's* hilt. The crackling power of her augmentations simmered in her blood, just beneath her palm and ready at a moment's notice.

The figure hovered, just past the porch railing, and went still. Its edges blurred into the towering tree behind it, and the depths of the woodland night swallowed it hole, as though it had never been there at all.

If she hadn't known to look for it, she might've even missed it entirely.

"I'm not in the mood for games," she warned it.

"Are you ever, Quinn Starling?" The wall of sound boomed through the forest. It hummed in her chest, overriding even her heartbeat, and the vibrations of each word thrummed through every muscle in her body.

Nocturne. Of course.

Her stance relaxed, and she took a cautious step closer to get a better view of the first dragon she had ever seen up close.

In the depths of the nearly invisible silhouette, a single eye opened. His eye, though black and smooth as a river rock, glowed with a dim, shimmering light of its own, like the soft haze on an early morning horizon. His iris narrowed as it focused on her, and she paused midstride under his scrutiny. Silky black scales along his neck blended with the darkness, such that only the occasional sheen from moonlight glinting off his body gave any indication he was even there. As his head hovered just beyond the porch railing, his long neck trailed into the darkness below.

"Will you run?"

Her heart skipped several gleeful beats as she did her best not to gape at him in awe. It took every ounce of self-control she possessed, but she managed to feign indifference. With a shrug, she leaned her back against the corner of the house, as close to him as she could get. "Would you chase me?"

Nocturne chuckled, and the raspy sound reminded her of Blaze. Her eyes drifted to the porch boards beneath her feet, and as much as she wished he were here with her, the vougel was safe back in Slaybourne.

"I would." The dragon's voice sent another wave of vibrations through her body. "But you will not try."

She smirked. "What makes you so confident?"

"Because I see through you." His head tilted, and his eye narrowed. "Now, of all the places in Saldia for you to be, why are you here?"

"Captives don't get much choice in the matter," she said dryly.

"Captive, are you?" Nocturne tilted his giant head, and his eye dilated as it focused on her.

She frowned and crossed her arms, but didn't answer. As majestic as this dragon was, he and Connor seemed to have some kind of bond. She couldn't risk letting him guess at anything the Wraithblade shouldn't know.

"Hmm." A biting wind rolled past, and the giant creature shivered. The shudder raced down his head and through the length of his neck. "You do not trust me."

"Should I?"

"Yes."

"I barely know you."

"Hmm." The soft growl floated through the forest. "A dragon's integrity is his most valuable asset and his greatest weapon. It is his lifeblood. On my honor, Quinn Starling, I swear not to divulge your secrets."

"How thoughtful." Quinn watched the legendary creature's face through the corner of her eye, still marveling as another ribbon of moonlight snaked across his scales.

The wind picked up, and a brief rush of air shook the leaves around them as the cold spring night dragged on. Somewhere out there, Connor stalked through the trees toward some unsuspecting bastards who were in for the most terrifying surprise of their life. Her thoughts wandered again to the boy fighting off Death in the house behind her.

"Why are you here?" she asked the dragon beside her. "You can fly anywhere, and yet you're taking us wherever he wants to go. You're a god, Nocturne, not a carriage."

The regal creature chuckled, and the leaves in front of his face fluttered with each grating rasp. "He made me a deal, just as he did for you."

"What kind of deal?"

Nocturne didn't answer. His flawless eyes narrowed, and in the thin moonlight, the edge of his mouth twisted slightly in what she could swear was a smirk.

"I guess that's fair." Quinn shrugged and hugged herself more tightly as the cold wind rushed by.

After all, she still hadn't answered his question. It made sense that he wouldn't answer hers.

She stared off into the forest, in the direction Connor had taken when he had left them all behind. "Do you think he can make good on all of these bargains?"

The dragon's head pivoted toward the ocean of leaves before them, staring at something she couldn't see, and several minutes passed in silence. As the cold wind howled, Quinn fought off a shiver. She summoned just enough of her Burnbane fires to warm her palms and held herself as her magic chased away the worst of the chill.

The dragon finally sighed and looked up at the moons. "I believe he thinks he can, but that is not a guarantee."

Fair point.

"If you can, you should lower your voice," she warned with a wary glance at the broken door. "The others might hear you, and they're not keen on others criticizing him."

"They are preoccupied," he assured her, but his tone quieted all the same. "Now, tell me what you know of dragons."

Quinn shrugged. "Just stories. I didn't think you still existed."

"What do these stories say?"

Images of raging beasts and feral monsters flew through her head, lighting castles on fire and unleashing the mighty chaos of the storms onto unsuspecting townsfolk. All the bedtime stories her father once told her bubbled just beneath the surface, rife with death and destruction while heroic Lightseers charged out to save the day.

"You don't want to know," she said.

"Hmm." The dragon's head inched over the railing, coming closer, and Quinn stiffened as his giant snout paused inches from her shoulder.

The urge to draw her sword burned within her, more an impulse than a conscious thought, and she fought off the instinct to punch him square between the eyes for coming this close. His hot breath rolled past her, warming her instantly, and the barest hint of charred smoke wafted across her neck as she waited to see what he would do.

"I see through lies." His soft, black gaze pinned her to the rickety wall. Though he spoke quietly, he was close enough that his voice still shook the floorboards beneath her feet. "But even I have been tricked before. What I see in Connor does not bode well for either of our homelands."

"He's cruel, then?" A crushing wave of disappointment washed through her, even as she fought to ignore it. "Deep down, I mean. He's hiding it? Is he really as terrible as all the others?"

"Not quite. He has honor in him," Nocturne corrected. "He has a noble heart, but for how long? Usually, the answer is clear, but with him, there is something else. Something *other* blocks my sight."

Quinn frowned as she pieced it together. "You're afraid that piece of him will take over. That he'll become just another warlord, like all the rest of them."

"It is of grave concern, yes."

She sighed and rubbed her eyes, her worst fears confirmed. "I thought you two had a bond. Why are you telling me this?"

The dragon's head inched closer. Her jaw tensed nervously as the creature's head hovered beside her, close enough to snap her in half with a quick twist of his neck, and she balled one hand into a fist as she prepared to summon her Burnbane fires.

Just in case.

"Because in you, I also see something *other*—it is new to me, and I cannot place it, but at least I can understand your intentions. This *other* part of you, whatever it is, has the power to challenge even him."

Her brows furrowed in confusion. "What do you mean?"

"I do not know," he confessed.

The dragon's massive head tilted as he studied her, and the tip of his giant nose rested against her arm. The smooth scales reminded her of silk, soft and subtle, and she leaned into him as she relished the sensation.

"I swore not to share your secrets, Quinn Starling, and that is in part because I do not fully understand them."

She narrowed her eyes in suspicion. "What do you see?"

"I see pain." His haunting voice swam through her mind, blending with her thoughts until she lost herself in his words. "I see a warrior who never belonged to the world she protects. Some wish to kill you. Others aspire to *be* you. Most of all, however, they all wish to use you in some way. They see what you can do for them, but not who you are. In you, I see a guardian searching for something to protect. You have lost your way, and not even you know what you really are."

She blinked rapidly to break his connection to her soul—or whatever the hell he was doing—and turned her back on him.

"It haunts you." The dragon's voice hummed in her chest. "But it has led you here. To Connor. To me."

As the cold night wore on, she took a steadying breath and waited for the regal dragon to continue.

"I rarely need to trust others," Nocturne admitted. "It is unnecessary when I can simply see the truth for myself. But with Connor, the stakes have changed. I must choose to either protect or destroy this man. It is my duty to guard the Dragonlands from war, even at the cost of my life, and the Wraith King has turned my people feral before. If Connor were to lose his way, he could do the same to me, and as a feral beast I would betray my homeland. I would lead them to my people and help him conquer them as well."

Quinn wrapped her arms tighter around her body as she listened to the regal creature speak. She hung on his every word, ensnared by power she didn't know the Wraithblade even had, and sparks of panic fizzled through her mind as she considered just how powerful this man could truly be.

Thus far, Connor hadn't been cruel to her—but, then again, neither had her father. A few good deeds did not make a good man, nor did it prove he had good intentions.

There were still so many unknowns. Connor stood in the center of all her and Nocturne's doubts.

"Perhaps I am right to worry," the dragon continued. "Or perhaps my fears are unwarranted. It is possible that soldiers like you and I simply lack the capacity to believe in someone who wields such raw power." Nocturne let out a weary sigh and shook his massive head. "Even if I left Saldia and abandoned my quest to find my lost brethren, there is no guarantee the Wraith King would not corrupt Connor in my absence. I need a failsafe. A means to ensure neither he nor the wraith will ever threaten my people."

In the lull that followed, she looked away.

"I wouldn't be here if I didn't see something in him," she confessed. "I just don't know what it is or how long it will last."

"Those are concerns you and I share," the dragon admitted. "Even good and honorable men can lose their duels with the darkness. Should he ever succumb to the Wraith King's greed, he would be a fearsome threat. If that day comes, I know I cannot win if I face him alone. That is why I have shared so much tonight, Quinn Starling. That is what I see in you. I see someone capable of defying the Fates to protect the greater good. I see enough power, between the two of us, to stop even Connor Magnuson."

Quinn's heart panged, and the jolt of surprise rooted her to the floor. The dragon had confessed so much, right down to her target's full name.

It left her speechless. All of it.

She sat with the weight of what he had said, with the burden of what he thought her capable of doing, and her mind went numb. As much as she had tried to shield herself against hoping one good man remained on this cursed continent. She needed to believe one existed. The devastating regret of all she had abandoned to be here—of all she had surrendered to learn the truth about this man everyone hunted—it all stuck to the roof of her mouth like sour milk, rancid and sharp.

"What if you're wrong?" she asked quietly.

"I hope I am," the regal creature admitted. He growled, and a ribbon of smoke shot out his nose. "I HOPE THAT, WITH TIME, I SEE IN HIM WHAT I SEE IN YOU—AN UNWAVERING FAITH IN THE GREATER GOOD. IT IS POSSIBLE, PERHAPS EVEN LIKELY, BUT IT IS NOT GUARANTEED. NOT YET, ANYWAY."

The great dragon's head tilted away from her, and he retreated into the shadows beyond the treehouse. Branches cracked and shifted as he disappeared into the darkness, and in a matter of seconds, he was gone.

"YOU STILL HAVE TIME," Nocturne said from the darkness. "BUT YOU MUST CHOOSE YOUR ALLIES SOON."

With that, the rustle of the forest's leaves drowned out any hint that he had ever been there.

Quinn set the back of her head on the wall behind her and shut her eyes. At first, she could only listen to the whistle of the wind around her and the distant croak of a creek frog's call. The night swam through her head, filling the numb gaps in her thoughts with sound and the crisp bite of springtime jasmine, but the peaceful void wouldn't last forever.

It couldn't. Not given all she had just learned.

When the numb prickle of her shock slowly faded, she didn't think of the life she had left behind. She didn't think of her mother brushing her hair when she was a young girl, in those days before her father allowed her to train as a Lightseer like her older sisters. She didn't imagine the soft fuzz on Blaze's face as her fingers wove through it, opening their connection. She didn't even think about *Aurora*, her one connection to the Lightseer code of honor and light she had sworn to uphold in these trying, deadly times.

No, oddly enough, she didn't think of her life at all. Instead, she remembered the rage on Connor's face when he'd climbed the crumbling ladder up to this very porch. With the girls missing and the men assumed dead, his grief had been all-consuming.

The thought of losing these people had killed a piece of him.

Cruel, selfish men didn't feel that level of pain. They iced their hearts until they felt very little at all. Quinn knew without a doubt that, somehow, Connor Magnuson had a good heart. Deadly and dangerous as he was, he still cared deeply about life. About justice. About protecting those who needed him.

But, like Nocturne, she had no proof it would last.

CHAPTER THIRTY-FOUR
CONNOR

Another day, gone.

Warm amber sunlight filtered through gaps in the shivering canopy as Connor led the small band of survivors through the Ancient Woods. The branches above them shook as several squirrels chittered and raced through the canopy. His eyes narrowed with suspicion as he watched them tail his group, no doubt looking for something to steal.

Furry thieves with fuzzy tails. That's all they were.

His bones ached. He had gotten a few hours of sleep, but it wasn't enough. Nothing was, anymore. His stomach gnawed at him from the inside out, demanding more food and water than the forest could provide. His head thumped with exhaustion, but he pushed through. He had to. For his new charges to be safe, they had to return to the treehouse by nightfall.

Up ahead, the ghoul slipped through the trees, visible for only seconds before he disappeared into a black cloud of smoke. It seemed pointless for the wraith to hide, since the survivors had all seen him last night, but Connor kept the undead king strategically occupied with scouting ahead to keep him from unsettling his new company.

An incessant itch tingled again along his scalp, and he brushed some of the caked filth from his hair with a haphazard shake of his head. As he had done so often on this trek, he glanced over one shoulder to study the survivors who had taken him up on his offer to join him in Slaybourne.

In the back, a cluster of three harried mothers ushered their five young children along the path. The poor women walked with their arms outstretched, herding the young ones like easily distracted sheep that kept trying to race through the nearest cluster of brambles. The kids—each no older than ten, he figured—kept trying to dart past their mothers and into the underbrush, just to see if they would come out unscathed. Fiona giggled along with the newcomers, twirling around with her new friends and cartwheeling across the uneven terrain with the first children her age she had ever met. As they played, their incessant giggles and lighthearted shrieks of delight pierced the otherwise silent air.

He let them make noise. The kids had to vent their energy one way or another, and he preferred laughter to the uncontrollable sobbing he'd heard last night. Most of them were too young to understand what they had witnessed, and if they could find joy on a tedious walk through the forest, he wouldn't stifle it.

Besides, nothing dangerous would venture out into the forest until after dark.

The only child who refused to play was Isabella. In somber silence, she walked between him and her mother. The little girl hugged herself tightly, her eyes on her tattered shoes as they marched, and Kiera kept one hand on the girl's back. Despite the uneven ground and the occasional need to climb fallen logs in their path, her hand never left the girl for long.

Sandwiched between the harried mothers and his small party at the front, two young women about his age walked in tight step with each other. The brunette clutched a shawl around her torso, and the blonde rubbed her bare arms as her hair hung in long curls over her shoulders. They whispered in hushed tones, mostly about the forest from what he'd overheard thus far. As he looked their way, however, their eyes darted toward him, and they went silent. The blonde grinned, slow and sultry. The brunette's cheeks flushed red as her chest stilled, like he had taken her breath away.

It hit him, then—the primal urge to have his way with them.

The insatiable lust started in his core and snaked down his thighs, like a lever flipping. Even in his tired state, his ravenous instinct demanded that he bend them both over the nearest log and have his way with them.

The desire—no, the *need*—hit him square in the chest.

His throat tightened as he fought the primal urge. Even the thought of it revitalized him and gave him a boost of energy he didn't think he had left in his reserves.

Either of them would be willing, the ghoul said. *Perhaps even at the same time. The brunette can barely breathe when you look at her. Watch.*

Instead of indulging the undead king's pent-up frustrations, Connor let out a steadying breath and returned his focus to the path ahead. He couldn't deny that the urges had gotten stronger the longer he tried to suppress them. He hated to think the wraith was right, but he didn't know how much longer he could fight these urges.

While the young women certainly seemed willing, it simply wasn't the right time to make an advance. For starters, they had to return to the treehouse by dark, and he wasn't about to bed a woman with witnesses just to sate a primal impulse. Most importantly, however, was the fact that those young women had nearly been sold into slavery. Trying anything now would be taking advantage of them both at a vulnerable time, and that wasn't the sort of man his father raised him to be.

He did his best to stuff down the sexual urge, but it persisted, like an irritating thought in the back of his mind that refused to die or let him focus.

The ghoul let out an infuriated growl. *You're going to drive us both mad, damn you.*

Connor shrugged.

He had plenty of choice words for the wraith, but he had opted for silence on the long trek back to the treehouse to keep from alarming those around him. He didn't want the women to think he was unhinged, even if the Wraith King sometimes made him question his sanity.

The trickle of a nearby stream blended with the distant crash of the waterfall as they got closer to the treehouse, and he let out a sigh of relief. They had made it with at least an hour of daylight to spare.

With the children derailing them so often along their route, it was something of a miracle.

Mixed with his relief, however, came a flood of dread. In just a few minutes, they would step into the clearing and find out if Sophia and Quinn had been able to rescue Ethan and Wesley, or if both men had lost their fights with Death.

He swallowed hard and steeled himself for the worst.

"I can't." Kiera paused in her tracks and turned her back on him. She sobbed and tugged on the frizzy braids of her hair, hiding her face even from Isabella as she trembled. "I can't go back, Connor. I just can't do it."

"Take a quick break, everyone." He gestured to the rest of the band to pause.

The adults nodded, and the children shrieked with glee at the chance to explore a bit. One of the boys darted off into the forest, yelling all the way, and his mother let out an exasperated groan as she watched him bolt.

"William, stay close!" The woman wiped her face with a dirty hand and lifted her skirts as she charged off into the bushes after her son.

The other two mothers, however, watched Kiera with pity. They huddled together by a cluster of aspens and whispered in hushed tones, but their eyes always darted back toward her. While they spoke, the two young women sat on a nearby log, and their conversation died. Both of them stared at the ground, and one leaned her elbows against her knees as her eyes slipped out of focus.

Walking kept them all from remembering, and their goal of reaching the treehouse by dark had propelled them forward. Whenever they paused, though, reality hit them again. He'd seen this every time they'd taken a break for water, but there was nothing he could do to help them.

Not with this.

Wordlessly, Isabella grabbed her mother's hand and looked up at her face. They had washed most of the blood from the girl's scar in one of the streams they had passed, but the bright mark still ran from her temple to her jaw. In the setting sunlight, it glowed, redder than ever.

As Kiera looked down at her daughter, her shoulders shook with tears she could no longer restrain.

Connor scratched at the back of his head as he debated how to best approach this. Isabella had already endured so much, and she didn't need to see her mother's pain, too.

Every child eventually realized their parents had flaws. Weaknesses.

Holes. That moment of realization scraped away at their perception of the world, and it left them wondering what was truly safe.

That was the moment the last of their innocence died, and if he could save a bit of Isabella's, he would try.

Connor knelt by the girl's side and subtly gestured to the two young women sitting on the log. "I think those two need a guardian, kid. I'm going to talk to your mother, so do me a favor, will you? Go make sure those ladies are alright."

Isabella frowned with concern, and she studied his face for a moment. Her eyes reminded him of an old woman's, then—far older and wiser than her frail little body. He wondered if she could see through his façade, but he didn't let his doubt show on his face.

After another moment, she nodded and silently trudged toward the blonde and brunette.

With Isabella distracted, he set his hand on Kiera's back. She trembled, her body shaking with each sobbing breath, but he resisted the impulse to tell her everything would be fine. It was a lie, and she would instantly see through it.

She needed to burn off the grief until she could face what awaited them both. He couldn't solve this for her, so he simply let her cry.

It was all he could do.

"When they dragged us away, I shattered," she said through shaky breaths. Her face flushed red with her tears as she hastily wiped them away. She stared out at the forest, up the gentle slope toward the waterfall hidden by the trees. "Right now, I can hope they're alive, but to go back and find out for certain… to see the aftermath… Connor, I just can't do it."

Yet again, he fought the urge to tell her about the healers treating both men. He didn't want to get her hopes up—or his own.

"Whatever you do, don't go into the treehouse," he said quietly. "There's no salvaging it."

She choked on a sob and shut her eyes as she buried her face in her hands once again.

"But," he continued, "there wasn't much carnage on the ground when

I left. My team will have cleaned up the worst of it by now, and I'll shield you and the girls from the rest as best I can."

"Your team?" She sniffled and wiped her nose on her sleeve.

He nodded.

"When did you get a team, Connor?"

"It's a long story," he said with a shrug. "I'll explain later."

"Okay," she said, her voice barely loud enough to hear. With a shaky breath, she nodded and surrendered to whatever awaited them in the clearing. "I'll do my best."

He gently squeezed her shoulder and whistled to the rest of the group. "We're almost there. Everyone, this way."

"Fiona," Kiera called. "Come here, darling. Isabella, you, too."

The youngest Finn daughter cartwheeled back to her mother, while Isabell ran over like the hounds of hell were after her. Both grabbed Kiera's hands and clung tightly at her side. Fiona's smile fell as she scanned the forest, as though she hadn't realized where they were. As though it had all come crashing back in that instant.

He led the way through the broken underbrush. As they neared, the creak of the treehouse swaying in the wind filtered through the trees. Kiera gasped softly, but her steps didn't falter.

In the distance, the muffled splash of water hitting skin filtered through the trees. Moments later, a man sighed happily. Just as quickly as it had come, though, the sigh faded into the rush of the waterfall. The man's voice had been a higher pitch than Murdoc's deep baritone, and despite his best efforts, Connor stiffened with hope that he had tried so hard not to indulge.

They were so close.

He sidestepped a large claw print filled with stagnant water. In his rush to get to the campsite, he almost ignored Nocturne's footprint. He almost pushed ahead.

Until a single, resonating thud shook the earth, and he remembered that he was the only one present who knew to expect the dragon.

Connor grimaced with irritation at himself as a second thud shook the earth. Around him, the survivors frowned as the ground stilled once again.

One of the mothers surveyed the canopy, while others stared off into the trees. Murmurs filtered through the small band as they asked each other if they had heard the same thing.

"Whatever happens, you're safe." He looked over his shoulder and briefly made eye contact with the six other adults in his band. "I have—"

The branches above them creaked and shifted, drowning out his voice as Nocturne's massive head broke through the canopy. The prince of dragons studied the small band that had joined Connor and nodded at them in welcome. "Good evening, my dear ladies."

They screamed.

Nocturne flinched, as though they had slapped him with their shrieks of terror.

"It's alright." Connor stepped between them and Nocturne. He raised his hands to soothe the clustered band of frightened survivors huddling together under the dragon's gaze. "He's on our side."

"I apologize for startling you." Nocturne's voice shook the earth, perhaps even more than his steps had moments before. "I mean no harm."

One of the children began to cry.

Connor let out a frustrated sigh, and he ran his hand through his hair as he tried to figure out how he could salvage this. Even with him close by, Kiera and Isabella held each other close, trembling as they stared up at the dragon.

But not Fiona. The youngest Finn child beamed with joy. As she stared up at the hulking behemoth, she giggled and clapped her hands, as if asking for the show to continue.

Despite the chaotic moment, Connor chuckled. Growing up in this forest had burned the fear out of her, just as it had done for him, but at least she could still enjoy its sunshine.

"He's safe," Connor promised everyone again, his tone firm and unyielding.

The clustered survivors began to slowly relax. Though most remained speechless, the braver among them muttered softly to themselves, their voices overlapping.

"...a dragon, Bethany..."

"…can't be…"

"…who is this man?"

At the last question, the young woman with a frizzy brown braid looked at him, and he cleared his throat uncomfortably.

"Come on," he said as he gestured for them to follow. "We don't have much daylight left."

Cautiously, the survivors obeyed, though they gave Nocturne a wide berth. The dragon thankfully understood their caution and retreated wordlessly into the forest. His thundering steps shook the canopy, and even the children stuck close behind Connor this time.

"A dragon?" Kiera hissed under her breath, glaring at Connor. "You could've warned us!"

"I know." He shot her a half-hearted grin. "Apologies."

Strange, how quickly a dragon had become commonplace.

Just before the edge of the clearing, he paused. The last row of low-hanging branches blocked most of his view of what lay beyond, and he took a settling breath before he shoved his way through the foliage.

At the base of the treehouse, Murdoc inspected one of the ladder rungs. As he poked it with his finger, a chunk of wood fell off into his hands. He stiffened and glanced around for witnesses before haphazardly trying to shove it back against the trunk.

Standing by the edge of the small lake, Quinn and Sophia spoke in hushed tones. Quinn's arms were crossed in front of her chest, while Sophia gestured repeatedly up to the treehouse. Their brows furrowed with anger, and whatever they were talking about, they barely paused long enough to glance his way as the survivors' steps crashed through the underbrush.

To Connor's relief, Wesley and Ethan both sat by the bank. Ethan sat on a rock beside his son, while Wesley knelt on the bank and scooped water from the lake with both hands. He splashed his face and sighed again, his eyes shutting with bliss as the cool water rolled over the bright pink scars on his neck.

Both Finns stared out at the water in a moment of shared silence, very much alive.

The tension in Connor's back disappeared in a rush. He briefly closed his eyes and thanked the Fates. Sophia was a miracle worker, and with this gift, he now owed her more than he could ever repay. Quinn had also kept her word, and he couldn't even articulate the depths of his gratitude for them both.

Kiera couldn't speak. Her eyes welled with tears, and she ran full bore across the clearing. Isabella and Fiona did their best to match her speed, and their tiny fists pumped at their sides as they tried to keep up. On the bank, Wesley peered over one shoulder and grinned broadly as he stood to greet them.

Ethan smiled and, as he remained seated on his rock, awkwardly shifted his weight. The movement revealed the nub of a leg that had survived his brush with death. He grabbed a branch off the ground and tried to stand, but Kiera reached him before he could make much progress. The five Finns hugged each other tightly, tears streaming down every face as they knelt around Ethan's rock, holding each other.

Behind Connor, the remaining survivors turned away. Most of them sniffled, and one of the mothers held one hand over her mouth as her shoulders shook. Tears welled in her eyes, and she gasped with pain as she turned her back on the Finns.

It was a reunion none of the other survivors would get.

This was why they had asked to come with him. None of them had anything left in Saldia. Their husbands, their fathers, their families, their homes, their farms, their animals—everything was gone.

Because of the slavers' cruelty, these women had nothing left but each other.

He cleared his throat, unable to look them in the eye. "Get some rest. I'll try to find some food, but the lake should be clean enough to drink."

They nodded, but didn't reply.

"Connor!" Ethan shouted. "Wesley, my boy, help me up."

The man wrapped one arm around Wesley's shoulder as the kid struggled to lift him to his feet. Kiera slipped under his other arm, and together they got him onto his remaining foot. Wesley gave him the gnarled branch with a curl wide enough to slip under his armpit, and he hobbled forward on the makeshift crutch.

"I've got it." Ethan pecked her on the cheek and forced a smile, though his eyes strained with pain. "I do, Kiera, really."

She kissed him roughly, right on the lips, and held his face in her hands. Their eyes locked, and for a while, they said nothing. She ignored Connor, ignored the meadow, ignored everything around her as she held him tightly. Her lip quivered as she set her forehead against his, and the two of them closed their eyes.

Reunited.

"I know you and Connor need to talk," she whispered, though Connor's enhanced senses easily picked up each word. "But I want your full attention the moment you're done."

Ethan smiled, his gaze roaming her face as he sighed happily, and he ran his thumb across her lip. "Yes, ma'am."

With her hands still cradling his face, Kiera lingered in the seconds that followed. She forced a strained smile and backed away, until she had no choice but to let him go, and reluctantly turned her back on him and Connor. She cast one more look of longing over her shoulder, but ultimately shifted her attention to Wesley. Isabella joined her, still hovering close by.

Fiona, however, didn't budge. The little girl stood at her father's side, frowning at his missing leg, and Ethan ruffled her hair with his free hand as he leaned on his crutch.

Kiera clicked her tongue. "Fiona, baby, let's give them a minute."

"Okay, Mama." Fiona squeezed her father's hand before joining her mother. As she retreated, however, she cast one last confused look over her shoulder, apparently still unsure what to make of his missing limb.

Connor walked over, keen to keep Ethan from trying to walk far, but the man seemed stubbornly determined to walk. Ethan limped over, and he grimaced with each halting step. The carpenter set his free hand flat against his chest and did his best to keep his balance. Though Connor quickly closed the distance between them, Ethan wouldn't stop trying to walk. His teeth clenched with every wobbly step.

For a moment, Connor wondered if he had done the right thing. Sophia had saved his life, sure, but now Ethan would live out the rest of his years in agonizing pain.

When he reached the man, Connor offered him a hand to shake. Ethan smacked it away and, instead, wrapped his free arm around Connor to pull him into a hug. He gripped Connor tightly, and the man sniffled.

"You came back." Ethan's voice cracked. He roughly cleared his throat, but he couldn't hide the water pooling in his eyes. "Fates above, Connor. I can't believe you came back."

"Of course," Connor said quietly. "Come on, sit. You shouldn't be on your—"

"—feet?" Ethan finished with a dry cackle, somewhere between a sarcastic laugh and a pained sob. "Only got one of those left, now."

Connor didn't respond, mostly because he didn't know what to say. He shook his head as he helped Ethan sit again on the boulder, and his chest tightened as he thought of how close he had come to losing these good people.

Staying away hadn't kept them safer, and he would never make that mistake again.

Ethan groaned with pain as he sat again on the rock, and he grabbed Connor's shoulder for balance as he settled in. Connor knelt, his forearm close by in case Ethan lost his balance again. The man leaned toward Connor's ear with a subtle twist of his head.

"Tell me you killed them," he whispered.

Connor stiffened, but Ethan's grip on his shoulder tightened. The man glared him dead in the eye as he waited for an answer.

As the waterfall crashed behind them, Connor nodded.

"All of them?"

"All but one."

Ethan shook his head in disappointment. "For what they did to us, I wanted them all dead."

"I did, too," Connor admitted.

In the lull that followed, he stole a quick glance at Isabella. The girl knelt on the bank and watched her rippling reflection. She tilted her head and ran her finger along the long red line on her cheek, but she didn't react. Her smooth features remained stoic and calm.

She was too brave for her own good.

At the tree line, Quinn stood with Sophia and Murdoc. Though his team were lost in a deep conversation, Quinn's gaze rested on Isabella. The Starling warrior's brows pinched with concern, and she ran a delicate finger over the scar in her palm, as though seeing Isabella's scar reminded her of her own.

"Go on," Ethan said, gesturing to the three warriors at the edge of the clearing. "They've been worried about you, son."

Son.

The word hit him in the chest with a soft pang, but Connor smiled and wordlessly stood. Kiera patted him on the arm as the rest of the Finns returned to Ethan's side and hugged him tightly once again.

As though they were all afraid to let go.

The soft murmur of conversation filled the air as he neared his team, and it took effort to resist looking over his shoulder as he left the Finns to talk amongst themselves. Murdoc grinned and smacked Connor hard on the shoulder in welcome, but Sophia's nose scrunched in disgust.

"You smell like a slaughterhouse," she said.

Connor laughed. "Hello to you as well, Sophia."

"Let me heal her," Quinn interrupted.

Connor's smile fell as he followed the Starling warrior's gaze across the lake to Isabella. "You'd be willing to do that?"

The Starling woman nodded stiffly.

He frowned as he debated whether or not to allow it. As far as he could tell, her concern seemed genuine. She had healed Wesley, true to her word, and he doubted she would do something reckless or destructive now.

"If you can heal her, give it all you've got," he said with a nod toward the girl.

Quinn slipped past him, but he grabbed her arm before she stepped out of range. She looked down at his hand on her bicep and raised one eyebrow in a silent challenge.

"Thank you," he said quietly, almost unwilling to believe he was saying it. "For everything."

The irritated creases in her forehead faded, and she offered him a thin smile. "Don't get used to me rescuing you, outlaw."

He chuckled and released her. She adjusted the bag on her shoulder, and when she reached the Finns, she knelt at Isabella's side. Kiera's eyes widened in surprise, and the woman gaped wordlessly at Quinn's trademark Starling hair. Quinn's back was to him as she rifled through her pack, and the soft hum of their quiet conversation blended with the waterfall as Connor resisted the urge to hover over her and watch her every move.

"Keep an eye on her, will you?" he asked the wraith under his breath.

The wraith groaned in irritation, but otherwise didn't reply. Connor took that as a reluctant yes.

"I owe you an apology." He crossed his arms and shifted his attention to Sophia.

The necromancer squinted at him in confusion. "Did you hit your head?"

He ignored the jibe.

"When I found them—" He cleared his throat, unwilling to say anything else about the horror he'd felt finding Ethan and Wesley's mutilated bodies. "I was unfair to you. What you did to save Ethan shows me exactly how powerful you are, Sophia. I cannot thank you enough."

"Yeah, you hit your head." She leaned her weight on one hip and set her hands on her waist. "Don't apologize. It's unnerving."

He closed his eyes in annoyance and crossed his arms, wishing that she could—for once—take this seriously. "Sophia, damn it—"

"No, I get it," she interrupted. "You were scared for their lives. I didn't take it personally."

"Good."

"Besides…" Her gaze shifted toward the Finns, and her shoulders relaxed. "When I was little, all I wanted was for someone to care about me that much."

The fading light cast soft orange glow across the clearing as she swallowed hard, refusing to look at him. Murdoc set one hand on her shoulder as the gentle murmur of conversation blended with the waterfall. The necromancer blinked rapidly, as though Murdoc's touch had snapped her from a daze.

"I care," Connor said firmly. "We're going to fix your augmentation, Sophia."

"I guess we'll see." With an awkward twitch of her head, she raised her chin defiantly and stalked off toward the treehouse, leaving Connor and Murdoc in stunned silence.

The former Blackguard watched her leave and sighed. "We can do it, right?"

Connor sighed. "I think so."

"She's been strange." Murdoc shook his head, his eyes glued to her as she retreated across the clearing. He set his hands on the back of his head, his elbows wide, and huffed in frustration. "The way she's been talking, Captain... I don't like it. I think she's going to bolt. After she's healed, I mean."

"She might." Connor studied the soldier's face as he let that thought settle on the air between them.

Murdoc swallowed hard and kicked a rock into the lake. It hit the water with a deep plop, and the former Blackguard glared at the lingering ripples. "I don't want her to go. I joke about her being my wife, but... but I'm not..."

"I know," Connor said quietly. "Look, you can't control her. Life is about what you let go of. What's real stays with you."

With a long, steady sigh, Murdoc shut his eyes and simply nodded. "A man can hope though, can't he?"

"Hope never did me much good."

"Good talk." Murdoc shot him an irritated sidelong glare.

Connor shrugged. "I'm not who you should come to for uplifting speeches."

"Clearly."

Branches shifted, distant at first but growing closer. Nocturne's steady footsteps thudded through the forest, and a flock of birds startled into the air as the steps circled around to the edge of the woodland behind Connor and Murdoc. The dragon poked his head out of the canopy, and as he did, snapped twigs rained down on them. Leaves tumbled in his exhale and floated up toward the ambling clouds.

"I DO NOT LIKE YOUR FORESTS," the dragon prince grumbled.

"*Our* forests?" Connor chuckled. "What exactly are yours like?"

"For starters, we have real trees." Nocturne snorted impatiently. "Tall ones, where I can walk between the trunks without getting smacked in the head."

Murdoc whistled, apparently impressed. "Those must be massive trees."

A giggle floated over the crashing water, and Connor looked over his shoulder to find Fiona clapping happily as she again stared up at the dragon.

"It seems you have an admirer." Connor smirked up at their prince of darkness.

"I did not expect you to return with guests," the dragon admitted, his booming voice a bit softer than normal.

"Nor did I," he admitted. "How many can you carry?"

Nocturne snorted in irritation, and a puff of black smoke rolled over them. "I am a prince, not a pack mule."

Little footsteps crunched across the dirt and gravel along the bank as Fiona ran toward them. She paused beside Connor and hopped anxiously on her tip-toes as she stared up at the legendary creature. A delighted grin spread across her face, so wide that her eyes strained from the effort.

"Mr. Dragon, sir?" she asked in a squeaky voice.

Nocturne lowered his head until he was right in front of her. "Yes, little one?"

"Can I pet you?" Fiona clapped her hands again.

Murdoc snorted and shook with laughter. "He's a dragon, not a cat."

The legendary prince tilted his head curiously as he examined the little girl, but ultimately nodded.

Fiona set her palm against the dragon's nose. His massive face dwarfed her tiny hand, and as he exhaled, his breath toyed with her loose blonde hair. She scratched her tiny fingernails against his scales, and the dragon's eyes dilated. He relaxed under her touch, and to Connor's surprise, a gentle purring filled the air.

The little girl giggled again and patted his nose. "Thank you, Mr. Dragon, sir!"

"You are welcome, child."

She skipped back along the bank toward her family. As she approached,

Quinn finally stood and slung her bag over her shoulder.

Nocturne's purr faded into the roar of the waterfall as he watched the little girl return to the cluster of Finns. "I ENJOY THAT ONE."

"That was definitely a purr." Murdoc laughed. "Maybe I was wrong—I think the term 'cat' suits you just fine."

"You're not ferocious at all, are you?" Connor added as he grinned up at the towering beast. "All that 'prince of dragons' nonsense is just a façade."

Nocturne shook his head in irritation but let out a resigned sigh. "YES, I CAN CARRY YOU ALL. IT WILL SLOW ME DOWN. WE MAY NEED ONE ADDITIONAL DAY, BUT IT IS DOABLE."

We have already lost so much time. The wraith's voice echoed through Connor's head, grim and dark as ever. *With Teagan Starling on the warpath, we cannot afford these delays, Magnuson.*

"I know." Connor's grin faded, and he stared up at the canopy as the last crimson shreds of daylight cast a deep red glow across the leaves.

He had saved the Finns, but it wasn't a victory he could savor for long. Their war with the Lightseers hadn't even begun, and his already impossible task had already become that much harder.

As Fiona leaned her head against her father's bulky arm, however, Connor smiled. Delays or not, this had been worth it—every lost second.

CHAPTER THIRTY-FIVE
OTMUND

In the mist-drenched moors of northern Saldia, an ancient city as old as the Fates themselves rose from emerald-green fields. Every building, from the castle to the smallest farmhouse, had been built with stones from the hillside. In the mornings, fog from the towering forest meandered through the wheat fields surrounding the tall gray walls that encased the city's core. At night, howls from the woodland reminded the locals of how much existed beyond the world they knew, most of which they would never understand.

Or so the legends claimed.

Otmund had never been one for stories, except perhaps when he was the one spinning the tales. Since Teagan had eyes in every corner of Saldia, Otmund had ordered heavy curtains to be hung over the carriage windows to ensure privacy along his journey. He lifted one and snuck a glance out the window at the horizon, trying to get one last view of the forest beyond Freymoor's inner walls, but the gray stone blocked most of his view. From here, he could see only the looming mist churning above the canopy. A flock of pigeons resting on the city's outer wall took to the air, their fluttering wings muffled by the carriage's thick windows.

It had always struck him as odd that the people had never cleared the forest growing by the city ramparts. The trees practically blended in with the stone, close enough to touch. Spring had come to Freymoor, but as always, a looming cluster of gray clouds drowned out the noon sky. Beautiful as this place was, the sun never seemed to shine on it.

On the main road, the people of Freymoor meandered at a leisurely pace through the shops' open doors. On occasion, the carriage passed a soldier wearing the white and gold uniform of the Oakenglen army, usually leaning against a wall with his eyes closed and his spear resting beside him.

Otmund huffed in disgust. Fat. Lazy. Bored out of their minds. The elite warriors in Oakenglen's army weren't sent to Freymoor. He'd heard the top brass used an assignment to Freymoor as punishment. One year in this place, and any decent soldier would be begging for relocation, no matter what it took to get out.

Across from him, two of the Nethervale elite sat with their backs straight as they held aside the curtains and scanned the world beyond the windows. Their eyes never settled on one thing for more than a second. Though dressed head to toe in the stolen Lightseer uniforms he had procured for them, they surveyed their surroundings with the withering scowls of two assassins sizing up their next mark.

"Stop frowning, damn it," Otmund grumbled. "No one's going to believe you're from Lunestone if you stare at them like you're going to steal the silver."

Only one of the necromancers looked at him, and the man's scowl only deepened.

"Ain't right," the other one grumbled, his gaze still locked on something out the window. "Wearin' a Lightseer's clothes. How many of us have those bastards killed this year alone, Lance?"

"Twenty." Lance crossed his arms and glared out the window.

"Twenty," the other necromancer echoed as his nose wrinkled with disgust. "Monsters, the lot of them. With what they did to my brother, it be a sin donnin' their clothes. Just ain't right."

"Shut your mouths, both of you." Otmund let out a frustrated sigh and peeked through the curtains as the first tower of Freymoor castle came into view. "I don't want to be in this mud-caked hellhole, either, but it's necessary. Focus. What else can you tell me about Freymoor? Have either of you been here?"

In unison, the two brooding necromancers shook their heads.

Otmund pinched the bridge of his nose to stifle yet another irritated sigh. In his chest, his heart thudded anxiously against his ribcage. Something had changed. The silent, obedient soldiers had been slowly corroding, bit by bit, since he'd found the informant. Nyx still hadn't returned from the decoy mission he had given her, and as far as he knew, she'd had no contact with her soldiers. Originally, he had figured this would work in his favor, but now he wondered if her elite fighters were getting sloppy without her around to strike terror into the withered husks of their hearts.

With no more tricks up his sleeve, these soldiers were Otmund's best chance at survival. Between these two and the fifteen others that would sneak over the walls tonight, he had a small army at his disposal even while the others remained in Mossvale to ensure the second half of his trap remained secure.

As long as they stayed close, he would be fine.

The carriage wheels rumbled over the oldest part of the city's ancient cobblestone road. That was his cue to tie back the curtains, as they had reached the city's inner-most walls. Sure enough, the main staircase and towering front doors of the fortress loomed ahead as the carriage neared.

This was it. Without a Rift in Freymoor—and with his influence over the Oakenglen castle corroding by the day—he had wasted almost a week traveling to this crumbling city. Whatever he had to do to convince the Lady of Freymoor to part with the Soulsprite, he needed to do it quickly. He sifted through his options, still debating between threatening her or pretending he could save her from impending doom. In the dozens of backdoor dealings he had secretly arranged over the years, he had quietly stripped enough of the kingdom's resources that either tactic would probably work.

His mind raced with possibilities, and his eyes glossed over as the carriage pulled to a stop. Still undecided on his method, he opted for charm to buy his soldiers time to hunt for answers.

The carriage door opened with a blinding rush of sunlight. Otmund winced as his eyes adjusted, but he stepped out of the carriage and wrapped his cloak tighter around him in the damp chill. Sprawling ivy covered the worn stone face of the castle, and the towering wooden doors opened just as Otmund's shoes hit the gravel. Two Oakenglen soldiers stood at the top of the main steps leading up to the grand hall. They frowned as he shivered, and without even a salute, they glared into the dark hallway as they held the doors open.

Otmund snorted in annoyance. These soldiers had forgotten their place in the world, and when he was finally king, it would fall to him to remind them.

Within moments, a stately gentleman with neatly combed hair emerged from the shadows beyond the open doors and trotted down the steps. Furs sewn into his leather cloak gave him the appearance of a king, and the bespoke collar covering his entire neck ended at his jawline in the classic style of the Freymoor upper class from the years before Henry's rule. A velvet red rope secured to his cloak with two golden pins were the only pop of color on his otherwise brown uniform.

Duncan Whitlock, advisor to the Lady of Freymoor and—as Otmund suspected, anyway—the true power behind what was left of the throne.

Their eyes met, and though Otmund refused to show the slightest hint of emotion, the man's brows furrowed with concern. A muscle in the man's jaw twitched, and he frowned deeply.

Otmund resisted a smile. These Freymoor fools always gave everything away. They couldn't hide their emotions, and therefore, he could always guess what they were thinking.

Making them dance was almost too easy. At least the Starlings posed a challenge.

Before the advisor could reach the bottom step, the Oakenglen soldiers retreated back into the castle. Another man brushed past them, however, and pushed through the closing doors as he jogged after Duncan. This one dressed in a modest black shirt with dark riding pants, and though he wore no cloak, he seemed entirely unaffected by the cold spring air. He reached the bottom of the staircase in seconds, and his gaze swept the Lightseer carriage without a hint of surprise. In fact, his smooth features betrayed nothing of his emotions at all—no doubt, no concern, no fear.

Nothing.

How curious. Otmund had never seen this one before. His attention lingered on the newcomer a second longer, trying to place his dark hair and stony gaze, but nothing came to mind.

"Lord Soulblud." Duncan frowned deeply and clasped his hands behind his back as he approached. "To what do we owe the pleasure of a visit from a Lightseer Regent?"

Otmund feigned a warm smile, grateful no word had spread of his shaky relationship with Teagan Starling. No one needed to know he was on thin ice with the reigning lord of fire.

"I require an audience with Lady Donahue." He scanned the castle windows, as if searching for her among the intricate stained glass of the timeless castle. "Where is she?"

"The Lady isn't well today. I'm afraid she can't be disturbed until—"

"Oh, but as a Lightseer Regent, I insist," Otmund interrupted. "It's an urgent matter, one I can only discuss with the city's rightful ruler."

Creases appeared in the advisor's forehead as the man's frown deepened, and his eyes narrowed in either suspicion or annoyance.

Maybe both.

"Very well, Lord Soulblud." Duncan turned on one heel and scanned the nearest row of windows as he spoke to the silent man behind him. "See to it the Regent's horses are fed and that his guards have adequate rooms."

The unspoken message was clear—*don't let them out of your sight.*

With a stiff nod, Duncan's assistant clicked his heels together with all the pomp of an army officer doing his best not to salute. Otmund studied the stranger with a bit more care this time as the man walked off toward the driver.

Though he couldn't spot a single weapon on the assistant's body, Otmund had studied warriors for most of his life, and the man carried himself like a soldier. Perhaps the rumors of a secret army in Freymoor had some merit after all.

From behind Otmund, Duncan cleared his throat. "This way, my Lord."

When Otmund returned his attention to the Lady's advisor, the man was already leading the way toward a vine-covered wall built at the far edge of the main courtyard. Emerald-green ivy strangled the gray stone archway built into the wall, and rows of bright yellow roses lined the path beyond it.

Otmund tilted his head toward the necromancers behind him and lowered his voice to an almost inaudible whisper. "Meet me in the gardens once you've gotten your rooms, but don't let anyone see you. And for the love of the Fates, try not to look like criminals while you do it."

The taller of them frowned in annoyance, but they both nodded.

Otmund marched after Duncan, and he had to move at a brisk walk to make up for the man's head start and longer stride.

As he passed beneath the archway into the gardens, the sweet perfume of the roses swam through the air like a heady drug—thick and dreamlike, one that stirred the clouds and reminded him of summer. Beds of fluffy pink asters littered every corner, and clusters of wisteria climbed every wall in the labyrinth of old stone pathways. Most of the original stone lay somewhere beneath the thousands of vines, and the stone walkway beneath his feet cracked under the power of the ancient roots that had made this garden home.

With a casual glance backward, Duncan disappeared through another archway up ahead. Otmund growled softly in frustration. Short of sprinting through the garden, he couldn't match the man's pace.

As Otmund rounded the bend, Duncan's quiet voice blended with the soft gurgle of bubbling water. A frail young woman sat on the edge of a fountain in the center of a rose garden. The advisor to the fallen royalty of Freymoor knelt at her side, speaking in a hushed tone, and even Otmund's augmented ears couldn't make out the man's words.

Damn it.

Patches of moss stained the fountain's central basin as water lapped against its side. The young woman held a white rose in her hands and leaned toward Duncan as he spoke. Her eyes glossed over as she listened, and the tips of her two slippered feet poked out from beneath the flowing hem of her royal blue dress as she fought to balance on her perch.

Otmund stepped into earshot, and he strained to catch any of what Duncan was saying.

"...but he insisted, my Lady."

"Forgive my intrusion, Lady Donahue," Otmund interrupted. He set one hand across his waist and gave an exaggerated bow usually reserved for royalty. "I need to speak with you immediately."

With a slight twitch of his eyebrow, Duncan stood and set one hand protectively on the Lady's shoulder.

"There is nothing to forgive, my Lord." As she released the rose into the fountain's rippling water, Dahlia Donahue offered him a warm but weary smile. Deep bags framed her eyes, as if she hadn't slept in days, and the thin creases in her forehead gave her the appearance of a woman far older than she truly was. It was as if she had aged a decade in the year or so since he had last visited. Her dark blonde hair flowed loose over her shoulders, and her naturally pale skin looked almost white.

How curious.

"I suggest you two speak at dinner," Duncan interjected. "In the meantime—"

"Nonsense." She waved away her advisor's concern with a flick of her frail wrist. "I rarely get visitors. Having company is quite a treat."

Beside her, Duncan's jaw tensed, but he said nothing.

Dahlia watched the white rose as it floated through the fountain's soft ripples. "How are you, Lord Soulblud?"

"Please, my dear, call me Otmund." He couldn't resist the briefest smirk of victory and a quick glance toward Duncan as he said it. "I'm well, but what I need to tell you is a sensitive matter. One we should discuss in private."

"Of course." She stood and brushed off her skirts. "Won't you walk with me through the garden? It's so lovely this time of year."

Given that her groundskeepers used a specially crafted Fieldmane potion to keep the roses blooming year-round, the comment gave Otmund pause. Her soft hair fell over her shoulders, unkept and unbraided, and for a moment, he was speechless. She had fallen further than he had expected into whatever twisted game Duncan was playing with her, and now Otmund wondered if she was, in fact, in danger.

If he were in the advisor's shoes, he would've slowly poisoned her until she was no longer of use. It seemed Duncan was, perhaps, a worthy opponent in this arena of unseen puppet masters.

Without a word and lost in thought as he contemplated how this changed his plans, Otmund offered her his arm. She took it, and her painfully pale hand glowed white in the low light of an overcast day. Together, they walked down the nearest lane of ivy-drenched walls and crimson blooms.

He cast a calculated glance over his shoulder to find Duncan trailing behind, just out of earshot.

Otmund lowered his voice to the barest whisper and leaned his mouth toward Dahlia's ear. "My Lady, you aren't safe."

She laughed, the sound airy and delightful, and it blended into the garden around them like a song. "Don't be ridiculous, dear sir. Oakenglen soldiers are here all the time. They help us keep the streets and castle safe."

In his shock at her sheer naivety, Otmund missed a step and shuffled sideways along the stone path. Her eyes went wide with concern as she reached for him, and he cleared his throat to cover his momentary lapse in judgement.

She gasped in surprise. "My Lord, are you—"

"I'm fine. Truly." He offered a reassuring smile as he adapted his approach. With someone this out of touch from the real world, the best way to manipulate her would be to simply play along with her fantasy. "But I'm afraid not even the Oakenglen soldiers stand a chance against the brutal assassin that's after you, Dahlia. Hell is coming to Freymoor, and it wants the Soulsprite."

She took an astonished step backward, and the last shreds of color drained from her face. The young woman blinked rapidly, her lips parting in shock, and she let out a shallow breath. "How do you know about the Soulsprite?"

"It has taken years," he admitted, mainly because the occasional truth made his lies more believable. "But my spies have alerted me to the danger that's on its way, and we do not have much time."

Her eyes glossed over, and this time, she resumed their walk without threading her arm through his. "Never fear, Lord Soulblud. The mists protect both me and the Soulsprite."

"I'm afraid what's coming for you won't be deterred by the Blood Bogs, my dear."

She paused midstride, but her gaze remained locked on the cracked stone path beneath her feet.

"What's coming for me?" she asked in a terrified whisper.

Otmund debated telling her at least something of the truth, but given her inexperience, she likely couldn't keep secrets. If he were to successfully wield the ghoul after he killed the peasant, he needed its origins to remain a mystery. "An assassin has stolen Henry's wraith, my Lady, and the criminal will not rest until he also has the Soulsprite. He will kill anyone who gets in his way, and he already has blood on his hands. Even with the legends surrounding the mists and your family's connection to this land, you are not safe from him."

The girl stumbled, as if standing on her own two feet had suddenly become too much to bear. She leaned her shoulder into the thick blanket of ivy coating the wall beside her, and she set a thin hand against her neck as her breaths came quicker and quicker.

Behind them, Duncan's footsteps thudded against the stone path.

Otmund had to act quickly. He grabbed the girl's arm, as if offering her support, but he used the moment to lean again toward her ear.

"I barely made it here in time," he hissed under his breath. "Let me help. Let me take the Soulsprite away from here and lead the danger to Mossvale instead. The assassin won't come for you if what he wants is gone."

Through thick locks of her frizzy blonde hair, her eyelids fluttered. Her green eyes slipped in and out of focus as she watched him. "Please—"

"That's enough," Duncan's booming baritone echoed through the quiet garden.

Within seconds, her advisor stood between them. He shoved Otmund aside and grabbed the young woman's waist as he helped her back to her feet. At his touch, her breath slowed, and she leaned into him.

The soft chatter of women's voices filled the air, and seconds later, two maids with their gray hair pinned to their heads rounded a corner farther down the path. They gasped when they saw the Lady leaning against Duncan and rushed to her side, their slippered feet shuffling across the stone with each anxious step. The servants wrapped one of the young woman's arms around each of their shoulders, and with their hands woven around her thin waist, they led her back down the path they had taken to reach her.

Duncan, however, remained at Otmund's side as they silently watched the Lady of Freymoor retreat from the gardens. Only the trickle of water somewhere in the labyrinth of stone walls and ivy filled the void between the two men, and with each of the young woman's retreating steps, the tension in the air thickened.

When she and the maids finally disappeared through the archway, Duncan's glare shifted to Otmund.

"I will only tell you this once," the advisor warned in a low, gravely tone. "I don't care if you are a Lightseer Regent. This is my kingdom, and if you threaten her, you threaten me."

Otmund raised one eyebrow and met the man's intense scowl. "I came with a warning, not a threat."

"How chivalrous," the advisor said dryly. "I suppose you insist on staying, then?"

"Very much so." He smiled at the man's discomfort. "As a gentleman, I must ensure she's safe and well."

The man grumbled under his breath and stalked off after the fallen princess. With his long stride and quick pace, it took mere seconds for him to walk through the same archway that the maids had taken moments before.

As Otmund watched the man vanish behind a towering wall of ivy, his feigned smile slowly fell.

In his hurry, he had erred. He expected her to whisper the secret to him, then and there. Given her tone, it seemed as though she had been close to doing exactly that. If Duncan hadn't intervened, he might already have what he wanted.

The air shifted behind him, and though he hadn't heard a footstep, the sensation of eyes on the back of his head sent a shiver of dread down his spine. Two shadows stretched across the ground at his feet, and he looked over one shoulder to find the two disguised necromancers standing behind him. Both men stared in the direction Duncan had taken, as though they could see through the very walls shielding the man from view.

"Follow him," Otmund ordered. "Find out everything you can about his control over this city. Observe how he interacts with the Lady, but don't kill him until I give the order."

One of the necromancers sighed in disappointment, but Otmund ignored it. For the time being, at least, he needed Duncan alive. It seemed the advisor had more access to Freymoor's secrets than Otmund had originally thought, and that could turn out to be quite useful, indeed.

CHAPTER THIRTY-SIX
QUINN

Back in Slaybourne, Quinn sat on a toppled pillar in a clearing by the lake on the far side of the valley. The way Murdoc told it, they'd come out here because this place had the fewest bones, and thus, it seemed like the best place to house Connor's new guests.

Whether he had liberated them or recruited a secret harem, she still couldn't tell.

Meadow grasses shivered in the rolling winds of yet another beautiful day in this haven of a valley that most people didn't know existed. Silent as ever, she merely studied the throng around her as everyone finally set down their packs from their long journey back to Connor's fortress.

A smattering of faded cobblestones, mostly eaten by moss and time, traced a meandering path through the clearing and into a small gap between the trees circling a massive lake. A small island riddled with boulders protruded from the center of the water. A fish leapt into the air, the sunlight glistening off its scales in much the same way as the moonlight always slid across Nocturne's sleek body.

The dragon had flown off to hunt shortly after they had landed, and now Connor sat on a boulder beside his father—or whoever these people were to him. The necromancer had slipped into the woods quite a while ago, and Murdoc lay on the grass to Quinn's left with his arm draped over his eyes. His pack lay beneath his head like a lumpy pillow, and one leg twitched as he shifted in his sleep.

Frankly, she couldn't tell if he was supposed to be guarding her or taking a nap.

In the shade by the edge of the forest line, Blaze lay on his back as two women and a few of their children scratched his belly. As a dozen hands scratched his head, neck, and stomach, his purring reached a crescendo. It hummed through the valley like low-hanging thunder.

Above him, a flock of birds took flight. Normally, he would've chased them, or at least batted at one or two to see if he could snare an easy lunch. This time, however, he merely leaned into the hands cradling his head as these newcomers petted the first vougel any of them had seen in their lives.

She grinned and shook her head. Her deadly mount, who had ridden with her on more missions than she could remember, had become nothing more than a kitten thanks to this lot.

Quinn stood and brushed the loose grass off her pants. As much as she enjoyed seeing Blaze happy, they had work to do.

"We're watching you, princess," Murdoc said, his arm still draped over his eyes. "Don't get comfortable."

"I'm not going to run." She resisted the urge to roll her eyes as he brought this up yet again. "Even if I were to bolt, where would I go?"

"That's not what I meant." He lifted his arm and squinted in the sudden brightness. His mouth curved downward in a disappointed frown, and he briefly glanced her over in the silence that followed.

At her side, her fingers coiled into a fist, and she didn't answer. He watched her for a few moments before returning to his nap. When he found a suitable position, he let out a contented sigh.

Don't get comfortable.

She wouldn't dare. Not among outlaws.

Grass crunched beneath her boots as she turned her back on Murdoc and headed toward Blaze. As she neared, the two women petting him paused and looked up at her in a blend of horror and awe. Their smiles fell. Their shoulders hunched. They grabbed their children's hands and backed slowly away, their eyes never leaving hers as they retreated along the edge of the forest line.

She almost told them to wait. To come back. To not look at her that way—like she would burn them at the stake for daring to touch what was hers—but their gaping expressions reminded her of Nocturne's warning.

I see a warrior, he had said, *who has never belonged to the world she protects.*

Quinn cleared her throat to hide the uncomfortable knot forming in it. Instead, she sat on the cold soil beside her vougel as he peered through one eye to see what had happened to all his worshipers.

"Some predator you are," she muttered to him.

He stretched his massive paws into the air, his teeth glistening as he yawned, and he growled happily in answer. Still on his back, he shuffled across the ground and inched closer to her in a silent request for her to continue what the others had started.

With a grin and a shake of her head, she scratched his chest. As her fingertips pressed into his fur, their connection opened once again, and a wave of peaceful bliss snaked up her fingers from him.

Warmth. Joy. Love.

Sometimes, she envied Blaze. Even all the money in her family's treasury couldn't buy the sort of peace and happiness he could get from a simple sunbeam. If not for their connection through the enchanted helm on his head, she wouldn't have even known the emotion existed.

As she stroked his soft fur, she scanned the peaceful valley. Several of the women Connor had rescued huddled on a couple of fallen logs at the edge of the forest, chatting in low tones as the children played nearby. The soft hum of muted conversations drifted through the air, tangling with birdsong and the breeze, and she closed her eyes as the southern wind hit her face.

A burst of maniacal giggling shattered the stillness. Fiona—the youngest daughter in the Wraithblade's family—raced barefoot down the cobblestone road, her loose hair fluttering behind her like an unfurled banner. Several seconds later, her mother trailed after her, muttering a string of curses under her breath as she fought to keep up with her child.

Quinn chuckled, but her smile faded as she once again remembered Murdoc's warning.

"You have a mission," she whispered to her pet.

He stiffened under her touch, and his body rumbled with a low growl as he awaited orders.

"I'm leaving again, and you have to stay here."

He whined in disappointment, and his heavy head plopped on the dirt at her feet. The great winged tiger looked up at her, his wide eyes watery, and his nose twitched.

"This time, it's different," she explained, so quietly her lips barely moved. "While I'm gone, it's your duty to protect these people. There are armies coming this way, and they will be scared. Keep them safe, Blaze. Keep them calm."

He rolled onto his stomach, and his eyes narrowed with silent concern. She forced a smile and ran her fingers along his jawline to soothe his worry, but a surge of protectiveness bled through their connection all the same.

"I'll come back," she promised. "You know I always come back."

The shuffle of bare feet over grass interrupted them, and Blaze shifted his attention to something behind Quinn. She followed his gaze to find Isabella, with her hands clasped behind her back, stiffly walking her way.

The long cut along the girl's face had faded to almost nothing, and without Quinn's Eyebright augmentation, she doubted she would've even been able to see it at all. She waited for the girl to walk closer, but all the while, Isabella never once met her eye. The child's gaze remained on the ground, and each of her steps kicked up a little cloud of dust as she dragged her feet across the dirt.

Without a word, she paused in front of Quinn and offered her a familiar bottle, now empty, that she had previously carried behind her back.

"Oh." Quinn took the empty Rectivane bottle and smiled, surprised it had been returned at all. "Thank you."

Though Isabella didn't speak, and though she still didn't meet Quinn's eye, the little girl nodded.

"You look well," Quinn added. "I'm glad to see there isn't a scar."

The child ran a fingertip gently over the line, perfectly tracing the barely-visible scar on her cheek. "It's there. I can still feel it."

Her voice snapped through the air like a whip, meek but still unexpected, and it took a moment for Quinn to rein in her surprise. Thus far, those were the first words she'd heard the girl speak.

"You gave me that potion." Isabella's sharp blue eyes darted toward

Quinn, and they never once wavered.

"I did."

The little girl stiffened. Her eyes shook, and a tear snaked down her cheek. "But I don't understand."

"What don't you understand?"

"You," Isabella admitted quietly. "Connor says I can't trust you, but you're so nice."

Quinn bit back a scathing retort and, instead, swallowed hard.

As Quinn sat on the ground, Isabella closed the gap between them until the Starling warrior had to crane her neck to look up at the child's face. Blaze leaned forward, ready to pounce the second she gave the word, but she clicked her tongue in a wordless order to stand down.

For a few moments, Isabella simply stood there, flexing and curling her fingers as she stiffly sucked in breath after shaky breath. She swallowed hard, her mouth opening and shutting a few times, as if she had so much to say but had somehow forgotten all the words.

"It's alright," Quinn said gently. "Breathe."

Isabella shut her eyes and took another deep breath. She didn't relax at all, but this time, she managed to squeak out a single word. "Why?"

Quinn's brows pinched together, and she tilted her head in confusion as she tried to understand the question. "Are you asking me why I chose to help you?"

Isabella nodded.

Though Quinn didn't let a trace of emotion show on her face, the question gutted her. These people—those who had no power, who needed the strong to speak for them—they had no voice, and she had always sought to give them one. To stand for them when they fell.

And yet, out here in this lawless land, the very people she had spent her life protecting feared her. They backed away slowly. They whispered hushed questions about what she was doing here and what it meant. They debated and discussed, but never to her face.

"How old are you, Isabella?" Quinn leaned forward and wove her fingers together as she met the girl's intense gaze.

"Eleven," the girl squeaked.

"*Eleven*. Fates above." Quinn's heart broke at the thought of someone this young having already seen so much horror. "I was afraid of that."

Isabella frowned, and her lips pursed with a soft pout. "Afraid of what?"

"When I look at you, I see a girl who grew up too fast." Quinn shifted her weight and settled onto her knees, adjusting until she and Isabella were eye to eye. "You've begun to see the cracks in the world. I gave you that potion because, when you look at yourself in the mirror, I don't want you to be reminded of the horrible things you've endured. I don't want you to see what you were, or how the world failed you. I want you to see what you can *become*."

Quinn gently set her hands on the girl's shoulders, knowing full well how fragile this girl was in mind and body.

Deep down, she wondered if she should keep her mouth shut. She debated stopping here, and though she felt someone watching her, she never wavered.

This advice had gotten her through her worst moments, and the time had come to give it to someone else. Someone who needed it more than she ever had.

"You are more than what has happened to you." Quinn lowered her voice to the barest whisper as she said the words her mother had told her so long ago. "We all are."

Isabella's blue eyes shook, and at first, Quinn thought she had made a mistake. That she had broken the girl she had tried to repair. That all the good she had done would backfire, and that the child's fragile little brain had finally fractured.

Instead, Isabella smiled, and her back straightened as she stood a little taller. "Thank you."

A surge of relief flooded Quinn, and she swallowed hard as she released her gentle hold on the girl's shoulders.

To her surprise, Isabella didn't shuffle away. The child launched at her and wrapped her thin arms around the back of Quinn's neck. She knelt there for a moment, the weight of a tiny human on her chest as the hug only tightened, and she sighed in surrender as she hugged the girl back.

This.

Moments like these gave her purpose. To know she had made a difference in even one good person's life—that was a worthy way of living.

Quinn had power, wealth, and influence across this continent, and until now, she had wielded it all for her father's benefit. For her family's name.

No more.

After she had uncovered her father's lies, she had lost faith in not just others, but herself. She had lost her way, and she had forgotten. It wasn't the Lightseers who gave her purpose, but rather people like Isabella.

As lost as Quinn had become in the betrayals and darkness of this world's underbelly, she had almost forgotten its light. There was still something to fight for, here, something more significant than coin or glory, and she wouldn't let people like Henry, the Wraith King, or even Teagan Starling himself snuff it out completely.

A shadow flew overhead, toward the lake, and she scanned the sky for the increasingly familiar silhouette of the only known dragon in existence. Nocturne circled the lake as he descended, and when he finally landed, the ground quaked beneath his massive feet.

Though everyone gathered in the field gaped up at the massive creature, Connor watched her from his perch by the lake. Even from his distance, his unwavering glare warned her to behave as she held a member of his family.

Their eyes met, and her grip on Isabella tightened. In her arms, oblivious to the brewing tension between Quinn and Connor, the little girl sighed happily.

CHAPTER THIRTY-SEVEN

CONNOR

Only ten days remain, Magnuson.

The wraith's voice echoed in Connor's mind, but the ghoul remained out of sight.

With a deep sigh, he leaned the back of his head against a sheer stone wall in the heart of Slaybourne. Exhausted, he rubbed one eye with the heel of his palm.

He needed a minute to himself.

It had taken four nights of travel, but they had flown through the gates of Death's Door shortly after dawn. He had slept for a few hours while on Nocturne's back, and he'd sighed with relief the moment he'd been able to change out of his decimated clothes stained with the blood of all those slavers. He now wore the bright blue tunic Sophia had forced him to buy back in Oakenglen, when they'd killed Richard Beaumont.

It had been nonstop bustle since they had returned. The survivors needed homes. The farmlands needed to be retaken from the overgrown forest, and the paths to the lake at the eastern edge of the valley needed to be repaired. It was more work than he and his team could manage before they left at dusk, but he would do his best to provide for those in his care.

At sunset, he and his team would leave for Quinn's augmentor, and his race against Teagan Starling would continue. For now, he had to wait for the cover of darkness.

Teagan's spies could be anywhere in Saldia—even in the Decay.

The soft twitter of birdsong filtered through the rustling leaves overhead, and he shut his eyes to savor the cool spring day. A gentle breeze rolled through the ancient woodland, and the crunch of a deer ripping grass from the dirt punctuated the mid-morning air.

He stood in the shade of a half-destroyed building. Its two remaining walls towered over the forest, and its imposing black stone cast a long shadow across the fallen leaves covering the uneven forest floor. His twin swords rested against his back in their sheaths, as they always did, but he could barely remember the last time he had drawn them for a fight.

Not even Beck Arbor's legendary design could compare to the wraith's blackfire blades.

Through a gap in the trees ahead of him, Quinn and her tiger-bird sat in the nearby field and enjoyed the sunshine. She rested her head on the vougel's stomach, her eyes closed and a thin smile on her face to absorb the warmth. Blaze craned his neck to look at her face and dangled the tip of his wing over her nose. Eyes still closed, she laughed and batted it away, as though it were a fly, and the vougel's wing shot just out of reach before she could brush its feathers.

Connor shook his head. He did *not* understand this woman.

He'd kept a close watch on her since they returned with the survivors, but her demeanor had shifted the moment she saw them. Though they mostly kept their distance, they went to her when they needed something—not him. He couldn't begrudge her for it, though, since a Starling was still a familiar sight among the chaos. To his surprise, she indulged their every request. Even her focus had shifted away from studying him and toward helping these complete strangers.

Nothing but a ploy to win their favor, according to Sophia's cynical mutterings. Connor, however, wasn't so sure.

The more she healed the survivors or listened to them as they relived their horrors, the more she seemed in her element. He would never admit it to her face, but she acted like the sort of person worthy of the Lightseer legends. Helpful. Caring. Compassionate.

Something told him Teagan Starling wouldn't be as concerned with the survivors' welfare when the Lightseer army reached Slaybourne.

Based on the original dates Quinn had given, they had only ten days before Teagan's earliest arrival window. Though he doubted even the Master General of the Lightseers could reach him so quickly, but he wanted to prepare for the worst-case scenario.

On the other side of the ruin wall, soft footsteps crunched against the dry leaves as someone approached. The rustle of skirts didn't do much to narrow down who it was, and he couldn't place the gait as the newcomer trekked at a steady pace despite the uneven terrain. A long shadow stretched across the decaying autumn leaves, and a familiar voice muttered quietly to herself as she sidestepped a branch lying on the ground.

Kiera.

With his head still resting against the ruin wall, Connor closed his eyes. "Over here."

The footsteps paused, and Kiera gasped in surprise. Seconds later, after a bit more shuffling and the continued rustle of skirt fabric, she let out an impatient sigh. "There you are. I've been looking everywhere for you."

"Is Ethan still sleeping?"

"Snoring loud as ever." She chuckled, and she leaned against the wall beside him. "I don't mind. Lets me know he's alive."

Connor didn't reply, except to open his eyes and stare out at the sunlit field beyond the forest.

"He's hurting, though," Kiera added softly. "Haven't seen him in this much pain since we lost Kenzie."

"I'll make it right," Connor promised. "I don't know how, but if the magic's out there, I'll find it."

She clicked her tongue. "You've given us so much already."

He shook his head. Nothing he had done so far seemed like enough.

"A Starling prisoner," Kiera gestured toward Quinn and her vougel. "An untouched haven behind a legendary gate. A ghoul tethered to you by magic I can't begin to understand, and a Lightseer army on the way."

"I've been busy," he said with a dry laugh.

Kiera didn't laugh along with him. She simply watched Quinn and the tiger-bird as they curled up together in the sunshine. "Are the Lightseers coming here for her?"

"Yes," Connor admitted. "And no. They're after the ghoul. They're after me. I think they're afraid of what I might become."

Though her lips pursed with unspoken questions, Kiera thankfully didn't ask anything else. He wanted to tell the Finns everything—what he was, and who the wraith had been in life—but this hardly seemed like the time.

"Murdoc and Sophia are finishing the safe room as we speak," Connor said to change the subject. "If all else fails, you need to get to the catacombs."

"You told us to stay out of the catacombs."

"You're right." He rubbed his tired eyes. "That's why you can only go there if the Lightseers breach the walls. We're doing our best to make it safe enough for you to ride out the worst of a siege, if it comes to that."

Kiera wrapped her arms tightly around herself, and the muscles in her neck tightened until he wondered if she could even breathe.

"I don't want you to leave again," she whispered.

A muscle in his jaw twitched, and he let out a pained sigh. He didn't know what to say.

"Isabella doesn't want you to go, either," Kiera added, though she didn't look at him as she spoke. "You know what she said when I told her?"

Connor's jaw tensed, and he watched her silently as he waited for her to continue.

"'Bad things happen when he leaves.'" The woman's voice broke, and she swallowed hard in a barely restrained attempt to strangle a sob.

Connor tilted his head to hide a pained grimace. His chest tightened, and the words hit him like a dagger in the heart.

"Worse things will happen if I don't," he explained.

Around the corner of the towering black ruin, muffled footsteps shuffled across the dirt. The swish and flutter of leaves sailing through the air suggested the newcomer was kicking them. Curious, Connor leaned forward and peered around Kiera to find Wesley meandering through the trees. The boy kicked at the leaves again, and a clump shot into the air. They drifted gently around him, as bright and vibrant as crimson feathers falling to the earth, and he shoved his hands in his pockets with a resigned sigh.

"He hasn't said two words," Kiera muttered under her breath. "Not since the reunion. He's taking it worse than any of us, but he won't talk to me. He won't talk to anyone."

"I'll see what I can do."

"Thank you." Kiera set a gentle hand on Connor's bicep and smiled up at him, though her eyes strained with worry.

Connor pushed off the ruin wall and rubbed the back of his head as he sifted through what he could possibly say to the kid. Though Wesley kicked and crashed through the underbrush, Connor's boots didn't make a sound. He caught up quickly, and for a while, they walked side by side in silence.

Sunbeams broke through the treetops, casting serene spotlights on the twisted roots that wove along the steep dirt slopes. In this section of the forest, the trees loomed overhead, with many of the lowest branches too high for even Connor to reach.

After a few minutes of their silent march, Wesley casually glanced up. The boy flinched in surprise as he finally noticed Connor walking beside him. He set a hand on his heart and doubled over, sucking in deep breaths as he fought to subdue the surge of panic.

"Damn it," Wesley muttered. "Don't do that to people!"

Connor chuckled. "I didn't mean to startle you."

"Wish I had that kind of stealth."

"It's possible. Sophia's brewing your Eyebright augmentation and will ink that before we leave tonight. She can give you a Prowlport augmentation, too, if you ask her soon."

Wesley scowled and shoved his hands in his pockets again. He kicked at the leaves and shook his head. "Don't waste the spellgust. I'm useless."

Connor frowned. "That's a hell of a thing to say about yourself, kid."

"It's the truth." The boy continued his trek through the woods, but he wouldn't look at Connor this time. "A lot of help I was when they attacked us."

"You were outnumbered."

"Wouldn't have mattered to you." Wesley shot him a sidelong glare and kicked a rock across the ground. "They hit us without warning. I barely had time to get a knife from the kitchen before they grabbed Fiona. I don't even remember most of what happened, just mother and the girls screaming. And then, when they cut off Father's leg, I—" Wesley's face turned red as he tried to swallow the tears, but the water welled in his eyes. "I just kept thinking none of this would've happened if you were there."

Connor winced. The comment cut deep, and he didn't know how to respond.

Two glowing green birds darted through the branches overhead, twittering to each other as they flew, and the emerald treetops swayed in Slaybourne's gentle breeze. The silent march continued, and Wesley's boots crunched across the dead leaves from last autumn while Connor easily sidestepped the worst of the debris on the forest floor.

"It wasn't long ago that I was in your shoes," Connor admitted. His fist tightened, and his knuckles cracked from the tension as he tried not to remember Kirkwall. "I know how you feel."

Wesley snorted derisively. "Doubt it."

"There's plenty of darkness in this world, kid. There are others who hurt, same as you, and listening to their pain can help you heal yours."

"What do you mean?"

Instead of answering, Connor drew one of the twin silver blades from the custom sheath strapped to his back and held it in front of him as they walked. Sunlight glinted off the blade, and Wesley watched it with a twinge of envy.

No, Connor realized—not envy, but desire. Longing. Like a wish he didn't dare speak out loud, for fear of not deserving it.

"My father didn't teach me to fight, you know." Connor tilted the sword and weighed it in his hand, letting the hilt rest on his fingertips with practiced ease as a glimmer of sunlight raced down the steel.

"Who did?"

"A man named Beck Arbor. He caught me hustling darts in a tavern and taught me everything he knew. He was in the King's Guard, and as a soldier, he traveled most of Saldia before retiring to the family homestead. He met every master blacksmith across every known kingdom, and over time, he used everything he had learned over the years to perfect the design for this pair of swords. They're even enchanted with a Strongman spell to make them more durable than a regular blade. I scrimped for years to pay for them, but he oversaw every part of the forging process to ensure they were perfect."

Connor paused midstride and adjusted his hold on the blade until he could offer the hilt to Wesley. The kid frowned and took a wary step backward, as though he couldn't believe he was allowed to even touch it.

"Go on," Connor prompted.

Delicately, Wesley set his fingertips under the blade and hilt. He smiled weakly at the masterpiece as he lifted it out of Connor's grip. The boy angled it this way and that, studying the light as it reflected across the metal, and his thin smile widened the longer he studied it. The lines in his brow faded, and his body relaxed. For a moment, he seemed to forget his pain.

"It's beautiful," the kid said reverently.

Connor grinned, and he knew without a doubt the swords had found a worthy new master. "It's yours."

"What?"

"They both are." He unbuckled the harness on his shoulders and slipped the twin sheaths off his back. The other sword remained in its scabbard, its simple leather hilt protruding from the leather casing, and he held it for Wesley to take.

The kid shook his head, eyes wide and mouth gaping. "I can't possibly take your swords."

"I tried to give them to you when I left the first time." Connor shrugged. "They've been yours for a while. I just held onto them for a bit."

Wesley adjusted his grip on the sword in his hands until he held it by the hilt, and he grabbed the second, sheathed sword with his free hand. "I don't deserve them, Connor."

"Of course you do." The Wraithblade crossed his arms over his chest as he watched the kid examine the perfect blades. "Every man needs a proper weapon."

The smile on Wesley's face faded, and he stared down at the ground. "I'm not a man, Connor. Not yet."

"Don't be ridiculous. After what you've endured, you're not a child anymore. It falls on you to protect your family. When the slavers attacked, that's exactly what you did."

"I failed, you mean."

"No, you did your best. That's all a man can ever do. His best."

Wesley sniffled, and eyebrows furrowed with anguish.

Connor let out a slow sigh as he tried to figure out what else to say. Grief burned holes in people, and he had lived with his own wounds for many years. One thing had helped him through the worst of his pain, and perhaps it would help Wesley, too.

"Hit that tree," he ordered.

Wesley scrunched his nose in confusion. "What?"

"Go on." Connor nodded to the nearest oak. "Hit it."

Wesley frowned, even more confused now, and looked down at the sword. "With this?"

Connor nodded.

"If you say so," Wesley muttered.

The young man raised the sword, and Connor used the opportunity to scan his stance. Wesley's center of gravity shifted too far to the back leg, and his grip on the sword needed serious work. He grunted with effort and swung the weapon as hard as he could at the oak, and the sleek blade sunk into the wood.

"Good." Connor pointed to the steel embedded in the bark. "This is how you test an enchanted sword. Most cut the bark, but a good one sinks deep."

Wesley gaped at the weapon, submerged almost entirely in the wood. "Wow."

"Do it again," Connor ordered. "This time, aim for the same spot and try not to miss."

Wesley tugged on the hilt, but the sword didn't budge. He grunted with effort, but it still didn't move. He set his foot on the tree and pulled harder, teeth clenched as he yanked on it with all his might.

This is painful to watch, the ghoul's voice resonated through Connor's head.

"Give him a break," Connor said under his breath. He scanned the forest, but thankfully, the wraith remained hidden for now.

Wesley yelled with effort, and this time, the sword popped free. He stumbled backward as he fought to catch his balance, the sword swinging wildly around him, and flashes of light glinted off the metal as he regained his footing.

The wraith sighed impatiently.

Wesley swung again, and the blade sank into the bark a good foot above the previous mark. He cursed under his breath and yanked it out, faster this time.

"Again," Connor ordered.

The young man swung, and chunks of bark sailed into the air as the blade skinned the tree. Connor didn't even have to say anything this time, and Wesley yanked the sword loose.

The young man swung again and again, missing every time.

Dust hovered in the sunbeams, stirring each time Wesley missed his mark. The young man's pinched brows became a furrowed scowl, and he yelled with effort every time he swung. The yells became strangled sobs, and before long, tears streamed down his face.

And yet, he didn't falter. The heavy thuds of the sword hitting the wood came at a steady pace, and even while sobbing, he whacked the tree, again and again. He focused on the trunk, not even looking Connor's way, and he lost himself in the exercise.

Connor knew that grief all too well. He stepped back to give the young man room to get it out.

"Put it to words," he ordered.

"Words?!" Wesley shouted through his tears. "There aren't words! I failed, Connor! You don't know what that's like! You could never know what that's like!"

Connor shut his eyes briefly against the memory of his father's head on a stake, but he didn't respond.

"I failed my mother!" The sword slammed into the tree, and Wesley yanked it out of the battered oak with a rough tug. "I failed my father!" The whack of steel on wood hit again, timed perfectly with the shout. "I failed my family!"

Wesley tried to swing again, but he collapsed to his knees. The sword clattered against the dirt as he buried his head in his hands. His shoulders shook, and he glared at the ground as he ran the back of his hand across his face.

"Sorry," he said, his words slurring as he sobbed. "I know a real man doesn't cry."

"To hell with that."

Wesley's head snapped up, and he frowned in confusion. "What?"

"You heard me." Connor crouched beside the young man and met his eye. "Cry. Grieve. Do it in private if that's what you need to do to make it yours, but let it out. A real man isn't scared of feeling things."

"I'm not afraid of that." Wesley sniffled and wiped his nose on his sleeve. "I'm furious."

"There's more to life than anger." Connor poked Wesley in the chest to emphasize his point. "Rage like that sits in a man's core until it rots him from the inside out, and then there's nothing left but the husk of what he could've been."

The young man stared at the ground, but didn't reply.

"Tell me what it was like."

Wesley shook his head. "I don't want to remember."

"You can remember it now or in your nightmares." Connor shrugged. "I've tried both, and this one works better."

Wesley sighed in resignation. "I thought I'd died. The last thing I remember was thinking, well, at least I went out doing my best. It was the closest thing to an honorable death that I could get, and there was some sort of... I don't know. Redemption, I guess, in going out that way. Now I'm back, and I know I should be grateful, but all I can think about is what a piss-poor job I did. I was useless, Connor. You had to save us, yet again. At least Father killed a few of them. I couldn't do a damn thing on my own!"

He yelled and punched the tree. His knuckles cracked, and he gritted his teeth in pain as he held his hand to his chest.

"Feel better?" Connor asked dryly.

Wesley laughed through his tears. "You know, I actually do."

Together, they let the chirping song of the forest fill the silence. Wesley had a chance to start over, but first, he needed to leave the battle behind.

"Mother won't tell me what happened after you saved her and the girls." The young man's voice dropped to a whisper. "But I know that face she made. She saw something horrible, and she's trying to protect me from it."

Connor frowned.

"You killed them, didn't you?" Wesley met his eye. "All of them?"

He rubbed his jaw, internally debating on how much to tell the young man, but he ultimately nodded.

"Good." Wesley spat on a nearby rock as though it were a slaver's face.

With a resigned sigh, Connor set one hand on the young man's shoulder. "I know this hatred, Wesley. I lived in it for years. I was lost to it. You don't want that life."

Wesley crossed his legs. "Mother says I should just move on, but I don't know what else to do."

"Anger doesn't work like that."

"No?"

Connor scratched at the stubble on his jaw as he tried to put it to words. "Anger's just a tool, like any emotion, but it's more destructive. Powerful, even."

"I don't understand."

"Think of it like a flame." Connor shifted his weight and sat on a fallen log nearby. He rested his elbows on his knees and gestured toward the young man sitting before him. "The thing is, you decide whether it's a cooking fire or an inferno. One, you control—but the other controls you. If you let it go unchecked, it becomes the only thing you think of. It becomes the only warmth in your life. That's not a life worth living, trust me."

"That's easy for you to say." Wesley gestured toward him. "I mean, look at you. I bet those slavers pissed themselves just seeing you for the first time."

"One of them did."

The young man smirked, and though he didn't look up, he nodded approvingly.

"You know the difference between us, though?" Connor leaned forward so that he could look Wesley in the eye. "My rage stays on the battlefield."

With a disgusted groan, the young man rested his chin on his fists.

"Think about what you're asking me to do—I can't just let it go. I could *never* let this go. What kind of man am I if I just move on? If I forgive the people who did something that awful?"

"You've got it all wrong." Connor shook his head. "Forgiveness isn't for them. It's for you. If you can't let it go, that's fine for now. The wound's still fresh, and sometimes it takes time. But you've got to learn to channel it into something better."

"How?"

"I'm not sure," he admitted with a shrug. "I don't pretend to have all the answers, and I don't know what to do. All I can do is tell you something my father told me."

Wesley leaned forward, and he waited with rapt attention for whatever came next.

With a small smile, Connor's eyes slipped out of focus as he remembered his father scratching away at his desk, sifting through sales numbers and inventory figures. "He said your soul is like a pot where you store all the things that make up who you are. When you make a mistake and you can't make it right, there's only one thing you can do—put it in the pot to make you braver. Use it to sustain you, because that's all it's good for at that point. The more you put in the pot, the stronger you get. Over time, you won't feel lost anymore. The shame burns away. The next time you face the thing you fear, you'll know what to do."

Connor paused, sitting with his father's wisdom, but he couldn't lie to himself or to Wesley. It took courage to live like that every day.

"You're not alone in this hatred, Wesley," he added. "I still haven't forgiven the person who got my family killed."

The young man's eyes widened in shock. He gaped at Connor for a while, apparently unable to speak, but Connor took a deep breath and stared off into the forest. If he ever saw Bryan again, he would run the man through—but he knew it wouldn't be enough. It wouldn't solve anything. Even killing the slavers didn't feel as satisfying as he had expected.

No amount of revenge absolved the bastards of what they had done, but it didn't make the world right, either.

"Sometimes you need the anger," he confessed. "It gets you through the hardest parts of life. Just don't let it burn away who you are."

Wesley's shoulders slumped, and he eventually nodded.

Connor glanced at the swords—one still in its sheath on the ground, in a heap of leather and silver buckles, and the other lying in the dirt. He pointed at Wesley and glared down at the young man over the bridge of his nose. "You'd better take damn good care of those blades. You hear me?"

Wesley grinned and, though he sniffled one last time, finally smiled. "I promise."

"Good." Connor stood and brushed off the stray wood chips that had settled onto his shirt. "Now, get on your feet. We have enough time for a quick lesson before I leave."

He offered Wesley a hand, and the young man took it. Once on his feet, Wesley wiped his forearm across his brow and grabbed the silver blade from the dirt.

"I won't let you down, Connor," he promised. "I'll make you proud."

The words hit home. Connor smiled as he remembered what his own father had always replied every time Connor had made that promise through the years.

"I'm already proud of you." His father's words echoed in the back of his mind, and he could almost hear the man's voice, clear as day. "Always have been, and always will be."

CHAPTER THIRTY-EIGHT

CONNOR

Sunset came too soon.

Connor leaned against Nocturne's neck as the dragon's wings snapped against the air. Far below, Slaybourne's forests whizzed past in a dizzying blend of green and brown.

He cast one last look over his shoulder. Four distant figures—two adults, and two children—still waved at him even as the others dispersed into the glowing green field. Wesley hadn't come to say his farewell, but Connor didn't mind. The young man could take his grief at his own pace.

Quinn, Sophia, and Murdoc sat against Nocturne's spines, clinging tightly to his back as they kept their heads low to protect themselves from the worst of the wind. In the distant sky, the amber sun scorched the clouds, and the mountain's long shadows stretched across the trees. Ahead, Slaybourne's striking black walls towered above the forest, and the imposing gates of Death's Door loomed ahead, closer with each passing second.

I will open the gates. The wraith's grim voice echoed through his head, and he merely nodded in answer.

As Nocturne approached the first of the two gates, a bolt of green light splintered through the massive black doors. The gates creaked open on ancient hinges, revealing the narrow channel that would take them to the exterior door. Despite the bright day, the looming walls on both sides of the cavern cut off the light and drowned the space in shadow.

The dragon barreled through the opening and into the darkness. A chill swept over them, and the deafening wind howled past, louder than ever as the tips of Nocturne's wings brushed both sides of the channel.

A thin ray of light stretched across the skeletons littered along the ground as the exterior gates opened, and the grating scream of iron on old hinges pierced the gale. Nocturne's wings slapped at the air one last time before he tucked them close to his body and barreled through the narrow opening.

The heat of the fading sun hit Connor's face as they left the icy shadows, and he closed his eyes to savor it.

With one last glance behind him, he spotted a lone figure standing on the wall near the top of the outer gate. The thin young man with blond hair waved both hands, and the two swords strapped to his back justled in their sheaths with each movement.

Wesley.

Connor smiled and, as they left the fortress behind, bid the young man farewell with a relaxed salute.

He wanted to believe the Finns were safe, even with the Lightseers on the way. The entire continent feared the Wraith King, and their terror was easily his greatest weapon right now—but even that wouldn't last.

Maybe that didn't matter. Perhaps he didn't *need* their fear.

His father had sometimes spoken of the line between cocky and confident, and of how blurred it could become.

The line is simple, son, his father had told him, once. *A cocky man is simply the one who can't follow through. If a man has to tell others how great he is, then he's probably not all that impressive.*

Connor chuckled softly to himself as he replayed the man's words in his head. He had always done his best to earn what he'd gotten in his life, and the tides had finally shifted in his favor. He had tamed a dragon and killed a horde of slavers, all with his own two hands.

Eventually, the time would come when he didn't need to rely on legend to keep Slaybourne safe. He was finally starting to understand what it meant to be power incarnate, but he knew one thing for certain: he hadn't even begun to test his true limits.

TEAGAN

With an exhausted groan, Teagan leaned back in his chair. His elbow rested on the leather seat's overstuffed arm, and he rubbed his tired eyes.

There had been too many Fates-damned delays. So many, in fact, that he had yet to hear from his assassin regarding the Wraithblade's weaknesses.

He and Colonel Freerock sat across from each other in the office of the elegant suite he owned in the heart of Lindow. His servants kept it ready for him at a moment's notice, given the city's strategic value along the southern road, but the worn wooden boards and the dusty tapestries on the wall served as a pale imitation of the grandeur available back home.

"Curse the Fates, Colonel, you found another burned hamlet?" With a deep groan easily mistaken for resignation, he managed to suppress the irritated growl that almost broke through the mask of firm but fair compassion he always wore around Rowan Freerock.

Teagan didn't give a damn about these people, but he did care about his public image—and by extension, his troops' morale. The vast cruelty and unjust death all across Saldia inspired new soldiers to join his ranks every day, and only a fool would've lost sight of what motivated them to pick up their first Lightseer sword. These people, many of whom began their careers as commoners looking for a way to make the world better, sacrificed more than just their lives in the name of embodying the Light.

And they did it all to protect the greater good.

To march by the injustice that had inspired them to join his ranks in the first place would rock their faith not just in their mission, but in him.

He couldn't risk it.

In his carefully laid timeline for their journey southward, he had budgeted for this. Any time his army left Lunestone for the Ancient Woods, he'd always had to save these people from the forest they had chosen as their home.

This time, however, he had underestimated the criminals of the southern woods. They were growing more brazen, especially in the years following Henry's slow retreat of forces from the main road.

"We're in a difficult position, Colonel," Teagan said as he inwardly debated whether or not the troops expected him to act on this one. If he could delegate the matter to the local lawmen, perhaps he didn't have to take on yet another delay. "Walking the line between defending the greater good and finishing the mission to the Decay."

Damn the peasants, he wanted to say, *and to hell with the greater good.*

With his legacy on the line, he was tempted to set fire to these helpless commoners' homes himself if they didn't stop begging for his help—and his money.

"Agreed, sir." In the chair on the other side of the desk, Colonel Freerock rubbed the back of his neck.

"It's important that we not rob the local lawmen of their right to protect their own home, Colonel. Why do you feel the Sheriff is incapable of handling this matter?"

"It's the survivors, sir. They—that is, they can't—" Freerock's voice caught, and he aggressively cleared his throat. Creases formed in his forehead as he scowled with barely restrained hatred. "Two young boys stumbled into town this morning. It's a miracle they made it through those woods alone."

"It is," Teagan agreed. "Not many children could survive out there on their own."

Inwardly, he grimaced. If a beast in the wood had merely eaten them, he wouldn't have to deal with this.

"Bandits attacked their homesteads." The colonel leaned forward, resting his elbows on his knees as he lowered his voice. "Slavers, by the sound of it. They took the boy's mother and aunt, as well as their neighbor's daughters. They killed everyone else. The men are all dead. Based on what I heard, these slavers are long gone by now, and it'll take an adept tracker to find them."

Teagan didn't reply. Instead, he studied the colonel who so foolishly thought of him as a surrogate father. His face relaxed, and the skin around his eyes creased with well-rehearsed concern.

"I respect you more than anyone alive or dead, sir," Freerock said as he stared at the floor. "Zander is my closest friend, and you know better than anyone that I've always thought of Quinn like a sister."

"But?" Teagan prompted.

"But they're warriors." Freerock's intense gaze snapped toward Teagan as the man bared his soul. "Even the worst we've ever faced is no match for them. They're alive, both of them. I know it. If Quinn were here, you and I both know what decision she would make."

Freerock had the sort of bleeding heart that attracted strays—man and mutt alike. His compassion had cost the Lightseers a hefty sum over the years, but it had also inspired countless others to join the cause. As with any worthwhile endeavor, Teagan benefited from it in the end.

Teagan's eyes narrowed as he let the man's words simmer on the air. In the ensuing silence, Freerock didn't move. He simply sat there, waiting for the words he—and, by extension, the other soldiers—wanted to hear.

"And Zander?" Teagan set his hands in his lap as he watched Freerock shift uncomfortably in the seat across from him. "What choice would the future Master General make in this position?"

Freerock's gaze returned to the floor, and he hung his head in resignation. "Remain focused on the task at hand, sir. The mission always comes first."

Good. At least Freerock's bleeding heart didn't blind him to the reality of what awaited them in the Decay.

Teagan leaned his elbows on the desk between them and, while he watched the young man in the stone-cold silence that followed, he studied every detail on the colonel's face. A muscle twitched in the soldier's jaw as he held Teagan's gaze. Tense and unyielding, he awaited the order he no doubt feared would come.

But there, buried in the slight tremble to his hands, hints of the young man's past resurfaced. Memories of a father who didn't return from war. Pain from losing a hero who had died the noblest death by defending their Master General in battle.

Damn it.

Best to get this over with, then.

"Very well, Colonel." Teagan stood and made a show of rubbing his face to stifle the surge of annoyance that followed. He rounded the desk and leaned against it. Arms crossed, he stared down at the young man who waited patiently for his verdict. "Clearance granted."

"Thank you, sir." Freerock jumped to his feet and saluted. "You won't regret this."

"I know, son." Tegan set his hand on the colonel's shoulder and looked him in the eye, as he so often did with Zander. "Take your unit and be back in two days. Understood?"

Freerock stood taller, and his mouth twitched as he fought a smile. "Yes, sir."

As the colonel left, Tegan turned his back on the door and set his fingertips on the desk's surface. The soft creak of squeaky hinges followed the colonel's almost imperceptible footsteps across the floorboards. The moment the door shut, Tegan's thin smile fell.

At least two more days lost. Possibly three, all to clean up Henry's mess. When he returned home, he would have to raid the Oakenglen coffers to pay for all of this.

These damned peasants were so *expensive*.

As he leaned against his desk, he stared down at his pack resting on the surface. The two bottles made of hand-carved spellgust waited inside, wrapped in their thick velvet cloths to ensure they didn't shatter in the heat of battle.

He fished one of them out of its wrapping and tilted the bottle this way and that, studying the facets in its surface despite having already memorized each one. A metal spike served as the bottle's cork, and its long, razor-sharp tip hovered just over the bottom. When the time came, it would pierce the Wraith King like a spear to the heart, rooting him forever in place.

Delicately, Tegan tugged the metallic stopper from the container and peered inside, still doubtful of this enchantment's power, despite his extensive research into the spells powering this priceless artifact.

As he stared into its depths, whispers floated past, so quiet they weren't even words—just voices, really. A bone-deep chill raced up his arm, and a pang of dread stirred in his chest like a brewing storm cloud. The whispers continued, thick with the promise of secrets no mortal man should ever know, if only he could understand.

Something swirled within the depths of the vial, and he squinted as he tried to figure out what it was. Smoke, maybe, like the soft swirl of fog rolling across a lake.

A gust of wind rolled past, and the hair on his arms stood on end. He shoved the metal spike back into the vial and let out a slow breath as he resolved to never do that again.

Even with the bottle now sealed, however, the soft breeze didn't fade.

He frowned and scanned the closed windows to find one of them ajar. A note rested on the windowsill, but he hadn't heard anyone enter.

Only one man could evade his notice like that.

Teagan slipped the bottle safely back into his bag and pressed his back to the wall by the window. Carefully, he snatched the note and peered outside. Loosely laid stones in the steep tavern wall provided a clear path to the window for any adept climber, and lights from the windows in the lower floors cast a soft orange glow to the flowerbeds below.

"I'll have to get that repaired," Teagan muttered under his breath.

He hated how often Charles revealed holes in his security, but at least the man served him and not the enemy.

At least he could finally find out what Charles had learned—and which of the Wraithblade's weaknesses Teagan could exploit to finally bend this infuriating peasant to his will.

CHAPTER THIRTY-NINE

TEAGAN

On the outskirts of Lindow, on an old farm his great-grandfather had quietly purchased shortly after the Unknown were first established, Teagan listened for footsteps in the cold spring night.

The steady hum of cicadas vibrated through the air. Stars blinked and faded in a churning sky full of silver clouds backlit by the twin moons. He set his palm on the barn doors, his ears straining to catch a hint of what awaited inside, but he heard only the muffled snort of a horse.

Without question, the site was secure. He'd already run a pass along the perimeter, as well as across the roof, and only two people waited for him inside. Most likely, he needed only to wear his mask for Charles, as the other person was either a captive to use as barter or, more likely, an informant who wouldn't survive the encounter. Given the secrecy demanded of the Unknown, his assassins didn't bring their informants to Teagan if they wanted to keep those informants alive.

No one in the organization knew each other's identities, save the sponsor who had called on them to take their place among the chosen, but they all feared one thing—what Teagan Starling would do to them if they ever betrayed the organization's interests.

They feared him more than death, as any sane man should.

He paused and dug his thumb into his left temple as he donned the facade best suited for Charles Jasper—confident, deadly, humorless. The muscles in his jaw tensed, and the lines in his brow deepened with grim focus and the barest hint of fury.

The rusted hinges on the barn doors creaked as Teagan swung them open. The stench of manure and cut pine rolled past, like a breath from the weathered structure itself. A soft nicker followed. In the nearest stall, the silhouette of a horse's perked ears flitted past the bars on the stall door, and a hoof hit the sawdust with a muted thud.

Every stall was closed, except for one at the far end. As the barn's main doors swung shut behind him, he strode through the center aisle and listened for any signs of an ambush even though he knew it wouldn't come.

After all, the Fates favored the prepared.

Only the soft whinnies of the horses and the quiet crunch of hay under hooves interrupted the steady whistle of wind somewhere through the rafters.

"How blessed we are to meet again," a familiar voice said from inside the open stall.

Charles.

In the silence that followed, the assassin waited for the other half of the Unknown's code. When Teagan reached the last stall in the row, he stood in the aisle and crossed his arms across his broad chest.

Two men waited inside. One sat, bound and gagged, on the floor. The other leaned against the flaking wooden wall, dressed in a muted brown tunic and mud-caked riding pants. Layers of dirt stained the knee-high boots as he pushed off the wall and set his hands on his waist. The smooth face and silky black hair reminded Teagan of a younger Lord Jasper, and he raised one skeptical eyebrow as he studied the young man's face.

"Here and tomorrow, Fates willing." Teagan frowned as he finished the coded phrase. "Your glamours are getting sloppy, Charles."

"A bit of vanity to relive my youth." The assassin said with a deep bow. "It won't happen again."

"Report."

"It was difficult, sir. Without a name, even I had trouble, but I managed."

"Brag to the whores who keep you company at night, but not to me." Teagan narrowed his eyes in warning. "You know better than to waste my time."

The assassin ran his finger along the skin above his mouth, toying absently with the moustache that wasn't there in his glamoured state, and nodded. "My apologies, sir. The Shade killed a group of slavers and freed the women they had kidnapped."

"Is that where you found this one?" Teagan nodded to the shackled man quietly trembling in the sawdust next to a pile of dung.

Charles nodded. "This is the lone survivor of the slaver contingent that has been causing so much trouble in the Ancient Woods over the last few months."

Teagan grunted, deeply skeptical of how accurate that information could be. "From what my soldiers have uncovered thus far, that unit is estimated to be seventy men strong. Maybe more. You're saying he took them all on at once? Why would he take that risk?"

"An excellent question, sir. It just so happens that the Shade followed them because they had something of his."

Teagan laughed dryly. "Were they stupid enough to steal from him?"

"In a fashion. They took his family. Two girls and their mother."

Teagan stiffened, and he resisted the urge to grin with victory. Every man had a weakness, and they had just found the Wraithblade's. "His wife and children?"

Charles shook his head. "Based on their ages, likely his sisters. He obviously reached them before I could, but I uncovered a surname. The Finns. Locals in Bradford gave me their names—Ethan, Kiera, Wesley, Isabella, and Fiona."

"The slavers killed the men, I suppose?"

"I couldn't find any evidence of that, but let's ask."

With a rough yank, Charles pulled out the gag in the prisoner's mouth. The spit-soaked rag slid over the man's chin and down his neck as his panicked gaze flitted from the assassin to the Master General and back. Long drips of dried blood flaked along his temple and down his jaw from an old gash on his scalp.

"P-please don't k-kill me," the man stuttered.

"Do what you're told, and maybe I won't," Teagan lied. "What did you do with the men?"

"Dead." The bandit nodded. "Hacked off one's leg and gutted the other. Left them for the wolves to eat. Roper's orders."

"And how did that turn out for you and Roper?" Teagan asked with a wry grin.

"Death." The color faded from the man's face, and the trembling worsened. The bandit's voice dropped to a horrified whisper, and he stared at the pile of dung at his feet as he relived the terror of whatever happened that night. "He fought like a demon from the forest, scarier than any beast I ever seen out there in the forest. Not afraid of the Ancient Woods like any sane man I know. Ain't afraid of being outnumbered, neither. Pissed myself, I did."

"How surprising," Teagan said dryly. "How did he approach your unit?"

"Came out of the woods. Alone." The slaver shook his head, as though he still couldn't believe what he had seen. "The lot of us thought he was mad. Had to be, right? Running around the woods at night like that. Mask over his face. All I could see was them eyes."

A masked vigilante, off delivering justice like he had the king's blessing. How irritating.

As he listened, a muscle in Teagan's jaw twitched. It intrigued him that the peasant's hateful glare carried so much power. Even Otmund had reported those eyes as the most identifying feature.

Teagan looked forward to the day this mess was finally behind him—when the Wraith King lay in Aeron's Tomb, speared and chained, with the Great Necromancer's other abominations.

"And that demon of a man had a…" the bandit's voice trailed off, and his brows twisted upward as his knuckles bleached white with the sheer force of his tight fist. "He had a creature with him, like Death itself floating at his side. A ghoul. A ghost."

The wraith.

Teagan's cold gaze shifted toward Charles, mostly to gauge the assassin's reaction. Charles had obviously interrogated the slaver already, and he'd had time to build the connections on his own. If he'd realized Henry's ghoul was actually the Wraith King himself, Charles never would've come to this meeting. That sort of damning evidence against the Lightseers would've ensured Charles never left this barn alive, and he wouldn't have taken the risk.

Calm, with his shoulders relaxed and his hands crossed over his chest, Charles merely waited for his next order. Teagan let the silence linger, using it to put pressure on the man's calm façade, but the assassin didn't flinch. He didn't fidget. He didn't so much as look away from the criminal at their feet.

Good. For now, at least, Charles had no idea of the truth.

"What else?" Teagan gestured to their prisoner as he regained control of the conversation. "I assume you brought me out here to discuss more than a piss-soaked bandit?"

The slaver whimpered.

"I did," the assassin said, ignoring their guest. "I tracked the Finns back to their piece of shit treehouse." Charles tugged an empty bottle out of his pocket and handed it to Teagan.

A potion vial, and definitely one of Quinn's. No question.

Teagan stared down at the empty vial in his palm. With no cork, its only significant feature was the hand-drawn cross on the label. His thumb brushed across the ink his daughter had once touched, and he clenched his jaw to snuff out his ever-growing hatred for the Wraithblade.

"No torture would ever force her to divulge which of her potions is which." Teagan sighed, long and heavy. "He must've used a Hackamore, and that means he has both funds and talent with a cauldron."

"Agreed, sir." Charles scratched his scalp and grimaced at the implications. "Unless he stole the regents he needed, of course."

Teagan considered it, and Charles had a point.

"Sir, if I may?"

"Go on," Teagan ordered.

"Are you sure he's some ordinary peasant? The more I find, the more the evidence suggests he's something…" The assassin paused, searching for the right word. "…more."

"What else did you find?" Teagan asked, intentionally sidestepping the man's question.

"Several other empty potion bottles suggested they were in a hurry and trying to tend to the wounded. The Shade, if I had to guess, since I figure he couldn't have gotten out of that scuffle without some serious wounds. Lots of blood on the mattresses, but the whole house was disgusting. Hard to tell what was recent and what was simply filth. No bodies, though the wolves could've eaten what was left."

"Well?" Teagan asked the bandit. "When he fought you, did he suffer injuries?"

"Can't say." The shackled man shook his head. "Covered in blood, he was, but I can't tell you whose."

Tegan almost demanded the criminal address him with his title to show proper respect, but it seemed like a waste of energy and time to teach a bandit manners.

"Hmm." He frowned. Before going into the battle against the Wraithblade, he needed to know if the peasant had sustained injuries in this fight with the slavers. If so, it meant he had quite a while to go before he truly mastered the Wraith King's power. If not, he would prove far more difficult—though not impossible—to kill. "The blood may have belonged to the father and—what was the boy's name? Wesley? Those two might have survived."

Charles' eyes slipped out of focus as he considered the idea. "Given—"

"We chopped off the big fella's leg," the bandit interrupted. "No way he survived that."

Teagan glared down at the peasant who had dared interject himself into a conversation more important than his life. The slaver gulped loudly and stared again at the pile of horse manure at his feet.

"Continue," the Master General ordered his assassin.

"Given the mess of footprints and sheer number of tracks around the base of the house, I can't be certain."

"Any on the perimeter?"

"Some." Charles leaned against the wall. "I tracked four sets of prints headed toward the treehouse. Two men, two women. We can assume one is the Shade, and one is probably Quinn. That leaves the potential for Zander to be traveling with them, as well as a second woman who could easily be the one making these potions if the Shade doesn't know how."

"Possible, but it's unlikely Zander or Quinn is traveling with him. Even shackled and powerless, they would make his life hell."

"Agreed, sir. I can confidently say, though, that the Shade left with more people than when he arrived."

"How recently?"

Charles let out a slow whistle, and his eyes glossed over as he slowly shook his head. "A week, at most, sir."

Damn the Fates straight to *hell*.

A furious growl built in his throat, nearly shattering his mask, and it took every ounce of willpower he possessed to keep from punching a hole through the stall's wide-plank wall.

If he hadn't wasted so many days saving these infuriating peasants from their own poor choices, he would've been in the area with near-perfect timing to intercept the Wraithblade himself. He could've captured the Shade before the man even had the chance to return to his stronghold.

The perfect opportunity—wasted on *peasants*.

He pinched the bridge of his nose and cleared his throat to regain his composure. Charles Jasper needed constant reminders of Teagan's superiority to remain loyal, and he couldn't let his mask fracture now.

Once his anger had settled again to cold fury, he glared at Charles with the full fire of his barely contained rage. "Which direction did they take?"

"Ah, yes." The assassin scratched the back of his neck in an uncharacteristically sheepish fashion. "That's unfortunately unclear because, well…"

"Spit it out, damn you."

Charles looked Teagan in the eye and shook his head in disbelief. "I also found dragon tracks, sir."

For the first time in a decade, something left Teagan speechless.

His eyes narrowed in disbelief as he watched his top assassin for tells of a lie, but the man didn't flinch. The vein in the man's right temple—which always pulsed whenever he grew nervous—was calm. The assassin's eye didn't twitch, nor did he fidget as he stood there, pinned under Teagan's glare.

The Lightseer Master General took a towering step forward and dropped his voice to a fierce whisper. "Did one of mine escape?"

If the Wraithblade had somehow managed to smuggle one of Teagan's own dragons off the small island just off Lunestone, Teagan would kill every man on that secluded island fortress and start fresh.

"It was the first thing I checked, sir." Charles let out a slow breath of relief. "And the answer is no. All the dragons on the isle are accounted for."

Teagan's shoulders relaxed, even if only a little, with relief. "How could the Shade possibly have one of his own? No new dragon has been sighted in centuries."

"I haven't the foggiest idea, sir."

"Then find out."

"D-dragons?" the slaver stuttered.

Lost in his thoughts, Teagan ignored their guest's interjection.

For the Wraithblade to fly a dragon unnoticed over Saldia, the man had to be traveling at night and keeping above the clouds.

Clever.

Teagan hated to admit it, but he rather envied the Wraithblade for having a dragon mount. No known conqueror had obtained one since the days of the Wraith King, and as much as Teagan would've loved to ride a dragon into battle, the damned beasts sometimes broke through the Bridletame helms designed to keep them obedient. Teagan couldn't risk one going rogue on a local town, nor did he have the means to steer one.

Even if he did, the common people thought of dragons as omens of death. The legends around dragon lore came from the time of the Wraith King himself, and any fool who rode one into battle might win the fight, but he would lose the long-term war of public opinion. Peasants would sooner side with a tyrant than rally behind a man riding the symbol of hellfire and damnation.

Thus, why the Starling horde remained a closely guarded secret—and why this news gave Teagan the advantage.

"I'm afraid I failed you, sir," Charles said. "You tasked me with delivering his weakness, and he got to them before I could."

"Quite the opposite." Teagan rubbed his jaw as he sifted through everything Charles had divulged about this emerging enemy. "He and his family are poor. I'm sure of it, now. Even with his newfound power, he left them alone in a decrepit treehouse. For the Fates' sake, a couple of slavers might've killed half of them." Teagan nodded to the useless bandit trembling at their feet.

Charles frowned. "But we have no idea where he's taken them."

"On the contrary." Teagan sneered as he pieced it together. "He could squirrel them away in safehouses along the western fork of the southern road, where we would never find them, but he won't. He's penniless, which means he doesn't have the wherewithal to take them someplace we won't think to look. Mark my words, he will take them to the Decay."

The assassin's brows furrowed in confusion. "Isn't that worse, sir?"

Teagan shook his head. "If he was willing to face a horde of slavers to save his family, it means he will do absolutely anything for them. He's getting cocky. I wager I can bait him into facing me head-on, even when outnumbered."

The Wraithblade thought he was untouchable, but Teagan worked best when he could twist a man's pride against him.

"There's one more thing, sir. A name." The assassin kicked the bandit in the side, and the man huffed with pain. "Go on. Tell him."

"Connor." The slaver spat blood onto the trampled sawdust. "I heard one of them ladies call him Connor."

So, the peasant had a name after all.

"I'm impressed," Teagan admitted with a well-earned nod of respect to Charles.

"Thank you, sir." A thin, prideful smile played at the edges of the assassin's mouth. "How else can I be of service?"

"Clean up the route between here and Charborough. You don't have to solve the southern farmers' problems, but for the love of the Fates, keep my soldiers from catching wind of any issues. This is our planned route, along with timeframe." He pulled a folded piece of parchment from his pocket and handed it to the assassin. "It's your job to ensure we make those milestones."

The assassin frowned as he opened the note and scanned the route Teagan had drawn earlier. "This is quite an undertaking, sir. May I request help from my colleagues?"

Teagan almost laughed as Charles referred to the other Unknown in code, likely in case the bandit was allowed to live.

How optimistic.

"I've already dispatched thirty others to help. You're in command until my troops reach the Decay. They're looking for a Master Roderick. Keep your hair black, but use a glamour that better disguises your face this time," Teagan added with a disappointed grimace. "First contact is tomorrow, in the usual place. Go."

Charles gestured to their chained company. "Shall I take care of our guest, sir?"

"Leave him."

The assassin raised one eyebrow in surprise, but nodded and bowed as he stepped past him on the way out of the stall. The man's footsteps made no sound as he retreated down the barn's center aisle, but the creak of the door hinges gave away his location as he finally left. The wooden exit slid gently shut, and the barn once more settled into the soft nickers as the horses in each stall munched their hay.

Teagan cracked his neck, and a rush of relief snaked down his spine as he finally dropped his mask. In his younger years, he had donned and dropped his personas with ease. The game had entertained him. Each long flight from town to town gave him time to dissect those around him as he had systematically uncovered the unique ways to make each person ever more loyal, ever more diligent, ever more dedicated to not just the Lightseer cause, but to him.

With age and time, however, the masks felt heavier. They took more energy to wear. For going on a decade, now, he had preferred Lunestone to the field for exactly this reason.

It all left him so very tired.

He shut his eyes and listened to the soft stomp of hooves on the sawdust. He leaned into the noise, letting his unique Hearhaven augmentation stretch beyond even what the most enhanced men could hear.

Enriched with the blood of dragons, Teagan's augmentations tested the limits of what magic could do.

The gentle thump of five hearts, each almost the size of his head, echoed in his ear. The wooden walls between him and the horses muffled each creature's heartbeat, but the slaver's heart sped with all the panicked terror of a rabbit running from a fox. Teagan even caught the tail end of the assassin's pulse, slow and steady as always, before the man walked out of earshot.

Dragon blood made Teagan a god. If he could sell the potions he used to create his augmentations, it would've brought him enough revenue by now to purchase the Oakenglen throne ten times over. His concoctions were stronger, lasted longer, and surpassed every recipe known to man.

That, more than wealth or influence, elevated the Starlings above the mortals. It secured their power and cemented them as superior in the eyes of the common man.

For this Connor fellow to have a dragon of his own put him on an even playing field. It sealed the peasant's fate, really, because no Master General had ever allowed a true rival to last for long.

The Lightseers lived by their motto, *duty above all else,* but the Master General and his chosen successor lived by another—*the superior man, unrivaled.* With that as their northern star, Master Generals throughout the ages had built the Starling name to something otherworldly and profound. Something revered and respected.

If the Wraithblade realized what he could do with dragon blood, the Starling legacy would unravel.

With a slow sigh, Teagan opened his eyes and stared down at the terrified outlaw before him. Even though this sniveling heathen was nothing more than a stain on the southern woods, he would get to witness something truly rare tonight. Something usually reserved for the people Teagan hated most.

This criminal would see the true Teagan Starling. The man behind the mask. The one no one saw until their dying moments, when it was too late to take back what they had done.

"Are you scared of demons?" he asked the sniveling criminal. "Of the monsters in the Ancient Woods?"

Quivering, his eyes shaking with fear, the man nodded.

Teagan crouched before the slaver and leaned his elbows on his knees. "And what scared you most about this man who calls himself the Shade?"

"He was brutal." The slaver's whisper cracked, like he'd tried and failed to speak louder. "Covered in blood. Walked into the firelight like the bogeyman from one of ma's old ghost stories. Didn't look human, neither. Looked like a god of war, or somethin' that drank blood instead of beer."

"Before I kill you, I want you to understand something." Teagan set his hand on the man's shoulder and stared him in the eye as the whimpering grew louder. "The most frightening demons in Saldia don't live in these woods."

The man gulped audibly. "N-n-no?"

Teagan shook his head and drew a knife from the sheath strapped to his thigh. He held the blade in front of the man's face, watching the bandit's reflection in its perfectly polished silver as his victim went cross-eyed to stare at it.

"Saldia's monsters—the real ones—live in Lunestone," Teagan explained. "And every last one of them calls me *sir*."

CHAPTER FORTY
CONNOR

Only six days left.

In the early morning hours of yet another day outside of Slaybourne's walls, Connor adjusted the cloth over his face. With his back pressed against a brick wall in Oakenglen's second interior, he listened to the night.

A dog barked in the distance, just once, and the steady orange glow from the dozens of lamps along the main road had given them precious few shadows in which to hide. Backlit by Saldia's twin moons, pale blue clouds churned through a rumbling sky as the flickering streetlights drowned out what little moonlight the night could offer.

Fates above, how he hated this place. It was too damn bright.

Will you lot move faster? the wraith asked him, not bothering to mask his irritation even as he remained mercifully out of sight. *Fates be damned, you move like snails.*

"We can't all disappear," Connor muttered under his breath. "Stay hidden and be patient."

Infuriating, the ghoul grumbled. *Utterly infuriating.*

Quinn crouched ahead of him, and he scowled at the back of her head as she peered out to check for soldiers. They waited in the darkest alley they'd found thus far, with crates and barrels lining the shadowy route between a bakery and a dress shop. While he would've preferred leading the mission, he had no idea where this augmentor of hers lived.

It was a risk, and at any moment, it could end with them all in a trap.

Though Nocturne had wanted to fly over the city to speed up the process, Connor hadn't allowed it. He couldn't risk a massive dragon being spotted, even though it had cost him roughly an hour of underground passages and hiding in alleys as they made their way toward Quinn's augmentor in the city's interior.

Sophia crouched behind him, breathing heavier now that they had finally paused for a short respite. As her ragged breaths broke the silence, he cast a concerned glance over his shoulder. The necromancer leaned her head against the wall, her shoulder pressed into the bricks, and her eyes were closed as she caught her breath.

If this augmentor couldn't help Sophia, they might not have time to take her to Freymoor. Their necromancer always put on such a brave front that the thought hadn't even occurred to him until now.

Quiet footsteps swept across the cobblestone behind them as Murdoc knelt behind Sophia. He leaned forward and lowered his voice to a whisper as he caught Connor's eye. "All clear."

Connor nodded. Good.

Quinn glared at the former Blackguard over her shoulder and held one finger to her lips.

"Do you even know where you're going?" Sophia hissed under her breath.

The Starling warrior's hazel eyes narrowed in annoyance, but as she opened her mouth to reply, the distant thud of a dozen footsteps on the stone streets interrupted her. Connor's ear twitched at the approaching danger, and from the muted clatter, he figured this had to be another patrol.

Though he had encountered many patrols on his last visit to Oakenglen, they had become far more frequent.

The perfect trap.

Without saying a word, he studied Quinn's face. Her eyes briefly glossed over, and she leaned ever so slightly toward the sound.

He had a few choices, but he opted to wait for her next move. He let the silence linger, dangling the bait to see how she would perform. In enemy territory, it would've been all too easy for her to lead them into an ambush.

With her precious vougel on the line, he doubted she would do it, but he wasn't going to risk his or his team's lives on that bet.

She held up one fist in an unspoken command for silence and turned her back on him. Carefully, she peered again around the corner and immediately darted back into the shadows.

"Guards," she whispered, signaling for everyone to slip back into the shadows. "Hide."

Interesting.

As his team retreated behind the stacked crates along the walls, the militant thud of boots on stone grew louder. Minutes later, they marched by in perfect formation. As Connor peered around the barrel he had chosen as a shield, one soldier in the middle of the cluster even swept his gaze across the alley as they passed. Quinn knelt behind a stacked pair of nearby crates, her head low, and the soldier's eyes lingered a second too long on her hiding place.

Connor tensed, and his fingertips pressed into his palm as he prepared to summon the blackfire blades. To fight Oakenglen soldiers in the wealthy interior circles of the city would be messy, but he would do it to protect his team.

As the soldier passed the alley, however, his eyes returned to the front. The man never missed a step, and as far as Connor could tell, they hadn't been spotted.

He let out a slow breath of relief.

When the footsteps finally faded, Quinn crept toward the exit once more and leaned carefully out into the street to watch them leave. After a second or two of silence, she gestured for Connor and his team to move, and she bolted in the opposite direction the guards had taken.

Connor followed, unwilling to let her get far, while Murdoc and Sophia kept close on his heels. Their pseudo-prisoner jogged down a side street and along a narrow path with no streetlights. As he stepped out of the orange glow on the main road, Connor's eyes instantly adjusted to the darkness. It took little effort to match her pace, and his gaze never left the back of her head.

He would never admit it out loud, but he wanted to trust her. Hell, he almost enjoyed her company. She had done right by him and the people he cared about, but she was still the enemy.

Their truce wouldn't last forever, and he couldn't let down his guard.

As the Starling warrior paused again at another corner, the gurgling rush of water filed the air. He peered around her shoulder to find its source. Beyond their path, four streetlights lit a massive courtyard lined with shops and window displays. In the center of the paved brick circle, a statue stood atop a fountain filled with frothing water and flowerbeds. Though he couldn't see much detail in the low light, the silhouette wore a crown and pointed a sword at the distant horizon.

"Where the hell are you taking us?" Sophia whispered as she and Murdoc reached them. "This isn't even the Spell Market. What decent augmentor has a shop outside the most prestigious magical bazaar in Oakenglen?"

"Mine," Quinn said with a terse glare over her shoulder.

She darted again into the quiet street and led them down a short hill. After passing several fabric shops and a butcher, Quinn finally paused outside of a small townhome at the end of the line. It shared one wall with a reagents shop, and its two windows had simple blue awnings above them. Overgrown hydrangea hung over the front stoop, nearly blocking the rows of drawings set on easels in the windows.

Quinn stared up at the roof. "Look away."

As they stood in the middle of the darkened street, Connor tilted his head in annoyance and frowned in a silent order for her to just get the hell on with it already.

When he didn't reply, she looked over one shoulder to find the three of them all glaring unflinchingly at her.

She grumbled under her breath. "Fine."

The Starling warrior wrapped her hand around a brick on the front of the building and quickly scaled the wall. Her fingertips deftly gripped the protruding blocks with ease on her way to the third-story roof, and Connor took a wary step forward as he prepared to follow her.

If she tried to lose him on a rooftop, his years of climbing trees to escape the blightwolves would make it effortless to follow.

Instead of trying to escape, however, she reached for a protruding roof tile and tugged something from underneath it. Without bothering to climb back down, she jumped easily to the brick path and trotted up the steps to the front door. In her hand, a flash of golden light snaked across the shaft of a key, and a small pinprick of green light radiated from the tiny spellgust gem embedded in its base.

"That's it?" Murdoc muttered under his breath.

She slid it into the lock. "What were you expecting?"

"You're a Starling." The former Blackguard shrugged. "I expected something… I don't know. Exciting."

"Not all magic has to be complicated." Quinn chuckled as she turned the key. The door popped open, and she reached up through the gap to silence the soft jingle of a bell as she entered.

The first floor is empty, the ghoul said before Connor could even give the order. *I hear someone on the second floor. Only one person, as far as I can tell.*

Connor took a settling breath to prepare himself for whatever they encountered inside. Breaking into an augmentor's house while they were asleep hardly seemed like the best way to make a good first impression, much less convince them to help strangers, but he had precious few options.

With the bell disabled, Quinn slipped into the dark store with ease and ushered them forward. He indulged her and stepped into the shop, taking it all in with a glance.

To his left, a golden throne sat on a raised platform against the wall, framed by white floor-to-ceiling bookshelves packed with various tomes and piles of scrolls. To his right, rows of shelves nailed to the wall held a colorful array of potions in bottles of every shape and size. Some glowed faintly green in the darkness, and a soft hum filled the air. On the far wall between them, a thick blue curtain closed off the shop from what he could only assume was the rest of the house.

Murdoc and Sophia slipped in after him, and Murdoc held the bell to silence its clapper as he quietly shut the door behind them.

The woman is asleep, the ghoul said. *I will check the cellar.*

Whisper-silent footsteps tapped above his head, and he tensed. His magic simmered in his blood, ready at a moment's notice. "Are you sure about that?"

What are you—

Already to the blue curtain, Quinn pulled it aside and hung the thick fabric on a hook nailed to the wall. The scent of rosemary and roasted chicken wafted past as the curtain rustled. She peered into a dark corridor, her head tilted to one side as she paused, midstride.

Listening.

A soft footstep came from the shadows, mere yards away from the Starling warrior who had led them through enemy territory.

With long, quick strides, Connor closed the distance between them in seconds. If Quinn noticed him approach, she didn't react. Instead, she stepped into the dark hallway and peered to the left, toward a darkened stairwell.

Curse the Fates, the wraith said. *She's fast.*

As Connor reached Quinn, a silhouette appeared at the top of the stairs. The gentle slosh of water followed, and glowing blue light pierced the darkness from above them.

Great.

This had gone even worse than he'd thought it would. There was no telling what augmentations a proper augmentor could give herself, and he wasn't about to take any chances if she decided to attack before he had a chance to talk her down.

With a twist of both hands, he summoned his swords, and the enchanted blackfire raged instantly to life. The silhouette raced toward them, taking the stairs two at a time. As the figure neared, her features came into sharp focus.

Dark hair, loose and flowing over her shoulders. Petite jaw. Thin frame. Piercing brown eyes. A rose tattooed on her neck, its lines glowing bright green with magic.

Halfway down the stairs, she paused, and her nose creased with anger. She glared at him, her thin eyebrows furrowed as she raised her hands in front of her. Water floated above her head, and blue light refracted through it as it bubbled with each twitch of her fingers.

"You must want to die." Her dark voice dripped with barely restrained fury, and her eyes narrowed as she spoke.

"Tove, wait!" Quinn bolted out of the darkness beside Connor and stood between him and the woman. The Starling warrior raised her palms to placate both of them before either could take the first swing.

The stranger's eyes widened in recognition, and though her shoulders relaxed, the water continued to swirl around her head. "Quinn? What in the Fates' name—"

"It's safe." The Starling's eyebrows shot up her forehead as she turned her back on Connor and focused her full attention on the woman she had called Tove. "I promise."

Tove's dark eyes shifted again toward Connor, and she pursed her lips as she quietly debated something. The water churned above her head, but the powerful blue glow slowly faded from its depths.

"I need a favor." Quinn relaxed, though her gaze never left Tove's face.

"A favor?" The augmentor raised one eyebrow and nodded toward Connor. "His wanted poster is everywhere! Not even you can involve me in whatever this is!"

The Starling rubbed her forehead and sighed. "Fine. Double pay, then."

"You know I can't be bought."

Connor smirked, impressed.

Quinn let out a slow breath and set her hands on her hips. "Look, Tove, put the water down. Let's talk."

"Have you lost your damn mind?" Tove stared at her incredulously. "You want me to put down my weapon and have a chat with a criminal?"

"Your weapon?" Quinn chuckled. "It's water. What were you going to do, splash us angrily?"

Tove frowned and flicked her finger toward Quinn. A small bubble of the glowing blue water above her head shot forward and hit Quinn square between the eyes.

Behind him, Sophia chuckled.

The Starling wiped her face on her sleeve and shot Sophia an irritated glare before returning her focus to the augmentor still standing in her nightgown on the stairs. "Please. Do it for me."

Tove bit her lip and closed her eyes. She let out a strangled little growl, like she couldn't believe what she was about to do, but her body finally relaxed. With a few graceful waves of her arms, the water floated back to the top of the stairs and splashed into a basin in the corner.

"Your turn," the augmentor said as her dark gaze snared him.

Still not at ease, Connor dismissed the blackfire blades without a word. Black shadows rolled over his arms as he studied the woman who had tried to attack him. Tove crossed her arms over her white nightgown and glared right back.

"I suppose you'll want tea," she groused.

Behind Connor, Sophia and Murdoc remained still. They watched her, Murdoc with his arms crossed and Sophia with her hands on her hips, both deathly silent.

Apparently, Tove took that as a yes.

The augmentor walked down the last few steps in silence and turned away from them, past several closed doors and toward the shadows in the back of her shop. Quinn let out a slow breath of relief.

Connor leaned toward the Starling. "Hope you're right about her."

"I am," Quinn whispered back.

"Did you know the Lightseers have been here, Quinn, asking about you?" Tove walked through a doorframe at the end of the hallway and grabbed something off a table by the wall.

Fire erupted along the short dagger, and she pointed it at something out of sight. Flames erupted in a hearth, casting a soft amber glow on the small table and two chairs placed in the center of the wide space. Tove blew out the flame on her Firestarter dagger before returning it to the table and walking deeper into the room, out of view.

"What did you tell them?" Quinn frowned and joined the augmentor in the kitchen as pots and pans clanked somewhere out of sight.

"Nothing, obviously. Give me a *little* credit," Tove said, exasperated.

Quinn leaned against the far wall and crossed her arms as she watched whatever Tove was doing.

Connor took a settling breath and leaned toward Sophia and Murdoc. "Don't get comfortable. She could still turn us in."

"No worries," Murdoc whispered, his glare never leaving the kitchen's doorframe. "Want me to keep watch on the front door?"

Connor nodded. "Sophia, you're with me. Wraith, make sure there's no one else here."

There isn't.

"Then keep an eye on the streets. I don't want anyone to catch us off guard."

You're trying to keep me occupied, Magnuson, and it won't work.

He smirked. "Yes, it will."

"What if you were followed tonight?" Tove asked, and the clatter of steel on porcelain followed as she fiddled with something Connor couldn't see from his vantage in the hallway. "What if they were watching my shop? What if the Lightseers or the King's Guard find out he was here? If I'm caught lying to a Lightseer, I'd lose my shop *and* my head."

Quinn's jaw tensed. "I'd never allow it."

As Connor and Sophia joined the two women in the kitchen at the rear of the house, his attention shifted to the Starling warrior. He'd caught the nuanced ribbon of fear on her face at the mere thought of losing this augmentor, and that wasn't the kind of protectiveness one felt for the people they hired.

That was *affection*.

Apparently, even the Starlings had weaknesses. For whatever reason, Quinn had led him right to hers.

When he stepped into the kitchen, he leaned against the wall closest to the door and studied the augmentor's every move. Waist-high tables sat against every wall, and she reached for a kettle on one of the overflowing shelves above each surface. Sophia sat at the small dining table as Tove placed five cups on gilded saucers. Steam rose from a teapot resting beside her, and Connor found himself wondering who this woman could truly be.

"Alright, tell me everything." Tove huffed and threw a towel over a basin propped on a wooden stool. "What is it you need this time, Quinn?"

"Don't pretend you don't enjoy my requests." A small smile played at the corner of Quinn's mouth. "I know you love a good challenge."

Tove raised one eyebrow and crossed her arms, still waiting for the Starling to answer her question.

"We need some potions," Quinn said, her voice softening. "There's also an augmentation that needs repair, if you can do it."

Tove huffed indignantly at the challenge. "What do you mean, *'if'* I can do it?"

"I said what I meant." Quinn barely restrained her smirk as she baited the augmentor. "It's nigh impossible, even for you."

Tove fidgeted, and her fingers tapped against her sleeve. Her eyes swept the ground, like she was trying to resist saying something, but it didn't last long. "What sort of challenge?"

Everyone had a price, and Tove's didn't seem to be money.

How interesting. Time to see just how far it went.

"Augmenting a dragon," Connor interjected.

Tove stood a little straighter, and her eyes shifted to him as her lips parted in awe. "What?"

"Yeah," Quinn echoed dryly as she glared at him. "What?"

"A dragon?" Tove's brows pinched as she slowly walked closer, studying his face for signs of a lie. "Are you serious?"

He nodded.

The augmentor's gaze shifted to Quinn, who gave a curt nod to confirm it.

Tove whistled softly as her attention returned to him. "No wonder the crown wants you in chains, Shade."

He frowned.

"You said you wanted potions." Tove raised her chin as she stared him down. "What exactly do you want me to brew?"

"Three Hackamores."

Quinn's eyes narrowed as he added one potion to the list without first speaking to her, but she didn't need to know that he intended to use the third one on Otmund.

Tove groaned and rubbed her eyes. "Quinn, what have you gotten yourself into?"

"You don't want to know," she admitted.

"There's more," Connor continued. "A friend of mine lost his leg. I need something that can help him walk again."

"That could be tricky." The augmentor leaned her weight on one hip as she looked him up and down. "Did you bring his blood, preserved?"

He gestured to Sophia. "She did."

"Good, then it'll be easy." Tove shrugged. "Is that it?"

Connor shifted his attention to the necromancer sitting at the table and gestured toward the augmentor in a silent command to chime in with her request.

Sophia got to her feet and walked toward the augmentor. Tove stiffened as Sophia lowered her mouth to the augmentor's ear and whispered.

Within seconds, Tove's eyes widened, and her lips parted in awe. "Show me."

Sophia frowned and glared at the others present. Given the augmentation's location between her breasts, Connor averted his eyes out of respect. Quinn, however, didn't move, and he reached over to lightly smack her arm. She groaned and turned her back on the duo by the teacups.

A faded green glow washed across the floor behind them.

Tove gasped in surprise. "Astonishing. I've heard about it in theory, of course, but to see it in person is something else entirely."

"Can you do it?" Sophia asked tersely.

The green glow disappeared, and Connor took that as his cue to turn back around. He stretched out his neck while he waited for the verdict.

Over by the basin and the still-empty teacups, Tove hesitated. She bit her lip and frowned, her gaze shifting again to Quinn, as though she wanted to say something but didn't know if she should. The Starling warrior turned around and, after a tense moment, nodded gently.

"You're not going to like it," Tove admitted in a hushed tone.

"I won't turn you in," Quinn promised. "Illegal magic or no."

The augmentor swallowed hard. "I've been studying death magic for most of my adult life." The words rushed out, as though the dam holding them back had been slowly corroding for years. "It's illegal, but bless the Fates is it fascinating. Every book I have is hidden where no raid would ever find it, and I can't stop collecting them. I never wanted you to know, Quinn, but there's a reason I can craft you the hexes and curses most potion masters won't touch."

"I figured," the Starling confessed, her tone far softer than Connor had expected.

"This will cost you a fortune," Tove's gaze shifted to him. "The bloody beauties alone—"

He grimaced. "I know."

"And you have the coin?" She glanced him up and down. "No offense."

No king suffers such an insult! the wraith growled in his head.

"Aren't you supposed to be keeping watch?" Connor muttered under his breath.

It's clear, the ghoul grumbled. *It's been clear. It will remain clear. It's the middle of the Fates-damned night.*

Connor ignored the wraith's outburst and refocused his attention on the negotiation in Tove's kitchen. Though Beck Arbor had taught him better than to agree to a bargain without clearcut terms and price, he was asking a lot of a complete stranger to even create these potions for him, much less do it in secret.

"I'm good for whatever it costs," he assured her.

She studied him, her toe tapping on the floorboards, but she sighed in defeat and shut her eyes tightly. "Give me the recipe for the dragon's augmentation."

He tugged the scroll out of his bag and handed it to her. Quinn watched the exchange, her eyes lingering on the parchment for a moment longer than he liked.

A possessive growl rumbled through his head, and dark smoke rolled across the floor from behind Tove. A hooded figure emerged from the wall, staring down at her with the intensity of Death coming to take a soul. She frowned at the smoke churning over her bare feet and looked over her shoulder to find the Wraith King's skeletal face looming above her.

She screamed and jumped backward.

Connor caught her before she could fall to the ground. With his hands on her shoulders and her back pressing into his chest, the honey-sweet fragrance of magnolia blooms drifted from her hair. Out of fear or reflex, she grabbed his forearm for balance, and her touch sent a jolt of energy through his body.

A powerful sexual urge hit him—*hard*. It was more intense this time than any thus far. Before he could stop himself, he lowered his nose to her hair and inhaled.

He gritted his teeth and tensed, fighting the primal demand of his overtaxed body as he carefully set her on her feet and released her.

Damn it all, he couldn't fight this much longer. He needed an outlet, and he needed one *soon*.

"What the hell is that?" she shouted.

"It's okay," Quinn said, her palms raised as she tried to soothe the augmentor's panic. "He's... uh, well, he's not a friend, but..."

"He won't hurt you," Connor assured her, though he glared at the wraith.

I promise nothing. The ghoul crossed his bony arms as his tattered cloak fluttered in the winds of the dead. The hollow holes of his eyes focused intently on the woman holding his priceless scroll.

"That's..." Tove leaned forward, her head tilting as she stared up at the Wraith King. "Isn't that..."

"No," Quinn interrupted.

Tove frowned and looked at the Starling warrior, and the unspoken urgency in Quinn's eyes said everything the augmentor needed to hear.

But Connor had still seen the exchange.

"Alright," Tove said under her breath.

With a wary glance at the Wraith King, she unrolled the parchment. Her eyes scanned the page, and the unease slowly faded from her tense shoulders with each passing second. Absently, she tapped her finger against her lip.

"I've never seen anything like this," she added breathlessly.

Nor will you again, the wraith grumbled.

"You cannot copy or recreate it," Connor said firmly as he pointed to the scroll. "That's part of the deal."

Tove pouted, but ultimately nodded. "It's not like I'll get the chance to do this again, regardless."

To his surprise, she sounded almost disappointed by the prospect.

"Sophia's augmentation is more urgent, but I can at least get the core brew started for... goodness, this one is intricate... oh, but what if..." Her mutterings faded to mumbled gibberish as she studied the scroll. She set it on a table and reached for a bottle of dried roots on one of the upper shelves. Her eyes glazed over as she finally tore herself away from it, and she lifted an iron cauldron from the corner as her brows furrowed with concentration.

"Do you need any help?" Connor asked.

She didn't answer, and only the crackle of the fire in the hearth filled the silence that followed. Tove still had her back to him, and though she held the heavy cauldron in both hands, she had barely looked up from the scroll since she had begun to read. She muttered again to herself, her eyes glossing over, and finally tore herself away from the parchment to set the iron cauldron on the open fire.

He frowned. "Do you need—"

"We've lost her." Quinn joined him as they watched the augmentor tug a jar of glowing green spellgust from a small chest beneath one of the kitchen's work surfaces.

I will ensure the scroll remains safe, the wraith announced, still hovering over the augmentor who had seemingly forgotten his presence.

"Then do it without her seeing," Connor ordered under his breath. "You're going to distract her."

Beside him, Quinn's head tilted ever so slightly toward him, but she didn't give any other indication that she'd heard him speak.

The ghoul grumbled, but he faded away into a cloud of black smoke.

"Remember, outlaw," Quinn lowered her voice to the barest whisper. "If any harm comes to her, you will answer to me."

"And if she fails to cure Sophia, you will be held responsible," he countered, lowering his voice to match her tone. "You made a lot of promises, Lightseer. I'll ensure you keep them."

Her hazel eyes drifted toward his face, and her neck tensed with the implications of what that would entail.

It didn't matter. He'd meant every word. If she betrayed them—or if any harm came to his team during this little detour of theirs—he had every intention of following through.

CHAPTER FORTY-ONE
OTMUND

Lost in thought as he rubbed his jaw, Otmund paced in front of the windows across from his borrowed bed. Stacks of parchment and an ink-stained quill sat on the nearby desk, and he debated penning yet another letter to the former princess of this fallen land. Flames crackled in the nearby fireplace in his suite at Freymoor Castle, but he barely heard the fizzle and pop of burning wood. He had already been here a week, and yet he hadn't had the opportunity to speak with the Lady since his first day.

Duncan kept the girl locked away, no doubt whispering lies and spinning tales to keep her complacent.

Otmund needed something he could use against the girl's advisor. Even a sliver of proof that he had been drugging her into submission would be enough to shift the situation back into his favor.

Otmund reached the far wall, his eyes still out of focus as he raced through scenario after scenario. He pivoted, ready to pace along his already well-worn trail in the carpet, but a man now stood in front of him.

He jumped in surprise and stumbled backward. With his back pressed against the wall and his hand on his thumping heart, he finally recognized one of the necromancers that had accompanied him on the journey into Freymoor.

"Curse the *Fates*." Otmund pinched the bridge of his nose as he tried to settle his racing pulse.

He hated it when they did that.

"Nothing new to report," the elite necromancer said with a bored tilt to his voice. The soldier crossed his arms over his narrow chest and stared out the window, as though he would rather be anywhere else. "Same routine as always. Same dinner, even. Nothing ever changes here."

Otmund cursed under his breath. "There has to be something we can use against Duncan. Anything at all that will make her lose faith in him for even a moment. That's all I need, damn it."

"Hmm." The necromancer absently scratched his jaw as his eyes slipped briefly out of focus. "There is the corridor."

Otmund raised one eyebrow in confusion as he waited for the necromancer to elaborate.

"He disappears," the soldier explained. "I don't know how he does it, but it always happens in a hallway on the north side of the castle. It's in a heavily guarded passageway, and none of us can track him through it without being seen. Every time I turn the corner, he's already gone. No secret doors that I can find. No hint at where he went. He simply vanishes."

"And you didn't think to tell me about this sooner?"

The man scowled and met the challenge by staring Otmund down. "Didn't have anything substantial to report."

Otmund shook his head in frustration. "Fine. Figure it out, and do it quickly. We need to leave as soon as possible. I want the Soulsprite by dawn."

"Suits me just fine," the necromancer said. He tugged his hood over his head and headed toward the exit.

Through the corner of Otmund's eye, something moved in the courtyard. He stared out the window just as a man in a black fur-lined cape and tall collar trotted down the central stairwell and tugged on his gloves. Though he walked with his head slightly turned, discussing something in detail with the man in black who never left his side, Otmund would recognize Duncan anywhere. The furs, the confident stride, the defiant act of dressing in the classic robes of a culture King Henry had tried to scrub from memory—Duncan *exuded* power.

"Wait," Otmund ordered.

A floorboard creaked, and the necromancer let out an impatient sigh.

The Lord of Mossvale grabbed a piece of parchment from the desk by the window and scribbled a quick note to the Lady. In his haste, his thumb smeared the still-drying ink, but he didn't care. With Duncan finally leaving the castle, this would likely be his only chance to secure an audience with her. "Slip this under the Lady's door on your way to the corridor, and don't let a soul see you."

He handed the note to the soldier, who slipped wordlessly out into the hallway. Another shadow passed by, and though Otmund didn't see a face, he figured it had to be one of the other necromancers who had snuck into the city since his arrival.

With a concerned frown, Otmund resumed his pacing by the window and mentally sifted through the dozens of presents he had already sent the girl to get her attention. Chocolates from the capital. Jewelry from Wildefaire. Fresh herbs from Dewcrest, given her love for the palace garden. Anything at all to make her feel cared for and adored. He needed her on his side, at least until she gave him the Soulsprite, and this sort of drivel always worked on the socialites in Oakenglen's inner rings.

And based on everything he'd seen so far, Dahlia would be even easier to control.

CONNOR

As sunshine glowed around the edges of the closed curtains along Tove's shopfront, Connor paced the full length of the floorboards across both of the front rooms.

Another day, gone. He was restless, and they had so little time left.

"How long is this going to take?" he grumbled.

Over by the gilded throne, Quinn gave a curt sigh as her fingers grazed a bottle on the top shelf. "Potions take time. I figured you of all people would know that by now."

Of course he knew. Knowing didn't make him any more patient.

Is the Starling woman's augmentor even capable of doing one thing at a time? The wraith huffed. *She needs to focus on the dragon's augmentation, not the Hackamores. Curse the Fates, how does she get anything done?*

Connor rubbed his eyes and stifled an irritated groan. Given his inexperience with a cauldron and Sophia's fading health, precious little progress had been made. At least Murdoc was out getting them supplies, though Connor figured most of the coin would be wasted on booze. Murdoc's was the only face Zander hadn't seen, and in case Quinn's brother had made it back to Lunestone alive, only their former Blackguard could venture into public.

"Where's that maidenhair tree bark?" Tove wandered into the front room from the kitchen, her nose still buried in a book as she expertly sidestepped a basket on the floor and rounded the corner toward the bookcases. "Quinn, check that bottom cupboard, will you?"

"Maidenhair bark? In a Hackamore?" Quinn clicked her tongue in disappointment and, as she reached again for the bottle on the top shelf of the bookcase, curled the fingers of her other hand into a tight fist. A quick gust of air shot through the room, and the magical burst of wind slid the bottle toward her palm. She grabbed it and shook the jar of dried mushrooms. "Use the death cap tops. They're better."

Tove snorted derisively. "I will obviously use those, Quinn, but those two ingredients don't even do the same thing."

"Sure they do. They both connect to the mind." The Starling frowned in annoyance. "Death cap heads weaken resolve, and with enough of them, no one can lie. That's how Father's potion works."

Connor stiffened, his brow creasing with surprise as she gave away something as vital as the key ingredient in one of Teagan's secret recipes.

"I don't like his formula." Tove shook her head and set her book down on the throne's black cushioned seat. "Besides, they don't do the same thing at all. Death cap mushroom heads weaken the mind, but maidenhair bark connects to it. There's nuance in how you can apply that in a potion."

Quinn pursed her lips in disagreement, but she didn't reply.

"Your father's potions are always so aggressive." Tove shuddered at the very thought. "It's all raw force and no nuance. With a Hackamore, you can't rely exclusively on the death cap heads. It's too harsh, and it's too easy to miscalculate your ingredients. Even the tiniest variation in your spellgust's quality can trigger a reaction that overpowers your subject's thought. Or, add one gram too much of the mushroom cap, and now you've left them too punch-drunk to be useful. That's why you balance it with maidenhair nuts and bark. Otherwise, your subject could simply forget to tell you an important detail, and you'll never know. The maidenhair might be a fairly common reagent, but I promise, it's the star of a good Hackamore."

Awestruck, Connor simply watched the augmentor in stunned silence.

Damn, the ghoul muttered. *She's good.*

Quinn frowned and crossed her arms, still holding the jar of dried mushrooms as she leaned against the wall. "How would you do it, then?"

"It's all about the maidenhair," Tove said, as though it were obvious. "The tree's nuts give you an instant connection to the mind, provided you don't destroy them with salt or oil first, and the bark connects the potion to the subject's memory. It preserves their accounts and ensures nothing is omitted, while the Everglade bloom relaxes them until they don't care enough to stop themselves."

Quinn scoffed. "Then how do you ensure they actually tell you everything?"

"Heart-leaved moonseed." Tove flashed a mischievous grin as she rifled through the bottom cupboard. "Its stems weaken willpower, while the roots weaken motivation. Maypop connects to the soul, and lucky for you I have both the petals and the fruits. Trust me, this Hackamore will be the best you've ever used."

"Maypop?" Quinn's eyebrows shot up her forehead. "How the hell did you get ahold of those on such short notice?"

"You're not the only influential person who owes me favors." Tove winked at the Starling.

Connor frowned. He wasn't sure he liked the sound of that.

"We don't have much longer before the wine and spellgust are done boiling." Tove picked up her book from the throne's seat and flipped a page. "Help me collect the last few things, will you? The death cap mushrooms are obviously important, so I need the heads and the stalks. I also need you to gather some fresh lionsmane mushrooms from the cellar."

"Fates above, you're so demanding." Quinn smiled, however, and she shook her head in surrender. "But you really are the best at what you do."

Tove laughed and nudged the Starling's side with her hip. "Talk about how great I am after you get me all those jars."

"Have it your way, then." Quinn knelt and opened a cupboard to reveal rows of bottles, each labeled with elegant script. She set her elbow on one knee and peered into the back of the shelves.

Tove's gaze shifted to Connor, and her smile fell. "Sophia's augmentation is taking a little longer than expected. To be honest, I'm still not certain what's wrong with her recipe. In theory, it should have worked."

He bristled. "Does that mean you don't—"

"I'm not giving up." Tove raised one palm to soothe his concerns. "I'm just warning you that it might take time."

"We don't have time."

"I'm sorry," she said with a delicate shrug of her shoulders. "I'm doing my best."

He frowned, but didn't reply.

"Yours is nearly done," she added, as though it was any consolation. "We can't augment you here, but I can brew the potion and distill it to ink before we leave. I'll add your blood and the dragon's in the few minutes before I augment you."

"Doesn't it need to boil?"

She tilted her head, and her brows pinched with confusion. "Wait… you didn't even read that scroll, did you?"

With Quinn almost always nearby and his preoccupation with their looming deadline, no. He sure hadn't.

His gaze darted toward the kitchen, but he didn't answer.

"Don't use your usual symbols." Quinn popped her head out of the cupboard. "They're too recognizable."

"Oh, good point." Tove pouted, and her shoulders slumped. "I hate to do less than my best."

"The alternative is to have the King's Guard come after you if they find him." Quinn said with a nod to Connor.

"Thanks for the vote of confidence," he said dryly.

"Well," Tove muttered. "When you put it that way…"

"Whatever you ink on me is fine," Connor interjected. "I don't care."

Fine? the wraith huffed, though he remained unseen. *A king's body is the temple with which he rules the lands he owns! At least one of your augmentations must be your coat of arms, you fool. It's tradition!*

"I don't have one," Connor countered.

Yet, the ghoul corrected. *But you will, even if I have to design it myself.*

Hmm. As Connor continued to pace the front rooms, he rubbed his jaw and thought about the prospect. Even if his kingdom was nothing more than a patch of ruins in the desert, perhaps having his own coat of arms wasn't the worst idea in the world. He didn't know the first thing about making one, but the wraith was guaranteed to insert plenty of unwanted opinions.

"Think about the design you'd like me to create," Tove said as she turned a page in her book.

He nodded.

The augmentor ran her finger down the open page and mumbled to herself again, already lost once more in the challenge ahead of her. He watched her leave, and her eyes darted briefly toward him. She paused midstride when she caught his lingering gaze. Her body tensed, and her eyes drifted to his mouth. He got the feeling she wanted to say something, but she didn't. After a tense and quiet moment, she softly cleared her throat and returned to the kitchen.

While she retreated down the hall, his gaze drifted to her hips before he could stop himself. He winced and shut his eyes as he steeled himself against the primal urge that followed. He tried not to imagine lifting her skirt, or the sensation of his palm against her inner thigh as he nipped at her neck.

He groaned in frustration and set his hands on his head as he turned his back on the hallway. Damn it all.

How interesting, the wraith said.

"Don't get any ideas," he warned the ghoul under his breath.

Instead of answering, the undead king's dark chuckle rumbled through his mind, and Connor let out an irritated breath of air as he finally shoved the urge aside.

CHAPTER FORTY-TWO

OTMUND

The time had finally come.

Otmund strode through the cold stone walls in Freymoor castle, following the two servants in plain brown cloaks that had summoned him to his audience with Dahlia. In the time they had already spent walking, however, neither had spoken a word or so much as glanced his way. His skin crawled with an ominous warning he couldn't place, and his hand slowly inched for the Bloodbane dagger hidden in a nondescript sheath on his waist.

He didn't draw it, but it gave him comfort to know it was there.

The two men led him through hall after hall, down one stairwell and up another, and he lost track of the route they took through the winding labyrinth of corridors. At first, he could at least guess at their location whenever he saw a window, but with time, the windows disappeared.

Strange. Freymoor Castle had seemed so much smaller from the outside.

They rounded another bend in the corridor and, this time, the hallway finally ended in two plain wooden doors. The hinges creaked as the men held them open, but the two servants stopped on the threshold. They waited, their eyes dead ahead, never so much as glancing his way as he walked past them. The moment he stepped over the threshold, the doors clanged shut behind him.

His eye twitched briefly as he looked over his shoulder at the closed exit, but he had to play nice if he wanted to keep his audience with the Lady of Freymoor.

He scanned the room to find a single wooden throne with a royal blue cushion sitting across from a set of iron doors barred with a thick wooden beam. Dahlia stood by a row of windows on the opposite wall, one hand pressed against the glass as she stared out onto the darkening gardens.

With her back still to him, he chanced another look at the iron doors. Barred and boarded like that, they had to be protecting something important—the Soulsprite, perhaps.

He cleared his throat, and a quiet gasp escaped her as she flinched with surprise. Her hands flew to her chest, and she spun around to face him. As soon as she saw him, though, she relaxed and smiled. Her eyes crinkled with delight, but not even that could mask the dark bags beneath her eyes.

"You look well," he lied.

"Thank you," she said with a modest curtsey. "And thank you as well for all the opulent gifts you've sent over the past few days. It was quite generous of you. I've never tasted chocolate so sweet."

"Of course." He gave her a deep bow, and though this insipid small talk tested his patience, he could practically taste victory. "There are still those who care for you, my dear, no matter what Henry did to your ancestral home. I wanted you to know that."

Her smile fell, and she clasped her hands in front of her as her gaze swept the floor. She had walked into his trap, and it was time for him to finally pounce.

"If I may…" He let his voice falter, employing all the false sincerity he had mastered over the years to feign interest in a naïve young woman who likely wouldn't survive another winter. "And, truly, I hope I don't sound rude, my dear, but you seem… tired."

"I am," she admitted with a gentle laugh. "I've never slept well, my Lord, but it's been worse since you came."

"Oh, uh… huh," he muttered, a bit taken aback by her honesty. "I apologize for being such a source of stress, my Lady."

"Oh, it's not that." She shook her head and looked again out the window. "I can't stop thinking about what you said. Freymoor may not be an independent kingdom anymore, but there's still so much to manage—too much for me, sometimes." She sighed and tucked a lock of hair behind one ear.

Otmund took the spare moment to steal another glance at the iron doors to size up any potential enchantments. If she proved difficult tonight, perhaps his necromancers could merely break in and steal the Soulsprite for him.

She slowly turned to face him, and Otmund used those precious seconds to don a mask of deep concern.

With her hands clasped before her, she stood a little taller and looked him dead in the eye. "I don't know you well, Lord Soulblud, but your reputation precedes you. My father may not have trusted the Lightseers, but I do."

Otmund's heart skipped a beat in anticipation. "A wise choice, my Lady. I take this to mean you'll let me lead the danger away from here?"

"Perhaps." Her shoulders rose as she took a deep and settling breath. "What I don't understand is why this assassin wants something as silly as the Soulsprite. It's just a trinket, something my father was fond of but which has almost no value beyond a sentimental keepsake. Why would this horrible man want it?"

"I'm afraid I don't know," Otmund lied. "All I know is dangerous people are after it and whomsoever possesses it."

Her lips pinched together in a soft pout. "And you have an army to keep you safe?"

Otmund nodded. "As soon as the threat is neutralized, I will return it to you. A simple keepsake or no, it's important for heirlooms to remain with their rightful families. I won't take that from you."

A lie, of course. Once he had the Soulsprite and the wraith, she would be powerless to get her little trinket back—unless, of course, she could offer him something of value.

She returned her gaze yet again to the window as the last rays of sunlight disappeared over the towering forest canopy beyond the walls. The soft orange light from the simple iron chandelier above them cast her reflection onto the glass, and she frowned with concern as she thought through his offer. He waited, wondering what final words she needed to hear.

Any minute now, and she would hand it over. All he needed to do was give her a nudge.

He took a few steady steps toward her, slow enough to guarantee she would see his reflection in the window, and he set his hands gently on her shoulders. Despite their difference in age, and despite the fact that they stood alone in the throne room where she had been forced to watch Henry behead her father all those years ago, she didn't flinch. The young woman remained motionless as he held her with all the false reassurance of a parent chasing away a child's nightmare.

"At your core, you are a princess," he reminded her in a gentle whisper. "A queen, really, even if Henry stripped the title from you. No one can care for your people like you do, my dear, and it is your duty to protect them. I ask you to do that now. To make this difficult choice for them. You *must* give me the Soulsprite."

"But Father…" Her pink lips pressed together, and she squeezed her eyes shut as though reliving a horrible memory. "He always… he always said…"

"Listen, Dahlia," Otmund interrupted, taking a risk even as he pushed her over the brink. "This assassin wants the Soulsprite, but you're a beautiful young woman. What will he do when he sees you? I can't even let myself imagine what goes through his depraved mind. I couldn't live with myself if that horrible man had his way with you, my dear, and I fear for what would remain of you when he grows bored of your screams."

Her fingernails dug into the windowsill as she balled one hand into a fist, but she didn't reply.

"Can you do what needs to be done?" Otmund squeezed her shoulders again, just once, to drive his point home. "Can your people rely on you to make that choice?"

She looked over her shoulder at him, and to his dismay, he couldn't read her expression. A jolt of surprise shot through him, and he barely contained his shock before it could show on his face.

All his life, he had read everyone in the room—Quinn, Celine, Henry, even Teagan. They played their parts, predictable down to their subtlest twitches, and he could usually guess what they would say before they said it. Truth be told, only Nyx could hide her emotions from him, and even then it happened rarely.

The comparison set his nerves on edge.

In seconds, the unreadable expression melted away. Her gaze swept across the floor, and her voice cracked as she spoke in a harsh whisper, as though the walls themselves could hear her. "I know Henry only left me alive because I was too young to be a threat. He knew the people would rebel without a member of the former royal family in this castle, and he knew I would never be strong enough to oppose him."

Otmund let her speak, surprised at her self-awareness. Though naïve, perhaps she saw a bit more of the real world than he had originally thought.

"I've suspected for some time now that I've lost what little control I had over this city." She swallowed hard. "I can see the traces of it—of someone plotting against me in my own home."

"Deep down, you know who it is. You just don't want to admit the truth."

"I've had dreams." Her ice-blue eyes darted toward him, and a muscle in her jaw twitched. "Horrible visions of what's coming to my home, and the Soulsprite is at the center of it all. I haven't known…"

As her voice trailed off, she stared at the set of iron doors across from the throne.

"I haven't known what to do," she admitted in a harsh whisper.

"Then let me help," he said.

He was so very close. He could *taste* it.

"Your arrival can't be a coincidence," she said without looking at him, as though she were speaking to herself. "It must be the Fates' doing, Otmund."

"It is," he lied.

"Protect it, will you?" Her gaze shifted back to him. "For my father's sake."

Jaw set, almost afraid that another word would change her mind, he merely nodded.

She walked to the doors, her footsteps echoing in the otherwise whisper-silent room, and she set a hand on the barrier blocking the massive doors. "All of the greatest treasures in Freymoor lie on the other side of this door, Otmund. It's a sight I've never showed anyone. Not even Duncan."

Otmund resisted the urge to smile. Perhaps he could find something else of value to take home along with the Soulsprite.

His newest little puppet danced *beautifully*.

She sighed and tapped her fingers on the barricade. "I'm afraid it's too heavy for me to lift. Shall I call a guard, or—"

"Not necessary, my dear." Otmund smiled as warmly as he could manage and stepped in front of her. He couldn't risk Duncan catching wind of this until he was already gone.

With a grunt of effort, he lifted the barricade. The heavy bar weighed on his hands, leaving imprints in his forearms from its sheer weight, and he huffed with the effort of lifting it. It felt like a full-grown man had sat on his chest, and he did his best to set it down without throwing out his back. It hit the floorboards hard, and he glanced at the entrance to the throne room in fear of the wrong person hearing the clatter.

He had to make this quick. A sharp pain shot up his spine, and he turned his head to hide a grimace as he stood.

Dahlia set her hands on the iron doors, but paused and looked at him over one shoulder. "You should do the honors, Lord Soulblud. The treasury is quite a sight to behold."

She stepped aside, and Otmund set his palms flat against the cold iron. It stung his palms like frost on a cold day, but he didn't linger. With a grunt of effort, he shoved the doors open, and they swung effortlessly outward on silent hinges.

His mind raced with the possibilities of what he would see in Freymoor's fabled treasury. Piles of gold, perhaps, or rows of artifacts in glass cases. Bejeweled statues. Glowing orbs hovering over silk pillows. All the legends of Freymoor's long-lost wealth simmered in his imagination like a fine tea, steeping to perfection as he waited for the doors to reveal what lay inside.

Instead of treasure, a thick fog rolled over his boots. The white mist obscured everything from view, as though the doors had opened onto a rolling bank of clouds.

In his confusion, he squinted into the murky void. She had mentioned that the mists protected her and the Soulsprite both, and perhaps this was what she had meant. Fog served as a suitable defense if one wanted to hide their greatest treasures. After all, a thief couldn't steal what he couldn't see.

Otmund looked over his shoulder, and instead of a lone girl in an empty room, a dozen men in blue tunics now stood behind him. Duncan stood beside Dahlia in front of the small army, and the towering man sneered as he held the heavy barricade effortlessly in his hands.

"What—" Otmund flinched in surprise and resisted the impulse to step backward, for fear of falling into the fog. He hadn't heard a footstep or a breath. Hell, the door hadn't even creaked. They couldn't have been here, and yet they all watched him with silent glares.

He simply vanishes, the necromancer had said.

Dahlia grinned and shifted her weight onto one hip as she studied his face. "Look at his face, Duncan. I think we broke him."

Her advisor chuckled. "It certainly seems that way."

Otmund didn't answer. In the numb horror that followed, he desperately tried to snap himself from his daze. He could only stare at the girl before him, at the young woman who had trembled with fear mere moments before, but who now watched him with all the cold-blooded indifference of a killer. The sickly girl was gone, replaced by a woman hardened under the years of a tyrant's rule.

"You put on quite a show," she admitted with a wicked little smile. "Perhaps I let this drag on a little too long, but I was simply having so much fun."

That, of all things, broke through his shocked stupor. Even though his breath came in shallow bursts, he scanned the wall of soldiers in front of him for any possible exit.

There wasn't one.

It seemed as though he needed to resort to threats, then.

"I am a Lightseer Regent." His nose flared with fear even as he stared Duncan down. "You will step aside at once, or—"

"Or?" Dahlia raised one skeptical eyebrow. "Tell me, dear Otmund, why a Lightseer Regent would come to my kingdom surrounded by necromancers?"

He swallowed hard, his last card played.

She snapped her fingers, and the soldiers behind her stepped aside. Her cold gaze never left Otmund as yet more guards stepped forward, each carrying a body draped in the dark robes of the necromancer elite.

Shit.

Her soldiers brushed past Otmund and chucked corpse after corpse into the mist. The fog churned as it swallowed each one, and only the heavy thuds of meat hitting the ground gave him any hint as to what waited beyond the iron doors.

Without a word, Dahlia held out one hand toward Duncan. His gaze darted toward her, and with a dutiful nod, he set the massive barrier in her open palm. Her biceps tensed as she lifted the heavy barricade with ease, and Otmund stifled a frustrated cry. The so-called sickly girl had hidden a Strongman augmentation from him all this time.

"Now he understands," she said as she read something in his face he hadn't meant to give away. "You saw what you wanted to see, my Lord. I just played my part better than you thought I could."

"You conned me," he seethed.

"I did." Dahlia took a step closer and adjusted her hold on the barrier in her hands as easily as if it were a twig. "You spoke of my royal lineage, and about that, at least, you're correct. Before my Father was murdered in this very room, he told me that people would do anything to obtain the artifacts hidden in our kingdom. He warned me it was my duty to protect them at any cost, even to myself. That was why Henry killed him—he lived by the principles he taught, and he sacrificed himself to protect the secrets of the bogs. It's why soulless charlatans like you have never been able to rape this land for its real treasures, try as you might."

"I haven't—"

"For once in your miserable life, stop *lying!*" she snapped.

A shiver snaked down Otmund's spine at her tone, and every man in the room shifted his gaze toward her. She bristled, her lips tight with her barely contained rage, and her grip on the barricade in her hands tightened.

"You *snake*," she seethed. "You come to my home and dare speak of my father as though you knew him. As though you cared when Henry—"

"Breathe," Duncan interrupted.

The Lady's advisor set his hand on her shoulder, and as if by some unseen tether not even magic could explain, his touch broke through her hate. She briefly closed her eyes, and with a settling breath, the lines in her forehead disappeared. She straightened her back and lifted her chin with all the regal poise of a queen.

When she opened her eyes again, she had regained her composure, and she now wore a mask of cool indifference.

But Otmund had seen the hatred. Emotion that intense always had strings for him to pull, if he could only get a firm hold on them.

As the cold fog coiled around his ankles, Dahlia's icy gaze swept over him.

"My dear—er, your Highness, listen to me." Otmund raised his hands in front of him as though he were speaking to a spooked horse. "What I said about the assassin, all of that is true. He's coming here, and he'll kill you. He will—"

"Celine sends her regards." Dahlia's cold voice hit him harder than any blow, and her words froze him.

Celine.

Celine had done this.

The retribution she had promised him should he fail to kill the wraith—she had followed through on every threat she had ever made.

And, just as she had warned him all those months ago, he had never seen it coming.

Dahlia swung the barrier, and it hit him hard in the chest. The blow kicked the air from his lungs and launched him backward. He hit the ground and rolled. The mist blurred and spun around him, swallowing him whole as he tumbled downward.

After what felt like an eternity, he skidded to a stop, but his head still spun. He tried to stand, and he staggered as he fought to get his balance. After a few blurry moments, his eyes finally refocused, and he found himself standing on a pile of yellow and red leaves. He looked around for a landmark, still unable to catch his breath as the fog rolled in. A bloodstained hand protruded from the wall of white fog that circled him. The mist obscured everything in sight as his heart thudded against his ribcage.

"I've been watching you." A voice boomed around him, eerily similar to Dahlia's, but the words echoed and overlapped like ripples on a pond.

"I listened as you muttered to yourself when you thought you were alone. You've taught me so much—about the Wraithblade, about the Starlings, and about everything at stake."

"I'll burn you alive!" he shouted into the fog. "I'll have my necromancers skin every one of your maids while you watch. I'll have them saw off your legs—"

The surreal voice giggled like a little girl watching a jester perform, and her haunting tone echoed further into the mist.

"I've been warned about people like you, Otmund," she explained. "The fools who say whatever must be said to get what they want. I learned to see through your kind years ago, and I know what you fear most—being discovered. You dread the day the world learns you're a fraud."

He scanned the mist. With her voice that close, that had to be real Dahlia. Somehow, she must've come down here with him.

She must've been just out of reach, toying with him.

Otmund set his hand on the hilt of the Bloodbane dagger, just waiting for the right moment to draw it. If he could capture her or stab her with the Bloodbane dagger, perhaps he could coax his way out of here alive.

"I see you for what you are," she added. "And the Blood Bogs cannot abide liars."

The Blood Bogs.

This was no treasury. He was in the dreaded fog that had claimed so many lives over the years.

His throat closed with the sheer terror of what she had said. The implications ate away at his plans and schemes. Try as he might, he couldn't fight the overwhelming urge to run, and the last shreds of his self-restraint withered away.

He had to get out of here.

A wave of panic drove him back up the hill he had fallen down moments before, and he clawed his way through the mud and lingering leaves to reach the door. He would break it down if he had to. He would claw at the wood until the nails ripped from his skin. He didn't care, so long as he made it out of this cursed woodland alive.

As he clambered up the hill, however, it never seemed to end. He passed the distance he had fallen, or so he thought, but the door had disappeared. All he could see were leaves and fog, and the mud caked to his hands as he climbed ever higher.

His foot slipped on a wet leaf, and he tumbled down the slope yet again. His head spun, and nausea burned the back of his throat as he choked back vomit. He tumbled, his shoulders slamming against the ground again and again on the long way down.

When he skidded to a stop, he laid there for a moment. Drenched in mud and sweat, he stared at the blurry leaves as he tried to regain his composure. If he could swallow his panic for even a second, perhaps he could think his way out of this.

Think, Otmund, he chided himself. *Get ahold of yourself!*

As he laid there, his head still spinning from his fall, he listened for Dahlia's voice. Any second now, she would taunt him. At any moment, he would hear the echoing giggle from that con artist as she tried to lead him deeper into the mist, and when that happened, he could figure out where she was.

But, it didn't come.

He lifted his head, just as a silhouette appeared ahead of him in the fog. The figure walked toward him, her dress dragging along the mud as she neared, and he reached again for the Bloodbane dagger. Though her feet made no sound, she walked steadily closer, teasing him as she hid just within the edge of the mist.

But this time, Otmund was ready.

Dahlia stepped into view, and she watched him with a cold smile. Before she could even open her mouth to speak, he jumped to his feet and drew the glowing green Bloodbane dagger. He drove it into her gut, chest heaving as he grinned with victory.

She couldn't escape this time. For all her tricks, he had finally won.

But the girl didn't flinch. She didn't even grimace in pain. She merely held his gaze—and smiled.

He gaped at her in confusion as the fog around him thinned. One by one, more silhouettes appeared in the mist. They stepped into view, each wearing the same blue cloak that she had worn in the throne room, and each sporting Dahlia's face and long, wavy curls. His jaw tensed in horror as two dozen Dahlias circled him, all of them watching him in stony silence.

"Interesting," Dahlia's voice echoed around him, even though none of the women's mouths moved. "I'm going to let you keep the dagger, Otmund. I want you to show me what it does."

The Dahlia he had stabbed merely stared at him with that cryptic smile, oblivious to the blade in her gut.

The bogs' tricks. It had to be.

"*Otmund,*" the women said in unison.

He went still as their voices hit him in the chest, and in his raw terror, he could barely breathe. He withdrew the Bloodbane from the woman's abdomen, and not a drop of blood came with it. She stood tall, unfazed, as though nothing had ever happened.

The women stretched out their arms, and their cloaks slid aside to reveal their slender arms as they glared him down.

"*The bogs are caked with conmen's lies;*
for the mists show who you truly be.
The wisps will carve out both your eyes
if they don't like what they see."

A flash of green light blinded him. He winced as he raised one arm to shield his eyes. When the light finally faded, he looked over his forearm to find two dozen wispy green lights hovering where each of the Dahlias had been moments before.

A shrill laugh echoed through the oppressive fog around him. The sound startled the wisps, and they instantly darted into the mist.

Just like that, he was alone.

Otmund stared down at the mud caking his fingers as he processed what he had just seen. Panting, soaked in filth and out of breath, he could only gape in horror at the ground as he relived the wisps' warning.

"I'm *fucked,*" he whispered.

CHAPTER FORTY-THREE
CONNOR

Connor needed sleep, but he couldn't even close his eyes.

In the spare bedroom on the second floor of Tove's shop, he laid on the narrow bed against one wall and stared at the ceiling. His hands rested on his chest as he lost himself in thought. He'd lost track of how long he had been staring at the speck of dirt right above his head. His only measure of time had come from the thin line of sunlight peering around the edge of the closed curtain as it slowly inched across the floorboards.

Just four days left.

The occasional buzz of muffled conversations filtered through the glass from outside as people wandered past Tove's shop, but no one had knocked. Whether it was because her curtains remained closed or because no one cared, not a soul had tried to enter all day.

The only chime of the door had come hours ago, when Murdoc had slipped out into the daylight to gather supplies for their trip north.

It didn't make sense. Tove clearly had talent. Hell, she had outright told Quinn Starling, of all people, that the Starling recipe was inadequate.

He chuckled. Confident, bold, and unafraid to offend powerful people. It suddenly made far more sense that Tove hadn't been offered a place in the Spell Market.

They'd have felt inferior.

Downstairs, the delicate bell above the main door chimed.

He bolted upright and threw his legs over the side of the bed. With his elbows on his knees, he tilted his head and listened through the floorboards, straining his ear as he tried to figure out who had walked into the shop.

A man's voice filtered through the floor, and a woman's followed. Calm. Steady. No panic in their tones, as far as he could tell. He curled his fingers, and his knuckles cracked from the tension in his bones as he waited to hear a scuffle, or the crash of glass breaking on the ground.

It didn't come.

Footsteps thumped up the stairs, muted by the closed bedroom door. Steady gait. Heavy footfalls. A man. Connor studied the cadence of the thuds, and it only took a second longer to recognize Murdoc's gait.

He relaxed and rubbed his tired eyes.

The door to the hallway swung open, and Murdoc stretched his arms above his head as he let out an exaggerated sigh. "I have returned, and I brought booze."

Connor stood and twisted his head until his neck cracked. "Did you get everything else I asked for?"

"I bought whiskey, if that's what you mean." Murdoc took a long swig of his flask. "A man like me can't live a dry life, Captain. We need proper stores back in Slaybourne."

"I'll work on it."

"I also found these." The former Blackguard pulled some folded papers out of his pocket and handed them over.

WANTED.

His shoulders ached with dread as he stared down at himself. The scarf across his nose and mouth hid most of his features, but those eyes glared back at him with all the hatred and spite of a man who wanted to watch the world burn.

No wonder Quinn had been so persistent in the beginning. If this was her first impression of him, it was only natural for her to assume the worst.

Connor's heart thudded against his chest as he rifled through the pages. Each featured his face under a sizeable reward, with instructions to notify the King's Guard at the first sighting. He paused as he stared at the worst of the drawings, and his nose wrinkled with disdain at the depiction of him as a hardened criminal.

Your face will be on every wall in every kingdom on the continent, Richard Beaumont had warned. *The world will hunt you down. You'll have nowhere to go.*

Nowhere to hide.

"That Otmund fellow has one hell of a memory." Murdoc pointed at the paper with his empty hand as he took another long drink from the flask. "It looks just like you."

"Thanks," Connor said dryly. "Any posters for you or Sophia?"

"None." The former Blackguard smacked his lips and let out a scratchy breath as the whiskey burned his throat. "Thank the Fates."

"But that would mean…" Connor scratched at the stubble on his jaw as he stared again at the poster.

He didn't dare hope that the blightwolves had actually killed Zander, but if he'd returned to Lunestone, the man would've spread the word about Connor's team by now.

"I also asked Tove to re-enchant my weapons." Murdoc patted the empty sheath on his waist.

"How do you plan on paying for that?"

"I'm not. You are, my fearless Captain."

Connor shook his head. "You're expensive."

"Yeah, but I'm pretty."

With a soft chuckle, he nodded to the bed. "All yours. Get some rest."

"Don't have to tell me twice."

As Murdoc collapsed on the bed, Connor strode out into the hall and swung the door shut behind him. Before he even reached the top of the stairs, a soft snoring filtered through the thin gap beneath the door.

Finally. The wraith's voice swam through his mind with a growl of frustration. *The Starling woman keeps trying to read the scroll, and I'm close to slitting her throat to make her stop.*

"Behave," Connor warned in a gravelly voice. "Has she tried to escape?"

Not yet, though she has eyed the door repeatedly.

When his boot hit the bottom stair, black smoke rolled across Connor's shoes. The ghoul emerged from the churning shadow, and the undead king crossed his bony arms across his chest. He stared into Connor's soul, as though waiting for a confession.

Without bothering to mask his impatience, Connor scratched the back of his head and gestured for the ghoul to speak. "Alright. Say it."

There's nothing to kill here, Magnuson. The undead king growled. *I am infuriatingly bored.*

"Are you, now?" Connor grinned. "It almost sounds like you enjoy the wilds to the city you tried to get me to conquer. Am I already rubbing off on you?"

Do not test me. The wraith's skull pivoted on his bony neck, and he raised his chin in defiance. *I am not in the mood.*

Connor just laughed.

Slippered feet shuffled over the kitchen floor, and he stood aside as Tove walked past him with her nose buried in yet another book. Her eyes darted briefly toward him and the wraith, but nothing else about her demeanor changed.

"Hold this, will you?" Without looking up from her book, she reached into her pocket and handed him a broken quill.

"What—" With his brows pinched in confusion, he held the destroyed instrument between two fingers.

Tove didn't pause long enough for him to finish his sentence. She flipped the page and marched out to the front rooms. Jars clinked, and the heavy thud of books hitting a shelf followed. Seconds later, she trekked back with two more tomes tucked under one arm as she continued reading the page she'd had open mere seconds ago.

Something is wrong with this one. The Wraith King's skull pivoted on his bony neck as they watched her pass.

"Tove," Connor said firmly.

At the sound of his voice, her head finally snapped up from the book. She blinked herself out of her daze, and her bleary eyes swept across his face. "Oh, hello."

He raised one eyebrow and held the broken quill in front of her. "Why did you give me this?"

She frowned and stared at it. "I have no idea."

The Wraith King sighed.

"It's good you're here, though." She continued down the hallway and beckoned him to join her with a tilt of her head. "Your dragon's augmentation is fascinating, but Sophia's project is unlike anything I've ever been able to work on in my life. The possibilities as to what went wrong and how to fix it are nearly endless! Everything should have been perfect according to the theories, so where was I supposed to start? Was there not enough energy in the initial body transfer? Was her chosen replacement weakened by an unknown disease or latent magical allergy? Perhaps, in the first event, she simply didn't kill enough people to properly open the channel to the death dimension. It's so hard to say."

I notice she's completely unfazed by that sentence, the wraith said with a nod of approval. *That's the mark of a talented augmentor.*

Instead of replying, Connor massaged his forehead. He didn't know what to make of that.

"Was the spellgust unrefined?" Tove continued, unaware of the exchange taking place behind her. "Or could she have used too little of the maypop flowers? I've been poring over my journals and notes since you all arrived, and I think I'm finally close to cracking it."

He followed her into the kitchen, only understanding about half of what she had said as she rambled on, but he couldn't deny the infectious excitement that lit up her face when she spoke about magic.

Quinn lounged at the two-person table by the hearth. Her elbow sat on the surface, and her head rested on one fist as her eyelids drooped. When Connor entered, she snapped upright and stretched her arms across the table, yawning into her shoulder as she spread her fingers wide.

"Nodding off?" he asked with a smirk.

Quinn sniffed and leaned back in her seat, blinking as she struggled to keep her eyes open. "Never."

Come fetch me when the augmentor starts making sense, the wraith growled. He disappeared into a puff of smoke, and Connor crossed his arms as he leaned against the wall to watch Tove work. Unaware of the world around her, the augmentor mumbled to herself and flipped through the various open books strewn across her kitchen surfaces.

"I mean, I have to be careful." Tove tapped one finger against her lip, and at this point, he couldn't tell if she was speaking to him or to herself. "This won't be like augmenting Quinn. With her, I have a margin of error, but Sophia is—"

"Tove," Quinn hissed, scowling.

Connor's eyes narrowed in suspicion, and his gaze drifted to the Starling warrior sitting at the table. "Margin of error?"

"Yes, exactly." Tove gestured to the Starling sitting at the table, though her focus remained on her books. "Quinn's augmentations always last longer than they should, even when I realize later that I made a small mistake or could've tweaked an ingredient. The impact spellgust has on her is fascinating, and I've never figured it out. Even though I always strive for perfection, I appreciate the wiggle room I have with her. Sophia is different. For her augmentation, everything has to be *flawless*."

Tove spun around, mouth open to continue, but her smile fell as her eyes darted between Connor and Quinn. "Oh, I didn't—I mean, I shouldn't have—"

The Starling warrior growled in frustration and pinched the bridge of her nose.

Connor let the silence settle on the air. He wasn't sure what to make of this interesting new piece of information, but he would have to figure it out later.

For now, Tove had a lot left to finish.

He nodded to the books. "Shouldn't you be working on—"

"No, the Hackamores are done." Tove pointed to three jars filled with an iridescent white liquid on one of the nearby shelves. She rested her hands on the edge of the nearest work surface and leaned over three of the nearest books. Her hair slid over one shoulder, and she began to mutter to herself once again.

"And the telepathic augmentation?"

"Brewing." Without turning around, she pointed to a cauldron in the hearth. "There's another eight hours to go on that one."

"And the new leg?"

"On its way." She flipped pages in two of the books before her. "I had to call in a favor for that one, but don't worry. Murdoc delivered the note for me during his errands and read it when he thought I wasn't looking. He can confirm that I gave precious few details and that I didn't inform the authorities."

Connor hesitated as he studied the woman before him who had done an impossible amount of work in just a few short days. "Have you slept?"

With her back still to him, Tove tapped her fingernails on the wooden surface and turned another page.

Never one to endure being overtly ignored, he walked up behind her and waited for her to reply. Quinn tensed in her seat by the hearth, but he ignored it. He towered over Tove, only a few inches away from her now, and yet the augmentor still didn't look up from the open pages in front of her.

"Tove," he said firmly.

The brunette gasped and spun around. First, her eyes landed on his muscled chest, and it took a moment for them to trail up toward his face.

"When did you sleep?" he asked again.

"I didn't," she confessed with a weak shrug. Her eyes lingered again on his chest, but she inched around him and headed for another of her books farther down the row of tables that sat against her kitchen walls. "I can sleep all I want once these potions are done. Besides, this is too fascinating. I couldn't sleep if I tried. I'd wake up thinking about it." She snapped her fingers, and her eyes slipped out of focus once again. "Oh, I'm going to need more maypop. Let me see what I have left in my stores."

She darted back into the hallway, and Quinn leaned back in her seat as she watched the augmentor disappear around the corner.

Connor pointed after Tove. "Is she always like this?"

Quinn nodded. "I told you she was the best."

"Ha!" Tove shouted from the other room.

"I guess she found the maypop," he muttered, mostly to himself.

Rapid footsteps pounded along the floor as Tove returned to the kitchen and slid the final few inches toward the nearest book. She shoved a jar of flower petals into Connor's hands and flipped through the pages, still muttering to herself.

"...but if we infuse an object this time, it can retain the power without draining... huh, if we don't get the fusion right, it could... or maybe I should... would that kill her?"

Connor scowled down at the augmentor leaning over her books. "Come again?"

"Sophia!" Tove shouted without looking away from the pages.

An impatient sigh filtered down the hallway as the necromancer joined them and leaned against the doorframe. "What in the Fates' name do you want now, woman? Do you somehow have *more* infernal questions for me?"

Tove smacked her palms against the open pages. "I've got it!"

Connor stood a little taller, almost unwilling to believe it, and waited for the augmentor to elaborate.

Quinn stood. "You're sure?"

"Positive." Tove slammed her book closed and turned around, beaming. "Sophia, I can fix your spell."

The necromancer went eerily still, and she hugged herself tighter as her chest stilled in awe. "How?"

"It won't be easy," Tove confessed. "Based on my research, you failed to account for the cost associated with moving a soul from body to body. You—"

"Don't be ridiculous," Sophia interrupted. "What do you think all that belladonna is even for? Between that, the bloody beauties, and the maypop, I couldn't possibly have done more to account for the wear on the new body."

"But that's just it," Tove said with unfettered excitement. "It doesn't just wear on the body, Sophia. It also wears on your *soul*."

The augmentor paused and scanned the faces of everyone present. She spread her arms wide, as though waiting for the three of them to applaud whatever the hell she was talking about.

Instead, they all stared at her with various expressions of confusion and simply waited for her to continue.

"Don't you see?" she asked, exasperated. "Every time you move bodies, it requires more power to pull the soul back from the death dimension. The bodies remain constant, but the soul becomes—how can I put this? Heavier,

I suppose. Without a tether to this world, the soul will naturally drift away, and it takes more and more magic to resist that pull. If you used another body without accounting for this nuance, there's no guarantee it would last as long as this one did. Hell, it might not even *work*."

"What's the alternative?" Sophia asked.

Instead of answering, Tove shifted her attention to Quinn. "I need to use the reserve."

The Starling warrior groaned and leaned back in her chair. "You can't be serious."

Connor frowned. "What reserve?"

"Please," Tove begged, ignoring him. "You want this to work, don't you?"

Quinn crossed her arms and drummed her fingers on her bicep. "You're absolutely sure there's no other way?"

"I can't think of a single alternative," Tove confessed. "And I couldn't possibly find one that big on such short notice."

"What reserves?" Connor repeated, more firmly this time.

"Fine," Quinn said with an irritated sigh. She pinched her eyes shut, as if this would hurt to watch. "Just take it."

"You won't regret this!" Tove disappeared into the hallway, and a door slammed. The distant scrape of rock on stone followed, and she returned moments later with a spellgust gem the size of her fist.

Connor's eyebrows shot up his forehead. "That's the biggest gem I've ever seen in my life."

"Solid spellgust," Tove said proudly. "Finest quality on the market."

"It must've cost a fortune," Sophia said softly.

"It did," Quinn snapped. "And it came out of my fortune. I expect to be repaid."

"This is how we save you." Tove held the spellgust stone in front of Sophia's face, and the glittering gem cast its dazzling green reflection in the necromancer's eyes. "You did the hard part with your initial spell's design, but this is what you were missing. You can't rely on your body to sustain you. You need something more. Something that can retain the sort of magic necessary to tether you to this world and fight off Death."

"Of course," Sophia whispered as it all finally made sense to her. "And if we hadn't come here... if we had gone to the mountain instead..."

Quinn gave the necromancer a sarcastic salute. "You're welcome."

"You need to change it every year." Tove wagged her finger in front of Sophia's nose. "To the *day*, Sophia. I mean it, and you need to come here to get it done. Don't you dare try to do it yourself."

Sophia huffed. "Why the hell not?"

"Because removing this will kill you for a time," Tove said matter-of-factly. "It's not ideal, but this is new magic, and it's the best we've got."

Connor pointed to the gem. "How exactly do you plan on getting that in her?"

"It will be excruciatingly painful," Tove admitted with a sheepish shrug. "Sedation will be necessary, no question. I'll carve out part of her chest to—"

"Tell me after." Sophia held up one palm. "I don't want to know until it's done."

"I don't like this." Connor took a looming step forward and frowned down at the augmentor. "Carving out her chest? Are you insane? You're going to kill her!"

"Yes, but not for *long*," Tove said with an irritated huff. "That's the point."

His furious glare shifted toward Sophia, who stared at the floor. She pursed her lips and shut her eyes, but ultimately, she relaxed. All the tension from the last few weeks faded, and any lingering concern dissolved entirely. "Connor, I haven't been able to refute a single thing this woman has said. You know I'm not one to trust others to do what I could do myself, but I think she's right."

"You've got to be joking," he said. "She's going to carve out part of your—"

"I know!" Sophia snapped, grimacing. "I know."

"Does that mean you're ready?" Tove's smile broadened. "Do you need to sleep on things?"

The necromancer shook her head. "I'll have plenty of time to sleep on it if you kill me."

"That's the spirit," Quinn said dryly.

"I can get everything ready in the cellar." With the massive spellgust gem in one hand, Tove used the other to close the remaining open books on the counter. "Meet me down there when you—"

Without a word of warning, Sophia spun on her heel and darted up the stairs. Connor frowned in confusion, staring after her, and took the stairs two at a time as he followed.

When he reached the top of the staircase, she had already thrown open the door to the spare bedroom and grabbed Murdoc by the collar. She pressed her lips roughly against his as he snapped awake, his hair askew and his eyes still half-shut in his exhaustion.

Before Murdoc could say a thing, she dropped him back on the mattress, took a settling breath, and stormed back out into the hallway.

Connor stepped aside and grinned down at her as he let her pass. "I knew you wanted him."

"Ass," she muttered when she walked by.

"What was that?" Murdoc sat upright, his eyelids drooping as he stared around him in a daze. "Did I die? Is this the afterlife? Because I like it."

Connor chuckled.

I will observe the operation, the wraith said as Connor headed back downstairs. *I suspect it will be quite interesting to witness.*

At the base of the steps, a door slammed. Muffled footsteps retreated down a stone staircase, and by the time he returned to the first floor, Tove and Sophia were gone. Only Quinn stood in the hallway, and she leaned against the wall as she stared at the closed cellar door in silence.

"This had better work," he said under his breath.

Quinn smirked. "Don't you trust me, outlaw?"

His jaw tensed, and he studied her face as he tried to decipher whether or not that had been a taunt. In the end, he chose not to reply, and they stood together in somber silence.

He had done all he could. Tove had to kill Sophia for this to work, and it fell on the necromancer to claw her way back from the dead.

And, to his frustration, all he could do was *wait*.

CHAPTER FORTY-FOUR
CONNOR

Several hours passed, and yet no one had emerged from the cellar. Late afternoon light framed the closed curtains of the lone window in Tove's kitchen. While a fire raged in the hearth beside him, Connor shifted his weight in his seat and leaned his forearms against the small two-person table. His fingertips tapped against the teacup in his palms, but he didn't drink. He had mostly poured it to warm his hands and give himself something to do.

Despite the muted chatter of the market outside the augmentor's shop, the house was still and relatively silent.

His eyelids drooped, and though he had fought his exhaustion for hours, he let them shut this time. The occasional creak of a floorboard filtered down the stairs from the spare bedroom where Murdoc waited for news on Sophia's procedure, and steady breaths from the front room suggested Quinn had fallen asleep in the augmentor's throne.

The scrape of pottery across wood cracked through the air like thunder.

He snapped awake. His grip reflexively tightened on the teacup in his hand, and he nearly shattered it. At the last second, he caught himself, and he stared down at the curls of steam rising from the honey-gold liquid. A plate of crumbs sat before him, the bread and fresh chicken long gone, but it was barely enough to whet his appetite. As he stared longingly at the platter, another pang of hunger twisted through his stomach.

With everything he had yet to face on his way back to Slaybourne, perhaps he needed to fully indulge his body's ravenous hunger before they left Oakenglen.

It is done.

The wraith's grim voice stirred his thoughts, and Connor sat upright as he waited in silence for more detail.

None came.

Slippers brushed against the steps leading up from the cellar, and he leaned forward as a door in the hallway swung open. Something wet splattered on the floorboards. When the door once again swung shut, Tove stood in the hall, holding a bloodstained cloth.

Bright crimson goo dripped from her delicate fingers, and the once-white fabric had been stained completely red. With a weary sigh, she rubbed her eyes on her shoulder and squinted in the harsh light filtering around the curtains.

His jaw tensed, and he stood. His chair scraped across the floorboards as he stared at her hands. "That's a lot of blood."

"She's fine." Completely calm and apparently unfazed by the scarlet smears all over her forearms, Tove offered him a tired smile. "Everything went exactly as I expected."

He sat back in his chair, but he didn't relax.

Stop fretting, you nattering old hen, the wraith chided. *The necromancer is alive. Drenched in blood, perhaps, but breathing.*

Connor let out a settling breath and reclined back in his seat. The tension in his core dissolved, and the tightness in his chest faded completely.

She died for a time, the wraith casually added. *The augmentor had a hell of a time dragging her back, but managed. It would've been a waste to lose such a wicked little thing.*

He grinned. Even the wraith was going soft on him.

Tove toweled off the last of the blood and tossed the rag in a bucket by the hearth. With an exhausted groan, she collapsed in the seat across from him. Her eyes fluttered shut, and her chest rose and fell in a steady rhythm as she relaxed into the chair.

"Here." He slid his untouched tea across the table and stood. "I want some whiskey, anyway."

She raised the cup toward him in an unspoken toast and took a sip as he rifled through a nearby chest that Murdoc had recently restocked with copious amounts of alcohol. He popped the cork out of a wide mouth bottle and poured it into a mug, relishing in the sweet tang of rye that spiraled into the air.

As he returned to the table, Tove watched him over the brim of her teacup. Its spiraling steam rolled across her face, and those dark brown eyes traced his every step. The intensity reminded him of the sultry look he'd gotten years ago on the morning after he'd spent his first night in a woman's bed. The arched eyebrows. The playful tilt of the head. The subtle twist of a smile at the corner of her soft lips.

The expression bubbled with insatiable curiosity—and thinly veiled lust.

A pang of ravenous desire snaked through his core, and he drowned it with a deep gulp of whiskey. She sipped her tea in unison, but she still refused to break eye contact.

Curious, he raised one eyebrow. "You look like you have questions."

"Some," she admitted as she set the teacup on the table. "Mostly, I'm just thinking about how much fun I've had these past few days."

"Fun?" He laughed. "Hosting outlaws and refining illegal magic is your idea of a good time?"

"I'm friends with Quinn Starling." Tove rested her cheek on one hand and shrugged, as if that was all the answer he needed. "What else did you expect?"

Ah. They weren't just colleagues, then, but friends. Quinn's protective nature made far more sense, now.

"Speaking of..." Tove leaned her elbows on the table and threaded her fingers together as she studied his face. "I'm not sure what's going on between the two of you. You've been clever not to leave us alone, and that's made it hard to get any details on this whole truce-prisoner thing you two have going on. Frankly, I don't expect either of you to tell me. Whether it's because I'm an incorrigible gossip or because she's trying to keep me safe, she never tells me anything. Fine. I get it. It's not my place to ask, and she knows what she's doing. However, there is one thing you absolutely need to know."

"Oh?" He sipped his whiskey, waiting for the inevitable threat.

"She's my best friend in the world," Tove said under her breath. "I'm no warrior, and I couldn't kill you if I tried. But if you hurt her, or k—" Tove swallowed hard, unable to finish the sentence. "If she dies on this expedition of yours, you won't make it to your next birthday. I don't care what it costs or what I must sacrifice to make it happen. I'll destroy everything you love."

He took a sip of his whiskey to hide the smirk of victory at having been right.

Everyone threatened him eventually, but for whatever reason, he'd hoped she would be different.

"I'm not sure I believe it," he admitted with a lazy shrug. "That seems a little dark for you."

"I'm serious." Her frown deepened, and she stared intently into his eyes. "Quinn is the closest thing to family I have left. I can't lose her, too."

Still hidden by the mug, his cocky grin fell.

That had hit a little too close to home.

SOPHIA

Every palpitation of Sophia's heart sent another shockwave of lightning through her veins. With each beat, the open wound in her chest sizzled with hellfire. It ached. It burned. It carved a hole in her chest and filled it with acid.

She couldn't see. She couldn't think. She couldn't even breathe.

The only thing she felt—the only thing she knew—was the pain.

She had never felt agony like this, not even during her many years of torment in Nethervale. The snap of broken bones paled in comparison. She had experienced the smoldering sear of a brand on her shoulder and the splintering agony of sharp blades cutting her open time and time again, and if her mouth would've cooperated, she would've begged for either of those instead. She had even survived the mind-shattering horror of a blightwolf descending on her once, long ago. Nyx had laughed while the beast's teeth had glimmered in the low light of the forest, inches away, and yet nothing even began to compare to the cataclysmic suffering ripping her apart right now.

Nothing.

Her lungs ached for air. She sucked in a deep breath, and the hole between her breasts blazed hotter. Bile shot up her throat with the sensation, and her cheeks flushed with nausea. A vile, sticky substance burned the base of her tongue, and she couldn't hold it back any longer.

Though she wanted to scream, her eyes snapped open seconds before she rolled over and vomited onto the floor.

The putrid stench of her half-digested beef wafted up from the large pot someone had placed beside her bed. Its metallic edges slipped in and out of focus as her vision blurred. The pounding ache in her head hammered against her skull.

With a disgusted groan, she wiped the back of her hand over her mouth and squinted at the world around her. Fuzzy streaks of red and black floated around her. Something orange flickered nearby, and she blinked rapidly as her eyes struggled to make sense of her environment.

Deep within her chest, something snapped. It was dull, like the pop of a log in a campfire, but present nonetheless. With it came a wave of relief, and the ache in her head dissolved as quickly as if an unseen muse had siphoned most of the pain from her body with a wave of one immortal hand. Only a lingering ache remained, and at last, Sophia could think.

Everything sharpened in a rush, and the blurs of color solidified in an instant. On one wall, a candle sputtered on a black table draped in dark silk. Red velvet lined the walls, and the thick fabric gathered over itself in perfectly spaced folds that reminded her of curtains on a stage. With the lone candle as the room's only light, long shadows stretched across the floor and engulfed each of the room's corners.

Dark, just the way she liked it.

A kiss of cool air rolled over her bare shoulders, and she glanced down to find a single white sheet draped over her naked body. The bright fabric pooled to one side, sliding bit by bit toward the ground with each passing second, and another breath of air rolled over her exposed thigh as it fell off of her. She grabbed it on impulse and tugged it to her chest as she scanned the room.

Memories hit her, then, like the chaotic cacophony of an orchestra tuning instruments before they played a masterpiece. The spellgust stone. The bubbling cauldron. The debates over how to tweak the recipe. That augmentor, seemingly too young to have a remote chance of doing this right, tucking a lock of hair behind her ear as the world went dark.

And yet, Sophia had awoken.

As her trembling hands held the sheet to her chest, a bright green glow pulsed to life from between her fingers. With a curious frown, she dropped the blanket, and the dazzling light filled the room.

Embedded in the skin between her breasts, the fist-sized spellgust stone shimmered like a star.

Her fingertips traced the edges of the gem, where its facets met the gold casing that secured it in her body. The metallic edges circled the spellgust in a perfectly smooth line, without so much as a divot or dent to suggest where the master augmentor had begun her bloody work. As Sophia gently touched it, the soft facets pressed against her skin like glass, and the flawless gem cast dazzling reflections onto her arm as she marveled at this new part of her.

Bit by bit, the last threads of sizzling pain faded to a dull ache in her chest. For however long she sat there—hours, maybe, or days—she could only stare at the spellgust stone keeping her alive.

This crazy plan of hers had worked.

To her astonishment, the fuzzy dizziness in her head was gone. She could move without losing her balance. She could sit upright without an icy chill burrowing its way into her core. She could curl her hands into a fist and hold it, all while knowing her blow would hurt anyone she chose to hit.

Her borrowed body felt solid. Certain. Once again, at long last, Sophia had complete control.

She curled just the tips of her fingers in a long-practiced motion, and on command, blisteringly cold ice pooled in her palm. It held, strong and sure, awaiting her next orders.

Her lips curled into a wicked little grin as she stared at the block of ice that had formed from nothing. It hovered above her skin as her magic froze the very air, more powerful than ever before. Fog rolled off her hand like a breath on a cold day, and the magic pulsing in her blood hummed with life.

Astonishing. Her other augmentations must've been drawing additional power from the stone infused with her body.

"I'm… I'm cured," she whispered.

The ice in her hand melted as she released the magic. A thin stream of water snaked down her forearm, crisp and cold as a northern spring, but she didn't care. With her hands in her hair, still not entirely sure this was real, she laughed. Her shoulders shook, and tears rolled down her face as she gave herself over to the relief.

Cured.

She laughed—and cried—even harder. That crazy woman had succeeded where even Sophia had failed, and they hadn't even needed to go to Aeron's Tomb. No books. No heists. Just one well-connected prisoner and a well-made bargain. As long as Sophia visited this augmentor each year and stole a high-quality spellgust stone for the procedure, she would finally be able to thrive in her new life.

A hot flash of jealousy snapped her from her celebration. No one else could have this augmentor. All anyone had to do to kill Sophia was murder Tove Warren, and she could never let that happen.

Nyx would've kidnapped the woman and kept her safe in a tower somewhere. Sophia briefly considered it, but her time with Connor had given her new ideas on how to influence people. Besides, imprisoning the person who would resurrect her each year probably wouldn't end well.

With her finger tapping along her jawline, Sophia looked up at the ceiling—toward Connor. At the thought of him, a gentle pang hit her in the chest. She tensed, prepared for another crushing wave of misery, but this softer twinge faded almost as quickly as it had come.

As she accepted that no pain would hit her this time, her shoulders relaxed. Her pulse settled, and as the brief panic faded, she racked her mind to place the sensation she had felt. It wasn't pain. It wasn't terror. It wasn't fear.

Her head snapped up as she finally recognized it. She hadn't felt this emotion in so long that she had almost forgotten what it was like.

Guilt.

Without knowing everything at stake, Connor had passed her test. If they had gone after the Soulsprite first, it would've been all the proof she needed that he would just let her die. She had braced herself for it, expected it even, and she had already made her plan. If he had chosen the Soulsprite, she would've disappeared into the night to heal herself and returned another day to slit Connor's throat as retribution.

Though he had held complete power over her life, he had delivered above and beyond anything she could have ever hoped for. To sweeten her victory, he had even strong-armed a Starling into helping Sophia survive.

With her hand still touching the spellgust stone, Sophia stared again at the pools of crimson fabric nailed across the walls and ceiling. Where she had once waited to see what choice he would make, she now faced one of her own: she could still disappear and leave them all behind, or she could remain with the men who had given her a renewed chance at life.

Originally, long ago when they had first struck their bargain, she had planned to leave at this point rather than give her new pseudo-ally a chance to betray her. Isolation had always been safer. Alone, she at least knew she could rely on her own wits and cunning to survive.

But Connor was different.

She grunted in frustration and tugged on the roots of her hair as she tried to figure out what to do. Logistically, the path seemed obvious: run. But she didn't have the words to explain what he and Murdoc meant to her. She couldn't articulate why she felt rooted in place.

With a heavy sigh, Sophia rubbed her eyes and set her face in her hands. Any other elite necromancer would've simply disappeared. Even with a ghoul wandering the house, they would've slipped out into the night like a ghost themselves and never looked back.

But she couldn't do it. Connor had ruined her.

Her shoulders relaxed as she finally accepted what she had, on some level, always known would happen. The tension in her back and legs finally faded as she surrendered to the truth. As she sat there, naked on a slab in an augmentor's cellar, she closed her eyes and let herself feel something she hadn't felt in ages.

Happiness.

Connor had ruined her, yes, but possibly for the better. Maybe it was time to finally pledge herself to a king and let herself have a team.

To let herself have a *home*.

CHAPTER FORTY-FIVE
CELINE

As the balcony doors clicked shut behind her, Celine watched yet another Wildefaire sunrise over the curved stone railing.

Below, the city's dazzling golden rooftops glimmered like gemstones in the morning sun. The homes stretched on seemingly forever in every direction with the castle at their center, like rays on the sun. Mountains circled the outer-most rim of the kingdom, their distant peaks still topped with the last patches of winter snow.

Her balcony jutted over the royal gardens. Pink and silver trees swayed in a gentle breeze as birds twittered their mating songs in the spring morning. With her bloodstained hands on the railing, she closed her eyes and waited for the awe she used to feel whenever she saw this view.

Nothing came. Not even a flicker of joy.

With a disappointed sigh, she sat in the silver throne her cousin had commissioned for her retirement. A butler stood beside her, nothing more to her than another piece of furniture as he held a tray with three rolled towels. He stared dead ahead, blinking rapidly as the silver tray trembled in his palm.

The blood from her hands had left crimson smears on the stone railing, so she took one of the towels to wipe her fingers clean. Red streaks stained the white fibers as she wiped away the evidence of how she had spent the dawn, and she rubbed the corner of the cloth into her cuticles to clear away every last blot.

Bored, she tossed the cloth onto the butler's arm. He flinched—subtly, but all the same—and she frowned in disappointment.

Weak. All of them.

"Tea," she ordered.

He bowed deeply, the tray still held aloft, and turned on one heel. His shoes clacked against the stone balcony, and each grating step pierced her eardrums like a mallet hitting a gong. She grimaced, but her patience for the common folk had long since eroded. Still, the more of them she killed, the less likely the survivors were to obey.

Patience. Strategy. Caution. She had to wield them all like weapons.

A half-dozen pairs of glass doors lined the long stretch of balcony along her wing of the castle, and each of them led to another of her rooms. Halfway down the balcony, a silver cart waited with several metal domes resting on both its shelves. A porcelain teapot with two ornate porcelain cups waited on the top tray of the cart, and steam spiraled from the opening in its slender white neck.

These past two weeks had revealed much of what awaited her in Oakenglen. So many players. So many lies. So many bodies disappearing into the night. Even Edgar, her sister's son and the only family to survive Henry's axe, had met his end trying to ascend the throne. With a frustrated shake of her head, she rubbed the pulsing ache in her forehead.

There was so little left in this world worth saving.

As her mind raced with the nuances and intricacies of what awaited her in Oakenglen, someone spoke in the room behind her. The closed doors muffled his voice, and the meaty thud of a fist hitting flesh followed.

The piercing clacks of the butler's footsteps pounded against her skull as he returned, and she gritted her teeth in irritation. If she stayed here much longer, she needed servants with a bit of stealth.

When he reached her, he bowed again and offered her another silver tray. This one held the teapot, a steaming cup of tea, and a letter sealed with dark blue wax. As she took her first sip of tea, she lifted the letter to examine it.

The outline of a wolf stared up at her from the wax—the Freymoor family crest.

"Finally," she muttered.

As the steam wafted from the cup in her left hand, its warmth leaving soft spots of dew along her red lips, she popped open the seal with her right thumb. The soothing brew carried hints of vanilla and lavender, and she let out a contented hum as it pooled on her tongue. The paper in her hand crinkled as it opened, and sloping letters written in black ink filled the page.

Your Majesty,

To my utter delight, you were entirely correct.

My scouts say Otmund has been spotted on the road between Oakenglen and Freymoor, and he travels with two companions we suspect are, in fact, necromancers. Whatever you did, however you got him to come here, I owe you an enormous debt.

He should arrive within a few days, and though no one has seen any strange green daggers on his person, we will of course notify you immediately if one is discovered.

And as for the dagger, I confess, I am still quite curious as to what makes it unique. However, I trust your judgement if you deign it unsafe to tell me quite yet.

Ever yours,

Dahlia Donahue, Lady of Freymoor

Celine scoffed. That sickly girl could barely hold a pen, much less manage her city. No, whomever Celine's contact truly was, they pulled the girl's strings with the sort of subtle art even Celine could admire. Freymoor would no doubt demand a ransom for the dagger, since they knew she wanted it, but it would find its way to her one way or another. If they properly obeyed, perhaps she would even reinstate the Freymoor monarchy. Having an ally with so much access to the old magicks would prove useful, provided they feared her enough to use them to her benefit.

Time would tell.

As she held the letter, the faded lines of more writing flashed briefly through the paper. She frowned and held it to the light. In barely legible script backlit by the rising sun, a second message appeared in the gap at the bottom stretch of the parchment.

I never thought I would thank the woman who married my father's murderer, but I must show you my gratitude for sending Otmund to me. Perhaps the old wrongs can be righted after all.

Celine scowled as she reread the lie. Freymoor didn't forget. The land of the Old Ways would never forgive old wrongs.

With another sip of tea, her eyes fell again to the comment about necromancers, and she grimaced in disgust. That old fool had sunk to a new low if he had truly gone to Nethervale for bodyguards. Not even the elite could protect him from a kingdom he had looted for so many years. Most of the Freymoor treasury had found its way to his, and all the while he had thought himself too clever for anyone to find out.

His schemes had caught up with him, and those he had played against themselves had discovered his treachery. He would not leave Freymoor alive, and she would see to it no one would go looking for him after he disappeared.

Through the door, the muffled snap of a bone blended with a stifled scream of agony. The servant, still standing at her side, whimpered. His hand shook as he held the empty tray, and her cold eyes narrowed with frustration at yet another interruption.

She set the letter on the tray and snapped her fingers in a wordless command for him to refill her teacup and just leave.

The honey-brown liquid trickled into her half-empty teacup as he re-poured her drink. When she waved him away, he bowed again and scurried across the balcony toward the cart. As he retreated, his thunderous footsteps carried through the air faster than before.

Just as the butler's footsteps finally receded, the latch behind her clicked. The curtained doors opened, and the whisper-quiet shuffle of cloth across skin circled her throne. Immobile, still sipping her tea, Celine listened to the birdsong twittering on the palace roof as her companion joined her.

The buttons at the top of his bloodstained shirt lay open, revealing a chest of dark hair. His rolled sleeves hid the curve of his biceps as he leaned his elbows against the edge of the railing and stared out at Wildefaire without a word.

Another sip of the jasmine tea slid past her delicate lips as she held her cup to her mouth, but she ignored the fragrant aroma and instead scanned what she could see of her guest's expression.

General Jensen Barrett rubbed his forehead, and his touch left dark red streaks across his sweaty brow. A long scar ran from his dark blue eyes, through the thick hair covering his jaw and all the way down his neck.

The wind rustled his once neatly combed hair, and he sighed. "You were right."

Still raised in front of her face, her teacup hid her smirk. "One day you will learn, General, that I always am."

He shook his head, still staring off at nothing. "I had no idea Davarius had corrupted the city to this degree, Celine."

Her eye twitched at his casual use of her name, but then again Henry had always insisted his generals be treated like family. She pursed her lips to restrain a scathing remark and instead drank the last bit of her tea.

"He wants me dead," Barrett whispered, clearly still in shock.

It took effort to restrain from rolling her eyes at him. Anyone with half a brain could have guessed Henry's two generals would go to war with each other once he died, but she needed this man on her side. "Did you uncover everything you needed to know?"

He bit the inside of his cheek, but eventually nodded. "Davarius and I had our differences, sure, but we always had the same goals—keep Oakenglen safe, and protect our king. I never thought… not once did I consider…"

"…that he would send an assassin after you?" she finished for him.

He clenched his jaw and froze as he stared down at his bloodstained hands. Only the subtle movement of his chest rising with each breath suggested he was still alive.

"Exactly," he eventually admitted.

As the general listened to the Wildefaire morning, Celine set her empty teacup on the wide seat of her throne and waited. Luring Barrett's assassin here and intercepting him for the general to interrogate had taken considerable work, but saving the general's life would secure his loyalty. With his attention to detail and deep-rooted influence across Saldia, he could squelch any lingering dissent among the noblemen and merchant classes to ensure her effortless return to power.

"It makes sense," she confessed, mostly to fill the silence and ensure he couldn't see through her intentions. "He wants the kingdom to himself, but you're the General of Defense. He may control the army, but you control the city, and you are also a man of law. He has no claim to the throne, and you would never allow him to take it. It was only a matter of time, General, until he came for you."

Barrett shook his head, and a lock of hair fell into his eye. "I wish I had your foresight, Celine."

"If you pledge yourself to me, as you did to Henry, then you will have my foresight and more for the rest of your days."

The general looked at her over one shoulder, those deep blue eyes sharp and clear, but he said nothing. He scanned her face, and she met his gaze without a trace of doubt.

Celine had planned this to the tiniest detail. She already knew what would happen, and she merely had to wait for him to play into her hands.

A pair of bluebirds sped by, the feathery flap of their wings on the air like a burst of applause in the calm morning sun, and that seemed to snap the general from his daze. His eyes swept the ground as the gears turned in his head, but his shoulders drooped.

The man turned his back on the sunrise and, facing her, lowered his chin to his chest. He set his pointer finger and thumb against his forehead as he closed his eyes, and he set his other hand flat against his heart. "I owe you my life, Your Majesty, and I am a man who pays his debts. Whatever you ask is yours for as long as I live."

Her lips twisted with a small, wicked little smile. "You know what I want, General."

He nodded, and he glared out at the road leading from the castle to Wildefaire's outer gates. "I assume you want to use the Rift to return to Oakenglen?"

"On the contrary." Celine stood and joined him at the railing, and together they stared out over her cousin's dazzling kingdom. "I want the people to see me. I want to remind Davarius and any lingering rebel in those walls that the people know I'm well. My return comes with hefty consequence to anyone who dares threaten me."

"That will delay us, then," he pointed out. "It's unsafe for anyone to travel these roads, much less our queen."

One of her feathery blades rested against her wrist, waiting for an opportunity to shine in the sunlight. "I'll manage."

"As you wish, Your Majesty." He pushed off the railing and wiped his bloody hands on his already destroyed shirt. "I can guarantee you safe passage to Oakenglen within thirty days."

She frowned. "Certainly you can do better than that? It only takes a week to travel to Oakenglen from here."

He grinned, and his eyes crinkled with his smile. "You'll learn that I like to give conservative estimates, Your Majesty, and over-deliver where I can. You will likely be home in less than two weeks, but I need to secure soldiers along the route and prepare the castle. We cannot risk Davarius trying anything on your journey or once you arrive."

"I suppose that's true." Her back straightened as she imagined the castle doors opening for her yet again. "You won't meet as much resistance as you think, Barrett. I doubt Davarius will even be in Oakenglen when you return."

Barrett tilted his head in surprise and studied her face, no doubt wondering what she had been up to.

"So many whispers have been going through Oakenglen lately, General." She clasped her delicate hands in front of her. "Apparently, Davarius was quite heavily involved in my late husband's death."

Through the corner of her eye, she saw him raise one eyebrow in surprise. He must have tasted the lie, but this would work in his benefit as well as hers. His chest puffed, and his jaw tensed with the questions that must've been swirling through his exceptional mind.

Celine waited, testing his resolve and the limit of his moral guidance. A man who honored the law to his degree could never break it, but the rules could, on occasion, bend. She needed to see for herself if his nobility made him untouchable, or if he could, in fact, be bought.

After another tense moment of waiting, Barrett cleared his throat. His Adam's apple bobbed as he swallowed his doubt and set one hand on the back of her throne.

Celine raised her chin, and though nothing shifted in her expression, the gleeful rush of another victory ricocheted through her very soul.

It was nice to feel *something*, even if the sensation didn't last.

"Is he still alive?" she asked with a nod toward the closed balcony doors.

Barrett nodded and rubbed the back of his neck with a resigned sigh. "I assumed you would want to speak with him before I finish things."

"You're a wise man, General Barrett." She lifted her skirts and walked around the throne.

"Would you like company?"

"I'm quite alright, thank you."

"Your Majesty?"

With her hand on the ornate doorhandle, Celine paused and looked back at her new general. With one hand on his waist, he rubbed his bearded jaw with the other and stared at the ground, as though he wasn't quite sure how to word what he wanted to say.

"General, I am not a patient woman."

"I often used to worry for your safety." He crossed his arms and glared down at her, and his eye twitched once as he met her gaze. "I would go to Henry with intelligence and warnings of what our enemies wanted to do to you to get to him, and he waved me away every time. I was told to give you space, to let you live as you wanted to live, and to treat you as I treated him."

"And?" She frowned, unaccustomed to not knowing what would be said next. If Henry had revealed any of the truth to Barrett, her plans had to change.

"In there, you were holding back." Barrett nodded to the closed doors and the rooms beyond. "I could see it in the way you held yourself, and now I think I understand why Henry wasn't scared for your wellbeing. To be honest, I always wondered if he secretly wanted you dead. I added extra patrols to protect you, just in case. And now…"

Celine didn't move. She didn't answer or fill in the silence that followed.

Barrett sighed and shook his head. "Everyone wants the crown because they don't know what it takes to keep it. You must know, by now, what it will take for you to control the throne without Henry. You must understand how many people you're going to have to kill. Are you sure you want this life?"

A fair question, and one he would never have asked if he had known the truth.

Her shoulders relaxed, and her grip on the door handle softened. "By now, General, you know I'm not delicate. I assure you there is no one more capable of doing what must be done."

Without waiting for him to reply, she threw open the double doors. On a rug by the fireplace, a man bound in chains lay on the floor. Crackling flames from the hearth cast an orange glow on the rivers of blood streaming from his nose and ears. Loose clumps of his greasy blond hair fell into his face as he looked up at her, and he stiffened with fear.

Her cold eyes narrowed, and she smiled down at him while the doors swung shut behind her.

CHAPTER FORTY-SIX
QUINN

Crickets sang their midnight lullaby, and the croak of frogs blended perfectly with their springtime song. Quinn's boots crunched along the dirt as she scanned the forest around her, ever vigilant, but nothing appeared in the depths of the shadows between the trees. Moonlight stained the dark leaves blue, and the thick hemlocks in this part of the Ancient Woods swallowed the orange glow of Oakenglen as she and her captors left civilization behind.

Connor Magnuson led the way into the forest, and she stole a glance at the back of his head every chance she got. He walked with his back to her, which would've made him a prime target for an attack if not for the fact his wraith had taken post behind her.

This man was cautious and careful. That alone had probably gotten him this far, but it wouldn't be enough to win against her father. Not even with whatever artifact he hoped to steal from Freymoor.

To her right, Tove kept their brisk pace with ease. Sophia and Murdoc had disappeared to the back of their procession, but with the wraith blocking her view, Quinn couldn't keep a clear eye on them.

She and Tove were surrounded.

Connor and his team had gotten most of what they needed from her, and for all she knew, the trips to Freymoor and Otmund's castle were decoys. If the Wraithblade were to turn on her, this would be his ideal moment to do it—kill Quinn, kidnap the master augmentor she had delivered to him on a silver platter, and escape into the night on his dragon.

In the rare chance this wasn't going to be an attempt on her life, however, Quinn couldn't attack first. Not with Blaze still held captive in Slaybourne.

She had to wait, and the waiting set her on edge.

Her palms thrummed with the simmering heat of her Burnbane fires, ready at a moment's notice, and the thin, pale hairs on her neck stood on end as she waited for the telltale whistle of Sophia's Nethervale darts. However much she wanted to believe Nocturne would intervene, should the fools attack, she hadn't agreed to anything. For all she knew, he would simply wait to see the outcome as a test of her ability.

Or, worse, perhaps Connor's bargain with the regal creature was too tempting for even a prince of dragons to resist.

"Quinn," Tove whispered, her voice almost inaudible.

Most wouldn't have been able to hear it, even with a Hearhaven augmentation of their own, but Tove had crafted her unique blend with Maypop petals. The flower reacted uniquely to the puffball mushrooms classic to the brew, which gave her and Quinn hyper-sensitive hearing that surpassed even the Starling family recipe.

Quinn tilted her head, only slightly—just enough to watch her friend from the corner of her eye.

The augmentor didn't look her way or make any indication she had spoken at all. "Take these."

Her coat pocket shifted as Tove stuffed something into it. Leather muffled the soft clink of glass, and Quinn kicked a stone across the ground to mask the sound. With her attention fixed on the back of Connor's neck, she refused to betray any hint of what had just happened and lowered the bag on her shoulder to ensure the wraith hovering behind them didn't see what they were up to.

With her bag covering her arm, she slipped her hand into her pocket to find three small glass jars. "What are these?"

"A few Rushmars," Tove's whisper remained steady and calm, even as the augmentor subtly nodded toward Connor. "I've seen the way you two look at each other, but I figure it's not in your plans to be a mother."

Before she could stop herself, Quinn's cheeks burned red with the implications of what her friend had just said.

Beside her, Tove just giggled.

"Take them back," Quinn hissed. "Right now."

"Not a chance."

"It—are you—I can't fathom—*ugh*." It took concentrated effort to remain calm, but Quinn somehow managed. She finally looked at her friend, her eyebrows pinched in a blend of horror and embarrassment. "The first time we met, he ran me through with a sword!"

Tove pursed her lips and shifted her attention to the back of Connor's head as he led them deeper into the woods. "Isn't that a kink for you Starlings?"

"No." Quinn's cheeks only burned hotter. "Drop the subject. It's never going to happen."

"You say that now, but it's really just a matter of time. I mean, look at you two." With a subtle twist of her hand, Tove gestured between Quinn and the outlaw leading their band of misfits through the forest. "I've never seen someone more likely to win a fight against you, and I figured you're like Gwen in that way."

"Gwen—well, she—" Quinn groaned in irritation. "She didn't want to marry. She held that contest because she figured no one could win a fight against her."

Tove scoffed and rolled her eyes. "You and I both watched her duel with Cade Vossen. I've never seen her more aroused in my life."

"That's my *sister* you're talking about."

"I'm just telling you what I saw." The augmentor smirked victoriously. "And what I'm seeing now."

"Bless the Fates, woman. What am I going to do with you?"

"Adore me." Tove beamed and tugged gently on her bustier. "Forever."

Quinn chuckled, and her eyes glossed over as she tried to recall the look on Gwen's face after the duel against Cade. Her smile slowly fell, however, as she sifted through the memories of that day. The duel itself stood out like a diamond in the sun—a brilliant illustration of war in all its artistry and perfection. The plumes of trademark Starling fire. The blinding light of Cade's Buzzbright augmentation. Then, the two of them on the ground, chests heaving, as he held his sword to her neck and looked her in the eye.

But Quinn couldn't, for the life of her, remember Gwen's face. In that moment, all she could see was her father's proud grin as a soldier finally won against the best warrior to come out of the family line thus far.

"Look, Tove," she whispered with a nod toward Connor. "Anyone who gets involved with a man like that is in for a world of pain."

"Yeah." The augmentor's gaze lingered on his broad shoulders, and she bit her lip as her eyes trailed down his muscled back. "You're probably right. No way that would end well, huh?"

Quinn raised one inquisitive eyebrow and studied her friend's face. It took effort to fight off a protective impulse to literally shake the idea out of Tove's head.

Falling for an outlaw—especially the Wraithblade, of all people—would only get Tove killed.

A low growl rumbled through the forest, too deep to be thunder. As the ground vibrated with the raw power of the sound, everyone froze in place. Tove, however, clapped her hands together as she stifled a happy squeal, her eyes wide as a child being given a new toy.

Ahead and slightly to the left, a cluster of shadows shifted. Despite the quiet air, the trees around it shivered. A single thump shook the ground, almost knocking Quinn off balance, and a massive head loomed toward them from the darkness. At first, there was only a flash of blue moonlight across black scales, and then silence.

In the depths of the darkness, two dark eyes opened, glowing with just enough light of their own to leave pale imprints on the air as they moved.

"It... what... Fates above and below, that's..." Tove's words came out as breathy, incoherent gasps, and she stilled as she drank in the scene. "Dragons are real. Quinn, dragons are *real!*"

"Very." Quinn let out a slow breath as Nocturne's gaze shifted toward her.

Connor reached the dragon first, and the magnificent creature lowered his head. Connor shot a wary glance at Quinn over his shoulder before turning his back on her again, and he spoke to the regal beast in hushed tones she couldn't make out from this distance.

Time to get closer.

As she took her first step, however, the great beast lifted his head and stared directly at Tove. Quinn impulsively set her hand on the pommel of her sheathed Firesword as a warning, and his dark eyes shifted again toward her.

It had all happened so quickly, so instinctively, that Tove didn't seem to notice. Quinn let out a sigh and, not wanting to make this worse, lifted her hand off the sword in silent surrender.

"Can… can I…" Tove wandered closer, unable to form words.

Quinn followed, but a cold hand grabbed her shoulder and rooted her in place. The chill snaked into her back, into her bones, and she glanced down to see bony fingers too close to her neck for comfort.

Her jaw tensed as she was forced to watch quietly as her only friend in this world walked toward a creature that could swallow her whole.

Entranced, without so much as a glance toward the Wraithblade as he stood beside the dragon, Tove stared at Nocturne's face until she stood before him. She cautiously raised one hand in front of his snout, and he moved his head forward until his massive nose pressed against her tiny palm. He huffed, and hot air tousled the augmentor's hair like a gale in a storm. She laughed, delighted, as though she could die happy now, with her life complete.

Nocturne, however, tilted his head and studied her with a single eye. His pupil dilated, just as it had when he had first stripped Quinn down and peered to the depths of her soul.

Fates be damned—not Tove, too.

If he and Connor bonded enough through this experience to open this newfound telepathic link to each other, there was no telling what secrets the dragon prince would share with Saldia's most wanted man.

She took a step forward, but the wraith's grip on her shoulder tightened. A jolt of pain shot up her neck, and she glared at the hooded abomination as he pulled her back to her original spot.

That damn *monstrosity*.

Unable to intervene, Quinn merely stood there as Nocturne inched ever closer to Tove. Her shoulders ached from the wraith's grip and the dread of what might happen to her friend, but she couldn't lie—deep down, even she wondered what he would see in Tove Warren.

It seemed like treason to even consider the thought, but the augmentor had far too many tricks up her sleeve to be an ordinary girl from the city.

"You need to ask before looking into someone's soul." Connor playfully nudged the dragon's side.

The nudge pushed Nocturne off balance, and he growled in annoyance as his back hit a tree. A sharp crack pierced the night, and the rush of air through leaves drowned out even the crickets' song. The dragon regained his composure just as the tree hit the ground with a shuddering thwack.

Nocturne shook out his body, and as the rumbling growl faded once more, he stared right at Quinn. She let out a tense sigh, but the dragon had made his point without uttering a single word.

Somehow, Connor was getting *stronger*.

MURDOC

As the quiet trill of the cicadas joined the croaking harmonies of distant frogs, Murdoc led Sophia farther from the clearing where the augmentor had set up her makeshift shop.

"Where the hell are we going *now*?" His future wife pushed aside a branch and let out a breathy little sigh. "Whatever you're going to say, Murdoc, just say it."

"Impatient, are we?" He shot her a playful grin over his shoulder. "We're almost there."

The gentle slosh of water over river rocks gurgled through the night air, and he squinted through the foliage around him until he spotted a sandy bank through a gap in the underbrush.

Oh, good. He'd begun to think he might've been wrong about where they were.

He shoved his way through a cluster of evergreen saplings and held aside the flexible trunks of new growth so that she could slip through after him. Her brows furrowed as she scanned the riverbank, and she rested one fist on her hip as she pointed to the stream. "You brought me all the way out here to look at a river? Murdoc, that's not exactly new."

"It's not just any river." He pointed upstream, toward the gaping tunnel where the city's sewer water joined the stream. "It's where I first learned who you are. *What* you are. This is where we came after you killed your cunt of a cousin."

As she followed his gaze, her scowl deepened. "Why would you ever remind me that he existed? After what he did, Murdoc, I just want to forget."

"I know," he said softly, and his jaw tensed as he scratched at his beard. "I didn't bring you out here to remind you of the horrors of your past, Sophia. I only wanted to show you how far you've come."

To his surprise, the words disarmed her. The creases in her forehead faded, and her gaze swept the ground as her anger dissolved. With a fluttery little sigh, she bit her ruby-red lip. "You were never supposed to know."

In the silence that followed, only the croaking frogs filled the void. She didn't look up from the patchy grass beneath their boots, and they had both apparently run out of things to say.

Never one for awkward pauses, he cleared his throat and scanned the water. When he found the steep bank he'd been looking for, he pointed at it. "And over there is where you called me an idiot."

Her dark gaze narrowed, and her eyes finally shifted toward him. "You *are* an idiot."

"Rude."

She rolled her eyes, but she couldn't hide the grin slowly inching over her face. She crossed her arms and turned her back on him as she stared out at the water. Her delicate hand swept her hair over one shoulder, and her bare neck practically glowed in contrast to her dark red dress.

He just couldn't resist. Not anymore.

Murdoc walked up behind her, close enough to touch. Instead of holding her, however, he let the last inch between them crackle with tension and lowered his mouth to her ear. "I think it's high time you explain that kiss."

She chuckled. "Don't get excited. It didn't mean anything."

"Of course not." He set his hands on her shoulders. "Or, just maybe, you're finally acknowledging the inevitable."

She stiffened under his touch, and he waited for her to squirm away. This had been their game since he had met her—the moment he got close, she elbowed him in the gut or insulted him to make him stop.

At first, he had enjoyed the sport of it. He knew she would never have him, but he had finally found a necromancer with enough power to be a real challenge in a duel. It seemed like the perfect plan. Flirt. Tease. Toy with her.

And, most importantly, irritate the lights out of her until she indulged his death wish.

Murdoc had egged her on and teased her at every opportunity, but he'd never expected her to actually give in.

He had never expected her to start to *like* it.

Well-hidden smiles. Laughter masked with an annoyed groan or impatient huff. A little more time spent at his side, when before she had found any excuse to get some space. All of the clues suggested she had, for whatever reason, begun to enjoy his company.

Now that she no longer needed Connor, however, it seemed inevitable that she would dart off into the night. That was what she did, after all.

Run.

Whatever they had—whatever he was to her—he was convinced he would lose it, just like he'd lost everything and everyone else.

With his hands gently cradling her arms, he waited for her to pull away. He waited for her to insult him, or perhaps try to throw him over her shoulder and into the stream. He tensed his core, ready to deflect whatever blow came next, but she simply stood there.

Eerily still, and unnervingly quiet.

"I can't imagine what you've endured," he confessed, his tone hushed to match the serene woodland night. "You're not even thirty, and—"

"I'm thirty-seven," she whispered.

His brows pinched together in disbelief. "You shouldn't lie to your future husband, dear."

Though he still couldn't see her face, she chuckled and shook her head. "This body is twenty-five, but if I were still Leah Beaumont, I would be thirty-seven."

"That's alright." He rested his chin on the top of her head. "I like older women."

She laughed. "Idiot."

The water bubbled past them, and an owl hooted in the distance. His smile slowly faded as he remembered what he'd been saying, and he wondered if he should continue.

No, he had to. He needed to get this out.

"You've endured hell," he said quietly. "I can't even begin to guess at what life is like in Nethervale, or what you had to do to survive."

At her side, her hands curled into fists.

Gently, he pressed his chest to her back and kissed the side of her head. "With what you've gone through, it must be impossible to trust anyone. Honestly, I didn't think you would stay."

"I almost didn't," she admitted.

His chest tightened, and he took a steady breath as they listened to the river. "You made the right choice, then."

"Time will tell."

"I'm not worried." He gently squeezed her arms. Though he wanted nothing more than to spin her around and hike her legs around his waist, he released her. "You'll figure it out eventually."

With a soft frown, she looked over her shoulder at him. "Figure what out?"

"That I'm marriage material." He flashed her mischievous grin and gestured to himself from head to toe. "You'll realize that I'm a man who would never hurt you—unless you tell me you want to play rough," he added with a roguish wink.

She playfully shook her head and rubbed her forehead, but she still couldn't hide the broad smile on those sultry lips of hers.

He headed back toward the clearing, knowing full well she would follow. Back in Tove's shop, in the hours after Sophia's operation had finished, he had nearly blown it. He'd laid awake in bed, staring at the ceiling, wondering if he should race down to the cellar and watch her every move to ensure she didn't leave him. It had taken every ounce of his willpower to not do something stupid, and in the end, it was Connor's advice that had steered him right.

What's real stays with you.

And, to Murdoc's delight, she had chosen to stay.

CHAPTER FORTY-SEVEN
QUINN

That infuriating wraith wouldn't let Quinn *listen* to the augmentation, much less *watch* it.

With the ghoul's icy grip on her shoulder seeping through her clothes, she now stood with her back to Nocturne, Connor, and Tove. The longer the ghost held her rooted in place, the more her body numbed under his grip.

She glared out at the forest, silently fuming, but she hadn't been able to see much of anything thanks to the irritating abomination behind her.

When enough time had passed that even the undead could grow bored, she slowly peered over her shoulder to catch a glimpse of the augmentation, mostly to ensure no one tried to harm Tove.

The bony grip on her shoulder tightened, and she sucked in a breath through her teeth as a fresh bolt of agony shot down her spine. Shadows coiled over her boots, almost masking them entirely from view, and the ghoul shoved her farther away from the dragon as punishment. The Wraith King guided her every step with the cold grip on her shoulder, and she had little choice but to comply.

Damn it all.

The gentle hum of Tove's enchanted needles joined the woodland chorus of trills and croaks, stopping and starting as the augmentation continued, but no one spoke. The painfully silent forest carried on, and she could only listen for clues as to how it was going.

Through it all, the ghoul kept her rooted in place. The longer she stood there, the deeper the chill of his touch sank into her bones. Not wanting to give him the satisfaction of seeing her discomfort, she swallowed hard to suppress a shiver as goosebumps raced up her arms.

Through the corner of her eye, two silhouettes darted through the trees. Quinn's head snapped toward them, but she only caught the tail end of the necromancer's scarlet dress slip into the darkness between the trunks. Her eyes narrowed in suspicion. She set her hands on her waist, careful to position her right hand as close to *Aurora's* hilt as possible, and once more scanned the forest for traces of an ambush.

They had isolated Tove. The wraith had her in his grip and could draw his sword at any time. If they planned to strike, like she suspected, it would happen soon.

Between the Volt, her Firesword, and the magic sizzling in her blood, Quinn would be ready.

Snippets of a hushed conversation bubbled past the wraith as he continued to block her view of Tove, and Quinn's ear twitched as she picked up as much of it as she could.

"…but your hide is too thick," Tove said.

Connor's now-familiar voice followed, but she couldn't make out the words.

"I will remove a scale."

Tove gasped. "Doesn't that hurt?"

"Not at all. In fact, you may keep it. Another will grow in due time."

"Quiet," Connor chided. "Both of you."

Quinn bristled as the outlaw dared give her friend orders, but the ghoul's hand only tightened with the movement. Ribbons of pain splintered down her back, and she gritted her teeth as her neck went slowly numb.

More hushed conversation followed, and Quinn chewed the tip of her nail as she strained to hear it all.

"…and I will control the conversation?"

She tensed as Nocturne asked a pivotal question, one she had asked herself more than once since learning about this link they would share. Thus far, she hadn't been able to understand why a prince of dragons would debase himself enough to merge his mind with someone he considered corruptible, but now, it made sense.

Nocturne hadn't done this as a sign of trust. Quite the opposite. It seemed the prince of dragons had agreed to this augmentation in order to keep a closer watch on his mark.

Their mark.

"Not quite," Tove answered, mercifully loud enough that Quinn could hear despite Connor's earlier warning. "Both of you have to open your mind to each other for it to work. It has quite a few limitations—"

Connor said something in a hushed tone, and Tove cleared her throat with an awkward little cough. They resumed their conversation, this time in quieter tones Quinn couldn't hear.

Damn it.

With a frustrated sigh, she set one hand on the hilt of her Firesword and scanned the forest around her as she listened for any additional clues as to an impending ambush. Sophia and Murdoc were still gone, and tension pooled in Quinn's back as she fought the constant urge to draw her sword.

Her Starling crest clinked against the Volt around her neck, and she absently stretched out her fingers at her side as she debated what lay ahead of them all. It was surreal to think of what awaited them in Freymoor, and she wondered if she could really follow through on her end of this bargain she had struck with an outlaw. To trek to the Fallen Kingdom and journey halfway across Saldia to smuggle him into Otmund's castle violated just about every Lightseer oath she had ever taken.

Perhaps hers was a worse betrayal than what her father had done to her. The thought nearly stopped her heart, and she shut her eyes briefly as the shame and guilt rolled through her like an ice-cold fog.

When she finally met Teagan Starling on the battlefield, she truly didn't know what she would do.

At this point, maybe nothing she said could redeem her in his eyes. He had sworn he would break her spirit if the Wraithblade didn't do it first. It didn't matter how many criminals she had detained over the years or how many successful missions she had completed—to him, she was a doll to marry off.

A possession.

Otmund was no different. The feud he had with Connor would no doubt end in death for at least one of them. Yet again, she would have to pick a side. Otmund had taught her most of what she knew about magic, and though he had been there through every summer of her life, now she wondered if any of his affection had been real.

Perhaps he had been conning her, all her life, just like everyone else.

"There," Tove announced. "Finished."

The wraith dissolved in a puff of smoke, and Quinn let out a long sigh of relief as the pressure on her shoulder finally faded. She stretched out her neck as a sharp tingle spread across her upper back. Mercifully, the oozing cold from the wraith's grip had already begun to fade.

In her periphery, someone stood, and she cast a sidelong glance in an effort to catch at least a glimpse of Tove's handiwork. The augmentor stood in front of a now-shirtless Connor with her palm resting on his chest as she applied a goopy salve to his torso. Each time she dug her fingers into the glass jar in her palm, Tove blushed.

The augmentor had never exactly been fond of rules, so perhaps it was only fitting that she could fall for an outlaw.

Glowing green lines cast an emerald hue across his skin and neck, and Quinn scanned the augmentation to ensure nothing in the artwork could be tied back to her friend. A coat of arms now glowed against his skin, and a black mark, dark as the shadows in a cave, marred the center of his chest.

Before she could help herself, her eyes drifted to the well-defined muscle along his arms, and the barest hint of heat crept up her neck.

His intense gaze shifted to her, and that snapped Quinn from her daze. At first, she met it with a glare of her own—until she remembered the glass potions Tove had stuffed into her pocket.

With a gentle huff of discomfort, she looked away.

"Thank you," he said quietly to the augmentor.

Through the corner of Quinn's eye, Tove's blush deepened to an almost painful pink. Her friend couldn't even look at him as she nodded.

"Five minutes." Connor tugged on his shirt once more, and Tove let out a barely audible sigh of disappointment as the fabric covered his muscles. "We need to make good use of the darkness, and that means getting to Freymoor by dawn. And Quinn—"

She watched him, waiting to see what he would do next.

Waiting to see if this was the moment it all unraveled, after all.

He gestured to Tove. "Make sure she has a safe way home."

Quinn blinked rapidly in surprise, but ultimately nodded. Connor turned his back on her and patted the dragon's side as he retreated toward his familiar bag, now sitting beneath a nearby tree.

One by one, Tove picked up the now-empty jars resting on a cloth at her feet and set them into her pack. The augmentor wrapped her needles in an ink-stained towel, her face still flushed as she snuck glances at the muscular man rifling through his own bag a short distance off.

Quinn knelt beside her friend to help pack the last of the tools and salves away, but she cast another wary glance across the forest in search of the two outlaws who had yet to return from their rendezvous in the trees.

Tove smiled broadly and let out a happy sigh as she looked up at the dragon. "This was fun."

"I won't implicate you in this any more than I already have," Quinn promised in a low whisper.

"Is this it, then?" Her friend grimaced, and the skin around her eyes creased with concern. "Is this goodbye?"

Maybe, Quinn wanted to say. *I don't know.*

Though she busied herself by sealing up the last few jars, she let the silence linger a little too long. It weighed on the air between them, until Tove gently squeezed her forearm.

Quinn forced a smile. "You should know me better than that. Whatever happens next, I'll be fine. It's hard to kill me."

Tove didn't laugh. "But it's not impossible."

The croaking frogs quieted as Quinn's smile fell, and she met her friend's gaze as they both sat with the weight of all they had left unsaid over the years they had known each other.

Footsteps crunched along the ground, and Quinn's head snapped toward the sound as her body tensed for the inevitable ambush. Her fingers wrapped around the hilt of her sword, and a thin flicker of flame licked her palm as her Burnbane fires ached to be freed.

Murdoc and Sophia emerged from the shadows without even a glance her way. Sophia crossed her arms when they reached Connor, and Murdoc rested his hand on the hilt of his sword as he silently shook his head.

"All clear," the former Blackguard said. "We weren't followed."

Connor's dark eyes darted toward Quinn, and he gestured for his team to follow him into the trees, likely to get out of earshot.

With a dragon and a ghoul keeping guard, he knew she wouldn't run.

Quinn let out a slow, settling breath as she released her grip on *Aurora's* hilt. She shook out her hand until the Burnbane fires eased back into her blood, and she sighed at her own antics.

Apparently her fears of an ambush had been unwarranted.

"I've never seen you like this," Tove whispered.

Quinn shrugged.

"Are you his prisoner, Quinn? Is that what this is? Why can't you tell me what's going on?"

"It's complicated." With a frustrated groan, she rubbed her face and set the last jar into Tove's bag.

"Isn't it always?"

"It doesn't matter." Quinn stood. "I'll wait until you get safely back into the tunnel, and then—"

Tove blew a raspberry and waved away the thought. "Quinn, I'm the one who told you about that entrance. There haven't been any blightwolf sightings in ages. Nothing dangerous ever comes this close to the city. I'll be fine."

"He did." Quinn said with a nod toward Connor.

The augmentor scratched the back of her head. "I suppose you're right."

"Stay safe, Tove." She raised one eyebrow. "And you can't tell a soul about any of this. I'm trusting you."

"I never share your secrets." The augmentor grinned. "I just tell you everyone else's."

They chuckled, and for a moment, this felt like the sendoff before any other mission. A bit of banter, a few potions, and an update on what had happened in her absence.

"Promise me you'll come back." Tove's smile slowly fell. "I don't have many friends, and I can't even imagine what it would do to me to hear you were—" She swallowed hard and briefly shut her eyes, unable to even say the word. "Swear to me that whatever this is won't kill you."

Quinn didn't answer. She wanted to say everything would be fine. More than anything, she wanted to assure Tove that there was no need to worry, but she didn't want to lie to her only friend in the world.

So she didn't say anything at all.

CONNOR

As he sat at the base of Nocturne's neck, Connor peered around to ensure no one was watching. Alone on the dragon's back, he pulled on his collar until he could get a glimpse of the new augmentation on his muscled chest.

The brilliant green lines on his skin cast a soft glow on his shirt. His body hummed with energy, as though the spellgust had infiltrated every vein.

There it was. His very first augmentation.

Since Henry had taken Kirkwall when Connor was still a boy and taxed the citizens to near-poverty, his family hadn't had the funds to give him the Hygenmix augmentation most Kirkwall boys received at age fourteen. Once in the Ancient Woods, he hadn't had the coin to waste on frivolous nonsense, and he'd given up the dream of ever having one.

Until now. With a bit of the wraith's help, he even had his own coat of arms.

It took willpower not to touch the emerald green lines inked into his skin as he stared down at the shield Tove had sketched into his body. Every inch of it had meaning, and it fit him perfectly.

The dual axes behind the shield honored the lessons he had learned from Ethan and Beck Arbor. The helmet above them represented the noble man his father had wanted him to be, and the dragon etched into the shield itself honored the dragons who had turned feral under the Wraith King's torment, all those centuries ago. Because he obeyed no one, Tove included a broken crown above the dragon's head.

On a banner beneath the shield, Tove had etched an old saying most outside of Slaybourne had never even heard.

The dead fear no mortal man.

A bit of drama added by the wraith, perhaps, but true nonetheless. Connor was a dead man walking, and he embraced it. If he had to have a mantra, this one spoke both to his inherent power and his duty to wield it wisely.

On the ground, Quinn and Tove stood. The Starling set her hand on the augmentor's shoulder, and Tove smiled weakly. His gaze shifted to the nape of Tove's neck, and another powerful urge hit him as he imagined flipping her onto her stomach and riding her from behind.

"Fates be *damned*," he muttered, shutting his eyes.

Maybe he was losing his resolve.

We could always come back for a visit. The wraith's voice echoed in his head, grim and gleeful. *Without anyone to bear witness, of course.*

Connor sucked in air through his teeth and shook his head, refusing to acknowledge that the ghoul had spoken at all.

Only three days remained, and now he had absolutely no hope of returning to Slaybourne before Teagan's earliest projected arrival. Every second mattered, and he couldn't waste time on urges.

With everything ahead of them, he had to focus. An enemy far more powerful than Zander was on the warpath to his home, and Connor was almost ready to face him.

CHAPTER FORTY-EIGHT

OTMUND

With no idea of how to escape Freymoor's deadly forest, Otmund wandered through the Blood Bogs. The fog churned around his ankles and pressed in from every direction, until the trees blurred into nothing but murky silhouettes in a dense blanket of never-ending white. The fog swallowed the sun and, with it, any hint of the world outside.

In the Blood Bogs, only his shaky breaths kept him company.

His toe caught on a root, and he stumbled forward. The mist parted in front of him as he fell, revealing a tree where there had once been nothing but churning white fog. His forehead rammed into the bark, and black dots covered his vision as his head swam from the blow. A burst of nausea burned his throat, and he swallowed hard to keep from vomiting what little food remained in his stomach.

With his heart thudding against his ribcage, he scanned the endless fog that stretched in every direction. He needed a hint. A sign of where to go, or who to stab.

He needed *something*, damn it.

Deep in the mists, someone laughed. The high-pitched voice echoed and blurred, distorted and twisted, as though a child were giggling somewhere underwater. It faded within seconds, but it reminded him that he was, in fact, not alone in this cursed woodland.

Not by a long shot.

He used the tree he'd hit moments before for balance and leaned against it as he stood. His chest heaved with panic, but he pressed his back against the trunk as he surveyed the thick fog. The bark scratched against his palms, but he held tight to his one anchor to the physical world. To the realm of what was real.

The rolling fog parted and, in the seconds that followed, a brief trail appeared through a cluster of slender silhouettes that could only be more trees.

"Don't go that way," something whispered in his ear.

He flinched and spun around, expecting to see the tree, but it was gone—swallowed by the mist.

Perhaps it had never existed in the first place. He couldn't tell anymore.

His chest rose and fell, faster and faster, as he fought to get ahold of himself. To slow his racing pulse. To catch his breath. To get a feel for how this blasted forest worked.

It was just a puzzle. Powerful as it was, even magic was bound by its own laws, and even the most complex enchantment could be dissected into simple limitations. Even the best glamours in Saldia couldn't make something just disappear.

No, beneath this haunting façade of a ghostly woodland, there had to be a man—or woman—pulling the strings of a well-orchestrated show. Tricks, that had to be what this was. A little smoke. A few well-trained assistants, perhaps. This performance wouldn't undo him. He could see through it all.

Otmund simply had to find the ringleader and force them to show him the way out.

"Follow me," another voice whispered from just within the fog.

He shut his eyes, refusing to even look in its direction. This forest wouldn't be the death of him. He had sacrificed too much to lose it all now.

"Who's that?" another voice whispered, farther away this time.

"Not sure," someone answered.

They spoke in hushed tones, in voices that reminded him of two servants who didn't want to be overheard. These voices hadn't been directed his way at all.

Curious, Otmund peered through one eye to see if he could pinpoint where they'd come from. At first, the mists refused to part, and he saw nothing.

No trees. No path. No wisps.

But then, slowly, something churned the fog. It rolled and coiled as someone passed through it, and Otmund went still as a statue. Seconds later, the whipping clouds split in half around a cluster of trees. A looming silhouette with broad shoulders walked between them, followed by two bright green wisps.

The voices, following another victim through the woods.

Otmund's jaw tensed, and he resisted the impulse to shout for the figure's attention. For all he knew, this could be a trick.

He had to be careful.

The stranger paused and looked over one shoulder, but the two wisps following him darted back into the fog before his head turned. He hesitated as he stared into the forest where they had been moments before, and the creak of skin on leather cut through the dead-silent air. He let out a short grunt of annoyance and continued through the mist, his footsteps too silent to hear.

Otmund narrowed his eyes in suspicion, but he had gotten lucky before. If those wisps didn't want this man to see them, it was a good sign that he was real.

Otmund crept closer, careful to keep the figure just on the edge of the fog as he inched toward the trees the stranger had just passed. When he reached them, he hid behind a pine and peered around its thick trunk to get a closer look.

The stranger paused again, his back still to Otmund. With his hands on his waist, the figure scanned the endless nothing around him and sighed in frustration. The mists thinned, and as they parted, the stranger's features came sharply into view.

It was the peasant.

Even without the mask over the man's mouth, no soul on this continent could ever forget those eyes.

Otmund stifled a gasp of surprise and hid again behind his tree. He shut his eyes as his heart thudded so loudly he feared the man would hear it, and he scanned the trees around him for signs of the wraith.

Nothing.

He gritted his teeth, his back tense with anticipation, and chanced another peek around the trunk. The peasant now sat on a boulder and rifled through his pack for something. The fog beyond him thinned even more, and across a dried creek bed, a ghoulish figure darted through the distant trees.

At this point, Otmund could barely think. The overpowering thud of his pulse in his ear drowned out even his own ragged breaths. He tugged the Bloodbane dagger from the sheath strapped around his waist, and though sweat licked his palms, he held tight to the familiar hilt. Each of his shallow breaths failed to deliver enough air.

A chill snaked down his spine at the thought of finally, at long last, finishing what he had started with this peasant who had gone too far. Who had stolen the wrong man's power. Who had dared defy the future king.

At this distance, with the peasant distracted and the wraith so far away, Otmund actually stood a chance of slitting the man's throat.

He would get only one opportunity to do this, which meant he could not miss. As he had done so many times before, he relived the night they killed Henry, recalling how Celine had waited for her husband to turn his back. How she had tugged the dagger from the sheath hidden in her skirts, so quietly he hadn't heard it. How she had set her fingers delicately on his shoulder, and how she had positioned the blade right over his heart—and how he had shifted at the last moment, as if on instinct, to keep the blade from instantly killing him.

If Otmund could succeed where she had failed, this would all finally end.

With the Bloodbane dagger in one hand, he crept out from behind his tree, careful to keep low to the ground in case he needed to disappear into the thick fog cover rolling across the blanket of decaying leaves. His gaze darted back and forth, again and again, between the peasant and the wraith in those distant trees. With each step, he expected the peasant to look over his shoulder. For this to all end, brutally and suddenly, in the peasant's favor.

And yet the man's back remained turned.

Each step brought Otmund closer—to fame, to wealth, to survival. With only a yard left between them, the peasant shifted in his seat and set his hands on his knees—to stand.

No.

If the peasant saw him now, it would all be over, and he would die.

As the man stood, Otmund sprinted the final distance and rammed the blade into the peasant's back.

The enchanted blade connected, and something splintered. Though it sounded almost like wood, the man arched his back, as if in pain.

In the distance, something inhuman screamed in agony.

A rush of thick fog rolled between Otmund and his prey, so dense it obscured the man's body. Otmund didn't care. He drew the dagger and stabbed again. And again. And again. Each time, the resounding thump of metal ripping into something solid broke the still air, and even the infamous Blood Bogs couldn't fake the sensation of a blade driving into a living thing.

Through it all, the man didn't scream. He didn't even grunt in pain. Otmund would've found that odd, perhaps, if Henry hadn't done the same thing in his final moments.

Heaving, his arms aching from the relentless stabbing, Otmund finally allowed himself to stop when he'd lost count of how many dozens of times he had stabbed the peasant. He fell to his knees, his heart pounding so hard it hurt, as the mist finally thinned again.

The peasant was gone.

Instead of a blood-soaked corpse, the Bloodbane dagger stuck out of a tree stump by the boulder. Shards of rotting wood lay on the ground around it.

Still on his knees, mouth gaping in disbelief, Otmund's forehead creased in confusion as he stared at the battered stump. Breathless and numb, he snatched his dagger and waited to understand.

Laughter echoed around him from the edges of the thinning mist. Three wisps floated at the edge of the fog, and as the laughter grew louder, ripples of golden light pulsed within their emerald-green bodies.

Otmund growled, and as he lost himself in his unfiltered hatred for these nuisances, the raspy snarl that escaped him didn't feel human. Heavy and grating, it crackled with everything he felt. Frustration. Despair. Anger. Disgust. Horror.

Fear.

As the emotions blurred within him, he fought back. Deep down, he knew he could still escape this place. In his core, in the depths of who he was and what he knew, Otmund was certain he could find the way out.

But with his augmentation on his arm fading, his power over his weaker self failed. He struggled to tap into the magic that stifled his feelings so that he could think with a clear head, and for a moment, it worked.

The fear dissolved. The disgust dimmed. But as the other emotions faded, one burned ever hotter, and his fury at these wisps built to a breaking point. Any of them could lead him out of here. Any of them had the power to show him a path to the edge of the forest, and yet they toyed with him. As lost as he was in their domain, they thought themselves superior.

And he would prove them *wrong*.

"I'll catch one of you bastards!" He grabbed the nearest shard of the tree trunk he had stabbed and chucked it at them. Their laughter faded as the wood passed harmlessly through one of them.

At least now he knew they could be silenced.

"You just wait." His tone dropped to a deadly octave, and he raised one finger in warning. "It won't be long, now. One of you will make a mistake, and I'll be there to catch you. Whatever you really are, I bet you still bleed."

His threat lingered on the forest's dead-silent air, and those glowing green bastards weren't laughing *now*.

As it had before, the broad-shouldered silhouette of the peasant shifted within the fog just behind the wisps. The shadow darkened until the man stepped into view, and this time, he crossed his arms as he stared Otmund down. The thief's eyebrows pinched together in a stern glare, like a disappointed father shaking his head at his children's antics, but Otmund didn't care.

The real peasant would've tried to kill him by now. No, this was yet another mirage. It had to be.

To the figure's left, another peasant stepped from the fog. And another. And another. Each strode from the mist carrying something different—a lantern, a map, a compass—and each watched him with the same stern expression, just waiting for him to act.

Waiting for him to *choose*.

"Which is real?" a voice whispered from somewhere in the dense mist.

"Better yet," another whisper asked, "are any of them real?"

The nearest peasant took a step forward and drew one of the silver swords from the twin sheaths on his back. A flash of silver light—moonlight, maybe, or swamp gas for all Otmund knew—glinted along the blade as the apparition swung it back and forth with lazy twists of his hand.

"Is anything real, my Lord?" the illusion asked, in the peasant's voice.

His jaw clenched and his heart racing, Otmund took a wary step away from the wall of mirages. They were all fake, without question, but he would keep hitting them every chance he got. He could see through them, now, and he wouldn't fall into their hands again. He would keep stabbing them, one by one, until they made a mistake. Whatever glamours they wore couldn't last forever, and when he finally caught one, he would force the damn thing to show him the way out.

As with everything in his life, it was only a matter of time until he got what he wanted. Once he escaped this hellhole, the fallen Princess of Freymoor would pay for her treason, and he would pillage her precious kingdom for every last coin hidden in its walls. Every artifact would end up in his fortress, and Dahlia's head would rot in the swamps of Nethervale.

And once he had bled this land for everything it was worth, he would burn these cursed bogs to the ground.

CHAPTER FORTY-NINE

CONNOR

Through the crisscrossed panes of a window on the first floor of Freymoor castle, silver clouds tumbled through a midnight sky. Two days left.

Connor stole through the night, blending with the shadows as he followed Quinn's fire-red hair through the darkness. She paused at a corner to a well-lit passage adjacent to theirs, and he pressed his back against the cold stone wall as they waited for the all-clear.

Beside him, a long row of windows gave him a glimpse of the castle's courtyard. A thin veil of mist rolled across the cobblestone road outside, and a lone lamp in the center cast an orange circle through the fog.

Outside, a soldier stepped into view and walked aimlessly across the cobblestones. The banner hanging from his spear carried the Oakenglen crest, but the guard used the weapon as a walking stick. He kicked a loose rock across the road, his back to them as he strode away, and he didn't even glance up at the castle as he wandered toward his station.

They've gotten lazy, the wraith said with an indignant huff.

Connor nodded. At least it worked in his favor.

Oakenglen had occupied Freymoor for over a decade, and that meant he couldn't simply knock on the front door. If he wanted to speak with Dahlia—and whomever truly ran this city, with her as their puppet—he needed to sneak his way in.

To save time, he'd debated asking Nocturne to drop them on the roof. As simple as it would've been, it would've caused more problems, as any sane human would've taken the dragon's presence as an attack. It wouldn't have made the best first impression, and he needed this fallen princess of Freymoor to like him.

Given his track record with Saldia's elite, however, he didn't have high hopes.

Quinn crouched at the corner to the next hallway with her fingers pressed against the carpet at their feet, and she tilted her head to listen to the silent building. Behind him, Sophia and Murdoc huddled in the shadows, waiting for the order to continue their hour-long trek toward Dahlia's chambers.

True to her word, the Starling warrior had gotten them past every blockade they had encountered. She knew her way around this place, even after so many years away. With each passing day, he learned something new about her, and she never seemed to run out of tricks.

An admirable trait in an ally, but not one he wanted in an enemy.

A soft green glow lit the carpet behind him, and he glanced over one shoulder to find the stunning green light radiating from Sophia's cleavage. If they weren't careful, the light of her powerful new augmentation would give them away.

He nudged her with his elbow and pointed to her chest in a silent command to hide the light, but she shrugged. Nothing to be done about it now, apparently.

Somewhere out of sight, the slow and steady thuds of a man's footsteps meandered down the torchlit corridor they needed to enter. The footsteps paused, and the hiss of a dying flame followed. The bright light in the corridor faded as the man put out one of the sconces. Seconds later, another hiss cut through the air, and the corridor dimmed further.

With Quinn keeping watch ahead of him, Connor tensed as he waited for the man to leave.

In the silence, he tried again to connect with Nocturne through their new connection. He still didn't like the idea of Nocturne waiting, alone, in the forests just outside the legendary Blood Bogs. Even for a dragon, it hardly seemed safe.

He closed his eyes, as Tove had instructed, and set his hand against the augmentation on his chest.

Nocturne, he called.

As the guard's footsteps wandered lazily away, the dragon didn't answer.

Tell me what you see.

Nothing.

Yet again, Nocturne refused to let him in.

Connor sighed in defeat and, instead of pressing the issue, let it be. It hardly surprised him, since they still didn't have much of a bond. Hell, they might never have one, and this obscenely expensive augmentation of theirs might never be used. Even on their trip to Freymoor, Nocturne hadn't once let him in, even to get directions.

I have always hated this place, the wraith growled.

On instinct, Connor scanned the hallway around them to ensure the wraith hadn't made himself known. The ghoul thankfully remained hidden, but he doubted the reprieve would last.

I warned Henry to leave it be, the specter continued with an irritated huff. *The man wouldn't listen. He was a stubborn ass, Magnuson, much like you.*

"Focus," he chided in a harsh whisper.

This city isn't right, the Wraith King continued, ignoring him. *The people look at me like they can see me. Do not underestimate this realm.*

"Clear," Quinn whispered, beckoning them forward. "This way. We're almost to the secret door."

She darted into the dimly lit hallway, and Connor followed. Only a third of the sconces along the walls remained lit, and it cast a surreal shadow across the carpeted corridor, like dusk.

Quinn didn't dally. She bolted past two hallways and slipped into a third. Only one sconce flickered in the darkness through this new corridor, all the way at the end, and the hazy outlines of tables against the wall would offer plenty of places to hide.

Good choice.

Deep in the darkness of this new hallway, the Starling warrior pressed her back against the wall. Connor and his team followed, each of them crouching to pause and listen to the night. He waited for an inevitable footstep or a muffled conversation to give away the next servant or soldier's location, but the quiet castle was only punctuated with the weak crackle of fire in the few sconces that remained lit.

"...this way, my lady," someone said, their voice almost too muffled and distant to hear.

His ear twitched, and he frowned as he leaned away from Quinn and toward the voice. Though she continued to survey the hallway they had just left, he peered down the darkened corridor behind them. His eyes adjusted, and the hazy outlines became waist-high tables covered in flowers or wooden bowls of fruit. Portraits dotted the ornate cerulean walls, and the paintings filled every available space between the half-dozen doors lining the hall.

"Did you hear that?" He looked back at Quinn, who frowned in confusion as she scanned his face.

She shook her head.

"This way." He gestured for them to follow, and the Starling warrior let out an exasperated huff even as she darted after him.

The four of them sped through the darkness, their steps whisper-silent as he craned his ear for another clue. For several moments, none came. The corridor ended in another darkened hallway, and the lone sconce on the far wall flickered and died as he reached it. A silver moonbeam cut across the carpet in the silent castle, but the clouds quickly swallowed the soft midnight light from outside.

"This is the wrong way," Quinn hissed under her breath.

He closed his eyes and held up one finger in an unspoken command to listen.

"...but, my Lady..."

At the woman's soft voice, his eyes snapped open, and Quinn's lips parted in surprise. He smirked down at her in victory, and she rolled her eyes.

Glasses clinked, and muffled footsteps slid across the carpet. Around the corner, a pair of simple wooden doors sat open, and a beam of orange light stretched across the floor from within. A single shadow passed through the amber beam of light, and the footsteps faded.

Two sconces framed the open doors, but for them to get closer, he needed darkness.

He looked over one shoulder at Quinn and nodded toward the lights. "Can you snuff them?"

Though she pursed her lips in annoyance at the order, she raised her palms in front of her and tightened them abruptly into fists. The green lines along her arms glowed with the movement, and her Airdrift augmentation sent a gust through the hallway.

The fires instantly snuffed out, and the hallway plunged into darkness.

As he peered around the corner again, the orange light streaming from the open doors glowed brighter in the sudden shadows. He waited for someone to notice or pass through the opening, but the conversation ended.

"Wraith," he whispered. "Tell me what you can see."

It irritates me when you give me orders.

"Just do it," Connor muttered.

The ghoul groaned in annoyance, and Connor's stomach lurched. The world around him shifted in a violent blur of color, and in seconds, he stood in a simple room with a row of windows across one wall. Orange light from the dozen sconces along the stone walls cast a warm glow over the floor.

His head pivoted, as though someone else controlled his movements. A simple throne sat on a raised platform to his left, and the runes carved into its dark rosewood glowed with dazzling green light. To his right, a pair of closed iron doors took up most of the wall.

A woman stood alone at the windows with her back to him. Draped in a flowing blue gown, she clasped her hands together and sighed deeply as she stared out at the night.

That had to be Dahlia.

He fell back into his body with the force of a thousand-foot fall. The vision faded, and he leaned one arm against the wall as a dull ache flooded his brain. The pain faded as quickly as it had come, and he rubbed his face as he refocused on the task at hand.

"I hate it when you do that," he quietly snapped at the ghoul.

The wraith just laughed.

"She's in there." Connor pivoted and pressed one knee against the floor as he surveyed the three people crouching behind him, awaiting orders. "She's alone, as far as I can tell."

"She's never alone," Quinn warned.

"I don't know what to tell you." He gestured over his shoulder at the door. "There's no one else in there."

The Starling pursed her lips, but didn't respond.

"You've seen Dahlia before, right?"

She nodded.

"Good," Connor said with a nod. "Once we're in there, tell me if it's really her. I need to know if they've put a doppelganger in her place."

Quinn sighed in defeat. "Alright."

He scanned her face, detecting the reservation in her tone. "What is it?"

"This is your last chance to abandon this ludicrous idea." Her eyes darted toward him. "Whatever artifact you're after, you're not going to get it. Especially not by infiltrating the castle like a *criminal*." Her nose wrinkled with disdain. "Whatever is brewing here—whoever is using her as their puppet—I promise you don't want to be involved. I need to keep you alive to get Blaze back, and we're treading into the sort of thing that gets people killed. This place isn't to be trifled with, and it never stays conquered for long."

"It's lucky I'm not here to conquer it, then," Connor said with a terse glare. "Murdoc, follow at the rear and close the doors behind us once we're inside."

The former Blackguard nodded.

Connor let out a settling breath and darted out into the darkened hallway. He inched toward the open doors and peered through the opening to find the woman still standing at the windows with her back to him. Her palms rested on the windowsill as she stared out at the moonlit night.

On the journey here, he had rehearsed what he would say. The world saw him as an outlaw, and he had invaded her home in the dead of night to ask for a family heirloom he doubted she wanted to give away. No amount of charm or bargaining could redeem the terrible first impression he was about to make, but he would simply have to adapt and make do.

As he stepped into the simple throne room, his boots passed silently over the floor. His team followed closely behind, and Murdoc cast a final, wary look into the hall as he gently slid the doorstops aside.

Connor's body tensed as the firelight from the sconces hit him, but he couldn't stay in the shadows forever.

As the doors shut behind them, the air shifted, much as it always did when the wraith appeared. This time, however, the twang of a bowstring followed the sensation. Something sailed toward Connor's head, and he snatched the arrow from the air right before it could embed into his skull.

Yet the woman by the windows didn't move.

A second bowstring twanged, and Quinn summoned her shield of light as another arrow raced toward her neck. Unwilling to take any chances, he grabbed it before it could hit her shield, and its painfully sharp tip scraped against the light she had summoned to protect herself.

Her hazel eyes darted toward him, but she didn't say anything.

Connor scanned the walls, wondering where the hell those could've come from, only to find thin slits carved into the mortar between the stone bricks.

Fates be damned. Freymoor had an army hiding in the walls.

"You could've thought to check for traps," Connor hissed at the wraith under his breath.

I'm looking now, the ghoul said with an indignant huff. *I've never seen such an elaborate network of secret passages. They're full, Magnuson. There are at least forty archers surrounding this room alone.*

Shit.

The only silver lining was that he and his team were still alive. Even he could be outnumbered, but these soldiers had yet to stuff him full of arrows.

He let out a slow breath and studied the woman who still had her back to him. This admittedly unpleasant surprise still didn't change anything. He had come to bargain, and she had left him alive long enough to start the negotiation.

"I'm not here to hurt you," Connor said firmly as he tossed the arrows onto the floor.

The woman rolled her shoulders back and turned to face them. Her neckline plunged to reveal a thin line of cleavage, and a lacy blue collar framed her chest as it climbed her shoulders and covered the back of her neck. Her dark blonde hair framed her delicate face with thick curls, and her blue eyes narrowed in fierce warning. Her pink lips pinched together as she studied him, unafraid.

"Lady Dahlia," Quinn said stiffly. "You're looking well."

Good. So this was, in fact, Dahlia Donahue.

The Lady's eye twitched in annoyance as her cold gaze darted toward Quinn, and her lips pursed as she bit back a retort. "Starling."

Tension crackled in the air as the two women glared at each other, and Connor fought the urge to shake his head in disappointment. It seemed as though he had underestimated Dahlia's hatred for the Lightseers. Maybe he should've locked Quinn in a cellar somewhere and done this without her.

Too late now.

With the posture of a queen, Dahlia clasped her hands in front of her and studied them in the silence that followed. Though Quinn had warned him that she would be a sick and feeble thing, nothing about her seemed even remotely weak.

How interesting.

"Clever." He grinned, admittedly impressed, and rubbed his jawline as he pieced it together. "You've never been sick, have you? It was all a show."

Her blue eyes shifted toward him. "Bravo, Wraithblade."

His smile fell at the unspoken implication of her calling him by his title. She knew of the Wraith King. She knew what he was.

And yet she remained unafraid.

"There isn't a shadow king here at all, is there?" Connor gestured to the throne room to emphasize his point. "There's no puppet master. There's no conspiracy. You made it all up."

"I let people believe what they want to believe." She lifted her chin in defiance. "It keeps them from interfering."

"And yet you're showing me the real you." He met her unflinching gaze. "To what do I owe the honor?"

"I debated playing the part for you," Dahlia admitted. She took a deep breath, and as her chest expanded, the line of her cleavage became more prominent. "But I felt it crucial that you know who you're up against."

He raised one eyebrow as he met her unspoken challenge. "And who is that?"

"A queen," she said simply. "I know why you're here, and you're only alive because you also happen to have something I want."

"What luck," he said dryly. "It sounds like we can strike a bargain after all."

"Perhaps," she said with a slight tilt of her head. "If you're able to survive, that is."

Connor's neck tensed at the threat. That sounded ominous, and he didn't like where this negotiation was headed.

Yet again, he tried to contact Nocturne. This woman saw far more than they had expected, and for all he knew, she had already discovered the dragon in her forest. He needed to warn Nocturne of the danger.

But that damned dragon still didn't reply.

CHAPTER FIFTY

NOCTURNE

The soft, fluid rustle of blue-black leaves shivering in an ancient canopy kept Nocturne company in the otherwise dead-silent night.

With a head that towered over the forest, he kept watch from a meadow. Tense, alert, and aware, he listened. His midnight scales melted into the shadows, the perfect camouflage for a being who could sit still enough to be mistaken for a statue.

Gnarled oaks and aspens circled the field, and mist rolled across the twisted roots. He eyed it, cautious of the fog, but he had little to control in this place. Even the air in Freymoor had weight to it. The enchantments on these trees sank deep to the soil, to the bones of those who had come before, and it knew Connor was here.

Whatever *it* was, it already knew.

Nearby, a patch of the slender meadow grass lay flattened from their landing. A thin trail cut toward the tree line and the dim orange light of the city beyond. Gray stone walls circled the lone castle on the highest hill in this stretch of flatlands, and a single light in the tallest tower flickered, too far away for even his enhanced vision to see as more than an amber speck.

Movement in his periphery caught his attention, and only his eyes shifted as trees creaked and branches swayed. A shadow stepped on four hooves from the darkness between the trunks. Brown fur. White spots. A slender head.

The deer ambled into the meadow and sniffed at a clover in the grass. Its ears twitched and shifted as it investigated its snack, but it didn't bolt. It didn't so much as look his way.

Eat.

A pang reverberated in his chest, as sharp and violent as a scream, and his predator instinct compelled him to swallow the deer whole. It longed to feel the hot tang of blood down his throat. The snap of bones between his teeth. The race of a dying beast's heart as it slowed to a stop.

But Nocturne didn't move.

Feral urges were a part of a dragon's life, and he had mastered his long ago. The predator in him would never be satiated, and hunger no longer fazed him. Besides, a meal in foreign territory risked distracting him from a threat, and he never allowed himself to eat while on duty unless he first secured the surrounding area.

With its twitching nose embedded in the grass, the deer nibbled at a patch of clovers for a few minutes. Nocturne watched in stone silence, his eyes shifting with the beast's movements as it wandered off into the woods once again.

Something heavy and strange pressed against his mind once again, like a human's fist against his skull, but he refused to let Connor into his head just yet. This attempt persisted, far longer than the others, but it carried no urgency. The attempts never did. He felt nothing, heard nothing, saw nothing at all while his wall remained firmly in place, and he preferred it this way.

The idea of an open passage into the Wraithblade's mind had intrigued Nocturne enough to allow the augmentation to happen, but only for his own benefit. Connor claimed he only wanted to use it while they flew, but Nocturne saw more—he saw a chance to peer into the man's soul to find the truths he hid even from himself.

Connor had potential. No one could deny that. Strong in body and in mind, the man would shift tides. In the dragonlands, a king like Connor would herald an unprecedented era of peace.

But Nocturne had spent enough time with humans to know they did not have a dragon's temperance or self-control. They were creatures of war. If Connor had been born a dragon, Nocturne would have fought and died for him. But as a human, his heart could be tempted. Twisted. Swayed.

Corrupted.

For a brief moment, he allowed himself to close his eyes as his silent debate raged on: to join Connor, or to kill him.

There would be no shades of gray in this choice.

His snout wrinkled in frustration. Extremes rarely served as the only option, but in this case, Connor's sheer power left little room for nuance. Regardless of the deal the man had offered, leaving such a powerful threat behind had never been an option.

Nocturne saw potential in Connor, but he had endorsed the wrong warrior before. Potential could sour. True potential always became greatness, but greatness was a spectrum that ranged from mercy and peace to cruelty and bloodlust.

Evil deeds—and wicked men—could still be remembered as great.

Connor Magnuson had the sort of power that could swallow continents whole, and that would either save or destroy Nocturne's people. Kings built alliances and respected their neighbors, but a warlord always sought a new land to conquer. The latter lived for the hunt, and no amount of land or power could satisfy their greed.

Nocturne would die before he allowed his people to lose even a scale to a war with mankind—if the dragonlands still existed, of course. If his people had survived at all in his absence.

His head shifted, and he stared at the ground in his shame. He had failed them, but he would make it right.

The night, calm and quiet, went on. The gentle hum of trilling beetles filled the gaps in the trees, and somewhere nearby, a bullfrog croaked. The last of winter had long ago melted away to spring, and the tail end of the season's warmth soothed the forest.

At the edge of the meadow, a tendril of fog broke through the tree line. He glared at it, not trusting the enchantments in this place, but another broke through the line to his right. Bit by bit, minute by minute, the mists crept closer.

He scanned the trees again, but nothing had joined him. He still sat alone in the field, as far as he could tell, but he didn't trust this place to tell him the truth. A soft rumble built in his chest—a quiet warning that could've been mistaken for distant thunder—and the pang of his feral self hit him again in the chest.

Defend, it commanded. *Fight.*

The fog coiled over the ground, spreading like frost on a windowpane, until it finally curled over his feet. It touched him with the gentle brush of a cool breath on his scales, but the sensation carried life.

In an instant, the air shifted. His horns tingled with warning and the weight of eyes on his face. From somewhere in the shadows, something watched.

The growl in his throat built, louder since he no longer needed to hide, and he waited for the watcher to show themselves.

Thus far, he had nothing to fight but the fog.

A whisper, soft and soothing, rolled past him like a breeze. The canopy at the edge of the meadow shivered. The wind built, slowly at first, until a strong gust rolled through the grass toward him and carried more voices with it.

Their words blurred together, but he recognized them all the same. Voices he remembered.

Voices of the dead.

Mother.

Father.

Coatl.

He snarled and spread his wings. They snapped open, and he shifted his weight onto his front claws. The blisteringly sharp talons dug into the dirt for balance as he summoned his feral power.

A rush of glee hummed through him like a vibrating string on a lute, and he silenced it with a snort of smoke through his nose. He commanded himself, not his feral side. He had control, always, regardless of its endless temptation.

His power crackled in the depths of his soul, a raging inferno none could tame, and lightning skittered across his scales as he dared the watcher to step forth. The sparks cast yellow bursts of light onto the pitch-black meadow, and the mists around his feet glowed like clouds in a thunderstorm.

The gale grew stronger. The trees bent and moaned from its strength. Leaves flew off their branches and swirled overhead, consumed by the brewing storm as he stood in its eye.

The voices rushed him again. They overlapped each other and blended with the wind until he couldn't tell which was louder.

"...*welcome*..."

"...*royal dragons*..."

"...*so much to say*..."

The whispers built to a crescendo, crashing into each other as they spoke, one after another, louder and louder as they fought the biting rush of wind. He growled, body tensing as he sifted through the noise, searching for the single voice that must be commanding them all.

"Show yourself," he demanded.

His voice resonated through the field, through the very earth, and it carried the command of a general. An order. A demand.

Obey.

The hum of overlapping chatter faded in an instant. The gale dissolved into a quiet breeze once again, and a single leaf tumbled past as it lost momentum. The buzzing energy in the meadow settled, stale and uncertain, but the weight of eyes in the shadows remained.

Threat, his feral instinct warned.

The growl in Nocturne's throat hummed louder, and several clicks followed. The clicks of a predator stalking prey.

A final warning.

Another gust of wind, gentler this time, fluttered toward him through the grass.

"...*you are safe*..." the voices promised in unison.

"Yes," he answered, his voice booming over the empty forest as he lowered his head and prepared to taste blood. "But are you?"

This time, the voices didn't reply.

In the darkness at the edge of the tree line, two red eyes appeared. They glowed with feral fire, and the dark slits in their centers settled on him.

He bristled. A feral dragon, *here*. One of his kin, lost to their rage, perhaps broken into submission just as the Wraith King had tried to do to him all those centuries ago.

The eyes swung side to side with the ambling gait of a circling predator, and they left fading trails of crimson light in the shadows as they moved. A silhouette appeared between the trees—just a snout, at first, but a head followed. Curling horns with silver stripes that glistened. Sapphire-blue scales, rich and dark.

All of it, familiar.

As the dragon stepped closer, Nocturne's eyes widened in surprise and recognition. His younger brother paused at the edge of the meadow, half his size and with his head somehow reattached.

Lie.

The Knowing hit him square in the chest, but he didn't need his regal powers to assume this creature wasn't real. Coatl's very existence, here in this meadow so far from home, could have only been a lie.

Nocturne snarled and stretched his wings even wider as he settled once more into his stance. "You are dead, little brother."

Coatl nodded, and Nocturne seethed with rage at this liar's brazen imitation of the brother he had so loved.

The imposter lowered his head as he calmly paced the edge of the field in a classic taunt. Circle. Watch. Wait for the other to strike.

Nocturne couldn't be so easily fooled. He remained rooted in place, unmoving except to follow the imposter's footsteps with his eyes.

"Your anger is justified," the imposter said, and his voice boomed over the meadow grass with all the command of a royal dragon.

Nocturne's heart panged with grief. With fury. With shame. This power, this strength, it was everything Coatl could have been.

To show him his dreams for his younger brother was not the mercy this fool thought it was.

"I needed you to listen," Coatl's voice stabbed at Nocturne's chest like a tail spike to the heart, yet he only snarled louder as the imposter spoke. "I needed you to understand."

"You have precious few seconds to speak, imposter," he warned.

Coatl paused mid-step, his clawed foot still raised as his eyes narrowed. "Very well, prince of dragons. You saw potential in Coatl—in me. You wanted me to ascend to my rightful place at your side as a warrior prince. It was my right, but Mother saw my weakness, when you saw only my potential. She knew I would be consumed in the Trials. She knew you would be the one to end me. She tried to save—."

Nocturne roared, and his voice drowned out the imposter's final words.

The utter *audacity*.

The sparks skittering over Nocturne's scales burned brighter. His claws dug deeper into the soil, snapping through roots as he fought with the guilt of what he had done. Of how he had failed.

Coatl paused and spread his glorious blue wings wide. "You understand, then, why I am here. You see how the past repeats itself."

Nocturne didn't move. Though tempted to glance back in the direction of the castle, toward Connor, he remained poised to strike. Still as stone, he glared at the imposter wearing his younger brother's face. "Tell me what magic this is."

"This is the land of the Old Ways," Coatl answered. "Here, the dead do not stay buried."

"Who are you, then?"

Coatl paused, his head tilted with thought as he watched Nocturne in silence. The wind picked up again, frothing as it shook the ring of trees around the meadow, and the feral dragon's form shifted. The edges blurred with the forest behind him, such that Nocturne couldn't see where his brother ended and the trees began. The dead prince bled into the shadows until only those glowing red eyes remained. They hovered in the darkness, watching him, until they, too, disappeared.

Nocturne snarled, hating this place's tricks. Its lies. Its brazen disrespect. He wanted nothing more than to burn it to the ground, and if it gave him any more reason, he would—his pact with Connor be damned.

His jaw snapped shut as he caught the subtle creep of his feral rage. He briefly shut his eyes and forced a settling breath to calm himself.

To remain in control.

Another silhouette appeared on the tree line, though this one was tiny.

It skipped into the field, its blonde curls bouncing, until its face appeared in the low light—a little girl. She smiled up at him with warmth as her delicate green dress settled around her legs.

Tiny nose. Hair as blonde as a field of wheat. Big blue eyes, and a wide smile as soft as the sun. Now, the imposter dressed as Fiona Finn, the child who had charmed him in the forest. The little bundle of light and joy, a reminder that humans could be pure, if only for a time.

Lie.

Nocturne took one step closer in warning. He'd had enough of these lies. Now, both he and his feral side hungered for retribution.

"You asked me who I am." The imposter tilted her head as she craned her neck to meet his eye. "I am a mask, nothing more than a familiar face the Blood Bogs wear to speak to mortals."

Truth.

He narrowed his eyes at the small child, still unwilling to trust. "To show me my brother—"

"Is cruel." She nodded once in apology. "But you needed to remember the fall that awaits your human should he fail. You've faced this all before, and Coatl nearly killed you. You nearly failed him twice. You must see the damage the Wraithblade could do to your home if he, too, lost his way."

Truth.

The growl in Nocturne's throat faded, and the sparks on his scales disappeared into the night. He watched the little girl in silence, and in suspicious awe of what the Blood Bogs knew.

Perhaps the imposter knew much more.

"What is left of my home?" he asked.

The little girl smiled, as gentle and calm as a timeless entity trapped in a child's body. "Much, but I cannot see it all. I will offer you what answers I have as payment if we first discuss the Wraithblade."

Nocturne snarled again in warning as the child taunted him with what he wanted most. "I cannot be bought."

"I'm aware, but this affects us both, Nocturne, Prince of Dragons, King of the Nightlands, Protector of warriors and monks alike."

His eyes narrowed in suspicion. Perhaps the mists knew entirely too much.

"I've seen what he will become if his will fractures even a little," she continued. "You've seen it for yourself, time and time again. You've watched your brothers—both in blood and in battle—lose themselves to their inner barbarian. They drowned in their power, and they took others with them. You've felt that pain before. Can you face it again?"

"SUCH IS MY DUTY!" He snapped at the air, and the chomp echoed through the painfully silent meadow. "IT IS CONSTANT AND ETERNAL. IT IS AND ALWAYS HAS BEEN MY BURDEN TO BEAR IN THIS LIFE. THIS IS YOUR LAST CHANCE, IMPOSTER. ASK WHAT YOU TRULY WANT TO KNOW, OR PREPARE TO FACE ME WITH MORE THAN LIES AND RIDDLES."

Static built in his throat as he prepared to roast the imposter alive. He didn't care the mask she wore or the lies she told.

The little girl set her small palm against the nearest tree as she met his glare. "I have seen what has become of good men who acquired immense power. Some remain pure, but most do not. I ask you, then, if you think he will lose his way—and if you could survive the final battle against him."

Nocturne's head snapped back in surprise, and his brows furrowed as he watched the little girl staring up at him with wide blue eyes. Though it was an inner debate he often had with himself, no one had ever questioned his might before. No one had ever asked him if he would lose, for it was his duty to win. To endure. To persevere against all odds to protect the homeland and its people.

His gaze drifted to the ground, but he could not lie to himself. Any lie gave his feral side a claw into his soul, and bit by bit, deception corroded his control.

In his battles with the giants of his past, he had on occasion risked losing. Each time, he had tapped into his feral bloodlust to win, and each time, he had almost lost himself to the raging beast within. If he were to duel Connor to the death, he would face the same choice—and it may require more of his feral power than he could reclaim.

Whether he lost the duel or lost himself to his feral side, he would still lose the war.

"I DO NOT KNOW," he confessed.

"I feared as much," the imposter admitted with a sad little sigh.

Nocturne's gaze shifted toward the castle, and he studied its spires as most of it blurred into the night. Even if he failed, there was another who stood a chance of success.

Perhaps.

The little girl tilted her head as she scanned his face. "Would you like to see for yourself what lies ahead?"

He scoffed. "You said yourself you know of the past. Of the dead. The Old Ways cannot speak of the future."

"True," she admitted. "I'm no selkie, but the future is so often a repeat of the past. Man changes so little, even as the forests grow tall around him. Is your faith in Connor unwavering, my dear Prince of Dragons, or can you stomach a glimpse of the death that awaits both our lands should he fail?"

Nocturne sat with the Blood Bog's offer. All those centuries ago, he'd had the utmost faith in Coatl, and he had chosen wrong. His brother had failed, and as much as he wanted to believe Connor could succeed, he didn't know for certain.

Following an imposter into the mist carried risk as well. He had been tricked before, but this place of magic knew more than any mortal ever could. He figured it could have dragged him into the mists, by now, if it had so chosen. To be given an offer showed its respect for him.

Still, his eyes narrowed in suspicion. "What tricks lie in wait for me if I were to follow?"

"None for you," she answered. "But many for him."

Truth.

He stared off into the forests, into the brewing mist churning in the distance as it all but swallowed the woodland whole.

"Show me," he demanded.

The imposter smiled, warm and gentle, and she skipped off into the trees. Mist churned over her ankles as she dissolved into the shadows between the trunks. The fog seeped out into the meadow and coiled over his scales, thicker than before.

With a huff of black smoke through his nose, Nocturne followed.

CHAPTER FIFTY-ONE

CONNOR

At any moment, this negotiation with the Lady of Freymoor could go south.

Given the forty-some archers hidden in the secret passages around her throne room, Connor needed to tread carefully.

With a subtle twist of his head, he scanned the room for a way out. The wooden doors into the hallway had already closed behind them, and he briefly calculated the odds of him and his team making it into the corridor without becoming pincushions in the process.

The odds weren't good.

Besides, getting to the hallway wouldn't guarantee their safety. If Dahlia had secret passages behind the throne room's walls, she could easily have more in the other areas of the castle. Even with the ghoul's power and his own considerable skill, their small band could still become outnumbered.

He would have to talk his way out of this one.

"It's clear you already know my name." Dahlia's piercing blue eyes swept across his body. "It's only courteous for you to tell me yours."

In answer, he simply frowned. He had expected better of her than to ask such a foolish question.

When he didn't reply, her lips curled into a thin smile that didn't reach her eyes, and she took another deep breath. Her chest moved with every inhale, drawing his eye each time. From the high collar to the plunging neckline, her dress perfectly framed her cleavage.

A tease, and a trap. She knew how to flaunt her beauty, and she wielded it like a weapon with every bit as much skill as Quinn did.

Tempting, but too deadly to indulge.

"I expected you sooner," the fallen princess admitted. "Were you delayed?"

Connor huffed impatiently. "Enough games, Dahlia."

The Lady of Freymoor paused, and with a little sigh, she relaxed. The stern creases in her brow faded, and her expression softened. "Perhaps I approached you too harshly, Wraithblade. My father always told me to be truthful with my allies, and I wanted you to understand our power."

She waved her hand, and what arrowheads he could see retreated back through the thin slits in the walls.

"Allies, are we?" Connor crossed his arms as he nodded to the arrows he had thrown onto the floor. "Do you often shoot at your friends?"

She smirked. "Only when I know they won't get hit."

"How endearing." He didn't bother to mask his sarcasm.

He didn't trust her. Not for a second. No matter what sweet words came out of those pink lips of hers, she had already proven herself to be a master of manipulation. This woman had feigned illness for a decade and created the facade of being manipulated, all to ensure that others underestimated her.

Frankly, he'd begun to doubt she had the *capacity* to tell the truth, much less the desire. If he didn't need the Soulsprite, he would've turned his back on this whole mess and simply left.

Dahlia snapped her fingers, and the wooden doors to the hallway swung open. Where before the corridor had been empty, a man dressed in a black fur cloak now stood with ten soldiers. Every one of his men carried a crossbow, and though the arrow tips remained pointed at the ground, each guard glared at Connor with an unmasked and unflinching desire to pull the trigger.

Delightful.

Servants filtered past the soldiers, and each maid carried various trays or chairs. Two men carried in a table, while one of the maids balanced a silver plate lined with empty teacups on her way into the room. Another carried in a pile of cookies coated in various jams in one hand and, in the other, held a silver teapot with steam billowing from its spout.

In less than a minute, the servants had erected a full tea service in the center of the throne room, complete with a place setting for Dahlia and each member of Connor's team.

"Come, now. Sit." With her back to the simple wooden throne, Dahlia took her place at the head of the table and poured herself a cup of tea. She reached for one of the cookies coated in bright red jam and took a delicate bite as she watched the four of them to see what they would do.

No sane human shot an arrow at a man's head and then invited him to tea.

Neither Connor nor any of his team moved. They stood there in silence, waiting for the catch. His stomach rumbled, and as the scent of rose and lavender swam through the air from her teacup, his throat tightened with thirst.

Still, he remained on his feet with his arms crossed, glaring at the woman who was clearly still playing games with him.

"Not one for pleasantries, I see." The fallen princess smiled, unfazed, and leaned back in her seat. "Very well. To business, then. I know why you're here. I've learned a fair bit about who you are, and I know what you've come here to retrieve. I don't, however, know why you want it, nor am I convinced you deserve to have it."

Beside him, Murdoc's hand rested on the hilt of his sword, and Sophia's hands glowed briefly blue as the soft crackle of ice across her skin pierced the otherwise silent air. Somewhere in the secret passages surrounding the room, a bowstring tightened.

He needed to intercede, or his team would get hurt.

Once, long ago as a brash young teenager, he'd nearly punched a King's Guardsman in the face when the man had insulted his family's shop. He'd known what the consequences would be, but as an idealistic young fool, he hadn't cared. Back then, his father had talked him down with seconds to spare, and in the end, all three were laughing at his father's jokes.

The whole episode had taught him that the best way to soften a conflict was with humor. If that didn't work, the second-best option was far simpler—don't be an asshole.

With a reluctant sigh, Connor grabbed the nearest chair and dragged it to the other end of the table. It would mean having his back to the iron doors opposite the throne, but he didn't care. If he was going to negotiate with Dahlia, he would sit across from her, in the spot that established him as her equal. Though he didn't have a plate or teacup, he sat in his new spot and set his elbows on the table as he stared at her down the length of it.

With a sidelong glance at Murdoc and Sophia, he gestured to the open chairs. "It's alright."

Sophia glared at the woman in blue, but ultimately took the nearest open seat. Murdoc rounded the table and sat beside Connor, leaving the chair beside Dahlia open for Quinn.

The Starling woman didn't budge.

"Sit," Connor said as he pointed to the chair.

Quinn's gaze never left Dahlia. With her arms crossed over her chest, she shook her head. "Freymoor has killed far too many Lightseers for me to sit at her table."

"It doesn't matter to me." Dahlia took a sip of her tea. "You weren't supposed to be here, Starling. Standing or sitting, I'm not interested in anything you have to say."

Quinn's eyes narrowed with contempt.

"I'm curious, Wraithblade." The Lady of Freymoor set her teacup on the table and, with her elbows on either side of the saucer, threaded her fingers together in front of her face. "I'd like to know what exactly you plan to do now that you've retaken Slaybourne."

The wraith growled. *How the blazes could she know that?*

Connor ignored the wraith's rumbling growl and instead met the fallen princess's gaze. "You certainly know a lot about me."

"I do." She nodded. "But you didn't answer my question."

"I want to be left alone," he admitted. "I want all of you rich folks to give me space and let me live in peace."

Her smile fell, and her brows pinched with confusion as the words disarmed her. "That's not possible for people like you and me, Wraithblade."

"You asked what I want, and I told you." He shrugged. "Now, what about you, Dahlia? What is it you want from me?"

"I want proof. Proof of who you are. Proof of your motives. Proof of your intentions."

"That's all?" he asked dubiously.

"That's *everything*." The noblewoman's gaze swept the untouched place settings before her. "It will give me answers. About you. About the wraith. It will explain what you serve to gain by killing Otmund. It will clarify what the Bloodbane daggers do, and why Celine wants one so badly. It will reveal what you plan to do with the Soulsprite, and what you plan to offer me in exchange."

Connor stilled, almost unable to believe she had revealed so much to him in such a short time. She knew far more than he thought she possibly could, and he truly didn't like where this was going.

In his periphery, Quinn's eyes darted toward him. Dahlia had revealed too much, and he didn't expect the Starling to keep any of this to herself. When they were negotiating her release, he would have to be careful to figure out exactly what she knew about the Soulsprite and how he planned to use it.

For now, he needed to focus on Dahlia.

The fallen princess leaned subtly forward, and her arms perfectly framed her chest as she stared him in the eye. "Once I understand what you want, I will finally know if you're worthy."

"Of the Soulsprite?"

"Yes, and no." Dahlia shrugged coyly. "The Soulsprite is safely stored in the Blood Bogs, and the mists will only give it to someone who can prove their worth. A Champion."

In Connor's periphery, Quinn stiffened. The Starling's hazel eyes closed, and her chest stilled as she held her breath.

"That sounds ominous," he admitted.

"I suppose." Dahlia eyes glossed over, and she leaned one cheek against her hands as she leaned her elbows on the table before her. "I held it, once, a long time ago. All that power, in a tiny little orb. It didn't seem possible, and yet, there it was."

Her words ached with longing and nostalgia. With loss. With pain. Either she was the best damn actress he had ever seen, or she was telling the truth.

He set one palm in his lap to hide his hand as he curled his fingers to ease the tension in his body. However much he needed the Soulsprite, he had to feign indifference to keep from losing what little advantage he had in this negotiation.

"You don't know what you're asking of us," Dahlia continued, almost wistfully. "My father used to tell me of the old days, when our magic was stronger. He told me of what we once were, of all the power we used to possess. How we were considered *other* by the outsiders. How they used to call us fae because they simply didn't understand the magic that seeped from our mists. All that magic came from the Soulsprite." Her eyes darted to him, crisp and clear. "That is what you're asking me to give you, Wraithblade. That is what you came here to take from me."

His jaw tensed, and though he held her gaze, he didn't reply. He wasn't dead, which meant she was in enough of a bind herself that she was at least willing to discuss his terms.

"It is a mightier treasure than any of you realize." Dahlia gestured to the lot of them with a flick of her delicate hand. "It comes from the land of the dead, and like your wraith, it does not belong here. It does not abide by mortal laws, and I do not offer it to you lightly. If you need it, you will pay a hefty price."

Need it.

The word choice must've been intentional, and the noblewoman was most likely trying to gauge his desperation, just as he sought to gauge hers.

Time for a little test to see how much she truly knew, as well as how much she had bluffed him thus far in their discussion.

"I don't need the Soulsprite," he lied. "I do, however, have use for it if we can come to an agreement."

"A word of advice." Her eyes narrowed in annoyance. "Don't lie to me with so much at stake."

"And you would do well to dispense with the charade." Unfazed, he pointed at her to emphasize his point. "You've barely told me a useful thing since I sat down, and if you want to actually get anywhere, you would do well to name that price you keep mentioning."

For a moment, she watched him in silence. Whatever she debated internally, her face remained stoic and calm, and only the soft rise and fall of her chest indicated that she was anything more than a statue.

"Very well," she said quietly. "I am well aware of your limited time. Though Teagan Starling was delayed in his journey south, you have mere days before he arrives at Death's Door. Your dragon can carry you fast enough to reach him, but only if you leave soon."

Connor sat in his chair, still as a stone as he tried to understand how she could know all of this. Not even Quinn had figured most of this out, and he couldn't fathom the spy network this fallen princess must've had at her disposal.

He was frankly envious.

She forced a thin smile. "Shall I continue?"

With a subtle nod, he gestured for her to speak. He liked it when his opponents couldn't stop talking—it gave him fodder to use against them.

"Suit yourself," she said. "I know you wouldn't be here, now, with everything at stake out there in the Decay, unless you absolutely needed the Soulsprite to power whatever monstrosity that wraith of yours built into his mountain. So be it. You want the Soulsprite, and I'm willing to give it to you."

His heart leapt in his chest, but he drowned the surge of hope with a cold dose of dread. She knew the value of what she offered, and the cost could bankrupt him if he wasn't careful—or worse. "And your price?"

"You must declare yourself as Freymoor's Champion." Dahlia pointed at the iron doors behind him. "You will step out into the Blood Bogs and prove yourself to the mists. And, if you pass its tests, you will have everything you desire."

He laughed and shook his head. "I'm not setting foot in those mists, woman. That's a death sentence."

"For some," she acknowledged. "Those who are invited, however, stand a far better chance of surviving."

"I don't take chances."

"To live is to take a risk," Dahlia said with a huff. "Every day is a gamble, especially for you."

"You want me to walk out there on your say-so?" He laughed again at the ludicrous request. "You're trying to con me into an early grave, Dahlia, and it won't work."

She crossed her arms. "If I wanted you dead, you wouldn't have made it into this room. I want my Champion, Wraithblade, and I don't have much time left to find him."

There.

A clue.

She was desperate, and now her willingness to give him the Soulsprite made more sense. Whatever she wanted this Champion to do, it could change the tides for her.

He had finally regained the upper hand in this discussion, and he planned on keeping it.

"Tell me something." He leaned his forearms on the table and stared her dead in the eye. "You have forty archers in this room, and I barely heard them. That means they're good. If they're that talented, it means you have at least one instructor capable of training them. If you have someone that skilled in your employ, you hardly need me. You clearly have an illegal army, Dahlia, one Oakenglen doesn't know about. With that kind of military power, why would you ever give away something as precious as the Soulsprite to this Champion you claim you need so badly?"

With a sidelong glare at Quinn, Dahlia's nose creased with disdain. "Because our magic only works in Freymoor, and the world has become so much larger than us. We are weaker than we have ever been."

"You didn't answer my question." He shrugged, not buying any of this. "I don't see how a single man can fix that."

"You misunderstand." Her chin lifted slightly in defiance. "I don't seek a single man to fight a war for me. That's not what the Champion does. He is an ally I can trust with my life. He is the one who can speak for me out there, where my power wanes." Her head pivoted toward the window, and the muscles in her neck tensed.

"That hardly seems like payment enough for the Soulsprite," he said, calling her bluff. "What else is this Champion supposed to do for you?"

A muscle in her jaw twitched, and she pursed her lips as the silence stretched between them.

He scoffed, astonished by her brazen entitlement. "Do you think any man would agree to be your Champion with no understanding of what's being asked of him?"

"Some of our magic was stolen from us," she said quietly, her eyes trained on the floor. "Long ago. It was corrupted, mutilated, and destroyed. Our Champion must replace it. He must heal that ancient scar, and in exchange, we will build his power." Her cold blue eyes shifted to him, softer now, and her thin eyebrows pinched together as she studied his face. "With time, we will build you so completely, so fully, that you will be able to return the Soulsprite to us—because you simply won't need it."

Impossible, the Wraith King snapped.

Connor ignored the ghoul, preferring instead to study the fallen princess's features. She watched him with an earnestness he hadn't seen in years. It was the sort of hope children felt when they listened to fairytales, and as much as she seemed to believe in the truth of what she said, he didn't.

He let out a long, slow breath as he chewed on everything she had said thus far, but this surpassed anything he had been willing to offer. He had enough hell to deal with just trying to secure Slaybourne, much less fight someone else's war.

Even for the Soulsprite.

"I'm not your man," he confessed.

Through the corner of his eye, Quinn's shoulders relaxed, and she let out a quiet breath of relief.

Dahlia smiled, and the skin around her eyes creased. "Saying that only convinces me otherwise."

"That doesn't make any sense," Sophia snapped.

"On the contrary." Dahlia gestured to the iron doors behind Connor. "Hundreds have come to me over the years, each certain he was the only choice, but none of them were worthy. None could prove themselves. They came not to protect the mists, but to exploit them."

"And what happened to those people?" Connor's voice lowered an octave as he sensed the unspoken threat.

"I don't know," Dahlia said softly as she stared at the iron doors. "Even if I did, it's not my place to tell you. All I can say is that you'll most likely see for yourself, out there in the fog."

"You must think I'm a damned fool." He stood and set his fists on the table as he glared at her from across the table. "Do you really think I'm going to march into the Blood Bogs simply because you ask me to?"

"No fool would've made it this far," she countered. Dahlia stood and leaned her own fists against the table, mirroring his stance. "And since you are clearly not a fool, you know full well you can't win this battle with Teagan unless you have the Soulsprite. Correct?"

His eyes narrowed, but he didn't answer.

"Precisely." Her voice dropped to a growl, and she pushed off the table as she made her point. "You need me. You need the Blood Bogs. You cannot win without us, just as we cannot reclaim our rightful place in this world without you. It is an unfortunate reality, but one we must come to terms with if either of us wants to claim what is rightfully ours."

Connor jabbed his pointer finger into the table. "I obey no one, princess."

"No Champion would." She shrugged, as though that were obvious. "You asked for my price, and I gave it to you. Now, what is your answer?"

With a frustrated groan, he shook his head. He didn't like any of this, but as much as he hated to admit it, the woman had a point.

Still, he wouldn't walk out into those mists without a clear understanding of the trials that awaited him.

"What makes you so certain I'm your man?" he asked.

"I've heard the whispers." Dahlia gestured toward the wall of windows beside them. "When I first heard about the Shade, I wondered if our time had finally come. A noble folk hero in the south? It seemed too fantastical to believe. I tried not to hope too hard, but then…" She sighed and rubbed her eyes. "But then the visions began. The glimpses. The memories. I've heard the tales of those you saved. I've seen your face, always masked, always hidden behind that cloth." Her eyes drifted to the fabric still covering his nose and mouth.

Yours is the most famous face we've never seen, Richard Beaumont had said the night they'd drugged him for answers, what already felt like a lifetime ago.

It's those eyes. I can tell you're feral just by looking at you, and you can't ever hide that.

"Of course, I couldn't let anyone know I was looking for you," Dahlia continued, "If anyone suspected I wanted an audience, Teagan would've sent his elite soldiers here to keep me company." She grimaced in disgust. "The Blood Bogs told me you would come for the Soulsprite, and I was warned to wait. Imagine my surprise when Otmund came for it first."

"Otmund was here?" Connor stiffened, and he crossed his arms over his thick chest to mask his jolt of surprise. "Where is he now?"

"I can't tell you."

"Can't?" Quinn asked. "Or won't?"

"Take your pick." Dahlia's eyes narrowed as she glared at the Starling warrior still standing apart from the rest of them.

This negotiation wasn't going the way he had planned. Connor rubbed the back of his neck and stood behind Murdoc's chair as he sifted through the ways this could go wrong.

Admittedly, there were a *lot*.

"Listen, Wraithblade." Dahlia clasped her hands in front of her, and she examined him intently as her shoulders relaxed. "I don't want a servant. I want an ally. I want a partnership."

Murdoc leaned backward and lowered his voice to a whisper. "I think she just propositioned you, Captain."

"Focus," Connor chided under his breath. He scratched at the stubble along his jaw and returned his attention to the fallen princess standing before him. "If I went through with this, what's waiting for us out there?"

Sophia set her face in her hands and groaned impatiently. "You can't be serious."

"I don't like it, Captain," Murdoc agreed.

"I don't, either." Connor raised one hand to silence their concerns. "But let's hear her out, at least."

Dahlia stiffened with hope. "Everyone experiences the mists differently, so I can't tell you what you'll see. I can warn you, however, that nothing in the mists is what it seems. The bog speaks in riddles, and though your eyes will deceive you, the voices never lie."

"Well, that sounds horrifying," Murdoc muttered.

"What else?" Connor prodded.

"As a contender, there's a grueling challenge ahead of you," she warned. "It was designed to break you. To corrode you. You won't leave the mists the same man you were when you entered. You'll be stronger."

"Or dead," Sophia snapped.

Dahlia cast an irritated frown at the necromancer, but quickly returned her attention to Connor. "If you want to defeat Teagan, you will need everything you find in the bogs—not just the Soulsprite, but also what you discover about yourself. It will test everything you love. It will test your resilience, your desire, and your drive. It will make you question what you know about yourself, your world, and your team."

"This is a con." Quinn shot him a sidelong glare and shook her head. "She's asking you to do the impossible."

"Am I, now?" Dahlia's heels clacked against the stone as she walked past him and toward the iron doors. Her thin fingers wove through the circular handles, and she pushed them open.

Thick coils of mist rolled over the hem of her gown. Beyond the doors was a thick fog lit from within by a soft white light. At the threshold, stones pushed up through the dirt. The flat rocks formed a makeshift path that popped up from the soil, one stone at a time, and led deep into the unknown.

"Good luck, Wraithblade." With her hands clasped before her, the fallen princess watched him over her shoulder. "For what little it must be worth to you, I do want you to succeed."

She lifted her skirts and stepped onto the first stone. In seconds, the fog swallowed her completely, and the Lady of Freymoor was gone.

Connor took an unintentional step forward, shocked at what had just happened while the mist churned in her wake.

A roar echoed through the fog, muted and distant, but familiar all the same. Connor's chest tightened with dread, and a gust blew through the room as the bellow rumbled through the air. Every sconce along the wall blew out at once, and the throne room plunged into darkness.

The only remaining light came from somewhere in the enchanting fog as it swirled beyond the doors, beckoning them to enter.

But that roar—he would know it anywhere.

Murdoc stood and set one hand on the hilt of his sword. "Did anyone else think that sounded like—"

"Nocturne," Connor confirmed.

Two figures darted through the mist, nothing but vague silhouettes in the blurred white light, and he squinted as he tried to make sense of them. Voices flooded from the fog, overlapping each other in harsh whispers until they blended into a single, swelling chant.

"Simple but not easy
is our task for you;
walk the path to find her,
and she will guide you true."

Their voices hit him in the chest like a banshee's scream in the night, and the bitter whispers stole his breath from his lungs.

Quinn drew her sword, and bright orange flame crackled to life across the blade.

Sophia snorted derisively. "Fire isn't going to do much good against fog."

"This is no ordinary fog," Quinn countered without even a sidelong glance at the necromancer.

"Still think this was a good idea, wraith?" Connor asked under his breath.

I suppose we will find out, the ghoul conceded.

"What's the plan, Captain?" Murdoc asked as he stared out through the doors.

"We're getting what we came here for." Connor walked to the edge of the fog and set his boot on the first stone in the path. "And if they touch one scale on that dragon's head, we'll burn this city off the map before we leave."

CHAPTER FIFTY-TWO
CONNOR

Connor led his team through the Blood Bogs.

They had already walked for what felt like hours, though it could have been mere minutes. The overbearing mist swallowed the sky, and he had no way to track the time. No moon. No sun. No stars.

Nothing.

To retain the element of surprise where he could still have it, he had opted against summoning his swords or shield until absolutely necessary. Beside him, Quinn's Firesword crackled, and its fires cast an orange glow across their feet. The mist burned amber with the sword's light, but it did little to chase away the oppressive shadows.

With every step, the enchanted stones at the edge of the mist pushed their way up through the soil, and the path continued to carve its way through the white haze obscuring their view. The trail meandered through the fog, aimless and wandering.

From somewhere far beyond what they could see, voices overlapped each other. The words rushed and faded, always too fast or too quiet for him to make out.

A dark shadow loomed ahead, and his fingers twitched as he prepared to summon his sword. As they neared, however, it solidified into an ancient pine.

Behind him, Murdoc let out a quiet breath of relief.

The tree's canopy pierced the white haze above them, and the path curved away from its trunk. They walked past without incident, and the mist swallowed it again.

Silhouettes stood along the edge of the mist, nothing but blurred outlines that shifted and sank into the white haze around them. They didn't remain in one place for more than a few seconds, and every time he tried to study their movements, their edges began to blur and shift.

Three figures darted through the edge of the fog, backlit by whatever light filtered through this place, and the chittering whispers intensified.

"Come this way," one said.

Connor gritted his teeth and glanced over his shoulder at his team. "Stay on the path."

"Obviously," Sophia muttered under her breath.

"Wraith, what can you see?" he asked.

Fog, the ghoul answered. *Figures. They see me, and they're beckoning me to follow.*

"Stay hidden, even if they can spot you." With a wary sidelong glance, he watched the silhouettes skitter just out of sight. "You might still be able to see something we can't."

Doubtful. I've never seen fog like this in the in-between.

"That's probably by design. I can't imagine the bogs are entirely fond of you."

They are not, the wraith confirmed.

Deep in the mist, something screamed. The shriek echoed through the wasteland, and the silhouettes froze. The whispers faded, and in the overbearing silence that followed, Connor could hear his own pulse.

To hell with this place.

As he and his team slowed to a stop, so did the stones at the edge of their field of vision. The sifting scrape of rock against dirt faded, and an eerie stillness settled into the air.

A low growl wandered through the thick white haze, and he summoned one blackfire blade as he listened for its source. The crackle of his and Quinn's swords roared in the quiet air, but nothing darted toward them through the mist.

The whispers started again, followed by the crunch of bark—or bones.

"I told you this was a bad idea," Quinn whispered to him.

"Can't change it now," he grumbled back. "Come on."

As he took another step along the path, the flagstones once again pushed their way out of the dirt. The trail continued to carve its way through the haze, always materializing at the edge of his vision. It led him deeper into a fog he didn't trust, and he had no choice but to follow.

Another shadow loomed ahead, tall and wide this time, like the side of a building or the edge of a wall. He slowed, cautious and wary, but it didn't move. Unlike the silhouettes, this shadow retained its shape as he stared up at it. With one last glance at his team to ensure they had all remained together, he steeled himself for the worst and led them forward.

The thick fog coiled over itself as they neared, and the looming shadow became an archway. The ancient stone broke through the mist, and most of its mortar had corroded over time. Loose stones lay in the soil around it, and moss had taken over most of the blocks. Vines dripped from its uneven edges, half of them torn or snapped at the ends. The top of the arch faded into the mists above them, but the stone path led through its frame to the patchy stretch of grass on the other side.

As far as he could tell, it seemed as though only this archway remained of whatever great structure had once covered this land. If a castle or road had stood here, once, the bogs had eaten it long ago.

"Stay close," he ordered.

"That's the plan, Captain," Murdoc said with a nervous laugh.

Connor raised his blackfire blade as he led them through the archway. Though Sophia and Quinn masked their steps with near perfection, the steady tap of Murdoc's boots against the stone mingled with the crackle of the flaming swords.

The air thickened. Each breath sucked in as much water as it did air, and Connor coughed violently to clear his throat. He spat onto the ground, trying to clear his lungs, and his sword's blackfire hissed as fiercely as if he'd submerged it in water.

But the footsteps behind him stopped, and the crackle of the Starling Firesword faded.

He looked over one shoulder to find himself on the other side of the looming archway, alone.

"Fates be damned," he muttered.

He charged back to the archway, and though the air thinned as he passed again beneath it, no one waited on the other side. He peered through, his boots never leaving the flagstones of the shifting path, but the enchanted stones now ended at the archway.

Only unending mist waited beyond—and those infernal silhouettes, always watching. Just waiting for him to step off the trail.

"Murdoc!" he shouted, not caring how many of the shadows heard him. "Sophia! Quinn! Where the hell are you?"

"I have them," a woman said.

That voice—it just wasn't right.

His body cringed at the sound of it, and he sucked in a breath through his teeth as he fought the surreal sensation of it burrowing into his mind, as though the sentence had claws to it. Other voices overlapped hers like waves on the sea, but a singular feminine voice overpowered the others.

Unnerved and unsettled, with the hair on his arms standing on end, Connor returned his attention to the path ahead as it sliced through the mist beyond the archway. Where before there had been only a white haze, a towering silhouette now stood just beyond the small stretch of what he could clearly see.

Impossibly tall, she loomed above him just as the archway had towered above as he had approached it through the fog. Her head tilted as he spotted her, but she otherwise didn't move. A long gown flared from her hips and disappeared into the mist at her feet.

He stiffened as a ribbon of dread snaked through his body. It wasn't just her voice that set him on edge, but the sensation of being watched. Her presence dissected him, much in the same way as Nocturne's gaze.

Though he had never seen her before, it all felt so... *familiar*.

"Can you feel that?" he quietly asked the ghoul.

Very much so. The wraith's voice tightened. *This place is flooded with magic. It is much like us, but stronger. None of this is right, Magnuson. This is what it was like when I died, and she reminds me too much of Death.*

"I am like Death, yes," the voice said. *"As are both of you."*

A pang of dread hit Connor hard in the chest. "You heard him speak?"

"*I did.*"

Shit, the wraith said.

"Then you aren't Dahlia." He pointed his finger at the silhouette and walked calmly toward her.

Though he walked toward her, he couldn't seem to close the distance between them. With every step closer, the edge of the fog receded, and her silhouette went with it.

Always out of reach. Forever just out of sight.

"*I am not,*" she answered.

"You're the source of Freymoor's power, aren't you?"

"*Correct, and I do not fear you.*" Her head pivoted slightly to the left, as though looking at something Connor couldn't see. "*Nor do I fear you, Wraith King. I know this power you possess. It is stolen, and it was never yours to have.*"

A trap.

His chest thrummed with disgust, but he wasn't going to go down without a fight.

He summoned his other blackfire blade and settled into his stance, daring her to attack. Ethereal entity being or no, she wouldn't take his power from him, and he would find a way to drag her to hell if that was what it took to survive.

"Try to take it," he growled.

"*I will not, Wraithblade.*" The silhouette raised one hand to placate him. "*It is not yours to have, but neither is it mine to take.*"

"Then tell me what you did with my team," he demanded, not believing a word she said. "When they're safe, I'll take the Soulsprite and be on my way."

"*They are already safe.*"

His eyes narrowed with warning. "Show me."

"*Soon,*" she promised with a flourish of her hand. "*For now, we have other matters to discuss.*"

"Such as?"

"*This one.*"

The silhouette gestured to his right, and the mist dispersed. A thicket of trees formed a walled tunnel that ended in a small clearing, and a woman with fiery red hair stood in its center.

Quinn.

Her Firesword blazed as she held it in front of her and settled into a cautious stance. She slowly circled, her eyes scanning the edge of the trees, but her gaze passed right over him.

She couldn't see him.

"Do you trust her?"

Quinn's head pivoted toward something he couldn't hear.

"Of course not." His chest tightened at the words, and he cleared his throat to relieve the tension.

"Nor do I," the figure said. *"She is a Lightseer. She is the enemy."*

"What has she done to you?"

"Her? Nothing—yet. But her father has caused us so much pain, and he has taken so many of our lives. She will become like him, one day. You will see."

Connor's mouth twitched in disagreement, but he didn't respond.

"I did not expect you to bring her here," the silhouette confessed. *"I do not like what she has seen. Let us simplify our bargain, Wraithblade. Kill her, and I will make you my Champion. Kill her, and you will have the Soulsprite."*

Take the deal, Magnuson, the wraith ordered.

"No," Connor said, his voice clear and firm as he answered them both with a single word. "She and I have a bargain."

"Then make a new one," the looming figure demanded. *"With me. Whatever you need from her, I can provide."*

"That's what you want?" he countered. "That's who you are? You'd have me betray someone to prove I'm worthy?"

"Yes," she answered. *"You must prove to me that you can make the difficult choices in the heat of the moment, when I am not there to watch. Prove to me you can do what must be done, even when it feels wrong."*

He paused, looking for the con, but Dahlia had warned him that no voice he heard in the mist would lie.

Do it, Magnuson. The Wraith King appeared in a rush of black smoke. The grim demand echoed through Connor's head as the specter's skeletal face loomed between him and Quinn. *Do it or I will.*

"Don't you dare." Connor's voice dropping an octave in warning.

Shove aside your foolish morals for one second and think, damn you! The wraith snapped. *Think about what is at stake. Think about those blasted mortals back in Slaybourne that you claim to care for. Think of how much blood you spilled to save them. Would you leave them to Teagan's mercy? And for what? All to uphold a deal made with your enemy's daughter, who will turn on you the moment her father gives the order?*

Connor glared at the ghoul in a silent command to stop talking.

The wraith loomed closer and pointed one bony finger in Connor's face. *Kingdoms are built on bones, you fool, and blood is the mortar that holds the bricks together. You will spill much more of it in your time as the Wraithblade, and you cannot lose your way now. Not when we're so close.*

"That's not the man my father raised me to be," Connor said quietly.

The tension in the air faded. Connor scanned the fog, but the towering silhouette was gone. His body relaxed, and the sensation of her eyes on him disappeared.

"I wonder if your team shares your morals, Wraithblade?" the entity asked, her voice muted and distant. *"Are they as loyal as you think?"*

"Get back here!" he roared. His voice echoed through the woodland.

At the end of the tunnel of trees, Quinn's head darted around, as though she heard him but couldn't place where the voice had come from.

"My offer stands." The entity's voice faded, almost indistinguishable from the crackle of blackfire across his swords.

You are a vainglorious halfwit. The specter's skeletal face snapped toward Connor, and he disappeared in a furious rush of black smoke.

As Connor stood on the path, alone once more, the flagstones popped up from the soil and led toward Quinn. He waited, glaring dead ahead, watching her as she raised her sword to the hazy bog. She said something to the mist, but from this far away, he couldn't distinguish the words.

With a resigned sigh, he rubbed his forehead as he internally debated what to do.

Despite what he wanted to believe, Dahlia had been right. Peace wouldn't come to him or to Slaybourne, and he had always known protecting it would require immense sacrifice. His blood, his sweat, his bones—those were the concessions he knew how to make. An honest man could make them. An honorable man.

A good man, like his father.

But kings carried burdens for their countries. They did terrible things, all to keep their land safe. If empires truly were built on bones, perhaps he would have to sacrifice more than just his desires.

Maybe some of his morals had to die, too.

His nose wrinkled at the thought, and he shook his head in disgust. Honor. Nobility. Morality. Those values alone had guided him through the most challenging moments of his life. He wouldn't even have the Wraith King if not for the self-sacrifice he had shown in the cathedral ruins, when Otmund and the King's Guard had tried to kill the Finns.

"We know all about the Finns," a voice said from the edge of the mist.

His eyes narrowed, and he looked up at the whisper that had dared mention their names.

Silhouettes darted through the fog. Their movements stirred the haze, and several of them gathered by the trees between him and Quinn.

"They need you," another said.

"What would you do to save them?" asked a third.

He growled and shut his eyes as a dull ache ripped through his skull.

"Just about anything," he admitted quietly, more to himself than to the shadows.

CHAPTER FIFTY-THREE

SOPHIA

Damn it all to *hell*.

As Sophia stood alone and glared into the churning mists, she summoned ice into her hands. Her magic swam through her veins, fueling the frost that inched over her fingers. The icy breath of the ball of ice in her palms rolled over her skin and mingled with the fog coiling over her ankles. Silhouettes towered overhead as the murky white haze rolled through a silent forest, and she spun in a slow circle as she tried to get her bearings.

She had only just gotten renewed life, and she didn't want to die *now*. She hadn't even wanted to come here.

Through the corner of her eye, something shifted. Though not even a footstep had broken the dead-silent forest, the very air shivered. The weight of eyes on the back of her head made the thin hairs on her neck stiffen, and she froze mid-step as she searched her peripheral vision for more evidence of her newfound company.

This sensation—she couldn't put it to words, but then again, nothing in this cursed old woodland made sense. Whoever or whatever had joined her felt foreign. Other, somehow. Unnatural.

Though this place set her nerves on fire, she tried to rationalize her way out of panicking. Quinn and Connor could've snuck up on her, but neither of them set her on edge the way this new presence did.

The silence stretched on. Nothing moved. No one spoke. The undead forest weighed on her, as heavy as a chain around her neck, waiting to see what she did next. Whomever had joined her didn't want her to know they were here, but that wouldn't stop her.

Nothing could. Not anymore.

Sophia tapped into her Rootrock augmentation to summon the vines from beneath the soil. She reached for them, her fingers stretching wide as she grappled to control them.

At her side, her hands rotated until her palms faced the canopy above. It was the silent command for the vines to spring to life.

None of the vines beneath her feet obeyed.

"*...silly necromancer...*" someone whispered from beyond the thick white haze.

"*...the bog is not yours to control...*" another whisper added.

She frowned.

Fine, she could still freeze them alive.

With all the deadly silence her elite training could provide, she hurled the ball of ice at her new foe. The moment the ice left her hand, she summoned her enchanted Nethervale dagger from the depths of her sleeve and hurled it after the ice with a practiced flourish.

Sophia Auclair didn't take prisoners.

The ice hit something solid with a hearty thwack. It crackled as it spread over her victim and, seconds later, the dagger thudded into her mark as well. The splintering thunder of a falling tree broke the silence, and overhead, the hanging moss strung through the drooping canopy shivered. Sophia flexed her fingers wide to summon the blade to her palm once again, and her enchanted dagger obeyed. Mist churned around the steel as it returned to her, and as the fog parted, a toppling oak cut through the haze.

Damn. She had missed.

Her dagger slid into the sheath affixed to her wrist as the tree slammed against the ground. Unfazed by her failure, she settled into her stance and scanned the fog. Whoever this was could apparently move fast, and she couldn't risk letting her guard down for even one moment.

Somewhere in the mists around her, a woman clicked her tongue in mock disappointment. "That was a dangerous choice, Leah Beaumont."

A jolt of panic rooted her to the ground as Nyx Osana spoke the long-dead name she had buried with her old body.

Everything in her screamed at her to run. Even with her newly enhanced power, she wouldn't stand a chance against her old mentor. Her eye twitched, and she scanned the small clearing for a way out.

No, she chided herself. *Snap out of it.*

Sophia's jaw clenched as she forced herself to take slow and steady breaths. Nyx wouldn't have followed her in here, of all places. Even that woman feared this place. This wasn't real. The mists were playing with her mind, and she wouldn't give Dahlia the satisfaction of seeing her tremble with terror at the mere thought that her old mentor had finally hunted her down.

"What if I was one of your teammates?" the imposter asked.

Simply hearing Nyx's voice induced yet another flare of panic. It took concentrated effort for Sophia to hold her ground as the stranger spoke.

A silhouette passed through the fog, and Sophia pivoted on impulse. This time, she gave it everything she had. With a frantic grunt of effort, she hurled both daggers into the mist, toward an oddly familiar shadow with broad shoulders and a mess of long hair.

But this time, it was Murdoc.

At the last second, she pulled on the unseen tethers between her and her blades—the connection that allowed her to control it midair—and altered the dagger's course. the steel sank deep into a tree trunk to the silhouette's left, and the shadow dissolved into the mist.

A trick, most likely, but she couldn't risk it.

"You've gone soft, Leah." From somewhere deep in the fog, Nyx laughed just as she had all those years ago, when Sophia had thought she would die as a rabid blightwolf's dinner. "You know better than anyone that necromancers can only love themselves."

Don't fall for this, she chided herself.

For just a second, Sophia allowed herself to close her eyes and recenter. Shoulders back, with her chest out and her chin held high, she took a settling breath. She was better than this. The magic in her chest gave her access to the loftiest realms of power, beyond anything she had known before, and she spread her fingers wide as she tapped into it.

The daggers whistled through the air as both returned to her palms, and she opened her eyes to face the fog once more. "I was never one for games, and you're boring me. If you have a point, you should get to it."

A chill snaked through the air, and she couldn't tell if it had come from her or the mists.

"Very well." The voice shifted in timber, and Nyx's voice blurred with a dozen others that spoke in unison. Their chatter overlapped like ripples hitting each other in a lake, and it seemed as though the Blood Bogs had finally dropped its façade. *"I don't want you here, necromancer, so I will make you a deal. I hear your kind always likes a good bargain."*

A wry smile tugged on the edges of her ruby red lips. "Provided you can trust us to keep our end of it."

Overhead, the long strings of moss in the canopy trembled like a cat bristling for a fight, but she didn't move. Her expression didn't change. She waited, listening and always scanning the edge of her vision for the next threat.

"Leave," the voices commanded. *"Let me have the others, and I will show you the way out. You will live, and I will be rid of you. We both win."*

Sophia frowned, her eyes narrowing with suspicion as she tried to dissect its lie.

"You don't believe me," the mists observed.

"Obviously," she said dryly.

For a moment, nothing happened. The fog didn't reply, and Sophia stood there in stone-cold silence, waiting to encounter something she could kill.

To her left, the mists churned. She shifted her weight and coiled, ready to aim her dagger yet again, but the fog parted to reveal a meandering path through the forest. Along the mossy ground, a smattering of walking stones led the way through the gnarled old oaks and twisted maples. The longer she watched, the more of the path appeared, until sunlight finally pierced the haze at the far end. White puffs of fog curled and coiled along the edges of the walkway, like a murky wall protecting her along the road to freedom.

Her breath quickened as the bogs offered a way out of this cursed woodland. All she had to do was take it.

A strong pang of longing, blurred heavily with guilt, hit her square in the gut as she gaped at her chance to escape.

To run.

At her side, her fingers drummed against her thigh. With a deep breath, she shut her eyes and turned away from the path. If it had only been her and Quinn Starling, then yes, she would have left in a heartbeat. Connor and Murdoc, however, she couldn't leave behind.

Slaybourne wasn't her home; they were.

"I don't care what you do with the Starling woman, but the men aren't yours to have." Sophia's neck tensed as she fought the impulse to bolt down the path and escape this cursed hellhole. "If you so much as touch them, I will find a way to burn you to the ground."

"Lofty threats to make against the immortal, child."

"If you know my name, then you know the two of us aren't as different as we seem." She scanned the canopy, still hunting for the source of the reverberating voices. "And you know full well what I'm capable of, maybe more than I do."

The mists didn't answer except to hum with curiosity. As the sound echoed through the little clearing, the foggy wall along her path to freedom broke like a popping bubble. The white haze swept over the stepping stones, swallowing them whole until there was nothing left to see.

She sighed with disappointment.

"Show me the way to them," Sophia commanded. Though she wanted nothing more than to sink her blade into the nearest living thing, she couldn't exactly get into a fistfight with whatever unholy creature lived in these woods. It played by different rules, and she would have to wait to satisfy her bloodlust.

"So many have betrayed you, Leah," the voices said, ignoring her demand. *"How foolish to put your life on the line for those who will only destroy you in the end."*

"They're different," she answered. "And so am I."

"Perhaps." The voices carried a lazy tilt this time, like they had heard this all before, and it set Sophia's nerves on fire. *"Or perhaps you're the same as every other sentimental fool who has lost himself in my domain."*

Over by where she had seen the silhouette, the fog parted, and a single footprint appeared on the ground. Cautiously, she inched her way toward the print and knelt, careful to glance around her as often as she could, just to be safe. This close to the ground, more footprints appeared in the retreating haze, and she recognized the boot print from all of her recent travels through the Ancient Woods.

Murdoc.

As she squatted by the footprints with one elbow leaning on her thigh, she glared off at the trail the boots had taken through the bogs. The mists had tricked her once already, and she couldn't bring herself to believe this clue had merit.

Still, it was all she had to go on, and she wouldn't let this forest eat her or her team alive. With a frustrated sigh, she pushed herself to her feet and walked along the trail of prints. As she set off into the woods, however, the mist's voice echoed through her thoughts. She tried to ignore it, but the more she resisted, the louder their conversation played in her head, over and over and over again.

How foolish, the mist had said. *They will destroy you in the end.*

Sophia swallowed hard as she followed the cold trail, and she couldn't help but wonder if it had, in fact, tricked her yet again—or if the land of the Old Ways could truly know what was to come.

CHAPTER FIFTY-FOUR
MURDOC

A ray of dew-drenched light gleamed across the blade of Murdoc's sword. He held it in front of him, squinting as he spun in slow circles through the mist. His boots churned the fog, dispersing it with each step as it crept closer, and the muscles in his neck tightened from the sensation of someone watching him.

His sword cut through the mists, but he took a careful step back as the murky wall approached. His core tensed with the anticipation of a brewing fight against something he couldn't even see. He scanned the lonely forest around him and hunted for any clue as to where the others had gone, but he stood alone in the small clearing.

The thick white fog swarmed him. It coiled and curled in on itself like waves on the ocean until it encased him in a cocoon of opaque mist. It swallowed the trees one by one until their silhouettes dissolved into the endless white, and its tendrils swept across the ground by his feet.

As it neared, closer to swallowing him whole with each passing second, Murdoc wanted nothing more than to hack at the fog with his sword. Sweat licked his palms as he gripped the hilt of his blade, and he gritted his teeth and tried to get ahold of himself.

But he couldn't. Not really. With his allergy to spellgust, his body recoiled from this place. Ingesting even a trace amount of the glowing green ore could kill him, and this place was burning him alive from the inside out.

Every breath in these woods clawed at his lungs. Magic seeped off every tree and every leaf. He could practically feel the enchantments leaking from the low-hanging moss overhead. The fog itself pulsed with power he didn't even recognize, and his body fought off the poison it so hated.

He needed out.

The hair on his neck stood on end in a silent warning that he was not alone. He froze mid-step as his gaze darted across the mist. A weight settled on his chest, like heavy air in a humid cave, and his throat tightened as it threatened to close entirely.

He didn't have much time left before this place killed him, but he had a job to do. Though the back of his tongue swelled, he forced a shaky breath and did his best to ignore the pain. Panic would only worsen his symptoms, and right now, he had to focus on whatever waited in the fog.

The sensation of being watched by something supernatural had no single word to describe it, but this gut instinct of his had saved his life more than once as a Blackguard soldier, back when he had hunted monsters through the darkness. His nose flared as he paused to listen, as clearheaded and focused as he could be in this state, and he waited for another clue as to who—or what—had joined him.

Any Blackguard who made the first move lost his head, and he'd learned long ago that patience served him best against those powerful enough to wield spellgust.

"Why are you out here, love?" a woman asked.

As her soft voice fluttered through the mist from somewhere behind him, he nearly jumped out of his skin in sheer surprise. His nerves fizzled with the need to kill something. He pivoted on one heel, his blade still raised in front of him, only to find the thick fog closing in.

"A scoundrel has no place here, I'm afraid," the woman said from the depths of the fog.

His eyes narrowed at the insult, but he refused to take the bait.

"Oh, my apologies." She laughed, the light and airy sound out of place in this otherwise grim and deadly forest. "That's a rude word now, isn't it? It's so hard to keep track, sometimes, as the years go on. I meant no offense."

"Sure you didn't," he muttered.

"My point still stands, my darling" she continued. "These lands are more potently magical than any spellgust mine, Murdoc Baynard. It's far too dangerous for you to be here."

"Cute trick." His voice hummed in his throat, deep and rough as his body rejected the very air around him, but he wanted nothing to do with her games. "I don't know how you figured out my name, but I'm not afraid of you. Show yourself."

"Huh." The gentle word rolled past him like a breeze. It carried curiosity with it and a hint of awe, something rarely directed toward him.

Fingers brushed through his hair. He flinched and slapped them away, but his hand hit his own head with a hearty thump. He winced in pain from hitting himself, but the sensation of unseen fingertips gently caressing his scalp continued.

"Stop that!" he demanded, still trying and failing to push them away.

"Sorry, love," the woman said again from the depths of the mist. "I rarely see a man with long hair like this. And to meet a brave one? You're the sort of hero I would've wanted in my bed, back when I was alive. I simply couldn't help myself."

Back when I was alive.

The phrase echoed through his mind, again and again.

It seemed surreal—but then again, his friendship with Connor had brought plenty of impossible oddities into his life.

At the edge of the churning white wall, a bare foot stepped through the fog. Long black curls appeared next, followed by a heart-shaped face and piercing brown eyes. A woman slipped through the mist and joined him in the clearing. The dazzling silver gown she wore hugged every curve and left little to the imagination, even as it glittered with an ethereal light of its own. The dress's neckline dipped low enough that he saw the full curves of her cleavage, but he only let his eyes linger for a moment.

He squared his shoulders and aimed his sword at her face in warning, unwilling to be duped even by a pair of excellent breasts. She smiled as their gazes met, her eyes crinkling with genuine joy, and she paused barely a foot away from the tip of his blade.

As he examined her face, however, a sliver of light flashed across her body. It reminded him of firelight on metal, quick and almost impossible to see, and he didn't know what to make of it.

Murdoc's brow furrowed in confusion as he scanned his new company. Though mud caked his boots from their trek through the woods, her feet didn't have a speck of dirt on them. No sweat licked her forehead, and her impossibly smooth skin glowed with the light of the moon in the mist's low light.

If the mists thought they could tempt him with a pretty young woman, they obviously hadn't dug far enough into his mind to truly understand him.

His skin creaked as his grip on the hilt of his sword tightened. "Who are you?"

In answer, her smile widened. "I'm a messenger for the Blood Bogs, my dear Murdoc. That's all. Don't be afraid."

He chuckled dryly. "Don't confuse caution with fear, dear lady."

The stranger set a delicate hand over her lips and giggled. Her eyes shut, and her shoulders shook with genuine mirth. "I won't hurt you, Murdoc."

"What a relief," he said, not bothering to mask his sarcasm as he scanned her delicate form.

She laughed again, louder this time. "I'm not even real, Murdoc. Go on, try to touch me."

With a frown, he took a tentative step closer. He extended his sword until the tip of his blade pressed lightly against her shoulder. She tilted her head and studied his face as she allowed the blade to rest against her skin, and he lightly pushed on his sword to test her claim that she was, in fact, not real.

His sword went clean through her shoulder, as though it had pierced a ghost, and he let out an irritated groan. He didn't stand much chance fighting something his sword couldn't even pierce.

"So, love, why are you here?" she asked, unfazed by the blade still jutting harmlessly through her shoulder.

He sheathed his sword, since he didn't have anything to fight anyway. With a grunt of annoyance, he set his hands on his waist as he examined the ghost of a woman in front of him, if he could even call her that. If she was truly a messenger for the bogs, he couldn't help but wonder how she had ended up here. She stood before him like a goddess visiting the mortal realm, glowing and impossibly beautiful, but he had no way of knowing what bits of her memory truly remained—or if she was just a marionette, with the bogs tugging on her strings.

Even as his throat swelled shut and his body screamed at him to demand the quickest way out of this swamp, he did his best to keep a level head.

Besides, a charming approach would serve him best, just as it always had with pretty women in the past.

Murdoc clapped his hands together and rubbed them as he scanned the fog. "As much as I would love to chat—and truly, my dear, you seem lovely—I need you to show me to my team."

Her lower lip quivered in an adorable little pout, and she crossed her thin arms beneath her breasts. "I'm afraid that's not possible, my darling, at least not yet. I have a job to do, after all. You still need to answer my questions."

Damn it.

A dull ache throbbed in his head, and he rubbed his forehead to soothe it as he tried to think of a plan. The mist had control, here, and if it wanted to test him, he had little choice but to indulge its games.

Fine.

"Alright." He spread his arms wide in surrender. "Ask away."

"Why are you here?"

"Because you lot separated me from my team."

She giggled. "No, you silly thing. Why did you come to the bogs? To Freymoor?"

Murdoc frowned, not altogether delighted by the idea of giving away information about Connor. His gaze swept the piercing wall of fog trapping him in the clearing, and he let out a frustrated sigh. "I'm here because my captain needs me."

"I see." She clasped her hands in front of her and paced the edge of their foggy cocoon. "You've thrust yourself into danger, all for his sake. Why does he deserve such loyalty?"

Murdoc squared his shoulders and bristled at the unspoken implications in her question. "He's a good man trying to do right by the world. We need more of those, in my opinion. Taking a hike through a swamp is hardly him asking too much of me."

At the mention of the word 'swamp,' her eyes flashed briefly white, and she froze mid-stride. Her delicate eyebrows creased with anger as she glared at him, and he took an unconscious step backward in surprise.

The stranger's eyes fluttered closed, and she sucked in a deep breath. As she exhaled, her anger dissolved, and she blinked rapidly as she studied his face once more with a calmer gaze. "I insulted you, I suppose, so it's only fair I forgive an insult in return."

He kept his mouth shut, but he made a mental note not to say the word again.

The woman tapped her finger gently on her lips, and she tilted her head in curiosity. "This captain of yours. Is he worth following to hell? Would you die for him?"

A muscle in Murdoc's jaw twitched as he studied her face, not liking the turn this conversation had taken. His eyes narrowed, but she had made it clear he wouldn't get out of here until he answered her questions.

He nodded once in answer.

The edge of her soft lips curved down into a disappointed frown, and the light in her eyes briefly faded. Her gaze drifted toward the wall of fog around them, and with a wave of her hand, the mist parted. Twisted roots clambered over each other along the forest floor, and towering fir trees cast strange shadows through the mist.

As the fog receded, Murdoc's throat relaxed, and the incessant stinging in his lungs quieted while the magic-drenched mist gave him space to breathe.

In the distance, at the far end of the narrow channel through the fog, another figure stepped into view. Tight pants and a bespoke jacket betrayed a feminine figure, and as he squinted to make out more details on the silhouette, Quinn's fire-red hair finally came into view.

He frowned with displeasure. "She's not really on my team, but I'll take it. Thank you, my dear."

Murdoc took a step, but something slithered under his boot. He grunted with surprise and looked down to find thick brown roots crawling toward him from every direction. One snaked up his leg.

He reached for his sword, but he didn't get the chance to unsheathe it.

More vines shot out of the ground from behind him and coiled around his arms, pinning them against his body. As he tried to fight them off, he glared over one shoulder to find the woman standing behind him, now. A lock of black hair fell in her face as she stared off at Quinn. With each passing second, more roots wrapped around his legs, locking him in place.

He couldn't move.

The roots climbed up his calves and over his shoulders. Murdoc wrestled against the ungodly grip on his arms, and though his fingernails clawed at the roots wrapped around him, the woman didn't acknowledge his struggle.

"Quinn!" he shouted, certain the Starling was close enough to hear him, even with all the fog. "Quinn, get your ass over—"

"None of that now, love." The ghost behind him covered his mouth with her delicate hand and lowered her lips to his ear. "You still haven't answered all of my questions."

With her hand over his mouth, he let out a muffled string of curses and glared back at her.

The apparition's eyes, however, never left Quinn. "Every man has his price, Murdoc. What's yours? For that matter, what's Connor's?"

It was a question Murdoc had asked himself once before, and truth be told, he still didn't have an answer.

He stilled and swallowed hard as he followed her gaze back into the mist. Another figure appeared in the fog, and this one stalked with a slow and steady gate toward Quinn. The man held two swords that crackled with black flame, and his broad shoulders towered over the forest floor.

Even with his back to Murdoc, it was impossible to mistake Connor for someone else.

"The Blood Bogs ordered your captain to kill the Starling woman," the ghost beside Murdoc explained. "He's supposed to slit her throat, here and now, and he will finally obtain the Soulsprite if he obeys. Is that a man you want to follow?"

A jolt of panic shot clear through Murdoc's heart. The bogs must've done something to Connor. Twisted his mind, perhaps, or tricked him. If the captain had been snared into some sort of enchanted daze, Murdoc had to do something to break the spell.

With Teagan barreling toward Slaybourne, desperate to get Quinn back, they couldn't let her die. Murdoc had to stop Connor from doing something that could destroy them all.

Murdoc yelled through the hand covering his mouth, but the muffled shouts didn't seem to reach Connor. The man didn't slow, and he only raised his swords higher as he neared Quinn Starling. Murdoc struggled against the ghost's impossibly strong grip, anxious to break free and smack some sense into his captain.

"Sorry, love," the beautiful ghost said softly in his ear. To her credit, the twinge of sorrow seemed genuine, and her grip on his mouth relaxed ever so slightly. "You and I can only watch."

CHAPTER FIFTY-FIVE

QUINN

Thick white fog cascaded over the crumbling stone archway on the path ahead. It dripped from the obscured branches above them and poured over the ancient stone like a waterfall made of clouds, blocking any glimpse of what lay beyond.

Quinn didn't like this. Not one bit.

Connor stepped through the archway and slowly faded into the fog on the other side. Though the ghoul hadn't shown itself since their arrival in Freymoor, the sensation of someone watching her set Quinn's nerves on edge. Another scan of the thick fog turned up nothing, save for Murdoc and Sophia behind her as the mist slowly swallowed them, too.

With no alternate route available, she tightened her hold on *Aurora's* hilt and stepped over the threshold. Connor's broad silhouette dissolved completely into the white haze, and she gritted her teeth in frustration.

They needed to stay together.

The gray gloom around her thickened. A pulse of green light shot through the fog, just out of sight, and a flash of heat followed. The enchanted flames along the blade of her sword dissolved with a violent hiss, and she froze in place as she fought to understand how that was even possible.

The magic in this place wasn't right.

Steam clung to her skin, weighing her down, and her hair stuck to her face. With every step, another bead of sweat dripped down her neck, until the humid haze filled her lungs and made every breath a struggle for real air.

Nothing croaked. No one spoke. Not even a scuffle of a boot across the dirt broke the long stretch of silence, but Quinn had had enough.

With a twitch of her wrist, flames roared back to life across *Aurora's* blade. They licked at the muggy cloud, and the air gently sizzled as the fire scorched the dewdrops that had formed on the steel.

"Stay close," she warned everyone as she scanned the gloom around them. "The mists are up to something."

She waited for the necromancer to make a snide remark, but no one answered.

Though her pulse thudded in her ear, her chest settled as her training kicked in. Her feet shuffled across the dirt in a well-practiced move, and in seconds, she spun in a tight circle to get a full view of her surroundings.

Nothing.

Lost in fog that obscured even the trees, she was alone.

"Of course," she muttered.

With *Aurora* at the ready, she sank into her stance and closed her eyes, since relying on vision in a place like this would only slow down her reactions. A soft amber light filtered through her closed eyelids as she took a settling breath and listened to the forest.

Nothing chirped. No birds sang. Not even the trees swayed, here, in this enchanted hellscape between life and death.

"*Quinn.*"

Her eyes snapped open as the whisper filtered past her, and a jolt of dread shot clear to her toes as she tried to place its source. The thick steam rolled past her as a clump of her hair stuck to her face, but nothing darted through the mist.

She frowned in confusion as she craned her ear, but not a single footstep hit the ground. No breaths. No sighs.

The haze churned, as though someone had swept their arm through it, and the putrid stench of rotting eggs followed. She wrinkled her nose in disgust as the stink wafted by like a fetid breeze.

Droplets of water from the humid fog pooled on her tongue, and though the moisture in the hot air nearly drowned her, she forced each breath to come slow and steady.

It all came down to control. In these situations, when the opponent had the upper hand, she had to remain calm. If a soldier lost their self-restraint, they had no hope of regaining command of the environment in which they fought.

It all comes down to control.

Her father had taught her that, years ago.

A cool gust rolled over her face, like a breath from a winter spirit, and she finally opened her eyes.

The steam had receded, and she now stood in a dirt clearing enclosed by a circle of barely visible trees. The fog clung to the edge of the glade like a roiling white wall, and a silhouette stood just beyond the edge of the mist. It remained there, so still she might've mistaken it for a statue if not for the voice she'd heard moments before.

As Quinn waited for the figure to speak, she raised her sword between them and listened again for hints of life. A footstep. A breath. A cracking knuckle, or snap of a twig.

But the longer this figure stood there, silent as a ghost, the more certain she became that it wasn't even real. The stench of sulfur faded, and with the figure so close, she expected the salty sting of their sweat to hit her enhanced senses.

It didn't. Only the musty whiff of moss and mud remained on the air.

How curious.

Real bodies had to sweat in a place like this, and even augmented bodies made noise. Whether a statue or some elaborate trick, the silhouette in the mist clearly wasn't alive.

But it didn't hurt to play along.

"Is that you, Dahlia?" Quinn used the moment to scan the rest of the fog to confirm she and the figure were alone. "I wondered when you would pay me a visit."

In the fog, the silhouette twitched. Quinn stifled a startled gasp and took a wary step backward.

She hadn't expected the damn thing to *move*.

It took a moment to regain her composure, but she forced her shoulders to relax and focused on the familiar crackle of *Aurora's* flames to soothe her nerves. "After all, now I know your secret."

"Yes, you do." Dahlia's voice echoed through the clearing.

Quinn did her best to stifle a cocky grin at correctly guessing her opponent, and she shrugged, as if all this was inevitable. "Were you surprised to see me?"

"Very," the haunting voice admitted. "I assumed the Wraithblade was intelligent until I realized he chose to trust you."

"No need to be rude." Quinn smirked as she played the game and dug under Dahlia's skin. "But I suppose I'm impressed. You let the world think Duncan controls you, and while they're distracted, you're left unhindered to do as you wish. It's clever," she admitted with a soft chuckle. "I can respect you for that, at least."

"I have never sought a Starling's respect."

"That's a shame." Quinn cast a subtle glance around the clearing once more to ensure nothing had crept up on her from behind during their little chat. "Maybe this would've gone differently if you did."

In the depths of the fog, the figure took its first step. Quinn adjusted her grip on her Firesword's hilt, just waiting for a chance to strike. She needed a target—a chest or, ideally, a head she could cleave off.

As the silhouette reached the edge of the murky haze, tendrils of mist rolled off the figure's curves. The fallen princess of Freymoor stood at the tree line with her hands clasped just below the line of her cleavage, and a thick plate of iron armor rested on each shoulder. Metal bars across her exposed chest anchored the armor in place and continued down her bodice, framing her thin waist. The effect gave her the air of not just a princess, but a warrior queen.

"You must know you won't make it out of here alive, Starling." The young woman lifted her chin in defiance. No fear. No doubt. Just a calm and calculating sovereign, stating the facts.

A thin sheen, like light across a painfully sharp blade, flashed across Dahlia's body. It was gone in an instant, but Quinn had seen it all the same. It confirmed for her that whatever stood before her was, in fact, not Dahlia

Donahue at all—but more likely a mirage, conjured by the bogs.

Thus far, her ploy had worked. Now, to trick the apparition into sharing something real.

"As much fun as this has been, I'm a busy woman." Quinn's free hand tugged on a dagger tucked in a hidden sheath on her upper thigh. Without breaking eye contact, she spun it lazily in the air and caught it by the hilt. "Tell me what you really are, and I won't kill you."

The illusion quirked one eyebrow. "What are you—"

Fed up with the games, Quinn hurled the dagger at the imposter's face. It landed perfectly between the apparition's eyes, only to sail clean through its head. The dull thunk of metal hitting wood followed shortly afterward.

"You may not be real, but you can still give me answers!" Quinn snapped as she called the apparition's bluff.

The illusion smiled, and even the skin along its eyes crinkled with genuine joy. Whoever crafted the mirage had done a truly masterful job. Dahlia clapped, and the slow applause cut through the otherwise whisper-silent air like a giant dropping something heavy, again and again.

"It took Otmund longer to figure it out," the ghost said.

"Otmund?" Quinn frowned with disbelief. "He was here?"

"Your Lightseer brethren, too." The apparition clicked her tongue in disappointment, as if Quinn hadn't said anything. "I don't understand how you can be both wildly observant and so incredibly blind."

"I saw through you."

"I suppose you did." The Dahlia-imposter raised one eyebrow in challenge. "But what about everyone else?"

The edges of the charlatan's body shimmered, and the metal sheen flashed across her skin again as her body widened. Her hair darkened and receded almost completely into her head, and her delicate fingers thickened. Her nose grew into a pronounced hook, and in seconds, Otmund stood where Dahlia had been moments before. His eyes narrowed, just as they always did when he was concocting a new plan, and Quinn's lips parted in surprise.

From every direction, silhouettes appeared in the fog. Zander stepped from the mist first, with blood coating his neck and arms. The thick locks of his fire-red hair stuck to his scalp, and blood bubbled from a long gouge down his neck that ran clear to his shoulder. He sneered at her, as though he didn't even notice his wounds.

"Hello, baby sister," he said.

Quinn sank into a wide stance and whipped her sword toward him, but that same metallic sheen raced over his body as she held *Aurora's* flame near his face.

Fake, just like Otmund. Just like Dahlia.

A stunning blonde woman stepped from the mist to Zander's left—her mother. Madeline Starling's brow creased with concern, but she didn't say anything as yet more silhouettes stepped forward.

Victoria. Gwen. Her father. One by one, they circled her, their arms crossed as they glared at her from the edge of the clearing. Quinn slowly spun in a circle as the apparitions of her family closed in, and one last figure loomed beyond the wall of fog.

She waited, already knowing Connor would step out next. Already prepared for what the mirage might say.

"They're not real," she reminded herself in a harsh whisper. "This is just a trick."

"We played you." The mirage of Otmund grinned and stretched his arms wide. "All you ever did was dance."

"We're all bored of this." Victoria gestured toward Quinn with a lazy wave of her hand. "Of you, playing war. Hang up your sword, you little harlot, and finally do something useful for the family."

"She's right." Zander stalked closer and leaned into her face, until they were almost nose to nose, and his fingertip hovered just below her chin. "You're no warrior. You're a bartering chip for me to play to my advantage." He scoffed, as though speaking to her had been a waste of time. "Honestly, baby sister, how could you possibly compete with me?"

"Enough," she seethed.

Her flash of anger hid the pang of shame that gutted her as she sat with what he said, knowing all along that he was right.

"Is that really all it took to break you?" Zander snorted derisively. "An insult from a superior fighter? Can our father's precious miracle child really not handle a bit of brutal honesty?"

"Pathetic." Her father shook his head in disappointment.

"I'm surprised it took her this long, honestly." Victoria brushed off her ornate green bodice and let out a bored sigh. "Our sweet baby sister. So innocent. So naïve. You should have known better, but Father sheltered you from the real world. It made you stupid."

Quinn looked at Gwen and her mother, but both of them simply stood there, letting this happen.

Just like always.

"You've been hunting for your place in this world." Dahlia's voice echoed through the fog, seemingly from every direction. "But have you considered you don't belong in it at all?"

"I said that's *enough!*" The fires in *Aurora's* blade burned hotter, and in her rage, Quinn summoned the magic in her blood.

She was ashamed that she'd let *apparitions* get under her skin, but her ire burned all the same.

This was a trick. A trap. A means for Dahlia to look into her soul and see things she didn't need to see.

And she had to stop this before the fallen princess saw anything more.

Quinn called on the dazzling augmentations inked into her skin, ready to scorch the earth if that was what it took to break the bogs' spell. Fire and air hummed beneath her skin. The comforting sturdiness of her Shieldspar waited, perfectly within reach. Every augmentation hummed to life—even the one she couldn't control.

As the magic blistered in her blood, a crackle snaked through her palm.

Oh, no.

In her anger, she had made a fatal mistake—she had summoned the crackling chaos of her Voltaic augmentation.

But it was too late.

Instead of a wall of perfectly controlled fire, lightning arced from her palm in a dazzling display. It flashed through the clearing, suspending everything in one blinding moment of frozen anarchy. Though most of the crackling light hit the ground, harmless, two of its erratic bolts nailed her father in the chest.

He didn't even flinch.

A zap of mind-numbing pain shot up her arm as she fought to rein in the feral magic, and after considerable effort, the light finally faded. The simmering power in her soul calmed, and she let out a string of curses as she shook out her hand.

Rarely did she lose control, but this forest had dug its blade in deep to her soul. Instead of tricking it into revealing the truth to her, she had betrayed something unforgiveable to it.

Unlike her father and brother, Quinn could still not control the lightning that came so easily to them. It was a point of shame that Zander exploited at every opportunity. While few warriors in history had ever tamed the Voltaic augmentation, the Starlings remembered in the legends always could.

It was yet more proof that she wasn't—and never had been—good enough.

Dahlia clicked her tongue in disappointment, and the irritating sound echoed through the forest.

"I'll *burn* you." Quinn's voice scratched against her throat, verging on more of a savage growl than words as she fumed.

"Please try," Dahlia said calmly. "It will show the Wraithblade who you truly are. It's only a matter of time, Quinn, before he realizes what a burden you are. His team despises you, and I will never ally with him while you're alive. You cannot be trusted. Your father has too much control over your broken little mind. The Wraithblade's work in this world will be much easier if you simply never escape this woodland. Don't you agree?"

A broad-shouldered silhouette wandered past, hidden by the mist, before it disappeared once again into the depths of the fog.

The air behind her shifted, and a soft breath rolled over the back of her neck.

"You can't play both sides any longer," A familiar voice said.

In a reflexive movement her father had taught her years ago, she pivoted and put several feet between her and whatever had closed in while she had been distracted.

Her father now stood behind her with his arms crossed over his chest, watching her intently as the other apparitions slowly dissolved into the mist lapping over their shoes. *Aurora's* flames snapped at the air between them as Quinn fought for every breath in the humid fog, and within seconds, only she and the mirage of her father remained in the clearing.

A series of voices bubbled from the mist, each of them overlapping such that she could only catch snippets of the conversation.

"*…they all have to die…*"

"*…she can't do it…*"

"*…weak, really…*"

"This isn't about you, Quinn." Her father set his hand on the hilt of his sword, still in its sheath on his waist. "When I come for him, you will stand aside."

"Can you kill him?" Connor's voice asked from the fog.

She scanned the mist again, and the blurry silhouette passed just out of sight. This time, the hint of a footstep followed—but as the voices clamored around her, they almost masked the sound.

"Yes, my dear, can you?" her father took a step toward her and spread his arms, silently inviting her to take her best shot. "Or are you afraid he will use you, too?"

"What if you're never anything more than someone's pawn?" Otmund asked from the depths of the mist.

Her father looked at her down the bridge of his nose, just as he had in her childhood any time he'd delivered a lecture about how she needed to improve. "When he's done, what will be left of you to discard?"

Of everything the apparitions had said, that dug the deepest.

"You can't break me," Quinn said quietly, speaking to the maestro hiding in the fog. "I know none of this is real, and I don't even care how you learned so much about me. You want to know why I'm here? I'll tell you, no tricks involved, because I'm not a coward like you are."

"*Then tell me,*" the voices answered in unison, each whisper overlapping the other.

"Because I will not sit idly by while any of you burn the world." Her gaze shifted to the apparition of her father. "Not even *him*."

She swung *Aurora* at the mirage, and he didn't flinch as the fiery blade cut through his neck. The specter faded, and a single green light shot into the canopy, safely out of reach from her sword.

"I've had enough of your games." Quinn scanned the wall of fog at the edge of the clearing. "Dahlia, you're no better than I am. You've let your people live under Henry's rule, and for twelve years, you've done nothing to liberate them. How many of them burned at the stake when Henry toppled your kingdom? How many lost their heads under the executioner's axe? All of them, even your father, could've safely hidden here in these mists if this swamp truly protected you. Or are the bogs afraid of mortal men, too?" She spat on the ground, disgusted with all of this. "They live and bleed and *die* in the crossfire of your wars, and none of you bastards care. Not Zander. Not my father. And certainly not *you*."

The silhouette again walked through the churning fog, just out of sight, and this time, she lost her patience.

"You think you know me," she said with a deadly calm. "But you have no idea what I can do to you. Let me show you, Dahlia. I want you to see for yourself."

With her free hand, she grabbed the Volt and aimed a piercing blast of lightning at the figure lurking in the haze. A burst of light crackled through the mist, and seconds later, the ear-splitting crack of shattering wood rocked the forest.

Another mirage. Another lie.

It didn't matter—Dahlia was no doubt watching, and she had seen it all. Quinn had accomplished what she'd set out to do, and Dahlia knew exactly what was at stake.

If she tried to kill Quinn, here and now, the Blood Bogs would *burn*.

"*Lightseer.*" The whisper hit her like an insult hurled from afar.

"*Pawn,*" another voice chided, this time from the opposite direction.

"*Starling,*" a third voice spat, like it was the worst slur of all.

The voices built to a cacophony, each talking over each other until the words blurred into a furious gale of nonsense and hate.

"*...can't be trusted...*"

"*...they own her...*"

"*...obedient little pawn...*"

"I obey no one," she said firmly, her back straightening against the insults.

They meant nothing, anymore. This place had no power over her, and she refused to let it taste her fear.

She stood in the center of the clearing, and *Aurora* crackled in the otherwise painfully silent air as she waited for the voices to speak yet again.

Behind her, something changed in the air, and she felt the eyes on the back of her head before anything else. The quiet thud of a boot on the dirt followed, and the musky hit of sweat on skin followed.

This one was real.

She pivoted on her heel, brows furrowed, and she gripped the hilt of her sword as she prepared to slaughter whatever had come for her this time.

Connor stood at the edge of the clearing, and she froze in place as his forehead creased with concern. Both of his shadow blades crackled in his grip, their blackfire raging. He didn't speak. He didn't even move. He just watched her with narrowed eyes, tense and wary, as if he were still debating what to do next.

Quinn didn't lower her blade. "What did you hear?"

"Enough," he admitted.

"*Look at him.*" A voice rang through the mist, distant and distorted.

Connor didn't flinch, and if he heard it at all, he didn't give any indication.

"*...swords drawn...*"

"*...ready to kill...*"

"*...why should we let you leave this forest?*"

Those blasted voices. She grimaced, firm in her stance, and did her best to tune them out. They had played her thus far, and she wouldn't fall prey to them again. They egged her on, no doubt wanting her to attack, but she wouldn't.

If she swung first, he would defend himself, and they would fight to the death.

With one of his blackfire blades, he gestured to the Volt on the tight chain around her neck. "That's how you escaped the Bluntmar collar, isn't it?"

She pursed her lips, not entirely interested in answering that, but she ultimately nodded.

He'd probably already seen its power for himself.

"Clever," he admitted. "Are you going to tell me why you let me capture you?"

"Don't see why I should." Despite the dire circumstances, her tone remained calm as she waited for his next move. "Is this where our tense agreement ends?"

His grip on his swords tightened, but otherwise, he remained still. His ear twitched, and though Quinn didn't hear anything, she suspected the mists or the wraith had some choice words to share about their predicament.

The two of them stood there, armed and waiting for the other to act, but she hadn't come this far to lose it all now.

He shook his head and let out a frustrated sigh. The swords in his hands disappeared with a rush of black smoke, but Quinn didn't move. He had tricked her before, and she wouldn't let him do it again.

"Relax." His deep baritone echoed through the fog. "I keep my bargains, Quinn. Even if I don't fully trust you, it looks like you keep your bargains, too."

"Interesting," a disembodied voice said.

He tensed and scanned the fog around them. Apparently, he'd heard it that time.

With a skeptical glance at his hands, Quinn lowered her Firesword and dismissed the crackling flame along its blade. "Truce?"

He nodded.

Cautiously, she sheathed her sword and wiped the sweat from her brow with the back of her hand. "I hate this place."

"Understandable." Connor paused, as though he wanted to say something else.

Again, she waited to see what he would do.

He cleared his throat uncomfortably and set one hand on his waist. He ran the other through his hair and sighed. "We should find Murdoc and Sophia."

"*This way,*" a voice said from somewhere in the mist. "*They're waiting for you.*"

The fog cleared, and the shifting stone path wove through the trees, leading deeper into this cursed swampland. Two silhouettes appeared in the distance, and Sophia's crimson dress cast a pale pink shadow on the fog around her.

"Think that's really them?" Connor asked, never taking his eyes off the figures.

Quinn studied his face, and for the first time since they had entered the mist, her shoulders relaxed. "We could stab the necromancer. That would tell us easily enough if she's real."

"Behave," he chided.

"Fine." She shrugged. "There's a sheen on the apparitions. That's the easiest way to tell if they're fake—though I think my way is more fun."

"Hmm." His eyes briefly glossed over, and he glared off into the fog. He focused on something in the depth of the white haze, but as she scanned the bogs around them, no figures emerged from the mist.

Whatever he stared at, she couldn't see it.

"What is it?" she asked.

He shook his head. "Nothing. Take point."

"And turn my back to you?" She scoffed. "Not likely."

With an impatient tilt of his head, he gestured to the path before them. "If I wanted you dead, Quinn, everything that just happened would've gone much differently."

A chill snaked down her spine at what he'd left unspoken, and it stole the breath from her lungs. That simple reassurance carried so much implication—if she could trust it at all.

Figures darted through the fog, nothing but blurred shadows in the churning white mist, and Quinn summoned fire into her palm to light the way. The ball of flame cast a dim orange glow on the forest around them.

"I've got your back." Connor pointed again to the route between them and the others. "Go ahead."

Hesitantly, she raised her hand. The flickering ball of fire in her palm cast an amber light across the roots of an ancient forest drowning in fog. With the Wraithblade behind her, watching her back, she took her first cautious step along the flagstones leading deeper into the woodland.

Together, she and the outlaw took the trail at a painfully slow pace. Quinn scanned the forest around them while Connor kept an eye on the silhouettes ahead. Every now and then, his gaze darted briefly toward her, and when he looked away, she snuck a glance at his hands to ensure he hadn't summoned a weapon.

Their uneasy truce was holding—for now.

Deep down, she wanted to believe the voice in the mist had been wrong. She wanted to believe that at least one man on this continent could keep his word. She wanted to believe their shaky bargain could persevere, even as he acquired more and more of what he wanted.

One way or another, she would find out soon enough.

CHAPTER FIFTY-SIX
CONNOR

Connor didn't have much patience left for the Blood Bogs or its tricks.

At the end of the stone path through a tunnel of trees, Murdoc and Sophia clustered at the edge of the fog. With every step, Connor fully expected them to slink forever backward, just as the towering entity had when he'd tried to get closer.

The final flagstone pushed out of the ground by the pair's feet, and their heads pivoted toward him and Quinn. The Starling's flame cast an orange glow on the hazy air, and Connor's knuckles cracked as he made a fist and prepared to break bones.

If this fog had done anything to his team, Dahlia would have a world of pain coming her way.

The mist around the duo cleared, and Sophia took a guarded step backward as he approached. Murdoc set his hand on the hilt of his sword, knees bent in a fighter's stance, and the two watched him with the same wary caution he felt.

A thick layer of frost spread across the necromancer's palms, and she raised her hands in warning. "Not another step."

"Can you tell if they're real?" Connor asked the wraith under his breath.

I cannot, the wraith admitted. *Nothing in this cursed bogland makes any sense to me.*

"Thanks," he muttered. "Very helpful."

He studied their faces for the telltale sheen Quinn had mentioned, but he had yet to see it for himself. Nothing on their bodies changed, and as far as he could tell, no metallic shimmer flashed across their features.

He shifted his attention to Quinn and nodded toward the duo. "Is that them?"

"Yes," she said with a curt nod. "They're real."

"It's me." He let out a quiet sigh of relief as he and Quinn finally reached them. "The real me."

"Well, an apparition would say that, wouldn't it?" Murdoc's grip tightened on the hilt of his sword, but he had yet to draw it.

"It certainly would." Sophia's voice grated on her throat as she glared at him. "Which only makes me doubt this one."

"Wait." Murdoc raised one hand in front of the necromancer as he squinted at Connor's face. "There's no sheen on him. Look."

Connor spread his hands wide and shifted his attention to Sophia. "Satisfied?"

Her jaw tensed, but she ultimately dismissed her frost magic with a few shakes of her hands. "We've got to get the hell out of this place."

Beneath their feet, more flagstones popped up from the ground. Sophia's boot slid to the side as the stones pushed past her. The trail carved its way through the grove and faded into the fog beyond.

"We've already come this far." Connor pointed to the path as it led deeper into the swamp. "Let's get what we came for."

"I don't know, Captain." Murdoc sighed with frustration. "I'm a real fan of the 'let's leave' suggestion."

"*...you had only to ask,*" a whisper said.

The trees around them shivered, and Connor studied the canopy as he waited for a gust of wind to hit them, but none came. The still air weighed on his shoulders, heavy and somber even as the rustle of leaves in the canopy grew louder.

"Oh, what *now*?" Quinn snaped as she stared up at the branches.

The ground rumbled, and Connor sank into his stance to keep from falling over. His team did the same, and everyone drew their weapons. Flames crackled to life across Quinn's Firesword, and Connor summoned one shadow blade as he prepared to slice open whatever was about to attack them.

Instead of a beast thundering through the fog, however, tree roots ripped from the soil. The long wooden tendrils writhed over each other like wooden eels. Many of them dove in and out of the earth, as though it were water. Chunks of soil splattered onto his boots, and small pebbles stung his arms as the ground churned before their very eyes. A thick brown haze settled on the small clearing as clumps of dirt launched into the air. He coughed to clear his lungs, and his team coughed along with him.

The forest shifted, the shadows blurring and changing, and at first, he couldn't process what he was seeing. It seemed wrong. Unnatural. More like a trick of the eye than an actual possibility.

The trees weren't just trembling—they were *moving*.

Trunks drifted sideways as their roots clambered over each other. The giant oaks and withered pines clustered together on the stone path, blocking any hope of continuing down it. The roots swallowed the enchanted flagstones as the trees replanted, one by one, until a thick wall of bark and wood blocked Connor from taking another step forward.

As the trees moved, however, a new path formed to his right. A tunnel framed by thick wisteria vines led toward a bright stretch of sunshine in the distance. Clusters of purple flowers hung from trellises along the new dirt path, and the fog slowly cleared. At the edge of the new trail, the sun shimmered upon glowing green fields. A bird flew through the sunlight and twittered a brilliant song.

For all intents and purposes, it seemed like a verdant paradise buried in the fog—but no flagstones led that direction. The route the mists had told them to take led away from this brilliant meadow and directly through the trees that had just blocked their path.

Now, Connor needed to decide exactly how much he trusted the Lady of Freymoor's word—and if the voices of the bogs could lie to him after all.

"I don't like this," Quinn said under her breath. "Not at all."

"*...come, now...*" a voice in the fog said.

"*...we've shown you a way out...*" another added.

"*...just like you wanted,*" whispered a third.

"I thought the voices told the truth," Murdoc said, his back tense as his gaze darted between the two routes.

Connor stood a little taller as he pieced the riddle together, and he grinned in victory. "Those voices said it was *a* way out, not *the* way out."

He returned his attention to the trees blocking his path and lifted his blackfire blade to see if its fire revealed anything along their bark. None of them had faces, but they'd had enough control to move into his path.

Either they were sentient—somehow—or the puppet master controlling them was close enough to hear him speak.

Time to find out.

"Move," he demanded, his voice firm.

"So rude." The clear voice came from somewhere directly in front of him, as though someone he couldn't see stood between him and the nearest oak. It sounded different from the whispers in the mist.

More real, almost, or more solid.

"So pushy," another voice agreed.

"A peasant," a third one added. "Acting like a king."

A jolt of irritation hit him hard in the chest as this place corroded the last of his patience, and his eye twitched as he did his best to rein in his frustration.

"Let me clarify," he said, a little louder this time. "Let us by, or you'll become kindling."

The branches above them shivered and huffed, like an old woman bristling at a child insulting the wrinkles on her face. "No need to be so unpleasant."

"A path veers right," another voice said pointedly, as though speaking to an entitled child. "Take that one. It's nicer."

"That's not *my* path." With the tip of his sword, Connor pointed at the flagstones swallowed by the trees' roots. "That one is."

"We're comfortable," one of the voices huffed. "What sane man asks a tree to move?"

"What a waste of air," another added.

"Hardly worthy," grumbled a third.

The voices overlapped, snickering and sighing, each with a strong opinion of every word he had spoken.

Their chittering burned off the last of his patience.

He shook his head. "Have it your way, then."

His bicep flexed, and he sliced through the nearest tree with his blackfire blade. A shrill scream echoed across the woodland as his sword cut effortlessly through the bark. A blistering crack thundered past as the oak toppled forward, its foundation cut in half. Thick blood, as red as any man's, bubbled from the wound and poured down the stump to the dirt beneath it.

Connor easily sidestepped the tree as it fell, and his team followed suit as the dead oak landed hard on the ground. Slowly, the bright crimson blood seeping from its exposed inner rings turned to sticky amber sap that dripped like honey from the stump.

The shivering trees stilled, and a tense silence followed.

"Anyone else still too comfortable to move?" he asked.

The leaves trembled, and the ground quaked once more as roots twisted from the soil. Clumps of dirt launched into the air again as the grove hastily shifted out of his way. In seconds, the flagstones appeared.

The oaks and pines formed a narrow path, only wide enough for them to walk in a single-file line, but it was enough to expose the flagstones their roots had swallowed moments before. Streaks of flattened dirt stained the path, but the stones remained otherwise unfazed and disappeared into the fog at the end of the grove.

"Much obliged," he said, not bothering to mask his sarcasm as he stepped around the severed oak's withered stump.

"Crude," Quinn muttered from behind him. "But effective."

He shrugged, hardly in the mood for a critique.

Connor led his team through the narrow tunnel of trunks and hanging moss, always keeping a wary eye on the canopy above as the trees shivered and muttered in hushed tones. Their indignant grumbles overlapped until the words blurred together and none of it made sense, but he didn't care.

Served them right.

The whispers swelled again, their voices overlapping, but he caught snippets of their warnings as he passed beneath their branches.

"...beware the company you keep..."

"...young Wraithblade..."

"...none are as they seem..."

He didn't respond. No mist or ancient magic could turn him against Murdoc or Sophia. They had followed him through hell, and he trusted them with his life.

Quinn, however, was another story.

He peered back at her as they walked, and he wondered what the bogs knew about her. Whatever they had shown her in the mist, it had gotten under her skin enough to set her on edge. They hadn't known each other long, in the scheme of things, but he had never seen her lose her composure. Even when he'd stabbed her that first night they'd met, she barely reacted.

Back there in the fog, she had snapped. It had only lasted a second, but it proved she had skeletons in her closet and, most likely, plenty of blood on her hands.

During their visit to Oakenglen, Tove had revealed there was something different about Quinn Starling. Something unique. Though he had survived every attempt on his life thus far, perhaps she had the power to succeed where everyone else had failed.

He didn't want to think so. He didn't hate her company as much as he'd expected he would. Given all she had done to help, he wanted to believe she was one of the few good ones left on this continent.

It seemed like a foolish thing to hope for.

Up ahead, the fog thinned, and the tunnel of trees ended in an open field shrouded with mist. As he stepped out of the forest, he expected a ray of sunlight to hit them, but the overcast sky drowned it out. Only the constant white glow from within the fog lit their way.

Shredded ribbons of white haze churned across the grass, and silhouettes appeared along the ground. Just shadows, at first, but their features slowly sharpened.

Bones.

Dozens of skeletons lay strewn across the large meadow. Their jaws gaped at the ground, as though something had pried them open, and vines protruded from most of the hollow skulls. Some of the bodies lay stretched across the grass, their skeletal fingers spread toward something just out of reach. Other skeletons curled around themselves, hugging their own withered knees tightly and still frozen in their moment of death.

"What the hell happened here?" Murdoc whispered.

"Something bad," Quinn replied.

"That's an understatement." Connor lifted one crackling blackfire blade in front of him as he scanned the carnage. "Everyone stay close."

At least now they knew how the Blood Bogs got their name.

CHAPTER FIFTY-SEVEN
CONNOR

The Blood Bogs had surprised him yet again, and Connor didn't like this one bit.

Dark flowers bloomed across the endless vines stretching across the open graveyard, their black petals a stark contrast to the time-bleached bones from which they grew. A soft purple light pulsed from the pollen stems at their centers. Hundreds of them covered the field, with at least three growing out of every corpse.

The fragrant perfume of honey twirled through the air, and the scent warmed him from within. It reminded him of summer and sunshine. Of happiness.

Of joy.

He frowned as a ribbon of ecstasy snaked through him from the flowers' perfume. Joy hardly had a place here, in this field where the dreary sky presided over an ocean of the unburied dead.

I'm impressed, the Wraith King said with a self-satisfied huff. *We should create something similar in Slaybourne, Magnuson. I could find a place for a graveyard like this near Death's Door.*

"Focus," he chided the old ghost.

Murdoc stood beside Connor and pointed at the nearest cluster of flowers. "Are those—"

"Bloody beauties," Sophia said breathlessly. She pushed her way to the front of the group and laughed in amazement as she scanned the open field worth a hundred kings' ransoms. "I've never seen so many in my life."

She set her eyes on the nearest grouping of black blooms and took a step off of the path, but Connor grabbed her arm. She glared back at him just as the mists shifted, and he finally got a clearer view of the ground.

Their enchanted trail curved through the field dead ahead of them, and the route led past the few skeletons with no flowers blooming on their graves.

"Those aren't for us," he said quietly.

"Connor, you're being ridiculous," Sophia snapped. "The magic I could do with even one of these—"

"They aren't for us," he repeated, more firmly this time.

"Don't touch them," Quinn agreed as she surveyed the field. "Everything about this feels like a well-baited trap."

"But…" Sophia's brows pinched with sadness as she stared out at the flowers, fighting between acknowledging the trap and drooling over the incredible lure the bogs had chosen.

Though Quinn's Firesword would've served as better light than his blackfire blades, Connor didn't like the look of this place, and he opted to lead the way. He raised his sword ahead of him and stepped onto the path as his sword cast a thin gray light onto the murky air. Every few steps, he cast a wary glance backward to ensure that Sophia didn't break rank to grab one of the bloody beauties.

Sophia walked behind him, and though her face contorted into a scowl, she kept her eyes trained on the back of his neck. Quinn followed behind her, and Murdoc guarded the rear of their small band.

"Connor," someone whispered.

Someone familiar.

His ear twitched, and he paused as he scanned the misty meadow. In the slowly churning haze, no one made their way toward his path. The scattered skeletons covered the ground, immobile and still, and only the delicate purple light at the center of each flower twinkled through the fog.

"Connor," the voice said again.

Dahlia had claimed not to know his name, but the Blood Bogs clearly knew too much about him. The figures in the mist could've easily overheard one of his team saying his name, or they could've even known it all along.

Either way, he refused to fall for their tricks.

This place had answers for him, and after what it had forced them to endure thus far, he would make a point to uncover them *all*.

As the fog shifted, it revealed a large flat rock up ahead. Their path curved toward it, and the flagstones ended at a few hand-hewn stairs carved into its base.

The boulder struck him as odd—as wide and long as the foundation of a house, it looked almost like a platform someone had built into the center of the field; and yet, its rounded edges and time-battered surface gave the effect of a natural formation as old and natural as the forest it called home.

Skeletons clung to the edges of the massive boulder, as though they had died trying to climb onto it. Hundreds of bloody beauties covered the stone like a dazzling floral carpet. Their vines dug into its surface, and their soft black petals shifted in a wind he couldn't feel.

He paused at the base of the weathered stairs carved into the rock, still waiting for their flagstones to continue through the field, but no more appeared. The path didn't continue past the boulder at all. If they wanted to remain on the enchanted stones, they had nowhere else to go.

"Look at all of them," Sophia whispered with awe as she stared up at the bloody beauties covering most of the boulder's surface. "Those are most definitely ours for the taking."

"I don't like it," Quinn muttered.

"You don't like anything," Sophia hissed back.

"Alright." Connor pointed up the stairwell. "Take a few, but let's focus on figuring out how to get out of here. Quinn's right. I don't like this at all."

The necromancer grabbed her skirts and bolted up the steps. Connor and the others followed behind, and his jaw tightened as he waited for something to charge out of the mist at them.

It seemed inevitable. No one would leave such glorious bait in this horrible place without intending to eat whatever flies fell into the web.

When he reached the top stair, he found Sophia already kneeling by a cluster of blooms. The necromancer ran her delicate finger along the midnight petals and smiled broadly. Specks of purple light floated into the air at her touch, like enchanted pollen, and a ribbon of light traced the path her fingertips took along the bloom. She slid her pack off her shoulder and set it on the platform beside her, already consumed in her task.

"Connor," the familiar voice said again. "Come here."

He stiffened, and his gaze followed the voice. Though bloody beauties covered much of the edges of the boulder, most of them clustered around a pool of dark water at its center. Pinpricks of light glowed from within the pitch-black liquid, and as ripples spread across its surface, the effect reminded him of stars in the night sky.

Serene. Soothing, almost.

He glanced up at the foggy sky, but the mist blocked everything. Whatever this pool was, it wasn't showing him a reflection.

Connor looked again at the water. The pond had a breathless beauty to its depths, and he couldn't help but stare into it.

Deeper, as the seconds passed.

Longer, as he tried to make out what lay in its depths. In fact, the longer he stared into it, the less he wanted to look away.

Something is wrong, the wraith said.

The ghoul's voice continued, but it became a confusing murmur, and Connor couldn't make out the words.

A silhouette lay in the depths of the pond, just out of sight. He squinted as he looked deeper into the dark pool and tried to make sense of it.

A faint warning hummed in the back of his mind—something urgent—but he forgot the details seconds after it came to him. The thought slipped away like dandelion seeds drifting off in a breeze, and he could only watch them fly away.

"Connor," the voice said again, louder now. "There you are. Goodness, my boy, how you've grown!"

It came to him, then, where he had heard the voice before.

It was his mother's.

He frowned with confusion and knelt by the pool as something shifted in its depths. A calm face appeared far below, drifting up toward him in the inky waves as it glowed with peaceful light. His mother smiled up at him through the water, calm and content.

Water. It seemed like a fitting place to be for someone who had died in all that fire and ash.

"Look at you." A second voice gurgled up through the pond as his younger sister floated from the murky depths. She smiled broadly as her eyes roamed his face. "I hardly recognize you."

"Ashlyn?" he said, his voice cracking with disbelief.

She giggled. "Who else?"

He reached for her. For them. He needed to touch them. He needed to know they were real.

"Don't," his father's voice demanded.

Connor froze in place, his hand outstretched and inches from the water's surface.

From the depths, a familiar man with a dark beard floated upward. The joyful creases around his blue eyes set Connor at ease, but the urgency in the man's tone rooted him in place.

"Why?" His eyebrows furrowed, but he obeyed the order.

"It's not your turn." Below the water, his father shook his head even as his smile widened. "It's not your *time*."

"Be patient," Ashlyn added with a playful wag of her finger. "Isn't that what you always told me? You'll get your turn to die, big brother."

"What..." A fog rolled through Connor's brain, and for a moment, he knew all of this was impossible. He knew none of this could be real.

The wraith's voice echoed somewhere just out of reach, but the ghoul's words blurred together into slurring nonsense.

"We're not in pain anymore," his mother promised. "There's no one for you to rescue on the other side."

A jolt of pain shot through his head, and he grimaced with discomfort. It was like a bolt of lightning hit him in the skull, and he sucked in a sharp breath through his teeth to fight it off.

He was so close to this making sense. He was so close to understanding.

Another jolt hit him square in the temple, and he growled with frustration as he pushed through the pain.

"Other side?" he asked. "What other side?"

"They won't show us much of the world we left," his father said with a shrug. "I wish I could see what you've been up to, my boy. I hope you've built a life for yourself. I hope you've built a home and a family of your own. You can't live in the past. You can't live in what was, only what's coming."

"I don't..." Connor grimaced again and squeezed his eyes shut as he fought to drown the heart-wrenching horror of it all.

"You need to move on from what was to what is," his father added. "We're waiting, but time moves differently here. You stay on that side for as long as you can, you hear me? There's so much beauty in your world that you can't get here, son. There's still too much left for you to do. Don't throw it away now."

"...*wrong*..." a voice said, its tone stiff and irritated. "...*silence*..."

Connor's eyes sharpened for only a moment, and their faces faded into the rippling waves of the pond.

His heart tightened with grief as he lost them all a second time, and the clarity didn't last.

In seconds, his eyes fogged over once more, and they were back.

Right there.

Just below the water.

"Go on, son." His father forced a thin smile, but his eyebrows curved upward with sadness.

With loss.

"I won't let you throw it all away," he continued. "Not for us. Not for *me*."

"No, this..." Connor swallowed hard and fought the murky haze in his mind. "This isn't..."

"See you another day, big brother." Down there in the inky black, Ashlyn sank into the darkness. She reached for him as she faded, and her frail hand was the last thing to disappear.

"Good luck, my boy." His mother's dark hair floated around her face as she, too, sank to the depths of the pool. She smiled up at him, soft and sad, but she was gone in seconds.

"Look at you, Connor." Though his father still smiled, he coughed to clear a knot from his throat as he hovered below, now alone in the darkness.

"To be here, talking to me through magic I didn't think existed—you're incredible, son. They've shown me some of what you've done, and I couldn't be more proud of the man you are."

"They?"

"The Fates." His father laughed, as though he couldn't believe it either. "I can't tell you more. I won't spoil the surprise."

"But—"

"Look, son," his father interrupted. "You're proof there are good people left in Saldia. There's still time for you to shift the tides."

"Father, wait," Connor demanded. "You can't leave ag—"

Get up.

His father's voice hit him square in the forehead, as much a memory as spoken word, and Connor careened backward. He hit the stone with a heavy thud, and agony ripped through his body as the blow bruised something in his spine. Gasping for air and groaning as the ache tore through him, he stared up at the fog above him.

For just a moment, three faded stars broke through the mist, and then the bogs swallowed the sky once again.

"No," he whispered to himself. "They're dead."

His father. His mother. Ashlyn. They were all long gone, and no magic he knew of could ever bring them back.

But Slaybourne wasn't rubble, yet, and the Finns' very lives depended on his return. As much as he wanted to be with his family again, he couldn't just give up and die.

Not now. Not when he was so close.

MAGNUSON! the Wraith King roared.

Connor jumped to his feet, one hand on his chest as he fought to catch his breath, and reality hit him like an arrow between the eyes. He sucked in air, but it was never enough to fill his lungs. A sharp ringing in his ears drowned out any other sound, and he winced as it slowly faded.

After he blinked himself from his daze, he found others staring into the dark pool. Though he had approached it alone, Quinn, Murdoc, and Sophia now surrounded the reservoir. Each of them watched its rippling surface in silence, lost in their own thoughts. As Sophia leaned forward, and her fingers flattened the black flowers lining the water's edge.

The dark pond rippled, and the pinpricks of starlight in its depths twinkled more violently than it had before. Enraptured, Murdoc reached for the glittering light, and something moved just below the surface.

Connor's chest tightened with dread. His father had stopped him from touching the water, and now he had mere seconds to stop his friends from doing the same.

CHAPTER FIFTY-EIGHT
CONNOR

In the gruesome field surrounded by moss-covered bones and priceless blooms, cool tendrils of mist snaked across the stone platform holding the mysterious pool of star-strewn water.

What the hell is wrong with you? the Wraith King asked with an indignant huff. *You weren't responding to—*

Connor tuned the old ghost out as Murdoc's hand hovered above the ripples. Something swam just below the surface, getting closer with each passing second.

"Murdoc!" He shouted as he grabbed his friend's shoulder. "Snap out of—"

Murdoc glared at him—but the former Blackguard's eyes weren't right. The irises had faded entirely, leaving only the whites behind. Those haunting, vacant eyes stared at him, empty and void.

How unsettling, the ghoul muttered.

Connor gritted his teeth as he tried to make sense of this mess. "Murdoc, what the hell's wrong with your—"

Before he could even finish, Murdoc drew his sword. Unblinking and unfazed, the former soldier stood. He didn't answer. He didn't flinch. In fact, he didn't seem to recognize Connor at all.

A glimmer of light snaked down the former Blackguard's steel, and he sliced at Connor's neck.

On instinct, Connor ducked. The sword cut through the air inches above his head.

For a moment, he could only watch in shock as his friend tried to kill him. He paused, one knee resting on the stone as Murdoc absently twirled the blade in one hand and scanned Connor's torso for a weak spot.

He finally snapped, the wraith said. *Shall we kill him, then?*

"He's enchanted," Connor snapped, trying to make the ghoul shut his damn mouth long enough for him to piece together a plan.

Despite the Murdoc trying to cut off his head, Connor took a quick glance at the two women by the pond. Quinn stood on the opposite bank, her head tilted in curiosity as she stared into the pond, while Sophia's palms flattened two bloody beauties growing by the water's edge.

And, instead of eyes, both women had the same blank white voids as Murdoc.

Whatever enchantment the bogs had put on this star pool, it had snared them all with its magic—and they would all try to kill him.

Delightful.

Without warning, Murdoc sliced again at Connor's nose. Connor leaned backward, and the tip of the steel blade passed directly in front of him. A blast of wind snapped against his face from the blow, but he remained otherwise unscathed.

The attack gave him a narrow window of opportunity to charge, and as Murdoc stepped into range, Connor took his chance.

He leapt forward and tackled the former Blackguard. With his right arm hooked around the man's chest, Connor dropped to one knee and used his own momentum to hurl his friend off the platform.

One way or another, he had to break this curse. Hopefully, all he needed to do was get them far enough from the pond to snap them out of their dazes.

Murdoc hit the stone hard and rolled toward the grassy field. His sword slipped from his hand, and with one final grunt of pain, he tumbled off the boulder and out of sight. The fog churned in the air above where the man had fallen. Something heavy hit the earth, and the crack of brittle bones shattered the meadow's surreal silence.

Connor waited with bated breath.

Still out of view, the soldier let loose a string of curses. A loose bone from one of the skeletons in the field launched into the air, carving through the fog. Murdoc popped his head over the edge of the platform, both palms flat against the stone, and glared at Connor with clear brown eyes.

"What the bloody hell was that for, damn it?!" the man shouted. "That hurt like a bitch, in case you were wondering!"

Good. Murdoc was back, and now Connor had a plan.

"We have to get them away from the star pool," he shouted. "Wraith, you take Sophia, and I'll…"

He trailed off as Sophia slipped her bag off her shoulder and set it beside the pond. Opposite the necromancer, Quinn leaned over the water and peered into its depths as the flames on *Aurora's* steel slowly died. The last of the Firesword's flickering orange light cast rippling shadows across the water.

Sophia inched toward the water's edge, and as she shifted her weight, her fingers dipped into the water. Waves of green light pulsed through the surface from her skin.

Shit.

He didn't have time to explain the plan to the wraith. He had to intervene—and he had to do it now.

Connor lunged at Sophia and hit her with the force of a boulder rolling downhill. They tumbled across the stone platform, flattening dozens of flowers as they toppled. Even as the blurring white haze tumbled around him, the crackle of ice snapped through the air.

Damn it. Not *again*.

He pushed her away just as her ice-blue hands reached for his neck. Her fingernails clawed at the air in front of his face, but he managed to shove her off him in the nick of time. He slid to a stop with his back to a boulder, and he looked up just as she drove her icy blue fist at his face. He tilted his head out of the way, and her blow cracked the stone where his skull had been. Ice splintered across the rock behind him, and he landed a swift kick in her gut to slow her down.

She groaned, the wind knocked out of her, but she glared at him through the loose locks of her dark hair. With her eyes still as white as the fog around them, she stumbled back to her feet and summoned more ice into her palms.

Enchanted, are they? the wraith muttered. *Are you certain they aren't simply fed up with you ordering them about all the time?*

"Will you get in here and *help*?" Connor shouted.

The ghoul clicked his tongue in disappointment, but didn't respond.

Sophia hurled two balls of ice at Connor's chest, one after the other. He summoned his shield, and the chilled blasts of magic sizzled across the enchanted metal as it protected him from a cold, miserable death.

When he lowered the shield, she had already turned her back on him and was marching with calm purpose toward the pool once more.

A short distance off, Quinn's Firesword slipped from her hand and clattered to the stone ground. The Lightseer knelt beside the water, enraptured by whatever she saw in the murky basin.

He couldn't stop them both by himself. Not with Quinn that close to the water.

"Wraith, get Sophia!" Connor shouted. "Now!"

You're the one who wanted to adopt this little team of yours, the specter grumbled. *I see no reason for me to save them from themselves.*

"Make yourself useful, damn it!" Connor pushed himself to his feet and charged toward Quinn. "Get Sophia away from the water!"

The ghoul groaned in annoyance. *Very well.*

Thick black shadows rolled across the water as the wraith appeared between the necromancer and the pond. His skeletal face emerged from the darkness, and Sophia summoned one of her Necromancer blades in response. She hurled the dart at his face, and he dissolved into smoke as it passed harmlessly through the gloom he left in his wake.

A bony hand reached from within the black haze and wrapped around her waist. Half-submerged in his own shadows, the ghoul grabbed her and pulled her roughly away from the pool. Her body flailed like a ragdoll as he dragged her to safety.

Her black hair whipped around her face, and though she clawed at the empty shadow around her, her vacant eyes glared back at Connor.

He couldn't care.

As he ran toward Quinn, Sophia threw her second dart at his head. He saw it in the nick of time, and he skidded to a stop just as the weapon impaled the nearest stone pillar between him and the pond.

With that, Sophia faded into the thickening white mist surrounding the stone platform on which he stood, and a string of her muffled cursing followed.

Good. That left only Quinn.

Kneeling in a bed of priceless black flowers, the Starling warrior set her palms on the stone and leaned toward the water.

Connor bolted again toward her, but with every step of his boots against the stone, she leaned ever closer to the surface.

Her long hair slid off her shoulder and hung around her face, and its fiery red strands hit the water. Ripples of green light pulsed outward, brighter than when Sophia had touched it, and the entire pond quickly filled with ever-expanding circles of glittering light.

A dark hand reached from the depths of the pond and toward her face. Its edges dripped from it, as though it were made of the same murky water as the star pool itself, and its fingers stretched wide. Quinn's vacant eyes closed, and she relaxed as she lowered her forehead toward it.

Connor slid the final few feet toward her. "Quinn, don't!"

She didn't respond.

He grabbed her arm and pulled as hard as he could. Her body skidded backward across the stone toward him, and the watery hand snatched at the air where her face had been. The dripping fingers slid through her hair, instead, and the fiery red color drained from whatever strands it touched. A soft lavender light glimmered briefly in its wake, like a film its touch had left behind, before her hair returned to normal.

He let out a sigh of relief and got to his feet, but Quinn wouldn't look at him. With her focus still on the pond, she wrenched herself free of his grip with an effortless twist of her hand. He growled in frustration, and he grabbed her shoulder this time to root her in place.

In a motion so quick he barely registered it, Quinn crouched and shifted her weight onto her palms. With a flawless kick, she swept his legs out from under him. He hit the ground hard, the air knocked from his lungs, while she stood with all the grace of a dancer.

When his head finally stopped spinning, he looked up just as her heel sailed toward his face. He rolled, and the stone shattered beneath her boot.

Apparently done with him, she turned away from him and slowly walked back toward the pond. The watery hand clawed at the bank, searching for her. Its fingertips swept across the black blooms growing on the stone, and petals shriveled at its mere touch.

"Quinn, snap out of it!" Connor pushed off the ground and sprinted toward her.

She knelt again, and he wrapped his arm around her neck in a chokehold. Her nails dug into his forearm as she squirmed in his grip, but he only tightened his hold on her.

With Murdoc, he'd been careful, but he doubted he could snap any of Quinn Starling's bones despite his incredible new strength. With all her augmentations, she could not be easily broken.

Her back pressed against his chest, and despite her struggling gasps for air, he tightened his right arm around her neck. Steadily, carefully, he pulled her backward and away from the water.

Not much farther, now, and he should be able to break whatever enchantment the pool had put on her.

Before he could reach the edge of the stone platform, however, she leaned her weight into him and hooked one leg around his. It threw him off balance—just a little, but that was apparently all she needed.

His center of gravity shifted, and she took full advantage of the momentary lapse of control. With her hands firmly gripping his forearm, she leaned forward and launched him over her shoulder. His stomach churned, but there was no way to stop it.

Damn, she was *good*.

He held tight to her neck, and together they rolled across the flattened flowers toward the pond. She gritted her teeth, her red hair flying around her face, and the world around him became blurred glimpses of the pond as they rolled nearer and nearer.

For the love of the *Fates*—she had hurled them directly at the water, and with enough force to send them both sliding into it.

He let out a strangled yell as he shoved his heel into the stone to slow their tumble across the stone. His shoe dug into the rock as they careened toward the water, leaving a carved trail through the platform as they slid, but it mercifully slowed their momentum.

Barely a yard from the rippling black surface, he let out a breath of relief.

Still squirming in his grip, Quinn elbowed him in the gut. He grunted, and a rush of nausea burned his throat as he fought the momentary lack of air. Stunned and breathless, he didn't see the golden edge of her light shield until it hit him square in the face. As his vision went temporarily black, he reflexively loosened his hold on her neck, and a chill swept across his chest as her warm body left his.

Something hot and wet dribbled from his temple, and his vision blurred when he tried to blink away the hazy fog left behind by her attack. She had rolled out of his grip him, and now only her leg remained within reach.

With a roar of pain and frustration, he grabbed her calf and pulled as hard as he could. She slid backward across the stone and flipped onto her back, glaring up at him with those vacant white eyes as the murky hand reached again for her.

He'd had enough of this.

When she was finally close enough, he pinned her to the ground with one hand on each of her wrists. He set his knees against her inner thighs to keep her from wriggling free yet again, and he glared down at her as he tried to figure out what the hell he could do to snap her out of this.

As she fought against him, writhing beneath his grip and close to breaking free, a drop of blood from the wound in his temple splattered against her cheek.

"QUINN!" he roared down at her.

Her eyes shut as she braced herself against the sheer force of his voice, and when they opened, the blank white void was gone. She stared up at him, dazed and bewildered, and her hazel eyes scanned his face.

Out of breath, his chest heaving as he fought for air, he let out a sigh of relief.

"What..." Still pinned to the ground beneath him, Quinn's hands curled into fists. She frantically looked around, surveying his expert hold as it rooted her to the stone beneath them. "What the hell are you doing?"

"Saving your life." He hesitated, not entirely sure what would happen when he released her, and his eyes narrowed in suspicion as he debated the best course of action to take from here.

He did *not* want to go through that again, and he couldn't risk the pond getting hold of her once more.

He looked back at the star pool, but the dripping hand was gone. Only a few puddles of water along the bank gave any indication it had been there at all.

"You saved my life?" she asked, her voice softened by her surprise.

Still breathing heavily, he simply nodded and released his hold on her wrists. He sat upright and tugged off the cloth covering his nose and mouth. Exhausted and fed up with this bog's infuriating tricks, he wiped the blood off his temple.

Quinn sat upright and propped one knee. She leaned her elbow on it as she studied his face. "Why?"

"Thanks for that vote of confidence, Lightseer." He scoffed as he finally caught his breath. "I figured you knew me better than that by now."

Her gaze drifted across the rocky platform and the trampled bloody beauties around the edge of the water. Her shoulders still heaved with every breath, but at least he'd been able to bring her back.

The air shifted, and the hair on his arms stood on end. He bristled, scanning the open field for an impending attack, but the churning mist only thickened. Murdoc and Sophia stood at the base of the platform, where the flagstones met the rocky outcrop, but no one would look at each other.

Whatever they had all seen in the depths of the pool had unnerved them just as much as it had unsettled him.

He stood, fists tightening, as the towering entity's looming silhouette appeared once again in the fog. She towered over them, her skirts flaring out from her hips as she spread her arms wide. This time, however, something grew from her head. The flailing tendrils reminded him of snakes, at first, until they solidified into horns as wide and interwoven as a stag's.

"*Well done,*" she said. "*All of you.*"

"You've seen more than enough!" Connor raised one finger up at her, and his voice rumbled in his chest as he dared her to play another game. "This ends now!"

"*Not quite yet, I'm afraid,*" she said, calm and unfazed by his threat. "*Though I do believe you've earned a reward for all you've endured thus far.*"

She faded into the fog, but the sensation of her eyes watching him never left.

The moment the entity disappeared, more flagstones pushed out of the dirt. The mist thinned, and the path carved its way through the skeletons, toward where the being stood moments before.

"What in the Fates' name was that?" Sophia asked, breathless.

"I have no idea," Connor admitted as he ran the back of his hand over his brow to wipe away the lingering sweat. "But I think she—it?—whatever it is, that's our way out of this place. Get your bags. We need to move."

He grabbed his pack from where he had dropped it by the pond. As much as he hated turning his back on something so dangerous, he couldn't risk getting snared by the enchantment again, and he refused to look at the pond as he slid his bag over one shoulder. As the rest of them gathered their packs and weapons, only Quinn remained seated. She stared at the ground and hugged her knee, her eyes fogging over with bewilderment.

"Quinn," he said gently, in case she was slipping back under the pond's spell.

She didn't budge.

With a resigned sigh, he grabbed her Firesword off the ground and set it beside her. He knelt and set one hand on her shoulder, still trying to check her eyes. "Hey, look at me."

She flinched, and her hazel eyes widened as they darted toward him.

He frowned. Jumpy, frightened, nervous, and a little insecure—this wasn't like her at all.

"I need you to focus," he said quietly. "Whatever you saw in there, it wasn't real. Remember that."

She stiffened and slowly shook her head. "It was all real, Connor. Every second of it."

His eyes narrowed in confusion as he studied her face, but she brushed his hand off her shoulder and stood. She ran her fingers through her fire-red hair and cleared her throat as she grabbed her Firesword. With one last look at him over her shoulder, she trekked back toward the others.

Connor rubbed his face and watched her retreat toward the flagstones. For whatever reason, the Blood Bogs seemed to be saving its cruelest tricks for her.

QUINN

Quinn led the way through the fog.

The flames crackling across her Firesword left an orange stain on the mist around her. She did her best to stay present. To focus. To leave the confrontation back there with all those dead men's bones.

But she couldn't.

The man she had been ordered to bring back to Lunestone in chains had saved her life.

Twice.

The weight of eyes on her neck distracted her, and she couldn't help but look over her shoulder one last time as the starry pool faded into the mist. Rolling fog swallowed the last fractured skull of the poor fools who hadn't escaped the pond's magic, and she thanked the Fates that Connor had snapped her from that daze.

"*This way*," something in the fog whispered, so quietly it felt almost like a dream.

Quinn paused midstride and lifted her sword, squinting as she scanned the wall of white around them, but nothing moved within it.

"What was that?" At her side, Connor summoned his blackfire blades. Dark shadows rolled across his arms as he followed her gaze. "Did you hear a voice?"

"I don't know," she admitted.

"Steady." The blades in his hands disappeared into another rush of smoke, and he patted her on the back. "We're better than the bog's games."

"Right." She swallowed hard, unsure of whether or not it was true.

She still couldn't fathom what she had seen back there in that starlit puddle. It had been fuzzy. Faint, like a forgotten thought dredged from the depths of her soul.

In the center of the water, she had seen snow. No people. No weapons. Just a wall of white, blended with blurs of green and brown.

Her throat tightened as she relived it yet again. Whatever it was, it had actually happened to her once. Long ago.

It wasn't a trick of the eye or a mirage, but a memory. She knew that deep in her bones, and no one would ever convince her otherwise.

Now that the long-lost moment had returned, it didn't want to die. She relived it, again and again, as their small band wandered through the enchanted fog.

A woman sobs.

An arrow thunks into a nearby tree.

A man speaks, but she can't understand what he says. She just knows that he is safety, and it frightens her that he is scared.

Someone holds her to their chest as a bowstring twangs, and the arrow lands with the wet squish of meat.

She falls, and the ground is cold. Something heavy presses her cheek into the icy dirt, and someone's final breath rolls across her neck.

Lying there, pinned to the frozen earth, she cries. The wails overtake her infant lungs, but no one comes to soothe her.

The ruthless shiver of winter gnaws at her bones, and her tiny little world goes black.

CHAPTER FIFTY-NINE
OTMUND

The heavy thunk of a blade hitting wood cut through the Blood Bogs. Otmund let out a feral growl—half frustration, half rage—as yet another mirage of the peasant who had stolen the wraith from him dissolved into thin air. A withered old oak now stood where the mirage had been seconds before, and he yanked the glowing Bloodbane dagger from the depths of the tree.

A distant laugh floated through the woodland, and he resisted the impulse to hurl his dagger in its general direction.

"Damn it!" he shouted.

He balled his hand into a fist and rammed it against the tree, and a burst of pain shot up his arm. He gritted his teeth and leaned his head into the trunk, seething as he rode out the waves of pain, but his grip on the Bloodbane dagger only tightened.

"You almost had it that time." The peasant's voice swam through the fog around him, from somewhere to his left.

He scanned the churning white mist as more silhouettes circled him, always just out of sight.

"So close," the man said again, this time from somewhere on his right.

"Try again," a third voice taunted him. "Maybe you'll get one of us this time."

He screamed with frustration and swung wildly at the fog. The shadows dodged and darted out of reach, some with only moments to spare, like a bird diving in front of a horse only to escape its hooves at the last second, like the twisted thing enjoyed the thrill of toying with death.

They were playing with him, like a cat playing with its food.

"You infuriating wretches!" he yelled.

The peasant's face appeared within the mist, disembodied and hovering in the air. He slashed at it, and the Bloodbane finally sliced through its skin. Instead of blood, however, the mirage merely flickered and faded into a dull green light.

Hovering. Immobile.

His heart skipped several beats as he dared to let himself hope he had finally caught one. He reached for it, not wanting to miss his chance, but the green wisp darted past him.

Laughing.

He shouted every obscenity he knew, and he did it as loud as he could. He barely even listened to himself as he slashed wildly into the fog, still trying to catch one of them. He only needed one, for the Fates' sake.

Just *one*.

Any one of these green bastards could show him a way out. If this Bloodbane dagger could kill a wraith, it could certainly kill whatever infuriating puff of magical smoke comprised these irritating creatures.

His dagger dug into yet another tree, and he set one foot against the trunk as he fought to yank it out. While he focused on his task, he stopped trying to scan his surroundings. He stopped listening for footsteps.

Nothing in this forest made any damn *sense*.

When he finally tugged the blade free, he stumbled backward and barely caught his balance. The fog around him thinned, revealing dozens of silhouettes in the depths of the white blanket that coated this infernal hellhole. As the shadows watched him, some shook their heads. Some laughed. Others sighed with boredom.

One by one, the silhouettes turned their backs on him. They walked away, the mist curling behind them as they faded into nothing, and even the laughter slowly died.

Apparently, they had grown bored of him.

"Come back here, you cowards!" he shouted. "I can handle anything you throw at me!"

"*Can you, now?*" a whisper asked, so close he could feel its breath on his neck.

Otmund spun around, ready to stab it, but he was alone.

He sucked in breath after breath, heaving, furious, desperate to kill something. Whatever games they were playing, he'd had enough. He scanned the edge of the clearing as he waited for another of them to step forward.

They always did, eventually.

After a few breathless moments of waiting, another silhouette walked forward, shrouded yet again in the depths of the fog. The edges on this one blurred and shimmered, and he squinted as he sought to make out its shape. It took a few moments, but eventually a slender figure materialized within the fog.

Wide hips. Tiny waist. A sword, held aloft.

As she neared, her fire-red hair came into sharp focus before any other feature. Before he could even see her face, he knew then who the bogs had sent him this time.

Quinn Starling paused at the edge of the clearing, and her eyebrows pinched together in confusion as the fire in her sword raged across its steel. The flames cast an orange glow across her features and brought out the golden highlights in her hair while she stared at him with a convincingly puzzled frown.

Perhaps the Blood Bogs expected Otmund to swoon. Maybe the master of these mists thought he cared about this girl, or that seeing her would spark some sort of confession as to his intentions.

More than anything, however, it confused him. She had nothing he wanted. Not anymore.

After everything he had endured in this hellish place, he simply laughed. He couldn't help it. The chuckle started gently at first, quietly, but it built to hysterical wheezing.

Every time he looked her in the eye, he only laughed harder. Her nose wrinkled in disgust, just as it did anytime she saw something that annoyed her, and he had to commend the bogs' attention to detail. It was a decent portrayal, but no amount of nuance could convince him she was real.

These wisps kept trying to weasel into his mind, but it all finally made sense.

At long last, he understood what was really going on. Granted, it had taken him far too long to figure it out, but now he knew what these bastards wanted.

All of this had been a test.

In the panic-drenched moments when he had first fallen into the mist, he'd ignored Dahlia's warning. He hadn't understood, back then, what it had meant. The bogs only wanted to know what he ultimately desired. They wanted to tease him with whatever he craved most and use that to lure him deeper into the forest.

That should've been obvious from the moment they showed him the Wraithblade. But by giving him Quinn Starling—the woman most men in Saldia wanted in their beds—these fools had finally shown their cards.

It was so damn simple that he almost hated himself for taking this long to figure it out.

As his laughter finally faded, he wiped a gleeful tear from his eye and sighed with relief. "It seems as though you all aren't as powerful as you think, eh?"

The mirage tilted her head in almost believable confusion as she studied him, but she didn't answer.

"Come on, now, out with the rest of you." He clicked his tongue in disappointment. Still holding the Bloodbane dagger, he scanned the empty fog bank and waited for the rest of them to come out of the woodwork yet again. "Come on, let's have it!"

"Otmund?" The mirage raised her blazing sword. Its orange light stretched across the clearing between them until it reached his feet.

He pinched the bridge of his nose and sighed impatiently. "Is that how it's going to be, then? You can't make the puppet master dance, you overblown toads!"

She took another cautious step closer, but she still wouldn't say anything.

"I've had enough of you lot." Otmund raised his finger at her in warning, and the mirage froze under his glare. "You all, with your laughing, your hallucinations, your trees. All of your damned *trees*."

The apparition glanced him up and down, like it didn't know what it was witnessing.

"Oh, just leave." He waved it away, fed up with its foolishness. "If you're going to try to taunt me with the things I desire most, then show me the Wraith King. I couldn't care less about the Starling girl. She couldn't even bring me the peasant. She's worthless."

With an indignant huff, the mirage arched its back. Something flickered, deep in its eyes, like a flash of understanding.

"She's worthless to you, is she?" the illusion asked.

"Of course." He brushed some loose tree bark off his shoulder with his free hand as he waited for this to end. "Why else would I send her after the peasant without the Bloodbane dagger to protect herself? She's expendable, like any other Starling."

"You raised her," the hallucination pointed out. "She spent every summer at Mossvale, hanging on your every word. You told her to call you Uncle, and then you asked her father for her hand. Was it all a game, then?"

"Uncle, right." He snorted as he mocked the apparition. "That girl was always so starved for love that it was easy to make her dance for me. Show a little affection, pretend to be proud of her, and just like that." He snapped his fingers for emphasis. "She's completely under my control."

The mirage bristled, but he'd had enough of this. He opened his mouth to speak, to chase it away again, but a better idea occurred to him before he could say a word.

His jaw snapped shut as he toyed with the idea.

If this moronic wisp wanted to chat, he could at least use this to his advantage. The longer he kept it talking, the better chance he had to inch closer. If he got near enough, perhaps he could catch this one.

With an exaggerated yawn, he stretched his arms above him. The glowing green Bloodbane dagger left streaks of emerald light on the dark forest air, and he used the moment to take a few cautious steps closer as he prepared his trap.

Freymoor hated the Starlings almost as much as he did, so perhaps the bogs wanted to know more about Teagan Starling's prized daughter. How fitting that the mist had tried to dangle what he wanted most, only to give him something he could use against it.

Fitting, really.

"Not many know this, of course," he began, his mind buzzing with the many ways he could spin this in his favor as he inched closer. "But Teagan molded her into a perfectly obedient soldier from day one. Her purpose—her duty—is to be predictable. Every choice she makes, every action, it's all by design. She does what she's supposed to do, even when she thinks she's making her own choices. He burned his essence right into her soul, so deep that she can't tell the difference between obedience and free will."

The apparition didn't move. Its expression didn't change. It didn't even blink. The imposter simply stood there, glaring at him, those almost-convincing eyes trailing each movement he took as the gap between them closed.

"Between you and me, I think she's dead." Otmund shrugged, using his genuine indifference to sneak a quick glance around the empty clearing for signs of another wisp. "I think the peasant killed her, and maybe it's for the best. I couldn't imagine getting stuck with her as my wife."

The creak of skin on leather cut through the crackle of the flames as the mirage tightened its grip on the Firesword.

It didn't matter. He had gotten as close as he needed to get, and the foolish wisp hadn't even tried to inch backward.

He attacked.

Just as he had with all the others, he drove his blade at its face. This time, however, he knew he could hit it. The damn thing was so close, and it hadn't even tried to run.

It had gotten cocky, and he would happily take advantage of that mistake.

As the glowing blade neared her left eye, the mirage grabbed his wrist with its free hand. Its impossible strength stopped the blow as his blade hovered inches in front of its face.

Those thin brows crinkled with overt hatred as their eyes met. The orange glow of the crackling Firesword cast long shadows across the mirage's features as a tendril of mist floated between them.

He frowned, confused. "What—how did you—"

The wisps never fought back. From what he could tell, they had no solid form to block a blow.

But if that was true, then…

…then she had to be…

…*real.*

Quinn Starling kicked him in the gut. Something snapped in his chest, and he couldn't breathe. Agony splintered through his core, and he hit the ground hard. He rolled through the clearing, kicking up leaves and dirt, and every tumble sent a fresh wave of pain through every vein in his body.

A twig stuck to his face as he slid to a stop. His cheeks flushed with nausea, and he nearly vomited what was left of his last meal, right then and there.

Trembling from the blistering bolts of pain still shooting through his chest, Otmund set his palms flat on the ground and stared up at her in shock. The emerald Bloodbane dagger lay on the ground between them, but she didn't acknowledge it.

The cold dread of what had happened slowly burned away his anger and fear until only cold disbelief remained.

He couldn't move.

He couldn't think.

He could only watch her, mouth gaping, as his mind struggled to piece together how the real Quinn Starling could have found her way here, of all places.

She had never been a mirage. The mist hadn't dangled anything in front of him. If anything, it had conned him—*again.*

From the blanket of thick fog behind her, an all-too-familiar silhouette emerged. The peasant paused at her side, his broad shoulders framed by the white mist behind him, and the orange light of her sword's fire cast a harsh glow on both their glowering faces.

"No," Otmund said firmly, as if that settled the matter. "This—you two—this isn't real. You wouldn't be together. If she was really here, that criminal would be in chains." He pointed a trembling finger at the peasant. "Quinn always does what she's told. She always delivers. She's always—"

"—predictable?" The muscles in her neck tightened, and fire erupted in her empty hand as she coiled it into a furious fist. "Naïve? Too *trusting*?"

Her voice kicked the last breath from his lungs. His lips parted, but he couldn't respond. The ice-cold dread of this moment chased away the last shreds of what he had thought he knew about this forest and its apparitions.

For the first time in decades, he didn't have a clever plan. He couldn't pivot, and he had no idea what to do. The effortless lies he had always relied upon to weave his puppets' strings didn't come, and he could only watch in horror as his brain struggled to craft a new strategy.

"Fuck," he whispered, his voice strangled to near-silence as bafflement froze him in place.

"Yes." Her hazel eyes narrowed as she glared down at him, and a chill snaked down his spine at the sheer hate radiating from her expression.

It reminded him of Teagan.

"You're no mastermind." Her revulsion dripped from every word, as though each breath spent talking to him was a waste of air. "You're nothing but a fraud."

His worst fear had come true.

He had lost the last of his puppets, and with her faith in him went his last hope of survival.

Long ago, his father had warned him of what happened to those consumed by their hunt for power. He'd thought the man was a sentimental old fool, back then, but now those words rang truer than ever.

Watch that greed of yours, son, he'd said. *It's a killer. It's a wolf. Its endless need for more may drive you onward, but you can never sate its hunger. Sooner or later, it will grow hungry enough to eat you from the inside out, and you will die—*

"—alone," he finished aloud, his breathless whisper barely audible above the crackle of Quinn's Firesword. "And not a soul will care."

CHAPTER SIXTY
CONNOR

O*tmund.*

Here.

In his stunned daze, Connor could only stare at the trembling nobleman lying in the dirt. The man's hand shook as he lifted it in front of his face, those beady eyes of his shifting between Connor and Quinn. The mist curled over Otmund's mud-stained shoes and the dirty hem of his cloak, but no glistening sheen glimmered across his body.

This was no apparition. By whatever fate had brought him here, Connor had finally come face-to-face with the real Otmund Soulblud.

And this time, Connor had everything he needed to finish what that cold-blooded coward had started.

A bright flash of green light broke his concentration, and he stiffened as he shifted his attention to the glowing Bloodbane dagger lying in a pile of leaves between him and Otmund.

With that, his mind cleared in a rush.

"You're a wretch," Quinn continued. She stood off to the side and slightly ahead of Connor, her shoulders tensing with every word. Slowly, she stalked through the fog toward the enemy.

No, this was too easy.

It felt like a trap.

Connor set one hand on her shoulder in a silent command for her to stop. She flinched at his touch, but to her credit, she paused. With a wary look at him over her shoulder, she waited for him to explain himself.

Cautiously, he scanned the path at their feet. The flagstones had led them to this clearing, but none carved through the circle of dirt and withered roots, nor did the trail lead them deeper into the forest. Just as it had when they found the stone platform among the skeletons, their path ended in this small outcropping of patchy grass surrounded by trees.

For whatever reason, the bogs wanted him to walk into this clearing. It wanted him to face Otmund, after all this time.

"What is it, Captain?" Murdoc asked from behind.

"Is it something I can kill?" Sophia added. "I heard a man's voice, but who knows what's real in this hellhole."

"Wait back there." Connor ignored her bloodlust as he signaled for them to stay on the path. "I need a minute."

To think and sift through the risks, because nothing in his life had never been this easy.

Black smoke rolled across the ground as the wraith materialized beside Connor. The old ghoul stared down at the quivering nobleman, who only trembled harder as the Wraith King appeared from the depths of shadow.

Dahlia mentioned this coward had come, the wraith said. *I thought she was lying.*

"So did I," Connor admitted under his breath. "Think it's a trap?"

"Or another test?" Quinn scanned his face as she, too, tried to piece together the clues.

Or a gift? The wraith shrugged, and his bone-white fingers stretched wide as he lazily gestured toward the path behind them. *The entity said you had earned a reward.*

His jaw set as he met Quinn's gaze, and he whistled softly in wonder.

This was one hell of a reward.

Connor stepped off the last flagstone, and his boot hit the dirt without a sound.

That broke something deep within Otmund, and though the man's breath quickened, he darted forward like a beetle being hunted by a bird. His manicured hands dug into the dirt as he lunged for the Bloodbane dagger.

How adorable.

Closer to the dagger and a hell of a lot faster than this withered old fart who used others to do his bidding, Connor snatched the enchanted knife off the ground with ease. A quiet moan, similar to one an animal made when cornered, escaped Otmund as the man froze with one hand outstretched. Gaping, he stared up at Connor in horror.

Good. After all the terrible things this man had had done to this world, Otmund's final moments deserved to be filled with fear.

"On the night we met, you ordered hardened soldiers to kill an innocent woman." Connor stalked forward, and Otmund crawled away as he tried to put distance between them. "You ordered those men to kill two defenseless little girls. Admit it. Say that out loud."

Otmund's eyes widened. "I… I didn't…"

With a sharp twist of his hip, Connor kicked Otmund in the face. The man's head snapped violently back, and blood splattered into the air. Otmund collapsed in a sweaty heap, and his shoulders heaved as he struggled for breath. Sharp whistles filled the quiet clearing on each of Otmund's inhales, and he let out a pained groan as he tenderly held his face.

That had felt *damn* good.

"Say it!" Connor demanded again.

"Yes," Otmund admitted in a hushed voice. "It was unfortunate, but no one could know where the wraith had—"

Connor kicked him again, and this time a bone snapped. Otmund writhed on the ground, his hands on his face, but it didn't feel rewarding that time.

All he could feel was unbridled hate for this vile little man.

"Here we are." Connor gave Quinn a pointed look over his shoulder. "You said you wouldn't help me kill him. After everything you just heard, have you had a change of heart?"

She didn't move. As shadows danced across her face from the Firesword in her hand, she merely studied the man who had set all of this into motion. Her jaw tensed, and she squeezed her eyes shut as the fire in her free hand dissolved with a sharp hiss.

"You were family to me, Otmund," she whispered, her voice cracking. "I trusted you."

"But you *can* trust me, Quinn." The nobleman sat upright, though his hooked nose now bent at an unnatural angle. "Everything I said about you, my dear, was just a lie to rile up the bogs. The mists want secrets about you, about all of the Starlings, and I had to concoct something horrible in order to—"

"Don't you dare lie to me again." Dark and low, her voice dripped with venom—the sort that could kick the air out of a man's lungs as effectively as any blow to the gut.

Her voice *ached*—with loss, with grief, with fury—and her stunning eyes narrowed with barely restrained loathing.

As blistering fire raged along her legendary blade, she looked every bit the part of an empress about to burn down her enemy's castle.

No one spoke. Murdoc and Sophia inched quietly toward the clearing, and though they watched from the shadows, they stayed on the path. Connor stood between Quinn and the man she had once thought of as an uncle, and in the stunned silence that followed, only the crackle of fire filled the air.

The Starling warrior took a menacing step forward as she met Otmund's eye. "Are you even capable of the truth, you sniveling traitor?"

If this is an act, it is a convincing one. The wraith hovered along the edge of the field, his bony hands behind his back as he observed the encounter.

Connor raised one eyebrow in silent curiosity.

It could be truth, or it could be a ploy. The ghoul gestured to the two nobles in the center of the field. *When outnumbered in a battle for South Haven's outward shore, I once feigned disgust with my top general. Much like this, I stalked toward him, threatening to slice off his head as my enemy watched. They thought they were witnessing a king's unraveling at the end of his life, and they found it entertaining. It was anything but. The tactic had been rehearsed many times prior to the war. Once I reached him, our backs were protected, and we decimated the survivors together.*

The corner of Connor's mouth twitched in concern, and his grip on the Bloodbane dagger in his hand tightened. To be safe, he stepped out of Quinn's range and slowly walked around Otmund until he stood behind the whimpering nobleman. With a subtle nod, he gestured for the ghoul to remain on the other side of the clearing.

It was a simple maneuver, done primarily to put some distance between him and Quinn. If this was a ploy, she couldn't be within range, and she couldn't be granted an opportunity to surprise him.

After all, he had seen her true potential back there by the star pool—she was fast, and he wasn't going to take any chances.

Not with her.

While the wraith hovered behind Quinn, Connor positioned himself behind Otmund. No traitor would escape this clearing alive.

Incredibly, Quinn didn't seem to notice his movements.

"I never would've believed it," she said, tears burning in her eyes as she stared down at Otmund. "Connor told me you had ordered the deaths of an innocent family, and I refused to believe him. Not you. Zander, maybe, to cover his tracks, but not *you*."

"Connor? Is that—" Otmund looked briefly behind him, as though it was the first time he'd heard Connor's name, before he returned his attention to the Starling. "He kicked me in the face, my dear. What did you expect me to say? I lied to make him stop. I would never—"

"And to kill your own soldier to open the Rift," she interrupted. "A guard who had been sent through to protect you."

"You don't have the whole story. He was going to—"

"Everything I knew about you was a lie," she spat. "Everything about you is *fake*."

"Stop this at once!" Otmund demanded, his tone firm even as air whistled through his broken nose. "I'm disarmed. I'm injured. You wouldn't—"

"I *would*." The flames on her sword blazed wildly as her grip on the hilt tightened. "And I *have*. For Father. For you. All because I thought I was doing the right thing. You played me. Is that all I was to you? A plaything?"

Otmund mumbled, but none of the words made sense.

"And him." Without breaking eye contact with her target, she gestured toward Connor with the tip of her flaming sword. "You twisted the truth about him and lied to the world about who he is. You told me he was dangerous, Otmund, but he's a better man than you could ever dream of becoming."

Connor raised one eyebrow in surprise, intrigued by the compliment. He hadn't expected her to ever say something like that.

Don't get excited, the wraith chided. *That sounded more like an insult to him than flattery to you.*

He frowned, but the ghoul had a point.

The Starling raised her sword, and the firelight cast a wide circle across the dirt. She glared down at Otmund and paused with the mighty blade above her head.

In the rare chance this was indeed a ploy, Connor shifted his weight onto the balls of his feet and prepared to fight Quinn Starling yet again. He stretched out his fingers, his magic simmering just beneath his skin, and he prepared to dodge any blow that came his way.

Behind her, Murdoc and Sophia waited just beyond the circle of trees, watching in tense silence. The wraith hovered behind Quinn with his bony hand resting on the hilt of his sword.

Waiting. Watching. Curious to discover what she would do next.

"You can't do it." Otmund's voice softened and became far gentler than Connor imagined was possible for someone so heartless and cruel. The loving words sounded almost like a caress, like the way a father soothes a child when she wakes, crying, in the night. "I'm not perfect, Quinn, but you're a good girl. You're—"

"You're not even worthy of the Code," she growled.

Before he could say another word, she swung. Her sword launched at Otmund faster than he could even react, and the steel sliced clean through his neck in a single blow.

Severed from his body, Otmund's head rolled across the dirt, his eyes wide with shock even in death. At Quinn's feet, his body collapsed onto the ground in a bleeding heap.

Though tears welled in the corners of her eyes, Quinn Starling didn't cry. Instead, she spun her sword through the air and drove the blade deep into the decapitated corpse's chest.

The skin around the steel turned black, and the chest collapsed in on itself as the body burned in the Firesword's enchantments. The pungent stench of burning flesh snaked into the air as a plume of smoke spiraled out of the corpse, and in seconds, nothing remained of Otmund Soulblud but his head and a pile of ash.

Connor's mouth parted in surprise, and a bewildered silence followed. Murdoc and Sophia stiffened at the edge of the clearing, and the wraith gestured at the Starling warrior with an irritated wave of his bony hand.

Damn it, the ghoul pouted. *I wanted to kill him.*

Truthfully, Connor felt the same. She had taken his kill, but if anything, it seemed like she needed the closure more.

Besides, he had acquired the second Bloodbane dagger—a more valuable treasure than any revenge. As long as Otmund was dead, it didn't matter who had killed him.

Whispers bubbled through the forest around them, from every direction, approaching them like a wind spiraling from the south. The chattering ghosts hit the clearing in a rush, each talking over the others as their voices built.

"*...his head...*"

"*...his eyes...*"

"*...we want them...*"

"I don't care." Quinn wiped her eyes on her sleeve as the fire in her blade died. "He's not worth anything to me."

The whispers continued, apparently unsatisfied with her answer.

"Take it," Connor said. "It's yours."

The voices faded in a rush, like a candle's flame snuffing out with a breath. In the light seeping from the thick fog that surrounded the clearing, a long arm draped in vines and moss reached out of the darkness by Otmund's head. Its claws dug into his eyes, and a long streak of blood dripped from the severed remains as the arm dragged what was left of the sniveling coward into the underbrush.

Murdoc shuddered, and even Sophia wrinkled her nose in disgust as they watched the arm disappear from sight. The leaves in the underbrush shook as the thing left the clearing, and with that, there was silence.

Quinn Starling intrigues me, the ghoul admitted.

Connor nodded. "Likewise."

Quinn's head tilted briefly toward him, but she didn't respond, and she refused to even look him in the eye.

He took a step toward her, but the thundering grate of shifting rock rumbled through the air before he could say a word. The ground stirred, and he slid into a deep stance as he scanned the world around them for the source of the noise.

At the edge of the clearing where the hand had disappeared, the trees shifted once again. Their roots wriggled through the air, snapping against the fog like whips, and the trunks shifted sideways as the forest's oaks and pines once more walked. The trees replanted, and the ground shook with each trunk that slammed itself back into the earth. Their branches formed a tunnel through the forest, and as the canopy thinned, they revealed an archway that had previously been buried within the thicket.

The imposing archway stood like a beacon in the mist. Vines hung from the ancient stone, and patches of glowing green moss coated its mortar. The path beyond the arch blurred with fog.

"That looks familiar," Murdoc grumbled.

As the echoing rumble faded and the trees finally stilled, more flagstones pushed up through the dirt. They curved around the pile of ash that had once been Otmund Soulblud and ambled toward the newfound tunnel of trees. After a few moments of shifting dirt, they finally ended at the arch.

A bellowing roar echoed from the depths of the fog, and Connor stood taller as he yet again recognized Nocturne's voice.

They were close.

"Think that means this is finally over?" Sophia asked.

"I'm not going to hold my breath," Connor admitted.

"It's probably going to separate us again." Quinn glared at the archway as though she hadn't just killed the man she once considered to be family.

Connor watched her for a moment, and though she wouldn't look at him, he set one hand on her shoulder. He didn't know what to say, and honestly, words weren't going to help, here.

She frowned and shifted her intense glare to him.

Instead of saying something she would inevitably take as a meaningless platitude, he gently squeezed her shoulder. It was a gentle act, a comforting one, and it said more than words ever could. Her furious gaze softened—just a little, but he saw it—and her body relaxed beneath his touch.

The bogs had put them all through hell, but she was a soldier, and she would push through. It was what they all had to do to get out of here alive.

"Ready?" he asked.

She nodded.

He released her as Murdoc and Sophia jogged down the path toward them.

"Connor?" Quinn asked.

With one eyebrow raised in curiosity, he looked back at her.

"Thank you," she said with a subtle nod.

"Don't thank me yet." He stared up at the looming archway and took a deep, settling breath. "I get the feeling this place has one more trick up its sleeve."

NYX

Nyx stared out at the waterfalls of Mossvale with her feet propped on the priceless mahogany table Otmund had inherited from his father two decades ago. She sipped wine stolen from his personal reserves, deep in the castle's cellars, and reclined against the silk pillows of the elegant sofa the servants had set out on the balcony for her.

Compared to the bogs and muck of Nethervale, this place was paradise. It had never made sense to her that Otmund spent so little time here in his constant quest for more power.

The tension in her scarred back eased as she reclined against the pillow, and she closed her eyes to enjoy the distant crash of the dozen waterfalls that lined the southern cliffs and fed into the glittering sea. The wind brought with it hints of seaweed and the tide, and for a moment, she almost smiled.

Almost.

Against her breast, nestled between her skin and the black fabric of her Nethervale tunic, the spellgust coin linked to Otmund shattered.

She bolted upright, her hand on her chest as it caught her by surprise. The broken gem scratched against her skin as pieces of it fell into the bandages supporting her breasts, and Nyx stiffened at the implications. Impulsively, she set her hand on the broken stone as bits of it fell through the layers in her shirt, and she pinched her eyes shut in disappointment.

Someone else had killed Otmund before she'd gotten the chance.

How unfortunate.

It was a lucky break that she had found the forgeries when she did. Otherwise, Otmund's little plan would have actually worked, and Teagan would've had a very convincing stack of evidence waiting for him when he returned from his scuffle with the Wraithblade.

In the end, however, this didn't change a thing.

Even if she hadn't been the one to kill him, Otmund was dead, and his forgeries had been destroyed. Only that mattered. Setbacks or no, she loved it when a plan came together.

Once again, she reclined in her seat, and this time it felt even more comfortable. For roughly a decade, Nyx had searched for a new foothold in Saldia, a puppet state she could control from anywhere on the continent, and it seemed as though an opportunity had finally presented itself.

With a wicked little grin, she took another sip of wine. Even if she hadn't gotten the chance to skin Otmund alive, this had ultimately worked out in her favor—and that always put her in a good mood.

CHAPTER SIXTY-ONE
CONNOR

Connor led the way through the fog, toward the towering archway surrounded by ancient trees.

Whispers floated through the mist, aimless and jumbled, overlapping like waves in the sea, and whatever warning they carried was lost as they each fought for dominance. With a quick scan of the ancient, mossy structure before him, Connor tensed and prepared for something to attack.

It seemed inevitable.

You fool, the wraith snapped.

Connor let out an impatient sigh and glared over his shoulder to find the ghoul hovering at the back of their small band. Murdoc stood between him and the undead king, his sword drawn and forehead scrunched in confusion as Connor paused. Behind the former Blackguard, Sophia surveyed the trees, her hands glowing softly blue with her icy magic. Quinn brought up the rear, her Firesword blazing as she, too, studied the looming forest around them for signs of a trap.

You turned your back on your enemy. The Wraith King gestured subtly toward Quinn, but she didn't seem to notice.

Connor simply shook his head.

Quinn Starling wasn't his enemy. Not anymore. In fact, the more he learned about her, the more he wondered if his enduring mistrust of her had been somewhat unwarranted.

"Stay close," he ordered as he returned his attention to the path. "All of you."

You infuriating ass, the wraith grumbled.

"Quiet," Connor chided. "Focus."

"But I didn't say anything," Murdoc whispered.

A brief smile tugged at Connor's mouth, and he briefly pointed back at the ghoul to explain who he had been talking to.

"Ah," the former Blackguard said under his breath. "That makes more sense."

"Hush," Sophia scolded.

The fog thickened with every step, and Connor braced himself as he reached the archway. Nothing appeared on the other side except more of the glowing white haze, and he'd had just about enough of this place.

If this led them into another test, by the Fates, he was going to start breaking things—otherworldly magic of the forest be damned.

"Here goes nothing," he muttered as he stepped beneath the arch.

Once he was through, he looked again over his shoulder. He knew his team would be gone, same as before, but his stomach still twisted with the hope that he would be wrong.

He wasn't.

Connor now stood alone in the mist, and he shook his head in frustration. He needed to get back to Slaybourne. To the Finns. To the survivors who would die without him there to protect them from Teagan.

He couldn't afford to waste another second in this fog.

"You've had your fun!" he roared into the mist. "What more could you possibly hope to discover? What else could you possibly want to know?"

"I do not revel in the suffering of others," a familiar voice said. Yet again, his body cringed at the sound of overlapping voices and the sensation of her voice burrowing into his mind.

Connor snorted derisively. "You could've—"

Before he could finish his thought, the ground gave out beneath him. The rumble of stone and crumbling soil deafened him, and his stomach churned as he dropped boots-first into the unknown. A steep slope guided him into the bowels of the bogs, deep into the earth, twisting and turning as he slid ever downward.

With his core tensed and his magic pulsing through his fingertips, he fought the impulse to slow his fall by driving his hands into the walls of soil surrounding him. Whatever waited for him at the bottom of this slope would either give him answers or try to kill him—hell, maybe both—and he wanted this to be done.

Better to face it like a man.

The tunnel of dirt ended abruptly, and gray smears whizzed past him in the seconds before his shoes hit rock. Fog rolled across his legs as he easily stood, ready for a fight.

Yet again, he was surrounded by a thick white haze, but this time, the glow from within the mist brightened until it nearly blinded him. He raised one hand to shield his eyes until it finally began to thin, and pieces of an underground cavern came slowly into view: soft gray walls on every side; thick vines covering half of the polished stone, each covered in brown and green leaves as they clung to their ancient perches; and a stream of glowing white water that carved through the gray rock at his feet.

The white river flowed around him, and as the last of the mist cleared, he found himself standing on a stepping-stone in the middle of its current. More smooth white stones led toward a rocky bank to his right.

"Where the hell are we?" he asked.

His voice echoed in the cavern, but no one replied.

He balled his hand into a fist as he waited for the ghoul to answer, but the grim voice didn't come. The silence reminded him of his time before the Wraith King, before he was the Wraithblade, when he would talk to himself during the long, frigid nights in the Ancient Woods.

Alone.

Shoulders tight and knuckles cracking, Connor cautiously stepped to the next stone in the water. The second his foot hit it, the stone glowed white, and a face appeared in the water by his shoe. He grunted in surprise, only for the strangely familiar face to smile at him as it faded back into the milky current.

The face of his father.

Unsettled and still trying to piece together whatever game the bogs had concocted now, Connor took another step onto the next stone. Two figures appeared in the water this time—him and Quinn, walking through the mists with her Firesword blazing in front of her.

A memory.

As before, it faded as quickly as it had appeared, and the current washed it away.

"I hate this place," he muttered under his breath.

As he took a final step to reach the rocky bank, a hand launched from the water and grabbed his leg.

A jolt of alarm shot through him, as cold and paralyzing as ice in his veins, and he summoned his shadow blade on reflex. Smoke rolled over his forearm as he sliced at the hand gripping his ankle. The blade passed harmlessly through the white water, but the disembodied fingers never loosened their grip.

Four more arms shot from the water.

Five.

Ten.

He slashed uselessly at the arms as they tightened their hold on his legs. They tugged—hard—and their tight grasp overpowered even him. His foot slipped, and his boot landed in the knee-deep river. Water seeped through the seams in his shoe, and his pant legs clung to his skin as the current crashed into him far stronger than he had expected.

The sensation of fingers tightening around his ankle only worsened. The hands spread to his toes, his calves, his knees. He slashed again and again, carving holes through the arms with lightning speed, but it didn't do a lick of good.

The more he fought, the tighter their hold became.

Stop resisting. The wraith's grim voice echoed through Connor's mind, but after the long stretch of silence, he didn't trust it.

"What the—what do you mean *stop*?" Connor glared at the cavern around him, wondering where that damned ghoul had gotten to, but he was still alone. "I'm not going to let them drag me under!"

'Stop' means you need to dismiss your damned sword, you stubborn ass! the

wraith snapped. *You're going to make it worse for both of us!*

Connor stifled a furious growl, and though the hands continued to launch from the river and root him to the rocky terrain below the water, he raised his arms above his head and dismissed the shadow blade in a rush of black smoke.

The hands stilled, but their rooting hold on his legs remained.

The fallen princess is coming, the wraith warned. *Try not to say anything stupid.*

A frustrated growl rumbled in Connor's chest, and he sucked in a breath through his teeth to bite back a scathing remark.

To his right, along the nearest wall, the vines covering the rock slowly retreated. As they slithered up toward the ceiling, he noticed a tunnel carved into the stone that had previously been hidden by the thick roots. The clack of heels echoed first through the quiet cave, and seconds later, a silhouette appeared within the darkness.

Dahlia.

The Lady of Freymoor emerged from the pitch-black tunnel, and her eyes narrowed as she stepped into the light. With her hands clasped in front of her, she studied his face.

To his surprise, her thin brows twisted upward with the barest hint of remorse, but she still raised her chin in defiance as she stared down at him. "You've done well. No one else has made it this far."

"You have ten seconds to explain what the hell is going on," Connor warned.

"Or?" She playfully smirked and glanced him over as he stood in the water, immobile.

"Behave, my dear," the feminine voice from the bogs chided.

Connor's head snapped upward, toward the sound, but he couldn't place where it had come from. It seemed to echo through the cavern, coming from everywhere and nowhere all at once.

In unison, nearly every vine along the walls began to move. They slithered over each other, retreating from their perches and kicking up dust as they gathered in the center of the underground room. Slowly, they took shape, rising over each other to form a skirt, and then a torso, and then shoulders, then arms. The writhing roots rose above him and Dahlia both, until a head emerged from the top of the looming figure. As it formed, the vines of its body shifted endlessly.

As the being's head emerged from the center of its broad green shoulders, butterflies made of white light flashed to life around its face. The trailing tendrils of light fluttered as the figure rose from nothing, and one landed on its outstretched finger. The silhouette stared down at it, watching in serene silence, before the butterfly took flight again.

All at once, a glowing green light flickered through every vine—like a pulse. The heartbeat rumbled, slow and steady, as two glowing green eyes appeared in its head.

Connor gaped up at the silhouette he had seen out in the fog. He had thought it was, perhaps, another of the swamp's games, but before him stood something impossible. Something unprecedented. Something he didn't think could exist.

Out there in the fog—the entity hadn't been a trick of the eye at all.

"You're..." He gaped at the dazzling entity before him, speechless in his shock. "You're real."

"I am." The figure nodded, and her slender neck tilted with all the grace of an empress.

No, not an empress.

Something far more powerful—a goddess. Something not of this world at all.

As he studied her writhing features, horns grew from her head, not unlike the antlers on a magnificent deer. Her back straightened with regal pride, and she wore the horns like a crown.

"The riddle." He grimaced as he finally understood. "We weren't supposed to find Dahlia. We were supposed to find you."

The being nodded again, and the last of the glowing white butterflies faded into the air around her.

"What are you?" he asked, astonished at the sheer force of her presence.

"I am the Antiquity," the being explained with an elegant wave of her hand, as though it were obvious. *"I am All That Was. I am the Master of Memory,* the Mother of Fallen Dynasties, and the Goddess of the Past."

As his unfiltered awe slowly faded, he blinked himself out of his surprised daze. Goddess or no, she still had his team captive somewhere in her bogs, and he would get them back "Where's the wraith? You clearly did something to him and my team."

"I cannot kill him, if that is your fear."

"You didn't answer my question."

Though the Antiquity had no mouth, her head tilted, and her eyes relaxed—as though she were smiling. *"He is safe, as are your friends."*

"Where are they?"

"The Wraith King is bound elsewhere in the in-between, where he will remain until I release him," she answered.

"That's it. We're done." Connor tried to rip his leg free from the hands holding him in the water, even as more arms launched from the current to grab him. "I've had enough of your tests!"

"I understand your impatience. Your homeland is under attack, but even now, you still do not realize what you are asking of us. Only a worthy Champion may obtain the Soulsprite, and one way or another, this will all be over soon."

He didn't like the sound of that.

"Take heart," she said calmly. *"This is your final task, and the most important of them all. There is nothing left for you to do, Connor Magnuson, as this challenge is one you can only watch unfold. A test not of what you can do, but of who you are—and what you have already done. Now, we will see whether those you lead will walk into hell for your cause, because that is what they will face, Wraithblade. It is what you will all face, time and time again."*

With a wave of her hand, one of the crystalline walls shivered. Its soft gray rock faded until it became transparent, like a diamond, and revealed a second cavern beyond it. In the far corner, a waterfall crashed into the same white river that snaked across both caverns. A hole in the ceiling gave him a perfect view of Saldia's twin moons, and their soft blue glow cast an azure spotlight across the cavern floor.

And there, standing in the center with his back to the river, was Nocturne.

The dragon's pronounced jaw was raised toward the sky, though his eyes were closed. With his wings tucked tightly against his back, he stood in statuesque silence. A low growl rumbled through the air, warbled and distant, but unmistakable.

Connor let out a quiet breath of relief.

He closed his eyes and pressed against the dragon's mind. Stubborn or not, the dark prince had to let him in.

They had to face this—together.

Though the dragon's ear twitched, he remained still. He didn't move. He didn't speak. And, unfortunately, he didn't let Connor in.

Connor frowned, confused. This wasn't the time for pride. They had to solve this and figure a way out of here.

Distant voices echoed through the cavern, too far away at first to make out, but drawing closer. It took another few seconds before Connor recognized Murdoc's string of cursing, and he scanned both rooms as he tried to place where it was coming from.

Moments later, vines along one of the walls in the other cavern retreated, and Murdoc tumbled out. He hit the ground hard, still rolling, and Sophia shot out of the tunnel next. She landed on top of him in a flurry of muffled yells and crimson skirts.

Quinn fell through the hole after them, but unlike the others, she effortlessly rolled to her feet without even breaking stride. She scowled up at the cavern with unrestrained fury and summoned a massive ball of fire into her palm.

"I have had ENOUGH!" she shouted.

Her voice echoed through the cave, and she hurled the ball of fire at the far wall, at something out of view. The ground shook from her rage as she stood by the edge of the flowing white water, glowering at the silent rock around her.

"Goddess, she's a Starling," Dahlia said softly. "Can't I kill her?"

Connor gritted his teeth and resisted the urge to fight his way out of the river to put the fallen princess in a headlock.

But the Antiquity answered before he could say anything. "*You may not, child. If he passes, that will be his choice to make.*"

"And if he fails?"

"I'm right here." Connor's eyes narrowed as he watched the two of him debate Quinn's life.

"If he fails, then yes, she is yours to dispose of," the Antiquity said, ignoring him. *"But be patient, Dahlia, and hope he succeeds, even if it means the Starling woman lives. Such is the compromise of allies—you will not always have your way."*

"I'm not a fan of how you treat your allies," Connor quipped.

"You aren't our ally," the Antiquity corrected. Her glowing green eyes darted toward him as she gestured to the next room. *"Not yet."*

With that, the vines composing her body dispersed. They snaked along the ground, and her body slowly unraveled as the roots affixed themselves to the walls once more.

"We are nearly done, Wraithblade." The Antiquity's voice resonated through the cave and hummed through his chest. *"The most painful challenge a man must face is to witness what others think of him—and be unable to interject. Today, I will witness firsthand the seeds you have sown thus far. It will show me who you truly are, more than any noble deed ever could."*

In the far cavern, his team dusted themselves off and surveyed their surroundings. None of them looked his way, and as far as he could tell, they couldn't see him.

A shadow darted past a hole in the cave wall, along the ceiling. He squinted as another darted past, and another, but he couldn't make sense of the movement.

Until, of course, one of the shadows stepped into the light. The man dressed in black furs—the one who had stood outside the throne room when Dahlia ordered tea—now waited in a secret passage, hidden high in the cave walls. The stranger frowned, glaring down at Connor's team, before disappearing again into the flickering shadows slowly filtering into position.

"Two hundred archers." Dahlia took a settling breath, and her eyes roved across the walls in the next room. "Completely invisible from the ground floor."

"Dahlia, stop this at once," Connor warned. "If you hurt them—"

"I won't," she interrupted. "Not unless they give me reason."

"What are you going to do?" He pulled again on the arms holding him in the stream, his dread burning away to fury as he was left wondering how this test of hers would end. "If those soldiers do anything to any one of them, I'll slit your throat, royalty or no!"

She bristled, and for a moment, she watched him with that same, cold expression she had worn the moment he entered the throne room.

"What would you do to save them, Wraithblade?" the Antiquity asked.

"Burn your swamp to the ground!" He ripped free from one of the clusters of arms, only for dozens more to grab his leg and anchor him back into the river.

A soft chuckle rumbled through the air, light and airy, but Dahlia's eyes widened with horror at what he had said. She whistled, and the stomp of a dozen men's boots on the stone followed as more soldiers funneled out of the tunnel she had used to enter.

The soldiers surrounded him, and some even jumped onto the stepping-stones he'd used to get closer to the bank. They aimed their crossbows at his head, each of them meeting his eye with stern, unwavering glares as he stared each of them down, one by one.

"Try it," he dared them.

"Don't fight," Dahlia warned from the bank. She clasped her hands before her, even as her expression softened. "Not even you can stop this now, Wraithblade. We have to finish what we started."

He shifted the full fury of his glare toward her and balled his hands into fists. He wanted to rip his way out of this river. He wanted to break necks and set fire to the bogs. He wanted nothing more than to kick down the wall separating him from his team, if that was what it took to save them.

"Death won't stop me," he warned her. "And you don't want to be my enemy, woman."

Despite the soldiers surrounding him, and despite the ancient magic of a goddess literally rooting him in place, the fallen princess swallowed hard with fear at the prospect of what he might do.

"Your quarrel is with me, not her." The Antiquity's calm and serene voice clashed with the chaos building in both caverns. *"As for your team, I merely set*

up the test. It is up to them what happens next. We will watch what they do when they think you cannot see them. We can hear everything, from this room—even the whispers they think are secret. Are you prepared to face the truth?"

Connor let out a furious growl and gritted his teeth, but he didn't reply.

Magnuson! the wraith shouted in his head. *Shut your Fates-damned mouth. You're making this worse.*

Eyes shut, Connor finally took a settling breath and forced himself to be still.

"Nocturne," Quinn said from the other cavern, her voice tense and wary as she stared up at the great dragon. "What is this place?"

"It has begun." The goddess's voice echoed in Connor's head. *"Let us watch, Wraithblade, and listen. You will discover how worthy you are of that which you desire most."*

Tense, furious, and unable to move, Connor stared out at the team he would murder the gods to protect.

Now, he would see if they truly felt the same.

CHAPTER SIXTY-TWO

QUINN

"I have had ENOUGH!"

Quinn's furious shout echoed through the massive cavern. As she waited for something—anything—to happen, her voice slowly faded into the crash of cascading waterfall in the corner. Soot singed the opposite wall, where her fireball had slammed into the glistening stone. She frowned, brows furrowed as she studied the towering room, but she had never seen anything like this before.

It was as if the entire cavern had been carved from a single diamond.

Murdoc groaned and sat up, his legs spread wide as he brushed pebbles from his hair. "I need a raise."

"Stop whining." Sophia pushed herself to her feet and stretched out her left shoulder as she scanned the cavern around them. "None of us get paid."

As Murdoc jumped to his feet, Quinn tried to tune them out as she studied the cavern for signs of life. Aside from Nocturne, who still sat behind her with his eyes closed, they were alone. The waterfall crashed into the narrow river that split the cave in two, and mist rolled from the milk-white waves lapping against the hand-carved bank.

A face appeared in the river's current, and a brief pang of surprise hit her right in the chest. Once she took a step closer to inspect it, however, the face vanished into the waves.

"Nocturne, what is this place?" she asked.

The dragon didn't answer. She looked at him over her shoulder to find the regal creature staring at the twin moons through a hole in the ceiling, and he let out a scratchy moan that reminded her of Blaze's wistful sighs.

"Nocturne." Her body tense and ready for another battle, Quinn set her hand on the hilt of her sword in case this was another trick of the bogs. Though they had left the misty woodland, she had no proof its magic had faded.

If anything, this new place set her more on edge than the forest.

"I've had enough of this hellhole." Sophia brushed off the skirts of her dress as she glared at the walls.

Though she never took her eyes off the dragon sitting with his back to her, Quinn nodded. "For once, we can agree on something."

"Oh, I get it." Murdoc picked his sword off the ground as he gaped at the towering walls around them. "We're dead, aren't we? That's what this is, isn't it? We died out there in that fog."

"No." Nocturne's voice echoed through the cavern. After the long stretch of his silence, the vibrations of even a single word from the legendary creature sang like a gong in the depths of Quinn's soul.

"Then where are we?" Sophia asked through gritted teeth. "I don't have an ounce of patience left for this place."

"This is one of Saldia's in-betweens." The dragon prince spoke calmly, without so much as a twitch of his tail, and remained perfectly immobile as he stared up at the moons. "The Blood Bogs exist in two worlds, yet belong to neither. It is a place of transition."

"How do you know that?" Quinn's intuition buzzed with foreboding.

This had to be another trick. Another *trap*.

"Do you know how Saldian magic works?" Nocturne tilted his head toward them, his eyes black as a river rock and soothing as the midnight sky.

Murdoc took a wary step backward, apparently sensing something off with the beast as well. He stiffened and held his sword in front of him, ready for a fight. To his left, Sophia curled her fingers, and the first hints of frost crept across her knuckles as she prepared for battle as well.

When no one answered him, Nocturne's gaze shifted to Quinn. "Do you?"

"Of course I know how magic works." She tilted her head in confusion as she tried to figure out where he was going with this. "I've made hundreds of potions in my life. The spellgust—"

"Not the spellgust." Nocturne shook his massive head in disappointment. "Have you never wondered where spellgust gets its power?"

"It simply is." Quinn shrugged. "Same as the color of the sky, or Saldia's twin moons. It is and always has been."

"It is more nuanced than that." The regal creature returned his attention to the glowing pockmarked orbs in the sky. "Magic comes from Death. From His domain. That is why these hosts of the in-between do not abide by the laws of Saldian magic. In these places, with Death's power, we can see so much more than what lies before us."

"What the hell is wrong with you?" Murdoc frowned and craned his head to get a good look at the dragon's face. "What does any of this have to do with finding Connor and getting out of here?"

"See for yourself." The dragon's wing stretched out from his side, and with the gesture, flashes of color snapped across the glimmering walls. Red and black streaks blended together, racing across every surface, and Quinn squinted as she tried to make sense of the cascading lights dancing in the depths of the diamond walls.

Fire.

Still wary of the milky white stream ambling through the cavern behind her, she took several steps backward and spun in a circle, not altogether certain of what she was witnessing. The flames stretched in every direction, on every wall, but no heat rolled off of what should have been a bonfire hot enough to cook them all. There was no crackle. No sparks. No fizzling pops. It raged, safe behind the stone, without a sound.

Sophia summoned ice into her palm and hurled it at the nearest flickering flame, but nothing changed. Even as the frost spread across the stone, the fires raged on, untouched and unaffected by her magic.

The necromancer settled into her stance, scowling in frustration as she watched her ice magic do nothing to impede the flames. "What is this?"

"A memory," the dragon answered. "The Blood Bogs are more than just a forest. It is a kingdom in its own right, separate even from Freymoor."

"Kingdoms have kings," Quinn said warily as she once more scanned the cavern for any hint of someone listening in on their conversation. "Who exactly rules this wasteland?"

"Show respect," the dragon chided. "This is the domain of the past. Of the truth. I have spoken with the goddess of this place—She Who Knows. The daughter of Death. She is the keeper of all that has happened to her people, and she collects their memories on their way out of this life. You are among them, now. We all are—from the moment we stepped into the bogs, a part of us belonged to her."

"I didn't agree to that!" Murdoc snapped.

"Nor did I," Quinn said tersely.

Nocturne didn't answer.

On the crystalline walls, silhouettes stepped into view amidst the painfully silent fires. The shadows stalked through the flame, and for a time, they were nothing but figures marching across the faceted stone. With time, however, a few of them stepped into the light. Men in dented helmets raised their bloodstained swords and shouted noiselessly into the blaze, at each other, before they charged. Swords hit. Helmets flew into the air with trails of red droplets flying behind them. Bodies crumpled to the ground, and sparks flashed as the quiet war raged on.

In the sky above the bonfires, a dragon soared through the memory. A man stood on its back, nothing but a silhouette backed by a blood-red sky as he raised his sword above the fray.

She squinted at the distant figure in disbelief. "Is that—"

"—the Wraith King," Nocturne answered.

"How…" She gaped at the memory, still not fully willing to believe what was right before her.

The mists had tried to trick them already, time and time again. It seemed unwise to simply believe them now.

"A young woman from ancient Freymoor, caught in the fray," Nocturne answered. "We are witnessing her most terrifying moment, just as she herself saw it."

On the wall, a young man dove through a flame and fell onto his back. His helmet rolled across the ground as his sword slid across the slick grass and disappeared into the nearest patch of fire. With his helmet gone, Quinn could see the soot-smeared detail on his young face. Barely eighteen, the boy gaped in horror after his lost weapon as a second figure jumped through the fires behind him. The second warrior, clad from head to toe in thick plates of black armor, raised his sword. Unarmed and pinned, with nowhere to go, the boy raised his hands over his head and mouthed words Quinn couldn't hear.

Begging for his life, no doubt.

"Stop this at once," Quinn demanded.

The second soldier drove his sword into the boy's stomach, and Quinn grimaced. She looked away, unable to help a long-dead boy, and she tried to bury the image of something she couldn't undo.

It didn't work.

Images of war and death surrounded her. Every wall played a different memory from the battle, from a different vantage. Some men crawled backward across the ground as they tried desperately to escape the warriors in black that hacked their way through every living thing. Others ran desperately through a burning field, racing toward a forest shrouded in fog.

Everywhere she looked, someone died. Men lost their heads or fell backward into the broiling bonfires of a lawless battleground, and never once did the destruction cease.

Even when she closed her eyes, the seared images replayed, again and again.

"Nocturne, enough of this!" She cautiously circled the massive dragon until she stood under his head, glaring up at him. "Explain yourself at once. You're talking like the mists, for the Fates' sake. You were supposed to wait in the forest, not join—"

"Do not chastise me." His massive black eyes darted toward her, and his horns glowed briefly gold. "I came here to learn the truth, and I've found it. This is the legacy of the Wraith King. As a man or as a simmering soul, he has always been a demon. He cannot change. Look at what this man has done, Quinn Starling." Dark smoke rolled from his nose as he scanned the walls around them. "Look at it!"

She didn't. She kept her gaze trained on Nocturne as he studied the hell and destruction replaying across the walls around them. His low growl filled the cavern, and another ribbon of golden light snaked across his scales.

"You're afraid," she said quietly, too softly for anyone but Nocturne to hear.

He snorted, and another wave of charred smoke hit her in the face. "And you are not?!"

"What did the mists do to you?" she asked, refusing to rise to the bait. "What did you hear it say?"

"The goddess shared many memories," he answered. "In the fog, we see the truth in ourselves, and I have witnessed the full legacy Connor inherited. I've seen the histories. I've seen the death. For every host that has fused with this abomination of a man, this is what they all become. What makes you think our friend will be immune? How do you know we will not lose him, too?"

Our friend.

Quinn flinched at the word, surprised by it. As she further studied the dragon's face, however, his strange behavior finally made sense.

Nocturne didn't *want* to kill Connor. He had never wanted that. He wanted to believe Connor would overcome, that he would be the first in history to control the Wraith King's bloodlust and succeed where every other host had failed.

Everything the dragon had said so far, everything he'd sought to uncover, even this hunt for a failsafe—it had all been done out of fear.

He didn't want to believe the bloody wars being relived on these walls could really happen, not to Connor. But as Quinn watched the battlefield unfold before them all, even she couldn't deny that it was possible.

After everything he'd done for her, and after all they had endured together, she hated herself for even entertaining the thought—but only a fool would ignore such a potent threat.

No living being could see the future, and they had no way to be certain of what would come.

If Connor would eventually succumb, like all the others, she had an obligation to stop him before he burned the world. To save him from himself before he became the darkness he so hated.

Quinn squeezed her eyes shut, and her knuckles popped as she clenched her fists. At every step of the way, Connor had proven himself to be different than the rest. At nearly every opportunity, he had chosen the higher ground.

But can he sustain it? she asked herself. *Can he resist the Wraith King's darkness forever?*

Internally, the war raged on—with herself, with her doubt, and with all the ways she had played into others' hands over the years.

She had been conned before, same as Nocturne. She had trusted the wrong man, and the consequences had nearly destroyed her.

Something darted through the blood-red sky on the diamond walls surrounding the cavern. Just wings, at first, and a distant tail, but as it came closer, the firelight reflected across its beautiful golden scales.

Another dragon, this one eons old and nothing but a memory.

A massive lance shot through the air and speared it through its chest. The dragon fell from the heavens. Its face contorted with misery and pain, though they couldn't hear its roar, and it fell to the earth and the raging inferno below. It thrashed, its tail and neck writhing in agony. In the moment before it disappeared into the fires, Quinn caught sight of its face, as its glowing red eyes matched the sky.

Nocturne snarled and jumped to his feet, and his wings spread wide as he seethed at the memory. "War. Betrayal. Blood. Death. My brothers, turned feral and broken. This devastation follows the simmering souls throughout the ages, every time, and I fear that Connor is doomed to live the same life. Look at the war brewing at the mere mention of his name. Look at the blood that has already spilled. It has already begun."

"Get ahold of yourself!" Murdoc shouted. "Why are you saying these things? You let him augment you, for the Fates' sake!"

Without even glancing his way, Quinn shook her head. "It was a precaution."

As she stared up at the carnal chaos on the walls around them, her words echoed in the silent air. The other three looked her way, but she didn't bother meeting their gazes. She could only stare at the war above her and wonder if Nocturne was right.

"A precaution against what, exactly?" Murdoc's tone took on a deadly edge.

Quinn met his furious glare and tapped her fingertips against the hilt of her own sword in a silent warning for him to stand down. "To keep watch over someone he fears."

Sophia snorted derisively. "He's a dragon. What does he have to fear?"

"Much," Nocturne interjected. "I fear the Wraithblade's power. I fear what he can become if left unchecked."

The flickering fires on the walls faded away, and mists replaced the flames. A silhouette appeared within the fog, the flames in her sword casting an orange glow on the haze around her. As her boot passed through the edge of the mist, she raised her Firesword and finally stepped into view.

Quinn's eyes went wide as she saw herself. The scowl. The skeptical tilt of her head. The steady eyes, focused and furious, as she stared at the memory's owner. But the only person who could've seen her like this was—

"Otmund," she whispered.

"His final moments," Nocturne confirmed.

In the memory, Quinn wrinkled her nose in disgust. A fist holding a glowing green dagger swung at her face, and she grabbed the wrist with her free hand. The scene shifted and shook as Otmund fell backward onto his ass, and she stiffened as she watched his final moments through his eyes.

Connor stepped from the fog beside her, and he watched her with unfettered hatred. Though she knew he was staring at Otmund, it still felt as though his murderous glare were focused on her.

As though he wanted *her* dead.

In the memory, Connor's mouth moved noiselessly as he spoke words the walls couldn't convey. He kicked Otmund in the face, his movement eerily similar to the armored warriors from the first memory, and Quinn reflexively held her own jaw as she closed her eyes.

"This," Nocturne said. "Is this who you three will follow to hell? Because he will take you there."

"Look, you scaly idiot," Sophia snapped. "This has—"

"Take care in how you address me, sorceress." Nocturne growled, and the warble echoed through the cavern.

"No. This has gone far enough." The necromancer waved away the dragon's warning with a flick of her slender wrist. "I can't believe we're even discussing this. You think I would be here if he was a normal man? If he was a coward or a warlord like all the others? He kept his bargain to me, even when it would've served him best not to keep his word."

Quinn crossed her arms and paced the length of the strange river as she tried to ignore them. Instead, she watched the ever-changing memories playing out across the walls, waiting each time to see what the bogs would show her next. Otmund's memory faded, swallowed by midnight shadows, and various scenes flashed across the walls. A woman running from a blood-soaked madman. Connor, wearing a bloodstained scarf across his nose and mouth, driving his sword into a man's stomach. Blightwolves darting through the underbrush, getting closer as a young woman ran for her life.

"...and this isn't him!" Murdoc's furious shout snapped Quinn out of her thoughts. "You haven't been with us long, but I figured even you knew him better than that by now. He saved my life. He gave me purpose again. He trusted me with the Wraith King's secret even though I was a Blackguard! He's one of the few good men left on this continent, and I will not let you stain his name!"

"You see what he is in this moment," Nocturne said sadly. "Do not let it blind you to what he can become."

"We don't have time for this nonsense!" Sophia's voice echoed off the walls. "We need to find him and get out of here. This place is a lost cause. The Soulsprite can't possibly be worth what we've already endured."

"I don't believe this." Murdoc gestured across the cavern, ignoring Sophia's concerns. "Quinn, he's saved your life twice, now. Are you going to say *anything*?"

She didn't reply. She could only stare at the carnage flashing across the walls around them as Connor stalked through a midnight forest, soaked in other men's blood. The cloth hiding most of his face only brought more attention to his eyes as they narrowed, focused on his next target. He raised his sword, and she stood eerily still as she relived the final moments of whomever he was about to kill.

"Why will none of you listen?" Nocturne snarled. "The Wraith King

ENSLAVED MY FELLOW DRAGONS, AND I WILL NOT PERMIT HIM TO DO IT AGAIN!"

Ah.

Now, it all made sense.

Quinn sighed and pinched the bridge of her nose. She turned her back on the memories and faced the fracturing remnants of Connor's team as they faced off without him here to keep them together. Sophia stood with her hands in front of her, frost already inching across her palms, and Murdoc lifted his sword in warning as he glared up at the dragon.

"This was never about Connor," she said quietly. "You want to trust him, but you can never bring yourself to trust the Wraith King. If the ghoul were gone, you wouldn't have a doubt in your mind about Connor's intentions."

Nocturne's head snapped toward her, and though the other two flinched, she remained rooted in place, shoulders relaxed and calm despite the massive dragon glaring at her with all the fury of hell.

"Say it," she demanded—calm, quiet, and unfazed by the legendary beast before her.

A plume of smoke rolled past her face as he huffed indignantly, but he shut his jet-black eyes and sighed.

"YES," he finally admitted. "I HAVE IGNORED MY BETTER JUDGEMENT BEFORE, AND THE DRAGONLANDS PAID DEARLY FOR MY MISTAKE. I CANNOT AFFORD TO BE WRONG AGAIN."

Before Quinn could reply, the creak of tightening arrow strings cut through the echoing roar of Nocturne's voice.

The Starling warrior drew her sword on impulse as she searched for where it had originated. By the roof of the cavern, hundreds of arrows pointed down at them through thin gaps in the rock she hadn't even noticed before. The arrows circled the cavern, roughly shoulder width apart, and her throat tightened with concern.

Their exit had disappeared. If those arrows fired, there would be nowhere to hide.

"This keeps getting better," Murdoc grumbled.

Quinn's fingers wrapped tightly around *Aurora's* hilt, and she nodded. "We really are lucky, aren't we?"

CHAPTER SIXTY-THREE
QUINN

"*Leave.*" The whisper echoed through the cavern until it sounded like several voices overlapping one another. The sensation sent an unnerving shiver down her back, as though the voices could crawl into her brain and live there.

Despite her best efforts, Quinn shuddered.

"Happily!" Murdoc quipped. "As soon as we find Connor, there's nothing we'd love more than to leave your precious little hellscape."

Sophia elbowed him hard in the side, and he grunted in pain.

"Please," he added with barely concealed irritation.

"*No,*" the whisper answered.

"Then it looks like we're at an impasse." The creak of skin on leather filled the silence as Murdoc's gaze swept the line of archers.

"We've played your game." Quinn's powerful voice dominated the cavern, and her nails dug into her palm as her body stiffened. "Show us where he is!"

"*Very well.*"

On the opposite bank of the narrow river that split the cavern in two, the sheen within the glimmering diamond wall faded until it was as clear as glass. Flashes of light shimmered within it, like a nearly perfect gemstone.

Through the iridescent wall, Connor stood knee-deep in a river not unlike theirs, though it cut through the cavern in the opposite direction. His hands rested on the back of his head as thirty archers surrounded him, each spaced perfectly apart so that every arrow would hit its mark with flawless precision. The soldiers all glared at him, unblinking, but Connor stared dead ahead—at Quinn.

As he scowled at her, they all waited with tense unease to see what would happen next.

The river sloshed around his legs, but the water didn't flow with the rhythmic pattern of a normal current. Quinn examined the milky white waves from afar, and as she stared at them, two hands made of the same white magic as the water snatched at his clothes, dragging him a little deeper into the stream.

Dismayed and disgusted, her heart fluttered in her chest. The bogs had called on the dead themselves to keep the Wraithblade pinned, and his ghoul was nowhere to be seen.

As Quinn watched the spectacle through the clear sheet of stone, Dahlia stepped from the shadows beside the Wraithblade. The fallen princess crossed her arms, her eyes narrowing as she studied them from the safety of the next room.

"Figures," Quinn fumed. "Freymoor played us."

Sophia growled in frustration. "Those two-timing bastards!"

"Sophia, dear," Murdoc whispered as he cast another glance around the archers. "How many of those do you think you can take?"

"Don't," Quinn quietly warned.

"You and your scaly friend can sit this one out." The necromancer glared at her over one shoulder. "We're not leaving Connor behind."

In Quinn's stunned surprise, she could only stare at the necromancer in disbelief. In her years at Lunestone, she had witnessed dozens of interrogations that betrayed the breadth and horror of Nethervale and the lives its necromancers lived. When she was little, the soldiers' confessions of slitting sleeping throats and the near-endless homicides in that swampland tower had given her nightmares. Survivors of the Nethervale Academy—those who inevitably became Nyx's elite soldiers—couldn't trust anyone else enough to have a friend, much less be loyal to anyone but themselves.

In Nethervale, devotion got people killed.

"We have to be smart about this," Murdoc whispered. "If you take the left row—"

"It's not enough," Sophia hissed back.

As the two of them deliberated, Quinn sighed in frustration and tuned them out. Their plan didn't matter. With only one magic user—even if that woman was a Nethervale elite—anything they did would fail.

Quinn again met Connor's gaze, and he watched her with that same intense expression he'd worn back in the Ancient Woods when they first met. Since then, he'd had several chances to be rid of her—someone who had relentlessly hunted him across the continent.

And yet, he hadn't taken any of them.

In the next room, Dahlia raised one hand. The archers around Connor tightened their holds on their crossbows, and his furious glare shifted to the nearest soldier's face.

Quinn's hand instinctively flew to the hilt of her sword, and she had to stop herself from drawing it so that she could first come up with a plan. A real one, before tensions got worse.

Every instinct told her to intercede. To stop this before something terrible happened. To defend Connor, same as the others, even though he embodied the darkness she had sworn to exterminate when she had knelt before her father and taken the Lightseer oath to earn her Firesword *Aurora*.

A lifetime of obedience to the Lightseers had imprinted ideals within her that were hard to ignore.

To her left, Nocturne's eyes burned amber. He snarled, the low growl filling the cavern. This situation clearly left him on edge, too. Like her, he wanted to intercede.

He just didn't know which move to make.

To her right, the necromancer and the former Blackguard debated their options in scratchy whispers, and it all seemed too surreal. Both of them had been in combat, and both had to know this would be suicide.

Yet neither of them seemed phased. They would truly die for him.

It didn't make sense for a Nethervale elite soldier to sacrifice herself to save someone with power she should, by all accounts, want for herself. A Blackguard soldier, even a former one, shouldn't have been willing to face an army far larger than a magicless scoundrel could possibly survive, all to defend the sort of magic his brotherhood had dedicated their lives to exterminating from the land.

Nocturne lowered his head until his eye was level with hers. She cast him an irritated sidelong glare before returning her attention to the brewing battle.

Deep in her soul, something snapped.

It was rough. Violent.

Painful.

Quinn held her hand to her chest as her pulse settled. The rush of pain slowly faded, and with it went her fears. Her doubts. Her uncertainty.

Her head cleared in a rush, and for the first time in years, she felt only the ice-cold clarity of what she knew had to be done.

Quinn Starling would protect the Wraithblade—with her life, if need be.

Options buzzed in the back of her mind as her defensive training took over. To salvage this, she needed to come up with a *damn* good plan, and she had to do it quickly. If possible, she needed to convince Nocturne to help.

"Hmm," the dragon said with the same gentle tone he had used back in the forest to mask his powerful voice. "That expression, that resolve—you have made a choice, and I must know what it is."

"You need to be a little more specific." Her bicep flexed, straining against her jacket as she scanned the walls for weaknesses. "My place in this battle? In this war?"

"In this world."

Her jaw tensed, and she looked the dragon dead in the eye.

"...agreed?" Sophia whispered. She smiled up at Murdoc, a hint of sadness in her expression.

Just a hint, but there all the same.

"Agreed," he whispered back with a gentle smile.

Quinn shook her head. "Look, Nocturne, this isn't the time—"

"It is the only time," he interrupted. "You saw through me, and I cannot lie to you or to myself. I respect him. If we can save him, if we can keep him on the path to protect the greater good, I will defend him to the ends of time. I must simply know if you and I can stop him, should the time come. I need to know you're willing to do what must be done, however devastating it will be for us both."

She wanted to tell him whatever he wanted her to say, just to make him help, but she couldn't lie—not to him, and not to herself.

Though furious at her father for what he had done to her and all the ways he'd manipulated her, she still didn't know if she could kill him. To face hell at someone's side made them family, and Connor had done so much for her and those around him. He had a good heart, and deep down, he was a good man.

If the time came and he lost himself to the Wraith King's greed, she didn't know if she would be able to see what he had become—just what he had been to her.

"It won't happen," she finally said under her breath. "He's a folk hero, for the Fates' sake! He's saved countless lives."

"But the death surrounding him—"

"You and I both know heroes don't have clean hands," she interjected. "Did the goddess show you the memories of the people I've killed? For all I know, I'm worse than he is."

"You are not."

"Of course I am." Furious, she glared at the dragon beside her. At how naïve someone with so much power could be—but then again, the same had been said about her. "I've assassinated hundreds of people, all in the name of the Lightseers. I took orders from my father and never questioned him because I believed he knew better than I ever could. Looking back, I've shattered lives, Nocturne. I've destroyed families. Who knows the depths of destruction I've caused, all while believing I had done the world good?"

Just out of earshot, Sophia stretched her fingers wide. Her focus swept across the rows of archers above. Frost coated her palm, and she took her first slow and careful step toward the wall dividing them all from Connor.

"Stay where you are!" a man's voice shouted. "Don't move!"

Sophia ignored him.

Quinn bristled, but it couldn't be stopped now. The more she studied the scene, the more arrowheads she discovered, at least a hundred strong. Maybe two hundred.

With the bows all strung and the archers at the ready, she needed Nocturne's help to stand a chance of salvaging this.

"Look, Nocturne, I need your help to win this," she confessed in a hushed tone. "Back at the treehouse, you asked me why I was there. Why I'd let him capture me. Well, here's your answer—I did it so that I could study him up close. I wanted to finally know who he is and what he wants. You might have some magical insight to the truth, Nocturne, but I've never had the luxury of knowing when someone is lying to me. I've been played, manipulated, and lied to all my life. I don't trust easily, but I've studied him longer than you have. I can let a man's actions speak for him, and he controls the Wraith King. Can't you see it? Can't you *feel* it?"

"Who controls whom?" Nocturne huffed. "Can't you see where his actions have led us? He returned to the Wraith King's home. He came here to steal an artifact from a goddess, all because the ghoul told him to do it."

"And what did the Wraith King tell him to do with you?" she countered.

Nocturne sighed in defeat, but he didn't reply.

Murdoc trekked after Sophia, and together, they reached the narrow river separating the two halves of the cavern. In the next room over, Dahlia's finger twitched as she studied the two people walking closer.

No ruler would let a threat get close to her. Those two had just seconds to live.

"Final warning!" a soldier shouted from above.

Furious that it had come to this, Quinn drummed her fingers against *Aurora's* hilt. All that damn necromancer had to do was listen and wait long enough for Quinn to convince Nocturne to intercede.

Nocturne studied her face, waiting to see what she would do. He could stop this in an instant—and, hell, maybe he *would*—but he was cutting it frightfully close.

On the opposite side of the cavern, Sophia turned her palms toward the ceiling and summoned two glowing blue balls of light into her palms. The ice shimmered like winter lights in a frigid sky.

The rushing water nearly drowned out the twang of an arrow sailing through the air. It had begun, and they were all going to die.

It infuriated Quinn, really, how much she cared about a necromancer's life.

She grabbed the Volt around her neck, and the tight chain pulled against her skin as she fired a single blast of lightning at the arrow. The bolt of sizzling light sailed over Sophia's head and collided with the arrow in the seconds before it pierced Sophia's skull. The shuddering boom from her pendant rocked the cavern, and even Sophia looked over her shoulder in numb shock as the cave went deadly silent.

For the first time since she had entered, Nocturne took a step. The floor shook with the weight of his massive body, and he stepped in front of Quinn, blocking her from moving forward. His massive head lowered until his towering face blocked her view of nearly everything else in the cavern. A blast of hot breath shot from his nose as he stared her down, his eyes glowing brilliantly amber, and only the crashing waterfall filled the silence that followed.

Behind him, in the stretch of cavern she could no longer see, footsteps echoed across the floor. The creak of tightening arrow strings and the muttered commands of a soldier blended with the cavern's thundering waterfall.

"Uh, Quinn?" Murdoc asked from somewhere beyond the dragon. "We could use more of that all-powerful Starling help right about now."

She was out of time, and frankly, so was Nocturne.

"You will stand aside," Quinn demanded of the dragon. She drew her Firesword and glowered at the regal beast as flames erupted along *Aurora's* blade. "Connor won't die today, even if I have to cut you down to save him."

The legendary creature's eyes narrowed in warning, and a soft clicking filled the air as he growled.

"You say you fear what he might become, but look at who you are, right now," Quinn admonished. "Look at the power you have over him in this moment, and look at what you're doing with it. Out of *fear*."

The predator's clicking trill slowly faded. Seconds later, the growl stopped as well.

And yet, his eyes never wavered as he listened, breathless, for the answer she still hadn't given him.

"As a Lightseer, I saw only good and evil." Quinn walked closer, daring the dragon to act, utterly lost in the breathtaking *freedom* as she finally broke through the chains that had shackled her to her old life.

To the Lightseers.

To her father.

"Tagging along with this group of ruffians shattered me," she said, her voice dark and deadly. "But I'm grateful. I finally found the line no good man crosses, and it's so simple it hurts—leave behind a better world when you die. That's all we have to do, and that's all Connor has done."

She closed the final step toward Nocturne, and a rush of smoke hit her square in the chest as she glared him down.

"And should he cross that line," she added in a grating whisper, knowing full well the dragon would see through any lie she told him. "If he becomes the Wraith King, like you fear? Then you and I will kill him. Together."

"Stay right where you are!" the officer shouted from somewhere above.

"You are bound," Nocturne warned. "It is an oath that cannot be broken. A burden you will carry to your dying day."

"Fine," she fiercely snapped, furious it had come to this. "Now help me or step aside!"

"Fire!" the commander shouted.

A jolt of dread shot clear to Quinn's toes, and she sprang into action before Nocturne had time to move. With her boots thudding against his skull, she scaled the dragon's head even as he raised it, and she ran along his neck as a black haze of arrows sailed toward Murdoc and Sophia.

Her sword wouldn't help her now, and she sheathed it as she ran.

With a brief glance, she confirmed that Dahlia had not yet released the arrows keeping Connor rooted in place. The Wraithblade watched in horror, the hands of the dead grabbing his legs and rooting him in place. He fought against them, ripping arms out of the river even as more reached for his limbs to hold him still. Muscles flexed as he fought to get free despite the arrows pointed at his head, he shouted wordlessly from behind the glass wall.

As Quinn leapt off of Nocturne's long neck, Sophia hurled a glittering ball of ice into the air.

Quinn's stomach churned as she fell toward the ground, but she summoned the air into her palms. Though she preferred fire, flame carried too much risk against arrows. She had to use her Airdrift augmentation to disrupt their trajectory.

As her fingers spread wide, a breeze that obeyed only her churned through the cave. Coils of dust swirled against the rocky wall, and her fiery hair whipped past her face in its torrent.

Unlike fire, however, air resisted control, and it always tested for weaknesses in its master's aim. As the air challenged her, Quinn gritted her teeth with the effort of controlling such a massive gale.

With a strangled scream of effort, her boots hit the ground, and she raised her hands above her head.

The gust shot into the barrage of arrows, dispersing Sophia's frost magic across them in a crashing burst of glowing blue light. The crackle of splintering ice mingled with the whistle of metal through the air, and the black haze shot violently upward. Some of the arrows embedded in the ceiling, while most hit the far wall harmlessly. They rained to the ground, out of range of their small band, and gathered in a pile on the floor.

Quinn bolted forward and leapt over the white river. She landed hard and rolled, still scanning the walls for another attack, and she jumped to her feet with ease.

Sophia gawked at her, and Murdoc raised one eyebrow in surprise as she joined them. Quinn drew her sword once more, and *Aurora's* flame ignited across the flawless blade as the last of the arrows fell harmlessly to the rocky terrain.

In the deafening silence that followed, she stood between Sophia and Murdoc, ready to take on an army if that was what it took to escape this place. Though she glared at Dahlia through the clear diamond wall, her companions still gaped at her in her peripheral vision.

"Stop this lunacy at *once!*" Her booming voice echoed through the cavern, just as powerful as the dragon's. "Put your weapons down now, or you will go through me. This time, I know exactly where you're hiding!"

Though Dahlia met her furious glare with one of her own, the woman's lips twitched—just once, but it betrayed a hint of doubt.

A hint of *fear.*

The cavern shook under Nocturne's feet as he joined them. Though Quinn didn't look back, sparks skittered over his faded reflection in the glass wall between them and Dahlia.

"*Nocturne, my dear,*" the grating whisper asked. "*Have you made your choice?*"

"I HAVE, GODDESS," the dragon announced. "YOU WARNED ME TO CONSIDER THE LEGACY HE INHERITED. I HAVE CONSIDERED, AND I HAVE CHOSEN. WE WILL LEAVE WITH THE WRAITHBLADE."

"*You are certain?*"

Quinn fought off a shudder as the words burrowed into her ear.

"I AM."

A soft sigh rushed past them, as quiet and soothing as a breeze through a forest, and it had a strange sense of longing attached to it. The emotion swam through Quinn's chest, as furious and raw as though it were her own.

Peace.

Hope.

Relief.

The clear wall between them shattered like glass, and Quinn summoned her Shieldspar augmentation to protect their small band. The dome of crisscrossing light sprang to life across her forearm, and she raised it over her head as the broken shards fell to the ground. Murdoc and Sophia ducked beneath the shield just as the first shard hit, but it splattered harmlessly across the woven light, like rain.

"Stand down," Dahlia ordered. "All of you."

The archers standing beside Connor lowered their crossbows and returned their arrows to the quivers on their backs. The milky white arms protruding from the water released their hold on his legs, and he let out a sigh of relief as he rolled onto the bank. Water dripped from his soaked pant legs.

Lying on his back, staring up at the ceiling, he rubbed his face as his chest rose and fell. Murdoc and Sophia bolted toward him without sparing a glance back at Quinn, but she waited with Nocturne.

After all, this wasn't her reunion, and she wasn't part of his team.

"How about you get off your ass, huh?" Murdoc grinned and offered the Wraithblade a hand.

The man chuckled and took it.

Sophia glared at Dahlia as she walked past. "And they call *me* a sorceress."

Instead of returning a stinging quip of her own, the fallen princess merely wrinkled her nose in disgust.

But Quinn didn't move. She could only watch the reunion from afar, still an outsider.

Always alone.

As she studied Dahlia's features, something Nocturne had said back in the Ancient Woods now made perfect sense. Even the gods feared the Wraithblade's power, and every muscle in her body tensed with the sheer weight of what that truly meant.

That is what I see in you, the dragon had said. *I see enough power, between the two of us, to stop even Connor Magnuson.*

"May the day never come," Nocturne said quietly.

Quinn let out a shaky sigh. "Agreed."

CHAPTER SIXTY-FOUR

CONNOR

Connor grabbed Murdoc's hand and stood, chest still heaving. He closed his eyes as relief flooded through him.

It was finally over.

As the Freymoor archers retreated down the long tunnel Dahlia had used to enter the cavern, Murdoc grabbed his shoulder and pulled him into a tight hug. Connor clapped the man on the back and let out a slow breath, still not entirely able to believe they were done with the bogs. Sophia stood a short ways off, her arms crossed, but her red lips twisted into a small smile.

"Thank you," he said quietly to them both.

"Right." Sophia looked at her nails and cleared her throat awkwardly. "Don't get used to us saving your ass, Wraithblade."

He grinned. "Noted."

Through the corner of his eye, he caught Dahlia watching him with a stiff expression he couldn't read. She stood by the water's edge, while Nocturne and Quinn remained rooted in place. Neither of them had moved since the wall fell. The dragon prince watched him in silence, those deep black eyes seeing more than Connor could even know, and the regal creature's neck curved in a graceful arch. Beside the dragon, Quinn sheathed her sword and hooked her thumb on her belt loop as she watched the reunion from afar.

His smile fell. After everything he'd heard tonight, he would have to have a little chat with them later.

"It is time, Connor Magnuson." Yet again, the Antiquity's voice echoed through the cavern, everywhere and nowhere all at once. *"We have much to discuss."*

To his left, a cluster of vines that had thus far remained in place now slithered across the wall. As they retreated, they revealed yet another tunnel carved into the stone.

"We're not done." He cracked his knuckles in warning as he stared up at the cave ceiling. "We're missing one."

"The ghoul shall remain where he is until you understand what it means for me to give you the Soulsprite. He can hear us, but I will not permit him to speak until we are done."

A muscle twitched in Connor's jaw as he tried and failed to find the goddess's face among the roots along the cavern walls. "I passed your tests. That makes us allies, and allies don't hold each other hostage."

"Please, Connor," Dahlia said gently. She gestured toward the tunnel with an open palm and waited, shoulders stiffening, for him to walk ahead of her. "Only you and I can see what's in here."

His eyes narrowed in suspicion. It seemed like a perfect way to isolate and trap him—except they had already done that, several times over. Even with every opportunity to kill him, they'd kept him alive.

"Are you insane?" Murdoc scoffed. "After everything you did, you think we would actually stay here and—"

"It's alright," Connor said.

The former Blackguard let out a long grumble, and in his escaping frustration, it briefly sounded like a snarl.

Connor patted the man on the back and walked into the tunnel. The clack of Dahlia's heels echoed behind him as she joined, but no other footsteps followed.

It was probably for the best. If the goddess didn't want the wraith present for this, whatever waited down here couldn't be good.

More vines covered every wall, and pulses of green light shot through each vine, like the heartbeat of the continent itself. Shriveled leaves dusted the floor, and he sidestepped them as best he could.

With a wary glance over his shoulder, he studied Dahlia's face—tense, furrowed, and focused.

Uneasy.

"You don't know what to expect either, do you?" he asked.

Though she pursed her lips, she shook her head.

"Have you been in here before?"

"Once," her sharp voice pierced the quiet tunnel. "When I was little."

Interesting. Apparently, even the heir to the throne wasn't invited here often.

"I apologize for the theatre," the fallen princess said softly. "Did you at least enjoy your gift?"

"Otmund?"

She nodded.

He cleared his throat. "I did, though I would've preferred to kill him myself."

"You aren't the only one," she said, and her voice took on a gravely edge he hadn't expected. "I don't suppose you'll let me have his Bloodbane dagger?"

"Not a chance." He laughed. "You never should've let him keep it."

"It was a difficult decision," she admitted. "But we needed to understand what it did."

"Did you figure it out?"

Her sharp eyes darted toward him, and she simply nodded.

He frowned. How delightful.

"Tell me something." He scratched at his cheek as they approached a sharp curve in the vine-covered tunnel. "Why all these tests?"

Dahlia swallowed hard, and for a moment, he figured she wouldn't answer.

Eventually, her eyelids fluttered closed, and she took a deep breath. "We had to know if you were worth the sacrifice we're about to make, Connor."

"Will you just give me a straight answer for once, damn it?" he snapped. "Just once. Curse the Fates, Dahlia."

"It's a breathtaking and awe-inspiring sight to behold," she said quietly, almost wistfully. "I would rather not ruin the surprise."

"I'm fused to an undead king," Connor said with an impatient huff. "It's hard to surprise me."

To her credit, the fallen princess smiled. It was brief, almost unnoticeable, but he caught it nonetheless.

As they took the curve in the tunnel, the rocky ceiling receded sharply upward, and they stepped into a grand circular room. Pulsing vines covered every wall and faded into the thickening mist far above their heads. A dazzling green glow pulsed through the room with each beat of the glowing heartbeat shooting through the roots.

"*I am more certain than ever.*" The Antiquity's voice boomed in the small room, and Connor winced at the sheer volume of sound. "*You have proven yourself worthy, Wraithblade, and you will make a fierce ally in this violent world.*"

Before he could speak, the vines along the wall retreated. They coiled around each other, thickening into a torso that grew quickly from the rocky floor. As before, the Antiquity appeared within the slithering roots, her head emerging from within the shoulders as her body formed. Her magnificent antlers grew from the crown of her head, and in mere moments, she loomed above them in the tall chamber.

The pulses of light centered in her chest, and as he watched in stunned silence as a goddess once more appeared before him, the vines in her torso receded like ribs snapping off a ribcage.

Deep in her chest, a hollowed hole held a nest strikingly similar to one a bird would make for her chicks: thick with brambles, dead leaves, and more of those glowing white butterflies. Within it, two glowing green orbs pulsed with the same brightness and rhythm as the thudding light in her chest.

The Soulsprite—and there were *two* of them.

In his shock, he took a wary step backward as he stared at the orbs. The light within them churned, much like clouds in a stormy sky, and their power electrified the very air. His body hummed with their magic. With their energy. With the lifeforce of the gods and all that he had yet to understand.

Each orb snared him, drawing him closer, piquing not just curiosity but reverence. Respect. Awe. Horror. They held within them the sort of power that could form worlds and melt bones.

They radiated not just life, but death.

"*You understand,*" the Antiquity said with a gentle tilt of her elegant head.

"What are they?" he asked. "I mean, what are they really? These aren't ordinary artifacts. No human made these."

"Correct. They were designed by Death, formed in the forges of both worlds, and He infused them with my soul when He created me, long ago."

A ribbon of surprise rooted Connor to the ground, and a twinge of numb disbelief buzzed in his fingertips as he processed what she had said. "Death created you?"

The goddess nodded, just once, and a glowing white butterfly fluttered past her face. She lifted one finger toward it as it hovered by her nose, and the sprouting tip of the root comprising her finger brushed against the little insect.

"Life and Death are one, my dear," the goddess said calmly. "Death is nothing without life to take. He is the master of both this world and the one that follows. The Creator and the Destroyer, even of the immortal. The Soulsprites are the blood of the gods, and they tether me to both worlds. I am one of the in-betweens. That is the one duty of all gods."

Connor rubbed his forehead as he absorbed everything he was hearing. "There are more of you?"

"There were," she said, and her voice hardened with the first anger he'd heard from her thus far. "A dozen of us, more or less, each with our own lands and our own people."

"Freymoor," he said, piecing it together. "They're not just a kingdom. They worship you."

"More than followers," the Antiquity corrected. "They are a part of me, as is every soul that passes through the bogs."

"It is a rite of passage," Dahlia explained, her voice soft compared to the mighty resonance of the goddess above them. "When we turn sixteen, we venture into the bogs to meet the goddess for ourselves." Her blue eyes briefly shifted out of focus, as though she were reliving a memory. "It changes us."

"All magic has limits," the goddess explained. "Even mine. I can see the memories of the dead, but only of those who have survived my mists—or died in them."

Connor quirked one eyebrow. "Which means my team and I—"

"Correct," she said. "You are all of Freymoor, now. You are one of us."

He bristled at the idea of his final moments, whenever they came, flashing across the crystal walls beyond this room. A man's final moments seemed too personal to broadcast for all to see.

"*We gods thrived, once,*" the Antiquity continued, "*And we lived out our purpose to Death. In our homelands, we were safe.*"

"That's why you live in the Blood Bogs?" Connor ran his hand through his hair as he sifted through what she was telling him. "It's not just your home, but an in-between?"

"*I do not live in the bogs, Wraithblade. I am the bogs.*"

He frowned.

"Aeron Zacharias killed the gods," Dahlia added. "He wanted the Soulsprites, and he murdered immortals to obtain them. He stole the orbs, one by one, until only two of Death's gods remained."

Connor went still, and he studied the fallen princess's face as he sat with how a man could've possibly killed a god.

"*With time, it became clear he sought not just to master Death, but to become Him,*" the Antiquity said with a weary sigh. "*I believe, at first, he had no idea of the harm he had caused. We surviving gods watched in horror as we witnessed the tides in this world change. With each simmering soul he brought to life, our light began to fade.*"

The statement hit Connor like a war hammer to the chest.

The Wraith King had been crafted from the stolen blood and magic of a fallen god.

Above him, the Antiquity reached into her hollowed heart and lifted one of the glowing green orbs into her palm. The moment it left its nest, the vibrant light inside faded, and the orb became black as ash. The inky spirals and ornate runes carved into its surface glittered briefly in the pulses of green light flooding through her body, like a flash of sunlight on obsidian, but it otherwise retreated into itself.

Dormant, but powerful as ever.

When she lifted it into the air, the vines in her chest closed tightly, as though afraid she would remove the last one as well. She held it above his head, and in the ensuing silence, she examined the magnificent artifact with her glowing green eyes. Though her wooden features masked her expression, her gaze lingered on it.

Lovingly.

Forlorn.

"Each of us gods came here with three." The Antiquity's resonant voice hummed with sadness. *"One of mine was stolen. One, now, is given. Only one remains."*

"Goddess," Dahlia whispered. "Are you sure about this? Must we truly weaken you so severely?"

"We must, child," the Antiquity said with a somber nod. *"It is not a price paid, but an investment in the future. In rebuilding our power."*

Dahlia hunched forward, and her dark blonde hair hid her face. She sniffled and turned her back to Connor.

The goddess lowered her hand, and offered him the dormant stone.

After all his hunting, the Soulsprite was nearly his. Everything he had endured had led him here, to an ancient artifact lying in her open palm, finally within reach.

He just had to take it.

As tempted as he was to grab it from her outstretched hand for everything they had put him and his team through, he finally understood the theatrics. The games. The vague riddles.

In this day and age, it was hard to know who could stab him in the back. Any trust given was hard-earned, especially for a people who had endured so much already. The Antiquity, Dahlia, and Freymoor itself weren't just giving him a family heirloom—they were giving him their last great chance at survival.

He sighed, and instead of reaching for the orb, he scratched at the stubble on his jaw. "What will happen to you if I take this?"

The goddess tilted her head, as though surprised, and her glowing green eyes narrowed slightly with barely masked pride. *"I will lose part of the bogs. They will shrink, and my tether to this domain will weaken."*

"Will it kill you?"

"It will not." The blackened Soulsprite inched toward him as the vines in her arm grew longer. *"One for life. Two for power. Three for protection. When acting as the beating heart of a god, that is how the Soulsprites work."*

Conflicted, he set his hands on the back of his head and stared down at the Soulsprite. It was everything he needed to preserve Slaybourne, but it came at a horrific cost to Freymoor.

"*When I find more, I will guide you to them,*" the Antiquity promised. "*It is my hope that, one day, you will rebuild my power. In exchange, I will make you and Slaybourne powerful beyond belief. I trust you will return this to me, one day. With luck and favor from the Fates, it will be one day soon.*"

"You have my word." He stared deep into the goddess's glowing green eyes and nodded.

"*Then all is well, and I give this freely.*" She lowered her great head toward him, and the closer she came, the brighter the glow of her pulsing green light became. "*Be warned, Connor Magnuson, that no being may possess more than three of these without a visit from Death. Zacharias acquired too many, and Death came to collect what He was owed. Never in my many centuries did I imagine my Champion would be fused to one of that heartless man's abominations, but the Wraith King has not corrupted you. If anything, it is you who corrupts him.*"

Connor squinted in confusion. "If that was a compliment, then thank you."

"*It was.*" The goddess chuckled, and a few more white butterflies sprang to life around her head. "*I confess, Wraithblade, to being something of a romantic. I watch history repeat itself year in and year out, with every generation, but I am renewed in those rare moments of true and lasting change. That change occurs when a truly great champion shifts the ripples of time in favor of a new future. I believe you are one of those great heroes, but that is my blind spot. My weakness—the hope for a brighter future, when all I know is the past.*"

Connor gave the immortal being a thin smile of gratitude, but his attention shifted to the Soulsprite in Her hand. To take it came with a grave responsibility, far more than he or the Wraith King could have ever fathomed.

But he had to do this. For the Finns. For his team. For Slaybourne.

He reached for the dull black orb.

"*To take it is to fully commit,*" the Antiquity warned. "*It is to accept your role in Freymoor's future, as we do in yours. This is not a gift, but a debt you must repay. A link between our worlds until we both fall. Do you understand?*"

He nodded confidently. "I do."

"You will fight for us when we cannot," the goddess added. "Where we cannot go, you will speak for us."

"I swear it," he said.

"Then the Soulsprite is yours."

He lifted the dull orb in his palms. Even silenced as it was, a pulse of magic shot through him at his touch. The sensation reminded him of roots, growing from his feet and delving deep into the earth.

It felt like an anchor—to this life and the next.

It felt like a piece of *home*, warm and safe in his palms.

Part of the mists had died to give him this power. Slaybourne and whoever lived in his new kingdom would thrive because of this alliance, and though it was a generous act, it had not been made selflessly. The time would come when the goddess would collect on this debt, and it was one he would gladly pay.

Slaybourne had its first ally—and a dangerous one, at that. Freymoor would fight for his emerging kingdom as much as he fought to restore theirs.

"*The wraith must never touch it.*" The goddess stood again, once more looming above him, and clasped her hands in front of her as she stared down at him. "*What he is—what Zacharias did to create the simmering souls—the wraith's magic will destroy it. Even one touch will shatter it, and we will both lose everything.*"

Connor swallowed hard at the prospect. "No pressure."

"Some pressure," Dahlia quipped from behind him.

He cast a glance over his shoulder as the fallen princess wrapped her hands around her torso, as though cold. Her focus remained on the goddess, and even as he watched her, she never so much as looked his way. She watched the Antiquity like a daughter studying her mother on her deathbed—terrified of what was to come, and of what she feared to be inevitable.

"*Take this,*" the goddess said.

As Connor returned his attention to the Antiquity, the ancient being offered him a box made of vines. She opened the lid to reveal a small indent in the cushion of leaves within it, and he set the Soulsprite inside.

"*This will protect the orb in your travels,*" the goddess explained as she handed him the box. "*We are allies to the end of Saldia, Connor Magnuson. I have hope for your lifetimes to come."*

He frowned with confusion. "What do you mean?"

"I thought you knew." The great being's head tilted in surprise. *"You are no longer a man, but neither are you a god. You are a hybrid, as much the in-between as I am. You are of both worlds, but welcome in neither. Before long, you will have to choose."*

"Choose what?"

"Your place," the goddess answered. *"And your role in the tides of time."*

His eyebrows shot up his forehead, and his mouth parted in surprise.

Dahlia's heels clacked against the stone as she walked up beside him, though her focus remained on the goddess above. "Should we tell him about the other active simmering soul?"

"Another one has fused to somebody?" Connor asked.

"I'm afraid so," the Antiquity said sadly. *"For now, do not worry yourself with these developments. We will monitor the situation, and should the newcomer become a threat, we will inform you of his plans."*

Connor tensed, not liking where this was headed. "Tell me."

"You have enough on your mind, my Champion," the Antiquity said gently, almost lovingly.

Like a mother, doting upon her child.

"Focus on your battle with Teagan," the immortal being continued. *"If Slaybourne falls, the other simmering souls will no longer matter."*

He bristled. After everything he had endured in the Blood Bogs, he hated the idea of more secrets. More games. More riddles.

But the goddess had a point.

"Fight one battle at a time, Wraithblade." The vines composing the goddess's towering form slowly retreated, writhing and slithering as she shrank again into nothing. *"We will speak again when you have secured Slaybourne. For now, rest and recover your strength. You will need it."*

Within moments, the goddess disappeared. Her vines traced up the wall and settled into their perches, still and silent as the pulse of her heartbeat shot through each root in a ribbon of brilliant green light.

A puff of black smoke rolled through the center of the room, and a familiar skeletal face emerged from the shadow.

Infuriating. Rude. How dare that goddess treat me—

"Calm the hell down," Connor snapped.

Calm down? The ghoul's bleached white face pivoted toward him as the black smoke slowly dispersed. *She had me trapped where I couldn't—*

"Show her respect." Connor nodded toward where the goddess had stood moments before. "You must've heard what she gave up for us. They kept their word. That's all that matters."

At least you have it. The ghoul growled, and his bony hands curled into fists at his side. He grumbled obscenities and disappeared again into a puff of smoke. *Ass.*

"Charming," Dahlia said dryly.

"You have no idea," Connor admitted.

"You should eat." The fallen princess gestured for him to walk ahead of her down the tunnel they had taken to enter. "The sun rises in less than an hour, so I'm afraid you'll have to stay for another day. You should use this time to rest and recover."

He sighed impatiently, but he couldn't refute the woman's logic. He had to be at full strength when he faced Teagan Starling, and damn it all, he wanted a hot meal and a bed.

"I hope you have enough coin to feed me," he said with a dry laugh. "And after that ordeal, I'm going to need all the wine and whiskey you've got. I might not be able to get drunk, but curse the Fates, I'm going to try."

CHAPTER SIXTY-FIVE

TEAGAN

A strong wind from the southeast carried thin spirals of sand across the Decay.

Teagan stood on a raised platform overlooking the vast desert beyond Charborough. The southern road, carved into the gnarled old oaks of the Ancient Woods long before the Wraith King salted this earth, ended abruptly in the sand. To the north and the south, the edge of the forest curved through the bleak hellscape like the bank of a river, stretching farther than even Teagan could see.

As the wind hit him, a surge of anger ignited within him, like a spark in the tarpit of his soul. He shut his eyes to snuff it out, and with a settling breath, the rage fizzled almost instantly. As always, only cold fury remained where the raw hatred had been moments before, and it cleared his head.

It had already taken seventeen precious days to assemble his forces and arrive at the edge of the Wraith King's domain. Rescuing peasants had cost him valuable time, but at least Charles had managed to keep any more calamities from reaching the soldiers. Whatever chaos the peasants here endured, they would have to deal with it on their own for now.

He had greater opponents to fight.

Below him, heads bobbed and wove through the throng of gathered soldiers. With its position next to a vast stretch of empty wasteland, Charborough often served his forces as a secured area to test new weapons, as well as new spells that might've otherwise flattened his fortress. A sprawling stretch of dusty stone buildings had taken over the edge of the desert over the past few decades, each dedicated in some capacity to the various needs of any military force stationed nearby.

From his position on the towering platform, Teagan had a clear view of the military city in every direction. Behind him, the buildings and dusty cobblestone streets built into the Decay led back toward his suite in the central fortress Henry had forced him to surrender twelve years ago. Due east, sixty tents arranged in militant rows covered the desert landscape below as his soldiers settled in for the next few days.

Most importantly, however, were the testing grounds to the south. A line of eight machines waited patiently along the fenced edge of the massive arena, each of them covered in a collection of mismatched tarps woven together.

The merlins.

The creak of wood interrupted his thoughts as someone climbed the long ladder affixed to the outpost's center beam. Far below, a man huffed and wheezed on his way up the ladder, while another man took even, measured breaths.

One soldier, most likely, and one civilian.

Teagan set his hands on the railing as he waited and used the time to study the covered row of machines. A stacked pile of hay bales waited two hundred yards from a stone circle they used as the launching base for siege artillery. An additional three hundred yards from that, bushes and sprouting underbrush spilled from the forest line as the Ancient Woods tried to reclaim what the Wraith King had long ago claimed for himself.

A foot hit the floor of the watch tower's platform as the first man stepped off the ladder. Meanwhile, the steady wheezes and creaks of the ladder continued as the second man struggled to hoist himself to the top.

"The lead engineer will be up in a moment, sir," Colonel Freerock said from behind him.

As Teagan pretended to study the desert, he used the moment to don the all-too-familiar mask he wore around one of his best soldiers. His cold fury fizzled away as he adopted the persona of a calm and confident father figure that could demand anything of the young man. "While we wait, Colonel, it's time to tell you of your next assignment."

"Anything, sir."

"You are to take two soldiers of your choice and trail behind the rest of the troops. As we move through the Decay, track our route. Set up markers to guide any reinforcements that may need to follow us."

"But—" Freerock cleared his throat as he stopped himself from saying something foolish. "That is, of course, sir."

Teagan raised one skeptical eyebrow and looked over his shoulder to find the man wearing his trademark scowl of disagreement.

"Speak your mind, Colonel."

"Forgive me, sir." Freerock let out a quiet groan of defeat as Teagan caught him red-handed. "But to trail behind you now, in the final moments of our mission, means I won't be there when you reach Slaybourne. I've always fought at your side, sir." His jaw twitched. "Just as my father did."

Teagan smiled, careful to ensure the skin around his eyes creased with what would appear as genuine pride. "Your father would be proud of the man you've become, Rowan."

The soldier stood a little taller and nodded in wordless thanks.

"That's why I need you to handle this assignment." As Teagan returned his attention to the soldiers assembled below, he shook his head to drive home his point. "It can only be done by someone competent. We can't risk our opponent discovering these markers. If he destroys even one, any reinforcements that follow us will be lost in the desert. We need to come up with a means of ensuring only my soldiers can find their way to Slaybourne, and I can only give this assignment to someone I trust completely."

"I'm honored, sir."

You should be, Teagan thought.

Instead of speaking his mind, however, he opted for silence.

In the desert below, a cluster of seven engineers in beige tunics tugged off the cloth tarp on one of the devices at the edge of the arena. The burnt orange rays of the setting sun glinted along the metal corners connecting the massive wooden beams along the merlin's base. Even from this distance, the massive spellgust stones affixed to each corner glittered in the fading light as their fresh Burnbane enchantments hummed with power.

Metal gears clanked and whirred as the engineers spun handles built into its edges, and in the center of the machine, a wooden frame tilted toward the sky. A long barrel, not unlike the central channel of an oversized crossbow, tilted upward toward the sun-stained clouds. Assembled and ready, the merlin shook as the seven men rolled it forward from the line, toward the trees.

"Bless the Fates," Freerock muttered. "It's beautiful."

With his back to the colonel and his face shielded from view, Teagan allowed himself a brief sneer of victory.

Beautiful didn't even begin to describe power like this.

In any other onslaught, Zander would've been up here with him. He and the future Master General of Lunestone would look out at their troops and the next generation of siege weapons, and together they would revel in the might of the Starling name.

Instead, only the howl of the southern wind and the breathless gasps of an overweight engineer filled the silence.

"Join me, son." Teagan patted the railing beside him.

Freerock sucked in an almost inaudible breath of surprise. Within seconds, the colonel stood beside him, his shoulders tense as he frowned in a barely suitable attempt to hide his beaming smile.

"Tell me, Colonel." Teagan scanned the rows of tents below as his Lightseers gathered to watch the show. "Do the soldiers know why we've stopped in Charborough?"

"No, sir," Freerock answered with a stiff shake of his head. "Everyone assumes you have a brilliant trick up your sleeve, though, and we've been dying to see it."

Teagan smirked. "Flattery never works on me, soldier."

"It's not flattery if it's the truth, sir."

With a chuckle, Teagan nodded to the merlin as the engineers rolled it onto the stone circle in the arena. "Take a guess at what that is."

"It almost looks like an enchanted ballista, sir."

"Not quite," Teagan explained. "I call it a merlin, and no siege weapon in history can rival this piece of art. See there?" He pointed to the Lightseers he had chosen for the test run as they climbed aboard the massive device.

"It takes five men to maneuver and aim, but it would take twenty-five of the most seasoned Lightseers to match its firepower."

"How?" the young man asked, breathless.

"Starling enchantments," Teagan admitted with a self-satisfied shrug. "Unique blends unrivaled by any kingdom, burned into the metal plates that hold it together. It's like facing our opponent with an army three times larger than what we have."

The wooden ladder behind them creaked, and a palm smacked against the watch tower's floor. The engineer wheezed and let out a long sigh of relief as he hauled himself onto the roof.

"Good day to you, Lord Starling," the master mason said between breaths.

Without turning around, Teagan gave a lazy wave of his hand to acknowledge that the man had spoken, but he didn't care if the wheezing engineer noticed. With as long as their journey had taken, he had little interest in formalities.

Beside him, Freerock did his best to hide a knowing smile and pretended to survey the horizon.

The railing behind them creaked as the engineer leaned against it to catch his breath and his balance. "I thank you again, sir, for lending us your soldiers for the demonstration. Our best strongmen still had a hell of a time with the firing tests."

"Let's skip the pleasantries, Mr. Cobalt." Still well aware of the mask he needed to wear for Freerock's benefit, Teagan stifled an annoyed grimace. "What has the range been in your tests?"

"Upwards of five hundred yards, sir. If I may be so bold, I must say this has been my favorite project to build in my entire career. Your designs are a marvel of magic and engineering, my Lord, truly. It's been an honor to build this."

"I expect great things," Teagan warned, ignoring yet more flattery.

"You'll be pleased," the engineer said with the hint of a smile in his voice. "I promise you."

I'd better be.

On the field below, a loud clink reverberated across the desert as two

Lightseers used a dual-prong wheel. On the angled barrel in the center of the device, a metal tray large enough for a man to lie in inched toward the back of the machine. Two more men lifted a boulder the size of one of the wheels, and as the chute finally came to a stop at the end of the tension ropes, the soldiers rolled the boulder into the harness with a grunt of effort loud enough to hear even over the wind. At the front of the merlin, stationed under a metal dome beneath the launching pad, a fifth man rested his hand on a glowing green lever.

With the merlin loaded, the gathered engineers waiting along the edge of the merlin turned toward the watchtower and waved their arms.

"It's ready, my Lord." Behind him, the lead engineer clapped his hands together in gleeful excitement. "Give the order whenever you're—"

"Fire!" Teagan's command thundered across the desert, as loud as a crack of lightning.

Green light splintered along the metal plates like a ripple through water. The gems along its base shined as brightly as the stars on a clear night. The flickering pulse of magic raced up the supports and shot down the long chute to the boulder. Within seconds, the rock boiled, red as the setting sun on the horizon, as the Burnbane fires superheated it.

A shuddering boom rocked the desert, and the boulder hurled into the air, almost too quickly for the eye to track.

Birds startled from the treetops across the Ancient Woods as the thunder echoed. The molten boulder careened over the hay bales and, instead, hit the tree line with a second shuddering boom. It flattened the trees in front of it, and an inferno erupted across the surviving oaks. A plume of black smoke rolled across the desert, choking the ground in a thick haze, and the crackle of a distant fire followed seconds later.

Three soldiers ran to the front of the merlin and raised their arms. The perfectly synchronized motion stirred the smoke as their Airdrift augmentations took control of the wind. The black haze thinned to a pale gray, and as the last of it dissolved into the air, a deafening cheer erupted from the spectators below.

In the wreckage, entire trees had been turned to ash. The boulder had melted, but a long gouge in the earth marked its path. More plumes of pitch-black smoke poured from the Ancient Woods as fire raged through the decimated underbrush.

Freerock laughed, speechless in his joy, and joined the applause from the troops gathered below. Delighted whistles pierced the air as the Lightseers manning the test jabbed their fists into the air in victory.

"And that's from a single shot, my Lord," the master engineer behind Teagan said with a hearty laugh. "Imagine what all nine will do when the last one's finished."

Teagan didn't answer. He merely watched the decimated forest line, stiff and unmoving, as a sinister smile spread across his face. It threatened the mask he wore for Freerock, but given the swelling cheers, he allowed the brief betrayal of his true self as he celebrated something truly extraordinary.

For the first time in years, Teagan felt true joy.

"Make sure everyone is prepared, Colonel," he ordered in a calm, even tone. "In ten days, I want to announce to the world that Slaybourne has finally been destroyed."

CHAPTER SIXTY-SIX
MURDOC

In a vast hall carved into a labyrinth of tunnels beneath Freymoor, Murdoc sat on a raised platform above rows of dining tables. Dahlia's soldiers clustered on the benches below, laughing as they drank from iron goblets and bit into the slices of chicken on their plates. After what they had endured in the mists, Murdoc had figured these soldiers would've stood watch over them, eyeing them with suspicion, or at least stared over at them on occasion. But, for the most part, the warriors gathered at the tables below paid him no mind as they ate.

He crossed his arms in front of him and leaned his elbows against the long wooden table as he stared down at the chicken bones on his plate. Though tempted to fill the empty goblet in front of him, he didn't want to stand. With each minute, he relived their time in the bogs, and he scratched at the hair on his jawline as his eyes glossed over yet again.

As the swelling in his throat finally faded completely, he could only stare out at the secret city in awe and wonder why they had been allowed to see it.

To Murdoc's left, Connor bit into his fourth roasted chicken of the night. Twelve empty goblets littered the table in front of him as he ate, and a half-finished tray of potatoes sat off to the side. Steam rolled off the spuds, and he could already taste the warm tang of the melted butter across their grilled skins as he imagined taking a bite.

Though Murdoc's stomach growled again at the thought of more food, Connor had already smacked his hand once tonight. Murdoc stretched out his fingers, still fighting the soreness of being whacked—however playfully—by a demigod.

Wordlessly, the captain ate. The man stared down at the food, his eyes out of focus as he barely paid attention to it. Whatever wheels turned in the man's mind, Murdoc figured his friend had endured even more hell than him out there in the marsh.

A flash of crimson caught Murdoc's eye, and he lifted his head just as Sophia returned with three more goblets of red wine. She paused on the opposite end of the table, her back to the crowd, and wrinkled her nose in disgust as she studied the three plates of chicken bones sitting in front of Connor.

"I was only gone for five minutes," she said as the goblets rested between her slender fingers. "How does all of that even fit in you?"

Connor chuckled and took another bite of meat, but he didn't answer. He merely reached for one of the goblets and nodded once in silent gratitude.

Sophia rolled her eyes and set the wine on the table. With a subtle motion, she slid one of them closer to Murdoc. He grinned up at her, and though she didn't smile back, her eyes creased with just a hint of pleasure.

It was enough, and his grin only widened. She couldn't hide it from him.

As she sat across from them, Murdoc raised the new goblet to his mouth to hide his lips and lowered his voice to a whisper. "Did you find Dahlia?"

With a subtle shake of her head, Sophia leaned her elbows on the table and raised her own goblet to shield her mouth from any prying eyes. "I suspect we'll see her when she wants to be seen."

"Most likely."

A nearby table burst into laughter, and one of the men slapped another heartily on his back. Wine sloshed from their raised glasses as they talked over each other in a language Murdoc couldn't recognize. While he watched them, however, one of the quieter men at the head of the table met his gaze. The Freymoor soldier's smile fell, and his eyes shifted toward Connor. His brow furrowed with concern, but his lips parted with awe. The blended expression reminded Murdoc of what he had felt the first time he saw Connor fight.

It was like watching a god among men.

Though he wanted nothing more than to feel the buzz of the wine slowly dull the memories of tonight, Murdoc set down his drink and rubbed his temples. None of this felt real. To sit in a secret city below a conquered kingdom, to hear them speak a language they had been forbidden to practice under Henry's rule, it all felt like they had traveled back in time.

He saw now why so many called Freymoor a land of the Old Ways—this place didn't change, and it didn't stay conquered.

With a groan, Murdoc rubbed his tired eyes with the heels of his palms. "Are we going to talk about it?"

No one answered, and when Murdoc finally blinked away the exhaustion, he found Sophia already watching him with pinched brows.

She tilted her head and glanced him up and down. "Talk about what?"

"I guess not." Murdoc ran his hand through his hair and sat back in his seat. The back of the chair pressed into his shoulder blades, and he looked everywhere but at her and Connor.

Perhaps it was better that they just forget.

"You're talking about the mists?" Connor's voice broke the tension, and Murdoc flinched in surprise at the first words his captain had said since they left the bogs.

Murdoc tapped his fingernail absently against the table, but eventually he nodded.

Connor let out a long sigh and set his chicken leg on the plate. He wiped his mouth with the back of his hand, and though he didn't speak, a pained look crossed his face.

That proved it, then. They had all seen hell in those mists.

A pang of grief and loss hit Murdoc hard in the gut, and he cleared his throat to keep the memories at bay. "Yeah, me too."

Sophia set down her goblet and ran her finger along the metal edge as she stared into the wine. She blinked rapidly as she examined her drink, and if Murdoc didn't know any better, he could've sworn he saw a hint of moisture at the corner of her eyes.

Astonishing. He had never seen her cry.

He stiffened and leaned forward, tempted to say something to ease her pain, but her lips parted. He waited, his own pain shoved aside as he watched her intently and gave her space to speak.

"In that pool of stars, I heard my mother," Sophia said softly as she stared into the goblet. Her eyes glossed over as her gaze followed her finger around the rim of the glass, almost like she was in a trance. "I heard her scream as I slit her throat. I heard her choking on her own blood. I saw her wide eyes again as they stared up at me, horrified at what I had done. I remembered how I thought I'd feel shame, or a bit of remorse, but all I could feel back then was hate. I didn't need her blood specifically, but I picked her as my sacrifice out of spite for everything she did to me. For everything she forced me to do. For her cruelty, when all I ever wanted was a better life."

Murdoc leaned toward her. His stomach pressed into the edge of the table, but he still slid his palm across the table toward her as he listened with rapt attention. Beside him, Connor rubbed the stubble on his jaw and shoved aside his plate. The man waited patiently for her to continue, his elbows on the table and his fingers intertwined as he watched her in silence.

"Everyone I've ever killed was down there," Sophia continued, still refusing to look at them. "Even Richard. Even the girl who once owned this body. I heard their voices in the pool, and they all said the same thing. That they're waiting. That it's inevitable I'll face them again when I die. They all said the same things they said in life—that I'm too ugly to be loved, that I'm not worth anything, that I was never good enough. And I believed them."

She pursed her lips as her eyes shook with barely restrained tears.

"It's that last bit that got me," she confessed in a harsh whisper. "The 'never good enough.' Nothing but a ghost in an undead carcass. It was my shame that drove me toward the pool. What withered remorse I still have in me wanted to make it right and absolve myself in one fluid moment. It was tempting. I wanted to end it. To be done with it all, finally, and just find a bit of peace." She sighed and rubbed her face. "But I see now that it wouldn't have fixed anything. It would've just handed over my problems to you."

Her dark eyes drifted upward, and as Murdoc met her gaze, she stole the breath from his lungs.

In the silence that followed, a table at the far end of the hall broke into song. They laughed and clinked their goblets together as they wrapped their arms around each other's shoulders and swayed along with the melody. One by one, boots thumped against the stone floor until their stomps became a thunderous drumline to go with the song. Men clapped in time with the rhythm as the soldiers in the back belted their hearts out in a language he still couldn't understand.

As the music swelled, louder than ever, Murdoc reached for her hand as it lay on the table beside her goblet. "Sophia—"

"Don't," she whispered.

He clenched his jaw and, seconds before he touched her, he curled his fingers into a fist. Though he wanted nothing more than to hold her tight and let her know things would turn out alright, her pride wouldn't let her accept his comfort.

Perhaps one day, but not now.

He absently tapped his fingertips against the wooden table beneath them as the tavern song filled the dining hall. "You're not the only one hurt by the mist, Sophia. Those bogs almost killed me. That much magic in the air—I could barely breathe." He swallowed reflexively, grateful for the air in his lungs now that they had escaped.

Connor frowned with concern. "Did you know that going in there would hurt you?"

"Not a clue," he confessed. "But I wouldn't have told you if I did. That's what it means to be a team. You face hell together, and you come out stronger for it. I learned that in the Blackguards."

"Murdoc, that's insane." Connor scowled at him.

"Maybe." He shrugged. "But it's what I know. When I was a kid, I thought I had no future. A scoundrel in a world that could kill him by accident? What chance did I have of being useful?" He shook his head, but as he remembered his childhood, he couldn't help but smile. "Running around with a rusty sword I found in the garbage paid off, though, and I got my chance to be something more. I was born in Pinella Pass, you see, way up in the Frost Forest, and those black unicorns always gave us hell. One stumbled into town, and I killed it. Took it down myself. Stupid little sixteen-year-old boy that I was, I'd never felt more proud. More heroic. It was glorious."

Beside him, Connor grinned and shook his head as he sipped from his goblet.

"That's what got me into the Blackguards. They saw a warrior where my parents saw a lost cause." As Murdoc lost himself in the memory, his smile slowly faded. "But those days of brotherhood are long gone, and in that pool, I also heard the dead, Sophia. I heard the men I lost in Norbury, the ones I led against the necromancers. I heard the words they never got the chance to tell me."

"What did they say?" Sophia asked, her voice almost too quiet to hear.

Murdoc hung his head and stared down at his hands. "That I killed them. That it was my fault from the start. That I don't deserve to be here, and you know what? I don't."

Connor shook his head. "Now, listen—"

"Sophia's right," Murdoc continued. Ordinarily, he never would've interrupted the captain, but he needed to get this out before he buried it deep down, in the darkest recesses of his soul where he stored the rest of his guilt. "It was my shame that drove me to the water. It weighed so heavily on me that I wanted nothing more than to wash it off."

Murdoc stared at the scars in his hands, each from a wound that healed slowly, naturally, without a drop of a Rectivane potion to help it along. Every scar reminded him of his weakness, of his limitations, and they forced him to remember where he had come from.

They reminded him, every day, of what he had left behind.

A heavy hand grabbed his shoulder, and he snapped from his daze to find Connor watching him with a solemn expression. The captain's eyes narrowed, intense and clear, and the hand on Murdoc's shoulder tightened reassuringly. "One day, I hope you finally forgive yourself for Norbury. You and I both know you couldn't have done a damn thing different. Once you let that go, you'll see what you're truly capable of. You may be a drunk with a death wish, but I count you among my friends—friends I never thought I would have."

Murdoc grinned and absently scratched at his neck, entirely unsure of what to say.

"And you," Connor added as his attention shifted toward Sophia. "You're history in the making. I know the choice you made back in Oakenglen. I know you chose to stay."

The thin muscles in her neck flexed as she watched him with wide eyes. Though her hand wrapped around the goblet in front of her, the rest went eerily still.

Connor raised one eyebrow as he examined her face. "Once Tove gave you your new augmentation, you could've left us behind and found yourself a decent life away from all this, but you chose to stay. You proved I could trust you, and that shows the sort of courage that I can respect."

Her gaze drifted again to the goblet as she traced its edges with her finger, but a small smile played at the corners of her mouth, and her shoulders finally relaxed.

In the silence that followed, Connor once again bit into his chicken. The conversation was done, and they didn't need to say anything else. Theirs was the sort of brotherhood forged in battle, and the bonds between the three of them couldn't have been clearer.

Connor and Sophia would always have Murdoc's back, just as he would have theirs. He finally, at long last, had a true team.

He tossed back his goblet and drank every drop of wine left in it. With a happy smack of his lips, he closed his eyes and let the warm buzz hit his brain. His wine goblet thudded hard against the table as he set it down, and he savored the spicy aroma of roasted chicken and warm potatoes that lingered in the air.

He wanted to be done with it, but one last question stoked the fires of his curiosity. He tilted the empty goblet back and forth as he fought the urge to ask, but in the end, he lost the battle with himself.

Murdoc cleared his throat. "What did you all see when we lost each other?"

Beside him, Connor stopped chewing. His eyes narrowed, and he looked away. Across from him, Sophia frowned and tossed her head back as she drank the last of her wine. No one looked at each other, and Murdoc nodded at the unspoken confession between them.

"The bogs tested me," he admitted. "Did it test you, too?"

Sophia sighed and pushed away her empty goblet. With her elbows on the table, she ran her hand through her hair and stared down at the wooden surface. "Damn it all, Murdoc, can we stop with the feelings?"

He chuckled.

The necromancer across the table from him shook her head, and her long black curls slid over her shoulders. "It offered me a way out, alright? It showed me the path out of the mist and said I could take it as long as I let it have you two."

Connor took the last bite of his chicken—the bones already picked clean—and pushed his plate away. "What did you do?"

"I told it to go to hell, obviously."

The captain grinned and rubbed the last bit of chicken off his hands. "You really are going soft."

She raised her middle finger at him, and the three of them laughed.

"What about you?" Connor asked as he shifted in his seat and turned his broad shoulders toward Murdoc. "What test did it give you?"

"It told me you weren't worth fighting for." Murdoc leaned to one side and studied his captain's face.

The man's smile faded in an instant, and his dark eyes narrowed with concern.

Murdoc's vision blurred as he relived the encounter in the fog. "There I was, barely able to breathe from all that damned enchanted fog, when a woman walked out of the mist and started asking me questions. She rooted me in place and made me watch your encounter with Quinn. I was told you were ordered to kill her."

"That's right." Connor leaned his left elbow on the table, and the wood creaked from carrying the weight of just his muscled forearm. The captain watched him with a stony expression, his eyes steady as he met the unspoken implication in Murdoc's confession.

"I tried to stop you," Murdoc admitted. "I couldn't move. You couldn't hear me. I could only watch. Even though the bogs tempted you with everything you wanted, you didn't do it. You let her live."

Connor nodded, still waiting for the last bit Murdoc had left unsaid.

Given the captain's somber expression, Murdoc wondered if perhaps he was milking this a bit too much. He grinned, and it dispelled the tension. "Thanks for proving me right."

The man laughed, his eyes crinkling with delight and relief, and he clapped Murdoc on the back. A blip of pain shot up his shoulder, and he grimaced from Connor's sheer strength.

"I don't know." Sophia looked over her shoulder.

Murdoc followed her gaze to find Quinn Starling leaning against the far wall. Above her, a balcony jutted out over the massive dining hall, and soft blue drapes lined the archways along its edge. The redhead crossed her arms and propped one foot against the stone wall behind her as she surveyed a world she wasn't meant to see.

A world her father would probably burn to the ground if he knew it existed.

"You think I chose wrong?" Lines formed in Connor's brow even as he studied the necromancer with relaxed shoulders and an unreadable expression on his face.

A question, or a challenge—Murdoc couldn't tell.

"Maybe," Sophia admitted as she turned her back on Quinn. "With her father on his way to Slaybourne, I guess we'll find out soon enough."

Connor frowned, and his intense glare shifted to the Starling woman as her eyes swept the ocean of faces before her. His brows furrowed with concern, and a muscle in his jaw twitched as he stared at the woman they had only begun to trust—and who might well be the death of them all.

CHAPTER SIXTY-SEVEN
QUINN

With the back of her head resting against the cold stone wall, Quinn propped one leg against the stone and crossed her arms. Down here, in the depths of a labyrinth she could only assume had been carved into the rock beneath Freymoor, she studied the secret world no Lightseer had ever seen.

The implications of what it meant for her to see this left her stomach in knots. Either Dahlia had no intention of letting her out of here alive, or whatever newfound truce she and Connor had established offered Quinn the sort of immunity she wouldn't have otherwise had.

In the weeks after she had left her surveillance post in Freymoor, rumors of a hidden city had circulated among the Lightseer elite. They had been mostly dismissed as bunk, but as more and more soldiers went missing on their surveillance missions, it had become evident Freymoor had the sort of secrets they would kill to protect.

Though a rowdy drinking song filled the high ceilings in the underground dining hall, the soldiers kept their bows and arrows within reach. Four wine caskets, each as tall as a house, lined the far wall, and yet barely anyone waited for a drink. Most of the warriors nursed their goblets, and more than one shot her wary glares over their cups.

A tense truce had been called, but not even she believed it would last.

Connor, Murdoc, and Sophia sat alone at the head table on a raised platform. They leaned in, talking about something dire judging by their furrowed brows and deep frowns, but she had opted against joining them.

Nocturne had gone for a spin through the moonlit clouds to clear his head, and Quinn waited on the outskirts of conversations, alone here just as she had always been alone back home in Lunestone.

Even in the face of death, so little ever changed.

Quinn's ear twitched as a slippered foot shuffled over the stone floor. The swish of skirts followed, and the subtle perfume of roses wafted past.

"Hello, Dahlia," she said in stilted welcome.

The Lady of Freymoor stepped into her periphery and set her hands behind her back as she looked out over the soldiers gathered among the dining tables. "Take a walk with me, Lady Starling."

It could've been a trap. After all, Quinn had now witnessed many of the secrets Freymoor had murdered her fellow Lightseers to protect.

Without moving, she tilted her head toward the young woman and raised one skeptical eyebrow. "I suppose this is where you slit my throat for seeing too much?"

Dahlia pursed her lips in annoyance. "As much as I loathe you, Lady Starling, that violates the terms to which Connor and I have agreed. As long as he is your ally, I cannot kill you."

Quinn smirked. "A pity."

The Lady of Freymoor lifted her chin in defiance and glared at Quinn down the bridge of her nose. "Are you coming or not?"

With one last look at Connor, Quinn tugged a small dagger out of a hilt hidden in her pocket and slid it up her sleeve. Suitably armed and ready for an ambush, regardless of the young woman's promises, she pushed off the wall and forced a smile as she joined the fallen princess.

Together, they left the chatter of the dining hall and strode down a wide passage lined with flickering sconces. Windows lined one wall, their glass glowing blue with the moonlight.

Neither she nor Dahlia looked at each other, and they simply walked in silence until the drinking songs faded to the quiet taps of Dahlia's slippers against the stone floor. Quinn matched the young woman's stride and kept a keen eye on their route in case she needed to return on her own, but for the most part, they kept to the main passage. It carried on for ages, bending here and there as hallways branched off in nearly every direction.

A true labyrinth.

Though she couldn't hear any breaths or tightening bowstrings, she doubted she and the young woman were truly alone. With every step, her shoulders tensed a little more for what felt like an inevitable fight.

"I was certain you were going to die in the mists," Dahlia confessed, finally breaking their silence.

How charming. Quinn bristled but didn't reply.

"Your father wouldn't have made it," the Lady of Freymoor continued. "That's the only reason the mists remain full of treasure."

"I didn't see much treasure," Quinn countered.

"Of course not." Dahlia smirked. "That was by design."

Though she wanted to put the girl in her place, Quinn bit back a scathing retort. Given that Connor had only just established a tense truce with this woman, she refused to let a few barbed insults shatter it now.

"I was certain he would kill you," Dahlia admitted. "After all, he was your quarry, once. It seems foolish for him to have put so much on the line for you, of all people."

"If you have a point, I suggest you arrive to it soon," Quinn warned.

"So impatient." To her surprise, the fallen princess chuckled. "My point is that I didn't want you to escape the mists. I made that clear to the goddess and to Connor, but both of them opted to keep you alive.

At her side, Quinn curled her fingers into a fist, and her knuckles cracked with the movement. "Is it me you hate, or my family?"

"Both. The Lightseers failed to stop Henry, despite my father giving them everything they needed to succeed. He sacrificed so much. He lost every—" Dahlia shut her eyes briefly and sucked in a deep breath. "Never mind. But yes, during your missions here, you were always the prickliest thorn in my side."

Skeptical, Quinn raised one eyebrow in challenge. "You knew I was here?"

Dahlia nodded. "My spies saw traces of you, and yet we never were able to contain you. I had no idea what you had seen until we captured and interrogated your replacements."

"You mean when you *killed* my replacements." A rush of anger burned deep in her core, and a flicker of flame snapped across Quinn's palm.

Dahlia paused midstride and stared her dead in the eye. "And what would you have done, Quinn, in my place? Who would you have murdered, rightfully or no, to protect the decades of secret work your family had undertaken? What would you have done to these foreigners who threatened everything you had built to protect your people? Would you have sent them home with a batch of fresh jam, then?"

Quinn let out an irritated sigh, but she couldn't hold Dahlia's gaze.

"Of course not," the fallen princess said with an indignant huff. "I've been a warrior queen since I was twelve, and I'm not proud of half the things I've done for this land and its people. But if I can give them back their home, then all my shame is worth it."

Dahlia resumed her walk, and for a moment, Quinn simply watched the young woman's back. The girl walked with purpose, and despite the thick skirts swishing against her ankles, she carried herself like a soldier. Arched back. Steady pace. Hands clasped at her waist, suspiciously close to the skirts where daggers could be hidden.

Perhaps the term "warrior queen" suited Dahlia Donahue more than Quinn had realized. With a quick glance around them to confirm they were indeed still alone, she jogged to catch up with her host and again matched the woman's stride.

The fallen princess took a deep breath, and her chest rose with the exaggerated movement. "Despite our history, you are not my enemy. Not at the moment, anyway. You survived because my new Champion wants you alive, despite whatever little pact you and the dragon made, and that's enough for me. I suppose time will tell if that was a mistake."

"You keep trying to trick me into revealing something." Quinn shook her head. "It's not going to work."

"No?" Dahlia tilted her head and snuck a sidelong glance at Quinn. "I heard everything you said in the mist."

Quinn's chest tightened, but she didn't say anything.

"All of it," the Lady of Freymoor continued. "I can only guess at what your precious father did to lose your loyalty, but I don't for one second believe you should be allowed to leave this fortress. My advisors and I all want to see you put to death, but the goddess intervened. You owe her and Connor your life." Dahlia swallowed hard, and her jaw tensed with irritation. "They don't realize what you are, Quinn Starling, but I see through you. I remember the way you looked at your father, years ago when we were girls, any time you lot came to Freymoor. I saw how you hung on his every word. Teagan Starling was your idol, once, and that sort of devotion doesn't change."

The comment stung like an arrow to the chest, and for a moment, it was harder to breathe. She cleared her throat in an attempt to banish the sharp tension in her lungs, but it didn't work.

Dahlia raised an eyebrow in surprise. "You didn't react to me saying I want you dead."

"It's not a shocking thing for you to want."

The fallen princess slowed her stride, and her brows pinched together in confusion. She studied Quinn's face, but Quinn watched her with the same mask of indifference she had worn since they began their little trek.

"What?" she snapped.

Dahlia shook her head—in disappointment or disdain, Quinn couldn't tell. "You're more like your father than you realize."

Quinn frowned, her nose crinkling with revulsion at a comparison she would once have welcomed with pride. "How so?"

"Isn't it obvious?" Dahlia took a menacing step closer, until they were nose to nose, and her palms rested against the skirts that could've hidden any number of weapons. "You both lie to get what you want. You both kill with abandon. You both wear masks, though I'll concede that he's the better liar."

"There you go again," Quinn said with an edge of warning in her tone. "Hurling insults without ever getting to your point."

"My point," Dahlia spat the word, as though it tasted foul. "It's this—when you meet him again, I wish you the one thing you've wanted all this time. I hope you get the truth. I wish for you to see through him to the withered husk inside. And if the truth doesn't destroy you—which I'm quite certain it will—then I wish you the strength to do what should have been done ages ago."

"And that is?" Quinn narrowed her eyes as she dared the infuriating noblewoman to keep talking.

"Kill him." Dahlia's harsh whisper stabbed at the air.

Reflexively, Quinn's finger curled and tapped against the dagger hidden in her sleeve, but she didn't reply.

"I think you're too weak to do it." Dahlia poked Quinn hard in the shoulder, but Quinn didn't budge even under the woman's enhanced strength. "I think when the time comes, you'll remember the good and forget the bad. You'll stumble, you'll falter, and you will fail. And in those moments, for that brief span of time when you hold his life in your hands, I want you to remember this moment. I want you to replay this in your head, over and over, and I want you to hear my voice in your ear."

The fallen princess paused, and the silent hallway weighed on them as Quinn glared with barely restrained hatred.

"Prove me wrong," Dahlia whispered. "Please, for the love of the Fates, prove me wrong."

Quinn flinched in surprise and studied the young woman's face for signs of a trick, but the Lady of Freymoor didn't linger. She lifted her skirts with a frustrated groan and shook her head as she stalked away.

"Enjoy the feast, Starling," she said without looking back.

As the young warrior queen rounded a corner and disappeared into the shadows, Quinn let out a sigh and slid the hidden dagger back into the sheath in her pocket. And, try as she might, she couldn't get Dahlia's words out of her head.

Prove me wrong.

CHAPTER SIXTY-EIGHT

CONNOR

In the sleepy rays of the morning sun, Connor sat on the roof of Freymoor castle and stared out over the moors.

Tendrils of fog swept across the rolling hills, weaving through the blades of grass as a cool wind raced across the distant fields beyond the city walls. To the east, the towering forest of the Blood Bogs circled Freymoor, and its thick mist dispersed above the canopy into the rising sun's rays.

It was peaceful, almost. From up here, anyway.

Dark smoke rolled over the roof tiles from behind him, and the air shifted in a now-familiar warning that he was no longer alone.

Where is it, Magnuson? the ghoul demanded.

"Good morning," Connor said dryly without looking back.

The Soulsprite, the ghost continued impatiently. *I saw the box in your suite of the castle, but no fool would leave such a valuable artifact on the floor to sightsee. I don't dare risk touching it to find out if you—*

"It's safe," he interrupted.

We're out of time, Magnuson, the ghost grumbled. *Teagan Starling marches on Slaybourne as we speak, and yet you're watching a sunrise. Did the bogs break you? Have you already lost your will to fight?*

"We can't fly during the day." Connor shrugged as the shivering sunlight stained the clouds pink. "Might as well rest."

But the ghoul's words echoed in his skull, loud and grim.

Out of time.

Though he lay on the warming tiles with his arms stretched above his head, the ominous threat haunted him.

Out of time.

From the moment they'd left the bogs, the thought had clung to him like blood after a battle. He didn't bother counting down to Quinn's earliest estimate, anymore. There was no way for Nocturne to make it back to Slaybourne by the cutoff, and that meant Teagan Starling could easily beat him to the fortress.

If he wasn't there already, of course.

The thought of facing Teagan Starling without Slaybourne's undead army left him on edge. Tense. Unable to sleep, and unable to fully prepare.

Worse even than that was the thought of the Finns standing on the walls, facing an approaching army without Connor there to protect them.

Beck Arbor had often told him of this sensation—of those somber moments before the troops gathered to face an enemy. The disquiet that left each man isolated in his own head, lost in his thoughts and anxious over the chaos to come. These were the quiet waters one sailed even as he watched a storm brew on the horizon, and his stomach churned with the dread of the unknown.

Of what was to come, and of how this would end.

What is your plan? The ghoul demanded. *We must have contingencies. We must know—*

"Will you give me one minute of peace?" Connor sat upright, and his boot slipped an inch across the sloping roof tiles as he glared at the undead king hovering behind him. "Just one, man. Just *one*. We went through hell in the bogs, and we're about to go through it again when we face Teagan. I'd like one Fates-damned peaceful sunrise before that happens."

The Wraith King mumbled obscenities, but he didn't say anything else.

Thank the Fates.

Connor turned his back on the specter, and another wave of black smoke rolled past him as the tension in the air faded.

You did what I could not, the wraith said.

Connor tensed and looked around, but the wraith was gone. He sat alone on the rooftop, and apparently whatever was left to be said between them wouldn't be done face-to-face. To his surprise, the ghoul's tone sounded almost remorseful. It carried weight to it, perhaps a hint of sadness—or respect.

Perhaps the goddess was right, the wraith continued. *Perhaps the tide truly has changed. We can only hope it has changed in our favor.*

"What does that mean?" Connor asked.

Only the howling wind answered, but the sensation of eyes on his back disappeared as Connor waited for the wraith to speak.

He shook his head. That damn ghost always had to have the last word.

As the minutes passed, Connor sat in silence and listened to the whistling wind. In his life before the wraith, he would've been shivering up here on this northern roof, but not a single chill snaked down his back. If anything, he wanted to take off his coat and soak in the sun.

It might be his last chance to do so.

As the thought weighed on him, his eyelids drooped. Keeping them open took more and more effort, but he didn't dare close them. Not yet. To avoid the nightmares that would inevitably come, he wanted to wait until he couldn't keep them open.

He had seen his family in the star pool. He had come so close to holding them again, and once more, he had walked away.

His jaw tensed, and a knot formed in his throat as he swallowed.

A sunbeam cut through the clouds and cast a spotlight on the top of a distant hill. He focused on it, preferring this moment of peace to the pain of his past, and he let himself enjoy the silence.

Peaceful sunrises seemed rare, lately. They came few and far between.

Behind him, the soft jingle of a roof tile interrupted his thoughts, and the barest hint of a footstep followed.

He only knew of a few people stealthy enough to make almost no sound, and he could only think of one of them who could've wanted his company at the moment.

"Good morning, Quinn," he said without turning around.

She chuckled and sat beside him. "So that's what it's like."

He raised one curious eyebrow and waited for her to elaborate.

"Usually I'm the one doing that to other people." She shrugged and scanned the moors around them. "I must admit, I'm not a fan of how it feels."

He grinned, but didn't reply.

They sat together in the calm morning on the rooftop, listening to the sky as the distant chatter of the nearest marketplace wandered up from the streets beyond the interior castle walls. Deep in the maze of hedges that comprised the palace gardens, a familiar blonde trekked expertly through the labyrinth.

He was content with the silence, and to his surprise, he didn't mind the company.

"I figured you'd have left," he admitted. "I haven't kept an eye on you since the bogs."

"And go where?"

"Home." He pointed off at the horizon, only vaguely familiar with the direction she would have to take to reach Lunestone. "Oakenglen, maybe. Anywhere else but with me."

He expected her to bluff. To lie. To sustain their charade a bit longer. To her credit, however, she merely watched the rolling hills.

He leaned back on his palms and studied her face. "Does this mean I finally get the truth?"

"Yeah," she said quietly, still not looking at him. "I think you've earned it."

"Damn right, I have."

She laughed, and her eyes creased with genuine joy. It surprised him, really, to see her happy—if only for a moment. Since they'd met, she had either hunted him or he'd held her captive. He had only ever seen the warrior, and she had thus far expertly worn a mask of indifference around him.

"First, I have to know something." Her smile slowly fell, and she hugged one knee close to her chest as she stared down at the garden. "Back there in the mist, when you found me…"

"How much did I hear?"

Her jaw tensed, and she nodded.

He let out a slow whistle and stared off at the towering forest beyond Freymoor. Watching her yell at the ghosts in the fog had been almost painful. He knew her as a soldier, one with a cool head and a steady hand—but out there, he had witnessed her cracking. He had seen her weaknesses.

To watch such a strong woman unravel had set him on edge.

"I heard everything," he admitted. "I heard what the apparitions said. Zander. Your father. Your sister. Otmund. I saw that you still can't control your lightning, but I didn't realize until now that you feel less than because of it. And down there in the caverns, I heard you promise Nocturne you would kill me if I ever went dark. I heard it all."

She sighed. "May the day never come, Wraithblade."

"Agreed," he said, echoing her own words to Nocturne.

His throat tightened at the thought of the dragon he had considered a friend making a pact with a woman he had once considered an enemy. They would need the Bloodbane daggers to do it, and if the time came, she might even try to steal them from him.

Hell, maybe he should simply give her one.

He didn't want to become like the other hosts the Wraith King had endured in his long, undead life. Those men had gone mad with their newfound power. They had butchered their own family and burned villages to the ground in their unchecked bloodlust, all in their insatiable hunt for *more*.

Regardless of the cost, he refused to let himself become that.

If he ever lost his way, perhaps it was best to have someone nearby to intervene—before he could become what he so hated.

"Damn it," Quinn said softly.

He peered at her through the corner of his eye, waiting for her to elaborate.

She didn't.

The Lightseer sat beside him, close enough to kill, and stared out at the endless fields surrounding Freymoor. She rested her chin on her knee, but she wouldn't look at him.

"We all have ghosts, Quinn," he said gently. "We all have regrets."

A soft little sigh escaped her. "I'm fine."

"You killed the man you once called Uncle," Connor prodded. "You can't tell me you're fine after that."

"Imagine how many people wanted to kill him," she said quietly. "He deserved a worse fate than what I gave him."

"He did," Connor agreed. "I had quite a few plans for him, myself."

She shook her head, and she grimaced with unrestrained disgust. "The hell he put you through, and for what? Did he want the Wraith King for himself?"

"That's my theory."

"And my father…" Quinn rubbed her face. "I can only imagine what he wanted to do with you once you were brought to him in chains."

"Slit my throat and bottle the ghoul." Connor shrugged. "That's what Richard Beaumont thought, anyway."

"So you did kill him?"

"Technically Sophia did, but yes, I was involved." He raised one eyebrow, daring her to do something about it. "Are you going to take me in, lawman?"

She laughed and shook her head. "You're an idiot."

He grinned.

"Good riddance," she said, her smile falling. "I always hated him."

Back in Richard Beaumont's office, after Connor and his team had drugged the former Lightseer Regent with a Hackamore, the man had confessed so much—including what he would've done to Quinn, if given the chance. Connor debated sharing what Richard had said, but he instead opted for silence.

It was best she didn't know.

"I always thought you nobles had it easy," he confessed. "Money. Comfort. Fame, in your case. I envied it when I was little. I loathed it as an adult. All that poverty in the Ancient Woods, all those good people dying because they can't afford something as simple as a Rectivane. And yet you rich folk have all this money up here, in your castles and cities, just sitting in your vaults. It always felt like a waste." He sighed and leaned forward to stretch out his arms as he spoke. "But you've never had an easy life, have you? Not really. Your father molded you into a weapon and tried to frame you on the wall. You had a prison, same as the rest of us. Yours merely had silk sheets."

"I had it better than most," she said. "I don't need your pity."

"Not pity."

"Then what?"

"Empathy." He frowned and looked her dead in the eye. "I take it that's new for you?"

Her soft pink lips parted in surprise, and her gaze briefly roamed his face. A few gentle creases appeared in her brow as she relaxed, however, and she nodded once in gratitude.

"Out there in the bogs, you fought for me." Connor propped one elbow on his knee and scanned her features. "In there, against that army of soldiers, you were willing to kill for me, if that's what it took. Bless the Fates, but I never thought a Starling would stick her neck out for me like you did."

Unable to meet his eye, Quinn returned her intense gaze to the moors far beyond the city. "Like I said, it was earned."

"Why are you so certain I won't go dark?"

"I want to believe there's still good in this world," she confessed quietly.

"Huh," he mumbled, not sure how to reply.

"Look." She ran her thin fingers through her long red hair and took a settling breath. "If you were going to betray me, there's a lot you could've done differently. I wanted to know the sort of man you are, and I got my answer. You're not that bad."

He grinned. "Not that bad, but still a little terrible?"

"Just enough to be decent." She chuckled. Her expression softened, and she tilted her head as she studied his face. "Is it really over? Do you trust me?"

"I do." He cast a sidelong glance her way. "Don't make me regret it."

Smiling, she leaned back on her palms and let out a slow breath. "Guess we don't need those Hackamores, then."

"Well, they were expensive. If you don't want yours, I'll keep it."

She laughed and shook her head, but didn't reply.

"You let me capture you." He adjusted in his seat and leaned back on one elbow as he lay on the roof tiles, facing her. "Anything else I should know about that?"

"If you truly heard what I told Nocturne, then no. Not really." Quinn absently coiled one of her auburn curls around her finger as she spoke. "I needed to know what you wanted. I needed to know what this world would be like if you continue on this path you've chosen."

"Did you figure it out?"

"I think so," she admitted. "You just want to survive, but no one will give you peace."

He snorted derisively. "At least someone understands."

"You'll never have it." Quinn rested her elbows on her knees and watched him carefully. "Dahlia was right, as much as I hate to say those words out loud. Peace just isn't sustainable for people like you and me. The world always wants something from us, and we will always live different lives than most people. Every night, there's a cost we must pay to see the sunrise. It can't be helped. It can't be changed."

He studied her in silence, but she ignored him and instead stared down at her palm. The thick, pale scar across her hand cast a sharp contrast to her otherwise flawless skin, and she swallowed hard as she curled her fingers into a fist.

"What happened to you?" he finally asked, still not certain he would get an answer. "How does someone like you, with all that money and all those potions, end up with a scar like that?"

She didn't look at him. For several minutes, she didn't answer. She just stared again at her mark as the silence lingered, and he let her have her quiet.

If she didn't want to answer, she didn't have to. In the end, it wasn't his business.

"I caught my father in a lie." The whistling wind nearly drowned out her soft voice as they sat on the castle roof. "He knows what you are, and he sent me after you without the weapons I needed to protect myself. He hoped you would break me. When he thought I couldn't hear him, he finally told the truth, and I didn't like what I heard. I left because I don't know who he is, anymore. If I'm being honest, I'm scared to find out."

Connor frowned as he watched her. He didn't know what to say.

"He's terrifying," she confessed in a harsh whisper. "Even the most talented people I know fear him. One time, I witnessed the King of Hazeltide piss himself under my father's glare. I've watched him torture Nethervale elite and cut down enemies on the battlefield, but he has always been kind to me. He has always loved me, or so I thought. I figured that meant the people who suffered his wrath—well, it's naïve, I suppose, but I always thought they must've deserved what he did to them. He was my idol."

The tendons in her neck tightened, and her shoulders stiffened as she stared down at her hand. She bit her lip, and Connor let her sit with the pain.

He couldn't fix this. He could only listen.

"Maybe he does love me," she continued. "Or maybe that's just another mask he wears to keep me obedient. I don't know anymore. I watched him manipulate Zander, and I always feared he loved Zander more than me. Even if that's the case, it's proof that no one is safe. No one is exempt. He knows what to say to make you do what he wants, and I realize now I was never immune." She scowled and rubbed her eyes in frustration. "I just want some justice, Connor. I want to have faith in people again."

"You and me both," he confessed.

She nodded toward the horizon. "Out there, when we face him, I don't know what will happen. Maybe someone just needs to shine light on his lies. If I tell the soldiers what you are, it will unravel the foundation the Lightseers are built upon. For the Fates' sake, our supposed destruction of the simmering souls all those centuries ago is the very lie we still use to recruit new soldiers. We are the champions of light, after all." She sneered in disgust. "That's what we were told. If it's all built on a lie, the blind faith corrodes. They'll realize they've been played. Maybe that's enough to stop this from getting worse."

"Or maybe it will make them hate me more," he countered.

"Maybe," she admitted. "Lightseers are idealistic. We have to believe we can extinguish the darkness. It's the only way we can keep facing it."

Connor slowly shook his head. "I don't like this plan."

"Do you have a better one?" she retorted.

He grimaced, but didn't reply. Short of risking his team's life when outnumbered by ruthless professional soldiers, no. He didn't.

"You're coming back to Slaybourne, then?" he asked.

"Of course. You have Blaze."

"I'll keep him safe, and you can have him when it's over," Connor promised.

"I'm coming," she said firmly. Her eyes briefly glossed over, and she shifted her full attention to him. "You're afraid I'll defect to his side, aren't you?"

"Not quite," he admitted. "I trust you, but I won't ask you to face your father on the battlefield."

"You're kind," she said softly. "But I have to do this."

"And before I let you on that battlefield, I have to know I won't regret it," Connor replied. "What will you do when you see him?"

She let out a shaky breath and examined her nails. "There's an unforgiveable act among the Lightseers. Something that, if done, guarantees banishment. In some cases, it has ended with the death sentence."

"And that is?"

"Defy the commander," she said flatly. "Disobey. Stand in his way. When we face him, I will lose my position as a Lightseer Elite before I can even say a word. I'll be an outcast and an outlaw, same as you. I'll lose everything." She looked at Connor and let the weight of her words settle on the air between them. "I'll lose it all in the name of doing what's right, but I can't stay quiet anymore."

"You don't have to," Connor pointed out. "You can stay here. You can feign ignorance. You can walk out of the rubble and side with whomever wins."

"That's the coward's way," she snapped, and her nose wrinkled with disgust. "I can't live with myself if I don't. I would rather die."

"You might."

"Yeah," she said quietly as she watched the horizon. "I might."

He rubbed his thumb against his palm as he tried to piece together his thoughts. It didn't feel right, asking family to fight on opposite sides of a war. And in the heat of the moment, even a soldier as strong as her could lose her nerve.

Once she faced her father, even she might crumble—like she did back there in the bogs. If his and his team's lives depended on her, he needed a guarantee she would have a steady hand.

"Could you kill him?" Connor asked. "If it came to it. If he doesn't listen to reason. If there's nothing good left in him."

"Could you, if the roles were reversed?" she countered.

Connor's jaw tensed, and he looked away. That had hit a little too close to home.

She paused. "I didn't mean to—"

"It's fine," he lied.

"You're a shit liar." Quinn rubbed her forehead and sighed. "But it's not my business."

No, it wasn't. He let the silence linger.

"I don't see a warrior when I look at him," she admitted. "I see the man who raised me, who lifted me on his shoulders when I was little and told me I was destined for greatness. The man who told me he was proud of me. His miracle child, the one Death gave back. The survivor. The fighter." She stared again at the scar on her hand. "But I think none of those memories are real. None of that is true. Out there, I'm not going to stop until I meet the real man. I might not be a Lightseer once I face him, but our creed has never rung truer."

Duty above all else—and in her case, even family.

"Saldia needs you," she said gently. "And if my father tries to take you from us, he will go through me."

"Thank you." Connor smiled, astonished it had come to this, and almost unable to believe she would fight her own family to defend him.

And yet, here they were.

Quinn, however, didn't smile back. She snared him with those hazel eyes and leaned forward, her intense gaze firm and strong as the wind howled past them. This close, a blended perfume of jasmine and honeysuckle wafted from her hair.

When he'd first met her, he had seen a woman who learned to weaponize her beauty. It must've distracted most men, and he had therefore suppressed any hint of desire for her.

But here, this close and where no other soul could see them, a powerful urge to pin her hands over her head nearly overtook him. In a flash of dominating need, he imagined pressing his mouth against hers and using his knees to spread her legs wide. He could nearly taste her. The sweat. The sweetness of her breath.

This time, the primal urges he had denied for so long nearly won in the budding war against his willpower.

"I'm betting everything I have on you, Connor."

Her voice broke the spell, and he gritted his teeth to swallow the raw craving to feel her body beneath his.

Fates be damned, the urges were getting more powerful—and more frequent.

"I'm gambling my fortune," she added. "My freedom. My name. My reputation. My family. I'll never see my mother again. Because I'm betting on you, I might lose it all."

"I know." He nodded. "And I'm grateful."

"Good. I know it's what needs to be done." Though her stiff tone carried the weight of an officer delivering an order, her eyes drifted briefly toward his mouth. "There's only so much I can do, out there. In the end, it will come down to you. When you face my father, I need you to do something for me."

His eyes narrowed, uncertain of what she could possibly want. Quinn leaned in, and he fought another surge of desire as she tread dangerously close.

"Prove to me that I made the right choice," she whispered.

With that, she stood and walked back up the roof, toward the overhang he'd used to climb up in the first place.

When her footsteps faded, Connor let out a slow breath and rubbed his eyes as the last of the overwhelming urges finally faded.

"That's the plan," he told the sun-kissed sky.

CHAPTER SIXTY-NINE
CONNOR

In the late afternoon light, Connor leaned his back against a towering oak deep in the forests outside Freymoor. He stared up into the cloudy sky as the twittering woodland chirped with life.

Though his eyes ached for rest, he couldn't. Every time he tried, he thought of Slaybourne. Of the Finns. Of the valley between the Black Keep Mountains, blazing with hellfire.

Since sleep had failed him, he instead tracked the obscured sun on its way toward the horizon and waited for the first signs of darkness.

He didn't have much longer to wait.

Tendrils of mist coiled over the thick green grasses beneath his feet, and he eyed the fog warily. Though his team had survived the Blood Bogs, he had no intention of going back in there anytime soon.

Or ever, if he was lucky.

A crude wooden table sat in the middle of the field, out of place among the mossy ruins spread across the grass like debris. Vines drooped from the chipped, uneven edges of the stones, and Dahlia's soldiers casually strode between the rocks as they surveyed the forest. Archers, still armed with those damned crossbows, perched high in the canopy.

This time, however, their focus remained on the forest—and not on him.

While he had waited for Dahlia and his team to arrive, he had spent the last few minutes trying to make sense of the ruins. Given their chaotic placement, they almost seemed organic until he noticed the carefully carved edges that could only come from a mason's cut. The pillars poked from the earth, leaning in some places and perfectly straight in others, and none of the stones connected at any point. Whatever they were, or whatever they had been, they didn't seem to form any cohesive structure.

A soft snore interrupted Connor's thoughts, and he shifted sideways as he stared around the largest block.

In the open field, nestled in the center of the stones and obscured by most of them, Nocturne curled around himself with his great wings tucked tightly against his back. The dragon's chest rose and fell in a sleepy rhythm as the day crept by, and a coil of black smoke shot through his nose as another gentle snore rumbled through the ground.

Connor watched the regal creature, who hadn't awoken since they'd left the mists, and debated what he would say when the time came to discuss what had happened in the bogs.

I heard you, perhaps.

Or, *would you really rip out my throat?*

The thought of his friend turning on him hurt worse than any wound ever could.

His eyes glossed over, and he sifted through his questions as he debated what to do with the dragon. As much as he needed Nocturne's help, perhaps it was best to send the beast home. He didn't need supposed teammates conspiring behind his back.

After all, a man could only trust his team if they were as loyal to him as he was to them.

Something pressed against his mind, gently at first, and he grimaced as he tried to figure out what it was. The sensation felt oddly familiar, like an old friend stopping by to pay a visit.

The augmentation in his chest buzzed, and the gentle vibrations rumbled through him like thunder.

His gaze shifted to the dragon. Though Nocturne hadn't moved, the princely creature had opened one jet-black eye and now watched him from afar.

Connor cracked his neck. Time to let the dragon in.

He shut his eyes and leaned into the sensation. His breath quickened, and his shoulders tensed as he leaned into the kind of magic he hadn't thought he would ever possess. Almost instantly, a flurry of energy snaked through his core, and it took a moment to register the sensation as the same one he got from flying.

Lightweight. Joyful.

Like *freedom*.

You feel betrayed.

Even though he was expecting it, Connor's head snapped abruptly up as Nocturne's voice echoed through his head.

The sensation of weightless joy intensified, and his pulse settled. The dragon's voice in his head felt like *home*, like happiness, and he didn't understand why.

I know you heard everything.

Connor squared his shoulders and shrugged, as though it didn't bother him.

I did, he thought back to the dragon.

The pact I made with Quinn, the dragon continued. All of it. You know what is at stake, should you ever lose your way.

Tension snaked down Connor's spine as he braced himself against imagining the two of them cutting off his head, just as Quinn had done to Otmund. *I hadn't realized you two were so close.*

She and I are alike, Nocturne replied with a soft growl. Guardians, but not welcome among those we protect. Never one of the many, and yet we have no purpose in life without them. We are islands, and neither of us has ever belonged.

You weren't my prisoner, Connor pointed out. *You could've left at any time to go back to your people.*

This was never about leaving or staying, the dragon explained. It was about knowing if my homeland was safe. As I witnessed your power grow, I saw a potential threat rising in a land far too close to mine. I've lost good souls to the darkness before, Wraithblade. Such is the way of we dragon warriors, and it is the risk we all take to defend our home. I needed to ensure no war would follow me when I returned.

You're leaving, then? he asked.

NOT YET.

Connor's eyes narrowed in suspicion.

I HAVE DWELT ON YOUR OFFER, the dragon continued. *AND I ACCEPT. I WILL ONLY LEAVE WHEN OUR BARGAIN IS FULFILLED. CONNOR MAGNUSON. YOU WILL HELP ME FIND THOSE THAT I LOST, AND I WILL HELP YOU SECURE YOUR PLACE IN THIS WORLD.*

After the stunt you pulled back there, I'm considering taking that deal off the table, Connor admitted with a sidelong glare at the thickening mists just beyond the meadow.

YOU COULD, the dragon said calmly. *BUT YOU WON'T.*

What makes you so sure?

A soft chuckle escaped the dragon. *BECAUSE WE NEED EACH OTHER.*

Connor sighed impatiently, and he crossed his arms as he stared up at the branches above him. A soldier's foot passed through a hole in the thick leaves, but the man gave no other indication he was there. No creak of the wood. No heavy breathing. Nothing at all.

These Freymoor soldiers were damn good.

WHEN I WAS NEARLY FERAL, I THREATENED YOUR HOME, Nocturne reminded him. *WAS THERE NOT A LINE THAT, IF CROSSED, WOULD HAVE ENDED WITH YOUR SWORD IN MY SKULL?*

A gentle breeze tumbled through the canopy, tussling the leaves, and Connor closed his eyes in resignation.

The dragon had a point.

LOYALTY CANNOT BE BLIND, CONNOR. Nocturne let out a long, somber sigh, and his gaze shifted to the grass. *I KNOW ALL TOO WELL THE DAMAGE THAT CAN DO.*

Arms crossed, Connor waited for the regal creature to continue.

LONG AGO, I WAS FORCED TO KILL MY OWN BROTHER, the dragon's eyes squeezed shut at the confession. *I REFUSED TO ACKNOWLEDGE HIS LIMITS, AND THOUGH HE WAS NOT READY TO JOIN OUR RANKS AS A WARRIOR, I ALLOWED HIM TO ATTEMPT THE TRIALS. IT DROVE HIM FERAL, AND HE TURNED HIS IMMENSE POWER ON OUR FAMILY. ON OUR FRIENDS. ON OUR HOME.*

Connor rubbed his eyes, and his shoulders drooped at the thought of what that must've been like for Nocturne to endure.

The loss.

The guilt.

The shame.

I FAILED MY BROTHER, BUT I WILL NOT FAIL MY PEOPLE. The dragon prince lifted his head and stared up into the cloudy sky. *AND I WILL NOT FAIL YOU, CONNOR. ANY MAN CAN LOSE HIS WAY, BUT THE PACT WITH QUINN IS NOTHING MORE THAN A CONTINGENCY I PRAY I WILL NEVER HAVE TO USE.*

YOU HAVE A GOOD HEART, Nocturne continued. *I SEE DRAGONFIRE IN YOUR SOUL, CONNOR. YOU ARE A NOBLE MAN WITH GOOD INTENTIONS, BUT THERE WILL ALWAYS BE DARKNESS IN YOU AS WELL. WITH MY HOMELAND AT STAKE, I HAD TO KNOW IF YOU COULD WIN AGAINST IT. I STUDIED YOU, BUT I COULD NOT DISCERN THE TRUTH—BECAUSE EVEN YOU DON'T KNOW, YET, WHERE YOUR POWER WILL TAKE YOU. I NEEDED A MEANS TO PROTECT MY PEOPLE, SAME AS YOU PROTECT YOURS. EVEN IF IT MEANT KILLING MY FRIEND.*

Connor massaged the back of his neck, and though exhaustion weighed heavily on his eyelids, he pushed through the weariness. *You can stay.*

HOW GENEROUS, WRAITHBLADE. The great dragon chuckled softly and curled up once more. *IT IS A WISE CHOICE.*

"Fates be damned," Connor muttered to himself. "It had better be."

What? the Wraith King asked, though he remained hidden. *Were you talking to yourself again, Magnuson?*

Apparently, the Wraith King couldn't listen in on the augmented conversations with Nocturne.

What a *relief.*

Connor stifled a mischievous grin. "Nothing."

An uneasy grumble rolled through his head, but the ghoul didn't reply.

The crash of feet through the underbrush broke the forest's silence, and Connor shifted his attention as the noise grew closer. Several of the guards in the canopy above him followed the movement of someone he couldn't see, and since they hadn't launched any of their arrows, he didn't draw his swords or stiffen for a fight.

Besides, it had to be Murdoc.

"If one more damned mosquito bites me, I swear to the Fates, I'll get a torch," the former Blackguard muttered as he stepped out of the woods. He swatted at an insect buzzing around his face and incoherently grumbled more halfhearted threats to the hovering bugs.

"You understand how to be stealthy," Connor chided. "I've seen you in action."

"And?" Murdoc's eyes narrowed in confusion, and the man tilted his head as he waited for Connor to get to the point.

He gestured toward the broken twigs the former Blackguard had snapped moments ago. "Then why the hell do you make so much noise?"

His friend shrugged. "We're in friendly territory. I have to be lazy whenever possible, Captain. It's the only way I stay sane."

Connor shook his head, but he grinned.

Fair enough.

The swish of a skirt snaked past, and Sophia slipped into the meadow seconds later without any other hint that she had been coming. A flash of red hair amongst the trees followed, and Quinn joined them within moments.

As he caught the Starling warrior's eye, his gaze lingered—and she watched him a moment longer than she normally would have.

Sophia huffed and crossed her arms. "Why did that woman want us to trek to the middle of nowhere?"

In the oak above Connor, one of Dahlia's soldiers sucked in a sharp breath through his teeth, as if biting back a scathing remark.

"Sophia, 'that woman' is our ally," Connor corrected, before the soldier could make things worse. "Show her some respect."

The necromancer rolled her eyes, but didn't respond. That was apparently the best she could do, and frankly, he would take it.

Given their introduction to the Lady of Freymoor, it was still an improvement.

In the distance, a twig cracked, and both he and Quinn briefly tilted their heads toward it. She glanced briefly at him, and he raised one eyebrow in a silent request that she behave herself.

They would have company, soon.

"Information," Quinn said.

Sophia's dark eyes swept toward the Starling warrior in a silent demand for context.

"We're here to get information." The Lightseer gestured toward the empty table. "Before you enter a warzone, you need to understand troop movements. It's standard procedure. With Dahlia's connections and resources, I can only assume she has spies littered throughout Saldia, and she likely has a significant amount of intelligence to share before we leave. Heading to Slaybourne without preparing first is suicide."

"You are correct, Starling." Dahlia's voice pierced the air, sharp and clear, from behind them.

Connor looked over his shoulder as Dahlia led a cluster of soldiers through the underbrush. The man in the cloak lined with thick furs walked beside her, carrying a cluster of rolled parchment under his arm. Behind him, several of the other soldiers carried saddle bags over their shoulders. Each of the various pockets puffed out, so full the buttons threatened to pop off.

Dahlia joined them, and she tilted her head toward the man in the black cloak. "This is my general, Duncan Whitlock."

"I remember you." Murdoc crossed his arms as he stared up at the towering man who had barred the doors back in Dahlia's throne room.

"Good," Duncan said dryly.

"None of that," the fallen princess chided in a quiet voice. "They've proven themselves."

His mouth pressed into a thin line, and though he glanced briefly down at her, his intense focus shifted instead to Quinn.

"We've brought you provisions," Dahlia said with a gesture toward the saddle bags. "Our Champion deserves more fanfare in his send-off, but with Oakenglen soldiers patrolling every street, I'm afraid this will have to do."

"It's more than enough, and far more than I was expecting." He briefly scanned the bags, wondering what she could've possibly given them to need so many packs. "Sophia, keep track of all this, will you?"

The necromancer grinned deviously and lifted the nearest bag onto her shoulder. "Reagents? Potions? What do we have?"

"Everything, including ten bloody beauties for you to use at our Champion's command." The fallen princess narrowed her eyes in an unspoken warning.

"Ten?" Quinn blinked rapidly in surprise.

"Ten," Dahlia echoed tersely. "I take care of my people, and he's one of us now."

Still holding the rolls of parchment under his arm, Duncan took several menacing steps toward Quinn. "She shouldn't be here. Not with what we have to discuss."

"She stays," Connor ordered.

Duncan paused midstride, and his glare shifted to Connor. Everyone else stilled, and a dozen pairs of eyes darted toward him. Unflinching, Connor met the general's steely gaze and dared him to protest further.

"Very well," Dahlia said, though her eye twitched in irritation. "The Starling stays."

Though he sighed impatiently, Duncan turned his back on Quinn and strode toward the table in the center of the meadow. An attendant trailed after him, easily keeping pace, and Duncan gave the man the cluster of rolled parchment he had been holding.

"This one, sir," the attendant said as he tugged out one of the rolls. "It's the southern map."

"Good, thank you," Duncan muttered as he unfurled the parchment. He set it on the table and leaned forward, his palms holding the map open as his eyes scanned the paper.

Connor followed, and he stared down at a carefully drawn sketch of the Ancient Woods and the Decay. The others joined them shortly, and before long, they all circled the out-of-place table in the center of an ancient ruin.

"Teagan was last spotted in the Lightseer's engineering zone outside of Charborough." Duncan tapped his thick finger on the edge of the Decay, where the eastern fork of the southern road met the desert. "It's a military testing grounds the Lightseers claimed centuries ago. Over the decades, they've constructed their own little village of warmongers."

Connor's heart panged with dread. "When was he last spotted?"

"Long enough to be irrelevant at this point." Duncan looked up at Connor, calm despite the devastating implication in what he had just said.

Damn it.

"Then he's in the Decay already," Connor set his fists on the table, his biceps bulging as he hung his head in defeat. "He's going to make it to Slaybourne before us."

"It appears so." Duncan pulled two daggers from a sheath on his leg and stabbed them into opposite corners of the map to keep the parchment from rolling closed. "Where is Slaybourne, so that we can estimate your travel time?"

Fates be damned, he didn't know. He had followed the ghoul out to the Decay.

With a sigh of resignation, Connor pinched the bridge of his nose. "You want to answer that one, Wraith King?"

A weary groan echoed through his mind, but the tension in the air shifted in answer. Black smoke rolled across the table, and a bony finger emerged from the inky void. The skeletal tip of a dead man's finger pressed against a large stretch of desert on the map, almost to the edge, and it disappeared seconds later.

Murdoc shuddered. "I hate it when he does that."

"Same," Dahlia and Sophia quipped in unison. The two women briefly looked at each other before returning their attention to the map.

Duncan, unfazed, set his finger where the ghost had pointed. His attendant tugged a stick of charcoal out of his pocket and marked the spot with a circle.

Freymoor had given him one of their greatest treasures, and the ghoul had shared the location of a long-lost fortress. For better or worse, the alliance was in full force.

"I would estimate five days, then, for him to reach Slaybourne," the general continued. "Provided the map is the correct scale, of course, and we believe it is. Given Teagan's load and numbers, that sounds about right. He will probably arrive at the Black Keep Mountains in three days."

"That fast?" Quinn's voice dropped to a whisper, and she gaped at the general. "That's a record."

Connor shook his head. "It's a four day flight."

"Then you'll have to hurry." The general shrugged. "When you face him, you won't just face an army. He's bringing something with him, Wraithblade. Something devastating. Something we've never seen before."

An icy chill snaked through the air, and for a moment, everyone went silent. Connor stiffened, lost in thought, and he quietly debated his options.

He had known facing Teagan Starling wouldn't be easy, but this was so much worse than he could've ever imagined.

Hell, it might even be *impossible*.

CHAPTER SEVENTY
CONNOR

Teagan Starling had already left for the Decay, and the odds of Connor reaching Slaybourne first weren't good.

"Give me a second," Connor said under his breath. "I need to come up with a plan."

"We're here to help," Duncan said firmly. "We work with what we have. It's all we can do."

Calmly. Confidently. Entirely focused on the facts. This was a man of war, and one clearly familiar with impossible odds.

Connor's jaw tensed, but he nodded for the Freymoor general to continue.

"Even at night, there's little chance of passing him without being spotted." Duncan lifted one hand, and his assistant put the stick of charcoal in his palm. The commander drew four thin black marks through the desert and tapped on each one as he made it. "However, five days of travel requires four nights of rest. That means an opportunity, each time, for an ambush."

"If he doesn't make it to Slaybourne first," Murdoc pointed out.

"True." With the stick of charcoal, Duncan tapped on the circle marking Connor's fortress. "You will either pass him in the desert or meet him at Slaybourne's walls, but you won't be able to avoid him. Not if you want to get there before he breaks through the walls."

Still hidden in the in-between, the Wraith King huffed in anger. *He underestimates Slaybourne's power.*

"Or he knows something we don't," Connor retorted in a hushed voice.

"Once we reach the edge of the Decay, we will fly day and

night," Nocturne interjected. "That will make up for lost time."

A few of the soldiers surrounding the table flinched at the dragon's sudden voice, but Connor simply shook his head. "I need you in that battle. Flying that long will exhaust you."

The great dragon chuckled. "I was bred for war, my friend. I can handle both."

"Wait a minute," Sophia said quietly as she tapped her fingertip against her ruby-red lips. "You said, 'considering his load.' What do you mean? Is he being slowed down by something?"

Duncan nodded and sighed in resignation as he rapped one knuckle on the table. "Long before he arrived in Charborough, the master engineers were building something. It was a flurry of activity for weeks, and it remains such even now."

"What are they building?" Murdoc hesitantly asked, as though he wasn't sure he really wanted to hear the answer.

"That's just it." Duncan shook his head. "We don't know. We've gleaned bits and pieces, but nothing of true substance. Lightseer security is notoriously good," he added with a sidelong glare at Quinn.

Though her eye twitched in irritation, she thankfully didn't rise to the bait.

"It's not all bleak." Dahlia leaned her palms against the table as she studied the map. "Our war-pigeons did return this morning with new intelligence."

"Tell me you're joking," Sophia said dryly.

Dahlia met the necromancer's incredulous glare. "About what, Miss Auclair?"

The necromancer raised one skeptical eyebrow, and her nose wrinkled with disdain. "War-pigeons?"

The fallen princess huffed impatiently. "They're one of the fastest birds alive, and they're always overlooked. Our pigeon master trains the fastest in Saldia. So, yes. War-pigeons."

Murdoc raised one hand to cover the broad smile on his face as he tried—and failed—to stifle his snorting laughter.

"War-pigeons," Connor said dubiously. "Alright, fine. What did you find out?"

"We know they're working on something big." Duncan gently stroked his beard as his eyes swept across the map. "It leaves behind the kind of devastation that can level a castle's walls. That's all we know. We haven't even been able to watch one fire, thanks to the impenetrable security around the area. Those engineers are fiercely loyal, and each new hire is more zealous than the last. We've been trying to infiltrate the compound for decades."

Teagan Starling plans on hurling rocks at us? The ghoul laughed derisively. *How primitive.*

Connor didn't reply. Teagan didn't seem like the sort of man to spend that much time on a basic siege weapon, and it seemed foolish to assume there wasn't more to this story than met the eye.

He shifted his attention to Quinn, who still hadn't spoken. She stared down at the map with lines of worry creased into her forehead, and her eyes had glossed over in thought.

With a frustrated groan, Connor began to pace the length of the table. "How can I make a plan to defeat him when I don't even know what weapons he has?"

We improvise, the Wraith King explained.

"Improvise?" Connor echoed. "That's not a plan!"

Dahlia raised her chin, and her gaze darted to something behind Connor. He looked over his shoulder, but no one was there.

She sees me, the ghoul said in a tense voice.

A thin smile spread across Dahlia's face, and she nodded.

"How?" Connor demanded.

The fallen princess's gaze shifted to him, and she relaxed somewhat. "It's a difficult skill to learn, but all those who enter the bogs can develop it with time."

"I suggest we remain focused," Duncan warned. "There's far more to discuss."

"Of course." Sophia closed her eyes as she waited to hear the worst of it. "Go on, then. Get it over with."

"There's a chance he has his assassins in tow," the general continued as his finger traced a line from Oakenglen to Charborough. "Several of our best spies went missing along the route to the Decay, which can only mean the Unknown are involved."

"Assassins?" Quinn interjected, finally breaking her silence. "The Unknown? What the hell are you talking about? The Lightseers are the most elite fighters in Saldia. We don't need assassins."

Everyone from Freymoor looked at her incredulously, as though they couldn't believe she had lied to them in their own land. Brows furrowed. Eyes narrowed. Some even gripped the hilts of their swords.

"Truth," Nocturne interjected.

"She can't possibly be telling the truth," Dahlia hissed under her breath.

"She is," the dragon confirmed.

"Of course I am." Quinn crossed her arms as her furious gaze swept across everyone present. "Your intelligence is wrong."

"He has secret assassins?" Connor asked as his head began to thump with a dull ache. "Assassins he hid from his own daughter?"

"Evidently," Dahlia said dryly.

"There's... there can't be..." Quinn stuttered, but the conviction in her tone began to fade as her gaze shifted to Nocturne.

"He lies to everyone, Quinn," Connor said gently. "Why wouldn't he lie to you about this?"

The muscles in her neck tightened, but her lips pinched closed as she glared down at the map and refused to respond.

"The Unknown are the most devastating force in Saldia," Duncan said, his voice low and gravelly as his furious glare lingered on her. "They're more deadly and more dangerous than any Lightseer I've ever met, and I was damned lucky that I was able to kill the one that came after me."

The rustle of leaves in the canopy filled the lull that followed, drowning out the choking silence as everyone watched Duncan—even as the general never once looked away from Quinn.

Teagan's daughter didn't reply. She merely watched him, waiting for him to continue like everyone else.

"Brutal fighter," Duncan finally continued. "She came after me in the middle of the night. I head into the privy and find a woman, dressed in black, with a knife at my throat. Still have the scars." He tilted his head to one side, and several long, silver lines snaked down his neck and into his shirt. "I killed her with a broom handle, and after she was dead, *she* became a *he*. It was a glamour, and a damn fine one at that. I recognized the corpse as a Lord who had spent his life in the Freymoor court, even in the years before Henry took over. The man who tried to kill me grew up here. He was a well-known merchant, for the Fates' sake, and he led a secret life of murder. We only pieced together the clues thanks to the Antiquity's help."

"The Unknown are everywhere." Though Dahlia stared directly at Quinn, the fallen princess gently set one hand on her general's arm. "They could be anyone. No name. No ranks. No residue. That's the point—no one knows how many there are or even who they are. Not even the members of the Unknown know each other. We've pieced most of this together bit by bit, year after year, from the trail of bodies they leave behind."

"Fuck," Murdoc whispered. He rubbed his face so hard his skin turned red.

"Are any of them traveling with the army?" Connor asked, fairly certain he already knew his answer.

"There's no way of knowing." Duncan pushed off the table and shrugged. "It's certainly possible. Everyone in the army is in a Lightseer uniform, but that doesn't mean anything."

"Alright." Connor took a settling breath as he leaned over the map. "With any plan, you start with the basics—what we know, what we don't, and what we're trying to accomplish."

"We know we're facing certain death," Sophia quipped with a lazy flick of her hand.

"Not helping." He shot her a warning glare through the corner of his eye.

"We know Teagan has a hundred-strong army." Duncan crossed his arms and nodded toward Quinn. "We know he mustered his best fighters to face you, and that he gathered them in record time."

"Thank you." He looked at Sophia and gestured toward the general in front of them. "See? *That* was helpful."

The necromancer set her hands on her hips with an impatient little huff, but didn't reply.

"We know they will likely arrive before you," Dahlia added.

"They have unknown weaponry capable of mass devastation," Connor added. "If it's strong enough to corrode the last of Slaybourne's enchantments, that means the Finns and everyone in that fortress are in danger."

His jaw tensed at the thought, but he couldn't dwell on it. He had to focus.

"My father will negotiate," Quinn added in a quiet voice.

A lull settled on the table as everyone present shifted their attention toward her.

"Care to elaborate?" Connor prodded.

Her hazel eyes darted briefly toward him, and she shrugged. "Over the years, I've often seen him negotiate. He always sets up his army first to showcase his power. Whether or not he begins the attack, however, depends on the opponent's strength and numbers. If they're a threat, he hits them hard until they've lost soldiers or the high ground."

"And if he doesn't consider them to be a threat?" Murdoc asked.

Quinn hesitated. "It depends on how generous he's feeling that day."

Connor frowned, his mind buzzing with all the ways this battle could go—and with how few of those scenarios ended in his favor.

"So," Dahlia interjected. "Let's review what we *don't* know."

"We don't know if we can get to Slaybourne first," Murdoc pointed out. "If he beats us there, we don't know if we can get to the gate in time to open it without letting in a hoard of Lightseers after us."

"We don't know what his weapons are, either," Sophia added. "Or if Slaybourne will even be there when we arrive."

"It will." Connor's voice cut through the air like a knife, and for a few moments, no one spoke.

He needed to believe it would be there. Anything less, and he wouldn't be able to focus on the fight that lay ahead of them.

"We know enough to acknowledge we know very little." In his frustration, Duncan rubbed the back of his head and sighed deeply. "That means we have barely enough information on which to build a solid plan. Whatever you decide now will likely change by the time you arrive."

Exactly, the wraith said, exasperated. *We will be forced to improvise.*

A sharp breath of air shot through Connor's nose. He hated to think the ghoul was right, but at this point, he didn't see many alternatives.

"You'd better come up with an amazing plan, Connor," Sophia warned.

"I don't know about amazing," he admitted. "But it's something."

"How comforting," Quinn said dryly.

Connor ignored the jibe, and he leaned over the map as his mind spun with ideas. "Our main objective is to get the Soulsprite into Slaybourne, and the only way to do that is to go through Death's Door."

You and I can go over the walls, the wraith reminded him.

Perhaps, but that meant leaving his team to die on the frontlines, and Connor refused to allow that to happen.

If he made it into Slaybourne, he'd ensure his team did, too.

With his arms crossed over his broad chest, he paced the length of the table. Lost in thought, his mind raced with possibilities. Through the corner of his eye, he noticed lingering gazes shifting toward him.

Apparently, he now had the stage.

Though the gathered Freymoor soldiers kept their backs to the table, the nearest man tilted his head slightly in surprise. Dahlia stood beside Duncan and the eerily silent assistant, and the three of them watched in tense silence as Connor took control of the conversation.

They had done all they could and shared all they knew. From here, he and his team had to finalize the plan.

"It's dangerous," he admitted. "If Teagan is already at Slaybourne by the time we arrive, it means the main gate will likely be swarmed. We're going to have to fly high and do our best to go unseen until the last moment. From the flight path, we're guaranteed to get there at night, which means we have a solid chance of going undetected long enough to reach the wall."

"But not to get through the gates." Duncan scowled. "If I were a betting man, I'd say Teagan's army will be focusing the heaviest firepower on the entrance."

"That's why we'll need to decimate whoever is at the gate," Connor said. "With night cover and a stealthy approach, we have a fair shot at getting inside before Teagan can send reinforcements."

"It's risky." Quinn shook her head. "They will pursue, and it won't take long for them to swarm us. I've watched Death's Door open and close, Connor. It's heavy, and that means it's slow. They have a hundred vougels that will attack within moments."

Murdoc smirked "But we have a dragon."

"Exactly," Connor pointed toward the former Blackguard. "Nocturne can outfly any vougel. We should be able to retain the element of surprise, even if they see us approaching. None of them should know dragons are real, much less that we have one."

"Wait. Look here." Quinn traced her finger over the map from Freymoor to Slaybourne. "There's a chance we won't see him in the Decay. We're approaching the fortress from a different angle than he is, provided he heads straight there from Charborough."

"True," Connor acknowledged. "Even if he does see us, Nocturne is faster. No matter what happens, we push through. Our success hinges on getting the Soulsprite in place. We have no other choice."

After a moment's hesitation, she nodded in agreement. "Every wall will be monitored. Every Lightseer contingent has a unit that specializes in speed and observation. If I had to guess, I'd wager my father took Unit-Seven with him, and that's the most talented of all the units he has. There's a chance we can approach unseen, but against a force this capable, it's unlikely."

Connor groaned in frustration as he sifted through the risks.

"Don't underestimate these soldiers," Quinn warned. "They're elite Lightseers. In an ordinary battle, it takes eight augmented fighters to overwhelm just *one* of them."

Them, she had said.

Not *us*.

Strangely, her ominous warning soothed some of his tension, if only because of the reassurance that she did, in fact, think of herself as no longer a Lightseer.

"Maybe," he admitted. "But how many of them would fight you?"

Her jaw tensed and her gaze shifted to the map. "Fair point."

"Do you think anyone will be on the walls?" Sophia asked. "What are the people inside going to do when the battle starts?"

"Hide," Connor said. "I told Ethan to get everyone into the catacombs the second the siege starts. No one will be on the walls."

"Wesley will be." Quinn stared at him intently, daring him to disagree.

With a dry laugh, Connor shook his head. "He may be an idealistic young man, but he's not foolhardy enough to stare death in the face."

"Of course he is." The Starling warrior snorted derisively. "He's more like you than you think."

"I won't bet on that."

"You should," she countered. "I've seen his type before. Just wait. He will be on the wall, waiting for you to return. And if you don't come back soon enough, he will try to fight off the Lightseer army himself."

Connor ran his tongue over his back molars as he debated the possibility. The wraith couldn't touch the Soulsprite because of what he was, but Wesley could. Still, Connor didn't want the Finns' only son to be on those walls to begin with, much less be involved in something as life-and-death as this.

Quinn seemed certain, but Connor wasn't going to rely on the slim chance that Wesley would be up there, waiting in a warzone.

He had to operate as if it wasn't going to happen.

"If he is there—and frankly, I doubt he will be," Connor added with a sidelong glance at Quinn. "Then yes, giving Wesley the Soulsprite is the logical choice, as long as we can find a way to get it over the wall."

"Does he know about the Soulsprite?" Sophia asked.

"No. None of them do." Connor sighed. "But he's smart. The wraith can show him where to go."

I'm not an errand boy, Magnuson, the ghoul grumbled.

"Then you're going to have to try something new," Connor retorted. "Or we all die."

"Great," Sophia muttered. "No chance of this backfiring."

"What if Teagan has already breached the walls?" Dahlia's calm voice pierced the air like a song. The fallen princess leaned her delicate hands against the table and watched him from across the map.

A lull followed, and though the forest breathed life around them, a flood of dread washed through Connor at the thought.

"Same plan," he eventually said. "We get in, and the Soulsprite goes into place."

"Can you focus?" Dahlia countered. "If he were to—"

"Yes," Connor interrupted. His eyes narrowed as he glared at her, daring her to disagree.

She pursed her lips and, for a while, she only watched him. Her expression shifted between compassion and doubt, in a strange blur of emotions he couldn't fully read, but she didn't elaborate.

"Connor," Nocturne said calmly. "She has a point."

He turned on his heel and looked the dragon in the eye, waiting for the regal creature to elaborate.

"Love is a strength, more than a weakness, but it can blind us," Nocturne warned. "We all saw the evidence of your battle with the slavers. You returned to us, drenched in other men's blood, and I can only imagine what you did to them. Though your family was gravely injured in that ordeal, they all survived. I hate to see the carnage that would follow should someone do the unspeakable to even one of them. I cannot imagine what that would do to *you*."

Connor's throat tightened, but he didn't reply. Though his features remained calm, he inwardly raged at the very idea. He couldn't let himself imagine all the blood he would spill if it came to that.

"Do you see any problems with the core plan?" He shifted his attention to Duncan. "Anything else we need to know?"

"That's everything." The general tugged his daggers out of the table, and the map curled in on itself. "Good luck, Wraithblade."

Connor nodded in gratitude and turned to face his team. "We have at most two hours before sunset. Make sure you're packed and ready. Eat what you can and prepare for a very long night. The second it's dark, we're leaving, and we won't stop until dawn."

"Aye, Captain." Murdoc saluted.

Beside the former Blackguard, Sophia let out a shaky sigh, but she nodded in agreement. Only Quinn remained silent, pacing as she tugged on the ends of her hair, and she stared off into the forest, lost in thought.

Hmm.

"I will hunt before our journey," Nocturne said before Connor could snap Quinn out of her daze. "I need to eat."

"Stay out of sight," he warned. "It's still light out. We can't let any of the Oakenglen guards see you."

"Of course."

The dragon launched into the air, and a gust from the beast's great wings hit Connor squarely in the back. Skirts fluttered and hair whipped around the faces of those gathered as Nocturne flew over the forest, low enough to keep to the bogs only Freymoor could tame.

As those gathered by the table slowly dispersed back into the trees, only Quinn, Connor, and Dahlia remained behind. The Lady of Freymoor tapped her nails against the wooden surface, and her cold blue eyes remained fixed on Connor.

"Yes?" he asked dryly.

The fallen princess tilted her head slightly toward Quinn, who let out an impatient sigh and walked off into the forest after Sophia and Murdoc.

Birds twittered in the silence that followed, and Dahlia remained rooted in place long after the last of the footsteps receded.

"I get the feeling I won't like whatever you're about to say," Connor admitted.

"You won't," Dahlia said firmly. "Quinn Starling stays here."

He scoffed. "After all your talk of killing her? You must be insane."

"No, just wary. A Starling shouldn't be on that battlefield with you, and you know it."

"I trust her," he said, though it tasted somewhat like a lie.

He *wanted* to trust her. It didn't mean he *should*.

"If she turns on you, you're dead," Dahlia said flatly. "The Soulsprite will be lost to our greatest living enemy, and everything we've done here in the bogs unravels. You went through the trials, Connor, so I cannot tell you what to do. The Soulsprite is yours, and I honor our agreement. All I can do is point out weaknesses in your armor."

He shook his head. "You're not thinking this through."

"Oh?" She tilted her head, not bothering to mask the annoyed tone in her voice. "Do continue, Wraithblade."

"What happens if I face Teagan without either of the two children he came to rescue?" He crossed his arms as he stared down at her. "How much bartering power do you think that gives me?"

Her lips pressed into a thin line, but she didn't answer.

"Exactly." Connor shrugged. "I don't like this either, Dahlia. It's a gamble, and either way, there's a solid chance I'll lose. Bringing Quinn is the less risky bet."

"I don't follow."

"Without Quinn there, Teagan won't be willing to talk," he pointed out. "I can only bluff an experienced general for so long before I need to show him proof. Her being there buys us time."

"And if she turns on you?"

"She might," he reluctantly admitted. "But after what she and I have been through, I doubt it. Quinn survived the Blood Bogs, same as the rest of us. I'd say you owe her some respect."

Dahlia's eyes pinched shut, as if she couldn't believe his stupidity. Though her lips parted, she ultimately pressed them closed and hung her head in defeat.

"If we're going to be allies, you need to trust me," he warned.

"We *are* allies, Wraithblade." Her blue eyes snapped open, and she snared him in her frigid gaze.

The fallen princess walked around the table, and though he didn't budge, he carefully studied her every movement as she neared. She stopped in front of him and raised her delicate face toward his.

Barely a breath apart, she leaned in, and her voice dropped to a whisper. "The survival of both our kingdoms now rests on you, Connor. You hold my fate in your hands. How's that for trust?"

He didn't answer, and she didn't leave.

"My father died because he trusted the wrong person." Dahlia's breath rolled over him, sweet as honey. "Freymoor can't survive if you make the same mistake."

"Neither can Slaybourne." He let out a steadying breath. "And the more enemies you make, the harder both our lives are going to be."

He stepped around her without waiting for her to reply and headed back to the entrance to the tunnels below the city.

Dahlia was wrong about Quinn, and he was about to stake his life on it.

CHAPTER SEVENTY-ONE
ETHAN

High on the cliffs overlooking the Decay, Ethan groaned as he shifted his weight on the stiff boulder he had chosen as a makeshift chair. Though a rocky outcrop to his left blocked some of his view of the desert beyond, this spot offered him the best blend of shade and visibility. He stared over the walls surrounding Slaybourne, his mind buzzing with worry. Somewhere out there, Connor was doing the impossible and chasing down the sort of monsters Ethan couldn't even dream of, all to keep this place safe.

To keep his family safe.

A sharp jolt of pain cut through the lingering dull ache in his stump of a leg. He breathed through it, his face flushing as the agony swelled around the still-healing stitches. This damned pain never went away. It faded sometimes, almost quiet enough for him to forget, but it refused to leave.

With a frustrated groan, he reached for the hand-carved crutch lying beside him and leaned his weight into it. He stretched out his leg, and his stump twitched uselessly beneath his knee. The crutch pressed against his armpit, and his knuckles bleached from his grip as he leaned into the pain.

The intense prickle around his stitches finally faded, and he let out a sigh of relief. The dull ache lingered and pulsed in time with his heart. He rubbed his eyes, his forehead throbbing from the effort of sitting upright, but he refused to lie in bed all day.

His thumb brushed against something rough on the crutch's handle. He peered around his shoulder and lifted his finger to find letters carved into the wood. Messy and unfinished, they looped too wide and cut off at jagged angles of an unpracticed wood worker.

Love you, Daddy, it said, in Fiona's adorably sloppy handwriting.

Though his eyes drooped with exhaustion, he smiled. The pain in his leg receded a little more, and his breath evened out.

Behind him, wings snapped against the air. The rustle of feathers and cloth broke the tranquil day, and he strained to peer over his shoulder without losing his balance on his rocky perch.

Blaze's blinding white wings cut through the sky, and Kiera waved at Ethan from the tiger-bird's back. She grinned like a young girl discovering the sun for the first time. Several loose blonde curls flew loose from her bun as they landed on a nearby stretch of black stone ground.

Ethan's grin widened. As he watched her eyes crinkle with age and joy, he forgot the pain in his leg entirely. He forgot the worry and the fear.

Her sunshine chased it all away.

Blaze landed with a soft thud of his paws on the black stone, and he knelt for Kiera to slip off his back. When her boots hit the ground, he snapped to attention and puffed out the fur around his neck and chest, staring straight ahead with his wings spread wide.

Kiera chuckled and scratched the base of his jaw. "Yes, you're a lovely steed. So brave! So strong!"

He purred happily, and his eyes fluttered shut as he leaned into her fingers in his fur.

Ethan laughed and shook his head. "You're ruining that animal, you know. The Starling Heiress is going to come back furious that he's gone soft in just a few weeks of you spoiling him."

"Oh, you." Kiera waved away his jibe and patted Blaze again on the neck. "Let me have my fun."

He chuckled.

His wife's boots shuffled over the ground as she neared, and as she reached his boulder, she stood behind him. Her delicate arms wrapped as far around his bulky shoulders as they could go, and together, the two of them stared out at the empty Decay.

Ethan patted her hand, grateful for her gentle touch after all these hours up here alone. "Have you come to join me in my watch?"

"More like drag you back to lunch." She clicked her tongue and kissed the side of his face. "Besides, I'm not sure why you come up here. All you do is stare out at the nothing for hours on end. Do you think he will come back faster if you worry hard enough?"

Ethan shrugged. "It makes me feel like I'm doing something useful."

She let out a soft little sigh, so quiet he almost missed it, and her grip around his shoulders tightened. Something twinged at the base of his stump, and he gritted his teeth to ride out the blip of pain.

"Ethan," she said softly.

In answer, he merely grunted. He didn't want to talk about it. Instead, he reached into his pocket for his whittling knife and the half-finished dragon he had been making for Fiona. The rough shape of some sort of animal lay in his palm, and though he had modeled it after his sketches of the dragon, it still hadn't quite taken shape. He set the knife, still sheathed, on the rock beside him as he examined the future toy and studied the shape it would take. It arched almost like a cat, and the initial outline of a roughly hewn tail poked from what would eventually become its rear. Though he liked the challenge of making a toy with wings, he figured they would likely have to be pinned against its back. Eventually, a little girl was guaranteed to break them off, and he wanted this toy to last a while.

With the toy in his left hand, he slid the whittling knife out of its sheath and pressed the blade against the block of wood. With his thumb against the safe edge, he slid his tool along the wood. His first shaving of the day curled along the blade as he added more definition to the dragon's neck.

"Ethan," Kiera said again, more gently this time. "You can't say you're not useful. You've done so much for—"

"Father!" Wesley shouted, his voice muffled by the rock.

Kiera's arms disappeared from his shoulders, and somewhere behind him, Blaze snorted in surprise. Ethan snapped upright at the sound of his son's voice, and another twinge shot up his leg with the sudden motion. With the knife and toy resting loosely in his palms, he scanned the walls around him, wondering where the boy had gotten off to this time.

"Father, he's back!" The thud of boots on the dusty rock raced toward them, and seconds later, Wesley rounded the corner with a wide grin on his face. Connor's blades sat in the crisscrossed sheath on his back, the harness still too big for him even after they had tightened it as far as it could go. One strap slid off his shoulder as he pointed at the horizon just out of view.

Ethan set down the knife and toy and grabbed his crutch. He hoisted himself to his good foot as Kiera set her hand on his back. She grabbed his free hand and coiled it around her shoulder for balance, and he fought back the urge to prove to himself he could do it alone.

Together, the three of them stared off into the distance toward a rising plume of dust that had been blocked moments before by the cliff.

Ethan's eyes strained as he stared at it, and the noon sun baked his neck as its blinding light reflected off the barren desert's cracked ground. The dust cloud blurred into the sky, so far off he could barely see it.

The wind howled past them as they waited, and somewhere nearby, Blaze ruffled his feathers. As the quiet minutes passed, however, the plume remained on the horizon. It didn't race toward them with the speed of hell behind it, like that breathtaking dragon did when it flew.

It moved slowly, like an approaching caravan.

The hair on Ethan's arms stood on end, and a chill raced down his spine. "That's not Connor, son."

Behind him, Blaze growled.

Ethan glanced over one shoulder to find the vougel watching the horizon. The tiger-bird's wings were tucked tightly against the beast's fuzzy back. The fur on his neck stood on end, and the soft rumble in his chest carried on the air like distant thunder.

"What?" Wesley chuckled and squinted as he stared at dust cloud. "It has to be. Who else even knows about this place?"

A muscle in Ethan's jaw twitched, and as he leaned more weight against his crutch, he struggled to breathe. He couldn't answer that question. Not after everything else his family had already endured. To let them see more carnage, more death, he just couldn't—

"Ethan."

He flinched as Kiera's stern voice broke through his thoughts, and he shut his eyes as he forced a settling breath.

His wife swallowed hard, and her voice shook as she tried to form words. "Is that… tell me it's not…"

Brows knit together, he frowned. They had been together long enough for her to read his expressions, and without a word, he could hint at the depth of hell headed their way.

She stiffened, her shoulders tense as her eyes went wide. He had hoped it wouldn't come to this—that Connor would've been back with time to spare—and he hated that his family would once more face a battle they were unprepared for.

He needed to think on his feet.

His gaze drifted to his stump of a leg, and a pang of exasperated resentment burned within him. He gritted his teeth and shuffled backward toward his boulder as his hips ached and his arms burned with fatigue.

Ethan sat with a grunt of pain and glared out at the Decay as he tried to come up with a plan. Even when he'd had both legs, he hadn't been able to fight off a few bandits in the woods. The thought of fighting Lightseers sent a jolt of terror clear to his bones.

He would lose this fight, but Connor wouldn't.

Whatever it took, they had to buy the man some more time. To do that, he needed to put the fear of the Fates themselves into one of the most powerful men on this continent.

It would take a damn clever plan to bluff his way out of this one, and he needed ideas. He needed something to work with.

Ethan pointed at his son. "Wesley, I know you've been exploring the old ruins and going closer to the catacombs than I said you could go. Tell me what you've found so far."

Wesley went white as a sheet. "I-I don't, uh—"

"It doesn't matter, son." Ethan impatiently waved away Wesley's fear of being caught. "Did you find anything useful?"

"No, sir," Wesley kicked at the dust on the rocky ground. "Just piles of rock, some weeds, a, uh…" He gulped and looked away, both clear signs of a lie. "A bit of rusted armor, some broken spears." He tapped his jaw as his eyes glossed over. "And a few stairwells, actually."

Wesley had lied about the armor, and that meant he'd found something else along with it. "C'mon, son. You're not in trouble, but I need the truth. The armor. How much of it?"

Wesley shrugged. "It's all in a big heap."

Ah.

Ethan grimaced. "Are there bones in the pile?"

Wesley's jaw tensed, and his eyes drifted to the ground. "Yes, sir."

"Skulls? Whole bodies?"

Wesley nodded again.

Ethan rubbed his temples. Massacre. Had to be. It probably had something to do with all the skeletons they had passed when they had first stepped through Death's Door.

Beside him, Kiera muttered under her breath and fanned her face, but Ethan had to focus.

"Wesley, go tell the children to gather firewood, and then lead the women to the pile. We will cremate the bodies later, but for now everyone needs to get every helmet, chest plate, and weapon up to the walls as soon as possible."

Kiera gasped. "Ethan, you don't mean—"

"They're not going to fight, Kiera," he snapped, a little more harshly than he had intended. He took a settling breath as the sands of time slipped away from them and stared out once more at the plume of dust on the horizon. "We need to make whoever that is think we have an army."

Wesley's eyes widened with understanding as he pieced together the loosely forming threads of Ethan's plan. "I'll take the stairs so that you and Mother can ride down on Blaze."

Ethan patted his son's shoulder and smiled with pride. "Good man."

Wesley bolted off, and Ethan strained to keep his smile until the boy disappeared around a rock. When Wesley's footsteps had faded into the rush of the wind across the black stone walls built into the mountainside, Ethan shifted his attention to Kiera. She stared off at the dust cloud, her hand on her chest as the color drained from her cheeks.

"Kiera," he said gently.

She gasped, and her soft blue eyes snapped toward him. Lines formed in her neck as she tensed, and her bottom lip quivered with fear.

He patted a stretch of empty rock beside him. She plopped onto the boulder, her shoulders slumped as tears brimmed in her eyes. He set one arm around her shoulders, and she leaned into him. Her body shook as she quietly sobbed into his neck.

As her tears stained the collar of his shirt, he held the back of her head with one hand. Her hair pooled in his palm, and the soft lilac perfume of their handmade soap washed over him. He closed his eyes, savoring it one more time in case this was the last chance he got.

He wanted to tell her it would be okay, that they would make it and everything would end up alright, but he had made a vow to her long ago not to lie.

"I just want my family to be safe," she said into his shirt. "Why is this happening to us again? Can't we find one patch of Saldia that's not on fire?"

"I don't know," he confessed.

She sobbed harder.

He stared off at the horizon, at the impending dust cloud of death and doom, and everything in him warned him to hurry. But as she cried, as her shoulders shook, he couldn't bring himself to do it.

"What if he doesn't come back?" Kiera asked breathlessly. "What if he's really gone forever this time?"

"Well, now, that's a question you've asked before." Ethan chuckled as he held her close. "And I've already been proven wrong once. Let's let him prove us wrong again, huh?"

She chuckled and wiped away a tear with the heel of her palm.

"Come on now, love," Ethan said as he squeezed her shoulder. "He's counting on us, and we don't have much time."

With a deep breath, she sat upright and nodded. "What do you need me to do?"

"Take Blaze and get the children to help you build fires. As many as we can build."

She chuckled as she wiped away a wayward tear. "You should know better than to trust children with fire."

He grinned. "That's why this is your task and not mine. You'll keep them all in line."

"What are you going to do?"

"I'm going to stay up here until the armor is set up. After we've done all we can do, we need to get everyone to the vault Connor prepared for us. If the walls don't hold, we want to be somewhere safe."

As she met his eye, her smile slowly fell. "Do you really think this will work?"

He shrugged. "We have to try something, Kiera."

Without another word, she kissed his cheek as she stood. Behind them, Blaze stared off at the horizon with his fuzzy ears alert. Though he knelt to let her on his back, his gaze never left the dust cloud on the edge of the Decay.

This vougel belonged to a Starling. This was a creature of war. Ethan could only imagine the carnage Blaze had seen. The tiger-bird likely smelled the brewing danger, but when reinforcements arrived, he didn't know if Quinn Starlin's mount would continue helping them or turn on them all.

"Keep them safe, will you?" Ethan asked, not entirely sure if the creature understood.

Blaze's sharp eyes darted toward him, and the creature nodded once. The beast's great wings spread wide, and he took to the safe skies within Slaybourne. The subsequent gust of air kicked up dust on the black stone path, and Ethan turned away to protect his eyes. He coughed to get it out of his lungs, but his makeshift plan was now in motion.

He could only hope it would be enough.

CONNOR

The sands of time poured through Connor's hands far too quickly.

Several days had passed, and he pushed both himself and his team to their limit. They took off at first darkness, and they flew until the first ray of morning sun fell across the Ancient Woods.

Ever since they had reached the Decay, however, they'd flown nonstop.

As the hot sun baked his face, Connor held tight to his dragon friend's neck as they sped across the Decay. The cracked soil whizzed by below, but everyone's focus remained on the horizon.

"Hang on, Ethan," Connor said under his breath. "I'm almost here."

But he couldn't fight the sinking dread in the pit of his stomach, nor could he silence the ominous thought that he wouldn't make it in time.

Deep down, in the part of his soul he rarely acknowledged, lay the gut-wrenching certainty that, when he arrived at Slaybourne, only rubble would remain.

CHAPTER SEVENTY-TWO
TEAGAN

On the hazy horizon, the pitch-black gates of Death's Door finally filtered through the flickering mirage burning at the edge of the setting sun.

Slaybourne. At last.

As dusk cast a surreal amber glow across the cracked and brittle desert, Teagan raised his fist in the unspoken command to halt. Behind him, a horn cut two deafening blasts across the desert.

Let the peasant hear it, and may he piss himself in fear.

The snap and flutter of a hundred vougel's wings on the air churned like a storm as they hovered above the dusty ground. He peered over one shoulder to ensure that the dust stirred up by the lower-flying vougels continued to mask the merlins at the rear of the contingent.

Good.

He pulled a spyglass from the pack affixed to Tempest's saddle and extended the device to its full length. In the blurry light of a desert sunset, the horizon shook and shimmered while the setting sun played tricks on the eye. Even with his enhanced vision, Teagan could make out precious few details.

Black walls seeped from the mirage like water through fingers. As the sun slowly set, its magic faded, and the towering peaks of the Black Keep Mountains gradually crept into view. The towering gates of Death's Door solidified in the distance, and only the toppled trunks of blackened trees—nothing but twigs compared to the massive gate—gave any hint to the doors' true size.

Along the manmade rampart that connected Death's Door to the Black

Keep Mountains, the silhouette of a single spear protruded into the red glow of the sunset behind it. With a strangled growl of frustration, Teagan adjusted his spyglass to better see the silhouette, and the world through its lens blurred momentarily as it refocused. It sharpened to reveal the outline of a helmet and chest plate, both of them black as night and glimmering in the day's dying light.

He scanned the wall, and sure enough, soldier after soldier stood at attention for as far as the eye could see.

Perfectly stationary. Focused and alert. The Wraithblade's soldiers waited, armed and ready for war.

How irritating.

That had always been a risk, of course. The longer Teagan took to mobilize, the longer his opponent had to gather forces of his own. That was how Henry had grown so powerful, after all—Teagan had spent several months preparing his forces, and his ultimate assault had failed.

It was a mistake he had learned from, and one he would not repeat with the peasant. In the end, the new Wraithblade's army changed little. Teagan hadn't given the man enough time to do much, and whatever defenses he had gathered ultimately wouldn't be enough to win.

Secured in the fortress, Teagan's opponent had the high ground—for now. When the dust cleared and the peasant saw the merlins, however, the tides would quickly change.

Teagan gave the signal to land, and the flurry of wings filled the air as his army descended. He, however, hovered in place and studied Slaybourne through his spyglass as the final aspects of his rapidly adjusting plan snapped into place.

He cast another broad scan across the mountains, and this time, a spiral of dark smoke wafted into the sky from deep beyond the walls. The corkscrew carved through the air, thin and almost too far away to see. He frowned and refocused the spyglass on that area, only to find a dozen more coils of smoke curling into the air.

With a frustrated groan, he collapsed the spyglass between his palms. "It seems you have spent your time wisely, peasant."

If Teagan assumed there were roughly ten men to a campfire, that meant the Wraithblade had easily three hundred men, not including those on the walls.

It didn't seem possible. In fact, he doubted it entirely.

He tapped his heels on Tempest's side, and the golden vougel descended to the cracked earth below. As he descended, his army formed militant rows and awaited his command. Only the soldiers carrying the merlins remained in flight, hovering in the rear guard and stirring the unnatural dust storm that masked his prized weapons.

The second Tempest's paws hit the ground, Teagan swung his leg over the saddle to dismount. His boots hit the dirt with a thud, and his armor clanked as he stalked toward the assembled rows of his officers.

They saluted.

"At ease," he ordered. He needed them to speak their minds as he considered potential flaws in his plan.

Starling pride never got in the way of winning a war.

The two-dozen soldiers relaxed, though they kept their stances wide and merely set their hands behind their backs. The assembled officers watched him in silence, their eyes sharp from beneath their azure helmets. A soft green glow slipped from around the necks of some of his more powerful soldiers, but every officer's armor masked the sort of augmentations most peasants—like their opponent—could hardly fathom.

The Wraithblade didn't stand a chance.

"Edgars, report," he snapped, already missing Freerock's presence.

One of the soldiers stepped forward, a sergeant who had often shadowed Colonel Freerock and who the young man had tapped to replace him in the interim. "The merlins are holding strong, sir. The vougels have been alternating to avoid exhaustion, and thus far no breaks in the dust storm have been noted."

"Good." Teagan let out an irritated sigh and nodded back to the ancient fortress behind him. "It would seem our opponent has acquired forces of his own. My rough estimates gauge his numbers between three- to four-hundred, but I think it's a ploy. If I had to guess, he likely has about a hundred."

Edgars nodded. "Agreed, sir. No one has heard anything about hundreds of soldiers making their way out here."

"Exactly." Teagan paced in front of the officers, his thumb brushing the stubble along his jaw as he sifted through the information they had gathered on their route. "Even if he did somehow manage to acquire those sorts of numbers, they could only be mercenaries. Poorly trained, if they've even held a sword before. He hasn't had enough time to build the sort of loyalty that could genuinely threaten our forces."

"Should we send a negotiation party, sir?" Edgars asked.

"Not yet." Teagan's armor weighed heavily on his shoulders, and he cracked his neck to release some of the tension in his spine as he finalized his new plan. "I want to show him what we're capable of first. It will reduce his negotiating power."

"Should we perhaps wait, sir?" a woman asked from behind him.

Teagan pivoted on his heel and watched a towering blonde as her eyes followed his every movement. "Elaborate, Major Halifax."

"Of course, sir." Unfazed, the soldier met his eye, and a thick scar across her cheek glowed briefly in the surreal desert light. "With us holding the desert, he can't possibly leave. Waiting to attack allows us to draw further reinforcements."

He frowned. "You've been talking to Freerock, haven't you?"

She lifted her chin ever so slightly, but her gaze drifted to the desert soil as she nodded.

"Hmm." Teagan pivoted on his heel and scanned the horizon as he once more debated the option. "To be fair, you and Freerock both have a valid point."

Behind him, the major let out the breath she'd been holding.

"We have our opponent trapped," Teagan continued. "As soon as Colonel Freerock rejoins us, we'll send word back along the trail that we need reinforcements. However, we have only a brief window to enjoy the element of surprise, and I want to test the merlins along the outer wall. Let's see what our new toys can do."

A gleeful snicker bubbled through the officers. He peered over his shoulder to gauge their reactions. Some narrowed their eyes as they stared off at the fortress, while others shook their heads in pity for what awaited the poor bastards on the other side of those wall.

"Don't get cocky," Teagan chided.

The laughter died instantly, and a few cleared their throats as they resumed staring dead ahead.

He'd said it more to himself than to them, but every soldier present needed to remember the danger they faced in this siege.

Though it rarely happened, even Lightseers could lose. With Slaybourne finally in sight and the most powerful army in Saldia at his back, Teagan wanted to charge. To rip the bricks from the walls and flatten the mountains.

But he had learned long ago to snuff out the impatience that came in these moments before a fight. Teagan wouldn't risk his life or those of his children, and he always considered the risks.

"Our enemy has the high ground in this battle." Teagan squared his shoulders and surveyed the officers gathered before him, as well as the rows of soldiers out of earshot behind them. "If he has, in fact, gathered hundreds of soldiers, then we are outnumbered four-to-one. A trifle, really, given what you're capable of."

He paused, letting the compliment sink into their skin. As expected, most of them stood a little taller, and a few of the younger officers couldn't resist a prideful smile.

Good.

"But this is not our land," Teagan continued, his voice tense with warning. "We don't know the traps he may have laid between here and the gates. We don't know what will fly over those walls, or if they're even still enchanted like the legends claim. We are powerful, but we are not fools. We know things about our enemy that he thinks are secret."

Like the damn fool's *dragon*.

As Teagan watched his troops, he pointed to the black mountains in the distance. "Long ago, the creatures of Saldian nightmares infested the bowels of Slaybourne. There's no telling what beasts our enemy might unleash on us tonight. Be ready for hell, boys, because that's what this place is."

The gathered soldiers glared at the horizon, each of them steeling themselves in their own way. Some gritted their teeth, while others stiffened with silent hatred for those who would dare threaten the light.

"We bring experience to this battle." Teagan stood taller and clasped his hands behind his back. "We bring the sort of war-hardened skill no mercenary can ever acquire. And though he must know we're here, we have control for the moment. Let his soldiers see us. Let them tremble as they watch us close in on them, and we will see how many still have the will to fight when the time comes."

As he turned his back to his officers, he allowed himself a brief, triumphant smirk. "Once we have full darkness to shield our approach, we will move forward and anchor the merlins. Until then, this distance is far enough back to make a secure camp. Unit-One!"

"Sir!" said a woman behind him. Her boots clicked together, and the clank of metal suggested she had saluted him.

"Everyone on your team has recently re-inked Rootrock augmentations?"

"Yes, sir."

"Good. Use what vines or roots are still alive under this soil to carve ditches to surround the campsite. Standard size so the vougels can fit if need be. You have full authority to call in Unit-Eight to help you, should the need arise."

"Right away, sir."

"You're dismissed," Teagan said with a curt nod. "Unit-Two!"

Another clink of metal suggested a second soldier had stepped forward. "Sir!"

"See to it the merlins stay hidden in that dust storm. Rotate the vougels more regularly to ensure none are too tired for the inevitable onslaught. Dismissed."

The retreating clatter and clink of metal indicated the two soldiers had jogged off to deliver orders to their soldiers.

"Unit-Seven," Teagan continued, no longer bothering to wait for the customary salute. "Take Unit-Three and Unit-Four. Set up a perimeter around the citadel. Slaybourne and its mountains are massive, but I want it locked and the surrounding area under my full control. Split your unit into pairs and scour everything you can access without stepping into the line of fire. For all we know, there are a dozen secret entrances littered around the base of the mountains. If you find any way in, I want to know immediately."

"Understood, sir!" a woman said.

"Dismissed. As for the rest of you, listen closely." With his back still to them, he pointed at the distant silhouette of Death's Door on the hazy, sunburnt horizon. "When the time comes to negotiate, Unit-Zero is to join me while the rest of you cease fire. Man your posts, and be prepared to fire at any moment. He's outmanned and out-magicked, which means he's probably going to try something desperate. If he's foolhardy enough to attack me during the negotiation, I want you to fire every merlin at once. Keep firing until the walls fall."

The remaining officers didn't reply, and he peered again over his shoulder to find them watching him in the tense silence that followed his orders. The lull suggested disagreement, but on this, they knew better than to voice it out loud.

They had seen Teagan fight. They had witnessed his raw power firsthand. As much as they didn't want to let their Master General take on a powerful opponent alone, they knew he was more than capable of facing the Shade by himself. With Unit-Zero at his side—eleven of the most seasoned captains in his army—the peasant didn't stand a chance.

For effect, he let the lull linger. He needed their best tonight, and that meant tapping into their greatest power—their unflinching loyalty for the greater good.

He clasped his hands behind his back. "When we are faced with mountains, what do we do?"

"Flatten them!" His officers snapped to attention and saluted him, their chins raised in perfect form as they recited the well-worn rallying cry his troops spoke before every battle.

"Impossible odds?" he asked, his voice louder as his speech built to a crescendo.

"Overcome!" they shouted, and their voices carried across the desert like an echo.

"It is the charge of the Lightseers to face the darkness even kings fear!" He returned his attention to the Black Keep Mountains to hide his wicked grin. "Let us remind this bastard of his place. Dismissed!"

As the stomp of boots on the dirt retreated toward the other soldiers gathered out of earshot, Teagan stared out at the distant fortress and the coils of smoke rising into the burnt-orange clouds. His jaw twitched with irritation, and his hand curled into a tight fist. With his soldiers gone, he cracked his neck to release the brewing tension in his spine. With the movement, the mask he wore for his soldiers crumbled away.

The Wraithblade would die tonight. He could *feel* it.

Before dawn, he would set this whole cursed landscape on fire. The abomination would be sealed away, and this infuriating peasant would finally be dead. Zander would return to his post in Lunestone, Quinn would retire her sword, and the world would be right again. Better yet, Teagan might even claim yet another dragon for his collection.

"It's time to get what I came for, peasant," he said under his breath. "Show me everything you've got."

CHAPTER SEVENTY-THREE
CONNOR

Curse the Fates straight to *hell*.

Connor was too late.

In the suffocating darkness of the cold desert night, a ball of fire careened across the horizon. It left a streak of orange light burned into the dark sky, and as it hit the Black Keep Mountain, it shattered. Flames spiraled into the stars, and a red glow briefly illuminated the rocky wall of Slaybourne. The muffled boom shot across the cracked earth, reaching him a second or two after impact.

"Throwing rocks, huh?" Connor said under his breath, mocking the wraith's dismissiveness around Teagan's mystery weapon. "How's that for primitive?"

Yes, fine, the ghoul grumbled. *You've made your point.*

Nocturne slowed his breakneck pace across the desert, and Connor leaned forward as he grit his teeth against the biting wind. His chest ached. His pulse thudded in his temple, and for a moment, only the shrill ringing in his ears could pierce his stunned silence.

The flash of light slowly faded, but a hundred torches fanning out from Death's Door still lit up the night. Backlit silhouettes darted across the parched earth, and from this distance, he couldn't make sense of the battlefront.

They were too far away.

He couldn't place all the vougels, nor could he count the total number of soldiers below, even with his enhanced vision. He couldn't even glean anything useful from the shadowy outlines of whatever monstrosities Teagan Starling had brought to his door.

The machines.

It didn't seem like Teagan Starling had seen Nocturne, yet, so that at least worked in their favor. None of the fire volleys shifted direction, nor did any shouts ripple through the soldiers.

For the moment, Connor still had the element of surprise—but it wouldn't last for long.

He briefly closed his eyes and pressed against the dragon's mind through their augmented connection. The mental barrier between them held for a moment, but in seconds, the regal creature let him in.

Get us above the battle, Nocturne, he ordered. *I need to get a clear view of Death's Door.*

There was still a slim chance his original plan might work, and he had to find out for sure.

In answer, the dragon shot upward. His wings snapped against the air, carrying them higher, and Connor peered behind him to ensure none of his team had fallen off. Murdoc and Sophia clung to the dragon's spines, tied to his back with rope, and both shivered in the cold gale as they stared down at the siege.

Quinn, however, didn't flinch. Eyes narrowed and jaw tense, she intently watched the fray. Though her red hair whipped around her face, she didn't seem to notice as she held tight to the dragon's back. Far below, an explosion of fire erupted in the darkness, and the flames reflected in her eyes.

War clearly didn't faze her.

"Wraith, scout ahead," Connor instructed. "Tell me what you see."

Already in progress, the ghoul snapped. *Stop distracting me.*

Connor grunted in annoyance, but opted not to reply.

Another fireball careened through the air, and this time, the soaring flames cast an ocean of orange light across the soldiers gathered far below. Vougels hovered in the air above three towering machines gathered by Death's Door.

As he got closer, Connor did his best to inspect the machines from afar.

In a strange way, they reminded him of the ballistas he'd read about as a boy. The contraptions cast long shadows across the ground as the fireball soared. Enchanting green light glittered along their wooden frames. The silhouette of six more machines stretched out around the fortress on either side, circling Death's Door and most of the northern-facing wall.

How strange. Instead of focusing his firepower on the main gate, Teagan had spread his machines too far apart from each other. With as large as the northern wall was, even an augmented soldier would waste a considerable amount of time running back and forth between the machines.

"He thinks we're inside," Connor muttered to himself.

Despite the devastating army at his front door, he relaxed. Teagan had made a critical error—his admittedly talented army had been divided across seven key areas. If Quinn was right about the scouting unit within Teagan's army, that meant there were at least eight divisions. Maybe even more.

He still had a chance to win this.

A fireball slammed against the enchanted gates built into Slaybourne's only entrance, and a flash of emerald light rippled from the point of impact. The deafening groan of twisting iron echoed across the desert, and Connor swallowed hard.

"That's not good!" Murdoc shouted, though the wind drowned out most of his voice.

The man had a point. Whatever slim odds they had of winning this wouldn't last long. Without the Soulsprite, Slaybourne couldn't survive much more of this.

At any moment, the walls might even fall.

Nocturne slowed. The howl of wind across Connor's face became a whistle, and he carefully inched backward toward Quinn, Murdoc, and Sophia.

"We have to destroy those machines," he said over the wind. "There's no telling how much time we have left."

"There's some." Quinn pointed to one of the contraptions as another fireball shot into the air. "Look at the firing pattern. Only one goes at a time, even along the fringes. He's testing for weaknesses and trying to flush you out. If the full assault had started, every one of them would be firing, one after another, in perfect sync."

"It doesn't matter what his plans are." Connor pointed to the ramparts beside the gate as a fireball neared its target. "Watch the wall when it hits."

The flaming rock splattered halfway up the steep black cliffs that served as Slaybourne's outer wall, and a chunk of the mountain split from the rock. Boulders thundered down the mountainside, kicking up dust as fires raged in their wake.

Quinn's head snapped back in surprise, and Sophia's lips parted in shock.

"I'm with the Captain," Murdoc said. "We've got to burn those sons of bitches."

"Any ideas?" Connor asked.

No one answered, and he sighed in exasperation.

"Me, neither," he admitted.

The walls have not been breached, the wraith interjected. *They're holding.*

"Thank the Fates," Connor muttered. At least there was a bit of good news.

Yet again, he scanned the battlefield in search of something useful he had missed before. Two rows of twelve Lightseers stood in front of the iron gates, and a torrent of fire erupted from their outstretched hands. The flames pummeled against Death's Door, and another strained groan of twisting metal ricocheted through the desert. The bonfire crashed against the enchanted iron, strong and furious, as the minutes passed.

A man's distant voice echoed through the night from the front line, and the siege of fire instantly ended.

"That's a bad sign." Quinn clicked her tongue. "They're already pulling units to hit the walls. They don't think there's a chance of being fired upon. They know you're not going to answer the battle call. They think you've retreated already."

"That also means we can't open the gates." Murdoc muttered obscenities, but the wind drowned out most of them.

Connor ran his hand through his hair as he stared down at the carnage, but his mind had gone blank. He tried to think of a plan, to improvise and adapt as the wraith had warned he would need to do, but no ideas came.

It seemed bleak.

Quinn grabbed his shoulder. "Connor, we need a plan."

"I'm thinking," he snapped. "Give me a minute."

"We don't have a lot of minutes to spare, Captain," Murdoc quipped as another fireball shot through the air below.

He'd suspected they would have to improvise, but these machines changed everything. Each second they spent firing was a massive drain on Slaybourne's already taxed reserves. At any moment, the walls could collapse entirely.

Magnuson, the wraith snapped. *We cannot let those machines continue to fire. We must destroy them.*

"How?" Connor gestured to the nearest machine as it launched a flaming boulder into the air. "I count at least eight Lightseers on each of them. We can't take them out from the ground, and they're too far apart to destroy them from the air before we're spotted."

"Can we use them on each other?" Sophia asked.

"Too risky." Quinn shook her head. "A ground assault means drawing a lot of attention, and we would be overrun almost instantly. Worse, there's no guarantee we could figure out how they work, or how to aim them."

"And splitting up is too risky," Connor added. Whatever we do, we do together."

"Right." Murdoc scratched absently at his scar. "Uh, Captain, this would be a great time to give us some of that improvisation you and the wraith were talking about."

"I'm working on it," Connor said through clenched teeth.

The dragon's wings beat against the air, propelling them forward, and Connor lowered his head toward the regal creature's neck as he scanned Slaybourne's walls. His eyes watered from the wind, but he kept them open as best he could so that he could monitor their approach. They raced above the soldiers, and he kept a careful watch as he waited for one of them to look upward.

Bless the Fates, they didn't.

Behind him, the sound of cloth over scales inched closer. He glanced over his shoulder just as Quinn grabbed the spine behind him and raised one arm above her face to shield her eyes from the wind.

"I don't see him!" she shouted, her voice almost completely consumed by the gale. "His vougel is also missing."

Teagan.

Connor frowned. That was a bad sign.

As another fireball soared through the air, higher this time, something on the nearest fortress wall glinted in the firelight. Confused, he squinted and studied the metallic flash of light, trying to make out what could be up there. The closer they came to the walls, the more flashes of silver and red light rippled across strange fingers looming in the darkness.

A fireball hit halfway up the fortress wall, and one of the silhouettes toppled. A helmet came into brief focus, and the orange glow briefly illuminated a hollow plate of armor.

Someone had set up empty armor as decoys along the wall.

"Ethan is a Fates-damned genius." Grinning, Connor wondered how much time that had bought them.

"Father must think you have an army." Quinn's voice oozed with relief, and she set her hand on her forehead as her shoulders relaxed somewhat. "That changes things."

Amidst the shadowy silhouettes of the decoys along the wall, however, one of them stepped forward. The figure emerged from the darkness, and a screaming ball of fire glinted across a metal plate of armor about two sizes too big. As the light neared, the figure raised a familiar silver sword, and a familiar mop of messy blond hair came into sharp focus.

Wesley.

The young man stood on the wall with one sword drawn, facing down an army he couldn't hope to beat alone. And, given the sheer look of determination on his face, he didn't give a damn about what happened to him.

Connor looked over his shoulder at Quinn, who smirked in victory.

"Alright," he conceded. "New plan. Do you still think your father is open to negotiation?"

She tilted her head as she watched the battlefield below and sucked in a sharp breath through her teeth. "Maybe."

"That's reassuring," Sophia said dryly.

Connor tapped his fingers against his thigh as he sifted through the risks associated with this rapidly evolving idea. "What would happen if I called for a discussion? What would he do?"

"I can only guess," Quinn admitted. "He wouldn't risk leaving the machines unmanned, so he won't come with the whole army. No one has fired on him, but it doesn't mean there aren't soldiers in there. He could think it's a ploy, and he will be prepared with fighters to return fire at a moment's notice. My guess is he will come alone, or with a small contingent."

"Wouldn't he just kill us?" Sophia asked incredulously. "Once he sees Quinn, we're fair game."

"Not necessarily," Connor disagreed. "He won't know where the wraith is. Teagan will most likely assume the ghoul will kill her if he tries anything."

"Right," Quinn said. "And he won't see Zander. If things go south, bluff him and say Zander's in Slaybourne."

"I love a good bluff," Connor admitted. "Will Teagan cease fire during the discussions?"

Quinn nodded. "Standard protocol."

"Good." Connor paused, not certain if his next question was even worth asking. "Think there's a chance of actually reaching an agreement with him?"

"I doubt it." With a weary sigh, she shook her head. "But we should still try."

That didn't sound promising. He would have to operate as though any negotiation would fail—but that didn't matter, since the only purpose would be to buy time.

"Wraith," Connor said, not even sure if the ghoul was close enough to hear.

I must focus, Magnuson. The depth of carnage down here is—

"I need your help."

A stunned silence followed, and for a moment, Connor wondered if the haunting specter had, in fact, slipped out of range.

What is it? the ghost finally asked.

"I'm going to throw the Soulsprite, and I need you to—"

You Fates-damned imbecile! the ghoul interrupted. *Every time I think you've finally figured out how to be a proper king, you go and say something stupid enough to—"*

"Will you shut your mouth and listen?" Connor snapped. "Block the spikes if they launch. We can't risk the Soulsprite breaking."

Magnuson, this is madness, the ghoul complained. *If you miss—*

"I won't."

But if—

"I won't," Connor repeated, more firmly this time. "Lead Wesley to the treasury. He can't find his way there on his own, and I don't have time to explain what to do. Only you can get him in there. As much as I want your help on the battlefield, you need to stay by his side until the Soulsprite is placed. We can't risk him getting hurt."

A furious, frustrated growl rumbled through Connor's head from the undead king.

"Please!" he shouted. "I can't do this without you, damn it!"

Fine, the wraith groused. *But you can't stray far. Given our range, you will have to remain as close to the walls as possible. This still limits you.*

"I know."

Perhaps it's better if you go with Wesley so that I can remain on the battlefield.

Connor watched Quinn through the corner of his eye. As she surveyed the chaos below, he shook his head. "It's better if I stay out here. We're trying to buy time, not slaughter everyone."

This is risky, Magnuson.

"It is," he agreed as the walls of Slaybourne grew ever closer. "Ready?"

As I'll ever be.

"This is your last chance," Connor shouted over his shoulder to Quinn. "Are you sure you don't want to sit this one out?"

Her red hair danced around her face, and she lifted her chin in defiance as she drew her Firesword. "No turning back now."

So be it, then.

Keeping low to the dragon's back, Connor tugged open the pack he had tied around the base of Nocturne's neck for safekeeping. Carefully, he pulled out the box protecting the Soulsprite and handed it to Quinn. She clung to the dragon's spine with one hand and, with the other, she gripped the box so tightly her knuckles went white.

Her eyes darted from him to the box and back. "What are you—"

But he didn't have time to explain.

Connor shook his head and lifted the box's lid. The jet-black Soulsprite waited inside, as smooth and perfect as when he had first set it inside. In the final moments before they could reach the wall, he lifted the priceless black orb and held it close to his chest.

"Wesley!" he shouted.

His voice carried across the battlefield, but it was a necessary risk to ensure the young man heard him.

Below, several Lightseers whipped their heads around as they tried to place where the voice had come from. Since the soldiers were on the ground, they were at a disadvantage. Wesley, however, was high enough to instantly spot them, and the young man smiled with relief.

Nocturne propelled them toward the wall at full speed, even as they got dangerously close.

YOU WILL HAVE ONE CHANCE, the dragon warned through his connection to Connor.

"That's all I need," Connor said under his breath, more to himself than to Nocturne. His intense focus remained on the wall as his grip on the Soulsprite tightened.

A hundred yards to go.

"Connor," Quinn said urgently.

Seventy.

"Uh, Captain?" Murdoc shouted from behind him.

Fifty.

The smile on Wesley's face fell, and his eyes narrowed with concern as he took a wary step backward.

Thirty.

"Now!" Connor shouted to the Wraith King.

He hurled the irreplaceable artifact through the air, over the fortress walls and toward the stunned young man watching in breathless horror as a dragon barreled toward him.

Connor watched the next few moments unfold with all-consuming dread. Everything he had done thus far hinged on this succeeding.

The Soulsprite flew over the walls. A spear launched from the rampart's enchanted edge, but a cloud of black smoke obscured the weapon and artifact both. His jaw clenched shut as the dragon abruptly banked to the left, but he couldn't wrench his eyes away from the churning black smoke that would decide the fate of their entire mission.

If the wraith touched the orb, even by mistake, this would all be over.

The jagged spear launched into the air at a twisted angle, shifted from its course by something unseen, and a pained grunt followed. The scrape of skin on dirt followed as the black cloud cleared.

Wesley lay on his back, staring up at the sky, with the Soulsprite safely in his hands.

"Oh thank the Fates," Quinn muttered. She closed her eyes and let out a shaky breath.

Murdoc whooped with excitement, and Sophia collapsed onto the dragon's back as she let loose a string of curses obscene enough to make a whore blush.

But they didn't have time to celebrate.

"Follow the wraith!" Connor shouted as Nocturne carried them back into the sky.

Below, soldiers shouted at each other, and a few briefly looked his way—though none of them reacted. If they had seen the exchange, they didn't know what to make of it.

What's next? Nocturne asked through their connection.

Quinn said it best, Connor explained. *Tegan is using this moment to display his power and test the walls for weaknesses. I'd say it's time we do the same.*

He summoned one of his shadow blades. The perfect sword rested easily in his palm, and its dark smoke faded almost instantly into the incessant wind.

The time had come to show Teagan Starling what happened to those foolish enough to knock on Death's Door.

CHAPTER SEVENTY-FOUR
WESLEY

The desert air crackled with fire.

Churning black clouds hid the stars. Flakes of ash floated through the Decay, carried skyward by a desolate wind as their singed edges burned with lingering orange light. The muffled roar of men barking orders mingled with the distant creak of wood.

A flash of green light sliced through the darkness, followed by a sharp pop. Seconds later, another ball of fire careened into the air. It arched, leaving red streaks on the night air in its wake.

As it hit the wall, the very ground trembled from its might. A burst of fire shot into the sky, and a thunderous rockslide drowned out the distant shouts of men.

Still lying on his back, Wesley groaned. Something heavy weighed on his chest, and he clutched it on instinct. Round and smooth, it hummed under his touch like a purring cat curled into a ball. It warmed his palm with all the heat of a summer sunshine.

A splitting headache pierced his skull, and his body ached as he forced himself to sit upright. Another jolt of pain shot down his neck, and he mumbled obscenities his mother would've smacked him for saying out loud.

The weight on his chest shifted into his palms as he righted himself, and he peered through one blurry eye to figure out what the hell Connor had thrown at him.

A dark gray orb rested between his palm and his torso. Black etchings along its surface depicted symbols he didn't recognize—sloping circles and runes that told a story he didn't understand. They looped over each other, intertwined in dazzling chaos, and he furrowed his brow as he inspected the lines.

He cradled the artifact between his palms, but he couldn't even get his fingers all the way around it. The etchings in its dark surface called to him, like a puzzle only he could solve. As he stared, the rumble beneath his feet faded, and the longer he inspected the artifact, the softer the screams beyond the walls became. Bit by bit, the world around him dwindled. The colors faded, and the silent song of this strange orb pulled him from the fray.

Something whacked him on the back of his head.

A jolt of pain shot down his neck, and he let out a string of curses as the chaos beyond the walls hit him like a wall of sound. The green and orange glow of the magic beyond Slaybourne's walls nearly blinded him, and he squinted as the artifact's spell on him broke.

As he rubbed the back of his head, he glared over his shoulder to see what the hell had hit him.

Along the stretch of jet black stone, dark smoke coiled over the ground. A cloak billowed in the wind atop Slaybourne's walls, blocking his view of everything else, and he craned his neck to follow the length of the figure's body. A pang of dread hit him square in the heart, and the backs of his eyes stung with fear.

White hands, rotted to the bone, curled into fists. Tattered ends on an ancient robe fluttered in a breeze softer than the gale blowing past the walls. A bleached skull creaked on its boney hinges and craned toward him as though its empty sockets could still see.

A ghostly specter. The thing of nightmares.

Eyes wide with terror, he froze.

The wraith pointed back toward Slaybourne, toward something blocked by its towering form, and the bones in its left hand clicked together with the motion. Nothing else about it moved, but the message was clear.

Come this way.

In a chaotic rhythm composed of primarily terror and panic, Wesley's heart thudded in his chest. The dark orb still weighed on his palms, but he refused to look at it out of fear that it might lure him into whatever spell had snared him moments before. He simply felt it, warm and smooth, cradled between his palms and chest.

Wesley had come up here to fight. To do his part and face whatever foes came for his family. He had come up here to redeem himself, but Connor had given him a job to do.

He peered over his shoulder at the night, but the dragon and its rider had disappeared into the midnight sky. If Connor wanted him to follow Death itself into the depths of Slaybourne, then fine. He refused to let the people in his life down again.

No matter what it cost him.

THE WRAITH KING

As the infuriating Finn boy finally took the first step down the dark stairwell, a nearby roar broke through the deafening explosions from beyond the wall.

The wraith's head tilted toward the sound.

He glided along the rock, along Slaybourne's rampart and back toward the cliff leading into the chasm between the two gates of Death's Door. As he approached the steep edge, he peered down into the abyss.

A lone beast stood at the exit, pacing the full length of the gates with its wings spread wide. The Starling woman's vougel snarled at the gates, and its tail twitched back and forth as it pawed at the closed gate.

Interesting.

The ghoul stared out into the battle in the desert beyond his homeland. A fireball launched in the air toward him, and the cluster of soldiers standing just outside the gates fired another volley at the very door Quinn's vougel so desperately wanted through.

Magnuson could use all the warriors at his disposal—even the furry ones.

Perhaps, should the opportunity arise, the Wraith King should send the Wraithblade a little present.

CHAPTER SEVENTY-FIVE
CONNOR

In a dark stretch of Slaybourne at the edge of his connection to the wraith, Connor stood on a hill and surveyed the battlefield below.

Choosing the location where he would face off against Teagan Starling had come with significant risk. His enemy controlled the most obvious stretches of land. Connor could hope he was close enough to Slaybourne for the wraith to take Wesley all the way to the treasury, but he couldn't possibly know for sure.

And once the negotiations began, he wouldn't be able to move.

Quinn stood beside him, shoulder to shoulder. Though her sword remained in its sheath, her fingers drummed impatiently against its hilt. The faint scent of jasmine rolled from her hair, followed by the barest hint of honeysuckle nectar. In the night winds, her hair danced around her face as they observed the battlefield together.

How surreal to face off against the Lightseers with her, of all people, at his side.

Behind them, Sophia rummaged through her bag. Bottles clinked delicately together amidst the thunderous rumbles of the battlefield. Murdoc had his hands on his head as he anxiously paced back and forth across the desert. He kicked a rock, and it flew off into the darkness.

As another fiery boulder hurled toward the walls, Connor clenched his teeth together so tightly that a jolt of pain shot down his spine. His back ached with tension, and every breath felt like fire as his mind raced with all the ways this could go wrong.

He hated waiting, especially when what they needed most was to buy Wesley time.

"Updates?" Quinn asked, though she didn't look away from the Lightseers below.

"Nothing," Connor said curtly. His eye twitched as he fought to stifle his growing impatience. "Trust me, Nocturne knows what's at stake. We only get one shot at this."

"I know," she said tersely.

Anxious. Tense. Every bit on edge as he was, and with just as much skin in his game.

"Murdoc. Sophia." Connor peered over his shoulder as the two of them paused and looked his way. "If Teagan attacks, help Nocturne. Quinn and I just need to isolate Teagan from the rest of them."

"Aye, Captain." Murdoc gave a curt nod and resumed his pacing.

Connor nodded toward Sophia's bag. "Did you find all the potions?"

"And then some." She closed her pack and tossed it over one shoulder. "I'll go set my traps. They won't be able to circle us."

He nodded, his shoulders aching with the tension building in the air, and she faded into the darkness as she got to work.

IT IS TIME. Nocturne's voice rumbled through Connor's mind, and he stood straighter.

Their moment had come.

Connor pressed against Nocturne's mind through their connection. *The stage is yours, Nocturne. Show them what a prince of dragons can do.*

The regal creature didn't reply, and for a few more seconds, only the shouts of Teagan's soldiers mingled with the whistle of fireballs through the air filled the desert. Connor took a cautious step forward, tense and waiting in the overwhelming lull of activity.

At the front gate, a man yelled a terse command. A distant wall of fire slammed against the iron, and Death's Door creaked as the elite soldiers' flame tested its enchantments.

"C'mon," Connor muttered under his breath. He made a fist with one hand and cracked his knuckles as his heart skipped beats.

The wall of fire ended, and the gates' twisted groan echoed through the desert like a creature's final scream.

And, as it faded, the Decay was chillingly silent for a single, perfect moment.

Before another machine could fire, a deafening roar broke across the mountains. The ground quaked with the sound's sheer force, and even Teagan's machines trembled as the scream shook the earth.

It stretched into the night, farther than Connor thought possible, longer than any one creature should have been able to sustain. The tremors grew stronger, and one of the boulders in a distant merlin fell from its firing channel. A woman shouted, urgency in her tone, as it careened toward two soldiers on the platform below. They jumped into a trench that had been dug around it just as the boulder crashed through the wooden foundation. Splintered planks shot into the air, and fire followed. The machine toppled to the left, and more shouts followed.

One machine down, just from Nocturne's voice. Connor beamed with pride.

As the roar dissolved into the night, the soldiers' chatter faded. The eerie silence stretched on as the Lightseers waited for something to appear, until only the crackle of a hundred fires and the gentle rush of the wind through Lightseer banners and filled the air.

Everyone listened. One by one, their heads turned toward the sky.

A shrill whistle filled the air, softly at first but growing stronger with each second, as though something large were falling from the heavens and toward the earth.

None of the soldiers panicked. The hardened warriors kept their gazes on the sky. Several summoned glowing balls of light into their hands as they prepared to fire into the still-empty air.

Hardened warriors, afraid of nothing—the sort of enemy no man wanted.

"I see you two favor theatrics," Quinn muttered.

"Like you don't." Connor glanced at her over his shoulder.

She shrugged.

A blinding blast of lightning ripped from the sky. It arced in a dozen directions, chaotic and wild, as the bursts rained down upon the soldiers.

Quinn raised one arm to shield her eyes from the light, but Connor watched the whole thing. Even as twisted lines of crackling energy still left imprints on his vision, he couldn't pull himself away.

It was magical. Brutal.

Brilliant.

Nocturne's savage lightning carved through the desert, kicking up fire and dust. Screams followed. Bolts of multi-colored light shot into the air from the fighters on the ground, but the thick cloud cover obscured the source of the lightning from everyone below.

And then, without even a hint of warning, the clouds parted.

A massive silhouette plummeted from the heavens, too fast for the eye to follow. Another roar shook the earth, rippling through the desert like the aftershock of an earthquake, and a second blinding crack of lightning ripped through the soldiers. Fire erupted into the air from every direction as Nocturne destroyed machines and men alike. Wheels splintered, and twisted plates of metal soared through the carnage.

As an arc of Nocturne's lightning hit the nearest machine, its foundations snapped. Thick wooden beams launched into the air—toward Connor and his team.

"Look out!" he stretched his arms wide to shield the others from debris, but the beam landed in a stretch of desert just in front of them.

In unison, he and Quinn sighed with relief.

"That was too close for comfort," she mumbled.

Focused as he was on the aftermath, Connor didn't reply. In the catastrophic fires that followed the attack, he couldn't even tell how many machines had survived.

Even as the dragon's receding shadow sped through the night, none of the Lightseers funneled through the destroyed machines after him. They remained at their posts, focused and unwavering.

No fear. No panic, and barely even a pause before they'd leapt into action—but the merlins had ceased fire, and Connor now had the soldiers' full attention.

It was a win, and one he had hoped for.

The dragon roared again, and even from this distance, the ground beneath Connor rumbled with the magnificent beast's raw power.

As Nocturne reached the end of the battlefield, he unleashed another dazzling arc of lightning across a rear flank of gathered vougels. The beasts screamed as the lightning vaporized them, and clouds of black smoke coiled from the faraway ground.

As they watched the slaughter, a strange, strangled sound escaped Quinn's throat. The tendons in her neck tightened until he thought they might snap, and she held her breath as Nocturne massacred the very soldiers who had once fought at her side.

The stream of lightning ended, but she didn't look away.

Connor gently nudged her. "The faster we end this, the more of them we can save."

"I know." She swallowed hard and shut her eyes to steel herself against the bloodshed.

In an abrupt change of direction, Nocturne snapped his wings against the air and darted back toward Connor. He sped closer, drawing the soldiers' fire as he passed above them. A volley of glowing light curved through the air toward him, but none hit.

His team had made his show of force, and by now, he undoubtedly had the Lightseers' full attention.

"TEAGAN!" Connor shouted.

His voice echoed through the desert, and the battlefield went still.

Nocturne sped closer, and as the great dragon finally reached them, he circled. The eerie whistle of an approaching projectile cut through the night, and the ground shook with a resonant boom as the regal creature landed hard in the desert behind them.

All according to plan.

If Connor had to face Teagan earlier than he'd originally intended, there was no greater bartering chip than a dragon looming overhead.

The blast of a war horn cut through the night, and a ripple of barked orders followed. Several quiet moments passed, but no more of the flaming boulders launched into the air.

A cease-fire. Thank the Fates.

"He will come," Quinn said quietly. "There's no way he would leave a summons like that unanswered."

"Good." At his side, Connor's hands balled into fists as he waited to meet the man whose family had hunted him from the start.

Now, it was time to see if he could negotiate with Teagan Starling—or if trying to buy Wesley some time would ultimately cost him the whole damn war.

CHAPTER SEVENTY-SIX
CONNOR

The crackle of fires raged in the darkness as Connor stood on the edge of the battlefield. With Quinn at his side, he summoned his shield and one of his shadow blades as he prepared to meet Teagan face-to-face.

As the oppressive silence weighed on the battlefield, shadows moved in the darkness beyond the smattered firelight. He tried to track their movements, but the crackling flames obscured what little he could see beyond the circle of orange light.

Several agonizing minutes crept by as Connor waited for his enemy to find him. A muscle twitched in his jaw, and he scanned the darkness for signs of an approaching attack. If the negotiations fell through, this position would put him at a disadvantage.

He was banking on Teagan Starling refusing to fight his own daughter, but time would tell if that was a good enough bluff.

Deep in the shadows beyond even what Connor's enhanced eyes could see, a man slowly clapped. Connor and Quinn tensed in unison, both of them staring into the night as they waited for something to sail through the darkness toward them. A fist, maybe, or fire.

Nothing came.

Instead, a man's silhouette appeared just beyond the circle of light. A soft growl rumbled past them as a towering vougel walked ahead of the figure. The winged tiger stalked closer, its eyes milky white, and the spellgust gem in its helm radiated with a brilliant green glow. The vougel's ears pinned menacingly against its head as it neared. Its eyes remained locked on Connor, and its lips curled upward as it snarled.

Moments later, the silhouette stepped into the light.

Taller even than Connor, the man's broad shoulders rivaled his own. Thick red hair covered his head despite the weathered creases around his eyes. A thin scar sliced across the man's cheek and into the beard covering his jawline. Quinn stood a little straighter at the mere sight of him.

Teagan Starling. It had to be.

"What an intriguing show of force." Teagan's eyes darted toward the dragon towering behind Connor, and the man crossed his thick arms as he paused a good distance away.

"Glad you enjoyed the show," Connor said dryly.

"I confess, I wasn't expecting you to meet me out on the battlefield." The Starling patriarch sized Connor up with a lazy glance. "You surprised me, and that doesn't happen often."

Connor didn't reply.

In the darkness behind Teagan, eleven soldiers flew over on vougels. They flanked their commander, and each armored fighter jumped off their mount with ease. The fighters drew their swords and fanned out in perfect sync as they quickly blocked each possible exit toward the battlefield, but every man remained within view.

That most likely had to do with the dragon, but Connor wasn't going to complain.

To be safe, he cast a wary glance over his shoulder at the darkness just as Sophia emerged from the shadows around them. She gave him a curt nod, and he let out a settling breath.

May the Fates take pity on the poor fool who stepped in her traps.

Magnuson, the ghoul said, his voice grim in Connor's head. *I'm sending you a present. Use it wisely.*

Before Connor could react, a brilliant flash of green light shot along the gates of Death's Door.

That imbecile.

Pinned in place and unable to shout at that infuriating wraith to stop,

Connor gritted his teeth as he watched the gates open. They parted only slightly, and within moments, they once more began to close.

But there was no telling how many soldiers would be able to slip inside.

"Edgars. Burns." Teagan nodded to the gates as he watched them close. "Inspect."

"Yes, sir," two men said in unison.

The two soldiers who had spoken jumped back onto their mounts and kicked the vougels sharply in the sides. The beasts launched into the air and careened toward the gates as they shut.

Connor hesitated as he watched the men leave, almost unable to believe Teagan had just revealed the chink in his own armor.

To send two of his soldiers off toward the gates meant no one else was already there. Perhaps Nocturne's arrival had sent even more of a ripple through the gathered army than Connor had originally thought.

With a cautious sidelong glance, he studied Quinn's face. She stood beside him, eerily still, watching her father with a stony expression he couldn't read. He had known she would face an impossible decision out here, and now it was time to see if his trust in her had paid off—or if she would become his greatest regret.

Frankly, outnumbered as he was, he didn't know if he could do this without her—especially if she switched sides and faced off against him.

"I take it you want to negotiate?" The Lightseer Master General nodded toward Quinn.

"That's right," Connor said. "And I can guess what you want."

"I very much doubt that." Teagan's intense glare shifted to Quinn, and his expression instantly softened. "Hello, my dear."

"Father," she said tersely.

"None of this was supposed to happen," he chided gently. "But I'm grateful you're alright."

A vein pulsed in her temple, and instead of answering, her hand tightened around *Aurora's* hilt.

"Very well, Connor. Let's negotiate." Teagan's gaze shifted back to Connor, and the man grinned as he spread his arms wide. "After all, you've been making quite a reputation for yourself."

He stiffened, and his nose flared with fury. "How do you know my name?"

"Oh, I know all about you." Teagan's grin widened as he drank in Connor's discomfort. "I know about the Finns. I know about your escapades as the Shade. I know everything."

He glared at Quinn, not bothering to mask his anger. "How does he—"

"I don't know," she hissed under her breath.

"Did you—"

"No," she snapped, glaring at him.

Connor let out a slow breath to settle his thundering heart, and he believed her. There hadn't been a chance for her to slip away on their route to Saldia.

It didn't make sense for Teagan to know these things, but he couldn't let the man get under his skin.

"I know the Finns are behind that gate." Teagan pointed to Death's Door. "It took courage for you to face me out here, peasant, but courage isn't enough to win against me. If you want the Finns to see the sunrise, you're going to do exactly what I tell you to do. Understood?"

"That's not how negotiations work." Slowly, carefully, Connor slid his left boot across the dirt as he settled into a subtle fighting stance that would give him the momentum he needed to launch the first attack.

The stairs down to the treasury took ages to clear, and Wesley couldn't even be halfway down yet.

They needed more time.

"You don't want to fight me," Teagan warned.

"I'd rather not," Connor bluffed, and he threw in a lazy shrug for good measure. "But I will if I have to."

Behind him, the creak of leather on skin told him Murdoc was ready, and the crackle of ice meant Sophia was, too. A low growl of warning rolled through the night from above him, and he could only imagine how most men would've pissed themselves in fear just looking at Nocturne.

Thus far, only Quinn hadn't moved.

Without answering, he cast a wary glance at the nine soldiers behind

Teagan. All of them had drawn their swords. Green light glowed from within the Lightseers' armor, and he could only guess the sheer number of augmentations each man had at his disposal. The vougels stood between each soldier, teeth bared and just as much a threat as any soldier present.

Everyone here was ready for blood. Without question, they would get it.

"Those machines of yours are impressive," Connor said, mostly to see if he could get Teagan to waste a bit of air bragging about them. "What do you call those?"

The man scowled, and his head tilted slightly as he studied Connor's face. "Merlins."

Short. Sweet. To the point.

Not what Connor had expected at all.

"In exchange for that valuable information, I'll take my daughter." Teagan gestured toward Quinn.

"Come, now." Connor shook his head. "That's hardly an even trade."

"I've had enough of this, peasant," Teagan snapped.

The Lightseer Master General took an ominous step forward, and everyone present sank into a fighting stance of some sort. Swords reflected firelight. Vougels growled. Nocturne roared, and the ear-splitting scream shook the ground beneath their feet. Connor's stance widened even as the quake tested his balance.

Not once, however, did any of the gathered Lightseers glance up at the dragon. Their eyes remained on Connor.

On the *real* threat.

The chaotic rush of movement ended as quickly as it had begun, but it spoke volumes of the tension in the air. Everyone was ready to slit throats at a moment's notice, and how this ended would come down to which of them could hit first.

"Here's how this works," Teagan's voice dropped an octave, and he pointed one thick finger at Connor's face. "You give me my children, you surrender, and I seal that specter of yours away in a green jar for the rest of eternity."

"Hmm." Still bluffing like a hustler in a tavern, Connor tilted his head. He hummed in thought, as though he were actually considering the option, and shrugged. "I have to admit, that doesn't sound entirely in my favor."

"You try my patience," Teagan Starling warned.

Connor met the man's eye, and his façade melted instantly away as he matched the man's intense glare with one of his own. "And you try mine."

An icy chill swept between them as both men waited for the other to speak first.

Silence had always been a classic means of negotiation Connor used in tense moments like these—but more than anything, it was a great tactic to squeeze every possible second out of the encounter.

"Give me back my daughter," Teagan demanded.

"Of course," Connor lied. "As soon as you disassemble those merlins of yours, you can have her back."

In his periphery, Quinn's gaze shot briefly toward him.

She hadn't seen through his bluff, which gave him hope that perhaps Teagan hadn't, either.

"You're new at this." Teagan set his hands on his waist and shook his head, laughing. "You don't bring the collateral into the negotiation if you don't want it taken."

For a moment, Connor merely studied Teagan's face, convinced he hadn't understood the man. It had sounded, for a second there, as if he had referred to his own daughter as property.

Teagan pointed at Quinn for emphasis. "If you had any idea what you were doing, she would be locked up in a cell in your fortress. You wouldn't have come out here to face me, nor would you have given Quinn her sword. You're either cocky, or you're stupid."

Connor didn't reply, even as his shoulders stiffened.

This wouldn't end well, and he had a feeling it would end soon. If Wesley didn't get the Soulsprite in place, he would lose everything.

Nocturne pressed against their connection, and Connor instantly let the dragon in.

We are nearly out of time, the dragon said.

It appears so, Connor admitted, though he didn't let the dread show on his face. *How many of them can you take?*

I am not entirely certain, but I believe Murdoc, Sophia, and I can isolate the nine soldiers and their mounts from Teagan. A vougel inched closer, and Nocturne snarled at it in warning. The beast paused, its milky eyes locked on the looming dragon. *That will allow you to isolate Teagan from the others.*

Connor could only hope that would be enough.

Remember, he told the dragon. *We don't have to finish this on our own. All we have to do is stall until Wesley reaches the treasury.*

"You're safe now, child." Teagan's voice snapped Connor's eyes back into focus. The man smiled warmly at Quinn and stretched out his hand toward her. "He's outnumbered, and not even his wraith can save him now. You can walk to me."

His shoulders tensed as he watched Quinn to see what she would do. Everything he had done, everything he had sacrificed, everything he had worked for to get here—it all depended on what she did next.

With her sword still in its sheath, Quinn took two steps forward. Connor's throat tightened with disbelief, but from this angle, he couldn't see her face. As the scattered fires of the destroyed merlins raged around them, he could only wait—and watch.

"I have a question for you, Father," she said quietly.

"A *question*?" Teagan's eyes narrowed, and in a flash, his face contorted with anger. "You failed your mission. You were captured. If you had merely come home and admitted defeat, we wouldn't even be here. All of this death? All of this carnage?" Teagan gestured to the massacre around them. "This spilled blood is your fault. You have proven to me beyond a shadow of a doubt that you have no place in the field, child, and you will not spend even one more day as a Lightseer. The last thing you get from me is an answer, here and now, when I am moments from cleaning up your mess!"

She flinched at the fury in his voice, but she otherwise didn't move.

"Speaking of messes." Teagan's furious glare shifted to Connor. "Where is my son?"

He didn't answer. It wasn't in his best interest to explain what had happened, and Connor would hold tight to every bartering chip he had.

"Fine," the Starling patriarch said with a frustrated grunt. "You probably can't control Zander as easily, is that it? Is he the real collateral, locked away somewhere in the fortress?"

Quinn bristled, and her empty hands curled into tight fists.

Teagan didn't notice, and his attention never shifted away from Connor. "You might get a chance for redemption, Quinn. It's time we deliver justice to the assassin and recover that brother of yours."

This was it.

Her ultimate test.

Have faith in her, Nocturne said through their connection. *Have faith in us, Wraithblade. You cannot do this alone—nor should you have to.*

Connor swallowed hard, but he didn't know how to reply. He cast another sweeping glance over the gathered soldiers, but things looked bleak.

If Quinn turned on them, the bluff would fracture, and Teagan would hit the walls with everything he had. They wouldn't just run out of time—everything would end suddenly, and with a lot of bloodstains in the dirt.

Magnuson. The ghoul's voice pierced his thoughts. *This is urgent. We are so close. I'm not certain if you can hear me at the edge of our connection, but I know one of my abilities that can survive even this distance.*

In a violent rush, the world around him shifted. His head spun. The sky became the ground, and he lost all sense of direction as the deadly warriors around him became a blur of color.

No.

Not *now*.

The landscape around him changed as the Wraith King took over his sight. In seconds, he saw the world through the wraith's eyes as, deep in the Black Keep Mountains, the specter hovered in the shadowy staircase deep in the mountainside. Wesley stood in front of him, and the ghoul merely pointed down the stairs with a single bony finger.

You must come closer, the Wraith King said. *Only I can open the treasury door, and you are too far away.*

But Connor didn't dare move. Not now. A single step would break the fragile tension in the air, and Teagan's soldiers would inevitably attack.

A loud crack snapped through Connor's head. His ears rang. A blinding light burned away the shadows, ripping him from the ghoul.

And with that, his world went dark.

CHAPTER SEVENTY-SEVEN
QUINN

A bead of sweat dripped down Quinn's temple as she breathlessly scanned the gathered soldiers. With each passing second, she weighed the ever-changing risks of each possible outcome, and few scenarios worked out in their favor.

Nine Lightseers stood beside her father, their silhouettes lit by the smoldering bonfires of the destroyed merlins. She had personally joined each of these men in at least one mission throughout her career.

She knew their names. She had met their families. She had nodded politely to their daughters in the king's court, and she done her best to ignore their sons' advances, rather than punch the young men in the face. She had done it all out of respect for these fine warriors and the legacies they had built alongside her father in battle.

Each man had roughly two decades of experience to his name. Each man had killed more people than most folks met in a year.

With an anxious little bounce, she shifted her weight back and forth, doing her best to mask the fidgeting as she waited for one of them to inevitably charge. The longer they stood here, talking, the sooner these hardened warriors would realize Connor was just stalling.

At her side, the Wraithblade went suddenly still. He paused, body tense, still as stone and barely breathing. With a confused frown, she snuck a glance at his face.

His eyes glowed green. He stared straight ahead, as though looking clear into Teagan Starling's soul.

Across from them, roughly three yards away, her father sneered in victory. He had told her once that all a soldier ever needed was patience, because then he could simply wait for his opponent to make an error and take advantage of the moment.

It was a philosophy that had served him well, time and time again.

White sparks snaked across Teagan's shoulders. Calmly, quietly, he raised one arm as the skittering light intensified. His eyes narrowed as he aimed for Connor's chest, and a flash of blistering lightning erupted in his palm.

It all happened so quickly. In less than a second, the Master General of the Lightseers fired a blinding shot at the man standing beside her.

Quinn did the only thing she could think of—she stepped in front of it.

In the moment before the blast hit, she drew her Firesword and summoned her Shieldspar charm to reinforce *Aurora's* enchantments. A crisscrossing dome of light erupted across the Firesword, blending with the lightning as it cut through the air toward her, and she braced herself to take the blow.

A bolt of lightning would temporarily weaken her blade, but it wouldn't break. She had done this a dozen times before when sparring with her father, and all those years of practice were about to bite him in the ass.

With her arm and sword crossed in front of her, the bolt hit with all the power of a storm.

Maddening pain coursed through her, through every vein, through every muscle, through every bone and clear down to her soul. Her metal sword groaned in protest as its enchantments took the brunt of the attack. A shrill buzzing built in her ear as her light shield threatened to fracture. Snippets of electrifying energy arced off of the main blast, nipping at her arms, and her neck strained as the crackling bolt rooted her to the ground.

Her teeth clenched shut as she stifled an agonized scream. The seconds became hours. The pain built to a crescendo, and she arched her back as she silently pleaded with the Fates for this to end.

The stream of lightning stopped, and she let out a strangled gasp as her body mercifully relaxed. Her chest heaved, her body desperate for air, and it took every ounce of strength she had left to keep her sword and forearm crossed in front of her in case he fired again.

She glared at her father through the crackling flames covering the stunning blade he had given her, all those years ago, to protect this land from those who would decimate it. Never in her life had she imagined she would use it against him.

Quinn had chosen her side, and it could never be undone.

The deep creases in her father's face and around his mouth cast long shadows over his features. His eyes narrowed, and sparks cracked across his broad shoulders as he glared at her with an expression she couldn't read. Hatred, maybe, or disbelief. Disgust.

Though she never took her eyes off of him, she carefully watched the other soldiers through the corner of her eye. None of them moved, and one even gaped at her in disbelief.

No one spoke. None of them dared break the tension between father and daughter.

"Thank you," Connor whispered behind her, his voice barely audible over the crackle of *Aurora's* flame.

She risked a brief look over her shoulder to find him watching Teagan, his eyes mercifully clear again, and she simply nodded in reply. He stood behind her, that blackfire blade raging as the two of them faced the most powerful man in Saldia together.

This wasn't supposed to be how it happened. She was supposed to talk to him first. To try reasoning with him before he became too furious to hear a word she said.

None of this had gone to plan, and that enraged her. Her father wanted blood, but she wouldn't let him have it.

"Please stop." Though she spoke calmly, it took everything in her to keep from shouting at the man who had forged her into an obedient little soldier.

To end this bloodshed, she had to swallow her pride, and that meant appealing to the man who had raised her, rather than the warrior standing before them now.

"None of this needs to happen." Her voice carried across the circle of soldiers, loud and clear. "Connor isn't going to raid Lunestone or conquer Oakenglen or commit any heinous crimes. I stake my name and my sword on it."

"He did something to you." Her father glanced her up and down, and for a moment, the anger became concern. "A Bridlecharge enchantment, is that right? It's hidden well. Maybe an augmentation—"

"There's no curse," she interrupted.

The Lightseers around her stiffened, and a terrified lull settled on the desert air. Crackling flames from her Firesword blended with the bonfires of the destroyed merlins, but no one spoke. Everyone went still with horror as Teagan's scowl deepened.

No one interrupted the Master General, especially not his children. Of all his soldiers, they had always showed him the most deference.

That was simply how things were done.

"Explain yourself, child," her father demanded, not bothering to mask the overt disgust in his tone.

She bristled at his audacity. The sheer nerve of this man—for *him* to be disgusted with *her*.

He had underestimated her ability at every turn, and now he would discover the hard way that his pawn no longer played his games.

"Explain myself?" She scoffed, the sound dry and hollow. "You turned Connor into a scapegoat for the king you killed, Father, and you dare demand I hold myself accountable to *you*?"

Fire crackled against the air in the stone-cold silence that followed. Part of her had hoped these noble men would've reacted to the revelation that their Master General had killed their king, but that part of her died as not a single one of them reacted.

They didn't even flinch.

"Come here." Teagan's eyes narrowed in warning, and he pointed to the ground at his feet. His tone dropped an octave, and the scratchy growl in his voice sent a shiver down her back. "At once."

Not long ago, his tone would have terrified her into submission. Few could make her tremble with fear, but her father had always held a special power over her that she had never understood.

Now, however, only the barest patter deep in her chest hinted at the terror she had expected to feel in this moment.

Every night since she had first unraveled his lies, she had rehearsed what she would say when this moment inevitably came. She had practiced steeling herself against the shame, against the rage, against the hurt and betrayal, against it all.

Whatever it took to speak without scorching the earth in her grief.

But, as those blazing white sparks raced along his body, a single sentence echoed through her mind. It spun in circles, refusing to let her think about anything else until she said it out loud.

"'Father, is this working?'" she asked quietly, quoting what Zander had said back in Lunestone.

Back when she had learned the painful truth.

"Is *what* working?" he spat. "What the hell are you—"

"'If the public finds out what the wraith is,'" she interrupted, "'it threatens everything we've built.'"

Teagan went still. The furious creases in his forehead relaxed, and his rage shifted into a smooth mask of indifference. His hand balled into a fist at his side, and the sparks along his shoulders faded into the darkness around him.

His eyes darted briefly toward Connor, but Quinn had seen this expression before. The cogs in his brain were turning as he tried to figure out how to spin this in his favor.

It wouldn't work. Not on her, anyway.

She wasn't going to let him lie to her ever again.

"All I wanted was for you to be proud of me." The grating whisper stung her throat. "I wanted your respect. I trusted you to tell me the truth, and you couldn't even do *that*."

Her father raised one palm in a silent command to simply stop. "You don't understand what's at stake, Quinn."

"I think I do." She lowered her sword and summoned the light shield in her free hand, ready to block another surprise blow should her father try to knock her out of the fight. "You lied about the simmering souls to protect your power. You sent me after a timeless horror without the means to defend myself, all in the hopes of breaking me. And for what? Was all of this bloodshed worth it?"

To her disappointment, none of the gathered soldiers moved, and not one of them spoke. Though some slightly lowered their weapons, they all remained poised to attack at a moment's notice.

She had suspected as much, of course, but the damning implications of what she had said still carried weight. More importantly, her words carried severe consequences for everyone on this battlefield.

"Quinn Starling, I strip you of your title." Teagan raised one finger in warning, and a panicked pang shot through her even as he did exactly what she had expected he would do. "You will give me your sword, and you will step aside."

"And if I refuse?" she asked, unfazed.

He drew *Sovereign*, and flames erupted across its enchanted steel. Her father settled into the wide stance he always adopted during their training sessions, usually before he was about to beat her bloody to prove a point.

He slowly pointed the deadly sharp tip of the Firesword at her throat. "Then I will remind you of your place in this world."

Her heart skipped several terrified beats in her chest, and though a flood of dread washed through every inch of her body, she didn't budge. Shoulders back, chin raised in defiance and armed with the blade he had given her to defend this land from the relentless darkness, she stood her ground.

It had come to this, then.

So be it.

"Teagan Starling lied." Though she never once took her eyes off her father, she spoke in a clear voice every soldier in the circle her could hear. "He lied to me and he lied to all of you."

"Don't." Her father balled his hand into a fist, and white sparks shot up his arm as light leaked from between his clenched fingers.

"The simmering souls were never destroyed," she continued, as though he hadn't spoken. "King Henry's wraith was none other than the Wraith King."

Behind her, Connor growled softly in frustration, but they had both expected this to happen. For better or worse, the great Lightseer secret was out.

Teagan's greatest fear had been realized, and now she simply had to wait to see if their plan would work.

She didn't have high hopes.

"You brazen little shit!" Teagan fired a bolt of lightning at her, and she sidestepped the blast with seconds to spare.

The soldiers around them shifted, ready to charge, but she and Connor raised their blades in warning. The entire confrontation lasted mere seconds, and it ended without a single blow.

"The Lightseers don't defend Saldia!" Her ears popped as she shouted, almost astonished at the power in her own voice as she waited for another jolt of lightning to fly her way. "We all suffer and kill and *die,* just to protect the Starling name!"

Behind her, the sizzling crackle of the lightning bolt faded until it dissolved entirely into the roar of the bonfires lighting the dark desert night. Her father shook his head in disgust, watching her as though she were an imposter he barely recognized. His nose flared, and the scowl on his face deepened with each passing second.

But it was done, and short of murdering everyone present, he could never contain the secret again.

"Do what's right!" she shouted into the darkness. "Defy him! Ask yourself what duty you hold superior—to the greater good, or to a selfish liar?"

In the silence that followed, she finally broke eye contact with her father to risk a brief scan of the faces around the circle. The soldiers watched her with deep scowls and furrowed brows. Some stretched and curled their fingers as they silently debated their options, while others just stared at the ground.

It was progress from the stone-cold quiet, but no man sheathed his sword, and none of the hardened warriors broke formation.

Loyal, to the end. It was the Lightseer way.

"Is that it?" Teagan raised one eyebrow and gestured to the soldiers around them. "You expected to give a little speech and watch my soldiers switch sides? This is true power, little girl, and it is reserved for your superiors."

Despite the dismissive insult, Quinn's grip tightened on *Aurora.* "It's power I don't need. I was merely giving them a chance to live out of my respect for their time served as men of honor."

His haughty expression faded, and his eye twitched as he silently glared at her once more. Quinn tensed her jaw and shifted her weight onto her toes as she prepared for the only logical outcome—an impossible battle against the man who had not just raised her, but who had taught her almost everything she knew. Facing her father alone would've been difficult enough, but outnumbered like this, they truly didn't stand a chance.

Though she hated to admit it, that damned wraith would've been helpful right about now.

CHAPTER SEVENTY-EIGHT
QUINN

Quinn's gaze swept across the gathered Lightseers in the hunt to figure out a way to separate Teagan from his soldiers. A half-destroyed merlin towered behind them, just beyond the nearest pile of burning rubble, and the first threads of a plan began to form. She didn't like it, and it would probably fail, but it was the closest thing to an idea she had.

If the Soulsprite failed to activate Slaybourne's defenses, they were all as good as dead.

Beside her, Connor took a careful step forward and briefly lowered his mouth to her ear. "We need to get closer to the wall and buy them more time."

She grimaced. At this point, there wasn't much more time left to buy.

With that, the Wraithblade stood beside her with his sword held high in challenge against the inevitable onslaught. Black fire roared across the otherworldly steel as he held his sword and shield at the ready, evidently just as aware as she was of the inevitable battle.

"Look at yourself," Teagan spat. "The Wraithblade whispers in your ear, poisoning your mind, and you let him? You actually listen?"

"At least he doesn't lie," she spat back.

A gentle, rumbling snarl floated through the air, and the crunch of a soft footstep followed from the darkness outside the circle. The sensation of someone watching her sent a wave of goosebumps down her arms, but she would recognize that growl anywhere.

Blaze.

It hit her, then. When Death's Door opened, the wraith must've let Blaze out into the fray.

It took effort to stifle the grateful smile that tugged on her lips. Perhaps the abomination wasn't as bad as she had thought.

She studied her father's face, trying to gauge what he would do as her loyal pet stalked closer, but he didn't so much as tilt his head in Blaze's direction. His ear didn't even twitch, and though he had undoubtedly heard it, he most likely figured it was one of his own vougels stalking through the night.

Beside him, Tempest glared into the darkness with those milky white eyes. Quinn's grip on her sword tightened, but her father's mount didn't make a move.

She needed to keep her father talking. The only way to buy both Blaze and Nocturne some time was to encourage the Master General to enjoy the sound of his own voice. When furious, he usually preferred breaking bones to talking, so she had to settle for the next best thing—giving him more chances to lie.

"I've relived that conversation every day," she admitted. "Listening to you talk to Zander about how I pretend to be a warrior. How, if this mission didn't break me, then you would." Her voice cracked, and she swallowed hard to clear the knot forming in her throat. "If I hadn't heard it myself, I never would've believed it."

"It's impossible for you to have heard that conversation." As the fires on *Sovereign's* steel crackled, Teagan scratched absently at his beard. "Those rooms are secured. I don't know what trick you're playing, child, but—"

"'I maintain the oath I made when we started this,'" she said, quoting her father this time. "'If this failed hunt of hers doesn't break her spirit, then yes. I will break it for her.'"

None of the soldiers spoke, but one did shift his attention toward Teagan. Captain Oliver, a good man with a good heart who had admittedly tried a little too hard to get Quinn to marry his eldest son.

It was the first time any of them had broken their focus on Connor, and she considered that to be a win.

If Teagan noticed, he didn't react. Her father tensed, still watching her with slack-jawed disbelief as she effortlessly recalled every bit of the conversation that had shattered her world.

"You sent me after the Wraith King," she snapped. "Did you want to break me or get me killed?"

He shrugged. "I could've brought you back."

Quinn ground her teeth together to stifle a furious scream as her grip on *Aurora* tightened.

Lightseers protected the natural order. Only a necromancer would dare bring back the dead.

Even though her father had just confessed to breaking the One Rule of the Lightseers and defying the fundamental belief every Lightseer lived by, not one of the soldiers broke rank. Not one of them voiced a concern. Not one of them even lowered his sword.

"Don't let him get under your skin," Connor said in a calm tone. "Focus."

Her gaze flitted briefly behind her, and though she still wanted to yell into her father's face, Connor's voice was enough to snap her out of her rage.

"You've lost your damn mind." Quinn gestured to the hellscape around them. "It doesn't have to become a war. I've investigated this man, Father, and he's not like Henry. He doesn't want conquest. He just wants to *live*."

"Why do you care if he lives?"

"Because he's more of a Lightseer than any of you!" she shouted. "He has defended others—defended me, even, someone who relentlessly hunted him at every turn—in the name of doing what's right. That's what I dedicated my life to upholding. That's why the Lightseers exist!"

"The Lightseers exist to protect the Starling name!" Her father fired another bolt of lightning at her.

As she lifted *Aurora*, however, Connor's shield slid in front of her, and his chest pressed against her back as his enchanted shield took the brunt of the blow. She grabbed his wrist, and the crisscrossing light of her Shieldspar augmentation sprang to life as she pressed it against the interior of the shield. Her magic reinforced his as jolts of pain shot down her arm. Together, they leaned into the shields, their heels carving lines through the dirt as Teagan's blow drove them backward.

Just as the blast of lightning faded, the glimmering light in her Shieldspar dome shattered yet again. Connor lowered his shield until he could glare over it, but she sidestepped it completely to look her father right in the eye.

At the edge of the light, the barest hint of white fur hovered just beyond the shadows. Claws extended from the familiar vougel's paws as he rooted himself into the soil. Her brilliant pet didn't so much as breathe as he settled into position, ready to spring at her first command.

"What do you think will happen next, Quinn?" Teagan pinched the bridge of his nose as he shook his head in disappointment. "The peasant isn't leaving this desert alive. Think hard about the choice you're making, child."

"Oh, I have." She clenched her teeth, and a single massive flame curled around her closed fist as she fought to control her raw fury.

"No, you haven't." Teagan swung *Sovereign* lazily, just once as he adjusted his grip on the weapon, and the enchanted sword's crackling fires left a lingering circle of orange light that faded slowly into the darkness behind him. "Let me make one thing clear. You are only alive, at this moment, because you are my daughter. We have not attacked simply because he could slit your throat at any time, but I'm losing my patience. Lower your Fates-damned sword, or I will break you here and now, just as I promised Zander I would when this whole mess began."

Standing there, in the middle of a circle of warriors who had murdered countless people to appease their Master General, Quinn was left speechless. Her brows tilted upward, and she slowly shook her head as she struggled to reconcile this monster before her with the man she had idolized her whole life.

"I can't even recognize you," she confessed in a scratchy whisper. "I don't know who you are, anymore."

"You try my patience," he warned.

"I need to get closer to the wall," Connor whispered to her. "When hell breaks loose, lead him toward me."

She didn't acknowledge that she had heard him speak. It wasn't possible for them to move without reigniting the battle.

It seemed they were at a stalemate.

"Show me." With her blazing Firesword, she gestured toward her father.

"I want to know the real you."

Teagan shook his head. "You don't."

"I'm as good as dead, aren't I?" She shrugged, and even she didn't know if that had been a bluff. "The least you can do is tell me the truth before I go."

Her father stilled, and he watched her with a strangely indifferent expression. He sighed, deep and slow, and the scar across his face nearly glowed in the firelight surrounding them.

Without warning, Teagan Starling cracked his neck. He grimaced, as though the pressure hurt his head, and his gaze shifted to the ground. He rubbed his eyes, and for a moment, his forearm blocked his features. In case it was a trick, Quinn stiffened and prepared to shield herself against yet another bolt of lightning.

What came next, however, hit her harder than any blow ever could.

When he finally lifted his head, he studied her with a cold and calculating gaze. He sized her up as though he could calculate the value of her life with a glance—as though her worth decreased with every passing second of his growing disappointment. The furrowed lines in his forehead faded away as he relaxed into an easy stance, and he watched her with chilling apathy.

In her lifetime, she had only seen him study criminals this way.

A shiver of terror fused her feet to the ground, and she couldn't have looked away even if she had wanted to. As much as she had tried to steel herself against whatever she faced on this battlefield, she hadn't been prepared for this.

His mask had finally come off.

As she had suspected all along, she had never known the real Teagan Starling. Her father, at his core, was more terrifying than she had ever imagined.

"You want the truth?" he asked calmly.

The muscles in her neck tightened, but she nodded—both to distract him, and because this was what she had told herself she had wanted all along.

"I'm not going to kill you, but part of you will absolutely die," he explained. His tone was steady and calm, as though he were giving a lecture on how to train a dog. "Quinn, breaking you will be easy. First, I'll gut this bastard." He pointed *Sovereign* at Connor, who bristled. "I'll break your legs and arms so that you can't do a damned thing but watch him die. I'll make it painful, far more than I had intended. Maybe I'll skin him alive, or maybe I'll take a finger at a time." Her father shrugged. "I'll decide in the moment, depending on how angry you make me."

The soldiers around him watched in stunned horror. Some lowered their swords. Others took a wary step backward, but no one interrupted him.

"As I torture him, I'll be watching you." Teagan's piercing gaze snared her, and she could barely breathe as her father continued. "I know you, so you won't scream. You won't beg. But your eyes, Quinn, they always give you away. I will only kill him when your soul finally snaps, and then I'll drag you home. You know what I have waiting for you there?"

She swallowed hard and shook her head.

"A cell," he said casually. "One in the darkest corner of Lunestone, in a wing only a few know exists. In the darkness, where no one will hear you begging for mercy, I'll starve you. I'll drown you to within an inch of your life and shatter your will to fight. I might kill you, but it won't matter. I can bring you back and do it all again."

A bead of sweat dripped down Quinn's face, and her eye twitched as she struggled to recognize the abomination standing before her.

"When you're fractured and broken, I will finally drug you into obedience," he finished with a lazy tilt of his sword. "You'll live in a haze, foggy and obedient, and over the years you'll forget who you were. You are a pawn, little girl. A chess piece. All of you are, and down there in the darkness, I'll remind you where you fit into my world. I'll beat the rebellion out of you, same as I'll rip the insubordination out of Zander when I find whatever is left of him. He will take my place, and you will burn and bleed until you forget you were ever a warrior. Until all of this is just a nightmare that makes you too scared to sleep."

Her and Teagan's Fireswords crackled in the silence that followed, and Quinn gaped at him in breathless horror. In the distance, a muffled boom echoed through the desert as one of the downed merlins erupted. Behind him, a ball of fire whizzed up toward the stars.

"Fucking hell," Connor muttered from somewhere behind her. "That's your *daughter*."

"I know what you fear, Quinn," Teagan said, as though Connor hadn't spoken. "Your worst death isn't on the battlefield. Out here, you get to die a hero, and I won't allow it. No, your worst death is to die in your sleep, old and gray, married off and forgotten while great men overshadow you. Your greatest fear is to live the life I chose for you the day you were born."

A pang hit her in the chest, but she refused to admit he was right.

"Why tell me I would be a legend, then?" She tried to yell at him, to maintain the strength in her voice she had managed to keep thus far, but it came out as the barest whisper. "Why turn me into a solider at all?"

"To make sure our enemies can't destroy the family line, damn you!" He gestured to Connor with a dismissive flick of his free hand. "Think for once, Quinn Starling, about your *future*. You were only trained to fight so that you could defend yourself, your children, and the family name. That is *it*!"

Her head began to shake, unbidden, as she listened to him finally tell her the truth. This was what she had wanted all along, and she hated every second of it.

"The worst of it is you could've been a legend at almost anything." He scowled at her wasted potential. "If you truly did overhear that conversation, then you know full well you could've been queen of Oakenglen."

"A doll," she seethed. "Just another puppet for you to play with."

"Still a queen." He pointed his finger at her in warning as sparks skittered across his arm. "You could've had a real future. You would've been revered by all who knew you. That's what Starling women do, Quinn. They preserve the family and make us stronger, for we have *nothing* without the brilliant women who make our family great. But you threw all of that away. And for what?" He gestured at Connor. "For a peasant?"

"For justice," she corrected him. "For duty."

A humorless laugh escaped her father, and he rubbed his eyes as though he had grown bored of them all. "I am the bringer of justice, Quinn and I decide a soldier's duty. We all have roles in this world, child, and yours was chosen for you long ago. Every death here is on your head, Quinn, not mine, no matter what you think of me. These soldiers' blood is on your hands. The secret that would destroy your family has been revealed, and all because of you."

It clicked for her, then, that these nine men would never leave the Decay alive if her father won this battle.

Everything he had said, back in that meeting room when he thought no one else could hear, was true. She had tried to rationalize his disrespect for the lives of others as a lack of context, but he had already proven he would kill with abandon.

She had been a fool, yes, and naïve—but only because she had blindly trusted those she thought had her best interest at heart.

And it would *never* happen again.

Quinn gestured to the burning desert around her. "If a bit of truth is all it takes to destroy us, then we aren't worth protecting."

Teagan tilted his head, and to her surprise, he didn't answer. His eyes narrowed, as though he were astonished by her reply, and the silence weighed between them.

The lull spoke volumes, not just of his disbelief that she would dare speak to him this way, but also of the unhealed fissure that divided them. Both refused to back down, and both believed without a question of a doubt that they were right.

This would not end well.

"We're done." Teagan's voice snapped against the air like a whip. "You have obligations to this world and to me. You will obey."

"No," she said quietly, not caring if he heard. "Never again."

She had done what Connor had asked, and she had bought them all the time they had to spare—but there was no telling if it would be enough.

"Take the Lightseers," Connor whispered in her ear. "As many as you can. I'll fend off Teagan until—"

"Tempest," Teagan said, his voice dwarfing Connor's. "Bring her to me, and make it bloody."

The vougel beside him roared, its teeth flashing in the firelight, and the massive beast charged.

Quinn summoned her Shieldspar dome, and as the light flashed into existence over her forearm, she whistled sharply.

At the command, Blaze roared and leapt from the darkness. His claws sank into the nearest soldier's side, and his wing landed hard against the back of the nearest vougel's head. The soldier's mount fell limp to the ground, and the man screamed in pain as Blaze tossed him aside. Her pet didn't falter, and in the seconds before Tempest could bite her, Blaze dug his teeth into the massive vougel's neck.

Tempest screamed in pain and slashed at Blaze's face. Blaze's wings spread wide for balance, and in that moment, the dueling beasts blocked her view of her father.

"The helm!" she shouted as she sank into her stance.

Her vougel snarled and dug his claws into the golden band around Tempest's forehead. In unison, Tempest's claws dug into Blaze's forehead and ripped his own helm from his face as well.

"No!" Teagan shouted.

It was too late.

The golden band ripped from both vougels' brows. Blaze's fell harmlessly to the ground, while splatters of Tempest's blood shot into the air. The blood-drenched spikes of her helm's interior twirled, and the band of gold thudded on the cracked dirt beside Blaze's.

Blaze growled softly, and he squinted as the helm's magic faded. Across from him, Tempest shook her head and blinked away the milky daze in her eyes. She backed up, snarling, but her wide wings still hid Quinn's father.

"Blaze," Quinn whispered.

His head snapped toward her, and his features relaxed as their eyes met. Though his ear twitched in irritation, he crouched low, even without the helm to enhance his already clever mind. The tip of his tail twitched as he waited for another attack, and the soldiers along the outer ring of the circle held their swords high as they waited to see what would happen.

Waiting for the next order, like the diligent soldiers they were.

Quinn scowled. How disgusting.

Tempest's eyes dilated as she scanned the circle of soldiers. She stared at Blaze and snarled. He roared back, his claws extending into the dirt, but

Tempest wasn't having it.

She launched into the sky, leaving Teagan behind while Blaze remained at Quinn's side.

As the vougel flew off, Quinn could once more see her father. He glared at her with that cold, steady gaze, but she grinned.

"That's loyalty, Father" she said haughtily. "And that's the only kind of power I care about."

"Maybe I won't just break your legs," he growled. "Maybe I'll rip them off."

"Try it," she dared.

Her father charged, and she met him halfway. They both swung, and their Fireswords hit with an earth-shattering clang that echoed across the burning desert. Leaning into her sword with all her strength, she glared at him over their crossed blades as waves of heat rolled off the fires from both swords.

From somewhere behind her father, a war horn blared. The sharp blasts cut through the night, deafeningly loud and all too familiar.

The order to attack.

This negotiation had evidently not gone according to her father's plan, but he'd come prepared. In the gathered army below, men shouted orders. Fires lit. Metal groaned, and three of the merlins fired at the wall in unison.

They had officially run out of time, and there was nothing left for any of them to buy from the Fates. Whatever happened and however this ended, there would be blood.

Lots of it.

"I idolized you," she seethed.

"I know." Her father watched her with that same dispassionate glare, like she was an irritating bug he couldn't squash.

In her periphery, the circle of Lightseers charged. Connor let out a string of curses, but Quinn never broke eye contact with her father. Men shouted, and the splintering crackle of ice mingled with the roasting sizzle of the destroyed merlins.

"Blaze, guard Connor!" she shouted. "Get him closer to the wall!"

Her vougel roared in answer, and he charged the soldiers in a flurry of feathers.

But it wouldn't be enough. Even with Connor's entire team, they were vastly outmanned.

As her father lifted his sword to swing again, she summoned a ball of fire and hurled it at the merlin. She blocked his blow and stumbled backward just as her fireball hit its mark.

The wooden structure fractured, and it careened through the air toward a cluster of four soldiers. It wouldn't be enough to kill them, but it would give Connor a momentary edge against the horde.

Teagan sliced at her, and this time, their Fireswords met. The clang of steel blended with the roar of the enchanted flames as they coiled together. A blast of heat singed her eyebrows as she leaned into her blade and glared at her father over the flames.

He shifted his weight, and though the subtle movement would've been easy to miss, he had nailed her in the gut too many times in practice for her to fall for it now. She twisted her hips at the last second, and his knee hit air.

Before he could regain his balance, she summoned fire into her palm and hurled the ball of flame at his face. He blocked it with an effortless twist of his sword, and the flames on *Sovereign's* steel erupted as they absorbed her attack.

Quinn rolled out of range, putting some distance between them as he swung the flat of his blade at the air where her face had been moments before.

"You made a mistake," she told him. "If all you wanted was a pawn, you should never have given me my sword."

With her free hand, she grabbed the Volt around her neck and unleashed a dazzling stream of lightning at his chest. It sliced through the air, and he barely twisted out of the way in time.

A wayward arc zapped him in the side, but the dazzling flash of light blinded her from whatever happened next. She winced and shielded her eyes until the blinding glare faded.

He stood before her, still as a stone. Smoke spiraled from a bloodstained hole in his shirt, and he winced. He lost his balance and fell to one knee. With one hand on his wound and the other holding *Sovereign*, his face was momentarily exposed.

The moment wouldn't last, and she didn't want to miss it.

With flawless precision, she summoned fire into her free hand and twisted her hips as she took her shot. Her fist smacked into his jaw. Pain broke across her knuckles, but she swallowed the agony.

After all, Starlings didn't cry. They punched things until they felt better.

His head snapped backward from the blow, and he hit the ground hard. She swung the flat of her blade, aiming for his skull, but he rolled out of the way and jumped effortlessly to his feet. Her blade smacked against the dirt with a muffled thud.

Teagan chuckled and stretched out his jaw. "Perfect technique, Quinn."

To her surprise, she felt nothing at hearing such a rare compliment from him. No flicker of joy. No burst of pride. Just the steady, boiling current of the simmering rage fueling her to do the impossible.

His flattery didn't work on her anymore.

With *Aurora* at the ready, Quinn and her father slowly circled each other to the blood-chilling melody of clashing steel and muffled screams. She had lost track of Connor in the fray, but he could handle himself.

As the flames erupted around them, her entire focus remained on her father. It killed part of her, for it to end like this, but she couldn't lie to herself any longer.

Only one of them would leave this desert alive.

CHAPTER SEVENTY-NINE
CONNOR

The moment the two Starlings took their first swings at each other, chaos erupted across the Decay.

Nocturne attacked Teagan's reinforcements, and an arc of lightning ripped through the nine Lightseers. Most of them leapt out of the way, but several vougels went down in a flurry of screams and feathers. Branching bolts of crackling light hit two of the men in the chest. Both shot backward into the darkness, instantly gone, while the remaining seven charged.

The sound that followed wasn't just a roar. Its earth-shattering rumble dwarfed the scream of any dying creature. It wasn't just the thunder of a storm, or the quake of Mother Nature rebelling against the mortals who walked her soil.

The raging fires in the debris around the wreckage cast surreal shadows over the dragon's hulking body. His horns glowed yellow as he snarled at the Lightseers now blocked from Connor's view.

The dragon's tail separated Connor, Quinn, and Teagan from the rest of the Lightseers, and Quinn held her own against her father even as sparks erupted into the night with each clang of steel. Slowly, steadily, she inched toward Slaybourne's walls.

This reprieve wouldn't last long. These hardened Lightseers would fight to their dying breath, and there was no telling how long his team could hold even nine of them at bay.

In unison, Murdoc and Sophia climbed easily up the dragon's legs and onto his back. Brilliant blue beams shot through the night, briefly illuminating

Sophia's face each time, while Murdoc hurled a dagger into the throng below.

Shouts blended with the thundering booms of rock smashing stone as flaming boulders rocketed toward Slaybourne. The first of them shattered against the very walls protecting Wesley's path toward the treasury. The sky rumbled with all the fury of hellfire, and his fortress had precious little time left before its strongest walls crumbled.

Magnuson! the wraith roared in his head. *Closer!*

Furious, blood pumping but unable to join the battle, Connor sprinted toward the walls. He had to get closer to ensure the wraith was able to open the door, but the moment he did, he would be back in the fray.

In the corner of his eye, a white blur darted toward him. He ducked instantly, prepared to slit a vougel's throat, but recognized the gold stripes on a familiar furry face. Blaze snarled, and the tiger-bird's wings spread wide as he skidded over the dirt. Connor grabbed the beast's neck and jumped onto his back, and the two of them raced across the Decay.

That's it. Relief oozed from the Wraith King's voice. *You're in range. I can work with this. We're so close, Magnuson. I will remain by the boy's side until the Soulsprite is placed, but try to save some bloodshed for me.*

"Finally," Connor said.

He pressed his hands against Blaze's neck and swung his leg over the vougel's side, landing in the dirt with ease. His boots left imprints on the soil, and he kicked up dust as he slid to a stop.

Blaze roared impatiently behind him, but Connor pointed at Quinn. "Cover her. Stay out of sight if you can."

The vougel shifted his attention to his master, and with a soft growl, darted into the darkness.

Kneeling, Connor narrowed his eyes as he focused on the dueling Starlings. Quinn circled her father as both of their Fireswords blazed. The enchanted flames raged across the legendary steel of both blades, and neither Starling looked away from the other.

Both waiting to see who would attack first, and eager for an opening.

She glanced at him—briefly, for barely a second—and their eyes met. He nodded in a silent signal that he was ready, and her stride lengthened as she lured her father closer to him.

They both knew they stood a better chance together than apart.

Cautiously, Connor patted the sheaths strapped to each of his calves. The two Bloodbane daggers waited, and a thin glow escaping from the leather casing on each of them.

Good.

The Bloodbane daggers had incapacitated Zander, and that meant they would do the same to Teagan. It had been a risk to bring them into the fight, instead of hurling them over the wall with the orb, and he was about to see if the risk would pay off.

Against an opponent like this, he needed all the help he could get.

In the chaos, Connor had lost his grip on both his sword and shield. He summoned them again, and black smoke rolled across the desert as he stood.

Impossible odds or no, he had to end this.

As the two Starlings circled, Teagan cast a wary glance over his shoulder toward Connor.

Their eyes met, and the bastard sneered with unearned victory.

A low growl built in Connor's chest. Teagan didn't see him or Quinn as a threat. Despite being isolated from the army, and even with a dragon fighting against him, Teagan Starling barely seemed fazed.

Quinn held her Firesword tightly. Her eyes shook, wet with the tears she refused to let free, and her glare focused intently on her father.

Connor studied his enemy's gait for signs of weakness. A slight limp, perhaps, or an old injury. But with every confident step, Teagan held himself with perfect poise. No weak side. No blind spots. No holes in his armor.

A perfect warrior, here to kill them both.

It would be in Teagan's benefit to keep them separated. As much as Connor wanted to charge, he had to time this perfectly. At any moment, Teagan would attack, and they stood a better chance against him if they could fight side by side.

Only then could they overwhelm him. Only then did they stand a chance.

"What a waste," Teagan said with a disappointed shake of his head. "You would've been so useful, Quinn. A master at swordplay, perhaps, or a lethal mentor to my top assassins. You had so much promise, but you failed me. Hell, you failed yourself."

"I'm fine with that." Her voice cracked, but she didn't falter.

"This is theatre." Her father gestured across the battleground. "You can't do it. You can't kill me. You could never see this through to the end, little girl." He smirked as he baited her. "You don't have the *balls*."

Her boots slid silently across the parched earth. "You're trying to taunt me, and it won't work."

"Of course it will." His eyes narrowed. "It always does."

As much as Connor hated to admit it, the Starling patriarch had a point. In this duel, she was fighting far more than just her father.

Her past. Her future. Her purpose.

In this duel, she was fighting—and losing—it all.

"This is madness." Her voice cracked again, and this time, it came out as the barest whisper. "Stop. Surrender. Admit that even you could be wrong. Admit that Connor isn't the villain you've conjured him to be. You're trying to kill someone who could become your greatest ally!"

As Teagan finally passed between him and Quinn, Connor took his first few steps closer. He kept his eye trained on the back of Teagan's neck, even as the man watched him through the corner of his eye.

Connor shifted his weight between both feet, just waiting for the right shot, while Teagan casually twirled his Firesword.

"You're wrong, my darling," Teagan chided. His tone dripped with disdain, as though he were speaking to an insolent child who didn't like the word *no*. "I can never allow a man to be my equal, and this Connor fellow of yours came dangerously close."

Connor shifted his weight to the balls of his feet. Any second now, and Quinn would circle back to him.

Any moment now, and they could charge him together.

At the last second, Teagan swung his Firesword at Quinn's neck. She blocked, but he didn't even pause. He twisted his blade and drove it toward her face. She leaned to the side as the inferno of enchanted steel stabbed at the air. Teagan made the smallest gesture with his empty hand, as though he were shaking water from his fingers, and a blast of air landed hard in her stomach. She doubled over and stumbled backward, desperately trying to put space between them. His Firesword swung at her exposed neck, and she lifted her own sword with barely a moment to spare.

Clang.

Clash.

Smack.

His fist cracked against her jaw, and a few drops of blood shot into the air. She fell, her red hair covering her face, and rolled across the ground.

"Quinn!" Connor shouted.

"Don't you fret, Wraithblade," Teagan said with a dark chuckle. "I raised her to take a harder hit than *that*."

With Teagan's main focus on his daughter as she tried to stand, Connor had an opening. He had to use this moment to his advantage.

"You're insane." Connor inched closer, more focused on the distance between him and Teagan than he was on his words. His blackfire blade crackled, and firelight glinted across the shield on his left forearm. "We could've come to an agreement."

"Haven't you been listening?" Teagan's nose wrinkled in disgust. "I would never make an agreement with the likes of you. You never stood a chance."

Teagan shifted his full attention to Connor as Quinn pushed herself upright. Her arms shook, and a shadow darted from the night beyond the firelight. Connor tensed, not sure he could reach her in time to help.

A familiar white and gold head emerged from the shadows, and Connor let out a slow breath as Blaze tended to her. The vougel held his own helm in his teeth and laid by Quinn's side. She grinned and took the gold circlet from his mouth as blood dripped from a gash on her face.

Good, she was alive.

Connor swung at Teagan. Their swords clashed, and sparks shot into the air from the two enchanted blades.

But Connor had expected that.

He instantly shifted his weight to his rear foot and rotated his wrist. In a simple, elegant motion, he knocked Teagan's Firesword aside and drove his own blade at Teagan's neck.

Teagan's smile fell. The man gritted his teeth with effort as he knocked the blackfire sword aside with the flat of his blade. Connor kicked Teagan in the stomach, and though the man grunted with pain, he grabbed Connor's ankle and twisted. Connor flipped, landing hard on his back, and Teagan swung at Connor's face. He lifted his shield, and it took the blow for him.

Clang.

Clang.

Swipe.

Teagan's sword stabbed into the dirt where Connor's leg had been a moment before. He shuffled backward as Teagan's Firesword burned streaks of flame into the night sky, swipe after swipe.

Though he avoided each blow, this position left him momentarily vulnerable.

Teagan took full advantage of that.

The Starling patriarch kicked him hard in the face, and Connor launched backward. He hit the ground hard and rolled, kicking up dust as he slid. When he finally skidded to a stop, he summoned his shadow blade in his left hand. Black smoke rolled across his legs, and he used the moment to subtly tug one of the Bloodbane daggers from its sheath around his calf.

The dark smoke only lasted a moment, but it was long enough. Careful to hide the weapon from Teagan as long as possible, Connor held the Bloodbane dagger so that the blade lay flat against the inside of his arm.

The whole encounter had lasted mere seconds, and the man wouldn't see it until it was too late.

In the distance, Quinn stood. Backlit by the flames, she was nothing but a silhouette as her Firesword erupted once again with its enchanted inferno.

"Just give up and die," Teagan spat.

Connor didn't answer. He didn't need to. Armed with the weapon that had disabled even Zander Starling, he dug his heel into the dirt for balance. With one more settling breath to brace himself for a world of pain, he launched at Teagan yet again.

Ready for more.

"I'm insulted, honestly." Teagan didn't flinch, even as Connor swung his blackfire blade at the man's face. "With the damage you've caused, I expected this to be more of a challenge."

Teagan leaned backward as Connor's blade passed harmlessly in front of his face. He spoke in a lazy drawl, as though they were having a chat during a calm walk through the woods.

Connor swung again, refusing to take the bait. The Starling Firesword cut through the air to meet him, and sparks fizzed into the night as their broadswords clashed again.

Clang.

Clang.

Crunch.

Teagan's fist broke across Connor's jaw. Flashes of red lit up the night as Connor stumbled backward, but he resisted the impulse to wipe the blood from his face. He glared at Teagan as his head cleared, and he tilted his left shoulder forward to ensure the Bloodbane dagger in his right hand remained hidden.

When it hit Teagan, he wanted to make damn sure it was a surprise.

"I didn't think you would face me alone." Teagan shook his head in disappointment as he cast a quick sidelong glance at his daughter, who stalked toward them as Blaze darted toward the dragon.

"I'm not alone," Connor pointed out.

"Her. Right." Teagan looked again over his shoulder as Quinn neared. "But you know what I meant. I thought your wraith would've at least made an appearance by now. Did you lose control of him already?"

"You can't faze me." Connor grinned, and he could taste the blood on his teeth. "You assholes have insulted me my whole life."

A humorless laugh escaped Teagan Starling. The man shrugged, as though admitting he should've seen that one coming.

Without warning, and with his full attention still on Connor, Teagan raised one hand behind him. His palm flattened against the air, and sparks skittered across his body.

"Look out!" Connor warned.

But it was too late.

Lightning powerful enough to down a dragon shot across the desert. Wild arcs hit everything, and Quinn summoned her dome of crisscrossing light just as one of them cracked against her. The blow launched her backward, and she rolled across the dirt.

As the volley of electricity ended, Teagan chuckled. He didn't bother checking to see if Quinn had gone down. Instead, he took several slow, confident steps as he slowly circled Connor.

Enough of these games.

Before Teagan could position himself between him and Quinn, Connor charged. He raised his left sword as though he were going to attack, and Teagan predictably blocked it.

At the last second, Connor knelt and skidded across the cracked earth. Teagan's Firesword passed harmlessly overhead, and Connor dismissed the shadow blade. A puff of black smoke rolled over them both, and Connor used the moment of distraction to drive the Bloodbane dagger deep into Teagan's gut.

Right into the man's stomach.

The Lightseer Master General let out a guttural grunt, but he didn't scream. He didn't even gasp with surprise. Instead, he grabbed Connor's wrist with his free hand and twisted it hard, so violently Connor thought it might snap. Though his fingers twitched, threatening to drop the dagger as Teagan stretched the tendons to their max, Connor gritted his teeth and fought through the pain. Ribbons of agony shot through his elbow.

Together, they fell to their knees, both men holding the dagger as they fought for dominance. Teagan sucked in a pained breath through his teeth as blood bubbled from his stomach, and the man lifted his Firesword overhead.

Nope. Not happening.

Connor punched the man in his throat. Teagan choked, and his eyes widened with surprise. The Firesword thudded to the ground, and its fire hissed as it died. The muscles in Teagan's neck tensed, and Connor's chin lifted in defiance as he held the man's gaze.

Evenly matched.

But Teagan's grip on Connor's other hand tightened, and he twisted harder. This time, something in Connor's wrist snapped.

Refusing to give the man the satisfaction of knowing how much that had hurt, Connor choked down the guttural yell that almost escaped him.

The Bloodbane dagger fell to the dirt, now fair game.

In their tussle, Teagan had turned his back to Quinn. She once again stood, and this time, she wiped the back of her hand across her bloody jaw.

Though backlit by the fires, she reached for something around her neck.

The Volt.

It was all the warning Connor needed.

He summoned his shield in a rush of black smoke, and Teagan took the bait. The man drove his Firesword into the metal, but Connor managed to wrench his hand free from Teagan's grip in the nick of time.

A deafening crackle snapped through the air, and Teagan spun around.

But not even the great Teagan Starling could move fast enough to avoid the Volt.

The streak of lightning nailed him squarely in the chest. His back arched, and he gritted his teeth as smoke spiraled from the point of impact. Connor used the momentary distraction to dive for the Bloodbane dagger, but a hand grabbed his ankle.

Scorching energy blistered up Connor's leg and into his lungs as Teagan dragged him backward. The man glared at him with a mask of frozen hatred on his face, unmoving, his grip tightening even as tiny sparks darted over his eyes.

"Damn it!" Quinn shouted.

The bolt of lightning mercifully ended, and Connor dug his hands into the dirt as he kicked Teagan in the face with his free leg. Connor's boot cracked against the man's temple.

And, damn it all, it hurt like *hell*.

It was like kicking a stone wall in bare feet. Pain shot up the back of Connor's leg, and though dark spots buzzed along the edges of his vision, he did his best to push through it. He wrenched himself free and dove again for the Bloodbane dagger.

But something shifted in the air. The hair on his arms stood on end, and everything in him warned against grabbing it.

At the last second, he rolled to the left, and a ball of fire crashed into the blade. The force shot the dagger off into the darkness, out of sight and out of reach.

Connor glared over his shoulder to find Teagan staring at him, chest heaving as smoke spiraled from his body.

And the bastard *grinned*.

CHAPTER EIGHTY

CONNOR

Connor's chest heaved. Every breath scratched against his throat as his body screamed for rest—or, hell, to just give up and die already. He glared at Teagan Starling as Quinn ran, full bore, toward them both.

To finish this.

To land the final blow.

With her Firesword blazing, Quinn brought the painfully sharp blade down on her father's head. He rolled out of range at the last moment, and her sword drove into the dirt where he had been.

Teagan used his momentum to jump to his feet, and he took several wary steps backward. His chest heaved with every laborious breath, and the tip of his own Firesword dragged through the desert soil. Carefully, cautiously, he studied the two of them from afar.

Finally, they had the upper hand.

Connor glanced back, looking for the Bloodbane dagger lost somewhere in the darkness, but he grunted in frustration and abandoned it. He would have to recover it once the battle was over.

Damn it all.

He pushed himself to his feet and quickly closed the gap between him and Quinn, just as she inched toward him.

Shoulder to shoulder, they would face Teagan Starling together.

The Master General of the Lightseers fished something out of his pocket. Firelight glinted across a glass vial as he popped the cork with his thumb. He downed it in a single gulp, all while his gaze shifted between the two of them.

Quinn muttered obscenities under her breath. "That's a Dazzledane."

Connor didn't know what the hell that meant, but it didn't sound good.

"Better." Teagan tossed the empty vial aside, and it crashed against the dirt. "It's a Dazzledane, blended with a Rectivane. Energy and healing, all in one. I had to keep these out of your reach, or your addiction would be much worse than it already is."

A guttural growl escaped her, and she gritted her teeth as she glared at him. "I'm not—"

"You are." He chuckled. "I allowed it. It kept you in line. Child, you can't hide anything from me. I know it all."

Quinn grabbed the Volt around her neck.

Teagan clicked his tongue in disappointment. "You already tried that, dear."

"And it hurt you," she snapped. "That's the point."

"I'm still standing." He spread his arms wide, and the blazing sword in his palm left streaks of light on the air. "You hit me, point-blank, and I got back up. Nothing you fire will take me down for long. I'm better than you in every way."

"You're stalling," Connor pointed out.

"Obviously." Teagan set his free hand on the bleeding gash left behind by the Bloodbane, but to his credit, he stayed on his feet. His body convulsed, just once, and his breath slowed as the potion worked its magic.

Fine. If Teagan was going to use the moment to stall, Connor intended to use it to his advantage as well. He slowly knelt and reached for the last Bloodbane dagger strapped around his calf.

With a careful twist of his shoulders, he hid his movements as he tugged the small blade from its sheath. With every second that passed, he studied his enemy and waited for the perfect opportunity to throw it.

"Neither of you will ever be my equal," Teagan spat. "Even together, you're not enough. Don't you want to know why?"

"I don't care why," Quinn said through clenched teeth.

"Of course you do." A dry laugh escaped him. "That's all you've wanted this whole time, isn't it? The truth. I'm surprised you haven't figured it out yet, Quinn. You'll never get the truth because our family is built on lies. No human can be as strong as I am on his own. Not even with our potions. Not even with blightwolf blood." Teagan cracked his neck and briefly closed his eyes as his breathing eased. "It's the dragon blood, Quinn. That's why this peasant can't be allowed to keep his beast. That thing belongs to me, same as every other dragon on this continent. Just like you, I'll drag it back to Lunestone and chain it with the others. Just like you, I'll make it suffer until it breaks. Just like you, it'll die, old and gray and useless after I've wrung every drop of magic from its body."

Her eyes widened with disbelief. "The island."

"Of course the island," he snapped.

"That's why you wouldn't let me go." She pinched her lips together. "You're a fool to tell me that, Father. I'll destroy it, and I'll free every dragon in there."

"No point. They're all feral." Teagan breathed a sigh of relief and rolled his neck on his shoulders. "Besides, you won't remember any of this after I'm through with you."

Teagan closed his eyes and smiled. His Firesword still hung limp in his grasp, and for a moment, the man let his guard down.

It was all Connor had needed.

He aimed at Teagan's heart and threw the second Bloodbane with every ounce of strength he had left. The blade spun on its way toward Teagan's chest, and in that single, suspended moment, sparks skittered across the Starling patriarch's shoulders.

As the blade sailed ever closer, Teagan's eyes opened. He raised one hand, and a blinding blast of lightning tore through the night.

They had both fallen in each other's trap, and this time, Connor didn't have time to dodge the blow.

Teagan stepped aside, and the dagger sailed harmlessly past him into the night.

Damn it.

Connor summoned his shield, but the black smoke coiled over his arm just as the lightning crashed into his chest. He flew backward. His stomach lurched. His ears rang. The stars above blurred into the black sky around him, and he lost all sense of up or down as he tumbled, over and over, into the darkness.

Into the worst of the carnage.

Toward Death.

He hit the ground hard, and for a while, he couldn't move. The smoky char of burning cloth choked him. The searing ache of roasted skin crept up and down his left side. He violently coughed and slowly blinked himself awake.

The world blurred again and again, even as he fought to make sense of the smears of color around him. Black. Brown. Silver. Red.

So much red.

In the distance, a woman screamed, and a jolt of dread shot through him.

Quinn.

He tried to stand, but his legs gave out on him, and he collapsed to the ground. He tried again, his arms shaking under his own weight, but he only slid forward on the soil.

Get up, a voice echoed in his head.

The ghoul, maybe, or a memory. He couldn't tell.

His vision cleared even as he lay there, immobile. He grunted as more mind-numbing pain ricocheted through his body, but he managed to lift his head this time. He squinted as he glared back at the battlefield where Quinn now faced her father alone.

Teagan held her, one hand on each of her biceps, and her feet dangled over the ground. Fire raged in his palms and spread to her sleeves. His sword waited beside him, stabbed into the earth, while his magic scorched her.

Her back arched, and her hair dangled behind her as an unholy scream clawed its way out of her. Whatever he had done, she now hung limply in his grasp. Her left wrist hung at an unnatural angle, and a crimson stream bubbled from a fresh gash across her neck. Her eyes squeezed shut, and Connor could barely recognize her under all the blood.

"Get up," Connor said to himself. His words slurred, but he didn't care.

He pushed himself to his feet and stumbled. Everything teetered, as though the ground tilted under his feet, and he staggered sideways until his shoulder slammed into a merlin. Smoke spiraled from his chest, and his lungs tightened as they briefly refused to work.

Yet again, he fell to the ground, and that sent a fresh shockwave of misery clear down his spine.

"You did this!" Teagan held her close to his face as he shouted over her scream. "It should've never come to this, child! You only had to obey!"

That *bastard*.

Again, Connor tried to stand. Something in his chest ripped open, and he gasped in the gut-wrenching agony that followed. His arms gave out on him, and yet again, he hit the ground hard.

Teagan released her, and she collapsed in a heap. Though her chest rose and fell with each shaky breath, she didn't move. Smoke coiled from her singed body, and she weakly lifted her head as her father snatched her sword off the ground.

"Don't." She choked on her words and spat a clump of blood into the dirt. "Not that. Anything but that."

"It's time I take back some of that power I paid for." Just out of her reach, Teagan examined her magnificent sword. "Besides, with what I have planned for you, you won't be needing this anymore."

"Father, don't," she pleaded, softer this time. Unable to move, broken and battered, she still tried and failed to reach for her blade.

Teagan set his foot against the tip of the legendary Firesword and held the hilt with one hand. Sparks skittered across his shoulders, and this time, he set his palm flat against the base of the sword, where the hilt met the blade.

Quinn once again reached for *Aurora*. A blinding flash of light swallowed everything, and a thunderous crack boomed through the desert. The ear-splitting shriek of twisting metal ripped across the battlefield.

Within seconds, the light faded, and Teagan tossed the Firesword aside. The hilt thudded to the dirt beside the shattered remnants of its blade. It lay there, broken, with a single surviving shard of steel poking from the hilt.

Though her enemy stood over her, Quinn stared at the broken Firesword. Her lips parted in shock, and she gaped at it in numb disbelief. Oblivious to the battlefield and unflinching at the threat looming over her.

Grieving.

Connor could see it, plain as day, on her face. She had shattered right alongside her blade.

Get up.

As the pain slowly receded, Connor grabbed the nearest splintered beam and pulled himself to his feet. He teetered, and though he had to hold tight to keep his footing, at least he managed to stay standing this time.

He limped closer. With every step, another jolt of pain shot up his spine. His pulse thudded in his ear, and he pushed through.

But he couldn't move fast enough.

Teagan grabbed Quinn by her neck and lifted her until her toes again dangled over the desert ground. Though her left arm rested at her side, limp and useless, she grabbed his wrist with her right hand. She choked with each strangled breath, but Teagan's grip only tightened.

"Count yourself lucky," Teagan said under his breath, so softly that Connor almost didn't hear it. "At least you get to live."

"That's not life," she choked. Her eyes rolled into the back of her head, and she dug her nails into his forearm as she fought for air.

"Stop." Connor forcefully coughed, and his demand came out as more of a half-garbled mumble. He'd meant to yell it, but his lungs still wouldn't work. He could only limp ahead, his clothes still smoking as embers burned through the fibers.

He had to stop this.

If only that damned wraith would hurry up and help. It should never have taken this long to begin with.

As Teagan held her neck with one hand, he set his palm against her stomach. With one final look into her eyes, he fired a bolt into her body at point-blank range.

In the second before the flash of lightning blinded Connor, she sailed backward through the air, farther away from him than any time before. The rumbling boom of the lightning bolt split across the desert, and Connor instinctively shielded his eyes with one arm.

When the light faded, Quinn lay beyond the orange circle of firelight.

Nothing more than a silhouette, she didn't move. From this distance, he couldn't even tell if she was breathing.

Teagan sighed, the sound long and slow and riddled with disappointment. He dusted off his hands and shifted his attention to Connor, even as blood dripped from the gash in his stomach. "Now that she has been dealt with, Wraithblade, I can kill you in peace."

"You rat bastard," Connor said through clenched teeth. "You're dead."

"No, I'm tired." The man yanked his own Firesword from the dirt and kicked aside the ruined shards of Quinn's blade. "I wanted to retire. I wanted my son to take over so I could run things from the comfort of my home, and now you've dragged me out into the battlefield. To make matters worse, you've destroyed an entire pillar of my legacy." Teagan gestured lazily at Quinn's limp silhouette. "You deserve worse than death, peasant, but I don't need the Bloodbane dagger to end you once and for all."

Another wave of agony shot up Connor's spine, and he grimaced as he fought off the pain. He wanted to check on Quinn, but he didn't have that luxury. He had to kill this madman, and he needed to be quick about it.

Flames crackled to life across Teagan's sword. "It's going to feel damn good to kill you, Wraithblade, but I need to lure that wraith of yours out here first." He tilted his head, and his eyes narrowed as he paused midstride. "You realized that, didn't you? You clever bastard. That's your game, isn't it? Are you protecting him to buy yourself a few more seconds of life?"

Connor tried to speak, but he could only grunt with pain as he held the singed wound in his chest. Blood coated his fingers, and he didn't know how deep the wound went or how bad things would get.

Frankly, he didn't care.

He'd had a good life. For one, brief moment, he'd made the world a little better. A little brighter. He'd made a difference, and that was more than most folks like him could say.

If this was where it ended, fine.

The least he could do was drag Teagan to hell with him on the way out.

CHAPTER EIGHTY-ONE
QUINN

The muted screams of dying men blended with the crack and thunder of lightning in the cold desert night. A putrid stench wafted by, like the charred aftermath of a bonfire blended with the rusty tang of metal on the tongue.

Even with her eyes closed, a dull red light fizzled through her eyelids. The shrill scream in her ear echoed through her battered skull and blended with the distant shouts from the battle that raged on without her. In the void between awake and unconscious, she forgot her name. She forgot what battle this was and why she was here.

A steady thud battered against her skull. A thick fog rolled through her brain and numbed every sensation, until she felt almost drunk. Her cheek rested on something hard, but even with it holding her in place, her head spun in endless circles. Something dripped off her eyelashes, hot and wet, and it plopped with a steady cadence off the tip of her nose.

With a pained groan, she forced her eyes open. Everything around her blurred into unrecognizable smears. Mostly orange, with some black. A hint of beige.

Her name came to her, then, and Quinn gasped as the memories hit her like a punch in the gut.

A wave of agony rolled through her. She pressed her forehead into the dirt as her body broke again in real time, as the pain ripped her apart, as every inch of her ached and screamed in misery.

The mind-shattering tremors in her thigh and chest suggested multiple broken bones. The muscles in her arms popped and spasmed, like they couldn't bear to cling to bone anymore.

And through it all, that steady pulse thumped in her head like a sick and twisted drumbeat. Her throat blistered with all the agonizing fire of a thousand metal shards slicing her apart from within. She tried to gasp, tried to scream, tried to make any noise at all, but the sound died in her throat.

She was alive, yes, but her body screamed at her for it—for not surrendering.

For not giving up, here and now, and just dying.

She lifted her head and squinted at the blurry chaos around her. An orange glow faded and flickered across the cracked ground, and for one blissful second, the world came into focus.

It didn't last.

The simple act of lifting her head sent a shockwave of pain down her spine. Her skull throbbed, harder now, threatening to take her under, and she sucked in air through her teeth as she fought to stay conscious.

A sharp jolt of pain splintered through her abdomen, and she set her hand on it to ease some of the pressure. As her fingers pressed against her stomach, however, they didn't press against skin. Her fingertips slid through the hole in her shirt and into the gaping wound beyond.

A gut-wrenching tremor of pain froze her in place.

She couldn't breathe. She couldn't think. She could only shove her face into the dirt to stifle her scream, and her entire body tensed until the flood of misery ebbed to a trickle.

When the worst of it finally faded, Quinn let out a slow and steady breath. She had meant for it to calm her, but it came out as pathetic whimper.

Her father might've actually won. Of everything that had happened tonight, she hated that the most.

Barely able to think, she lay there, trying to summon the sheer force of will required to move. She had no idea the extent of the damage done or how many bones he had broken.

Resolute, determined to die fighting, she set one hand on the ground and tried again to lift her head. Instead of offering her a stable foundation, however, her palm slipped across a thick layer of goop. She squinted through the bloodstained clumps of her hair to find a pool of blood underneath her so thick that her fingertips disappeared into the puddle.

Is this how I die? she thought.

She had wanted to ask the Fates that question, to speak the words out loud, but the rusty bite of her own blood pooled on her tongue. Talking required more effort than she could spare.

Unbidden and with no warning, a fresh round of anguish boiled through her like a bonfire, scorching every vein, from her toes to the tips of her ears.

Here?

She wanted to scream.

Like this?

None of this seemed right.

Is this really all I've earned from you?

The Fates couldn't betray her like this. She refused to believe it could really end here, at her father's hand.

Something bright flashed in the corner of her eye, and she winced at the sudden light. It sparkled again, brighter this time, and she tenderly lifted her head to see what it was. Blood rolled down her face and dripped from the tip of her chin as she fought to make sense of the blurred landscape.

There, just ahead, something bright and green glimmered in the darkness. She blinked until it came into focus. Slowly, the shifting edges sharpened into the outline of a familiar dagger with a blade that glowed like an emerald sun.

The Bloodbane dagger.

At this point, rational thought challenged what little energy she had left. Wounded and isolated, she needed a weapon.

This would do.

She set her hands flat on the ground and pushed, trying to get up, but her arms shook. Her torso lifted, albeit slightly, and she collapsed back onto the ground as her arms gave out on her. She gritted her teeth as she tried to ignore the pain.

Fine. She could still crawl.

Tenderly, carefully, she pushed against the ground with the tips of her feet and dragged herself forward with her hands. Every now and then, she managed a slight rotation in her hips that pushed her ever so slightly farther, but even the slightest movement ignited a fresh wave of agony.

Her nails clawed at the soil, digging up small rocks on her way, inching ever closer to the only weapon within sight.

When she finally got close enough, her hand shook as she reached for it. Her fingers finally wrapped around the hilt, and she let out a sigh of relief. Having something sturdy in her palm settled the shake, and she let out a string of curses as another wave of pain tore her apart from the inside out.

Somewhere nearby, a man grunted in pain, and a body hit the ground hard.

Quinn lifted her head, brows pinched together as she tried to make sense of the chaos. Another jolt of agony ripped down her spine, but she forced herself to ignore it.

In the distance, a burst of fire shot into the air, its yellow and orange plumes igniting the sky, and she winced as the light momentarily blinded her.

As the light faded, her eyes slowly readjusted to the patchy darkness.

In the firelight of a burning merlin, Connor lay on the ground. The creases in his forehead deepened as he focused on a man who had his back to her. The Wraithblade lifted his brilliant shield just as the second man swung a blazing Firesword. Metal clanged, piercing and raw, as the two collided. Quinn winced from the shrill gong just as Connor let out a muffled yell of pain.

The man with his back to her stepped into the light, and his blazing red hair almost blended into the raging inferno around him.

"Connor," she whispered.

Her eyelids grew heavy as her body begged her to sleep. She struggled to stay conscious, to watch the fight, to help in some way, but the corners of her vision went dark.

Teagan Starling said something, his voice just quiet enough that she couldn't make sense of the words, and she grimaced as she tried desperately to stay awake.

Another clang of metal. Another muffled yell.

A flash of anger cleared her head, if only for a second. She wasn't the only one her father had manipulated into doing his bidding. He had conned the whole continent. The common people looked to him as a beacon of justice and light, but it was all a farce. Everyone—even her, even Zander—existed solely for his purposes.

All her life, she had never been more than a chess piece on the board. One of his favorites, perhaps, but a piece nonetheless.

Tears burned in the corners of her eyes, and she clenched her teeth to keep from screaming as her arms shook with the simple effort of trying to sit upright. She didn't know which hurt more—the hole in her stomach, or the gaping void in her heart where her love for her father had once burned brighter than anything else in her life.

The man who had lifted her onto his shoulders when she was a little girl had never existed. The man who had read her stories of heroes and righteousness, who had waxed poetic about the legendary woman she would become, had been nothing more than a mask an evil man wore so that she would do his bidding without question.

Everything she had ever known about her existence was a lie, right down to the man who had brought her into this world.

She gritted her teeth, furious, fuming, broken and shattered, unable to believe this monster was the man she had idolized her whole life. For over two decades, she had wanted to be like him. She would've—and had—done whatever it took to make him happy. To make him proud. To watch him smile as he clapped her on the back for a job well done.

He had been her champion.

And now, he wanted to burn the life out of her until there was nothing left that could resist him. He would carve her into a soulless husk, just like him.

Her plan to reason with him had been doomed to fail from the start, primarily because there was nothing in him to reason with. She and her family could never go back to the way things were.

They would never be a *real* family.

If Teagan Starling was allowed to walk away from this battle, he would only return with more soldiers and a bigger lie—this time, about her.

And everyone would believe whatever he said.

A lump formed in her throat, and the stinging in her eyes worsened. It might've been tears, or it might've been the blood—she didn't care. The void in her chest spread down her arms, until her fingertips went cold and numb, and she craned her head until she could see her father again.

With Connor on his back and Teagan looming above him, the Lightseer Master General raised his brilliant Firesword to strike again. He stepped to the side, just enough that she could see his face, and *Sovereign's* flame briefly illuminated his terrifying sneer.

Eyes bright with excitement, he laughed as Connor raised his shield again to block the blow.

That bastard was enjoying this.

Quinn's grip impulsively tightened around the Bloodbane dagger. Struggling to breathe, she simply stared at it and wondered if she could really follow through.

If she could really kill her own father.

Prove me wrong, Dahlia had said. *Please, for the love of the Fates, prove me wrong.*

A soft growl rolled past her, and the crunch of paws cut through the air like a knife. She rolled onto her side and tuned out her body's pained protests as she craned her head over her shoulder. She needed to get a view of whatever was stalking her before it could take its first bite.

In her current state, she didn't move fast enough.

By the time she finally lifted her head, a white tiger hovered above her. The golden stripes on the beast's familiar face shimmered in the low light as the first dark purple threads of dawn broke across the horizon behind him.

"Blaze." Her head fell backward and rested against the earth as she let out a sigh of relief.

He nudged her shoulder, and something plopped onto the ground beside her. She grimaced at the loud sound and adjusted until she could crane her aching neck to see what he had dropped.

A battle-worn leather bag now lay beside her, and she grinned with gratitude at her pet's foresight. He nudged her face gently, and she rested one bloodstained palm against his jaw. As her touch left red streaks across his fur, their connection opened, and a flurry of his emotions came through.

Concern. Desperation. Fear for her life.

"Good boy," she whispered.

He forced his head under her arm, and she held tight to his neck as he lifted her into a sitting position. The hole in her stomach ripped open with the movement, and she bit down on her lip until she drew blood to stifle the scream.

Blaze sat beside her, and she leaned her body into his warm hide. His wing stretched out and around, cradling her in a cocoon of feathers and fur. Again, her eyes drooped as she relished in the kind of warmth and safety she hadn't felt for quite some time.

But if she slept now, she would never wake up, and Connor would die.

With a miserable groan, she flipped open the flap on her bag. Quinn still gripped the Bloodbane as though it were a tether to this life, and she rifled through the bag with her other hand until her knuckles bumped weakly against the potions stored inside.

To her immense relief, only two of her decoy potions had cracked. That was by design, of course, given the protective coverings she always wrapped around each vial, but she was grateful nonetheless.

It didn't take long to tug one of her lingering Rectivanes out of its cloth pouch. With her thumb, she popped the cork and threw her head back to drain the whole damn thing.

The potion took control of her body. Her vision went dark, and she collapsed back against Blaze as the magic burrowed into the worst of her injuries. The potion blistered and fizzed through her bones, healing everything it touched, and orgasmic ripples of simultaneous pleasure and pain shot through her like waves crashing on a shore, again and again.

Bit by bit, the potion stitched her body back together, and she gritted her teeth to ride it out. Tremors shook her legs as her shattered knee fused together. The blistering ache shocked her brain, drowning her in anguish, and she bit down on her own shoulder when she could no longer stifle the scream of agony.

In the distance, Nocturne roared. Men barked orders. Fires raged, and the clang of metal on metal blurred together in a cacophony of bloodshed. Lightning crackled through the clouds, though she couldn't tell if it belonged to the dragon or a growing storm.

On the horizon, purple and orange clouds slowly ate away the midnight sky. First light would hit them soon, and once it did, Connor's team wouldn't be able to keep the Lightseers at bay.

With the dawn, her allies wouldn't have any shadows left to hide in, and their momentary advantage would disappear.

Exhausted, weak, and with barely enough energy to sit upright, Quinn glared out at the warzone as she reluctantly waited for her body to heal. The pops in her joints slowed, but they didn't stop. Rather than fading completely, the mind-numbing ache in her body zapped what little energy she had left.

Even a Starling Rectivane took time to work, but it was time she didn't have. She needed something stronger, something robust enough to power her through even as the Rectivane worked on her from within.

An idea hit her so suddenly that she sat upright, and the motion sent another shockwave of pain down her spine.

Grimacing, she rifled again through her pack until she found her Dazzledane. Only one sip, and only once per day—it was all she had ever allowed herself. Addiction to a substance like this corroded minds, but with so much at stake, she wasn't sure she cared anymore.

She tugged it out of its pouch and eyed the half-filled bottle warily, still not altogether certain this was a good idea. As she stared at it, Connor's agonized yell pierced the air, and Teagan Starling laughed.

It was all the incentive she needed.

Quinn scowled and, without another moment's pause, threw back her head as she drank the entire bottle.

The magic hit her in a sudden rush, and it hit her *hard*.

Her body hummed with life. With power. With hope. With light. Every inch of her buzzed and breathed in a steady cadence that matched her pulse. The ribbons of pain in her bones bled away to a steady numbness, prickly and light. In seconds, even that faded, and then she couldn't feel anything.

No pain. No exhaustion.

No fear.

Only the void in her chest remained. It hovered like a ghost burrowing into her soul. Aside from the numb nothingness, she could only feel the hollow disbelief at what she was about to do to the man who had once been her hero.

CHAPTER EIGHTY-TWO
QUINN

In the darkness, on the fringe of the bloody battlefield outside Slaybourne, Quinn set her palm on the ground and tried to stand.

Though she managed to get on her feet this time, she teetered, about to fall.

Blaze lowered his head in front of her, and she pressed her bloodstained fingers into his beautiful fur as he helped her catch her balance. She let out a slow breath and let her gratitude seep into him through their connection to conserve the energy she would've otherwise spent talking.

He lifted her to her feet, and Quinn paused as she settled into her stance. She took a wary step as her vougel hovered nearby, ready to catch her in case she fell again, but her boot settled into the dirt with ease.

In her tenure at Lunestone, Quinn had often done what no one else had managed to do—she surprised her father. She could walk beside him without him hearing her approach, and it was the one skill she had always lorded over Zander.

Her stealth was the stuff of legends, and it would now be put to the test.

"Stay here, Blaze," she whispered, without even the energy to look him in the eye as she walked forward. "Stay safe."

He moaned softly, but obeyed.

Thanks to the potions, a little more of her strength returned with each careful step forward. The Dazzledane mercifully numbed the pain that would've otherwise had her writhing on the ground. With every passing second, the blended potions worked their glorious magic, and they fueled her limping path across the cracked, crimson earth.

At some point, Connor had gotten back on his feet. He and Teagan slashed at each other in a dazzling array—two gods among mortals. Black flames coiled with red fire as the blades collided again and again.

In the lingering shadows of an encroaching dawn, neither man looked her way.

Ordinarily, her father would've kept an eye on her. He would never turn his back to her, but he had broken her. He had burned her to within an inch of her life, and after a battering like that, he must've expected even a Starling to stay down.

Yet again, he had underestimated her—but this time, it would not work out in his favor.

Thirty yards to go.

Masked by the night and drenched in her own blood, no one would see her until it was too late. The Bloodbane dagger weighed on her palm, her grip just tight enough to keep a hold of it in her numb daze.

Her boots passed across the ground without a noise, and her lifetime of stealth training brought her ever closer to the dueling pair who had no idea she was even still alive.

Twenty yards left.

Her father swung at Connor's head, and the Wraithblade barely ducked in time. Quinn saw Teagan's trick before Connor could react, however, and her father landed a left jab hard into the man's temple.

Connor landed on the ground, and blood streamed down his face from the fresh gash her father left behind. His blade and shield disappeared in a rush of thick black smoke as he tucked and rolled across the ground. Knocked on all fours, the Wraithblade muttered obscenities and stumbled as he tried to get back on his feet.

Ten yards, now.

She finally stepped into earshot, and the soft rumble of her father's voice became words.

"...and I'll add that dragon of yours to my personal collection." With his back to her, Teagan cracked his neck and stared down at Connor. "With all that power, I think it'll easily become my favorite. But don't fret, peasant. I won't kill it unless it can't be broken."

His dark and deadly tone brought her back to her childhood, to those terrifying moments of mind-numbing horror when she had knelt before him, small and helpless, doing her best to steel herself against his wrath. The warning in his tone had always hinted of consequences she didn't want to suffer, and as a little girl, she had done whatever it took to ensure he never spoke to her like that again.

But the past couldn't be changed, and Quinn pressed onward.

Almost there.

Connor got to one knee, about to stand, when Teagan landed a hard kick to the Wraithblade's throat. Connor curled in on himself, but her father didn't pause to let the man breathe. His boot nailed Connor in the jaw, so hard it shot him backward. Blood shot into the air, and the Wraithblade tumbled across the dirt as Teagan quickly closed the gap between them.

"Take comfort in knowing that you've at least been a challenge." The Master General swung *Sovereign* in a lazy circle, and the sword's enchanted flame left imprints on the darkness. "You even turned one of my children against me, which I never thought was possible."

With her father's back still to her, Quinn stepped into the circle of orange light radiating across the desert from the nearby bonfires. Numb, dazed, and broken, her grip on the Bloodbane dagger finally tightened.

Connor glared up at Teagan, and rivers of blood seeped from both his temple and his mouth. Undeterred, the man summoned the blackfire blade into his right hand.

A fighter, to the end. Quinn could respect that.

Before he attacked, however, Connor's gaze darted toward her. It flicked briefly, at first, and then his gaze shifted back, as though he couldn't believe what he was seeing. His eyes widened ever so slightly in barely restrained surprise.

Their eyes met, and if he could even recognize her under all the blood, she hoped he understood the desperate plea in her gaze.

Distract him.

"It didn't have to be like this." Connor wiped the back of his hand across his bloody face to hide his momentary surprise. With his gaze trained on the ground, he coughed and stumbled as he tried to stand. He fell to one knee, chest heaving, and glared up at Teagan. "I don't want your wealth, your power, or anything else. All I want is to be left alone."

Her father paused, finally standing still, and Quinn held her breath as she raised the dagger. Her body tensed as she prepared to drive the Bloodbane into his right lung.

Somewhere deep beneath the numb blanket of the Dazzledane potion, her body screamed at her to just give up and die already.

"You belong to an abomination," Teagan spat. "You don't get to—"

Quinn plunged the dagger into his back, right between his shoulder blades. At the last second, she twisted the knife and sliced right—just as he had taught her years ago.

Puncture a lung, and even the strongest soldier won't last long.

Teagan arched his back and let out a strangled scream of pain. Blood shot from his mouth. He pivoted on his heel, his face twisting in his fury, and he raised his sword to decapitate the fool who had stabbed him in the back.

Quinn didn't care. She drove it deeper with all her strength, and the dagger ripped open muscle as blood streamed from the wound.

"How?" he demanded, his voice choking as he spat blood, and the single word vibrated through her arms as if he had roared.

She didn't answer. Though she had so much she wanted to say, she didn't dare speak a word of it.

Her resilience had surprised him yet again.

Teagan's arm twitched involuntarily, and his grip on *Sovereign* loosened. The Firesword hit the ground with a heavy thud.

Their eyes met, and she braced herself for the expression that just might kill her. The one that would haunt her, every night, for however long she had left to live.

The betrayal.

The shame.

The sadness.

But there was no grief in his twisted features. There was no loss. There wasn't even a trace of disappointment.

To her dismay, he only wrinkled his nose in disgust.

In the suspended moment when his eyes narrowed in understanding—when he finally realized what had happened, and who had done it—he glanced her over as though she were a whore he had thrown in the gutter. As though she had less value than dung on the bottom of a shoe.

To think this was what he truly thought of her, deep down, gutted her most of all.

Blood spurted from her father's mouth as he tried to speak, but he swallowed it. "You miserable waste of—"

A black blade protruded from his back, missing Quinn by inches. Its midnight fire burned away the threads of Teagan's shirt, and the sickly sizzle of burning flesh filled her lungs like rancid water.

Teagan let out a quiet gurgle, like air bubbles popping in a stream, and white sparks danced across his body. He grabbed Connor's forearm, but Quinn had seen him use this technique before.

This close, with that level of contact, that would be a death blow even for a man as powerful as the Wraithblade.

She grabbed her father's wrist and bent it backward, ripping his hand off of Connor mere seconds before a burst of lightning snapped through the air. The pale hair on her arms stood on end, and a soft crackle of energy shot up her arm as Teagan's hand aimed harmlessly into the darkness.

"You're dead to me." Blood trickled through her father's bloodstained teeth, but he didn't seem to notice. He glared at her with unfettered hatred.

"I know," she said softly.

The bones in his wrist cracked as she snapped his hand back against his forearm, and he let out an agonized yell as he fell to his knees.

The blackfire blade disappeared from Teagan's back, and Connor kicked Teagan hard in the chest. Her father fell to the ground beside her and scooted backward, one hand on the bubbling wound in his abdomen as he scowled up at them both.

A knot formed in her throat, and that aching void in her chest finally overpowered even the numb haze of the Dazzledane.

"I wanted to save you!" Tears burned at the edges of her eyes. Though she wiped them away with the back of her hand, she only smeared blood across her face. "To save *us!*"

His chest heaved as he held his wound, and he shook his head as if he couldn't believe she hadn't figured it all out yet. "There never was an 'us' to save, child," he said through ragged breaths. "There has only ever been *me*."

She cocked her arm to throw the Bloodbane dagger, but he acted first. Sparks skittered down his arm, and he raised his palm as he unleashed a chaotic blast of lightning.

This charge wasn't aimed at anyone or anything. It shattered the air, nothing more than the desperate attack of a man inches from death who no longer cared what he hit or who he killed.

A man who had finally lost control.

Quinn didn't block it. Numb to everything but the hole in her heart, she didn't care if she died. Not anymore. Even as the light blinded her, she stared at where her father had been moments before.

Numb to it all, and broken.

Someone grabbed her shoulder and yanked her to the ground. Her knees hit the dirt, and a rock pressed into her once-shattered kneecap. A tremor of pain followed, but the all-consuming numbness of the Dazzledane swallowed it seconds later. A metal shield appeared in front of her as the person grabbed her shoulder and held her close to his chest.

The lightning snapped against the shield. Metal creaked and groaned under the assault.

Quinn looked up. With his head inches from hers, Connor gritted his teeth as he held the shield in front of them. His eyes squeezed shut as sparks snaked through the metal and up his arm. The tendons in his neck tightened painfully, and he stifled an agonized yell.

She grabbed his wrist and summoned her own Shieldspar charm to reinforce his shield. His body relaxed into hers, and he let out a breath of relief even as Teagan's relentless stream of lightning continued.

A distant screech filled the air. The flutter of wings quickly approached, and a single blast of the Lightseer war horn cut through the night.

"That's the rest of his army," Quinn said through the pooling blood in her mouth. "Even if we kill him, we're going to die."

"Any second now, we'll have an army," he said in her ear. "We just need a little more time."

"We don't have any." Her throat tightened as she sat with the weight of what she was about to ask him to do. "I can't finish this, Connor. I don't even think I can stand."

"You have to." His fierce eyes pierced her foggy haze, and for a moment, her head cleared.

"I can't." She swallowed hard. "But you can."

A muscle in his jaw twitched, but he didn't move even as lightning arched above his head and collided with a metal plate nailed to the destroyed merlin behind him.

"You have to kill him," she whispered. "I'll hold him off with the—" She grimaced as a jolt of pain shot down her spine, and her teeth clenched tight as she stifled a pained sob. "I'll hold him off with the Volt. I'll draw his attention. You only get one shot at this."

"I'm not letting you be bait. He'll kill you."

"He'll kill everyone," she snapped. "Wesley. Isabella. Fiona. Everyone. Let me do this, Connor. I have enough of the Rectivane in me that I'll survive."

It was a lie, but she didn't care. There was a chance it would work, however slim that chance might've been, and that was good enough for her.

He cursed under his breath as the volley of lightning continued, and though his brows furrowed with frustration, he eventually nodded.

Quinn let out a breath of relief.

Good. At least this wouldn't all be a waste.

If this was really how she died, at least her last moments would have meaning.

"He can't last much longer," she said as the lightning crackled against their combined shields. "The second the lightning ends, we lower the shields, and I will fire the Volt while you charge."

Connor nodded.

The blistering light continued, and she swallowed the blood pooling in her mouth. "Good luck, Wraithblade."

"This isn't over, Quinn." He shook his head. "Don't you dare die."

She grinned, exhausted, but didn't respond.

All at once, the blinding light around the shield faded. The groan of tortured metal stopped. Connor's shield disappeared in a rush of black smoke, and hers fractured as she released her hold on it.

Through the dark haze, she focused her full attention on the spot where her father had been.

The black fog thinned, and the second their eyes met, she grabbed her Volt and fired. In the same moment, he unleashed another bolt of lightning, this time straight into her chest.

Connor shouted, but over the thunderous crack from the lightning, she couldn't make out the words. Her lightning ripped a hole through her father's shoulder, and his blast of electric energy instantly faded.

But no one could stop the crackling bolt he had already unleashed.

Her free hand twisted impulsively to summon her light shield. The enchanted magic solidified just as the lightning hit it, and the resulting impact shot her backward over the cracked desert ground.

The sky became the ground became the clouds, and as her broken body rolled across the dirt, none of it made sense.

She lost track of how long and how far she tumbled. Her head smacked against the dirt, again and again, and the ringing in her ears grew to a deafening roar.

When she finally slid to a stop, she simply lay there. She willed her body to move, even if it was just a twitch of her finger, but she couldn't, and the void in her chest grew.

Finally, her eyelids became too heavy to open, and Quinn let herself sleep.

CHAPTER EIGHTY-THREE
WESLEY

*G*old.

Everywhere Wesley looked, piles of gold littered every corner. The money spilled from their piles, carelessly strewn across the floor, and they glittered in the glowing green light that cast a soft glow across the cavern.

As Wesley crossed a bridge leading over an endless void somewhere in the depths of Slaybourne, he kept his eyes trained on the pedestal at the far end to avoid thinking about what would happen if he fell into the shadows below. He tried not to think about dropping the sunbaked stone as he clutched it to his chest. The longer he held it, the more he feared it slipping out of his grip, and the tighter his hold became. His knuckles bleached white from the effort, and though his arms ached, he didn't care.

"Focus," he told himself. "Breathe."

The ghoul hovered behind him, those skeletal hands clacking impatiently against his bony arms, and Wesley tried to ignore the weight of the undead ghoul's stare on the back of his neck.

He did his best to ignore the skeletons guarding the door behind him and the dead person hanging in a cage over the abyss. He did everything he could think of to disregard the pebbles falling from the ceiling as yet another boom rocked the cavern. He tried not to imagine the walls breaking, or a sword piercing Connor's heart.

Instead, he tried to keep his attention on the lone pedestal surrounded by piles of coin at the far end. He had never seen this much money in his life, and he in fact hadn't ever thought it possible to have this much in one place. He figured even a king's treasury only had a bit at a time, but he had been wrong. As another thundering crash shook the mountain, a few gold pieces slid down their piles and fell into the chasm.

"Eyes front," he warned himself as the far end of the bridge mercifully neared. "Almost there."

As it stood in the center of the gold, with stairs leading to it, the pedestal had to be where this strange orb needed to go. He didn't understand any of this, but he had done as Connor had asked and followed the ghoul—and the wraith had pointed to this strange platform.

Hopefully, Wesley had pieced it all together correctly. With such a massive army at the door, he doubted he had the luxury of making even a single error.

Though the weight of eyes on his back remained, the ghoul hadn't followed him into the cavern. Wesley didn't look back, and honestly, he preferred the thought of it disappearing altogether.

It wouldn't, of course, but a man could dream.

As he finally stepped off the bridge, he let out a shaky sigh of relief. He paused, taking just a minute to gather his wits about him.

Through the corner of his eye, something slid along the nearest pile of gold. He yelled in surprise and jumped, nearly popping out of his skin. Still clutching the orb to his chest, he watched in paralyzed terror as something large slid down the biggest pile of coin.

As it slowed, the streaks of gold and green became nothing more than a crown. It hit the stone floor with a thunk as lingering pieces of sliding gold clinked against it.

For a few moments, Wesley could only stare at it with relief as his heartrate settled.

"Get it together, man." His furious whisper echoed through the cavern, and he shuddered.

A thunderous boom shook the mountain. The ground beneath him trembled, and vibrations shook more coin loose from the piles. Wesley lost his balance. He toppled, heart frozen in fear of dropping the dark orb clutched to his chest, and his knee slammed against the stone. He gritted his teeth and sucked in air as pain shot up his leg, and he let out a furious string of curses as the sharp jolts of pain slowly faded to a dull ache.

Damn it all.

He glared up at the pedestal and used one hand to push himself to his feet. He limped for a few steps, the ache in his knee sizzling each time his boot hit the ground, but his pain couldn't begin to match what Connor must've been going through.

As his foot hit the first stair at the base of the pedestal, the orb in his palms burned a little hotter. With each step, it sizzled, until his palms nearly burned with the heat that comes from putting a hand too close to an open fire. He swallowed hard, refusing to drop it. refusing to fail.

When he reached the top of the steps, Wesley lifted the orb and raised it over the pedestal. He didn't know what to expect. Perhaps it would explode. Maybe it would blind him with a burst of light, or throw him backward into the abyss.

It didn't matter. Not with everyone else's safety on the line.

With a pained grimace, he braced himself for the worst and turned his head away. As he shut his eyes, he set the orb in the small divot atop the podium.

Eyes still shut, he waited for light. For pain. For a shrill scream, or to be shot backward through the air. As the seconds ticked by, he waited, bracing himself more and more to the unknown.

Nothing happened.

With a frown, he peered through one eye to find the dark orb sitting on the pedestal, immobile.

His breath quickened, and he scanned the artifact for signs of a fracture. He must've broken it, somehow, or missed some crucial step to make this work.

A soft tone pierced the air, like a distant windchime, and the soothing hum rang through the cavern like a song. The black lines on the dark orb glowed gold—softly at first, but with more strength the longer he stared at it. Fractures of light split across the artifact's surface, and chunks of the dark exterior burned away like ash. The black flecks rolled off the orb like leaves carried on a breeze until only the glow remained.

Slowly, the orb raised into the air, as if carried by unseen hands. The dazzling light pulsed, steady and strong, from its core. The solid depths of the orb faded until only the symbols remained, glowing with all the brilliance of a sun around a hollow shell of what the orb had once been.

A flash of light snapped through the cavern. Wesley flinched and raised his arm to shield his eyes. Its radiance lit up the cavern and cast dazzling reflections on the dark ceiling far above, swallowing the darkness whole. In its wake, it left only a golden haze.

The rush of light faded to a soft glow, and he peered through his fingers to find the orb rotating above the pedestal. Only the etched symbols remained of the once-dark orb, and they burned with sunlight. Though he longed to touch it, to see what sunshine felt like up close, he buried his hands in his pockets.

At the entrance to the cavern, the wraith faded into a cloud of black smoke. The worst of the tension in the room dispersed, even as the hollow thuds of the battle beyond the walls continued.

And just like that, Wesley was left alone, hoping he had done enough—and that he wasn't too late.

CHAPTER EIGHTY-FOUR
CONNOR

For the record, Connor hated this plan.

He just didn't have a better one.

Time slowed, but his mind raced. Teagan's blast of lightning landed hard in Quinn's chest, and she snapped backward with all the force of a raging bull dragging her into the darkness. She faded into the shadows, and this time, he couldn't see even the hint of her figure in the darkness.

But Starlings were hard to kill. Like Zander, he refused to believe she was gone.

A deafening pang of loss ripped through his core, so much worse than he had expected. It swallowed his pain. It numbed every ripple down his spine until he couldn't feel anything.

Until all he felt was *hate*.

However much he wanted to make sure she was alive, he'd made a promise, and he couldn't chase after her.

Instead, he bolted toward Teagan, determined to finally end this.

As he ran, he couldn't think about what was happening to her, out there in the darkness, where she faced Death—alone. He couldn't think about whether or not he would find anything left of her when this was over. He couldn't think about the ally she might've been, or what would happen to his home when the sun finally rose.

They'd struck a deal, and he would make good on his end of it.

Quinn's blow landed on her father's chest with a meaty thud, and Teagan Starling launched backward. When the blinding light faded, a chunk of his shoulder was missing. White bone poked through the bloody divot in his bicep, and the Starling patriarch sucked in air through bloody teeth as he cradled the wound. Crimson rivers poured through his fingers, and though he tried to stand, he stumbled sideways. He lost his balance, and his wounded shoulder slammed into a wooden beam. His head snapped upward as he stifled an agonized yell.

But Connor was already closing the gap between them.

In his blood-red rage, he ran faster than he'd ever run in his life. He closed the gap between him and Teagan with record time, before the man even had a chance to stand.

He swung his blackfire blade at Teagan's throat, and an enchanted dome identical to Quinn's blocked the blow. Where hers had fractured under the blackfire blade's power, however, Teagan's held. Black smoke rolled over Teagan's Shieldspar as the dragon blood in the man's augmentations reinforced it, even against Connor's enchanted blades.

The two men glared at each other through the crisscrossing beams of light, each determined to finally kill the other, once and for all.

The war horn blared again through the night as the rest of Teagan's reinforcements waged their war against a dragon prince. The furious snap of wings on the air grew to a deafening clatter as rows and rows of soldiers approached on their vougels. The silhouettes drew every closer, and Connor didn't have a moment to lose.

Quinn was right. Without the undead army of Slaybourne, killing Teagan wouldn't be enough to end this battle, and they would all die.

"You've lost." Teagan laughed. Blood bubbled through his teeth as his grin widened, and his laughter only grew louder.

But deep in Connor's chest, something shifted.

The sensation was like a changing tide at sea—sudden, violent, and powerful. It swept through him, all-consuming as it funneled through his soul, and it delivered to him the power of a *god*.

A thick beam of green light erupted in the night. The emerald glow carved through the desert in a perfect circle, with Slaybourne at its center. Teagan didn't look at it, nor did any of the mounted soldiers. The Starling patriarch laughed with relief, already convinced he'd won, and no one realized how dramatically the current had just shifted in Slaybourne's favor.

No one but Connor, of course.

Wesley had done it. After all that blood, Slaybourne's full power had finally awoken.

Instantly, Connor became aware of the vast world beneath his feet. He could sense every corpse in the ground, as far down as they went, as easily as though they had whispered to him from afar. Deep in the soil, their fingers twitched. Their heads turned on their rotting necks.

One by one, the buried warriors pivoted to face him. They waited, obedient even in death, for his first order as their king.

A grim cackle echoed in his mind, louder even than Teagan's laughter, as the wraith reveled in the sizzling power of Slaybourne's full potential.

Kill them all, Magnuson! the Wraith King yelled in his ear. *Drown them in their own blood!*

Normally, he would've gone out of his way to curb the wraith's rampant bloodlust.

But not here. Not tonight.

Not with Teagan Starling.

His instinct fueled him, same as it did any time he leaned into the magic imparted to him by his connection to the Wraith King. The tendrils of his soul reached into the ground, connecting with every undead soldier buried in the dirt, and he focused his full attention on Teagan. On the Lightseers. He pictured them in his mind.

The enemy.

Defend your homeland, he ordered.

And the dead happily obeyed.

At Teagan's feet, bony hands broke through the soil. The tattered shreds of a half-rotten sleeve clung to Teagan's boot, and the skeletal hands snared his ankles.

The Starling patriarch's laughter faded abruptly. Even as he held his shield against Connor's blade, he stared down at his feet in disbelief.

In *disgust*.

More hands ripped from the ground, all of them rooting Teagan in place. The Lightseer Master General grabbed a dagger from the sheath on his thigh and slashed at the bones. It cut through a finger, but even as the bone plopped to the earth, the hand didn't falter. The undead soldiers' grip on him tightened, and he gritted his teeth as the skeletal arms forced him to his knees.

In Connor's periphery, black smoke rolled through a cluster of Lightseers that had surrounded Murdoc. Seconds later, the Wraith King emerged from the inky blackness, and the soldiers shouted in panic. His sword sliced through one man's neck, and he drove his hand clean through another's chest.

"What have you done?" Teagan asked in a horrified whisper.

"I distracted you," Connor said darkly, unable to resist the urge to gloat. "It's all we were trying to do from the beginning."

"You Fates-damned bastard, I'll—"

Teagan's shield shattered as more undead hands grabbed his arms. Connor's new soldiers popped up through the ground. The soil churned as their heads and helmets appeared one by one. Clumps of dirt fell from the gaps in their bones as they stood. Dazzling green light pulsed in their ribcages, where their hearts should have been, and their hollowed eyes stared with intent purpose at Teagan.

At their mark.

Connor relaxed as he loomed above Teagan. The Master General of the Lightseers knelt before him, chained to the ground by the hands of the dead. Sparks skittered over his shoulders, but the dozens of hands rooting him in place tightened around his many wounds. He stifled a strangled scream of pain, and the sparks faded.

Immobile, the man could only glare defiantly up at him. For what must've been the first time in the man's life, Teagan Starling was at someone else's mercy.

Dark fog rolled over Connor's boots, and a ghostly face emerged from the shadow beside him. The Wraith King stood at his side, staring down at the most powerful man in Saldia. The undead king set the tip of his own sword on Teagan's chest.

The time had come.

"Quinn was right, you know." Connor's blackfire blade crackled as he set the tip of it against Teagan's chest. "None of this needed to happen. You're a selfish, heartless cunt, Teagan Starling, and this world is too good for you."

"Peasant," Teagan's gaze shifted behind him, and he sneered. Buying time, no doubt. Trying to distract Connor with meaningless insults.

The fool.

"You can't win this," the man said. The muscles in the man's good arm flexed as he tried and failed to break free from the undead soldiers' grip. "I can't be killed by the likes of you. You're nothing but a peasant who's in over his head. That's all you will ever be, you damned imbecile. You will never be my equal."

"You're right." Connor's eyes narrowed. "I'm the Fates-damned Wraithblade, and that makes me *superior*."

In unison, he and the wraith drove their swords into Teagan's chest. The man's eyes went wide as Connor's steel pierced his heart. He choked, and blood bubbled out of his mouth as he leaned gently to one side. The undead hands pinning him to the ground rooted him in place, keeping him upright even as his body went limp, and Connor held Teagan's gaze until the last light faded from the Starling patriarch's eyes.

Behind him, the earth rumbled. Men shouted. Vibrations rippled through the soil as the dead rose from the very ground that had once eaten away at their bodies. They had waited, ever patient, for centuries in hopes of this second chance at life.

Connor let out a slow breath and dismissed his blackfire blade. The wraith withdrew his sword from Teagan's corpse and the Lightseer Master General slumped forward. The undead hands released him, and he collapsed face-first into the dirt. His blood poured into the earth, feeding life back into the parched land.

The Lightseers were too late to save their general.

A lull settled over the battleground. In the silent hush that followed, something else shifted at the edge of the glowing circle that only he could see.

Something big.

He frowned with confusion as he tried to make sense of it. Deep in the earth, two figures writhed in their dirt prisons. Their massive bulk coiled and stretched through the dirt as Slaybourne's magic gave them new life. One of them flicked its tail toward the sky, and a line of tilled earth carved through the ground in the distance.

It hit Connor, then, and he shifted his gaze to the Wraith King. "Tell me you didn't—"

Oh, I very much did. The undead king chuckled darkly.

The two figures clawed at the soil, and the desert quaked with their unquenched bloodlust. The roar of the shuddering desert grew to a deafening clamor, and he surveyed the battlefield as the ground quaked with the fury of the dead. Hundreds of hands clawed their way out of the soil, but he waited for the two figures at the edge of the battlefield, about to breach.

In the distance, a massive claw broke through the cracked dirt. Rocks flew into the air. Another claw followed and, moments later, a dragon's skull broke through the soil. Clumps of dirt sailed in every direction as the beast climbed out of its tomb.

The undead dragon snapped its wings open and screeched an ear-shattering roar.

A second dragon breached moments later, and the two stood side-by-side as they surveyed the warzone. Light seeped through holes in the leathery hide of their wings, and with just a cursory scan of the battlefield, they leapt into the air.

Connor watched them fly, mystified by their beauty even as he stood in the middle of an invading army. The dragons roared at the nearest cluster of Lightseers. Teagan's surviving soldiers hurled balls of fire, but not even the Lightseer elite stood a chance.

Through Connor's connection to Nocturne, the dragon bristled with anger. *I WILL KILL THE WRAITH KING MYSELF.*

That would kill me, too, Connor pointed out. *I suggest we discuss this later. For now, get Sophia and Murdoc into the air. You have to find Quinn. Make sure she's alright.*

The dragon growled, but in the distance, the regal black creature launched into the sky. A blast of fire chased after him, missing his tail by inches, and the current from his powerful wings fanned the nearest inferno. Its flames raged, hotter than ever, as he flew off with two figures on his back.

Pale amber light broke across the horizon, and the dawn cast a gentle golden glow across the burning desert. With the first hints of sunshine, however, came the grim reality of the night's massacre. Tendrils of thick gray smoke coiled from piles of burning wood that had once been merlins. A few of the structures still stood amidst the dozens of charred corpses and fallen vougels. Smoking bodies lay draped over the splintered wooden beams. Feathers sailed by on the breeze, stained gray from the soot in the air.

The survivors didn't know it yet, but the battle was over. The Lightseers had lost, and the massacre had begun.

QUINN

Quinn lay on her back in the desert, and she lost all sense of time.

She slept, on and off, sometimes aware of the screams of dying men and sometimes lost in her nightmares about them.

Perhaps days went by, or years. Maybe she was dead, and this was hell. Or perhaps she was clinging to life, alone in the aftermath, as Death made her wait her turn among the fallen.

She didn't know, and frankly, she didn't care.

During one of the worst nightmares, as she stabbed her father in the back again and again, something nudged her shoulder.

The sensation startled her awake, but even when she opened her eyes, she couldn't see. The darkness swallowed everything, and she couldn't hear a thing over the shrill ringing in her ears.

Blind and broken, she figured she should've been afraid. Her head reeled, aching with every new thought, and even fear required more energy than she had to spare.

Her visitor nudged her again. They sniffed at her face, the breath hot and warm on her bloodstained cheek. Someone tried to lift her upright, and though she tried to move, her hand hung limply from her wrist.

Quinn.

Maybe it was a voice, or maybe it was a dream.

She couldn't tell.

Her name echoed, and the whisper reminded her of the voices in the Blood Bogs. For a second, she wondered if she was still there. Perhaps the hazy visions of war and her brutal, bloodstained father had all been another mirage. Nothing but a cruel trick played on her by the fallen princess who hated everything Quinn stood for.

Up we go.

How strange.

There was that voice again.

Her body shifted, unbidden, and she groaned in pain with the sudden movement. Her head rolled until her chin hit her chest. Her neck stretched farther than it should have gone. The hand on her shoulder moved upward, until it cradled the base of her battered skull.

"It's done?" the voice said—or maybe that was her talking, that time.

"Almost," a man answered.

The darkness faded, and she blinked away the lingering black spots as her vision returned. The air nipped at her eyes, and she winced as she adjusted to the sudden light. A white haze sat beside her, blocking most of her view of the cracked desert, and a soft purple blur stained the fading night with the first hints of sunrise.

Though someone held her, the first thing she saw as her vision sharpened was a distant body lying in the dirt. She couldn't make out much detail from this distance, but his broad chest looked familiar, even with a hole carved out of one shoulder.

A thread of panic shot through her as a single name resonated through her head.

Connor.

"You didn't!" she screamed. "I'll kill you myself!"

A hand grabbed her shoulder. Fire erupted across her palms as she prepared to burn her attacker alive.

Her father would pay for this.

He would burn in the deepest circle of hell for—

"Whoa," a familiar voice said.

As her head finally cleared, she looked up at the person holding her. Blurry and bloodstained, Connor knelt beside her. Eyes wide with surprise, he raised one hand to soothe her, as though he were trying to calm a startled horse.

She let out a sigh of relief and sank back into his arms.

"Don't move," he ordered. "Let me go find your bag."

As he gently returned her head to the soil, she didn't answer. She just stared at the sky while the clouds turned pink with the dawn.

It hit her, then. The bloody corpse must've been her father.

The numb void in her chest worsened. The ringing in her ear grew louder, and all she could do was stare at the twin moons above as they faded into the brightening sky.

The chasm in her chest spread like the roots of a vine, digging deeper with every breath as her twisted heart grieved for what had become of their family. Of what had become of her home.

Of what she had done, justified or not, to the man she had once loved more than anyone.

CHAPTER EIGHTY-FIVE
FREEROCK

Colonel Rowan Freerock lay on his stomach, one eye pinched shut as he stared through the spyglass his surrogate father had given him long ago. His thumb rested on the Starling crest engraved into its wood, and a knot formed in his throat as he stared at the carnage spread across the Decay.

The ember-orange glow of burning wood cast flickering shadows across the ground. Morning sunlight glinted off armored bodies, strewn across the soil and still as death. Plumes of smoke rolled like fog across the blood-stained dirt.

Worst of all, skeletal abominations raised silver swords, and even from this distance, their ribcages glowed green with the sort of enchantments he'd never seen before. One of the abominations swung at a Lightseer's neck, and a spray of blood shot into the air.

His body went numb. Shattered with disbelief, he could only stare at it all in half-mad horror.

A churning cloud of sickening dread roiled through his chest like a storm through a forest, rooting him in place and rendering him utterly speechless. Chilled to the bone from the slaughter he saw through the spyglass, he fought the drowning surge of hopeless desperation at the sheer power of the devastating threat they now faced.

The two soldiers he had chosen to accompany him on this mission lay on the ground on either side of him. Their soft, whisper-silent breaths mingled with the steady whistle of the southern wind as they waited, perfectly obedient, for his report.

"This isn't possible," he whispered.

Freerock lowered the spyglass and stared at the desert ground before him. The device clattered to the ground, and he set his head in his hands as he watched it roll away.

His decades of training in Lunestone's elite arenas warned him to move, to act, to regain the high ground and make sense of the devastation later, but he couldn't.

He could only shake his head in disbelief.

The Lightseers had brought their best, and the Shade had leveled them. Nothing remained but a thinning force that would die before he could even reach them and a handful of charred merlins.

Everything Teagan had built, everything they had spent a third of a season assembling, had been destroyed in a single night.

If only Teagan had listened to him, all those weeks ago.

If only they had *waited*.

"Colonel?" the soldier to his left asked.

Freerock cleared his throat and lifted his head. He had a job to do. He needed to focus, and he had to remain in control—if not for himself, then for the soldiers left in his care.

To his left, Sergeant Finley's delicate eyebrows pinched together as she watched him warily. A loose strand of blonde hair slipped out of her braid and fluttered in the gale whizzing by them as the silence stretched on.

"They're dead or dying." Freerock's voice cracked, and he couldn't bring himself to look at her when he said it.

He couldn't even move.

"How many?" the sergeant asked.

Freerock's voice broke. "All of them."

"That's impossible," the soldier to his right said. Rodger Hutton, Freerock's longtime friend and confidant, snatched the spyglass off the dirt and peered through it.

The longer Hutton stared into the lens, the less he moved. The painful seconds trickled by, but the man couldn't speak. He stiffened, and a vein pulsed in his forehead as he forcefully cleared his throat, again and again.

He opened his mouth to speak, but instead vomited into the dirt beside him. The rotten odor coiled past them.

"But the Master General..." Sergeant Finley shook her head, like she couldn't believe what the two of them were saying. "Nothing can... not to *him*..."

Freerock shut his eyes and took a deep settling breath as he prepared to say the words he had never thought he would say aloud. "The enemy has killed Teagan Starling. Our Master General is dead."

The two soldiers beside him went eerily silent, and when he finally scanned each of their faces, they both watched him in numb shock.

"We're not going to panic." Freerock's glare shifted to the carnage on the horizon. "Light works differently in this desert than it does on most open stretches of land. As we were setting up each marker on the way here, I paid attention to the skyline. At this time of day, we're nothing but a mirage to them. We're far enough away that I doubt they've seen us. We can safely retreat."

He cast a quick glance over his shoulder to check on the vougels. The three beasts still remained low to the ground with their ears pinned to their heads as they waited for the command to fly.

Good. They hadn't given anything away.

Freerock glared at the dirt, and his hand coiled into a tight fist as his training took over. The pain seeped away, locked in a box deep in his soul, and that cleared his mind enough for him to focus on what had to be done.

Death was the cost of war. In his lifetime as a Lightseer, he had lost friend and family alike on the battlefield. Before he'd even come of age, his father had died protecting Teagan Starling. Now, Freerock had lost that great man as well.

Loss was a part of life, and his hatred for the darkness that had stolen so much from him would only fuel him forward.

"Quickly and quietly, we're going to leave," he ordered. "We have less than ten minutes before we lose the cover of the horizon's mirage."

Finley balked. "But the survivors—"

"Look at the aftermath," Freerock snapped as he shoved the spyglass in her hands. "You look at that and tell me if you think our new opponent left any survivors, Sergeant."

The moment she raised the spyglass to her eye, the tendons in her neck tightened to a painful degree. The color drained from her face, and she swallowed hard. What felt like lifetimes later, she finally lowered it and shook her head as she fought back tears.

"We're all that's left." Freerock bowed his head in respect for his dead friends out there in the desert. "We can't change that now, which means we must retreat. We get to Lunestone, and we return to this cesspit with every available soldier. It will take time, and he will get stronger in our absence, but so will we."

The joints in Hutton's wrists cracked as his body tensed with hatred, and Finley's blue eyes narrowed with all the hellfire of a woman about to burn the world.

"The next time we march on Slaybourne, we won't just kill the Shade." Freerock cracked his neck, but not even that relieved the brewing tension in his shoulders. "When we see this place again, we'll flatten the whole damn *mountain*."

CONNOR

By noon, not a single Lightseer would remain.

With his back to Death's Door and the Wraith King hovering at his side, Connor watched the massacre. Teagan's surviving forces cast torrents of fire and ice at the undead warriors who obeyed Connor's every command. The Lightseers swung their dazzling swords, void of any blood as they fought creatures they couldn't kill, and grabbed whatever they could reach to keep the Slaybourne army at bay. Decayed bones flew into the air, dismembered from wild swings of the survivors' blades as their numbers steadily dropped.

But none of them slowed, even as the skeletal forces closed in on them.

They know their fate, the wraith said. *But I can admire a soldier that fights to the end, even when he knows death is inevitable.*

Connor didn't answer. These men and women had come to his home, determined to kill him and slaughter everyone in Slaybourne at the command of a power-mad liar. They fought to their deaths not for the common good or righteousness, but out of overzealous loyalty to the man who had brought war to Connor's door.

He didn't have much sympathy—or respect—for any of them.

Overhead, the undead dragons flew in a tight formation and banked over the warzone. As they circled, looking for their next mark, one spat a half-eaten corpse from its mouth. The headless torso careened toward the earth.

Brilliant, aren't they? the wraith asked. *Efficient. Brutal. Obedient.*

"The perfect soldiers," Connor said dryly.

As the headless body hit the ground, a plume of dust shot into the air from the site of impact.

A thought occurred, just then. Something foggy. Fuzzy. A little distant through all the bloodlust of the battle, but there all the same. It took a moment for the idea to solidify, but when it did, it hit him like an arrow in the throat.

Kiera's look of horror, back when he had stood over the last slaver and decided the man's fate. She had listened to the massacre, and though he had told her not to watch, she had seen enough to fear for her and her children's lives.

And in that suspended moment, she had been afraid of *him*.

The memory snapped him from his bloodlust, and his head cleared in a rush. Quinn had once been his enemy, and he wondered how many of these Lightseers had only come to his home because they believed it would extinguish the darkness—just as she had, once.

His new power as the Wraithblade held significance and weight. Nocturne and Quinn had made a pact to kill him if he lost his way, and today, he had come dangerously close.

These soldiers before him didn't need to die, but he'd wanted them to hurt for Teagan's sins.

It wasn't right.

This—the bloodlust, the rage, the hatred—it wasn't who he would let himself become.

"Enough." Connor grimaced, his head thumping with disgust as he watched these people kill themselves in the name of their fanatical loyalty to a diabolical liar. "That's enough!"

His voice carried across the battlefield, even over the war cries of the Lightseers who thought they would meet Death today.

In unison, every undead soldier paused mid-swing. Their swords glinted in the dawning sun as they held their weapons over the Lightseers. A few of Teagan's remaining warriors spun around in tight circles, chests heaving as they scanned each undead fighter's hollowed skull. A few of the survivors lopped off undead heads, and a torrent of fire shot into the air at the rear edge of the battlefield.

Magnuson. The wraith's tone dripped with warning. *Think carefully about what you're doing.*

"I have," he answered in a gravelly voice.

Force them to surrender, Connor ordered his army. *But don't kill any more of them.*

Brought to life by his command, the Slaybourne soldiers sheathed their weapons. Even those without heads grabbed the Lightseers, and before long, ten undead warriors swarmed each of the survivors.

He turned his back on the war zone and silently ordered the two undead dragons to land between him and Death's Door. They instantly banked toward him.

With the undead dragons close by, he figured it would be best to keep the living prince of beasts as far away as possible to avoid yet another conflict between Nocturne and the Wraith King.

I have a job for you, Connor said, pressing on the dragon's mind. *Can you hear me?*

I can, the dragon prince answered.

Find any lingering scouts along the other walls, will you? Connor set his hands on his head as his pulse slowly settled, but his chest still heaved for air from his harrowing duel with Tegan.

Consider it done.

You might need help, he added. *I'll order some of my soldiers to follow you.*

With his arms crossed over his chest, Connor glared out at the Lightseers as his undead fighters systematically disarmed them. Teagan's survivors were forced to their knees or knocked unconscious with the hilts of chipped swords, and one by one, they stopped fighting.

You cannot let them live, Magnuson, the wraith warned. *Whether they die here or in a cell, every Lightseer present can never leave this land. They have seen too much, and their zealous nature will only end with a knife in your throat.*

Connor didn't answer. He needed a moment to think this through, and he couldn't do that while he watched them all die.

Bring them to me, he ordered his army. *Alive.*

CHAPTER EIGHTY-SIX
CONNOR

In the bloody aftermath of a brutal warzone, Connor stood with his back to the dawn. His shadow stretched across the dirt as he stared at Death's Door, which remained shut until he made the final call as to what to do with the survivors.

The two undead dragons stood before him, growling softly as they scanned the horizon, and he suppressed a gleeful smile as he stared up at the magnificent beasts.

He had to be careful, though. If Nocturne saw him marveling, he would suffer the kind of furious lecture that could last days. As stunning as they were, he wouldn't be able to keep these creatures if he wanted to keep his living dragon happy.

A shame and a waste, but it seemed inevitable.

His eyes closed, and he set his hand on his chest as blood seeped from the wounds along his torso and arms. He could still taste the blood in his mouth, and he spat the worst of it onto the soil at his feet. The parched dirt drank it in, absorbing it instantly as his blood stained the desert red.

The sensation of a thousand corpses trudging through the desert skittered through his body. He felt each of them, every movement, every tilt of the head. The connection transcended anything he could've imagined.

Just as the wraith had said, not so long ago, this magic didn't obey Saldian law. This wasn't the result of reagents and potions. This was Death's world, brought to a land where it barely belonged.

And it was his to control.

A boot kicked the dirt beside him, and his eyes snapped open on instinct. Murdoc shifted his weight as he stared out at the handful of remaining Lightseers gathered behind Connor. The former Blackguard kept his hand on the hilt of his sheathed sword and studied them intently, despite the thick bandage wrapped around his torso and head. Dried blood caked along his neck and jaw from a gash in his cheek, but he hardly seemed fazed.

Opposite Murdoc, Sophia stood with her arms crossed over her chest, and her dark eyes narrowed with suspicion as she scanned the survivors.

Bruised and bloody, his team had survived. They had faced hell, as the Antiquity had predicted, and they had both emerged from the worst of it to fight another day.

His shoulders relaxed, and he scratched at the back of his head to hide his deep sigh of gratitude from his prisoners.

The steady march of undead feet through the desert slowly faded as they brought him every surviving Lightseer. Every man and woman in Teagan's army gathered behind him, and each elite soldier had seven undead fighters to guard them.

Only turn your back on someone who can't kill you, boy, Beck Arbor had told him once. *If you can't see the blow coming, you're as good as dead.*

Everyone present knew what it meant for him to keep his back to them. They were his prisoners, and they were vastly outnumbered. Surrounded as they were by the undead soldiers who would slit their throat before they could even summon a spell, these elite warriors were no longer a threat.

What a surreal thought. He almost didn't trust it.

Though he felt more of the undead approaching, he still didn't turn around to face the gathered crowd. He couldn't. Not yet. He stood with his hands on his hips, waffling back and forth as he fought to decide what to do with the fifty-odd survivors and forty-some vougels.

He had to choose—spare them, or slaughter them all.

Even though his army outnumbered them, taking them as prisoners posed significant risk. It would mean coming up with enough food to sustain them, all while finding a place to keep them where they couldn't cause any harm. If even one of them escaped, they could wreak havoc on Slaybourne and those who had chosen to make this place home. A Lightseer, even without their weapons, could easily take hostages or even murder someone if the right opportunity presented itself.

It was a risk he didn't want to take.

Beyond even that, these hardened soldiers would look for weaknesses in his fortress. Clues. Insights. Intelligence. Secrets. If they were ever released, they would know far more than any enemy should.

Then again, he'd had the same thought about Quinn.

He shook his head and stared out at the desert, toward where he'd left her to grieve her father. It might've helped to have her here to earn the Lightseers' respect, but he didn't want her present in case he ultimately had to kill them all.

This is your last chance to fix your mistake, the wraith said in a grim tone. *Choose your next words wisely.*

The ghoul appeared beside him in a puff of dark smoke. The specter surveyed the prisoners with the hollowed sockets that used to be his eyes.

With a frustrated groan, Connor rubbed one eye with the heel of his palm and finally turned around to face his prisoners.

He knew what he had to do. Most of his team wouldn't like it, but it was the choice that would let him sleep soundly at night.

An ocean of Lightseers stretched out before him. The chipped steel of the undead soldiers' swords pressed into the living warriors' throats, but the Slaybourne army remained otherwise still as stone. Though some of the Lightseers watched the undead fighters with disgust or horror, most of Teagan's surviving army stared up at him.

Studying his every move.

Hawking his every step, as though just waiting for the chance to kill him.

Connor scanned the crowd, searching until he found the nearest one that watched him without even the barest trace of fear. When he found the man, he pointed at him. "You."

Four undead had their bony hands locked around the man's arms, while three others held him at sword point. The soldier's eyes narrowed as their gazes met, but he didn't say a word.

"What would you Lightseers do, in my position?" Connor gestured to the army gathered in front of him. "You've outnumbered your greatest enemy. You gathered the survivors, and you have them on their knees. They are at your mercy, and you will ultimately decide their fate. Would you take them prisoner, or slit their throats?"

The soldier swallowed hard, but to his credit, his gaze didn't falter. They both knew the answer, and this was all for show.

Death.

"There's been enough blood spilled today," Connor continued. He raised his voice so that everyone could hear. "And unless you do something stupid, this won't be the day you die."

Magnuson, the wraith said, his voice dripping with warning. *Your ridiculous, noble heart can't win this war. Don't be a fool.*

"Connor," Sophia hissed under her breath, almost in unison with the ghoul. Her dark eyes darted toward him, and her mouth barely moved as she did her best not to undermine him in front of prisoners. "What the hell are you doing?"

"The right thing," he answered.

"She has a point, Captain," Murdoc leaned his head toward Connor's ear and dropped his voice to a whisper. "Where are we even going to put them all?"

Connor shrugged. "Slaybourne has plenty of dungeons."

"This is a mistake," Sophia whispered as she took a few cautious steps closer, but her eyes scanned the crowd once more.

Listen to the necromancer, damn it, the wraith added. *At least she's making sense!*

"Why in the Fates' name would you keep them alive?" Sophia hissed under her breath as she neared.

"Because I'm not what they think I am," he answered, loud enough for everyone to hear. "Quinn switched sides when she realized that. You think these soldiers don't have good hearts, too?"

"Ah," Murdoc said. He sighed and looked out over the Lightseers, but he slowly shook his head. "Nope, I still don't like it."

"That's fine." Connor patted the man on the back, and Murdoc let out a grunt of pain. "I'm still right."

Sophia scoffed impatiently.

No, you're an imbecile. The wraith crossed his arms indignantly. His skull pivoted on his spine, following Connor's every movement.

Connor dismissed the wraith's comment with a lazy wave of his hand. "You're just upset because I won't let you kill anyone."

Obviously, the wraith said with a broad gesture across the gathered soldiers. *But my point remains valid.*

"Don't bother," the nearest Lightseer said. "It won't work."

The man's voice carried over the desert, crisp and clear.

Connor crossed his arms and stared down at the soldier. "What won't work?"

"This plan of yours." The man nodded to the ghoul. "You can't trick us into sharing Lightseer secrets. You can't convince us you're somehow the victim, here. And when that fails, when you realize what a waste of time it was, you won't be able to torture anything out of us, either. No amount of starvation or psychological pain will work. We've been through it all, and it doesn't faze us. You might as well kill us all and save yourself the trouble."

"See?" Sophia gestured to the man, as he proved her point.

Connor cast a sidelong glare at her in a silent order to be quiet. Though she pursed her lips in annoyance, she threw her hands up in exasperated surrender.

"Listen closely, soldier." He returned his attention to the prisoner at his feet. "Right now, I don't give a damn about any secret you have, and torturing people is more his forte than mine." He nodded to the ghoul.

The soldier's brows furrowed in confusion, and that clearly wasn't the answer he'd been expecting.

Connor didn't care. He'd meant what he said. There was more than enough bloodstains in this dirt, and he didn't want any more added.

In the back of his mind, Nocturne pressed against their connection. With a subtle tilt of his head, Connor relaxed and closed his eyes as he let the dragon in.

The southern mountain range is clear, the regal creature informed him. *Your soldiers found seven more Lightseers, but they've been contained. Any lingering scouts have been captured. I'm returning now.*

Good, Connor answered back. *Check on Quinn. I'll meet you there.*

The dragon paused. *How is she?*

We killed her father. Connor's jaw tensed, and his eyes snapped open. *How do you think she's doing?*

Hmm. With that, the weight of the dragon's mind faded, and Connor let out a settling breath.

He stared out at the horizon, far beyond the gathered soldiers, where a hazy shimmer of flickering light rolled across the distant soil. For all he knew, Teagan already had reinforcements on the way. Based on Quinn's initial estimates, it seemed like every Lightseer in Teagan's army was accounted for, but he had no way of knowing that for certain.

Word would trickle back to Lunestone, one way or another. He wasn't a fool, and the inevitable conflicts would only worsen.

For now, he couldn't dwell on the repercussions of killing Teagan Starling. After such a grueling battle and the tense flight here, he was hungry, exhausted, and could easily sleep for days. For now, it was best that he get some rest and prepare for the next fight.

After all, hell would always be after him—and he was finally getting used to the idea that he could handle whatever came his way.

CHAPTER EIGHTY-SEVEN
QUINN

As the early morning light cast a warm honey glow across the Decay, long shadows stretched from each of the fallen soldiers littered across the battlefield. Undead skeletons in tattered black robes lumbered across the desert at a steady pace, carrying bodies and salvaged crates or tents back toward the open gates of Slaybourne.

The aftermath of the battle breathed new life into the bloodstained land, but Quinn could only kneel beside her father's corpse.

Numb.

From the moment she could move again, she had been here, just staring at him in surreal silence. His legendary sword lay beside him, gathered at some point in the chaos after the battle, and its green gem still glowed with life.

She had lost track of how much time had passed, and she had spent it all watching his blood seep into the dry earth. Even as her Dazzledane began to fade, she couldn't feel a thing.

The original Rectivane had done all it could, and Connor had forced her to take a second one before he had allowed her to stand. Flashes of pain still ignited in her stomach each time she shifted her weight even a little, but she barely registered them.

Blaze moaned softly next to her, but she didn't move. She knelt before Teagan Starling's corpse, her hands in her lap. Her pet pressed his cold nose into her open palm, same as he did every time he wanted her to scratch his ears, but she couldn't bring herself to even turn her head.

Her father's milky eyes stared back at her, his expression frozen in his final moment of disgust. He stared vacantly out at the forgotten desert, almost angry, like the idea he might lose hadn't occurred to him until the second before he died.

The two shards that remained of *Aurora* lay before her, as well, but she didn't remember how they had gotten there. Connor, maybe, or Blaze. The green gem still glowed in the hilt of her beautiful sword, but the shattered bottom half no longer contained any magic.

She slid her hand under the hilt and closed her fingers around the worn leather wrap that had always given her a better grip. It shifted in her palm, the balance off with most of it missing, and she almost let it clatter back to the ground out of her grief.

Aurora would never be mended. Without the Master General's approval and access to areas of Lunestone not even she could see, it could never be done.

Her brilliant sword was gone.

With a flick of her wrist, she summoned *Aurora's* fire one last time. Smoke sputtered from the shattered steel as flame sparked weakly to life, but the inferno built with each passing second until it almost rivaled a Firesword's true flame.

Almost.

She stared at the blaze until it left dancing orange imprints in her vision. When she returned her attention to her father's body, the orange lights still flittered across everything she saw.

Without bothering to recite the Lightseer Code, and not certain this would even work, she drove her shattered sword into his corpse.

The skin around the blade slowly turned black as *Aurora's* enchantment dissolved his body to ash. The vile odor of burning flesh practically drowned her, and it brought back memories of the criminals she had killed in her career as a Lightseer.

It took longer than it should have, but flames eventually snapped to life across Teagan's body. They consumed his corpse like a wildfire, and she wrinkled her nose in disgust at the stench. The crackle of burning bones fizzled, and she scowled until the last fizzling pops faded into the howling wind as it crossed the plains.

Her father burned away to ash, and when the enchantment was done with him, all that remained was a pile of soot and a bloodstained sword.

Still numb, still waiting to wake up from this awful dream, she stared out at the horizon. She figured she would've felt sick, or angry, or ashamed.

After the Dazzledane had worn off, she figured she would've felt *something*.

Quinn released what was left of *Aurora*, and the broken blade landed in the pile of ash with a muted thud. Soot smeared the green stone, but not enough to dull its shine.

The wind ambled by, stealing a few grains of her father's ashes here and there, and she let it whisk him away. Her throat ached as she watched her legendary father fade to nothing.

To something worse than memory.

She swallowed hard to clear the ball in her throat, but that only made the painful lump worse. Her eyes ached for rest or release, and something wet rolled down her face.

She rubbed it off with the back of her hand, expecting more blood, but a droplet of water rolled across the clumps of dirt on her freckled skin. Another wet bead rolled down her cheek, and she sniffled as the stinging in her eyes worsened.

Starlings don't cry.

Her father's voice echoed in her head, just as irritated as he had been the last day he had said that to her, back when she was just a girl who didn't understand what being a Starling truly meant.

A sob escaped her, and she pressed her wrist against her mouth to choke it down. The pain in her throat fought her, though, and the tears began to roll down her face in a steady stream. Her shoulders shook, gently at first, but the tremors came more and more violently as she surrendered control.

For the first time in well over a decade, Quinn Starling let herself cry.

It didn't matter that she had the grime of war on her hands. She buried her face in her palms and let herself go. She sobbed, not caring who heard her.

For once, she held nothing back.

She grieved for the father she had loved, even if he hadn't been real.

She mourned the person he could have been if he hadn't hidden behind masks and lies.

The man he *should* have been, not just to her, but to the world.

As the hot tears rolled down her face, she wanted to scream. She wanted to be as angry as he was anytime she failed to do her forms perfectly, or any time she missed a target by a fraction of an inch. She wanted to shout into his ashes that it didn't have to be this way, that his greed had corrupted him, that he was wrong, that all these people today had died to protect nothing more than his Fates-damned pride.

But the anger was just another mask. Her own lie. Beneath it was a deep, painful sadness, and yelling at the dead wouldn't fix a thing.

So she wept.

She cried until a thundering ache pounded in her skull. She let the tears fall until the numbness crawled back into her chest, and until there was nothing left in her to let go of.

As she stared down at the last, small pile of his ashes that the wind had left behind, she shook her head.

"It didn't have to end like this," she told him, knowing full well he would never have agreed.

Her vougel growled softly, and his cold nose nudged her cheek. She leaned into his furry face, grateful to feel something besides hot tears and the sprawling void in her chest. He licked her jaw, and the gentle bumps along his tongue tickled her chin.

"Thank you, Blaze," she whispered to him. "At least I'll always have you."

He growled happily, and a flurry of protective pride rumbled through their connection as she gently scratched his ears.

Leathery wings snapped against the air, and the ground shook as something massive landed on the cracked earth behind her. The ground shook, and a gust of wind hit her in the back. Blaze peered over her shoulder at the newcomer, but Quinn didn't bother.

Only one creature she knew of could make an entrance like *that*.

A shadow fell across her as she knelt on the patched earth, her toes tingling and numb from how long she had been there. A cold chill replaced the gentle warmth of the budding day as Nocturne blocked the sun.

"I, too, know grief." The dragon sighed, and a puff of gray smoke rolled past her like a murky fog. "In centuries of life, it is inevitable. For what it is worth, I understand your pain."

Though his soothing voice vibrated deep in her bones, she didn't reply.

"You are not alone." He gently nudged the back of her head. "Not anymore."

"I know." Her voice cracked, her throat still raw.

Boots crunched along the desert ground, and Quinn's ear twitched as she tried to identify the gait. Light steps. Confident, steady stride. Stealthy and almost impossible to hear over the mild winds.

Connor.

Quinn lifted her head to find the Wraithblade walking toward her, and the open gates of Death's Door perfectly framed him as he neared. His duel with Teagan had left his shirt a tattered mess, and bloodstained muscle poked through the long gouges in the cloth as he rubbed his tired eyes.

He wasn't in earshot, yet.

Good.

"I hope he's worth it," she said quietly to Nocturne.

"I believe he is," the dragon prince said under his breath.

Moments later, Connor groaned and plopped onto the ground next to her. He leaned one elbow on his propped knee and, instead of saying anything at all, he merely scanned the desert around them for a while. He didn't look at her, nor did he acknowledge the legendary Fireswords at her feet.

Together, they listened to the whistling wind as more and more of his undead soldiers marched across the battlefield, salvaging what they could from the wreckage.

The twinkling light in *Sovereign's* spellgust gemstone drew her eye, and she lifted the famous sword in front of her to inspect it more closely. It weighed heavily on her hands, even with her augmented strength, but now she understood the truth behind why her father had been able to wield it so effortlessly.

Augmentations and potions crafted with dragon's blood had given him and Zander an edge over everyone else, further weaving the timeless myth that Starlings were simply superior.

But it was just another lie. Even she had fallen for it, surrendering to Zander as the chosen heir because of his age and inherent ability, but they weren't superior at all.

They never had been—and they never would be—anything but ordinary men.

"It's still beautiful," she confessed as she stared at it. "The first time he let me hold his sword, I thought I would melt from pride. To think my father trusted me enough to let me touch this made me want his approval even more."

In her periphery, Connor tilted his head toward her, but he mercifully didn't say anything.

"It was summer." Her eyes glossed over as she recalled the sweet aroma of the honeysuckle in the garden. "I remember it so clearly. I summoned a flame bigger than his, even as a child, and he twirled me through the air with a big grin on his face. Mother was sitting in the garden with a look of horror on her face, but I'd never seen Father so happy. That was the first time he said he was proud of me. He said it was proof I was a gift from the Fates. The perfect miracle child, destined for greatness. Destined to follow in his footsteps." Her voice shook, and she swallowed hard to hide it. "All my life, that was all I ever wanted. To be like him."

A hot breath rolled down her neck, and Nocturne's silky soft scales gently brushed the back of her head as Blaze moaned tenderly at her side.

Though she couldn't look him in the eye, Quinn offered the sword to Connor. "Let this be a reminder, more than a trophy."

He frowned as he grabbed the hilt. "A reminder of what?"

"Of what a man can become when he thinks he's untouchable."

The Wraithblade sighed and stabbed the renowned sword into the ground beside him. "Thank you."

She merely nodded. There was nothing left to say.

As the silence dragged on, she watched Connor in her periphery. Though he didn't look at her, he curled his hand into a fist. The muscle in his forearm tightened in much the same way it did whenever he summoned his blackfire blades.

Interesting.

"I killed your father, Quinn," he said flatly. "Are you and I... alright?"

"You're terrible at this."

Connor shot an irritated glare at the looming behemoth behind her.

"I told you to do it," she reminded him.

The Wraithblade clicked his tongue in disagreement. "Doesn't mean you won't hate me."

"That's fair." She rubbed the exhaustion from her eyes and waited for the flood of tears to return, but she had nothing left in her to give to her grief. "We couldn't let him walk out of this desert, no matter who he was to me."

Connor rubbed his jaw and shut his eyes, as though he didn't know how to respond to that.

The silence suited her just fine.

"I'm grateful you didn't turn on me," he admitted as he scanned the desert around them. "I was worried there, for a bit. I thought... never mind. It doesn't matter. Here."

The swish of metal on leather broke through the whistling gale, and a bright green glow fell against her thigh. Though her head still ached, she shifted her attention toward Connor as he pulled the Bloodbane dagger from a sheath on his waist. Its blade had been mercifully cleaned of Teagan's blood, and the weapon glimmered as he offered it to her.

She stared at the enchanted blade resting on his open palm. This dagger was something Otmund had probably killed people to obtain, and something that probably cost more than the fortune in a king's vault to create.

"I don't want it," she said flatly.

Nocturne smacked the back of her head with his wing, and she glared back at the dragon looming over her. His shimmering black scales glistened in the morning light, and he subtly nodded his head toward the blade in a quiet command to take the damn thing.

"I'm not giving you a choice." Connor set the blade at her feet and pointed to it. "Look, going into yesterday's battle, I didn't know what you would do. I didn't fully trust you. When you took those first steps toward your father,

I thought for a second that you might turn on us after all."

She didn't respond.

He let out a long, slow breath. "But what you did back there—I'm grateful. I can't imagine what it must've been like to have to defend yourself against the people who usually fight at your side."

Her jaw clenched, and she looked down at her hands as the Bloodbane dagger cast its emerald glow across her boots.

Connor ran a hand through his hair. "You said I'm more of a Lightseer than your father was. I think that's bullshit, personally, but I understand what you were trying to say. I protect people. I try to do what's right, even at a cost to myself. That's what a Lightseer is supposed to be."

"It is," she agreed.

"Right. So, if I'm a Lightseer, then you're just as much the Shade as I am. You protect Saldia. You've sacrificed as much as I have. You faced death, and you won—again, I guess, depending on what happened to you when you were born. I've never heard that story."

A dull ache blistered behind one of her eyes, and she swallowed hard. "It's for the best."

"Fair enough," he said quietly. "Look, you're a good soldier, Quinn, and you know what? Maybe you and Nocturne are right to worry about me. Maybe I will lose my way, some day. If I do, you're the only one I trust enough to do what has to be done."

She frowned, and for the first time since dawn had broken over the desert, she felt something.

This time, however, it was a sharp pang of dread that shot through her like ice.

They watched each other, both waiting for the other to speak first, and her lips parted in surprise as she tried to come up with something to say.

The comment—and his faith in her—left her speechless.

Connor Magnuson quirked one eyebrow and pointed at the enchanted weapon on the ground between them. "Take it."

Cautiously, carefully, she lifted the Bloodbane dagger into her hands and stared down at it, much in the same way as she had stared down at her father's corpse.

"Thank you," she said.

"Don't make me regret doing that," Connor added with a chuckle. "The wraith is on my ass for giving it up. Be grateful you can't hear him right now."

A dry laugh escaped her, and the void in her chest momentarily shrank.

What felt like a lifetime ago, back in the forest outside of Oakenglen, she had warned Tove that anyone involved with an outlaw like Connor would be in for a world of pain—and she had been right.

For the first time in her life, Quinn didn't have a plan. She had no idea what would happen next, but without question, a world of pain was headed their way.

Connor pushed himself to his feet and tugged *Sovereign* out of the dirt. He offered her his hand, and when she took it, he pulled her to her feet.

"Welcome to the team, Quinn Starling." A slight grin tugged on the corner of his mouth. "Fair warning—we're all dead men walking."

"Yeah." She scanned the undead soldiers stalking through the desert around them. "I suppose that's fitting."

CHAPTER EIGHTY-EIGHT
CONNOR

A day had passed since Teagan's siege, and much had changed.

Connor stood on the walls and stared out into the Decay. Nocturne loomed behind him, and the regal arch of the dragon's neck cast a long shadow across the ground. Quinn paced nearby, restless and silent. Her eyes out of focus as she stared off at the desert.

Waiting, like everyone else.

Murdoc sat on a nearby boulder with one elbow resting on his knee as he systematically tore apart a blade of grass. Though Sophia had insisted she didn't need to be here for this, the former Blackguard had refused to miss the spectacle.

Death's Door sat open below them, and half of the undead soldiers from the Wraith King's fallen army stood in perfect militant rows in the desert beyond the gate. The ghoulish warriors faced the horizon, ready for any threat that dared tread into the Decay. The glowing green circle of light pulsed in the distance as it carved through the cracked ground, surrounding Slaybourne in a perfect circle that only he and the wraith could see.

Slaybourne and its people now had the means to defend themselves against the threat of invasion. His home was finally safe.

Connor had gambled everything to his name, and then some. He had come dangerously close to losing it all, but he had won this battle.

More would come, but such was the life of the Wraithblade.

On either side of the open gates, the Wraith King's undead dragons sat with their tattered wings tucked against their backs, in an almost identical pose to Nocturne whenever the princely beast was waiting patiently for something to happen.

The char of smoking wood wafted past, and Connor glanced behind him as the funeral pyres burned in the verdant valley between the Black Keep Mountains. Ethan had offered to oversee the Lightseers' funerals, so Connor allowed the soldiers to say farewell to the friends they had lost in the night.

It was a battle that shouldn't have happened in the first place, but most of the Lightseers still didn't believe that.

Come sunset, the prisoners would return to Slaybourne's dungeons, isolated in the various cells and monitored at all times by his undead warriors. While the funeral pyres burned, Connor had ordered half of his army to remain inside the walls, ready to stop any attempted uprising before it could happen.

A puff of midnight smoke rolled across the ground as a void opened in the air between Connor and the desert. The Wraith King emerged from the inky depths, and the great ghoul sighed with resignation as he appeared.

The death fires are all lit, the wraith grumbled. *I still think you're an imbecile for letting the survivors live, but you keep proving me wrong. I suppose with this matter, time will tell.*

Connor chuckled, but he didn't reply.

You realize what Teagan was trying to do, don't you? The specter crossed his bony arms across his hollow chest. *The glowing green vials we found in his tent. Have you figured out what they are?*

"I've been a little busy," Connor said with a nod to the funeral pyres behind him. "I've barely had a chance to see the Finns, much less sift through everything the soldiers recovered from Teagan's camp."

The ghoul sighed impatiently, but Connor didn't take the bait. A lecture would inevitably follow, and he did his best to wait patiently for it.

Two green bottles made of spellgust, the wraith continued, as though it were obvious. *Clearly enchanted with a spell that could contain me. If you were killed and that bottle was open, I would've been dragged into it instead of into a new host.*

Connor tensed, and though he didn't take his gaze off the horizon, he sat with the weight of what the ghoul had said.

They both look similar to the bottle Aeron Zacharias first used to confine me, the wraith explained. *And I have been confined in something similar twice before.*

"That means the Starlings can make more," Connor added.

Quinn paused midstride and looked at him, waiting for him to continue, but he gently shook his head.

She shrugged and continued her pacing.

They can, the ghoul confirmed. *And they will.*

Connor frowned. Good to know.

Why haven't you gone to visit the Soulsprite? the wraith asked. *It is something truly awe-inspiring to behold, resting there in all its majesty. Powering a kingdom. Yours to control.*

"There's time for that later," Connor said. "For now, I need to focus on the more urgent matters."

Such as?

Instead of answering, Connor shifted his attention to Quinn. "Think we'll see more Starlings soon?"

She looked up again, and this time, he was already watching her face in a clear indication that he was speaking to her.

"In other circumstances, I would've led the charge," Quinn admitted. "I would've even obeyed Zander's every command, if that was what it took to complete the campaign and get my revenge. So, yes. You will see more Starlings, or at least what few of us are left." She swallowed hard. "If Zander is dead, Gwen will lead the charge, and Victoria will supply them with the sort of devastating firepower you can't even fathom."

"And if he's alive?" Murdoc asked.

A sharp breath shot through her nose, and she shook her head. "Then he will be back, and he won't underestimate you again."

"Where do you think he is?" Connor asked.

"Hopefully, rotting in a blightwolf's stomach." Her nose wrinkled with disgust. "But I doubt it. Wherever he is, one of three things has happened—he's dead, he's still recovering, or he finally learned patience. That last one scares me the most." Her hazel eyes darted toward Connor. "You're a match for him. Aside from Father, no one has ever had enough power to be Zander's equal. Not even me."

"Let's hope he's dead, then," Connor muttered.

But he wasn't going to hold his breath. A man like Zander was hard to kill, and everyone on this wall knew it wasn't likely.

"It is time," Nocturne's voice boomed through the air. "I ask that we finally set my brethren free. You swore you would."

"I did." He peered up at the dragon as the regal creature glared at the two undead beasts guarding the gates. "And I'm a man of my word. Be patient."

Nocturne growled restlessly, but didn't respond.

This is foolish, the Wraith King snapped. *These beasts abandoned the dragonlands long ago. We should not be forced to surrender them to Death simply to appease a glorified pack mule.*

"That's enough." Connor glared at the wraith, more grateful than ever that the two couldn't hear each other. "I've already decided, and I won't disrespect a dragon prince so that you can keep your toys."

The ghoul simply shook his head in frustration. *You don't want to get rid of them. I can tell.*

"Obviously," Connor said, though he chose his words carefully to ensure Nocturne lacked context for the conversation.

It was a compromise. Just as the Antiquity had explained to Dahlia in the Blood Bogs, such was the compromise of allies—a leader didn't always get to have his way.

Nocturne was right. It was time.

Connor briefly closed his eyes and listened to the surreal sensation in his chest that told him where every soldier stood. He reached for the dragons—and for a lone figure already standing at the open gates, far below.

A woman, nothing but bones after all these years, who still wore her crown.

"As for your request, Wraith King…" Connor hesitated as he struggled to find the right words. "Are you sure?"

The ghoul stilled, and his attention shifted to the Decay. *I am.*

"Are you going to tell me why you want this?"

The wraith pointed to the distant green circle that encased Slaybourne.

I assume you have taken note of the border?

Connor nodded.

Only we and the soldiers can see it. It is the line past which Slaybourne's magic fades. I salted the earth beyond the fortress to kill the land, to give the impression that our domain stretches farther than it does, but this is the extent to which the enchantments here can operate. Anything beyond it fades. I want you to witness what happens to the soldiers that travel beyond our borders.

Connor frowned. "Is it really that, or do you want to finally let her go?"

A quiet growl rumbled through his mind, but the specter didn't answer.

Fair enough.

With the Soulsprite's power churning through every nook and cranny of Slaybourne, Connor willed the dragons and the lone figure toward the edge of his kingdom's land.

Be at peace, he ordered.

The dragons tilted their heads toward him, like statues coming to life. He nodded, and with his blessing, they spread their great wings wide. The creatures took flight, kicking up dust as their massive shadows flew across the militant rows of soldiers standing outside of the gates.

They raced toward the outer ring of Slaybourne's domain—toward Death, and toward their freedom.

The ghoul lifted his bony head and watched the sky above them, his head following something Connor couldn't see, and the great specter stiffened.

With fear.

Below, a solitary figure walked through the rows of gathered soldiers. Her tattered dress fluttered in the desert wind, and her lone shadow filtered over the statuesque warriors on her way toward the boundary. The dragons raced ahead of her while she walked with slow and steady strides, and she didn't once look back.

When the undead dragons reached the border, they didn't hesitate. Both flew into the emerald light. Their decayed bodies collided with something Connor couldn't see, as though there was an invisible wall stretching into the heavens, and they faded instantly to dust. They didn't scream. They didn't flinch. They flew with determined purpose into Death's domain, and their ashes scattered on the southern wind.

Behind Connor, Nocturne let out a slow sigh of relief.

With the dragons gone, all eyes fell to the lone figure on her slow and steady trek toward the next life. When she finally neared the border, Connor took a wary step forward and strained his enhanced eyes to better see into the distance. Sunlight glinted off the crown atop her head as she staggered forward.

However, when she reached the line, she paused at the last moment. The figure cast one last glance behind her, toward Slaybourne.

Toward the ghoul.

The undead king stiffened, and he rose slightly into the air under her gaze.

The long lost queen of Slaybourne raised her chin in defiance, and she took her first step over the border. She, too, faded instantly to dust. She leaned into Death, embracing it.

As the last of her faded away, her crown clattered to the dirt.

Even after she was gone, no one moved. A weight settled on the air as Connor studied the undead king hovering before him, at the once-man who stared out into the desert where the one love of his life had faded into nothing.

"To new legacies, my friend," Connor said quietly.

At first, the wraith didn't respond, and it seemed as though he perhaps hadn't even heard the words. The undead king hovered above the Decay long after his queen had faded to dust, and the bones of his left hand curled into a tight fist.

Yes, the Wraith King eventually said. *And I believe mine is long overdue.*

CHAPTER EIGHTY-NINE
CELINE

In the heart of Oakenglen, Celine's carriage rumbled over the cobblestone. She leaned one elbow on the ledge by the window, her eyes glossed over in thought as she ignored the hundreds gathering along the street to witness her parade.

Servants. Pomp. Propriety. It bored her.

Aidan sat across from her and cleared his throat gently, timidly, as though he were afraid to succeed at getting her attention.

Good. At least this little pawn of hers feared her.

"Do you know why I chose you?" She set her hands on her lap, her back straight as she studied his face.

He shook his head. The edge of his mouth twitched, and a bead of sweat rolled down his neck. With her enhanced senses, she could practically taste his fear.

"Because you have ambition." Celine leaned forward, careful to let just a hint of her cleavage show with the movement as she held his gaze. His eyes darted briefly to her chest, and she resisted the impulse to sigh impatiently as yet another pawn played into her hands.

Predictable. All of them.

"You crave power," she explained. "What's more, you wisely attach yourself to those who can give it to you. In just five years, you ascended to the inner circles of the Wildefaire elite. My cousin watched you rise, and in all that time, she saw your potential."

"Queen Whitney—me?" He stuttered, and a dopey grin played at the edge of his mouth as he briefly looked out the window, in the general direction of Wildefaire.

"She did," Celine admitted. "And she was reluctant to give you to me, but she knew I needed a clever and loyal man upon my return home."

He stilled, studying her face, and his lips parted with shock. "Your Majesty, I don't know what to say."

Celine reclined in her seat. "Gratitude is usually the best place to start."

"Yes, of course." He laughed and closed the book in his lap with a gentle snap of paper hitting paper. "I can't begin to thank—"

"What do you want more than anything in this world, Aidan?"

"To serve—"

"No," she snapped, her eyes narrowing in warning. "I've begun to teach you my rules, but the one thing you must never do to me is lie. Tell me what I don't want to hear if you must, but never—not once—will I allow you to lie to my face."

He blinked rapidly as the color drained from his face, and he swallowed hard. An audible gulp pierced the silence that followed, but he took a steadying breath and squared his shoulders.

"Well?" she prodded.

His gaze drifted to the floor, and he tilted his head as though he were embarrassed to admit the truth out loud. "I wish to be a lord, Your Majesty."

"Considering your background, that is quite ambitious indeed."

He nodded. Fish merchants' sons rarely ascended to such heights, but this one had a silver tongue. From Whitney's reports, he knew how to speak to commoner and lord alike. He could spin tales, shift allegiances, and stir loyalty from the bottom ranks even if those at the top resisted.

He was perfect.

With her elbow still resting against the window ledge, Celine set her chin on her palm and set her delicate fingers against the side of her face. "Impress me, Aidan. Be useful. Remain loyal. Please me, and I won't just make you a lord. You will be Lord of Mossvale. You will live out your days with more women than you can bed and more wealth than you know how to spend."

His brows knit together in confusion. "But Otmund Soulblud controls

Mossvale. Are you implying…"

She smiled and raised one eyebrow to stir his imagination, and his eyes widened as he pieced together the unspoken implications.

"I will not fail you," he promised in an earnest whisper.

"No wise man would. May that serve as a reminder to you, Aidan, of what will happen if you cease to be useful."

His smile fell, and he clutched his closed journal more tightly as she studied his face. His jaw clenched, and he quietly nodded. This time, he simply sat there, waiting for her next command.

How marvelous. She already liked this one better than Otmund. Hopefully, Whitney was right about that silver tongue of his, or Oakenglen Castle would eat him whole.

Through the window, her palace came into view. Its stone-gray spires rose over the high walls that protected it from the other four rings of the city. "You know what to do when we arrive?"

"Yes, your Majesty."

As the carriage rumbled into the innermost ring of the city, she peered again through the window.

The show had begun.

Along the polished cobblestone streets, every face pivoted toward her. Women in layered dresses and ridiculous hats curtseyed, and many of the precarious headdresses wobbled as they threatened to fall entirely. Gentlemen bowed, until every head lowered in deference.

To her.

As her subjects paid their respects, Celine caught glimpses of familiar faces. Everyone who lived in the innermost ring was connected in some way to the titans of industry that kept Oakenglen afloat. Most of these entrepreneurs had earned their wealth under Henry, and all of them remembered a time before the crown's tax structure supported the city's merchant class.

These merchants who would fall in line, like everyone else.

The smiling faces disappeared as the castle gate opened to trumpeting fanfare. Her carriage banked to the right, around the ornate fountain in the central courtyard. Peach trees planted along the edges framed a path that led deeper into the royal gardens, and she stared longingly at the stairwell that disappeared into a lush rose garden.

A pang of loss hit her in the chest, and her stony mask faltered. In the distance, a pink rose shivered in a breeze off the lake, and for a moment, she could imagine walking those white brick paths with Henry at her side. He had planted that garden for her, along a stretch of cliff overlooking the lake, as an escape for them both.

From war. From blood. From the carnage.

She blinked away her daze as the carriage rounded the bend and sat taller in her seat as the driver delivered her to a grand staircase leading into the castle. The great wooden doors already stood open, and a red carpet spilled across the steps. Maids stood on either side of it as attendants in sharp white coats rolled the remainder of the carpet out to her coach.

The door opened, its handle held by a gloved attendant, and she lifted her skirts to step down onto the rug. Every servant bowed in perfect unison, their obedience long rehearsed, but she didn't bother looking at them.

Celine didn't even want to be here. The castle, the servants, the carpet she had selected herself to honor her king—it all reminded her of Henry, of the love she had lost to the Wraith King's corruption.

Perhaps she would find Henry again in the next life. When all was said and done, with the simmering souls destroyed and the continent on fire, she would look for whatever was left of the man she had once loved. Maybe he still had the piece of her soul—the joy, the happiness, the light—that he had taken with him to the grave.

With a quick flutter of her eyelids, she strangled the daydream. The Fates had never been so kind to her before, and she wouldn't let herself hope for happy endings in the next life.

This life needed her attention, and she had much to do before Death came for her, too.

CHAPTER NINETY
CONNOR

In the brilliant sunshine of a spring afternoon, Connor sat by the lake deep within Slaybourne. The gentle slope below him meandered deeper into the valley, through the lush forests and toward the ruins that had once been a bustling city. With a contented sigh, he reclined on the grass and savored the heat of the sun on his face. He smiled.

Finally, he was home.

Beside him, Quinn lay on the grass with one arm draped over her eyes as she slept. Her red hair sprawled across the ground, and her chest rose in a steady rhythm as she drank in the warmth of the day.

Admittedly, he watched her a moment longer than he should have.

Cloth rustled against skin as, nearby, Sophia stretched out on the blanket Murdoc had laid out for the two of them. The former Blackguard sat beside her, rifling through a wicker basket Kiera had packed to the brim with dried meat, berries from the forest, and freshly baked bread.

With a mischievous grin, Connor watched Murdoc hunt through the basket. "Looking for something specific?"

"You ate them all didn't you?" Murdoc pointed an accusatory finger at him. "They're gone. All of them."

Connor chuckled and settled back against the grass. "I have no idea what you're talking about, Murdoc."

"Don't lie to me, Wraithblade."

"You're talking about Kiera's breakfast rolls?" Quinn sat up and draped one arm over her propped knee. "The ones with the sausage in them, right?"

"Exactly!" Murdoc threw his hands up in exasperation as he stared down at the basket. "I saved four of them because Connor always beats me to them. Every time."

Quinn lowered her voice, and her hazel eyes shifted to Connor. "You took them, didn't you?"

"Cover for me," he whispered back, quiet enough that only the two of them could hear.

She chuckled.

"Every damn day!" Murdoc set the basket on the ground. "You beat me to them *every damn day*."

With a shrug of feigned ignorance, Connor closed his eyes. "I really don't know what you're talking about."

"I didn't realize there would be this much talking," Sophia grumbled. "I would've stayed in bed."

"It's almost noon," Connor pointed out.

Sophia huffed. "I've been up late making all those Bluntmar collars for the prisoners. *Your* prisoners, might I add."

A lull settled between them, and Connor peered through one eye to find Sophia and Quinn both watching him. The Starling warrior's smile fell, and she awkwardly cleared her throat.

"I think you killed the mood, dear," Murdoc told Sophia in a harsh whisper.

"Good," she snapped as she closed her eyes once more. "Maybe I can get some sleep now."

"On the contrary." Connor sat upright. "Since you brought it up, how long until you're done?"

"Today." A cloud passed by, and Sophia hummed happily as a fresh sunbeam fell on her face. "Though I'm not sure why we're bothering. You have ten of your undead guards watching each prisoner. We can't let any of them have access to their magic until we know they're not a threat."

"Or until Connor figures out what the hell to do with them," Murdoc muttered.

Connor frowned and glared at his friend, who shrugged sheepishly in reply.

"At least we found a place to hold them all," Quinn said under her breath. "Those catacombs go on forever, don't they?"

Tell her yes, the wraith said. *I don't want her to know Slaybourne's limitations.*

Connor sighed impatiently as the ghoul popped into his head, unbidden, once again. "Didn't you say you were keeping an eye on the soldiers?"

I am, the Wraith King said defiantly. *I can keep an eye on many things at once.*

In answer, Connor just rubbed his tired eyes.

"There you are!" a familiar voice shouted from the bottom of the hill.

Connor's gaze swept across the field as Ethan trudged up the grassy knoll toward them. The carpenter's leg rested in the enchanted casing Tove had crafted for him, and the spellgust stone in the joint at his knee glittered in the sunlight. The bulky man waved, smiling broadly. Even though he was missing a leg, Tove's contraption let him walk with a perfectly steady gait.

"Tove's a miracle worker," Connor said under his breath.

"She is." Quinn nodded, her eyes trailing after Ethan's every step.

If only you had invited her to join us in Slaybourne, the ghoul interjected again. *Then, we would have a proper augmentor—and you would finally bed a woman.*

"Will you shut your damn mouth?" Connor hissed under his breath.

The ghoul chuckled deviously, and Connor cast a sidelong glance at Quinn.

Honestly, Magnuson, the Wraith King continued. *I cannot take much more of this celibacy nonsense. You're going to drive me insane.*

"You already are insane," Connor countered.

For the Fates' sake, man, look at you, the ghoul muttered. *Any one of the surviving women from the slavers attack would happily bed you. Take your pick and ravage her until you get this out of your system. They will love it.*

The thought had crossed his mind, of course, given how the young women had looked at him on their journey back to Slaybourne. Still, it wasn't right. After all they had endured, those women needed someone to provide for them. To take care of them as more than just their king.

He couldn't be what they needed, and he wasn't going to use their bodies or break their hearts just to appease these primal urges.

"Bless the Fates, it's good to be walking again." Ethan let out a happy chuckle as he reached them, chest heaving from the effort of walking uphill. He set his hands on his waist as he fought to catch his breath. "I'm a bit out of practice, though."

"It's good to have you back." Connor stood and brushed the loose blades of grass off his hands.

As Connor stood, the rooftops of three log cabins at the base of the hill came into view between the trees, and a dirt path worn into the grass from thousands of footsteps connected the structures.

"You've clearly been busy," he added with a gesture toward all the new homes.

Ethan shrugged modestly. "A lot of the rooms are still empty, but the structures are up, and that's what counts."

A peasant's hovel, the ghoul complained. *If you dare claim one of those for yourself, I will smother you in your sleep.*

Connor sighed in irritation and scratched the back of his head, but he ultimately chose not to reply.

"Can I have a word, son?" Ethan nodded toward the path back down the hill.

"Of course."

The two meandered down the hill, and Connor waited patiently as Ethan took his time. The man inched down the steepest part sideways, but for the most part, he kept perfect balance despite the uneven terrain.

Connor cast one last glance over his shoulder at Quinn, who had already reclined back against the grass. She draped her arm over her eyes again, and her chest rose in a steady rhythm.

When he and Ethan finally reached the base of the hill, they followed the winding path toward the valley. The road turned, leading them farther away from the lake, and his team disappeared behind a cluster of trees.

Safely out of Murdoc's sight, Connor fished the last of Kiera's breakfast rolls out of his pocket and took a massive bite.

"I'm proud of you." Ethan clapped Connor on the back. With each step, the man's prosthetic foot clacked against the half-buried cobblestone road that remained from the Wraith King's time.

Connor finished the roll and clapped his hands together to dust off the crumbs on his fingers. "For what?"

"For—" Ethan laughed so hard he doubled over, and the man shook his head as he wiped a tear from his eye. "For what? Son, look at what you've created here. This is all because of you."

He gestured to the forest. To the birds twittering through the canopy. To two of the women Connor had saved from the slavers. The two mothers stood at the edge of the forest, smiling as they held baskets of twigs to their hips and chatted away in the sunshine—smiling, happy, and safe.

"You built the houses, Ethan."

"And you made sure we could live here in peace." The carpenter poked Connor's chest with one finger and raised his eyebrow to emphasize his point. "None of the decisions you've made thus far have been easy, and those are just the ones I know about. You bled for us, and we're grateful. All a man can do is protect his family and his home, even when it's not easy to do what's right. Even when he suffers for it."

They calmly strode along the path as Connor simmered on what Ethan had said. The two women chatting by the forest's edge waved at them as they passed, and Connor nodded respectfully back to them.

"Thank you," he eventually said. "But this isn't the kind of thing anyone can do alone. Your trick with the armor on the walls was brilliant. It bought us much needed time."

Ethan smirked. "It was pretty damn clever, wasn't it? I'm proud of myself for that one."

"You should be." Connor watched the carpenter through the corner of his eye, waiting for a tell.

For a sign, or for some indication as to how a supposed carpenter could think on his feet like that when facing down an army.

Ethan hummed quietly to himself and smiled as he lifted his face toward the sun.

"You really aren't going to tell me?" Connor asked.

With a frustrated grunt, Ethan shoved his hands in his pockets and surveyed the nearby trees. "I'm clever when I want to be, son."

"And?"

"And that's all."

"Come on, now, Ethan." Connor shook his head. "I haven't pressed you for much since we met, but you know more about survival and battle strategy than any carpenter can pick up in his trade."

"How do you figure?"

"How does a carpenter learn to survive for a decade in the Ancient Woods?" Connor shrugged. "It's hard enough to survive in a normal forest, but the Ancient Woods is brutal, and it's home to more predators than anywhere else in Saldia. And how does a carpenter know to use decoy soldiers, or how to arrange them, or what an invading army will think when the sun sets and the decoys look like men standing on the walls?"

Ethan scratched absently at his beard, and his gaze swept across the ground as they walked. "You're a smart man, Connor. I figured I would have to tell you eventually."

He tensed, wondering who Ethan Finn really was and what he had missed thus far. "King's guard?"

"What? No, son. Not even remotely." A dry laugh escaped Ethan as he dismissed the idea with a flick of his hand. "Back in Ludlow, before we left the city, I wasn't just a carpenter. That's what I wanted to do with my life, of course, but I didn't have much choice in the matter. With a build like mine, a man doesn't get to explore his passions." He sighed in defeat. "You protect your city. The sheriff convinced me to join the ranks early on. I was a lawman."

Ah.

Connor shut his eyes to shield himself against the irony as he pieced it altogether. "And when the sheriff refused to go after the man that killed your eldest daughter…"

"It was like being betrayed by my own family." Ethan slowly shook his head, his eyes out of focus. "We had proof. I saw the evidence. I interrogated the witnesses myself. I had everything I needed to see the man hanged, but the sheriff destroyed it all. That soulless man ain't a man of the law at all. He's bought and paid for."

"I'm sorry, Ethan." Connor sighed. "No father should ever have to live through what you endured."

"My family is safe, and Kenzie would've liked it here." Ethan smiled, though his eyes narrowed with strained grief. "That's good enough for me."

Piercing giggles floated by like bubbles on the wind, and Connor paused as they rounded another bend in the path.

Ahead, a field stretched over a nearby hill. Blades of tall grass rippled in the wind, glowing faintly even in the bright sun, while Isabella chased Fiona through the meadow. Kiera sat on a nearby log, stitching away at a stretch of fabric pinned in a wooden frame on her lap. Behind her, in the shade of a nearby tree, Wesley leaned against the bark with his arms crossed as he watched his sisters play. A small smile tugged at the corner of his mouth, and for the first time since he had arrived in Slaybourne, the young man looked at peace.

"This is a haven, Connor," Ethan said quietly as they watched the girls play.

A massive shadow darted past, and Connor stared upward just as Nocturne shot into the clouds. The black dragon spun in graceful circles, his wings tucked close, and a happy growl rumbled through the sky.

"It is," Connor agreed. "And I won't let anyone change that."

EPILOGUE
ZANDER

A crack of lightning tore through the storm clouds above a cottage, deep in the heart of the Ancient Woods. The only light filtered through the front window as backlit silhouettes passed by. Their long shadows stretched over the grass, exaggerated and unnatural in the suffocating darkness of a moonless night.

The main road didn't reach this part of the forest, and the folks in this stretch of the woodland isolated themselves with intention. Criminals lived out here to hide from the law. Deserters built homesteads, hoping the crown wouldn't care enough to hunt them down. Any given farmer, out here in the nothing, likely had enough blood on his hands to drown someone.

No amount of hiding in the woods could wash those stains clean.

A winding path carved its way up the small hill to the cottage at its peak. As he left the forest behind, another bolt of lightning snapped through the sky. The forest froze, suspended in that moment in time, before the torrential rain washed the moment away.

Droplets of rain broke on Zander's face, and the frigid downpour soaked him to the bone. His clothes clung to his body, fused to his skin from all the blood and grime of his travels with the blightwolves, and his footprints through the muddy puddles left ribbons of dark red blood swirling in his wake.

The storm cleared his head. Around him, the trees bent in heavy gusts as the southern wind stirred the canopy. With the rush of clattering leaves came the soothing swell of fresh grass. The stirring sweetness of honeysuckle. And, most importantly, the heady aroma of roasting meat.

His mouth watered as the aroma swam through his senses. The sharp pangs of his insatiable appetite rumbled with the storm. His eyes stung with exhaustion, and his throat cracked with thirst, but nothing hurt worse than the *hunger*.

The rusty tang of blood wafted through the air. It hung on the wind. Heavy. Thick. Plentiful. That metallic stench of death rolled through this place like an intoxicating fog, omnipresent and overwhelming.

It had drawn him here. It had told him more than his eyes ever could. Dozens had died here, today, and that could only mean one thing.

Bandits.

Anyone who had lived in that cottage was already dead, and no one alive in that house was worth saving.

Muffled laughter floated through the closed front door, and another dark silhouette passed by the window. Zander's boots squished through the mud, ruined beyond repair from his journey.

Astonishingly, he didn't care how he looked. He didn't care that he would appear to most as a homeless vagabond, covered in dirt and sweat.

He only cared about *food*.

I smell nine of them inside. The grim voice echoed in his head. It burrowed into his thoughts, into his very soul, and he didn't bother to hide the shudder of disgust at the Feral King's presence in his mind.

A shiver raced down Zander's spine, and he paused to cast a wary glance at the empty path behind him. A low growl rolled through the air, and only the brief flash of eyes in the darkness between two oaks gave any hint that the blightwolves waited in the forest beyond.

Yet, the Feral King was nowhere to be seen. It lived in Zander, perhaps, tucked away in his head until it saw fit to walk the forest like the rest of them.

A parasite.

"Eleven," Zander corrected. He sniffed the air as he resumed his march toward the cottage. "Two dead."

You're getting better. A dark chuckle rumbled through his head, indiscernible from the heavy thunder above. *Will you demand I stay hidden?*

"No point." No use explaining himself, especially not to the abomination.

Besides, he didn't have the energy to waste words.

You don't care if these men see me with you?

"No." Zander's stomach gnawed at him as he finally reached the house. His hunger ate away at him, as though his stomach would rather consume itself than let the pain continue for even one second more.

It didn't matter what these bandits saw tonight. They wouldn't live to talk about it.

As another burst of thunder rumbled through the sky, Zander kicked open the door. The laughter stopped the second it slammed against the wall. He stared through the blood-soaked locks of his sopping wet hair at the nine men gathered around a dining table that only had two chairs.

Most of all, he stared at the feast laid out before him. Whole chickens, their skin browned to perfection from the fires, covered the table. Slabs of seared steak sat right on the wooden boards. Drips of yellow fat oozed along the half-eaten bodies of whole turkeys, and mugs of frothing ale covered the gaps between meats.

Lamb. Steak. Poultry. Though they had clearly run out of serving platters after the fourth chicken, the feast itself rivaled what he could've had back home.

The edges of his vision went dark, but he managed to catch sight of at least some of the men in his periphery. They gaped at him, one with a half-eaten turkey leg raised to his mouth. The ones with half a brain had already dropped their food and watched him with their hands on the pommels of their swords.

The dull thud of his boots on the floorboards filled the stone-cold silence as he stalked toward the table. His decades of training kicked in, and despite his hunger, he scanned the room again. In the darkness beyond the candles, a limp arm reached from the shadow of the nearest doorframe. A woman's delicate fingers stretched across the ground, her nails perfectly aligned to several long gouges in the floorboards.

One of the original owners, he assumed.

Zander didn't wait. He grabbed the nearest chunk of steak and bit into it. The seared juice dripped from the corners of his mouth, and though he ate like a starved vagrant, he didn't pause. In the time it took the stunned bandits to finally mutter amongst themselves, he inhaled it, and another, and a third.

One of the bandits peered out the window, squinting as he surveyed the darkness, but the man frowned with confusion.

Looking for other Lightseers, no doubt.

The nearest bandit had managed to find a plate, and an untouched rack of lamb waited on the bone-riddled platter. Zander grabbed it.

"I was saving that!" The man reached for Zander's wrist.

The fool.

Zander grabbed the bandit's arm and snapped it in half. The resounding crack shattered the air, louder than the thunder. White bone stuck out of the torn red muscle, and the man shrieked as he stumbled backward. He stared at it in horror, still screaming, until his back hit the wall behind him.

Another man, one of only two with a chair and sitting at the head of the table, snapped his fingers. Though his eyes never left Zander, he gestured toward the screaming bandit. "Get him out of here."

The shrill scream continued, splitting Zander's enhanced ears, but he didn't care. He ate the entire rack of lamb in the time it took two of the other bandits to grab the injured man by his shoulders and haul him into the next room. One covered the screaming bandit's mouth to stifle the shriek, and for a moment, there was a reprieve from the irritating sound. The other stepped on the dead woman's fingers, and a softer crack, like the pop of a fire, followed.

"I know who you are." The man at the head of the table set his elbows on either side of his plate and wove his fingers together. He studied Zander over his knuckles and ran his tongue over his cracked lips as he apparently debated what else to say.

Zander didn't answer. He just bit into another slab of steak. He couldn't even taste it anymore. The dripping fat and seared blood blended together on his tongue, and only the next bite mattered.

He'd never been this hungry in his life. It didn't seem *possible*.

"...only reason you're not dead," the lead bandit continued.

Oh. Apparently, he was still talking.

Impatient and irritated, Zander's furious glare shifted toward the man who wouldn't shut his damn mouth. The remaining bandits flinched, and one took a wary step backward.

The smart one, apparently.

"Let's be honest, Lord Starling." The bandit let out a slow and steady breath, but his stiff shoulders and shaking hands betrayed his fear. "Nine-to-one aren't good odds, even for you. How about we make a deal?"

Zander barely heard him. The words made sense, but he just didn't care. As he finished another chunk of lamb meat, he reached for a whole chicken and bit into its hide without so much as breaking off the wings. Bones crunched between his teeth, not altogether unpleasant, like the soft crunch of celery on a hot summer's day.

"Eat with us," the leader continued. "Enjoy this feast and don't worry about where it came from. Once we're all happy and full, we will go our separate ways. How does that—"

The air shifted, and the hair on Zander's neck stood on end. A hazy warning wriggled through his mind from his years of training as someone else joined them, but his hunger drowned most of it out. A puff of black smoke rolled past his boot, and as the dark shadow sucked the light from the room, the leader's trembling gaze darted to the space above Zander's head.

As Zander took another bite, he peered carelessly over his shoulder to find a swirling mass of shadow hovering by the open door. Rain pelted the entry as the Feral King's yellow eyes appeared within the darkness.

Once, he had frozen in horror at witnessing the abomination stepping from another world into theirs. Now, he shook his head with impatience at the damned thing's love for theatre.

It didn't have to appear this way. It chose to milk the moment for all it could.

Anything to stir the terror in those present. The theatre. The drama.

How painfully predictable.

While horrified mutterings rippled through the gathered men, Zander ignored the atrocity of nature and instead focused on devouring the last of the chicken in his hands. No matter what he ate, he needed *more*. It baffled him.

How the Wraithblade managed to do anything while this hungry, Zander might never know.

Through the half-starved fog in Zander's mind, he managed to catch snippets of the world around him. Some of them prayed under their breath. Others couldn't move.

To his surprise, however, the Feral King didn't attack. It let the seconds pass, and with each moment, another of the men came to his senses. The leader stood, and his chair slammed against the floorboards as it toppled over.

It could've bitten their heads off with ease, and yet the abomination didn't move.

How very interesting.

Zander swallowed the last of the chicken and tossed the hollow corpse back onto the table. The fat-drenched bones skidded through the lingering juices on the table, and as it finally slid to a stop, he ripped a turkey leg off the nearest bird.

"You all should run," he suggested.

The second chair toppled over. Men slammed each other into walls. Their terrified shouts blended with the thunder outside.

In their desperate bid for the door, they trampled each other. The swish of metal on cloth filled the air as half of them drew their swords, and with an impatient sigh, he set his back against the wall to ensure none of them tried anything foolish.

The man with the broken arm was the last to charge into the rain, holding his shattered injury close. Zander finished his turkey leg as the panicked voices mingled with the downpour, and to his surprise, the Feral King only watched from the depths of its shadow.

It still hadn't moved.

Boots splashed through the puddles outside, and the corner of Zander's mouth twisted into a sinister grin. Those men didn't realize the blightwolves waited in the dark, and this he *had* to see.

With the nine men finally gone, he ripped off another turkey leg and leaned against the open doorframe. The men scattered, and though some ran down the muddy path, half of them splintered off and raced for gaps in the tree line instead. Their voices faded, and with time, only the distant snap of twigs gave him clues as to where they had gone.

The pelting rain pattered against the roof, and Zander bit once more into the turkey leg as he waited.

Any second now.

Sure enough, a howl pierced the night. A shrill scream followed. Incoherent babbling came next as the distant rip of meat punctuated the gaps between the rumbling thunder. Zander bit a chunk of burned meat off the turkey leg, and as three more screams echoed from the forest, his hunger only grew.

It hit him, then, what the Feral King had waited for. It enjoyed a fair bit of theatre, sure, and its actions implied it enjoyed a good performance, but an undercurrent of something else entirely punctuated everything it did. Every choice. Every act.

Something far more significant than a bit of drama.

Terrified screams cut through the air, and Zander frowned as he picked the last meat off the turkey bone in his hand. His eyes narrowed as he debated silently with himself, and he tossed the bone aside.

It hit him, then. The word. The undercurrent. The thing the Feral King wanted most of all.

Fear.

Made in the USA
Middletown, DE
09 October 2023